THE HAWTHORNE UNIVERSITY WITCH SERIES, BOOKS 1-3

A. L. HAWKE

PHANTOM HEART, LLC

ISBN: 9781953919090

ISBN: 9781953919021 (ebook)

This is a work of fiction. It comes directly from the author's imagination. Witchcraft is included to infuse a sense of realism to the novel, but in no way is it supposed to represent actual practicing witchcraft, witches or the religion of Wicca. The book also includes fictitious names, characters, places, and incidents. Any public names are used solely for creative purposes. Any resemblance to actual people, living or dead, or to companies, institutions, or locales is entirely coincidental or accidental.

Line edited by Stephanie Ward

Proofread by Eliza Dee of Clio Editing Services

Cover Design © 2021 by Regina Wamba of MaeIDesign.com

Published by Phantom Heart, LLC

27702 Crown Valley Pkwy, Suite D4, #201

Ladera Ranch, CA 92694

Printed and bound in the United States of America

First printing 2021

Learn more about A.L. Hawke at www.alhawke.com

Correspondence: contact@alhawke.com

❀ Created with Vellum

In memory of my mother
Your candle shines bright in my heart

BROOMSTICK

BOOK I

$$1$$

HER AFFLICTION

I feel a chill in the air. But the sunlight flickers between fall leaves warming me as I walk across campus with my best friend, Madison. It will be winter soon, but for now, the last days of autumn in Georgia seem so peaceful. I glimpse at patches of blue through the canopy of trees. The sky is like ... so perfect. I love fall, I really do.

But Maddie doesn't seem interested in Mother Nature. She's been acting like a witch since we got up, which is a bit odd because my BFF is one of the most energetic and cheery girls I know. I already asked her what's wrong, but she won't tell me.

We pass the dorms and climb the grassy hill at the center of campus. At the summit is the tallest building at Hawthorne University: our library. But we're not checking out books. A line of students snakes its way through a bunch of cute tables with burgundy umbrellas to the counter of our university coffee shop. I think the wait takes Maddie over the edge.

She finally starts spitting out the events of her evening. "I went out on a date with Patrick. You know, the guy in my film studies class." She told me about him before, emphasizing how tall and cute he is, but now she looks as if she bit into something sour. "I knew there was trouble the minute he picked me up in that filthy, dilapidated flatbed truck." (I'm not surprised. She's not a very good judge of character, you know). "We had this great tilapia chili dish and lime-green margaritas and everything was going fine until he reached under my skirt and touched my vagina." I look around me, biting my lip nervously. We're still standing in line, and she said the word *vagina* really loud. People are turning to look. Then Maddie tells me she hit him on the head. Patrick, acting like he was the victim, jumped up from their booth, ran, and left her the bill.

Anyway, Maddie's busy telling me this story about her date copping a feel—and saying the word *vagina* real loud—when, right before my eyes, she walks into the store and just grabs a drink off the counter. We haven't ordered anything yet. It looks like a latte, but I'm not sure. I'm not so sure she knows either. Then she grabs my arm and we make a hasty exit. Maddie is like a total kleptomaniac.

As we walk down a cement path paralleling the grassy hill, I stare at her and she flashes a really sweet grin, raising her cup as if in a toast. "Anyway, fuck him."

I'm thinking, *At least she was asked out on a date.*

She looks at the brew in her stolen cup, puzzled. Then she throws her long hair back and cocks her head toward me very earnestly, saying, "Alondra wants to meet you."

I'm still looking at her in shock.

"Why not?" Maddie asks. "It'll be fun."

But I'm not thinking about Alondra. I point at her cup.

"It's really good," she says with a chuckle. "I think it has soy. Want some? I don't usually order soy but...this isn't bad. Look, Katie..." (People call me Katie a lot, even though my name is Cadence.) "Alondra says she wants to meet you outside of class. Just come with me to her house."

"I don't know," I say. "I don't like the look of her."

Now we're dodging bodies on the crowded lawn, heading to the main hall of the university. The main drag of Hawthorne is a white paved sidewalk surrounded by grass and trees, with brick buildings on both sides— and even more college bodies. The classroom buildings are spread out through the fields and under the tall trees. The leaves are so pretty in red and orange. Fall is my favorite time of year because I love the colors.

Hawthorne University is in Georgia. It's a really nice college, and I'm lucky to have been accepted here. So is Maddie. Everyone has a book tucked under their arm or is carrying a backpack. I have a pink backpack decorated with a unicorn. Maddie has always thought it's a little too cute, but I think it's whimsical. It even has purple swirls around the straps. Maddie's carrying a small book, but I'm pretty sure she won't read it. She's not the best student.

"You should go," Maddie says again, sipping her stolen drink. She runs her free hand through her hair, which is long and black like mine. I reach for my hair and realize I put it in a bun this morning, so I just pat the top of my head like an idiot. Then I think about Maddie's being a poor judge of character and think to myself, *No. No way am I going to Alondra's.*

"Why do you do that?" I point to her cup.

Then she drinks some more with a large grin. Again, she offers me some, but I don't have a chance to taste it because a nerdy-looking boy with glasses sprints between us, nearly knocking down her mysterious drink.

"Hey!" Maddie yells. "Watch where the fuck you're going!" Then she turns back to me. "It's busy, Kate. We should have gone into town like I told you."

I shrug. "I thought we'd just spend the afternoon on the grass studying for midterms."

I must look hurt because Maddie giggles and runs her hand down my back. "Whatever. Whatever you want." Then she leans closer to me. "Just come with me tonight. Please. It'll be a lot of fun. Alondra's really nice. And I have a surprise."

"I don't know."

"Well..." Maddie walks off and stands under a really large tree. "You have to. For the surprise."

"Yeah? What?"

"Bryce will be there."

"So?"

"Whaddaya mean *so?*" she says. "You can't stop talking about him."

Of course Bryce will be there. He's my teaching assistant and is really hot. "You're just scared," I say. "Now you're trying to bribe me."

"I'm not scared, Cadence."

She plops down on the lawn, puts her book on her chest, and closes her eyes. I catch a glimpse of the book's cover. It features a burly man with rippling muscles and the title *Complete Me*. She's not studying.

"Just come," she says with her eyes closed. "I'll meet you back in our dorm at six to get ready."

"Are we eating there?"

"Yeah." Maddie laughs with her eyes still closed. "Alondra always has plenty to eat. Too much. She knows just how to fatten you up."

Dr. Alondra Johansen has a house in the middle of a thick forest, only a couple of miles from the university. It's rumored to have been built during the Civil War. I believe it. It's a white-columned two-story mansion with a large shaded patio and a beautiful paved walkway. It makes me think Scarlett O'Hara from *Gone with the Wind* is going to run down the steps, any minute, to greet us. Surrounding the walkway is a field of grass and tall trees, along with a garden full of white and red lilies. I like lilies. I don't like taking care of them, or any flowers for that matter, but I like looking at them. Especially in the wild. I like the outdoors. Always have.

A small wooden carriage, painted red, sits on a modern paved driveway alongside the property. Parked behind it is Dr. Johansen's dark gray Jaguar XJ. How does she own all this stuff? Some say she's the descendant of an old wealthy family. It can't be from her salary. She's my history professor.

There are others walking up the dirt walkway, mostly girls I recognize from class.

With all the grandeur of the mansion, I'm surprised to see Alondra herself greet us at the door. A long pitch-black cape is draped over a darker black silk shirt and slacks. She has long black hair like mine, hanging loosely in waves. This time I'm wearing my long hair down too. And like the times I've seen her in class, I'm struck by her eyes. Alondra has bright jade eyes, like jewels. Her skin is pale, much paler than mine, and for a moment I imagine that she's a vampire. It would certainly fit her affinity for the nineteenth century.

But her smile isn't sinister; it's sweet. She's always nice—too nice. She has a bright grin and seems thrilled to see me. "Cadence Hawthorne, come in." I'm a little surprised she remembers my name. "I'm so glad you came. Are you considering our project?"

"I'm thinking about it, Dr. Johansen."

Standing beside Alondra is her teaching assistant, the irresistibly yummy guy Maddie used to bribe me to come. Bryce's suit doesn't hide his muscular, athletic physique. He's looking down into my eyes too. But his eyes are blue—gorgeous blue. I'm reminded of the cover of that trashy romance novel my best friend was reading. The model was like a bulkier version of Bryce, but Bryce is the real deal—and incredibly hot.

Now I'm blushing.

"Cadence," Bryce says, taking my hand formally and tipping his head.

I'm cherry red.

Bryce turns to my friend. "Madison."

"Hi, Bryce," Maddie says. Then she looks at me and struggles not to laugh.

I look away.

The foyer is grand. Above me is this amazing chandelier. It's made of a hundred tiny crystals reflecting light. It's the most beautiful chandelier I've ever seen. I almost feel dizzy looking up at the twinkling crystals. But that doesn't do justice to the rest of the house. The hallway, including the wooden-railed stairway, is white, and marble columns frame the front door. Enormous windows extend from the ceilings to the travertine floor. The hallway leads to the kitchen, where everyone has gathered, their voices echoing through the house.

Dr. Johansen greets me as we linger just inside the doorway. "Please, call me Alondra." Oh yeah, my professor is still greeting me. Watching me. She's still looking at me with her mesmerizing green eyes. I completely forgot about her. I'm a little surprised she didn't say hello to Maddie. "You can reserve calling me by my title for when we're in class, Cadence," she says with a nod. "But here, please relax. Call me Alondra."

Oh shit, do I not look relaxed?

My eyes fall on Maddie. My BFF bitch has the largest grimace I've seen in weeks.

"Come in, you two," Alondra says. "Make yourselves at home."

Make yourselves at home. And Alondra really seems to mean it. Bryce leads me to the kitchen, leaving the other two behind.

The kitchen is just as lovely as the entryway, with steel stoves, and marble—like *real* marble—countertops. It's all tidy and neat. About fifteen people are gathered in a small adjoining dining room, talking and laughing, their voices echoing through the large open spaces.

"You can help me with the trays," Bryce says with this amused smile. I catch his eyes straying along my shoulders and down my elegant black dress. It looks like he's thinking of something other than the trays.

What's on your mind, Bryce? ... Hope it's me.

"Sure," I say.

He collects glasses already full of champagne and places them on two trays. "How do you like our class?" he asks.

"It's good. I especially like ancient history and medieval times."

"Yeah," he says. "You know, I used to be interested in engineering, but that changed when I saw how much math I'd need to know." He chuckles. I ogle his lips and that to-die-for strong jawline as he laughs. I freeze for a second. I fight off a blush and hope he doesn't notice. "I suppose that's what fascinates me about witch trials," he says.

"It's all...fascinating," I say. "You really seem to be into Dr. Johansen's research."

He lifts the tray and places it in my hands. I'm extra careful, because my heart is beating so fast staring at those thick biceps, and the last thing I want to do is drop the tray. But Bryce is so cute.

"Yeah, I am," Bryce says.

"What? Do you like the...subject matter? Or is it all Dr. Johansen's choice?"

"Well, Alondra loves it. I follow whatever she and Bill want me to study." He lifts his tray and gestures for me to follow him. "Come. Let's eat."

We walk into the dining room. Everyone's now sitting, laughing, and talking around a giant antique oak table. Another floor-to-ceiling window looks out onto Alondra's forest acreage. It's another mix of traditional and modern—a classic oak table in an open modern room. And in the center of the table is a series of silver containers, likely holding our dinner. Small candles are lined up on a formal white table mat. Most of them are unlit. The silverware, which looks like real polished silver, is laid out beside the pristine white china. It's so elegant. So classy. So chic.

As I walk in, I nearly step on a small gray cat. It meows and scurries away. That gets Alondra's attention.

"Ah, champagne." Alondra looks at me. "Cadence, would you be a dear and help Bryce hand out the drinks?"

"Sure." *Why does she keep addressing me? Why not Maddie?* I came here for Maddie, right? But Alondra practically ignored her when we entered her house. That was weird.

Maddie and Alondra are the only ones with open seats beside them —a seat for me and a seat for Bryce. Everyone is looking at us. Why? Do I look nervous again?

As we walk along the table, serving drinks, I pass a girl with long black hair, heavy eye shadow, and black lips—the total 1990s goth look. She's wearing a short skirt with black stockings. She has a large silver lip ring with tattoos lining her forearms and neck. The tattoos are creepy red-and-black skeletons and demons—really dark stuff. She sort of rolls her eyes at me when I nod hello.

Then there's an older gentleman dressed in a suit. This must be Dr. Reardon, another history professor at Hawthorne University. I've never met him before. He's wearing a black suit and thin spectacles. He's bald with a goatee on his gaunt, wrinkled face. He's sitting to the left of Alondra. I pass drinks to a few more girls. I see an Asian student, a senior I recognize from class—Jason. He nods. He's a nice guy. I see him talking to Bryce a lot in school. I think he's friends with my Prince Charming.

Prince Charming sits on the other side of Alondra. I catch his eyes wandering toward me. (Or maybe I'm the one who keeps looking at him; I don't know.) I finish making my rounds of the table, and I serve a drink to my best friend and sit down next to her. Maddie touches my arm for a moment. I turn and she seems almost giddy.

What's so funny?

She's probably thinking about Bryce. I told her how good looking I think he is. I remember him handing out assignments on the first day of class. Even on the first day, Tall, Dark, and Handsome was smiling at me.

He's really cute, you know, with really adorable dimples. He always brushes his hair to perfection. If it's early in the morning, he slicks it back with gel. His skin is flawless, with a perfect tan. And those eyes, those bright baby-blue eyes. Sometimes... And, anyway...

"Everyone has their champagne?" Alondra's staring at me again. "Good." I just nod. "Now let's toast." Her voice is commanding and, like in class, everyone is silent before her. "To life."

Everyone sips some champagne. Then Alondra turns to Maddie and me and says, "Can one of you grace us with a blessing before we eat?"

For the first time since walking into Alondra's mansion, Maddie looks uneasy. Her mouth even gapes open for a moment.

Apparently, Dr. Johansen has never met Maddie's family. She doesn't have any parents. She lives with her aunt Jane, who has a house not far from the school. And Jane's atheistic, progressive ways hardly lend themselves to prayer. And as for me ...

"Sure, I'll do it," mutters Maddie.

That prompts many around the table to nod and look down in prayer. But not Professor Reardon. Or Alondra. Alondra tilts her head and squints, seeming to study Maddie. I know Maddie has never said a prayer in her life, and I think Alondra is on to her little secret. Then Alondra looks over at me. So does Professor Reardon. It's weird; it's like they're examining us. I quickly look down at the table.

"Lord bless us for what we are about to have," says Maddie, her voice echoing in the small room. I try not to laugh at her hypocrisy. It's almost more blasphemous than if she hadn't said anything at all. "We should feel grateful." There. That's it. True enough.

But everyone seems to expect more. They all stare at us. At me.

Maddie falls silent.

"Amen," says Alondra, almost derisively.

"Before we eat," Alondra says, "I want to thank those of you who are new. I know midterm exams will be in a week, and it's time for many of you to start studying." Some people laugh. "So coming to my little party on such short notice is a personal honor to me. Doctor Reardon"—she points at him and he sort of tips his head—"is also really happy you've come. I'd love it if, before we start supper, those of you who are new could just say a word or two about yourselves."

Shit. Shit. SHIT! I hate, absolutely hate, talking in front of people. I'm not the shyest girl, but there's something about talking in front of a group that makes my bowels turn. And just as Dr. Johansen is saying this, Bryce is staring right at me. This time I don't care for his grin. Even my favorite of favorite boys looking at me in encouragement is not enough to relax my stomach. I run my hand through my hair, bite my lip, and look down.

My friend rescues me. "I'm Madison. Call me Maddie. I was born and raised in Atlanta. I'm a diehard Braves fan. I like picnicking under the stars...especially with boys..." People laugh. "I'm a Pisces. I favor Scorpio. I'm also a major sci fi buff. I like *Star Trek*, *Doctor Who*, and all the other nerdy stuff. I also like my share of scary movies, especially in the arms of a handsome man." More laughing. "That's why I like Dr. Johansen's class. Learning about magic and witchcraft mixed with history is totally cool."

"Thank you, Maddie," Alondra says with smile.

"Sure, Professor..." A few more chuckles erupt. "And, I don't know ..." Maddie turns to me. "Let's see..." She puts a finger to her face in thought; then she touches my back. "And my best friend in the whole wide world is sitting here next to me today, Ms. Cadence Hawthorne."

Shit! That's my cue to speak.

"Well, we already know you, Madison," Alondra says reflectively, smiling at my friend. Alondra has a way of putting people in their place with her smile. It's almost worse than if she directly insulted you. "I said those of you who are *new*." Then she looks right at me.

Double shit!

"I'm kinda new, Alondra," retorts Maddie.

"Yes." But Alondra doesn't turn from me.

When I still remain silent, she looks at the rest of the table, disappointed, and nods. "Okay, I suppose I'll go. You all know me as Dr. Johansen from your metaphysical history class. Outside of school I would very much like you to call me Alondra. I have three cats named Whiskers, Pete, and George. I love opera, so if any of you have tickets to a show downtown, please invite me... I like the Braves too, Madison. And... hmm." She laughs and I laugh too. Then she stares at me. "Why don't one of you newer folks tell us about yourself?"

"So we can eat," interrupts the doom-and-gloom goth girl across the table. She offers a wry smile then looks at the window.

"My name is Helen," says a bald black girl at the other side of the table. "I'm new to Hawthorne University—from Phoenix. Just came here this semester. I..."

Helen tells us about herself and I'm relieved. Then a girl named Katelyn speaks up, followed by a girl named Abby. Finally they circle back to me, and my professor's looking at me with her annoying smile. She's inviting me to speak as if nothing that comes out of my mouth could possibly be wrong, but I don't have the nerve. I don't say a damn word.

Alondra turns away from me. "Why don't you open the trays, Bryce. Mira's right. We should eat."

The food is still steaming in the metallic trays as they're opened. It's a large roast garnished with vegetables and potatoes. There are three of them—plenty for the twenty of us. It looks like a meal fit for a fancy five-star restaurant. And there are rolls and mashed potatoes and salad too.

Maddie whispers into my ear teasingly with a giggle. "I didn't know Bryce would be here."

Fucking bitch.

We eat, talking among ourselves. I start thinking how cool my teacher is. She seems so laid-back, as if she's just happy that we're all together. At times, Professor Reardon leans over and quietly says something to her. Once I even see them looking at me. I don't like that. He's got this sly grin, as if he's up to something. I'm a pretty good judge of character, and I just don't like Reardon. He seems the complete opposite of Alondra. She is so caring and welcoming. He seems to be self-absorbed, aloof, and angry. But the two teachers seem close.

Bryce is looking at me. And it seems every time he does, my BFF nudges me, which is kind of annoying.

By the time we're halfway through dinner, Alondra clicks her wine-glass with a fork. There's nothing in it, but she uses it to get everyone's attention. "Now that you're all fattened up, perhaps we can talk a little bit about the project. Many of you are from my class. Others were personally invited by Professor Reardon." She looks at the old man and gestures to him.

Dr. Reardon removes his spectacles, takes his burgundy cloth napkin, and wipes his mouth and his thin gray goatee. Then he waves the napkin in front of him. With a whoosh of red cloth, it bursts into flame. He throws the burning napkin down on his plate, and it remains a bright flame. A couple of students gasp in excitement. He smirks with satisfaction over his stupid parlor trick.

Maddie leans over and whispers in my ear. "I hear he can do a lot more."

I roll my eyes. I figure he put sulfur or something on the napkin. I think I smell it. With his sharp beard and mostly hairless head, shifty eyes, and nasty grin, he'd do well around sulfur and hellfire.

I'm not a stranger to magic, you know. My uncle Ray was a professional magician. He even taught me a trick or two with coins and cards. But this trick is so trivial that it doesn't impress me. It just verifies that the old man is creepy. And he's not done. He tosses something from his hand and the flame changes from red to blue.

"I'm Doctor William Reardon," he says with a dry chuckle. "You're all here because of your interest in magic and sorcery. As you know, Alondra is a history professor whose primary focus is on ancient black magic. Those who are in her class know of her interest in teaching ancient rites, the darker corners of Crowley and Baphomet, and the ancient wizards from ancient Egypt to the Middle Ages. My personal specialty involves the more pleasurable centers of the human body." I squirm at that. He looks like a real pervert too.

I'm thinking Alondra should be saying this. She has a knack for discussing things, in class, that are uncomfortable. But this guy is so mechanical about it. He looks away as he talks, rarely meeting anybody's gaze.

He coughs. Then he turns back and his shifty eyes fall right on me. "We explore our initiates in fine detail."

I slide down in Alondra's uncomfortable wooden dining room chair.

The old man looks out the window for a moment as if he wasn't talking to anyone. He's pensive for a long time. Everyone at the table is attentively watching him or the blue flame still flickering under him. Then he says, "The nature of our work forces us to set a few rules, of course. If you join, you will have to abide by them. I will explain each as best I can. Number one: you will be safe, but uncomfortable. Be warned. We can assure your physical well-being, but not your emotional well-being. You might even desire to leave or forfeit your position. There are, of course, provisions we can make to allow you to leave, but it's much better that you are committed when you sign. Number two: you will never unveil to others what we do. This is the most binding rule. In fact, if you choose to join us, you will have to sign a confidentiality waiver. Number three: there are..." He pauses for a moment and looks at Alondra. She simply nods reassuringly. "There are things that you will find morally repugnant. I warn you now, this is a study of human behavior. We are applying past theorems to the modern era. If you hold beliefs, religious or otherwise, that are so entrenched that you feel you cannot break with them, do not join us. Please leave now. Dr. Johansen and I have handpicked you because of your free minds."

I'm looking at Maddie and she's looking at me, and I'm thinking, *What the fuck?* Then I'm thinking, *What has she gotten me into?* And of course I'm not going to sign a damn thing—Tall, Dark, and Handsome or not.

Then, would you believe it? Of all the people at the table, shy little me—who wouldn't even introduce myself—finally opens her mouth. "Sir...Dr. Reardon, what do you mean by religious? I was told this project is for a dissertation in the metaphysical techniques of history and our ancient past. What does that have to do with our religious beliefs?"

"Cadence," says Alondra with her now-infamous reassuring smile, "this really doesn't apply to you. This applies to girls who go to church. Who hold superstitious beliefs about God that get in the way of modern views. Magic, black or white, can stir up fears in some who worship the cross. If you are too busy going to church or Sunday school, it is believed—"

"Alondra," Dr. Reardon interrupts, raising his hand. "She has not yet signed."

"It's all right, Bill. She needs to understand." Then she turns back to me. "Our ways may be so distressing that a participant might leave, and that would interfere with the project." Then she smiles. "But I don't think that applies to you, Cadence. You're not very religious. Neither is your friend Maddie."

So I guess she noticed my friend's blessing wasn't very orthodox.

"Am I wrong about this, Cadence?" Then Alondra turns to the rest of the people at the table. "For all of you—am I wrong about this? Are any of you so morally locked in your beliefs that you are unwilling to explore another viewpoint with open minds? Because if you are averse to the metaphysical, we won't let you in."

No one says a word, but Maddie looks at me again. She's really spooked now too, very different from her usual bubbly self.

"Number four," continues Reardon.

There's a number four?

"Those of you who complete your dissertations will be promised high marks from the university. Each of you will write your own thesis, which I will review, and if you are able to complete it, you will be far ahead of your counterparts. Few universities will reject you, upon graduation from any liberal arts graduate school, after completing this project. It's a great honor—not unlike a doctoral dissertation. But you must complete a year with our group. Even after the class is over, you must remain in the program for a year if she is to grant you this special commendation. Some of you, like Mira, are even returning for your second year."

The weird goth bitch nods.

"For those of you who wish to participate in our research, there will be a sign-up sheet at the front door. Please leave your name, phone number, and email so I can contact you. The rest of you, enjoy yourselves. Alondra likes company, and it's her pleasure to entertain you. So... there is no pressure." He coughs again. "What I would suggest is that you talk with those around the table who partook in the experiments last year. And our teaching assistant, Bryce Wallace. They can reassure you about, or recommend against, working with us."

"Good," says Alondra with a big grin. "Thank you, Bill."

The stodgy old man waves a hand over his plate, and the blue flame is doused.

There are a few more *oohs* and *ahs*. I roll my eyes again. I think he notices.

Then Alondra turns to Bryce. "Now, shall we have dessert?"

2

―――――

WORKING OUT

There's something wonderful about sweating your ass off in comfy gray activewear while running as hard as you can, as fast as you can, and staring through floor-to-ceiling windows at the thick wilderness, all the while listening to System of a Down blaring through your cell phone earbuds. Our campus gym has a breathtaking view of the trees. Between the sweat and the view, I find the whole thing exhilarating. Working out is a rush. It's also a good way to put your problems to the side. That's why I exercise so often.

My mother's sick. Well, she's been sick for years. She has MS—multiple sclerosis. It's a demyelinating disease affecting the neurons. First it takes your dignity. (It made her pee on herself at my high school graduation.) Then it takes your mobility and your mental faculties. It's really awful. Dad spends every day he can, back home in Atlanta, caring for her. He keeps telling me that she's not doing well. He's always taking her to the hospital.

So I'm breathing heavily on the treadmill, trying to run a mile in nine minutes, and I'm thinking about Mom.

And then I'm thinking about Bryce. I thought of him last night, you know. Bryce. All night. I couldn't sleep. I kept imagining that stubble against my cheek. And his short, perfectly kempt brown hair. I can't stop thinking of him. And I think he likes me too. I mean, he was looking at me a lot, and he asked me to help him out in the kitchen. *Me.* Why'd he do that? He must like me, right? I don't know.

Anyway, now I'm moving on to leg lifts. I'm lifting a lot of weight as the music has changed to *"Fuck the System."* Maddie always laughs when she hears the heavy shit I listen to. She's more into Taylor Swift.

I gaze out the window again. I love to get lost looking out at the shadows of the tall trees. I can just make out the shimmering lake through all the foliage.

There are a lot of students walking a dirt path about fifty yards down, leaving campus or coming in, barely visible through the dense woods. They're just shadows through the trees. It's a sunny day outside, but there are so many trees that it's always a bit shadier here. There are bugs out there too—a bit too many for an early October afternoon. They're out with the humidity as it's oddly hot this afternoon. It was sixty yesterday. Birds flutter around the window, obscuring the light of the sun, but I can't hear them with the music blaring in my ears.

So I'm puffing my cheeks and lifting over a hundred pounds when, in the periphery of my view, I glimpse a tall boy wearing a tank top and matching blue shorts. He's standing beside a bench press with a friend, looking over at me. Two other exercisers are on my right, near him, but I notice this boy keeps looking my way. And why wouldn't he? It's Bryce. Bryce and his Asian friend Jason, who I saw the other night.

He walks over. *Holy shit!*

He says something to me. I can't hear, so I pull out an earbud.

"Cadence?" he asks again.

I'm puffing out more air, struggling to lift the weight. I look up and try to act like I didn't see him, but I think he saw me looking over.

"Hi, Bryce."

I pull out the earbud from my other ear and switch off the music.

"It's good seeing you," he says with a grin.

Sixth lift. "Yeah." *Breathe out more. Wipe my mouth to make sure I'm not spitting in front of this Adonis.* "You too. I don't usually see you here," I say. It's late afternoon. I'm not an early riser. I figure maybe he is.

"My head feels like it's gonna explode," he says, rubbing his temples.

"That's why I'm exercising this late. I'm usually up at dawn. I had a little too much to drink at a party last night." He smiles again.

Ninth lift. And...tenth. Somehow the weight feels heavier under those gorgeous blue eyes.

I grab a towel and wipe my face. "Maybe you shouldn't drink so much," I say with a shrug. I'm being a little bitchy, but I've learned that boys love that. But I falter a little when I look up into those baby blues again.

"I didn't drink *that* much, Cadence." Then he looks down and chuckles. "Or...maybe I did."

He stands awkwardly over me. The silence is a lot more uncomfortable than it was the other day when we were at Alondra's house, surrounded by chatter. This time, he's hovering over me, and the cling and clang of exercise equipment is the only thing between us. He says quickly, "Listen, you want to go to one of our parties this weekend? It's at the Billington House."

"Hmm?" Of course I want to go. But I can't. I might be traveling back home to see Mom. "I'm not sure I can make it this weekend, Bryce. But I can probably make the next one."

"Well, we're having a party this weekend. It's to celebrate the end of midterms."

"Drinking more? At your haunted house?"

The Billington House is haunted. Everyone knows that. I'm not even sure anymore who told me about it, but you can't be a student at Hawthorne without hearing of the curse surrounding the Billington House. In the very late hours, people say a candle lights by itself before the central window, and some even say the ghost of the voodoo witch Escoba stands by the glass, silhouetted by candlelight and staring wide-eyed outside. But I've been to the house a few times for frat parties and have yet to see a witch or candle by the window.

"Um-hmm." He smiles. "Love to see you. I admit it's kinda creepy there. But the fact that it's haunted makes it a great place around Halloween. We're even planning a séance. I hope you can make it."

"I'll try."

"And...listen, you wouldn't mind if I call you sometime?"

Call me? Are you kidding! Call me anytime, Tall, Dark, and Handsome.

"Ummm...I guess. My number..." I reach down for my bag. I'm so flustered that I can't remember my own phone number. Then I can't find my phone.

"I know your number, Cadence."

"I gave it to you?" I can't remember.

"Alondra gave it to me."

3

———

THE FRAT PARTY

MADDIE AND I ARE TREKKING UP A FOREST PATH TO AN OLD HOUSE SITTING by its lonesome atop a hill of witchgrass and weeds. It's on the highest summit of Hawthorne. Surrounded by dead twigs and hollowed-out branches, it looms above thousands of trees, making it seem isolated. Turning back and looking down through the oaks and elms, I can still make out the evening lights of the university. The Billington House is the oldest house on campus. It's even older than Alondra's. Probably older than anything in a five-hundred-mile radius. Maddie and I are walking hand in hand. I'm not sure if it's out of affection or because the dark path up to the haunted house is giving me the heebie-jeebies.

I feel silly being so scared, but the tree branches tap each other and the wind howls under moonlight. I hear the evening creatures scurrying —probably squirrels—and the distinct sound of an owl. It's like right out of a horror movie. I think that's part of the house's charm, especially around Halloween.

"I don't like it," I say as we walk. I'm really just making conversation, trying to get my mind off the surroundings.

"Whatcha mean, Katie?" Maddie asks. She seems calm.

"It's dark and creepy."

"It's haunted," Maddie says with a chuckle. She winks at me.

She's acting like it's a joke, but she isn't fooling me. I know her well enough to know she's nervous too.

"Can you blame Abigail for consulting a witch?" I ask. "It's sad in a way."

"Yeah, I probably would have fucking cut Josiah's balls off," she says with a nod. "But I don't think it's sad. Abigail deserved it."

Honestly, I could care less about the Billingtons' curse, but talking about it, talking about something—anything right now—gets my mind off the dreary hilltop.

Let me tell you what I've gathered about the curse, attending Hawthorne University over the past year. I think it's a real sad story.

Josiah Billington, a Quaker from Scotland, was married to Abigail, a lovely girl from Tallahassee with long dark hair and pretty green eyes. They built their haunted house on the highest hilltop in the forest—the one we're climbing now. They lived a normal, mundane life until Josiah fell in love with another woman living on the neighbor's plantation. Then rumor claimed that there was an illegitimate child, Maverick—and not only was the baby illegitimate, he was brown-skinned. Josiah tried to cover it up and forget the disgrace, but the girl from Tallahassee could never forget.

Abigail consulted a witch named Escoba Hawthorne, a local voodoo queen who had recently moved from New Orleans. After agreeing on payment, Escoba asked Abigail to get something from Mr. Billington that only he possessed. Abigail cut a lock of her husband's brown hair. Then the witch cooked a foul-smelling bloody stew outside her shack while chanting magic charms. Only Escoba didn't curse Josiah—she cursed Abigail. Because Josiah was Escoba's lover.

"Escoba didn't really do anything," I say to Maddie. "Spells aren't real."

"The two boys died from consumption." Maddie lets go of my hand—I wish she hadn't—and then she touches her fingers as if relating a list. "The girl died from the school roof falling on her head. And Josiah was rammed by a bull. Everyone died a month after the witch brewed Abigail's hex. I'd say that proves curses *are* real, Cadence."

I hear something in the bushes and grab her hand again. She chuckles but doesn't pull away. She's acting all brave, but I know she's creeped out. As I look back, we're far enough from the campus lights that it's only getting darker, except for occasional strobing lights emanating from the house at the top of the hill.

"It's a hex, Katie," Maddie insists.

The story goes that while Abigail was busy walking around the witch's house of mysteries, touching her shrunken heads, shells, gems, and cauldrons, Escoba cut a lock from Abigail's long hair. She didn't add Josiah's hair to the cauldron—she added Abigail's.

"Well, Escoba didn't cast a spell because spells aren't real. Maybe she just killed them. Then she stole the house."

"Fine, Kate," Maddie says. "But if it that's true, we should still be scared of the house. A murderer makes a pretty evil ghost too."

Right. Exactly. And that's not making me feel any better.

We walk up to the front door alone, and I'm shaking a little from the cold, or maybe from the Billington curse. Actually, I'm still seriously creeped out, even with strobe lights flashing through the central window, reminding us of the party inside. The full moon is shining above us, lighting the path up to the door. Flies are buzzing around, and I swat at one near my face. Maddie clutches my other hand a little more tightly. I knew she was scared. I don't think she likes the look of the front of the house in the darkness either. When we reach a wooden gate, I put my hand on the latch. That's when Maddie touches my hand and screams in my ear.

"Fucking stop!" I yell.

Maddie bursts into laughter and embraces me more tightly. "Happy Halloween, bitch," she says, still lost in uncontrollable laughter.

When the front door creaks open, this tall, geeky redhead with pimples, carrying a red plastic cup of beer, gestures for us to enter, and all my ghostly fears leave me. The sound of music helps break the spell. But my stomach is still turning—in a good sort of way, because I'm thinking of Bryce.

The inside of the Billington House is much different than the creepy exterior. It's a typical frat house with boys sitting in recliners and beanbag chairs drinking beer, ladies swaying to music, and boys playing pool. Posters of half-naked girls are spoiling the classy antique walls, and lots of leftover antique furniture, frosty glass windowpanes, and vases fill the house.

I'm looking for Bryce, but he's not there. Nick is. Nick rushes over, hugs Maddie, and plants a long kiss on her cheek. That doesn't surprise me. Then he says hi to me. Hi, Nick.

I've known him since we took an anthropology course together last year. For a while he and my BFF were just friends. But apparently, since her fallout with Patrick, they're getting closer.

Nick has on a simple white button-down and black slacks. He's in a really good mood. He always is. He starts introducing me to all sorts of friends. I kind of get lost in the shuffle.

Soon I even lose Maddie. I pick up a beer from an ice chest and sit myself down on a beat-up leather recliner in the living room. A few girls are drunk, practically drooling or comatose, on a nearby sofa. The music is loud. It's some kind of heavy shit; I'm not sure what. But I like it.

There before me is a large frosted-glass window, probably from the nineteenth century, overlooking the fields. I can barely see the university buildings through the trees, but I know they're down the hill. This must be the infamous window at the center of the house where Escoba stands at night. I look for the candle but don't see it. And I remember the story as I'm sipping my beer by my lonesome.

That's when Bryce walks over. He always dresses so nicely. He's wearing a black silk shirt with jeans. He has a little bit of brown stubble along his cheeks, which looks really yummy, but his dark brown hair is combed back perfectly. I nervously run my hand through my own hair.

"Hi, Cadence."

"Hi." I'm trying to act really cool and nonchalant.

He sips his beer and looks at me with his famous wry smile. It's like he's always amused by me. That's kind of annoying. But those bright blue eyes looking down at me make it worth it. I'm sinking into them.

"Sucks you decided not to join us," he says.

"I'm just so busy with studies, you know," I lie.

"Well, I can tell you personally that Alondra was really disappointed."

"She seems to be," I say with a nod. "She seems so distant lately."

"She is." He nods and sips again. "She's busy too. We're busy. And...I think she's disappointed. You would have done well in our honors program."

We both turn to the window. He seems uncomfortable with the silence between us, but I don't really mind, I like just sitting beside him.

"But we welcome you anytime you change your mind, Cadence."

"Thanks."

"Well, enjoy the party." He starts to walk away.

Wait! That's it?

"Are you a member of Psi Kappa Psi?" I blurt out like a stupid child. That's the chapter that lives here at the Billington House.

It stops him.

"Was," he replies. Then he stiffens and gestures to his chest. "Before I graduated. I'm an honoree, Cadence. Since I graduated, I come by once in a while. Especially for annual back-to-school parties."

"I...I didn't know I'd ever get to meet an *honoree*," I say sarcastically. Then I resume sucking my beer bottle.

He smiles.

He doesn't go. He hovers over me hesitantly.

Then we're both staring at that infamous window again. I'm wondering if, after the party, candlelight will be shining.

He drinks more beer. So do I.

I like sitting beside him. I really do. Even though we don't say anything, I like just being near him. It sort of sends tingles down my back, you know, like in a lovesick schoolgirl sort of way. I know, it's stupid. But I also know that I'm starting to like him. I wonder if he likes me.

I turn for a moment and catch Maddie. She's talking with Nick but flashing me a huge grin.

Bitch!

"You stayed in this house?" I ask Bryce, trying to break our silence.

He nods. He pulls over a large beanbag chair and plops down near me. "Yeah. When I was a student. What's wrong with it?"

"Nothing. It's haunted. That window..." I point with a beer bottle in my hand. "It's lit up every night by a ghost. Escoba's ghost. You know the story."

"Yeah." He chuckles. "I know the tale, Cadence. But, between you and me, it's just a ghost story. And it's not Escoba who haunts that window. It's Abigail."

"Huh?"

"Who told you it was Escoba?" Bryce asks, furrowing his brow. "Escoba's been seen in the halls, but Abigail likes the window. Don't you know what Abigail did to Escoba?"

Honestly, looking into his mesmerizing eyes, I really don't care.

"You don't know about Abigail's ghost?" Bryce repeats. "After the Billington family was cursed, Escoba and Maverick took up residence in this house."

"I know."

He shakes his head and, with the hand holding his beer, he points to the window. "But Abigail began showing up with a lit candle by that window every night. It shone in the evening, even when Escoba didn't have company." He looks at me incredulously. "You really don't know about Abigail's ghost, Cadence? That's the best part of the story."

"I just know that Escoba got rid of Abigail and her whole family so she and Maverick could get the town."

"No, she didn't get rid of Abigail." He shakes his head. He seems to get more excited at the prospect of telling me more. It's like he's teaching me again and he loves it. "After the Billington family died, Escoba's eight-year-old son, Maverick—Josiah's illegitimate son—started seeing Abigail's ghost. One night the boy saw her standing here in the living room, with her back turned toward him, by the window. She was just sort of staring out into the woods. And Maverick began seeing repeated visions of her, screaming every night, waking Escoba from her sleep."

"So the house was haunted even before Escoba died?" I ask.

"Yeah. Abigail."

"I thought the ghost was Escoba," I say with a shrug.

"No. One day, Escoba saw Abigail's ghost too. In the middle of the night—when all was quiet and dark in her bedroom, as her son slept calmly beside her—Escoba turned and looked with one eye at an open window. The drapes were moving, as if in a slow breeze. But there was no wind. Perhaps the shutters had moved. So Escoba closed her eyes. But then she heard a noise from the side of the bed her son slept on.

"In the doorway to the hall stood an apparition. It was a pale woman with long black hair. She held a curved knife in one hand and a candle in the other. She stood over Maverick with malice as he slept calmly. Escoba screamed. Holding the candle over the child, the ghost did not move or lose her smile.

"The next morning, Escoba consulted her grimoire in order to oust the apparition from their home. She used items the Billingtons had left behind, in a chest in the basement, to serve as a connection with the ghost. Then she concocted another brew, in the grassy field around the home, spewing curses and spitting in a cauldron.

"Escoba's body was found three days later, sitting in a rocking chair, upstairs in her bedroom. She was holding a crucifix, and a knife had been stuck into her chest. Even in death her eyes were wide open, staring toward the hallway in terror. It was assumed that her death was from suicide."

"Then the ghost at the window could still be Escoba?"

"Abigail was found a year later," he says, shaking his head, "on neighbor Jesse M. Davis's farm, grazing naked like an animal, still catatonic, not saying a word. Everyone was overjoyed to know she was alive, but it's said that she never spoke a word again. Some say she was committed to the local sanitarium—at the time, a fate not much better than death. Others say she committed suicide in the forest. And others claim her spirit still haunts the halls of the Billington House today.

"And many still see a candle burning in the downstairs window, in the middle of the night, along with Abigail, *not* Escoba. Cadence, *Abigail* holds a long curved knife, staring out the window with wild eyes. Abigail."

God, that's even creepier than the original story.

I lean back in the old recliner. We both sip more beer and look out the window together. I hear the music again. It's really loud and comforting because it's not scary. I really don't want to hear any more ghost stories.

"It's just a story," he says with a chuckle. But he's totally creeping me out again.

"It sounds like a true story," I say. "I've seen their graves."

"Well, if it really happened, just like the story said, then the house really isn't haunted, is it? It was just occupied by a witch and a madwoman. But you know, you should come here next week. We have a great party on Halloween every year. The stories only make it more fun."

"Yeah, I know." I shrug. "I was here last year on Halloween." I look up at him, tapping my beer bottle with a fingernail.

"Want a tour of our haunted house?" he asks.

Uh...yeah.

He laughs, gets up, and reaches out toward me. I jump up and grab his hand, probably a little too eagerly. He laughs again. I feel like I've lost my cool act and am now acting really geeky. Then I find myself about two inches from his face.

Holy shit!

I can't breathe. I even feel the breath from his mouth. And for a moment, just a moment, Mr. Calm looks nervous too. He runs a hand gently through my hair. Then he grins and tugs my hand. "Come on, I'll show you around our haunted house." Meanwhile, I'm probably looking like a total buffoon, staring into those dreamy blue eyes.

"Yeah, okay," I say, trying to act cool again.

Show me. I'd love a tour of your run-down ghost shack.

And he does. He shows me everything, from the basement to a creaky wooden hallway leading to a room with a balcony. We're alone, but we're not alone. It feels intimate even though every room of the house is crawling with frat boys and their dates.

I love the way he incorporates history into every room. It actually feels like my history TA is teaching. He talks about the Civil War and how the house was occupied by the Confederate army before the Battle of Atlanta. It was on one of the highest peaks for miles and was a perfect lookout for the military. Then he shows me a bed warmer that's still stowed away in one of the rickety wooden closets. I love it.

"And there is the master bedroom," he says, gesturing to the end of the hallway. He's got a gaping smile and is still holding my hand. His hand feels so warm. It makes me tingle all over. We're dodging bodies along the hallway to get there. I see a couple lying in each other's arms on the floor, either comatose or too drunk to move.

When we get to the bedroom, I'm disappointed. From the tale, I was expecting to see a great big antique bed and large windows. Now I'm picturing Bryce's story of Abigail standing over Maverick with her curved knife, dressed in a white gown, with a wild stare. But there are three bunkbeds, using every bit of space possible in the large room. The walls still have white plaster. "I wonder if this is the same color it was two hundred years ago." I touch a wall.

Bryce tells me it is.

There are two desks in the room and, like in the rest of the house, the walls are decorated with posters of ladies in G-strings holding up beer.

"This is where Abigail stood over her victim," says Bryce with pride. Then he turns to one of the desks. "And there, according to legend"—he points to a wall—"is where Escoba sat for days with a curved dagger in the center of her chest."

How the hell does he know where Escoba sat? But I love how he acts so sure of himself.

"Doesn't look that way anymore," I reply with a stupid smile.

"Grisly isn't it?"

Bryce is still holding my hand. He refuses to let go, even when we're weaving around people in the crowd. We're sweating a little, but neither of us lets go. That's so cute.

"I stayed in this very room last year," he says.

"Really?"

"Yeah." Then he gently touches my chin and looks down into my eyes again. "When the wind blows and it's dark, I can swear I hear screams. I think it's Escoba."

I'm waiting for him to yell into my ears stupidly, like Maddie did at the fence, but he doesn't. He just grimaces. But, honestly, we're more lost in each other's eyes than giving a fuck about poor Abigail and any ghosts.

I raise an eyelid. "You said...you thought it wasn't real." I force myself to sip some beer and find it difficult to swallow.

He shrugs and we walk on. "Let me show you something."

Okay.

We walk back down the stairs, across a room full of drunken dancers, and through a creaky door. It leads down a flight of wooden stairs into the basement. This is where we're finally truly alone.

I'm a little apprehensive as we walk down the steps of the old wooden stairwell. The wood creaks terribly with every step, and I'm scared it's going to crack under my feet. But we make it to the bottom.

He takes out a lighter and lights a candle on the wall. It's dim, but it casts shadows throughout the small room. The wooden walls and rafters are dank and dusty. And now I'm beginning to freak out. Bryce's candle barely lights the room.

I sneeze.

Bryce tightens his grip around my fingers, almost as if he knew I'd be afraid. He leads me to a large chest.

"Perhaps we should go back," I say.

He chuckles. "Don't worry, Cadence. You have to see this. I found it last year when I was at a party like tonight's. It's really cool. You're gonna love this."

He lets go of my hand. I really don't like that. In the shadows, it was his hand that comforted me. But he needs both hands to open the heavy wooden chest. It reminds me of something you'd find in a pirate ship. Then he flashes the candlelight over the opening. The yellow light outlines his face, which looks a little spooky in the darkness. His hard jawline and those bushy eyebrows. His blue eyes, now flickering in the candlelight, looking down at the chest and staring back at me. He smiles. Damn, he's so hot.

I sneeze again.

"Go ahead," he says. He moves the candle closer to the chest and gestures for me to explore.

Inside the chest are a bunch of old things with thick dust covering most of them. There's a portrait the size of my hand. I pick it up and he shines the flickering light over it. It's a drawing of a girl. I'm guessing it's Abigail's daughter? Or Abigail? Or a friend? Or...who knows? It could be anyone. But her dress is long and formal and appears to be from the early nineteenth century. There's also a very beautiful necklace and a small mirror. It reflects a shadow of me in the flickering light, which really creeps me out, and I quickly put it back. There's also a pile of very old clothing at the bottom. I rummage through a scarf, a light coat, and a dress. It's all caked in dust. Then I see a drawing of a woman wearing a bandana, bright gold rings on her fingers and ears, and a long black dress —Escoba? I don't know.

While I'm exploring the contents of the chest, I catch Bryce staring at me. I look up at him, and he places a hand on my shoulder and smiles.

"I found this last year. Great, isn't it?"

"Sure."

"I knew you'd appreciate it because you love history so much, Cadence. It's never left the room. I don't think it's worth much, but it's history, you know? I was gonna show Alondra...if she doesn't already know. You like it?"

"Yeah." I do. I love it. It's like looking in a museum.

I take out the scarf. I think it's purple, but it's so covered with dust that I'm not sure. Then I start sneezing terribly.

"Sorry... Sorry, Bryce. I'm allergic to dust."

"Oh." He gently moves me away. "I'll close it then." He closes the heavy chest and takes my hand again. A cloud of dust forms, and my nose becomes worse. I just can't stop sneezing.

"This might sound silly, but you always seem so interested in class. I think you have a love for history more than most students."

"I've always liked it." I sneeze again. "It's like peering through a window into the past. It's like a journey, you know. Their story. Their journey. But a real story."

"Yes, I know. That's why I like it too."

Somehow it sounds to me like he said, "*That's why I like you too.*"

He brings my hand up to his lips and kisses it. I don't see much of him. Only a hint of his hard chin and kind smile under the flickering light. But I feel the whiskers of his unshaven skin. That makes me giggle a little. I giggle nervously. Then I sneeze again.

"Can I kiss you on the lips, Cadence?"

KISS? Hell yeah!

I giggle again. I sneeze halfway through the giggle.

"Okay. But you...better...hurry before I"—I sneeze again—"can't stand still for you."

In a flash, Bryce has his lips on mine. I can't see much. It's like the whole world is literally Bryce and me. His hands move from holding mine to embracing my body. My fear of being alone in the dark in the haunted house is lifted. All I think of is Bryce, his strong arms squeezing me tightly. I'm sort of lost in him. I inhale the scent of his cologne and rub my fingers along his short hair. He pushes his lips more firmly against mine, then gently moves his tongue into my mouth, tasting me. I let him.

But then I sneeze again, ruining everything.

"I think," he says, pulling back slowly, "that I need to take you back upstairs."

Gallant Bryce. I'm really starting to like this guy.

"Yeah," I say, his voice having a hypnotic effect on me. But I really don't want to.

He takes my hand.

I sneeze again.

The insulation in the basement is thick, and I can't hear much music until we open the rickety wooden door again. Then the party is louder than ever. Bryce leads me toward the kitchen. He's finally forced to let go of my hand when Maddie grabs me by the arm.

"Katie, come on!" She points to the living room. "We're playing a game."

"All right."

I look back, but Bryce is gone, lost in bodies. I'm not sure what happened to him.

Now it's Maddie who's taking my arm and guiding me, around frat boys, to the living room. I see a few girls from Kappa Alpha Kappa. Maddie sees them too and gives them a dirty look. They stupidly sit around on couches and chairs wearing matching red T-shirts, with their Greek letters in gold, and matching pants: elegant black slacks. If they didn't act so snooty, it might be cute. Well, Maddie and I never liked their chapter.

There are only four fraternity chapters and one sorority at Hawthorne University. Sororities never caught on for one reason or another, and only the most affluent kids end up in it. Maddie and I never even tried—well, Maddie's forbidden to join after joining Dr. Johansen's honor club. Anyway, the only fraternity worth its weight, to me, is Psi Kappa Psi, and that's only because of Tall, Dark, and Handsome.

So we pass the sorority snoots and walk into a large, dimly lit room.

About twenty people are standing around a dining room table covered with an elegant red cloth. In the center of the table is a crystal ball—yeah, an actual crystal ball—illuminated by a row of candles. That's pretty cool.

I sneeze again. The room is obviously full of dusty antique stuff. I look toward the door, and there's a wood cabinet about the age of the house and some dusty lamps.

People are sitting at the table holding unlit candles. The windows are covered in thick dark drapes. All we see is the yellow light emanating from the candles on the table.

Next to the crystal ball is a large board. And on top of that is a white plastic triangular-shaped thing with a central opening. It's a Ouija board. It looks like it's new, from Mattel. Maddie sits with me next to the board, and another five boys sit near us. I look at the large crystal ball again and even touch it. It's covered with dust.

"We're gonna play with the Ouija board." Maddie seems excited. Across from her is Nick, who seems equally enthusiastic. "Have you ever played, Katie?" Maddie asks.

"Yeah, when I was a little girl."

"Well, Cadence," says Nick, "we've been playing with it for a few weeks now, and I promise you it's nothing like you've ever played before. There's a vital energy here. This house has so much paranormal energy from the spirit realm. There's—"

Some girl shushes him. "Place your fingers over the planchette."

I'm still staring at the magnificent crystal ball. I can see reflections of everybody in it. It looks old. I wonder if it was Escoba's. I run my finger along the glass. It's so cold.

"Place your fingers over the planchette," the girl snaps at me.

I look up and am surprised to see that I recognize this girl. It's that weird goth girl I saw at Dr. Johansen's party. She's wearing a long black cloak, black lace gloves, and a very tight black dress showing a lot of cleavage. The candlelight is reflected by her large metallic nose ring, and her skeleton and serpent tattoos seem to dance in the light. She creeps me out.

I shrug, thinking this whole thing is stupid. Then I place a couple of fingers over the central device and look at the board.

"Spirit," the goth girl says, closing her eyes. Her face is serious. "Spirit, we call on you. Here in the house of Escoba and Abigail. Spirit, if you are here, please answer us."

Six people have a finger or two on this central device, the *planchette*: the goth freak, who's leading this Mattel séance, Nick, Maddie, a few boys I don't know, and me. But nothing is happening. I turn from the board and look at the crystal ball again. I marvel at it. I'm taken by it, just like the time I went to the Smithsonian and gazed at the Hope Diamond. It must be expensive. It looks expensive.

"Cadence!" hisses Goth Girl. "You have to concentrate! You're messing up the energy. Either concentrate or get the fuck out!"

"Hey!" cries Maddie. "If Katie goes, I go."

"It's all right," I say with a chuckle. "I'll play."

So I'm back to touching the *planchette*, as the goth girl calls it. Then the goth girl starts acting weird—really weird. She starts swaying and moving up and down while touching the white piece of plastic, closing her eyes really hard. She's so focused. I look at her, then at the boys, then back at her again. I realize her movements, up and down, up and down, actually appear lewd. It's as if she's orgasming over the table. The boys love it. They can't take their eyes off her. And being overweight, her tight clothes put her large breasts on display. I think the boys are more focused on her bosom than the board.

"Come to us, spirits! Come and join us in this room. Talk to us through the board. Enter from the spirit world and speak to us. We are here to speak with you."

The white plastic thingy, the *planchette*, seems to move a little. With my other hand, I take my half-drunk beer and take a sip. Goth bitch opens her eyes and stares right at me with venom. "Focus! I say focus or leave us, Cadence!" she hisses at me.

"Christ, Mira!" cries my best friend. "Leave Katie alone!"

Mira lets go of the planchette and slams her hands on the table. "You wanted her to be here, Maddie! If she's here, she joins. Otherwise..." She turns to me. "She needs to get the fuck out!"

I get up, embarrassed. All the others look up, feeling pity for me. That makes me angrier.

"It's okay, Cadence." Maddie smiles, grabbing my arms and pulling me back down. Then she glares at Mira. "Mira can be a real bitch, Katie, but she's nice when you get to know her. Sometimes. Forget her. Come, come play with us."

I sit back down, irate. I'm staying for my friend, and only for her, but I scowl at goth bitch. Mira takes a deep breath and touches the white plastic thingy again. She closes her eyes. With one hand, I drink more beer. She opens a sliver of an eye, but then she closes her eyes tightly again, ignoring my transgression.

"Spirits," she says. Then she takes a few deep breaths and opens her eyes. They seem wild. Then she looks at each of us. "Repeat after me. Spirits." We repeat it. "Spirits, come to us. In this house." She speaks slowly, and we repeat every word. I play along, but I still take a swig or two of beer in rebellion. "Spirits, move the planchette and show us you are here. If you have come to us, move the planchette to *YES*. You who remain in the spirit world. You who preside with the witch Escoba and the ghost Abigail. Come to us. Come to us, Escoba and Abigail. Show that you are with us tonight." She starts doing that up-and-down motion again, with her eyes closed. The boys are staring at her again.

And then...the plastic thingy moves. It moves slowly over the word *YES*.

We all smile, and I hear murmuring, for the first time, from the spectators behind us. There must be ten to twenty people gathered in the room. But everyone is quiet. Everyone is here for Mira's séance.

Mira is ecstatic. "Good. Good! Now, tell us, spirit. Tell us. Send us a message."

The plastic thingy moves to the letter *I*. It sort of vibrates under my hand. I wonder if Mira is moving it, or maybe Maddie. It moves again. First it circles around the board; then it slides over another letter: *L*.

"Excellent," cries Mira. "Excellent. I ... L ..."

The planchette moves to the letter *U*. And then *V*. And then *U*.

Nick mouths the letters. He writes them on a notepad. Then he chuckles and says, "I love you. It says *I love you!*"

I'm rolling my eyes. Maddie catches me and gestures for me to shut it.

"All right," says Mira. "You love us. Who? Who are you? Identify yourself, spirit."

The planchette moves again. It circles around and around the board.

Then it lands on letters. It starts moving faster, and now I'm sure someone is moving it.

The next letters come down in a fury. Nick jots down each letter on a piece of paper:

E M I L Y H A W T H O R N E

I lift my fingers and stare at my best friend with rage. *Emily Hawthorne. Emily.* Emily is my mother's name. The only one in the room who knows that is Maddie.

"What are you doing!" I yell.

"Nothing," Maddie says innocently.

I jump up. "What kind of a joke is this!" I cry, hitting the table with a fist. "It's not funny!"

"Sit down, Cadence!" shouts Mira. "You're disrupting the energy!"

I'm not amused. Maddie shakes her head again.

The rest of the goth bohemians stupidly believe they've stumbled on Abigail's family tree. They're excited. But no one except my best friend knows the name of my mother—and why I'm beyond pissed—my dear mother who is very ill at the moment and in the hospital. I don't get it. It's not like Madison to play such a sick practical joke.

"Is this a fucking joke?" I snap at Maddie. "What are you doing?"

"Katie, no! It's not me. I swear." She's shaking her head desperately. I'm ready to deck her. My own best friend. I want to kill her for this.

"Then who is it?" I'm pointing at her. I'm accusing her, and I'm only getting angrier that she's playing dumb.

"It's just a game," Maddie says. "I didn't do anything, Kate. I swear."

"Will you sit down!" shouts Mira.

"Forget you and your game!" I shout at Mira. "You're all a bunch of creeps!" Then I turn to my so-called best friend. "And you... it's not funny!"

I storm out of the room.

"What's the matter with her?" Nick asks as I leave.

I'm set on walking back to my dorm when Bryce, of all people, stops me by the exit. He's holding a red plastic cup. "Got you one," he says with a big smile. He tries to hand the drink to me, but I don't take it. He looks in the direction I'm heading and watches me throw on my long black coat. He looks disappointed. "Going somewhere?"

"I have to go, Bryce. I... I forgot I have a paper due Monday." But now that Mr. Handsome is here, I falter in my resolve.

"Oh, all right. Well, it was really great seeing you, Cadence."

"You too."

And he touches my hand. His hand. For a flash, it reminds me of the basement, but my feet sort of push me toward the door. I just nod and smile at him as best I can.

I'm not only angry and confused as to why my BFF would spoil the little Mattel séance for me; I'm also totally freaked out. The whole thing was super creepy. And now, as I walk down the hill alone, under the full moon, I'm even more spooked. I hear an owl and imagine a wolf's howl. The trees cast shadows in the moonlight all the way down the path back to the university and my dormitory.

Then my cell phone rings. It's my mom and dad's number.

"What?" I snap.

"Cadence," says my father. He sounds terrible.

"Yeah, Dad?"

"Cadence...your mother... She's...she died."

4

___

FALL LEAVES

In every movie I've ever seen, when a loved one has died, it's a gloomy, cloudy day with a mist blowing and all these morose mourners walking in single file, wiping tears from their eyes with white laced hand-kerchiefs and shaky white-gloved fingers—and black umbrellas; people usually have black umbrellas too. They're dressed in dark double-breasted suits or lovely flowing black dresses. Everyone's hugging each other and looking down at the ground, bawling their eyes out. But they all look beautiful for the dead.

Why? She's dead. Get over it.

I don't look pretty. I'm not even wearing makeup.

I'm too dainty and thin to carry the mahogany casket—or maybe I just don't care to. Instead I walk beside it while my brother, uncle, and mom's older friends, wearing T-shirts and shorts, carry the casket. It's hot outside. Fall's coming late this year.

I don't cry. I never cry. I never do.

It's raining. But it's figurative rain, you know, water dripping inside my brain. It's not actually raining. Outside, on the fields of the cemetery, it's hot and muggy. It's a lovely day in Atlanta. The sky is a beautiful cerulean blue. The bluebirds are singing. It's not raining at all. Only in my heart. In my chest. There it feels tight and constricted, and it kind of weighs me down as I walk beside the coffin. Inside is where the tears are. Inside there's this fog, shrouding all the pretty birds and lovely trees, and the scene looks just like those funerals in the movies.

But water actually does drip down my face. Sweat is dripping down my forehead.

I have on a lovely black dress. It once belonged to Mother. I liked it even before she died.

I don't want to mourn. Just like I don't want to cry.

The thing is, I have to get back to school.

The ceremony is really short. My brother and I say a lovely eulogy. He wrote it, and I nervously intone a couple of sentences from a sheet of paper I'm holding with a shaky hand.

Then it's over. I get in my cheap twenty-year-old Honda Accord and drive the one hundred miles back to Hawthorne University.

You see, Mom was dying anyway. And I think everyone saw it coming.

I could be sad. I see a bumper sticker and it says *CRY*. That finally makes me cry a little on my drive back to Hawthorne.

I can't concentrate in class. I study. I'm really smart, you know. I always get good grades. But I can't drop the images of the hot and sweaty funeral from my mind. Such a lovely day. Such a fucked-up lovely day. Such an awful feeling. I still feel it. That tightness. I want it to leave me, but it won't.

In Alondra's metaphysical history class, I take an exam on the various torture techniques utilized throughout the Middle Ages. I know I'm gonna get an A, because I studied all the required reading and even the optional materials before I left for the weekend.

5

AFTER CLASS

"I NEED A WEEK OFF FROM SCHOOL, DR. JOHANSEN."

Alondra is stuffing a MacBook laptop and a folder full of papers into her black bag. She seems in a real pissy mood.

"All right, Cadence," she says with disinterest.

We're at the front of the lecture hall, and all the students are leaving. I know Maddie is waiting for me outside.

Alondra has been aloof over the last few weeks. She used to smile at me a lot. Now it seems she doesn't want to give me the time of day. Of course I didn't sign up for her research freak show. Maddie did. Maybe that's it?

"You did well on the test, Cadence." Alondra stuffs a laser pointer into her bag.

"Thanks. I thought the witch hunts were interesting. Particularly the method of judging the witches. It seems so stupid."

"It proves how stupid men are," Alondra says with a shrug and a faint smile.

"Will we be getting our papers back soon, Dr. Johansen?"

"Excuse me, Cadence, but I really have to go," she says rudely, practically hitting my shoulder with her bag. "If you need a week off, you can just let Administration know. You needn't tell me."

"I know, but my mother died, Alondra."

I don't know why I said it. I tried to avoid saying it. Then I just said it.

Alondra stops in her tracks for a moment. I watch her pale hand rest on the podium, and she nods and cocks her head back. "How terrible. I'm sure you were close, right?"

And that's just as awkward.

"She was like my mother." It was meant as a joke, but it sounds like I'm mocking my teacher. I chuckle stupidly but Alondra doesn't laugh. She looks down. She seems genuinely upset.

"I'm sorry for you," she says.

I feel that tightness again. Somehow, it seems even worse in front of her.

"That's why I need time. I need to, you know, mourn, I guess."

Isn't that what people do? How should I know? My granddad died when I was four. I never knew him. That's all I knew about death—until Mom. People need time—right?—to feel shitty and sad.

Dr. Johansen turns around with a sad smile. She lays down her heavy bag for a moment.

"I'm so sorry for you, Cadence."

A tear runs down my cheek. I don't know why. I haven't cried at all since I saw that stupid bumper sticker but, somehow, for someone to acknowledge me makes me feel awful. Particularly Alondra, whose sweet smile always puts me at ease. Her kindness hurts.

"I'm so sorry," she says again. "You know, I really hoped I could work more closely with you. You're at the top of your class. That was the other reason you were invited for dinner."

"I thought it was because I'm an atheist," I say with a stupid grin. I'm still trying to be funny, but it's even more awkward now. I'm brushing tears from my cheek.

"Are you an atheist?" she says, surprised. I don't know why it surprises her. "That's not the profile I was looking for."

"I think I am."

"I don't think you're an atheist, Cadence... I'm so sorry to hear about your mother." She looks down for a moment; then she looks deeply into my eyes and puts a hand on my shoulder. "It is this pain that I study. It's this thing that we all turn from: pain. But it's an energy, just like joy, that we carry with us all our lives. I research nature's energy. Pain and pleasure. Even pain is a part of nature. But your ghosts are always so deep..." She looks down for a moment; then she nods. "Of course, of course you can have a week...but I can't speak for your other professors. You should let the provost know."

"I already have."

"That's good."

Alondra gently raises my chin and smiles. Her green eyes seem to pierce right through my soul. Then she brushes her hand along my hair like...like my mother. This reminder almost puts me over the edge.

"Please, don't worry about a thing. If you'd like, it would please me if you can come again to my house this Friday. I know you haven't signed up, but you can come for our initiation meeting. I want to make an exception for you. I think you will find it's not as scary as you might have believed. And our coven always honors those who have recently passed. I think it will help you through this. I'd really like to do this for you, Cadence."

"I'll see."

"Come if you wish. Anyway, I'm so fortunate to have someone as bright as you in class, whatever you decide."

"Thanks, Dr. Johansen," I reply with a smile. She's so nice.

"Please. Call me Alondra."

6

THE CEREMONY

I TAKE ALONDRA UP ON HER OFFER AND RIDE BACK TO HER HOUSE ALONE, IN my beat-up Honda, on Friday night. I'm very late. I made a tactful decision earlier not to tell Maddie I was coming. I didn't want her to know. We've made up since the party—I can't stay mad at Maddie for long—but I warned her never to mention the séance again.

Anyway, I'm crossing Alondra's gorgeous manicured front lawn, meandering along the dirt path to the door. It's a drab, gloomy day, and there's not much visibility. Looking back, I can't even make out my car. It's too foggy. In front of me the fog seems to amplify the yellow light coming from Alondra's old mansion. I shiver in my thin black cotton sweater; I forgot my coat at the dorm. Winter is coming. Soon the trees will turn their lovely red and yellow autumn colors to brown and it will be cold.

I knock on her door. She has a large antique metal knocker. I smile at its old-fashioned look. It's very Alondra.

Then I wait. I wait a long time, staring out at the trees under the mist.

"Hey, Cadence." It's Bryce. Normally I'd be shy, but I'm not in the mood for shyness.

"Hi, Bryce."

He gives me a gentle hug. "I heard about your mom," he says. "I'm so sorry."

"She's dead."

He loses his smile for a moment.

Well, she is dead, so get over it. Is dwelling on it going to make things better?

He places his hand gently on my shoulder. I think he would have preferred to hold my hand, but he's cautious. Then, just as he did many weeks ago, he walks beside me down Alondra's gorgeous hall. I expect to head straight to the kitchen like last time, but we don't. Instead we head into a room that looks like a den, with a sliding glass door.

I'm admiring her home. It's so chic. As much as she adores history, the interior is ultramodern. As Bryce works the lock to the glass door, I look at the stonemasonry on the chimney. Everything is in sharp angles and very chic. The white leather sofas surround a soft, furry white carpet with white wood around its perimeter. A flat-screen TV is mounted to one of the walls, which are painted light coffee-brown. How can she afford all this stuff?

Bryce finally yanks open the sliding door. "I told her she should have left it open. It keeps jamming. Anyway, come on, we're waiting for you."

Waiting for me?

Everyone is gathered around a blazing bonfire, the height of a person, in the center of Alondra's huge backyard. It's in a large open field of wild grass, like that surrounding the Billington House, with giant trees. Unlike the front yard, none of her backyard is manicured. In fact, it blends in with the surrounding forest.

Eleven people are gathered around the flames, surrounded by a circle of large white stones. They're all wearing these weird black hooded cloaks, like the clothes ancient druids wore. Alondra's hood is down, and her long black hair is hanging over it. Beside Alondra is my friend Maddie. I can't make out Maddie's face under her cloak, but I recognize her pants underneath. Dr. Reardon is there. He's wearing a button-down and slacks. His cloak is over his face, but I recognize him from his old-person clothes. Then I recognize Mira and a shy girl, Hannah, who I met at Alondra's party.

Bryce and I approach the circle around the fire and, for some reason, the walk seems to take a long time. It's like everything is in slow motion.

As we draw closer, I realize they're all holding hands and chanting quietly. It's not English.

"They're waiting for you," Bryce repeats. "Don't be afraid."

I look up into his eyes. He smiles sweetly. Then his hand tightens over mine.

I'm not afraid. I'd never be afraid in those hands.

All right, I'm a little afraid. But the tightness in my chest has been lifted. Now I feel butterflies rather than dread, but I'm still nervous. What is this freak club all about? I'm thinking of walking out.

"Cadence, you made it." Alondra gets up. She has that infamous smile of hers. "We built this fire for you. Please, sit."

She looks weird. Under her cloak, her pants are old-fashioned. It looks like she found them in the basement of the Billington home. And she has on really thick black makeup. Her mascara's like Mira's everyday dark makeup.

I sit down next to Bryce.

We're all sitting in cheap white plastic chairs around Alondra's bonfire. The odd thing that strikes me—aside from my professor's attire, and everything else—is the fire. There's no outdoor pit. Just a pile of wood thrown down on her lawn and ignited into a big conflagration. That's weird. Well, the whole thing is weird.

"Everyone knows what's happened to your mother, Cadence," says Alondra. She looks creepy, but with her gentle smile, it seems okay. She sits back down. Her face turns grave, and her speech is slow and measured. "I would like to perform a ceremony in her honor. If you let us, it might ease some of your pain. But more importantly, it will benefit your mother. It's up to you. If, at any time, you feel uncomfortable, we can stop. The coven is just happy to have the opportunity to be with you tonight. And...it is a special night because we are initiating Hannah, Tammy, and your friend Madison."

"Okay," I say. But I don't know if it's okay. And Alondra pauses for a moment to check if I'm sure. I don't say anything else. I just sit there watching everybody stare at me.

"We are here to pray for you," Alondra says with another comforting grin. "It is our hope that your mother passes swiftly to the higher realm. I, and many of the others here, believe the spirit moves to the Summerland. Then the soul moves on to inhabit another body in another place. With this ceremony, we can help her on her journey. Without our efforts, sometimes the soul can get stuck. Then it can become a ghost."

"Like Abigail," Maddie says.

"No," Alondra says with a chuckle. Then she turns grave. "This is quite serious, Madison. I'm not talking ghost stories."

"Okay," Maddie says. Then she gives me a comforting smile. It's a pitying smile, and knowing my BFF so well, it makes me a little sad.

Alondra reaches under her plastic chair and picks up a photograph and a candle. "We have this memorial candle. And your friend Maddie brought me a picture of your mother. We'd like to light the candle in memory of her, if you will permit us."

"Sure. All right." *I'm game. Why the hell not?*

I turn to Maddie. She surprises me. I expected to see her whimsical, fun face, but she's very serious.

"Katie," Alondra says to me, calling me by my nickname. "If you can hold hands, we will all begin."

I laugh. No one else does. "All right, but...I really don't believe in any of this," I say. "But thanks for all your trouble."

"It doesn't matter if you believe, Cadence," Bryce says. He grabs my hand. "What matters is that you are here. And we are here for you."

"Exactly, Bryce," says Alondra.

My left hand is holding Maddie's, and my right is holding my handsome TA's. I look at Alondra again and she nods, trying to comfort me, and closes her eyes. She closes them tightly, just like Mira did. Then I look over at Mira. The girl's copying Alondra, and I suddenly realize how her mannerisms seem to mimic my professor's. Then I think about the Ouija board, and for a moment I get a little upset and unnerved. I confronted Maddie about the incident, and she swears that she never told anyone my mother's name.

Everyone bows their heads down. I don't. I just gaze at the flickering flames.

I like the touch of my best friend's and boyfriend's hands. Their closeness is comforting. I also like that all these people are doing whatever they're doing for me. But I still feel uneasy.

Then Dr. Reardon speaks. I had forgotten all about him. "We who have been taught to follow a false god, taught to love all people, even those who hurt us, to listen to fools, to follow those who are misaligned or stupid, to live in guilt over our pleasures and live in pain—you who sit in this circle need do this no longer. None of us in the circle need do this any longer. We are protected, just as the darkness shades light. By Baphomet, the holy one. Through darkness roams the hunter. Through the hunter comes the sacrifice. We follow truth and believe in shadows, under the embrace of Gaia, that shall guide us toward our salvation."

"Atman," says Alondra.

"Atman," say the others.

"And for Emily." Dr. Reardon looks at me. I shudder. His goatee is shadowed by the dancing flames. He looks almost like a demon. "Allow her to pass over. Allow Cadence's mother to pass over to the Summerland and then beyond. Let her not remain as a ghost or vapor. Let her move on to her next life."

"Atman," says Alondra.

"Atman," say the others.

"So eloquently said," Alondra says, addressing Dr. Reardon.

I look up at the moon. The clouds have dispersed, and I can even see glimpses of stars. If the fog completely lifts, it will be a beautiful night. With the fire, it's the perfect temperature. It warms me and I think about removing my black sweater, but I'm reminded of Mira. I think that any such move will break the weird spell surrounding me, so I do nothing. I sit quietly. Then I look around the fire.

The others begin to raise their hands, and some of them say similar words. Many of their speeches are cloaked in this weird quasireligious shit. I'm not sure what they're referring to. Alondra seems to understand. Hope, one of the older initiates from last year—she stayed, just like Mira —recites a long dirge in a strange language. As she speaks, everyone looks down as if in prayer. Everyone except Alondra. Alondra is staring at me. And when I see her, she nods reassuringly.

I look into the fire. The red and yellow dances and the wood crackles.

Alondra rises. She lifts up her hands to the sky and gazes at the stars. All the fog has lifted. Then Alondra stands before us, addressing us, like she would do in class. Her smile has left her. Everyone opens their eyes, and Bryce and Maddie let go of my hands.

"We are here," Alondra says, "to mourn the passing of Cadence Hawthorne's mother, Emily. We know that her passing was timely. I thank the stars for that. Emily suffered terribly the last years of her life with a debilitating disease. No one should suffer pain. We, here in the circle, are here for the pleasure given to us by the earth. Emily's ailments caused her problems with vision and hearing. She couldn't walk. Because she couldn't see, she even suffered a terrible fall. She finally succumbed to a heart attack. We mourn the death of Cadence's mother, for we know how it has affected our sister Cadence so terribly. And we know how that love, though the bond may not ever be truly severed by death—the greatest illusion—has disturbed Cadence. Please take Emily and have her pass to a happier plane."

"Atman," says Professor Reardon.

"Atman," say the others in unison.

Alondra walks over to me and hands me the candle.

"Cadence," she says, smiling again, "can you light your candle by the fire, please? After you light it, take it back home with you. Let it stay lit as long as it will. Then one day it will burn out. If you wish, you may light it again whenever you feel pain over the loss of your mother. Know that she loved you and that the light from this candle not only represents her, but is her. It's the energy of her in you that shall never burn out. It resides within you, and unlike fire in the physical realm, it will never die. Ultimately, you control where and when such energy will manifest itself. Her love now resides in you and always will. The power of her flame lies in your soul. When you discover that light within, through love and hate, through black and white magic, you shall finally be reborn in full wisdom."

For the first time, I think of the Ouija board. And I think of the words *I luv u.* At the time I shuddered. Now, looking into Alondra's mesmerizing eyes, I think how beautiful the message was. Particularly, I think of how it was meant for me. If it actually was my mother, it was beautiful. It was a message to me right after her death.

And with that, I falter over the fire. Bryce grabs me before I fall. I open up and start crying terribly.

So does the rest of the circle. My grief seems to spread around the fire, and everyone starts crying. Even Mira, who I always thought hated me, bursts into tears. Even stoic and dark Dr. Reardon sheds tears. There are tears from everyone.

Bryce and Maddie help me slowly back to my seat. They hold the candle over my fingers.

Alondra walks over and kneels beside me. She gently lifts my chin and says, "Release your pain, Cadence. There is no reason to be sad any longer. Your mother has been freed to the Summerland. Your love just freed her."

I look up at her. She seems so sure of her words. Then I'm touched by the tears that have streamed down her face.

"Thank you," I say quietly. "Thank you."

Alondra smiles sweetly. "The rest of the evening is secret. You have not signed on. I'm afraid you need to return home... But know that the coven prays for you, Cadence. We are here for you, our sister."

"Thank you," I say softly again.

Everyone looks at me. They all smile sweetly.

I turn and leave.

No one escorts me out. As I reach the sliding glass door, I look back. Once again, around the circle, the group is holding hands. They're chanting something that I cannot understand. Even Bryce is completely immersed in the moment. And this time it's Doctor Reardon, not Alondra, who leads the group. The fire eerily dies down and, in shadows, the group dances around it, following Reardon, circling as if in a trance, mesmerized by the dying flames. I try to close the glass door. A few times. But it won't budge.

I walk back to my car alone. And then I drive home.

7

CRYING

I'm curled up in a ball, in bed, crying my eyes out. It's the middle of the night when I hear the lock turn and Maddie walk in. She's initially cautious not to wake me, creeping slowly to her side of the room, but when she hears me crying, she kneels beside the head of my bed. I feel her fingers run through my hair and rub my neck and back.

"Oh, Cadence."

I don't say anything. I just cry. It seems strange that I didn't do this before. And as much as I liked crying at Alondra's house, I really don't like it now.

"Oh, Kate."

Maddie can't really say much more. She just runs her hand along my dark hair.

I catch a whiff from her arm. It smells strange. It's an outdoor smell of juniper mixed with lavender. And there's an earthen smell. I turn quietly and look at my friend. Only the sliver of light from the door shines over us—she hasn't closed the door yet, nor has she turned on the light. I jump at the sight of her hair. Her hair is a complete mess. And the black mascara from her eyes is running. Her face is smudged with dirt, and there are small leaves stuck in her hair.

"What...what the hell happened to you?" I ask. Even her clothes, the formal black dress and stockings she's wearing, are torn up. Then I catch a few scratches and scrapes at the nape of her neck. "Maddie, what happened?"

I forget all about me. My friend looks like she was assaulted. Then I'm even more surprised when Maddie chuckles.

"Nothing, Cadence. Don't worry. I'm fine. I'm more worried about you."

Now I've spent time with Madison every day since first year orientation. There has never been a secret between us. Now there plainly is. Something did happen to her, but it's clear that she has no intention of telling me. And yet, as awful as she looks, it doesn't seem to bother her.

"Don't worry 'bout me, Cadence. I'm fine. What about you? How are you holding up?"

"Terrible," I say, turning away from her into my pillow. I suppress another sob. "I was so proud of myself for not crying. Now, ever since Alondra's little ceremony, the tears won't fucking stop flowing."

"But that's good, Katie," she says, rubbing my back. "You need to mourn. You'll feel better later."

I shrug. "That's shit, Maddie. That's complete bullshit. There's no reason I need to cry for anything. I just feel miserable."

"I thought you seemed relieved at the candle ceremony."

Did I? I don't even know.

She runs a hand along my cheek. Then she says, "You want me to sit here with you tonight? Or in bed? I can hold you."

It's not gay. It sounds gay, but from her tone I know it isn't. The funny thing is her affection suddenly makes me start crying more.

I don't know how long I cry, but it seems like hours. And all the while, my friend lies beside me. She's trying to sleep in my arms. That's cute. The funny thing is, I think her affection only makes me cry harder.

By morning, Maddie is sleeping like a log, impossible to disturb. Unlike Yours Truly, who feels like crap and has had no interest in sleeping since I got the news about Mom. I move out of my friend's arms and slip on some slippers. I marvel that she hasn't woken up due to our cheap, creaky bedsprings. It's cold and the window is frosted. The morning dew has formed icicles on the leaves on the bushes and trees outside my window.

I walk to the dresser and take out a shirt and pants to change from my white negligee. Then I turn on the Keurig and brew two cups of coffee, one for me and one for Maddie.

Maddie is still sleeping like death on my bed. I've never seen her look so awful. It looks as if she was attacked, and I'm not going to let her get out of it as easily as she did last night. I'm gonna find out who did it, where it happened, and why. It looks like I should call the police or something. And yet, besides her disheveled brown hair and dirty, torn-up dress, she looks completely at peace. Her smile is angelic.

The Keurig is loud enough to wake my roommate. She stirs, draws out her arms, and yawns. Then she opens her eyes and smiles at me.

I sip some hot coffee, then walk to her with her Donald Duck mug.

"Morning," Maddie says.

"Hi."

I lean against the wall and look at her. Maddie stretches again and sits up in bed.

"You feeling better?" she asks.

I'm still staring at her. And no, I have no interest in crying anymore. I've had quite enough of that. I just look at her and don't say a word.

"What?" Maddie asks. She sips some coffee. "What is it? ...You know, this shit sucks. What happened to those pods Nick gave me?"

"Drank 'em all," I reply with a shrug.

"Oh. Well, this tastes like water. Water mixed with a faint flavor of coffee."

But she still drinks it.

"So?" I ask.

"Hmm? So what? It's water." Maddie sips more. She leans her forehead against her hand, and light shines on her and all her train-wrecked glory.

"No. I mean, what *the fuck* happened to you?"

"I told you not to worry about it." Then Maddie laughs. "But you know..." She looks down at her tattered dress. "I really should change."

I'm staring at her. She avoids my gaze as she gets up, walks to her dresser, and pulls out some clothes. "I suppose this will have to be disposed of. Pity, it was my best dress."

"Tell me. Tell me now."

"Don't start, Cadence," she warns, pulling off her mud-laden, torn-up dress. It angers me to think she was wearing that in bed with me. Not because she dirtied up the sheets, but because something was obviously wrong. I was too messed up last night to address it. Now I feel better. A little.

Something's wrong. Really wrong.

"Just forget it, okay?" Maddie says.

"Tell me right *now*, Maddie. Tell me, or I'll call the cops."

"Stop it, Cadence," she says, waving a hand. She changes into a campus sweatshirt and jeans. Then she walks back to my bed and pulls on her socks and shoes. "Just forget it, Cadence. I'm just happy you seem better."

Maddie's tying her shoes. I sit next to her and lift her face—as she's been known to do to me, many times before—but she pulls away.

"Cadence, forget it."

"No. We're friends. Tell me what happened."

"I can't," she says, shaking her head. "You know I can't."

"What do you mean, you can't?"

"I'm sworn," she says, averting her eyes from mine. She just raises her eyebrows and figures that's enough. Then she resumes pulling on her shoes.

"It looks as if someone hurt you."

"Nobody hurt me, Cadence," she says with her head turned down.

"Your clothes say otherwise."

"Katie." She looks back at me with a sad smile. "Katie," she says again. "It was the initiation. Nobody hurt me. No one hurts anyone there without consent. Everything is done with consent. I promise. You must believe me."

"The initiation? What the hell do they do at the initiation?"

"I can't tell you that."

I give up. Or rather, my body gives up. I feel like a chair has landed on me, and I sort of fall on the bed. I'm exhausted. I haven't slept in days.

"Katie, don't worry about me. Take care of yourself. Just rest." She pats my back again. "I tell you what. I'll go to your professors today and get your homework, 'kay? You can just stay in bed today and get some sleep."

"All right." How can I argue with that? I can barely keep my eyes open.

"Great."

"Swell," I say sarcastically.

"Keen," she adds.

I laugh at her mockery of my fifties language. The situation isn't funny, but exchanging dumb words is. Just being friends together, you know.

But I want to know. I want to know what happened to her. I'm worried about her.

I felt good after leaving Alondra's mansion. I felt like her heart was there for me. I felt so good that I even considered joining their club. But not now. Not after seeing what she did to my friend.

And what's so good about some charm to make you cry all night, anyway?

"You want me to get you breakfast at the dining commons?" Maddie says.

"No. I'll try to go."

"Sure?"

I nod.

Then she puts her finger to her chin for a moment. She looks around and finds something on the dresser beside the door. It's the mourning candle from last night.

"You forgot this. Alondra wanted to make sure you got it."

It was only partially lit last night. It's still a fully lightable candle.

"Thanks." I touch her arm and look at her very seriously. "But please tell me, Maddie, is everything all right? Please. Are you okay?"

"Cadence, believe me, I've never been happier."

8

———

THE T.A.

A FEW DAYS AFTER ALONDRA'S CEREMONY, MADDIE FINALLY CONVINCES ME to go to class. It's early in the morning, and she knows I'm not a morning person. But I think it was after I laughed at her stupid comment, "Bryce'll be there," that I capitulated. Of course Bryce will be there. It's his class.

I'm majorly behind in my studies. The point of TA classes is to brush up on things, not to teach. Bryce usually just reviews Alondra's lectures and I, being the stellar super-smart gal that I am, often raises my hand just to regurgitate information both of us already know, just to see Mr. Handsome's infamous wry smile. But today I actually have to pay attention. At eight in the morning.

We walk through the quad. It's empty. Everyone is sleeping or recovering from their weekend hangovers, but I know Bryce's ancient history class will be full. It's one of the most popular classes in school. Apparently, that's why he can meet so early. At eight in the morning. As Maddie leans on my shoulder, telling me how she just dumped that dickhead playboy Nick (she's been telling me all week), I yawn and struggle to move forward to my boyfriend's class.

Just as I thought, the class is full. It's small, like a high school classroom, with about twenty people. Mr. Handsome is pulling out his laptop from a brown leather briefcase on the desk at the front. He's wearing pressed slacks, loafers, and a button-down shirt—left open ever so slightly to show the stud's chest hairs. Who dresses him? His clothes are to die for.

We sit in the back since the room is already full. Then Maddie pulls out her laptop from her bag. I forgot mine.

We wait. For a moment, I recall why I haven't slept in over a week. I feel that constricting feeling in my chest. But then I'm saved by the vision at the front of the class.

"Let's talk about Amarna," says my tall hunk. He looks down the rows and sees me. I win that smile, and I feel my heart bounce a little. "Ancient Egypt. Dr. Johansen spoke of Nefertiti and Akhenaten. This is, of course, well into the time of the pyramids. Do you know the son of this famous couple?"

"Tut," says a redheaded girl in the front row.

"Right. King Tut. Know that. And know of the mystery of his father, Akhenaten. Dr. Johansen will not want you to tell me what every kindergartener knows of Tut. She will want you to give me information on his parents. What's important here is Akhenaten, Amenhotep IV of the Eighteenth Dynasty, who changed his name to Akhenaten and created a religion based on monotheism, worshipping the sun disk. Have you seen statues of Akhenaten?" It's a rhetorical question. Bryce doesn't wait for an answer. "They're grotesque. The man has some of the weirdest features of any pharaoh. He doesn't look human. His wife, too, has been depicted in statues and hieroglyphs that look odd. But then there is also a famous bust that many believe to be the true bust of the Egyptian queen. She is beautiful—*nefer*, meaning, in ancient Egyptian, beauty."

He looks around the room. Everyone is intently focused on him. Then his eyes fall on me, and I can swear he flashes that smile again. At me. That irresistible smile. *Holy shit, he's hot!*

Then Maddie ruins it by hitting my shoulder. I turn and she has the exact same wry smile, making fun of me.

Bitch.

"You all need to know of Amarna," continues Bryce. "You see Akhenaten, not only being from another world, in my opinion..." I hear a lot of murmuring over that. "See, Akhenaten started a revolution. It was only upon his death that statues and paintings were defaced in order to cover up his rule and return to the ways of the past...because this is what people do to the unknown. People cannot deal with mysteries, and their fear and prejudice make them eliminate them."

Bryce looks at his PC. He moves the cursor around and types a little. The room is silent until he gathers his thoughts.

"Those of you who brought your computer or have access on your phone, open the file on our website on mummification. For others, I'll write the most important steps on the board. Know the following and memorize it. It will be on the test. If Dr. Johansen doesn't see them on your essays, know that you're not going to squeak by with much more than a C. She grades tough, but you already know that. "

"The following is done to the dead in the mummification process." He starts writing on the whiteboard:

1. *The brain is removed in pieces by a hook through the nostrils.*
2. *The organs are removed through a cut in the chest at the left side of the abdomen (sparing the heart) and placed in jars later buried with the mummy.*
3. *The body is dried out with natron, a salt substance. NATRON. Remember that.*
4. *The body is wrapped.*
5. *The mummy is placed in a coffin in an ornate tomb.*

"The whole process takes up to two months. Know the steps. But if you want an A, Dr. Johansen will want to know the details."

"How detailed?" asks a guy in the front row.

Bryce leans against his desk and recites, as if reading from a book:

"*The first step in preparing the dead is embalming, after which a hole is punched into the ethmoid bone of the skull not far from the nose. It is hammered in with pieces of the brain, meninges, and spinal fluid, adhering to a stick, as the priest thrusts in and out. In and out. After many thrusts—in and out—the fatty goo flows from the hole. But this never removes the entire brain. As much as possible is scooped out...* That detailed. Got it?"

The boy nods.

"Know your steps. Know your instruments. If you were in class, you would have seen the pictures." There are a few groans from the students. I'm sorry I missed it. "Now let's move on to Babylon and Hammurabi."

I start doing what I really shouldn't be doing in Bryce's class: daydreaming. The problem is, Bryce doesn't hold my attention the way Alondra does. He sort of spits out information. That's great for getting As on exams, but it won't work well for keeping me awake at eight in the morning after a restless sleep. I'm drifting off, getting some much-needed rest, when I suddenly hear my name.

"Cadence, can you expound on the Code of Hammurabi relating to witchcraft?"

I can. I learned this a couple of weeks ago, when we were learning of Salem and witchcraft in medieval times. He knew this, the sneaky, irresistible fucker.

"Yeah." I sit up, clearing my throat. He flashes that infamous grin. It irritates me a little this time. "The code is one of the first of its kind throughout history," I continue with pride. "It states that if someone accuses a witch of a harmful spell, the witch shall be thrown in a sacred river. If the witch dies, the accuser shall know she was guilty and take her possessions. But if the witch lives, the accuser shall be put to death, and the witch shall obtain all their possessions... It's stupid, and I can see why the dunking of witches has been made the butt of jokes ever since."

The class laughs and I pat my ego on the back. Bryce knew I would know the answer. I really like this guy.

"Right," he says. "Except the law is not stupid, Cadence, if you believe in the sacred river. I suppose, if you don't believe in magic, then it may seem stupid. But I think you're being stupid if you make fun of a law just because you don't believe in witchcraft."

Oh.

"And also, the law pertains to men, not just women. You said *she.* What makes you think witches can't be men?"

I'm sinking in my seat. It sounds like he's reprimanding me. It's like he's challenging me in front of the whole class, and I'm really embarrassed. Maybe he's not such a swell guy after all.

After I don't answer him, he goes back to Babylon, and the rest of the class is a complete blur. I'm pretty sure I sleep through most of it. But I need sleep. And I decide that if he calls on me again, I'll ignore him.

At the end of class, Maddie gets up and takes me by the arm. I'm not sure what she's up to until she plops me right in front of Mr. Handsome.

"I'm so glad you came, Cadence," Bryce says, stuffing his computer in his bag.

"Well, you didn't have to embarrass her," Maddie snaps.

"He didn't embarrass me," I say.

"Did I?" he asks surprised. He picks up his bag. "Don't be silly. I knew Cadence would know that." He turns to me. "You did outstandingly, as you always do. I just didn't agree with your mockery of magic and witchcraft."

"I wasn't making fun of magic. I was explaining—"

"You don't believe in it. If you did, the law wouldn't seem so ridiculous to you."

"I think she's just upset over how you corrected her in front of the whole class," Maddie says, chiming in. I look at her. She's not smiling. She's defending me, as always.

"I'm not upset," I say.

"You two are quite a pair," he says. "You fit so well. You're like sisters."

"That's why I know when she's hurt," Maddie adds.

And that pisses me off. Nobody's hurt. Maddie is going too far.

"Cadence," he says, hauling his man-bag over his shoulder, "I would love to be of assistance to you during these hard times. I can review the lesson plan further with you—"

"So you can prepare to embarrass her more?" quips my friend.

"Can you leave us for a second, Maddie?" I ask.

Maddie looks confused. "Yeah...all right," she says. Then she turns back to Bryce before she goes. "Take better care of my best friend next time, okay?"

Bryce doesn't say anything. He just stares at me with those baby-blue eyes.

"I would love to review the *lesson plan*," I say, knowing full well he intends to do much more.

Maddie's gone.

"Great, Cadence," he says with a glowing dimple-laden smile. Then he turns serious and touches my shoulder. "How about Wednesday in the library?"

"Okay."

He nods and walks with me to the exit. The classroom's empty now. Maddie's slipped out of sight, knowing when to leave us alone. I'm kinda cheerier walking beside Bryce. Or maybe I'm just more awake. I'm laughing inside about how my BFF was defending me.

Bryce seems preoccupied. He loses his smile. I'm thinking maybe he's still a little mad about Maddie's accusation. He cocks his head as we walk and says, "Look, Cadence, we all really care about you. The whole circle. Alondra wants you to know that. You have our heart and our blessing."

"Huh?"

He chuckles.

"Oh," I say when his words register in my sluggish head. "I don't care much for your circle, whatever the hell the *circle* is. But thanks, Bryce."

He nods. We walk down a cement walkway between two buildings, near the main drag of campus. There are a lot more students out now, carrying their backpacks, laughing, or walking alone to their next classes. Bryce is oddly quiet, but I don't mind. I just like walking beside him.

It's funny because neither of us knows where the other one is going. But somehow, the minute one of us drifts, the other follows. So we're kinda just dancing our way to the main walkway in the center of campus together.

"Incidentally, why Nefertiti?" I ask, fishing for something to say. "I don't get it. Why is Alondra teaching about Nefertiti and Aken...whatever his name is? It has nothing to do with mummification, does it?"

"Alondra and I are fascinated with his sun disk cult. That's one reason."

We reach the quad together. I suddenly realize what's happening. I'm walking with my teacher, but not because he's my teacher. It's just to be with him. And he's here to be with me. And there's still no push or pull for us to go our separate ways. For a moment, I consider meeting with him *now* in the library. I wouldn't mind his company for the rest of the day, "studying."

"The other," he continues, holding me back from being run over by an idiot on a bike, "is the lesson plan. As much as Alondra would love to teach the arts and the paranormal, the university expects us to actually teach ancient history too. And anyway, you find Nefertiti fascinating, don't you?"

"Sure, I guess."

"I don't doubt it. Because her name stands for beauty. I would think you'd be very familiar with that, Cadence."

Ooh, I didn't know you could be suave, Bryce. You're full of surprises, aren't you?

"Are you trying to say you find me pretty?" I ask casually, twirling a strand of my hair like a complete idiot.

He takes my hand and pulls me closer to him, and we stop for a moment. There's a lot of traffic back and forth, but I cease to notice. It's just me and him.

When I looked in the mirror this morning, I thought the glass would crack. My skin looked chapped and the skin beneath my eyes was sagging. My hair looked like a bird's nest. But judging from the way Bryce is looking at me, what he sees is quite different.

"Well?" I swallow a lump in my throat. "What are you trying to say, Bryce?"

"If we weren't on campus right now," he mutters almost in a whisper, looking into my eyes, "I would swoop down and lose complete control of myself, Ms. Cadence Hawthorne. You are very, very pretty. In fact, I would say quite irresistible."

I giggle nervously. It breaks his stare.

"My ..." I say. "Well, then, perhaps we need to meet outside of school instead of in the library."

"No," he says, mustering a chuckle. "The library's safer."

Safer?

He smiles and takes my hand. He rubs my fingers, and I feel shocks through my whole body.

We're walking again; now we're holding hands. I truly believe he refrained before because he was worried about rumors spreading throughout the school, but he doesn't seem to care anymore.

We're near a cement stage. During the summer, plays are performed here. Today, it's just a beautiful sitting area where a few students have their eyes glued to their phones or laptops. Everyone's wearing jackets or coats. I'm not. I've been so flustered lately that I forgot one. I try to hold back a shiver as I walk with my favorite TA.

He pats my hand with his other palm as we walk. "How about seven on Wednesday?"

"Seven in the morning?" I quip stupidly.

"Seven at night, Cadence," he says. "I'll see you at seven in the library?"

"I will be wearing my best T-shirt and jeans."

"Wear whatever you'd like." He runs his hand over my cheek, and I just about die. Then he says very seriously, "Take care of yourself, all right, Cadence? I mean it. We're worried about you."

"Okay."

"Bye."

"Bye, Bryce. Bye."

My hearts races as I watch him dip through another pathway and behind a building. *Aren't I supposed to be upset about something?* My conscience answers, *Cadence, your mother just died.* Oh yeah. *But, Mom, you need to meet Bryce. He is sooo hot! You'd like him.*

If Mom were alive, I would call her and tell her.

But she isn't. So I just walk a few long arcs around campus thinking of him. Then, when I want to snap out of it, I just think of Mom again.

I'm...confused. So confused. The tightness in my chest has grown, and I don't even know what it means anymore.

I need sleep—desperately.

I go back home, lie in my bed, and close my eyes. I think of the funeral and the rain. Did it rain at Mom's funeral? I can't remember anymore.

Then I think of Bryce. He said he can't control himself around me. He said I'm irresistible. Well, he obviously likes me. No, he loves me. I think I'm in love.

9

THE GIFT

The Jonathan Brewster Taylor Library, better known as the Taylor Building, is the most modern building on the entire campus. It was built a few years ago, replacing a very old, ugly three-story brick building. The old building had small rooms with low ceilings. The only modern feature was an escalator in the back. The new Taylor Building has floor-to-ceiling windows, two mall-like escalators, and tall vaulted ceilings. And it has five stories, not three. There is plenty of room to study, and there's even a coffee shop that opens onto an outside court—where Maddie stole her latte a month ago.

So I'm on the escalator, heading to one of the study lounges upstairs, when Nick, of all people, walks up to me. I like Nick. I always have, ever since we had an astronomy class together last year. He's a nice guy. He's kind of like Bryce, but he's more flamboyant and brash. "Hey, Cadence."

He's dressed in a Hawthorne basketball T-shirt. He was on the team last year. His pants are tacky. They're gray sweatpants.

"Hi, Nick," I say, cocking my head his way. I stay planted, waiting to exit.

"How is she?"

"How is who?" I ask, acting dumb.

"How is she? Tell me. She won't return my calls."

"Maybe you should forget about her," I say with a shrug. Then I walk away, and he follows me.

"Look...can you send her a message? Just tell her I miss her. Tell her I'm sorry about her car. She was right. I'd had too much to drink. I was stupid."

I start thinking about the night I went to Alondra's. Maddie looked like she'd been manhandled. Was it Nick? A car accident? Maddie never told me why she suddenly hated Nick, but she did tell me she was having car trouble.

"I think you should just leave her alone."

"Wait...Cadence, just give her a message."

I stop at the top of the stairs and throw my hair back. For a moment, in the silence, I look out the windows. They span both floors, and I can see the half-moon in the distance. The autumn leaves have fallen from the trees, leaving bare branches. It might be cold, but it's a clear night.

I sigh and look at Nick. "What?" I can't help but be mad at him. I don't know why, but Maddie and I are just that close. We have some sort of unwritten pact that if one of us is hurt by someone, the other responds the same way.

"Just...please ask her to call me," he pleads. "Please. Or...tell her I'll call her and ask that she just picks up. Ask her to give me another chance. Damn it, I miss her."

He's falling apart. It makes me smile and, for a second, the old Nick is back. He smiles too. That seems to reenergize his normal manic self.

"I'll tell her."

"Promise?"

"Promise."

"Look, if she stays mad, maybe...you know, you and I can hang out and—"

"I'll talk to her," I snap. Then I think of changing my mind. The nerve of that bastard!

Nick finally leaves, and I make my way into the study room. It has the same floor-to-ceiling windows and is furnished with thick carpets and brown leather couches. There's no one there. Why would there be? Everyone waits until finals to study.

I sit on a couch facing the large window. I take out my laptop from my unicorn backpack. Then I sit and look at the half-moon and the view of campus. A few people are traipsing along the walkways, lined by quaint streetlamps.

I take my iPhone from my pocket. It's 7:10 p.m. I thought *I* was late.

I don't want to read. I don't even really want to study. I know in my heart that I'm not here to learn anything. I'm waiting to see Mr. Handsome and enjoy his company.

But what if he stands me up? What if he never comes?

He comes.

He's wearing the same clothes he wore during his class on Monday. I'm not. I'm wearing a short, tight black skirt. My hair is up in a rather elaborate chignon. Maddie helped me with it. I have on dark mascara and burgundy lipstick. I'm wearing high heels. I look like I'm dressed for a steak restaurant. Well, at least I'm being honest. Bryce isn't gonna teach me anything tonight—not related to ancient Egyptian history anyway.

I stand up.

"Hi, Cadence."

"Hi." I wave, acting all suave like I did at the party.

He cracks a grin and sits in a brown leather recliner beside my couch. We're both facing the window. He puts down his large leather bag and hands me a small white box with a pink bow. My heart leaps a few times in my chest.

"What's this?" I ask.

"A gift. Something for us." He smiles his infamous smile. "I know we're here to study, but I want you to have this."

I start to open it, but he stops me.

"Not yet. Open it at home. Read the instructions and try it. I think you'll like it."

I look at him oddly, but then I just nod.

"I know we're here to go over what you've missed," he says with a chuckle, "but I couldn't help giving you something. It's a gift. Think of me when you use it."

"All right."

Here's an idea: how 'bout we dispense with the lesson and move on to the gift and us?

"Now, with everything going on with you, Cadence, have you even had time to read the passages in the handouts?"

I guess we're dispensing with us *at the moment.*

"Yeah. I read them. Maddie showed me where we are. I went through it."

"Great."

I'm a week behind in my studies. But the fact is, between you and me, most of the other students are always a week behind. In fact, many are ten weeks behind, planning to cram before their finals. Maddie's like this, except when it comes to Alondra's class. Her involvement in Alondra's club makes her an A student. This is a change for my BFF. She's really a C student.

So I know, and Bryce knows, that this study session is all a bunch of bullshit. But I play along and nod at him again. He leans forward, more intent. "All right. Well, I'm not Alondra, but I'll try to add facts that she's given us in class. 'Kay?"

"Sure."

I'm looking at his large hands. He's folding them, but he keeps twitching a finger or two. I want to hold them. But then I look at his eyes again. He's in his serious teacher mode.

"The pyramid structure is a marvel in construction. Cadence, even in today's age, we could not replicate the perfect measurements involved in the hallways of these structures." He points at me. "Know about the Sphinx—and the new one. A new one was recently discovered. Know that for the test. And know about ..."

I cease listening to a word my TA is saying. Instead, I just look at his mouth. And his lips. I want to touch those soft lips, and I can't help but believe he's thinking the same about mine. I know I look gorgeous. It was intentional.

I feel so good around him. I look at his short, wavy dark hair. There are curls near his ears, and I want to straighten them. Then I look at his shirt. There are buttons I want to unbutton. He's also wearing these well-worn brown loafers. That's cute. And his face is a little unshaven. Oh, how I'd love to touch the stubble on his chin.

He doesn't stop talking. I've already read the notes, and he's not telling me much about ancient Egypt that I don't already know, but far be it from me to stop him. I love his intense eyes. And his posture. He's sitting forward, so intent on teaching me. I just watch him.

"Cadence, are you listening?"

"Aha."

"No, you're not," he says, leaning back in his chair.

"I know most of this stuff already, Bryce," I say with a chuckle.

"Okay, then there's no reason to be here."

"Right." But then I flash a sly smile, and he chuckles again. He grabs my hand and strokes it.

"Cadence... I..."

"Yes, Bryce?"

He laughs again. I'm not sure what's so funny.

I look around the room. We're the only ones here. Then I turn back to him. He's leaning toward me again. I want to kiss his lips—just like I did at his frat house. I really want to just lean into him. But he grasps my hand in both of his and says, "Open my gift when you get home, all right?"

I nod.

"I think I should go."

What! No, wait.

He gets up.

"So soon?"

"Cadence, we've covered most of the lecture."

"You just got here."

He pulls out his cell phone and shakes his head. "I've been talking to you for half an hour. I think you know enough for class now."

"Oh." *Shit, has it already been a half an hour? It felt like three minutes.*

"Are you gonna make it to her lecture tomorrow?"

"Yeah," I say. But I really haven't thought about it. Alondra's lectures are at ten in the morning. I've really started getting used to getting up at eleven.

"Okay... Then can I have a goodbye hug?" he asks.

Of course you can have a hug.

We embrace ... for a very long time, and he touches my cheek. The room is still vacant. I suppose if there were students studying, they'd be looking at us. Then he finally lets me go. He heaves his bag over his shoulder and turns hesitantly toward the exit. I can't believe he's leaving. I'm actually a little hurt. Even if this wasn't technically a date, I figured he'd buy me a latte or something.

"I'll see you tomorrow, Cadence."

"Um-hmm."

He looks down into my eyes and kisses me gently on the lips. I almost fall. He holds me with a chuckle. Then he holds me tighter and kisses me once more. I feel him enter my mouth with his tongue, gliding it around mine and then sucking on my top lip. He leans into me, and the erection in his pants brushes against my leg. I yearn for him. I want him.

He lets go of me.

"Tomorrow."

"Yeah," I whisper. "Sure. Tomorrow."

"What a fucking tease," says Maddie, back at our dorm. We're sitting together on my bed. I'm still decked out in my dress clothes. I'm frowning a little.

"He's nice."

"Sure. So was Nick."

"Yeah," I say, "what happened to Nick? You know I saw him. He's desperate to talk to you."

Maddie's face lights up a little, but then she turns sour. "Nick, my dear, has the opposite problem as Bryce."

"Oh...seems you have that effect on a lot of boys." I regret saying that the moment it comes out of my mouth. It's like I just accused my BFF of being a whore. I cover my mouth and turn away.

"Well, this isn't about me," Maddie says with a laugh. "So...tell me, what was the kiss like?"

"Good."

We laugh again, like stupid grade school girls.

"He's really cute," Maddie says. She looks me over. I see her in my periphery, but my eyes are focused on the foot of my bed. "And...did he... touch you anywhere else?"

"No!" I snap.

"I'm just asking," Maddie says with a chuckle. "You don't have to get so defensive." Then she touches my hands. "Anyway, it's good to see you're back in the game, Cadence." Maddie knows I haven't really dated anyone since high school. I've been on a handful of dates at Hawthorne, but they always seem to fall flat. Somehow my library "date" was the best one so far.

In high school, I had a boyfriend for a year and a half. His name was Albert Selzer. He was Jewish and was one of the student leaders at our school. He had a really good heart. He was really shy, like me, and unlike Bryce, he rarely even tried to kiss me. He usually just gave me a peck on the lips. I liked him a lot, but after prom, we sort of went our separate ways. Then he moved and I never saw him again. I never scored with Al. It got hot and heavy in the back of his car once, but never a home run. Maddie knows all that. That's why she has this stupid smirk on her face at this very moment.

"Well, I'd be careful with Bryce, Cadence." Maddie leans back on the mattress.

"Why?"

"Because he's obviously an idiot. Anyone meeting a single, available girl looking as hot as you and not doing much more than kissing you on the lips must have a screw loose."

"Shut up, Maddie."

We giggle stupidly again.

Maddie picks up his gift. "Can I open it?"

"Sure. Why not."

Maddie pulls off the pink lace bow and opens the box on her lap. There's a handwritten two-page note inside. Then there are various herbs. I smell the odor from Maddie's lap.

"What the hell?" I say. I snatch the note from my friend.

Dearest Cadence,

Thank you for taking time out of your evening to spend with me. If you are reading this, it means things did not go so badly. I am well aware that our meeting was for us to get to know each other on a different level from a student/teacher relationship. But if, somehow, I have misread you on this, please do not read any further...

Good. If I still have your attention, I would like you to try an incantation for me. I think it will rejuvenate you.

"What does he say?" Maddie asks.

"Shh! He wrote to me. Just shut up!"

"Obviously. A bit too overdone, don't you think? What does it say?"

"Shut up, Maddie!"

Allow me to introduce you to an ancient method of communing with someone of the opposite sex. It involves bathing. If you follow the steps below, I think you will be pleased at the end. The one thing I ask is that you meditate on your memory of me. Remember my appearance and my presence. Remember me always as you follow these steps. But DO NOT do this during menstruation.

1. *Wash your bathtub with white vinegar. Ensure it is completely clean.*
2. *Draw a warm bath, not too hot but not too cold.*
3. *Cover up your mirrors. Your reflection could ruin everything.*
4. *Empty the contents of this bag, containing damiana, jasmine, and red and pink flower petals, into the water. Mix it rapidly with your fingers.*
5. *Undress yourself. Do it slowly and methodically, paying close attention to touching each part of your body.*
6. *Slowly enter the tub naked and face the moon. (But DO NOT do this if it is a full moon.)*
7. *Lean back against the tub and try to relax. Take three deep breaths. Try to rid yourself of all thoughts. Meditate on nothing except me. Remember me. Remember me in complete relaxation as you breathe. Imagine that my very presence is with you, Cadence.*
8. *Relax. When you are fully relaxed, repeat the following mantra addressing the goddess Venus:*

EGO SUM VENUS; EGO SUM VENUS; EGO SUM VENUS.

If you must, repeat it out loud. Repeat it again and again, feeling the goddess Venus enter you. If you do all these elaborate steps, you won't regret it. Let me know. I await the results of my gift!

Your not-so-secret admirer, Bryce.

Maddie is standing over me, trying to read over my shoulder. I turn to her and drop the sheet of paper by the box.

"You all are so fucking weird," I say. She laughs. I don't. "Why can't I find a normal man, Maddie?"

"I think it's cute."

I jump up and shove the small box at my friend. "You go do this shit, then. You like it, right? It's like a part of your cult, right?"

"Cadence, if you'd only seen what I've seen," she says with wide-open eyes.

"What? What have you seen?"

Maddie is smiling at me. I'm getting upset with that smirk.

I had been looking forward to this "date" with Bryce for days. Now I'm left disappointed. All I have to show for it is a "spell."

"Are you going to do it?" Maddie asks.

"Why don't you do it?" I ask, pushing the box at her again.

"I can't," Maddie says with a shrug. "It's not a spell for me."

"Oh, come on! Be serious."

"Guess your man isn't such a tease after all." Maddie jumps up and pats my back. "You've got nothing to lose, Katie. I think you should try it."

I just lift an eyebrow. I take a deep breath and stare at the floor. Then I cock my head up. "Where do we even have a tub?" We don't have a tub —not for ourselves anyway. The bathroom in the dormitory has communal showers.

"Well," Maddie says, "Alondra has a tub."

"Oh, come on!" I snap, whirling around. "Be serious."

"Now, wait..." She raises her hand. "Hear me out, Katie. I know Alondra. She cares about you. I know for a fact she wouldn't mind."

"*No*," I say with my eyes wide.

"All right," Maddie says with a shrug.

"You take it," I say again. "You go take a bath at Alondra's."

"Katie," Maddie says, falling back on my bed, "this is a love spell. It's for you. Why would I want it? Bryce gave it to you. He obviously likes you —*a lot.*"

"I don't believe in this shit."

"Well, you'll never know unless you try. I got it!" Maddie says, hitting her leg excitedly. "The Billington House. You can use one of their spare bathrooms."

I shake my head like crazy. "Creepy."

"Come on, Katie. Give it a try."

"Well...I could try your aunt Jane's house. It's not too far from here." Maddie was raised by her aunt Jane ever since she was a little girl. Their house is about thirty miles from campus. She's basically her mom, but Maddie's been known to call her "aunt Jane" to her friends.

"Great idea! You can come to our house tomorrow night."

She's ecstatic. I'm not. I have that same sinking feeling I get whenever I visit Alondra's house. "Wonderful," I say sarcastically.

She gives me a tight hug and laughs.

Maddie decorates the hallway bathroom of her house with scented jasmine candles in red glass candleholders. She also strews red rose petals in and around the sinks. Since Jane doesn't have a shower curtain, a long black curtain has been hung over the mirror. A statue of a naked woman adorns an altar between the two sinks. Maddie says it's Venus.

Jane's not even home. She's visiting her grandchildren in Omaha, Nebraska. So we have the house to ourselves. It's frigid outside and we've just had the first snowfall. I'm thankful for Jane's central heating. Her house is always more climate-controlled than our dorm.

I stand by the door to the bathroom. Everything is ready. Maddie even helped me draw the bath.

"You'll have to add the herbs," she says with a smile. She's giddy over the whole thing. I'm not. I'm kind of freaked out. But I'm glad I thought of

Madison's house. The haunted Billington House would have taken me over the edge.

"This is stupid. I feel like an idiot."

"Okay, I have to go." Maddie hugs me, ignoring my comment. I'm in my bathrobe; Maddie is dressed and still wearing a jacket.

"Wait! Where are you going?"

"I have to go, Katie," she says with a chuckle. "The spell will be broken if I'm here."

"How do you know that? The instructions didn't say anything about company."

"I just know."

Maddie doesn't wait any longer. She closes the door behind her, and I'm left in the flickering red light. I feel like an absolute idiot. I pick up Bryce's instructions and read them again. *"Empty the contents with your fingers. Mix them rapidly."*

I follow the instructions, mixing the herbs. Then I try to think of Bryce, but it's hard. I can't stop feeling stupid.

I prepare to just drop my robe on the floor, but then I recall the instructions. *"Undress slowly and methodically."* I really don't like this part. It feels perverted—wait, the whole thing feels perverted—but I let the robe slowly slide from my shoulders. The cotton glides along the nape of my neck and over my naked breasts. Then I untie it and push it slowly over my belly button and down over my hips. I'm not wearing panties or shoes. I am now completely naked. Then I put my finger to my chin, trying to remember where the moon is tonight.

Maddie already told me. She told me to face away from the door.

I enter the tub. It feels sooo good. Thanks to my friend, the temperature is perfect. There aren't any bubbles, so I can see my naked feet and legs. I readjust and lean back on the white porcelain. Then I try to relax. That's the hard part. I haven't relaxed in two weeks. Not since my mother passed.

I try to remember Bryce. That's not so hard now, as I close my eyes. I recall his hard jawline and his bright blue eyes. I think of the stubble along his chin and cheeks. Then I think of his chest.

I think of how I wanted to unfasten a button. Just one. I imagine doing it.

I lean back. The red glow of the room soothes me. The aroma of the herbs intoxicates me, making my skin more attentive to the warm water. It's so relaxing.

What were the words I have to chant? I can't recall. I should have brought the paper over.

EGO ... SUM ... VENUS; EGO SUM ... VENUS; EGO SUM VENUS.

I start saying the words out loud. I'm not ashamed and I no longer feel it's weird. I seem to have accepted the spell—it would be ridiculous not to. I'm committed. And I know Maddie left. She promised. I know she's devious, but she'd never be deceptive about her witchcraft. I know I'm alone.

EGO SUM VENUS.

I look at my naked feet. Then I run my right hand along my arm and stomach. I slowly move it over to my breast, cupping it. I feel my hard nipples, and I'm aroused. But nothing special is happening.

I think of Bryce again. I lean back and sink further, feeling my long hair float behind me. I'm supposed to think of him. My mind starts swooning, and I think of Bryce and speak the enchantment. I think of Bryce's hands. Those strong fingers. The touch of his fingers. His eyes. It's not so hard to think of him, actually. I can picture his blue eyes hypnotizing me and entering my mind. Then I remember his body and his warmth. And I think about the bulge I felt down there. I think of him. And soon my skin seems to feel him.

I don't know if I fall asleep. I seem to. But the mantra keeps being repeated, whether it's from my lips or my mind, over and over again.

Then something really weird happens. Smoke starts filling the room. It's as if the water in the bathtub were scalding hot, but it isn't. I imagine that if I hadn't covered the mirrors, they'd be covered in mist now.

In time, I hear the door. It doesn't bother me. I don't even turn. It just creaks open. And I know who's there.

He's wearing the same clothes he wore in class and at the library. He walks to the tub and kneels before me. His eyes are a little glassy, as if he's in a trance, but those blues look right at me. Then he reaches out for my hand and kisses the back of it.

"Cadence," Bryce says. "Cadence."

I don't respond. I keep repeating my mantra.

He's still holding my hand, but I turn from him, repeating the words. *EGO SUM VENUS.*

"Cadence. Cadence."

He says my name while I say my incantation. I feel as if we're saying the same thing.

I reach over and run my palm along his fingers. I feel tingly all over. Then I feel tightness between my legs. I look up at his eyes. He has his famous grin, but he looks hungry.

I move him closer and pull at his top button. I unbutton it, like I've been meaning to do for weeks. Then I reach down to unbutton the others. Just like I did with my robe, he ever so slowly pulls off his navy-blue button-down; then he lifts his T-shirt. I run my hand along the brown hairs at the center of his hard chest. Then I wander down over his well-developed abs. I look into his glorious blue eyes and he smiles again.

He reaches down and kisses me, just like at the library, but it's less guarded and more intimate. He sucks at my lower lip this time and runs his tongue over mine. Then he grabs my wet hair from behind, tugs it a little hard, then slowly, gently runs his fingers down my mane while massaging my back. It feels sooo good as he presses his fingers against my upper back muscles and the back of my neck, licking and sucking with his mouth again and again.

Then, after a time, he stands up straight. He pulls down his pants and underwear. Apparently, there's no delay anymore and I don't mind. His long, hard penis is throbbing before me. I touch the tip. It's wet. I've never seen a man's penis before. Not like this. I rub the tip and he closes his eyes and moans.

After I touch him, he reaches down into the water and touches my legs. He gently glides his fingers over my pubic hair and slowly rubs up and down my clitoris. I know under the water I'm wet. I want him. I want him sooo bad.

But then he releases me. He grabs a large yellow sponge from the edge of the tub and rubs it along my cheek, squeezing the scented water over my lips. I stick out my tongue and taste it as if it's a magical elixir of the gods. But the elixir is me. It's my body. I'm touching my lips to myself. Like my inner goddess or something.

EGO SUM VENUS.

I'm not saying it anymore. At least I don't think I am. The words seem to be echoing around us from someplace else.

He slowly makes his way around the curves of my breasts and rubs the sponge over the tips of my nipples. Then he follows the curves of my breasts again and trails down my back to the crack of my ass. It's like he's washing me, and it's unbelievably erotic. I lurch up just from the touch of his hand. He strokes and touches from behind too.

I look at his penis again. I want to taste it. I've never done that before, but I want it in my mouth. I want to suck his dick. Yes, I know it's wrong, but I want to try it. Somehow, knowing it's wrong drives me even more crazy.

He seems to know, and he moves closer to my face. Soon I have his penis fully in my mouth, exploring it with my tongue, just as I sucked his tongue when I French-kissed him. I bob up and down on his dick, sucking and pressing my mouth against it. He moans again. Up and down, I touch and lick him. But I want him. And now I want him inside me. I reach down and touch my groin again as I suck. He moans more and I chuckle.

I want him to jump into the tub with me. I so desire this! I want him to fall in and join me, but he won't. Every time I pull him, he shakes his head, refusing.

I close my eyes. I feel him touching me down below again. He's pressing up and down along my pussy with one hand, and I'm shaking in joy. Then, with two fingers, he enters me. At first it hurts. There's a sharp pain. But the pain only takes me over the edge. I come in the water. But he doesn't stop. I feel him pressing in and out, in and out. He keeps doing this with ever-increasing intensity. I so want him in the tub with me, but he keeps pushing me away. I want him inside me. He refuses. Instead he keeps pressing in and out with his fingers.

I come again. The water splashes around me like a wave.

EGO SUM VENUS!!!

The words shout out like a clap of thunder, literally shaking the whole room. The room quakes, knocking down candles and causing the statue of Venus to fall off its altar and hit the tile floor. I lurch back with a shot of ecstasy, splashing in the tub. I feel spent, but so satisfied.

Then the spell ends. I know it's all over. Bryce is gone. I'm alone inside the tub. And the only evidence I have of the magic is the small statue now lying on the floor.

I look down at my groin. There's a little blood around my vagina in the water.

I jump up from the tub. I feel ashamed and a little violated. I've never even touched myself like that before.

10

RUN CADENCE

I'M RUNNING.

I'm feeling alone.

As I dodge a couple of branches that nearly poke my eyes out, I push the leaves away and leap over a mud puddle. I look up at the canopy of trees surrounding me. The red and yellow leaves arch over me like a domed ceiling, and I feel small, like an insignificant bug. That's really not such a bad feeling right now. I feel unimportant and that's a good escape for me. I wish I could just shrink down to nothing.

The clouds above are shifting, with white and gray mixing over the misty sky. A stream meanders near my dirt path. The water trails along with me, rushing over rocks, as I run. I feel one with nature. That's good. I like the forest—always have. I don't have much company otherwise.

I nearly twist my leg on some uneven ground, but it doesn't slow me down.

I start puffing a bit harder, climbing up an incline.

I know this trail. It wanders far into the nearby mountains. Some say it even connects to caves, but here I can still catch a glimpse of the brick buildings of Hawthorne University.

I stop to catch a breath. There's a brown bird with a red breast—don't know what kind, maybe a robin—on a nearby branch, singing. I reach out a finger and it lets me touch its feathers. I'm surprised. I thought it would fly away before I could touch it. I run my finger over its head. Touching the bird puts me at ease. Then my finger brushes its wing, and it finally takes off.

I kneel down beside the rushing water. It smells clean.

I think of taking out my cell phone and calling Dad. He'd welcome the call. I've already made out the whole conversation in my head. It would go something like this:

"Hi, Dad."

"Hi, squirt." His voice has energy, but I can still hear his depression over Mom.

"I'm leaving."

"Hmm? What do you mean?"

"Hawthorne University." I start crying. It's the right moment, you know. "I'm leaving."

"Why? What's the matter?" he asks.

"It's...it's really weird here. Everyone's so weird. I don't feel like I fit in. I want to go home."

There's a pause. Dad's thinking of what to say. I keep whimpering.

"You can come home anytime you like," he says, but he sounds really down.

"I'm sorry. I know so much—"

"Baby, I just want you to be all right," he says.

Of course he'd say something like that. And he'd mean it. He really loves me.

I brush some sweat from my forehead and lean against a thick tree trunk. Of course I don't reach for my phone. I know the conversation would be something like that, but I'm more the kind of girl who will just drive home if I want to.

That I could do. I could drive home. I could take my battered Honda and just head home. It's only two hours. It seems so far away, but it's close enough. Still, it's not the right time. It would be unfair to Dad.

I could also just cry. But I'm not the crying type either (except that night at Alondra's—I'm not sure what the hell got into me there).

I start running again.

There aren't many people out today. It snowed a few days ago and rained the other night. But today, bundled up in a thick jacket, I can run.

I'm not sleeping during the day anymore. I guess that's better. Instead, I'm working out incessantly. I go to the gym twice a day now, once in the late morning and again after dinner. I'm running so much that I worry my calves are gonna look too big.

The path winds back so I'm approaching a hilltop close to campus. It's the highest point in Hawthorne aside from the outlook at the Billington House. I reach a plateau, covered in weeds, where several dirt paths converge. It's quite beautiful. Trees form a ring around a grassy knoll, and I feel at home here.

I run to the hilltop and look down at the surrounding forests. In the very far distance, I can see the mountains. In the other direction, I just see trees. And more trees. I also see the nearby river meandering into the lake. If I followed the river, it would take me down into the valley and over to Dr. Johansen's house. Alondra has prime real estate. Then, on the other side, at the other tallest peak, I can see the Billington House. Campus is not far below. I put my hands on my hips, breathing heavily, just looking at all this stuff.

The sky is heavy with the sort of dark clouds that look ready to open up in a downpour. I wouldn't mind so much. A little cold mist would do me some good. It's humid enough already that a calm wind brushes a cold vapor against my cheeks and wet hair.

My eyes wander along the wild grass. That's when I notice something very odd in the weeds: a pile of charred logs. I walk closer. A slightly torn black cloak is lying nearby. I step back. I know this cloak. It's part of Alondra's freaky "honors club." They were all wearing them at the initiation. Did they come here too? It's not that far from the other side of campus, maybe a ten-minute walk.

So they were here. They were on this hilltop. Why? I suppose they came at night; this hilltop must offer a spectacular view of the town in the moonlight—and a better view of the stars. They must have been worshipping, doing their hedonistic pleasure shit under the moonlight. That's what they were doing. Then I shudder. I remember Maddie. Perhaps she was wearing this torn cloak.

I walk back down the hill on a meandering dirt trail. Near a stream, the trail converges with a paved path leading me back to campus. I jog past classrooms and, even though it's Saturday, pass a few people carrying backpacks. The clouds are thick enough that I can see some light coming from the central library. I pass Tammy, another girl from Alondra's club. She waves and gives me a genuinely kind smile. I just keep running. They're always smiling. What do all of them find so amusing about me?

When I return to my dorm room, I unlock the door and walk in. Then I throw my drenched sweatshirt and pants in the hamper and head for the communal showers.

As I stand under the soothing hot water, my mind wanders to fantasy again. I'm thinking of the cloak. I'm picturing Alondra and my best friend and the others walking up to the knoll and bowing to the moon. Fucking weirdos.

I shower—fast (not slowly as my pervert TA might instruct me to do). Then I get in a skirt and sweater, preparing to head to the library. I switch off the light, and before I close the door, I stop cold. I turn and see a dim light. It's the candle that Alondra gave me. I placed it near the window a week ago. It's lit. It doesn't look much smaller than it did when Alondra gave it to me, so it must have just been relit.

Boy, Maddie's gonna get it. This is really not funny.

I turn to leave. I think of snuffing it out, but who cares—it's on Maddie's side of the room anyway.

I turn back to the room. The yellow candlelight still flickers.

I feel scared. My chest tightens like it did that night with the Ouija board. What if Maddie didn't light it?

11

DINNER

It's Taco Tuesday and the college always puts out a taco bar in the dining commons. It's my favorite. The food isn't half-bad, and I can put lots of shredded cheese all over the shredded beef and tortillas. And now that I'm working out incessantly, I don't have to worry about my waistline—well, not as much. So I can add sour cream too.

It's six o'clock, peak rush hour, so the dining room is crowded. I sit down alone, and a few girls give me snooty looks. I feel a little lonely, but I'm hungry so I really don't care.

I empty a packet of sugar into my iced tea. It's my ritual, you know—cafeteria food washed down with a glass of iced tea. Usually I'm eating with Maddie. Not now. Not today. We're fighting again.

"Cadence?" I don't recognize the voice. I look up. Standing over me is an overweight goth girl with thick black makeup, her hair tied up in ugly curls, wearing a giant metal nose ring. I stare at the red-and-black demon skeletons along her neck and arms. It's Mira. Mira just sort of squints at me with a deadpan expression. "Is this seat taken?"

Are you serious?

I look around, still surprised that she's talking to me. My table for four is empty.

"No... Have a seat."

"Thanks." She sits down across from me.

Mira has a healthy plate of lettuce, carrots and tomatoes. It makes me feel a little guilty about the tacos. She's even drinking orange juice.

But she looks like death. She leans her head in her hands and rubs her temples, her thick black eyeliner, mascara, and squinting eyes exuding a dismal aura. She seems to be constantly squinting in contempt at everybody around her.

"So..." Mira stabs her fork into the lettuce. It doesn't look like she wants to eat. "How you holding up, Cadence?"

I really don't think it's any of her business, but I offer a fake smile. "Mom's dead," I say with a shrug.

Mira puts her hand on my arm between shoveling a few leaves and, without looking at me, says, "Sorry."

"Yeah." I bite into a taco. It's really good. I gain some satisfaction knowing that my meal is much tastier than hers.

Then she raises her fork, holding a long strip of lettuce, and points it at me. "I don't usually eat here. I try to go out and eat healthier food."

"Oh, all right." *So can you, like, leave?*

"Yeah, but I figured you'd be here ... I mean, you're really cute and all." She throws more leaves in her mouth and continues with her mouth full. "But, if you really knew me, Katie, you'd know that I don't really like joining anybody for dinner. Even someone pretty like you."

I don't like her calling me Katie. And I really don't like her calling me pretty. I'm getting annoyed that I'm eating my taco in the company of such a gloomy goth bitch. Then I nearly lose my appetite when she actually winks at me.

"I'm here for you, Little Bo-Peep," she adds, "but I don't really give a shit what others think of me. I say fuck 'em, you know? So..." She shrugs and tries a smile again. "Don't think I'm here to have dinner with you. I don't really like eating with anyone."

O-kay??

On that note, I pick up my taco and eat again, watching a music video on the TV screen. I try my best to ignore her...because, after all, she doesn't really care about anybody anyway.

"So the real question, Cadence, is why am I here?"

"Yeah, why are you here?"

"To warn you."

I put my taco down and wipe my face with a paper napkin. "What?"

"A lot of changes are coming, Katie. Be ready."

"Please don't call me that."

"What?"

"Katie."

"Why?" She seems amused. "Isn't that what your friends call you?"

"Yeah, but—"

"I'm not your friend," she says dismally. "I understand."

She's so depressing!

"Okay, Cadence, or whatever the fuck people call you." She points her fork at me again. "Now that Madison's one with the coven, you need to know that she won't be your friend either."

"What do you mean?"

Mira smiles again with this mischievous, almost lewd, gaze into my eyes, and I can't help but think that her lips are curling in a way that seems more sensual than kind. I feel sick again.

"Madison answers to Alondra now," she explains. "That's more important than your friendship." She examines me as if trying to be sure what she's saying is sinking in. Then she shakes her head. "Don't look at me like that. You're acting like I'm full of shit. I guarantee you, Little Bo-Peep, that I know, after being a member longer than most, what I'm talking about with regard to the coven. I know you two were close, but you have to accept now that Maddie's a member of our family, not just your friend."

"I don't see how my friend is your business."

"She is"—she takes a swig of her orange juice—"when she's my sister."

I go back to eating my taco and staring up at the TV.

Mira chuckles contemptuously. "And Bryce. Bryce is our family too."

I nearly spit out my food. This is getting personal.

"Perhaps I should go," I snap, getting up. "Sorry, but I'm really not interested in talking to you."

"How rude," she says with a smirk. But there's actually a hint of offense in her voice.

"I just don't like people talking about my business."

"Bryce? He's *our* business, Cadence." She stabs more leaves, staring at her salad. "You need to join. If you join the coven, all this will make sense."

"I don't think my friends are any of your business."

"Sit down, will you?" She looks up at me curiously. "I said, they are when they're my brother and sister. They're members of the coven."

I reluctantly sit.

"You know I don't really care what you think about me," Mira says. Then she chews on more lettuce with an empty expression, almost to prove it. "Bryce ..." she finally mutters with her mouth full.

"What about him?" I snap. "Bryce is my teacher. So what?"

"Your *teacher*?" she says with a cackle. "Seriously? Is that all? He's part of the coven. When he came to you as an incubus, he broke our pact."

"Incubus?"

She rolls her eyes at me. "If you were one with the coven, you'd know. All you have to do is join. If you don't, you'll suffer...but you liked it when he came to you, didn't you, Cadence? He made you feel good?" She smiles that wicked smile again. Then she whispers, "When you sucked his dick."

I jump up. "Enough!" People turn, startled by my outburst. "Just stay away from me."

"Sorry," she says, raising a hand. "But you asked what an incubus is. An incubus is a demon spirit that comes to fuck you. Bryce came to you as a spirit that night to fuck you. That black magic shit actually kinda pissed Alondra off. Wizard Reardon taught him how to do that. He came as a demon spirit to fuck you, Cadence. He's quite smitten by you."

"You're really disgusting, you know that?" I snap. It doesn't seem to faze her. Even all the students still staring at us don't seem to bother her much. She chuckles. Then she gets up too.

"I'll go. I've said enough. I'm just warning you, that's all. If you don't join, things will stay confused. If you enter our circle, it will be a lot clearer."

"Why are *you* telling me all this?"

She picks up her tray, stands up, and cocks her head. Then she nods. "Because Alondra asked me to."

12

SHOPPING

MADDIE'S WITH ME, SHOPLIFTING AT VICTORIA'S SECRET IN DOWNTOWN Atlanta. She has a list of outfits she needs to get and a bunch of things she aims to stow away in her pockets. When I snatch the note from her hand, I gasp in disbelief.

1. *Burgundy pair of lace stockings*
2. *Burgundy lace bras*
3. *Burgundy panties*
4. *Burgundy silk scarf or tie*

Burgundy this, burgundy that; what's with burgundy?

1. *A black or white silk negligee with a matching bra and panties*
2. *Four G-strings (color is unimportant)*

Maddie grabs a pair of purple panties from the shelf and quickly sticks it in her pants pocket. I think she was only a few seconds away from being spotted by the clerk at the desk, but she's a pro.

"What's this?" I say in a forced whisper, shoving the paper into her chest.

Maddie grabs it and laughs.

"Is it kinky shit for Nick?"

"Yeah," Maddie responds sarcastically. "For Nick." Then she steals another pair of panties and closes a small wooden drawer. Of course it's not for Nick. Why would Nick need four G-strings?

I'm thinking she's preparing for a pornographic movie or something. Maddie has a basket of items in one hand and a few other things in the inside pockets of her jeans.

"I can't tell you," she says. "Just don't worry 'bout it, Katie."

"What can't you tell me?"

We're BFFs, you know. There's nothing we've ever kept from each other. But I back off a little. It's been good to be with my friend again, and I don't want to spoil our peace.

"Can't tell you," Maddie says and browses some more.

I lean against another white oak table covered with underwear. I've got nothing slutty to buy in this place. The only boy I can even think of is Bryce, and I haven't been thinking much of him either as of late.

"If it's for another frat party, count me out."

"Okay," Maddie says with a chuckle. Then she resumes her whore attire hunt.

She's looking at a pretty black silk negligee. She's picks it up and touches the material. It looks expensive. She's probably thinking about how she can stow it in her pocket without being caught and realizing it's too big. Especially since, by now, her pockets are pretty full. She lays it over my chest and says, "Can you try this on for me, Katie?"

"What? Why?"

"Try it on, Cadence. I want to see what it looks like on you. I want to see it on someone else before I buy it."

It feels soft. It's silky smooth. The black is as black as you can get.

"I think it'd look better on you. I can wait here if you want me to."

"Come on. Try it on, Katie. I've got some other stuff for you to try on too."

So we head over to the changing room, and I'm trying on this black negligee, but it's really not a negligee. It reminds me of something an S&M pervert would wear with tight leather clothes and boots while holding a whip. But Maddie's looking very earnestly at my get-up.

"Hurry," I say, rolling my eyes.

She chuckles. Then she starts tying these laces, which I didn't even know existed, on my back.

"You're kinda scaring me." *Is she turning gay? Maybe that's what Mira meant when she talked about their "coven."* "Why do you want me to try it on for you?"

"Looks good," Maddie says with a nod, ignoring my question. "Here's another." She pushes a burgundy one to me and then, before I can try the red one on, she presses a black silk bra over my chest.

"We're not here for me," I say with a sigh.

Maddie laughs. "It's the last one."

It's not the last one. She hands me another, but this silk negligee is white. There's something even more sinful about that. Being white, it looks like it fits under a wedding dress.

"So why are you getting all this kinky shit, anyway?" I ask, trying on the last garment.

But she's ignoring me. She's looking me over really carefully for some reason.

"You buying this for me?" I ask. "You want me to wear this when we're spending a nice quiet night at home alone together watching a movie?"

"Shh ..." Maddie says. "Don't be stupid, Cadence." She's so focused. She raises an eyebrow. Then she shakes her head. "Not bad. White. Goes well with your darker complexion. Definitely not burgundy. Nor the black one. Only white."

"Okay. Then I can take it off?"

"Sure," she says with a laugh.

"So," I say as I quickly untie the laces, "how's Nick? You two hit a home run yet?"

"A long time ago, Katie," she says, shaking her head contemptuously.

I don't like that. I don't like how my friend always acts like I'm so prudish. She's only six months older than me. And anyway, it's just sexual intercourse. What's so special? It's just sex. It's no big deal.

I've never had sex before. Maddie knows that. But she acts like it's some special accomplishment that makes her more mature than me.

I did have that weird encounter with Bryce. It seemed so sinful and wrong. The whole thing makes me uncomfortable when I think about it. It's why I've been avoiding Bryce ever since.

I start throwing on my blue cotton T-shirt and hand silk panties back to Maddie. She wanted me to try it on with the white outfit. There was no way I was gonna do that.

She finally turns away.

"You becoming a perv, Maddie?"

"Fuck off, Katie. But thanks for trying it on. I needed to shop for someone about your size."

"For Alondra's club? You having an orgy?"

"Fuck off again."

She swings open the dressing room door.

"Did you two find everything you were looking for?" asks the sales-clerk, who's been waiting for us. She's got a warm smile. She seems nice.

"Sure did," I say. Then I stick my tongue out at Maddie when the girl takes the articles of clothing we don't want.

We walk to the cashier. Maddie somehow manages to pay for most of it, but she stows away the rest. Then she turns to me. She has a big grin and hooks my arm into hers.

"Come on, girlfriend. Let's have lunch before your boring dad comes."

"Okay."

So, we're eating fast-food hamburgers together, and I'm savoring a tasty hot fry when I notice that my friend's ordered a Caesar salad. That's odd. She usually eats unhealthier food than I do.

Red and green are all over the food court because it's the yuletide season. Christmas is coming, and I reflect on how odd Hawthorne University is. Everywhere in this mall there are pictures of Santa Claus and his helpers, Christmas trees, stockings, sleds, fake snow—everything that tells everybody that Christmas is coming. But not at Hawthorne. Our college pushes Christmas to the side. I've been told it's for political reasons. In order not to offend people, the university chose not to cele-brate anything tied to religion. They could have celebrated Hanukkah,

Kwanzaa, and everything else during December, but instead they chose to celebrate nothing. That's probably why Halloween is always such a big hit at the Billington House. Anyway, Mother Nature tells you when it's the yuletide season in Hawthorne with leafless branches and frigid weather.

It was the same way last year. But not in Atlanta. Here, especially at the shopping center, Christmas is all over the place.

"Want one?" I ask, offering a French fry.

"No."

"They're good."

"Sorry, can't."

Maddie turns on her iPhone and starts texting somebody. She's typing quickly.

"I really should be shopping for something for your aunt Jane."

"Huh?" she asks.

"Jane. Your mom."

"What?" she asks again, staring at her phone irritably. She keeps typing away.

I look around the food court. Few of the tables and chairs are empty. If it weren't for the holiday season, it would probably be a ghost town this time of the week.

A large glass dome provides light to all the fast food restaurants. I look up at the cloudy sky. I think it might rain today. Maybe snow again.

"Shit!" Maddie says.

"What's the matter?"

"Hmm?" Maddie asks with a fake smile. "Nothing."

I unwrap my burger and take a giant bite. Maddie's still staring at her phone, not too interested in her salad. It reminds me of Mira. Obviously, their weird sex cult involves eating leaves. I find it funny how much they seem to hate doing it.

"Want some?" I offer my burger.

She just shoos me away with her hand. She's glued to her phone.

"Who are you texting?"

"Jesus, Cadence," Maddie says, looking up. "You're so nosy."

"Just wondering. And...what's with you not liking fresh, hot French fries? You know they're the best food in the world."

"Alondra..." Maddie shakes her head and looks back down at her phone. "Now please, leave me alone so I can send this important message."

"Can I ask you a question?"

"Hmm?" But she's still texting.

"Can I ask you a question?"

"What?"

"Can you stop lighting my mother's candle? I wish you wouldn't do that. I'd rather leave it unlit. When it's lit, it reminds me of losing her. I don't like that."

Maddie's still looking down at her phone. She shakes her head. "I haven't. I haven't lit your candle, Katie."

"What?"

"Hmm?" Maddie's pressing in all the letters carefully now. I look over her shoulder, mostly as a joke, but that really pisses her off. She jumps back. "Stop it, Cadence!"

"What do you mean you haven't lit it? Then who has?"

"What are you talking about?" Maddie asks. "I've never seen it lit, Kate." Then she hits the table. "Shit!"

"What's the matter?"

"Cadence," she snaps. "I..." She wavers for a moment. "There's just things I can't tell you, 'kay? I've sworn. I told you this before."

She puts her phone down and gives me a pouty face. "Don't look like that, Katie. You know I've joined Alondra's coven." There's that word again. "I swore secrecy."

"We've never kept anything from one another before." I'm surprised at how sad those words sound.

"You're so cute," she says, touching my arm. "But that was before I signed."

"And what happens if you disobey? You die?"

"No." But then she smiles and touches my arm again. "Don't worry 'bout it."

"Okay. But...what about my candle? If you didn't light it, then who did?"

Maddie shrugs. She presses a few more buttons and then stuffs some lettuce into her mouth. "Where's your dad, anyway?"

13

———

DAD

MY DAD DOESN'T LOOK ANY BETTER THAN WHEN I LEFT HIM AT THE funeral. He's thin and gaunt. Mom did that to him, even before she passed. And he looks depressing as hell, but I know when he interacts with people he hides it. I see him hiding it when he spots Maddie from across the mall. But even with his fake smile, he still looks sad. It reminds me a little bit of Mira, but that makes me hate Mira, because she doesn't have any reason for her depression. Dad does.

When our paths finally merge, Dad loses his melancholy and lights up at the sight of me. And his smile is real. He walks up and gives me a tight hug.

"Cadence."

"Hi, Dad."

Dad turns to my friend. "Hi, Madison."

"Hi, Mr. Hawthorne."

"You're looking good, Madison."

Madison's holding the pink Victoria Secret bag. Dad glances at it curiously. Thank God *she's* holding it.

No matter how much he smiles, I can feel his pain. And I think Maddie can too.

"I thought we'd meet for lunch," he says.

"We just ate," I say.

"Oh," he says. And for a moment, under his bushy eyebrows, his forlorn gray eyes nearly reveal his sadness. But then he recovers with a smile. "Well, I can just grab something. Perhaps we can go shopping?"

"I need to get back to school, Mr. Hawthorne," Maddie says.

"Oh. You're welcome to come with us and stay in our house," Dad says.

"That's okay. I really have to get back."

I wonder if it has something to do with Alondra's club. For a moment, Maddie flashes a disapproving glance, probably guessing my thoughts. I don't want her to go yet. The fact is, now that we're back to being friends, I haven't even begun to drill her regarding Alondra's mysteries.

"All right. Well, thanks for taking care of my baby." Dad gives Maddie a hug. But no one takes care of me. That kind of pisses me off.

"Bye, Maddie. I'll see you Monday," I say.

"All right, Katie." Then she winks and says, "Thanks for helping me with my shopping."

Bitch.

Maddie pecks me on my cheek and gives me a hug. Then she's off, turning her iPhone on again and texting as she walks briskly away.

"Nice friend," Dad says.

"Yeah."

"She's always been good to you, Cadence. She's a keeper."

"Sure is."

As we're heading outside to the parking lot, Dad cocks his head and says seriously, "I thought you'd want to take a break from school for a while. It will be good for me to have some company this weekend. And it'll give you time to think. And... rest... now that Mom's gone. I've made your bed in your room."

I don't know why, but everything—from seeing him walking toward me and Maddie with his head down to his holding my hand and circling the parking lot under the dark, cloudy sky—strikes me as really fucking depressing. I don't like it. I suddenly have an urge to call Maddie to pick me up and rescue me. But then my sweet dad looks right into my eyes with those gray eyes and says, "Whatever you need, whatever you want, squirt, I'll get you. You and your brother are what's important now. I think Mom passed too early. And it makes me angry that she had to go."

"I know."

"She shouldn't have left us so soon," he adds, clenching his teeth.

"I know. I don't want to talk about it."

"Oh...sure, Cadence. Neither do I."

Dad drives me home in silence.

Home isn't home. It's a mausoleum for Mom. Mom's favorite scented candles and the perfume she wore every day of my life linger in the halls. And it's the last thing I want. Really. I want to just forget the whole thing.

So I leave as early as I can on Saturday. And then I feel guilty. I feel bad for Dad. He's so lonely. But I can't stay in that house. Not with the smells. Not with the pictures and the memories. Not with the memories of Mom.

I call Maddie. She drives me home. But she lets me drive most of the way back while she texts on her iPhone.

14

THE SACRIFICE

I'm walking to my English lit class, passing a few bodies along a covered sidewalk—it's raining, so everybody's crowded under the ugly metal awning—and somebody taps me on the back of my shoulder. I turn and it's a boy wearing a white T-shirt and gray slacks and carrying a large brown leather bag. His hair is brushed back, and he looks too clean to be one of the students. It's Bryce. He comes up to me as the walkway descends down a few stairs.

"Cadence," he says, sounding a little desperate, "I called, but you didn't answer." We dodge some more bodies. Not only is it raining, it's around 11:30 rush hour. Most of the other students are like me and don't go to school in the wee hours of the morning. I haven't been to Bryce's class in two weeks.

"Just busy," I say with a fake grin. "How are you, Bryce?"

"Great." After being a gentleman and waiting for an elderly woman with a cane to walk down the stairs, he jumps over the last steps to keep up with me. "Did I do something wrong?"

I look at his eyes. Damn, those baby blues! How could he ever do anything wrong? I could get lost in those blues. But I don't. I won't. I don't want to be a part of his hedonistic shit. And my best friend's coven. But... he's...so...cute.

I'm not mad. Or am I? I don't even know. All I know is that after the strange bath ceremony, I really don't want to see him anymore.

"Nor have you come to class," he says.

Damn, he's persistent. And he's referring to *his* class. I never miss Alondra's.

It's pouring rain, and we're at the end of the antique steel awning. I take out an umbrella. He grabs it out of my hand, saying, "Allow me."

I snatch it back. "It's all right," I say. "I'm fine."

"Well, I was hoping we could meet again," he says. Now he's getting wet while I'm shielded by my giant red umbrella. He doesn't give up. "Well? Did I do something?"

Yeah, you had sex with me under a magical demon spell. And... What was it Mira called it? ...an incubus.

I finally stop at just the right moment to watch him getting drenched. Then we just stand there together.

"This is really weird, Bryce," I say after some uncomfortable silence.

"What? Weird?"

"The package you gave me. It was really weird."

"Oh. Sorry. But is that why you're not answering your calls?"

Uhh...yeah. I roll my eyes.

"Wait," he says, gripping my arm like a vise. "Did you...try it, then?"

I would have thought he knew, being that he was there. I look at him as if to say, *Are you for real?* What does he mean, did I try it? It was his hands rubbing my naked ass. Indeed, there's a hint of deception in his gaze. I smile back at him, on to his lie. All the while, his nicely combed hair is dripping.

To be honest with you, I actually like how he's acting desperate to see me. I'm being a real bitch, but I can't help but be mad.

"Don't play with me," I say. But I don't pull away my arm or walk away. I look down. That gets me madder because it feels weak. But we're alone now. And as much as I'm acting pissed, I don't want him to go.

People pass us, leaving the shelter of the awning, walking fast. We're the only ones standing out in the rain getting drenched.

He doesn't respond. But he doesn't move away either.

"I don't want to play with spells or voodoo shit," I explain finally, forcing my eyes to meet his.

"All right," he says. "No more spells. I promise." And then that infernal handsome smile.

"If you want to spend time with me, don't do that again," I add.

"Sure."

"Right."

I'm searching his eyes. Shit, I'm hooked! I'm mesmerized. He is too. He's just letting the water drip down his forehead, and he doesn't even care about the rain. We're just staring at each other like high school sweethearts. And neither one of us wants to go.

"Here," I say, putting my umbrella over him. "You're really getting wet."

"It's okay. As long as you're talking to me." *Damn, don't say stuff like that!*

He gives me a stupid smile. I finally walk toward the quad and he follows.

"May I ask you out to dinner, Cadence?" he asks. He's so suave about it. I laugh, and it seems to hurt his feelings a little.

"Why not?" I say with a nod. I'm trying to cover him with my umbrella. "Where?"

"How about Lacey's?" Lacey's is a quaint steak house a few miles from campus.

"'Kay."

"Great, I'll pick you up tonight at seven." He's super excited and it's cute.

"Wait! *Tonight?*"

"Yeah. Why not?"

How rude. Who asks someone out on a date on the same night? How arrogant. Then again, who has sex in a bathtub using devil spells?

"I have a test tomorrow," I lie.

"Then we can make it Thursday."

"Hmm...I'd rather see you on the weekend. I'm freer, without any tests from my teachers or...*you.*"

He chuckles. "I can't this weekend. There's a meeting with the coven at Alondra's on Friday and Saturday. Unless you're referring to Sunday. But Sunday is before Monday, isn't it? You probably have a test then, you little bookworm."

"Okay, I'll call you when I'm free, then. Bye, Bryce."

And then I rush away, leaving him in the pouring rain. I look back. The poor boy's drenched.

Why did I do that? I don't know. He creeps me out, I suppose. But it gives me time to think about him. Maybe talk it over with Maddie. No, she's a part of their voodoo club too.

Do I want to spend time with him? I don't know.

He's so hot. Yeah, of course I want to see him.

I do what I really shouldn't do. I go to Alondra's house Friday evening. It's not because I've been invited to some sort of party or initiation or because I've finally decided to sign Dr. Reardon's consent forms to join their pagan club. And it isn't because I plan on seeing Bryce there—though I know he'll be there. It's because of my friend Maddie. Maddie's been missing for the past two days.

She's been coming home late lately, but her not showing up at all really upsets me. I figure she'll be at Alondra's, or at least Alondra has some idea of where my best friend's gone.

I walk up the familiar path. It's still raining and cold, and I have a thick coat and my giant red umbrella. I think of how wet Bryce was and how he was trying to woo me—just like Nick did for Maddie in the library. That was cute. But I still haven't called him.

I rap on the door using that huge knocker. Then I close my umbrella under the ancient white wooden awning of Alondra's mansion. No one answers. But I hear them. Or I hear something. There's singing or chanting and the clanging of tambourines and drums. It's coming from the backyard. I force myself to swallow and walk around the house to sneak a peek.

From behind a thick tree beside the wall, I crouch down and watch. There's a bonfire in the backyard, but this time the group, or *coven* as they call themselves, is dancing around the flames. And they're naked. They've left those black cloaks on the ground, and they're dancing and chanting in the nude. They must be freezing under the icy rain, but it doesn't seem to bother them. I turn away. But then I recall why I've come. I'm looking for Maddie.

In some ways, I don't want to find her. I'd rather tell myself that she's not involved in this weird stuff. But I see her. At least, I think I see her. A woman about her size, wearing camouflage paint on her face and body, is dancing naked with her eyes rolled back. She seems drugged. It's very frightening. I've never seen Maddie in such a state.

I don't recognize the girl standing in front of Maddie, but I recognize the black-skinned girl behind her: Tammy. And then I see Mira. Mira's also naked, but with all her tattoos it's hard to tell. She seems to be leading the circle.

I try not to look, but my eyes are glued to them. Then I see men. Two men, one old and one young, dancing together in the circle. The older one is Dr. Reardon, and the young man is Bryce. They're naked too, with their privates flapping about, as they dance with the women. And, like the women, they're wearing thick camouflage makeup.

Another figure emerges from the back of the house. I glimpse long hair under the hood of her black cloak. She pulls a cart by a rope toward the circle. On the cart is an animal, squirming, tied down with ropes. It looks like a young calf or sheep, or maybe a dog. I can't tell from this distance. The woman stops before the fire and raises her palm to the sky, a large metal charm dangling from her hand. An old man, I'm guessing Reardon, falls to the ground before the charm with his arms wide, dancing on his knees. The others seem to come more alive, like ants suddenly stirred into a frenzy, raising their arms as they circle around the Reardon and the woman in the cloak. It's like they're worshipping.

Then the woman unsheathes a long curved knife inside her cloak. I see her profile as she turns, and I can clearly spot her breasts, hips, and legs. She's naked too, under the cloak. The woman raises her knife and thrusts it into the animal, which utters a terrible cry. Then the circle cries out too, and their voices echo throughout the grounds. I nearly fall back into the bush in a panic.

The woman in the cloak turns and looks straight at me. The others are totally oblivious, lost in their drugged furor, but the leader seems to see me. Then she smiles. A shiver runs down my back as I realize not only have I been found by their leader, but the leader who's found me is

Alondra. I would recognize that smug smile anywhere. My legs move against my will and I almost run, but I'm afraid the others will see me. So I'm left frozen, still watching the bizarre spectacle before me.

With the knife, Alondra slices the back of her arm. She allows the blood to slowly drip over the animal while the others circle around her, with their eyes rolled back, flinging their bodies about in drugged revelry. But Alondra seems sober. She moves with her usual grace and focus as she looks down at the animal. She runs a bloody hand—her blood—over the creature. Then she thrusts the knife into the animal again. She thrusts again and again. The naked worshippers cry out along with the animal until it stops moving. I hear one last scream—an odd animal scream. And when it's done, one of the ladies from the circle hands Alondra a towel. She wipes her bloody hands.

Then Alondra turns and looks at me. She smiles her infamous smile once more. It's all too much for me. I run for it.

15

OFFICE HOURS

Dr. Johansen's office hours are Mondays and Fridays between seven and nine in the morning. Her office is always packed with students, despite the early hours, because her class is so popular. I never go, but after the events of the weekend, I force myself to go now. I'm determined to confront her. I want to know what this is all about, not just for myself but for my friend. Maddie was upsettingly tight-lipped when she returned home yesterday. She even denied having been there on Friday, even though I'm sure I saw her.

I'm one of the last students in line. (You can't expect me to get up this early in the morning, can you?) There are still three students ahead of me. Alondra walks out in her formal white silk blouse, leather jacket, and slacks and looks at the three of us.

"Sorry, guys," Alondra says. "If it's short, you can see me after class and ask...or next week."

Everyone's disappointed. Then she closes the door on me. I'm enraged. She didn't even acknowledge my presence, though I'm sure she saw me.

Everybody leaves the hallway. I don't. I knock. Nothing. I knock again. Still nothing.

I'm resolved not to move. She'll either have to make an exit out her window or run into me. I wait nearly thirty minutes, knocking intermittently. Then she opens the door.

"Oh, hi, Cadence," she says, acting as if she didn't see or hear me.

"I need to speak with you, Dr. Johansen."

"Is it regarding the Inquisition? Egypt?" Her evasiveness is almost sarcastic. Before, I always found her smile endearing; today it seems so fake and infuriating.

"What's going on?" I snap. "What have you done to my friend! What—"

"Keep your voice down," she hollers back. Her anger surprises me. I've never seen her angry, and her voice is commanding. Then she looks down the hall, impatiently shakes her head, and opens the door wider. "Come in." It's not a suggestion; it's a demand.

Dr. Johansen's office is very small but immaculate. Two cheap red suede chairs face a dark mahogany desk. We're on the second floor, and there's a really nice view of the quad. I sit on one of the red suede chairs. Alondra drapes her leather jacket on the large leather chair, sits down, and leans back. She puts her finger to her chin. Then she says— nothing.

"I saw you," I say. "I saw all of you dancing naked around the fire."

"Close the door," she says impassively.

I had forgotten about the door. I get up and oblige; then I sit down. I'm uneasy before her. I'm not accustomed to an angry Alondra. I'm used to her sweet professor persona.

"What did you say?" Alondra is deadpan, still leaning back in her chair, making me feel stupid.

"I saw you and the honors students dancing naked around a fire." Again I feel really weird hearing it come out of my mouth.

She squints and leans forward. "Do you have any idea how ridiculous that sounds?"

"What's happening? What's going on with my friend? Maddie was gone for days last week."

"I don't know what you're talking about, Cadence. How should I know?"

"I saw you. And I know you saw me."

She looks up for a moment. "Well, I'm very busy, Ms. Hawthorne. I have to review quizzes. If this isn't a question about class, I would prefer you leave."

I stand up. "I can tell Administration. There are a lot of weird things going on at your house. Who knows, you could even be abusing the students."

"There's nothing hurtful going on at my house. I can assure you of that."

"Tell that to the animal you killed."

Alondra smiles. It's a sly, wicked smile. "Please leave."

"No. Tell me what you're doing. You looked right at me! Stop acting like nothing happened, because I know it did. I saw you with my own eyes."

"If you believe your eyes, then something indeed happened, Cadence. I'm not refuting that. You saw what you saw, but that has nothing to do with you leaving my office. Office hours are over. Get out."

"What does that mean?"

"It means what I said."

Tears start streaming from my eyes, surprising both of us. I'm not one to cry, but I'm furious. "I trusted you," I mutter. I jump up and make my way to the door.

"I trusted you, Cadence," she says as my hand touches the doorknob. "I asked you to join, but you refused. Do you think I can tell you anything? Even if I want to?"

I'm frozen, with my hand still on the doorknob, looking down at her drab brown carpet.

"Mira told me you sent her." I'm still looking down at the floor. "Is that true? Can you at least tell me that?"

"Yes. I sent her to speak to you." I whirl around, and she doesn't have that infernal self-assured smirk on her lips anymore. She looks concerned.

"Why?"

"Because I wanted you to join. You're a smart girl, and now that your best friend is one with the coven, I thought things would be easier if you joined. Things like this would not be so hard on you."

"You're all witches, aren't you ... Like Wicca?"

She smiles and gestures for me to sit, but I remain standing. Then she shakes her head. "Not Wicca. I see you've learned from class. But I don't affiliate myself with any formal group, Cadence."

"But you are a witch?"

"Yes, Cadence, I am a witch."

"A good witch or a bad witch?"

She laughs, and for the first time the tension in the room is lifted. "I think I'm a pretty good person. Don't you?"

"It didn't look that way last night."

"Sit down, Cadence." She gestures with a broad sweep of her arm. I feel like she's about to cast a spell. I sit back down, anxious.

"Where did you see me and this animal I supposedly killed?"

"At your house. In your yard."

"What were you doing in my yard, Cadence?"

She's not accusing me. She's giving me a welcoming smile, and I have to admit I feel better. I brush the tears from my eyes.

"Maddie's been missing. So has Bryce. So I figured they'd be at your house. I knocked on your door, but no one answered, so I walked around. That's where I saw the fire—"

"The bonfire?" she asks. "The pyre, like you saw when we honored your mother?"

"Yeah."

"And what was I doing with—"

"Don't play games with me."

"I'm not playing games." She earnestly shakes her head. Then she opens a desk drawer and takes out a very large metal object. It's a five-pointed star with a circle around it, the size of her palm. It's the charm she cast over the animal before killing it. She puts it on the desk and leans back, waiting to hear more from me.

"What's that?" I ask.

"A pentagram."

"Why do you have it...in your desk?" *What the hell?* But I'm actually not that surprised.

She smiles again. I wish she'd stop doing that. "Does it frighten you? You're not a practicing Christian. Christians fear it as a sign of the devil. Of Satan. But if I recall, you told me you were an atheist. And anyway, the pentagram was used by early Christians to symbolize the five wounds of

Christ. But if I turn it"—she turns it so that one point is pointing downward—"it becomes the symbol for Satan and for devil worshippers. Just as if I turned a cross over. All it takes is one turn." She turns the pentagram back. "There, now it's back to being safe again. This is good, and this"—once again, she turns it backward—"is evil. Good Christian faith, bad Satanic worship. That is how quickly one can turn. Perhaps a construct, perhaps not?"

I can't help but feel like she's teaching again. I almost have an idiotic urge to open my backpack and take notes.

"I can teach you a lot more than history," Alondra says, her face now quite serious, "but you have to swear secrecy. If you can't do that, then I can't allay your suspicions regarding your friends. Or me. I told Mira to tell you that."

"And which way do you prefer?" I ask with my own sly smile. I turn the pentagram back. Facing her, it is evil; facing me, it is good.

"You won't know until you join, Cadence. Until you can trust me."

"I told you, I don't want to join."

"Why are you afraid?" She turns the medallion around again. "They say in the Buddhist religion, evil is ignorance. The word *witch* means wisdom. Perhaps if you will allow me to impart wisdom, you will not see me as evil anymore."

"I don't think you're evil." But after I mutter the words, I'm unsure.

"Then why not join?"

"I...I don't know."

I bite my lip. She's staring at me, seeing my frizzled morning hair, the bags under my eyes, and my casual attire: a university sweatshirt and jeans. I look outside the window to avoid her penetrating green eyes. It's like she could hypnotize me with one look. And now that she admits to being a witch, I wonder if she can cast a spell just looking at me with those jade eyes.

"I will deny everything," Alondra says, finally averting her gaze. "I have to in order to protect the coven... Did you record this spectacle you say you saw? Perhaps record it with your phone?"

"No."

"Then you have no proof," she says. "And every member of the coven will deny it. We have all sworn to maintain secrecy and protect each other."

"Why?"

"Because people are just as scared as you are, Cadence." Alondra takes a deep breath. "People fear the unknown. And they persecute those who are different. They have been doing that since Salem. Since before Salem."

I merely nod.

"Do you know what happened twenty years ago to a daycare teacher?" she asks. "It was like Salem. There was a man who practiced witchcraft in Minnesota. One of the kids he was caring for told her parents that he'd touched her. Authorities investigated. Then another student claimed wrongdoing. Then another. One said that the teacher was forcing them to eat their own shit." I don't like it when Dr. Johansen cusses. She seems to notice and pauses for a second. Then she looks back into my eyes and makes it worse. "Another claimed he touched her vagina and rammed a pencil up it. There was no proof, but when it was found out that the teacher was a practitioner of Wicca, it was all over. The teacher was arrested. He was actually jailed for a couple of years, until it was found that he was completely innocent."

"I wouldn't tell anybody anything about you."

"Cadence," she says, leaning forward and raising her eyebrows, "you said a minute ago that you were gonna tell Administration on me."

Oops.

"Cadence," she says, recovering her smile, "I know you're under tremendous stress right now. I respect that. I told you how sorry I was to hear about your mother. But you have to understand my position. As much as I care about you, and you are one of my favorite students, I can't risk everything and tell you our secrets. Unless you join."

I nod.

"I think you should give us a try. All your friends have joined. Why don't you?"

"Can I leave? Can I leave once I join?"

Alondra nods, and there's a sudden look of triumph on her face. "If you swear secrecy, you can return to your normal life at any time. I don't think you'll want to. It's just that you must never tell anyone about us if you go."

"I only care about Maddie. I want to join to help her."

"All right." But Alondra didn't believe that was the only reason. And I wasn't sure I believed it myself.

"What if I tell?" I ask.

She turns the pentagram backwards in front of me, but her face is impassive. The meaning is clear enough.

"Why do you want me to join so badly?"

She shrugs. "Your best friend and boyfriend are members."

"Bryce isn't my boyfriend," I say with a chuckle.

"He gave you a love spell. He sure seems to think there's something between you."

He does? Of course he does. He was so anxious to see me again. And I haven't answered one call or text.

How does Alondra know? Of course she knows. It was a spell. She must know everything about her group. Her *coven*.

I look at her bookshelves. All her books are on ancient cultures, many regarding magic. It all makes sense. She's a witch. She's teaching all this stuff about history and magic because it's a part of what she does, her real job. Her work as a professor is just cover. Outside school she's a bona fide witch.

"I can leave at any time?"

She nods.

"Will I have to dance naked around a fire?"

She laughs. "Only if you want to."

16

A DATE

Bryce is taking out a confidentiality agreement for me to sign, but even in the dimly lit restaurant, I'm distracted by those bushy eyebrows, well-kempt hair, and baby-blue eyes. He's so excited that I'm signing. I'm not. I still have my reservations about Alondra's cult. But I'm also really curious. And I keep telling myself that Maddie needs me to save her. She doesn't, but I keep telling myself that.

I'm wearing a really pretty blue dress with a golden brooch pinned to the shoulder. It kind of makes me look like a goddess—like Diana or something. I even braided my hair all formal and Greek-like. But I don't think Bryce can see much. Lacey's is a small steak house encompassing one very dark room. Either they're trying to save on their electric bill or they think pitch-black darkness is romantic. There are booths on the side and candles lighting every table, so I can see Bryce in the flickering flame. He's wearing a T-shirt and jeans. He looks way underdressed, but he's so clean shaven and neat that it doesn't matter. And anyway, I can see those pecs and I'm reminded of what lies underneath his clothes.

"Just sign the last three pages, okay?" he says with a smile. He butters some bread and hands it to me. That's so adorable. "Got it?"

"Aha."

"I think it's a good decision, Katie. You won't be out of the loop anymore."

I sigh and raise my glass of wine as if in a toast. It's a really big glass. It tastes sweet and quite lovely.

"So...it might snow next week," I say. "Are you guys still going to get on your brooms and fly around naked?" I often try to be funny when I'm nervous.

He smiles. "You'll know after you sign," he says, waving his hand over the document.

I pick up a pen. I'm surprised at how much legal jargon there is. It's actually a bit intimidating.

I look up. "So...you sue me if I tell?" Then I'm staring back down at the document. I turn two pages because there's no way I'm actually going to read it.

"It's a formality, Cadence. It's more binding through magic than by law. But the secrecy is quite real for the coven."

I sign the document. He takes it from me, looking elated. Then I feel regret. I feel like I just signed away my soul to the devil.

"On Friday, Cadence, we'll initiate you."

"Great." That seemed simple enough. I sip more wine.

The waitress comes and takes our order. She's wearing a formal suit. I can barely see the suit because it's so dark. Then I take a bite of the sourdough bread and wonder if it has mold on it. I'd never know because it's so dark, but it tastes quite warm and fresh.

We order steaks, cooked medium, with baked potatoes. Then I sit back with my wineglass and smile at my hunk of a date. I'm amused by the fact that we've been chasing each other back and forth for the last couple of months, but this is our first actual date. And then I wonder if that's my prime reason for joining.

"Well, now that that's over." Bryce raises his wineglass and looks up thoughtfully. "You know it's not often I take my students out to dinner."

"It's not often I go out on dates with my teachers."

Then we're quiet. I butter more bread and turn to the windows, which are draped in red and impossible to see out of.

What I really want to ask him about is our encounter, but I don't know how to broach the subject. It was so weird, and I'm worried that bringing it up will just spook me again. But if we ever want to go beyond our date tonight, I should bring it up. But then I think about the contract again, and I wonder if I'm a complete idiot for signing it.

"You're such a mystery, Cadence," he says with a chuckle.

"What do you mean?"

"You're always thinking. What're you thinking about right now?"

"That I shouldn't have signed my soul away to the devil."

He laughs. "I can tear it up."

And now's my chance. What a perfect time to ask him about—

"Why don't you tell me about your mother," he says. "Whenever we mourn for someone, in a way that person becomes a part of us, or at the very least, a part of our family. Emily's now a part of the coven. What was she like?"

I don't want to talk about my mother. He seems to sense it, and he puts a hand up. "I'm just—"

"No, Bryce. Tell me about yourself. Did you grow up in Georgia?"

"I grew up in Missouri...Springfield, Missouri. My family has a farm out there."

"How'd you get interested in history?"

"For the same reason as you." He sips his wine. "I love stories. And I love learning of the past. Ever since I was a child. I used to play with Civil War soldiers. I learned about all the battles."

I smile, imagining Bryce as an adorable little boy.

"I imagined I was fighting the Battle of Bull Run or Gettysburg. So even in elementary school I read books about the nineteenth century. I came to Hawthorne University because of its emphasis on historical studies. Then I was as mesmerized as you probably were with Dr. Johansen. I loved her passion for her work. Her subject matter—the dark arts—put me off at first—as it probably did you—but then I understood the reason for it. She studies it because she seeks to cure evil. She's a very bright blue light, Cadence. Her personality is of the clearest water. She is good, but so many misunderstand her. She's probably better than anyone I know. But of course she creeped me out at first too—you know, her obsession with shadowy dark magic."

"Which you can now tell me all about, since I signed that stupid document, right?"

"Sure." He leans forward. "But it's just a legal document. Your agreement—with your blood, at your initiation—will be more binding."

I gulp my wine down harder.

"What would you like to know?" he asks, amused by my reaction.

"Blood?"

"Alondra will take a dagger to your arm." I'm remembering when I saw her do it to herself. I find myself shaking my head, and my eyes are probably bulging. I'm picturing myself as their sacrificial animal.

Bryce grabs my hand. "Don't worry, Cadence. Everything will go slow. Alondra is the greatest leader any coven could ever have."

"I don't want anyone to stab my arm."

"You will," he says reassuringly. "When you see the rewards, you'll bear all the costs. Just as a pregnant woman bears pain."

Shit. Now I'm about ready to ask for the documents back.

"Cadence," he says, rubbing my hand, "there's nothing anyone will ever force you to do against your will. You'll have every right to refuse the blood sacrifice."

"I can't even get my blood drawn at the doctor's office."

He laughs and I laugh too. Then he looks around. "There are herbs that Alondra will give you. Some will let you see more clearly than you've ever seen before. Some ..."

He keeps talking, and I'm struck by his passion for the whole thing. He loves this cult as much as Alondra loves to teach ancient history. He doesn't have this much passion for being a TA. The coven is so important to him, and he seems desperate to get me to feel the same way. But I stop listening. I'm thinking about that curved knife and blood.

"Trust me," he says finally, rubbing my hand more sensually than protectively. I blush a little.

I pick up my wineglass, and I'm surprised to see my hand shaking a little.

"Cadence," he says, watching my hand, "you must believe me. I won't let anyone ever harm you. I swear it."

And I look into his eyes and he means it. I force down some wine.

"What...what did you mean water? You called Alondra a water personality."

"The whole universe," he explains, opening his hands—again quite passionately, "is made up of four elements: fire, water, air, and earth. And then there is another energy binding it all. Everyone's personality can be described based on these elements. Alondra is very sensitive and empathetic. She's also psychic. It's what makes her such an amazing leader. She's like water."

"What am I, then?"

"You are," he says with a chuckle, "an earther. Your personality includes pragmatism. And you're also very stubborn."

I laugh too. He's right about that.

"So these elemental personalities are like astrology signs?" I ask.

"Yes, exactly. In fact, an earth element corresponds to Taurus, Virgo, and Capricorn. What sign are you, Cadence?"

"Capricorn."

Bryce extends his arms in a gesture meaning *see?*

"Okay, genius, what are you, then?"

"Hmm, what do you think I am, Cadence?"

"I don't know all this sign bullshit yet."

He shakes his head. "I really wish you believed a little more in magic, Katie. But that also goes with your sign... Anyway, I'm like fire and my sign is Leo and, accordingly, we are totally incompatible."

We both laugh again.

The waitress brings our food. It looks delightful, with some lovely garnishes embellishing the steak sauce. I bite into the tender steak and it's delicious.

"The tarot cards corresponding to earth are Pentacles and Coins," Bryce says with his mouth full. "Your corresponding card would probably be Queen of Pentacles, but really Wizard Reardon is the expert in cards."

"Wizard?"

"Yeah. He's the leading wizard, or warlock, of the coven."

"Oh," I say.

He chuckles again. "Alondra will expect you to know all this like the back of your hand. You'll need it to cast spells."

"Cast spells?" I raise my eyebrows.

"Yes. Spells. We're witches. We cast spells."

"So you're a witch?"

"Yes, and after you get initiated, you will be too."

"Fantastic."

He laughs. Then he scoops up some potato, swallows it quickly, and says, "Cadence, I've been dying to ask you this. Your last name is Hawthorne. Are you related to the Hawthorne family?"

"Dad probably was, but I don't know. But it helped in my admission interview."

"I'm sure it did."

"We don't really know our family tree for sure."

"Hmm. Maybe...maybe he's a descendant of Escoba's?"

He laughs, as if acknowledging how silly this is, but I have a feeling he's been thinking it.

"Or maybe Abigail, Bryce. I really don't know."

"You should check. Being that you'll be a graduate—and if you continue in the honors program, I'm sure Alondra will want to keep you as a graduate student—you should find out your connection."

"I don't know where to look."

"The archives. You could check in D.C." I think he wants to know more than I do.

I eat some more steak. It gives me a break from Tall, Dark, and Handsome. But I catch a few glimpses of him chewing his steak. He keeps looking at me. My dress is a success, I suppose.

"Let me ask you something." I say seriously. I feel like now is the time.

"Hmm?"

"That night, that night you came to me. Or...did you come to me? I don't even know." My skin feels hot, and I probably brighten as red as a tomato.

All of a sudden, he becomes very serious. He nods. "I shouldn't have, Cadence. I'm sorry. I broke the rule of the coven. I used left-handed magic without Alondra's permission. Alondra was furious."

"Left-handed?"

"Yes," Bryce says sheepishly. He looks down for a moment. "Bill taught it to me. It's a manipulative and deceptive conjuring, not white magic. Of course Reardon says there is no left or right, white or black magic. To him, casting any spell that satisfies the flesh is fair game. But not to Alondra. When Alondra found out I conjured up an incubus, she threw me out of the circle for a week. She made an offhand remark about it being because I was a man."

At this point, I have no idea what the fuck he's talking about. Nor do I care. What I really want to know is—

"Actually, I didn't even know if it would work," he adds, more to himself than to me. "I thought, at the very least, it would make you believe in magic. But it was forbidden."

"I don't care about rules, Bryce. Did you... Were you ..." I can't even think of how to ask it.

"Yes. I was there, Cadence."

I feel uncomfortable, almost violated. And my mind is mixed up. Can I even believe it? If it's true, I had sex with him. And in such a weird way. I look at him and he seems uncomfortable too.

"I told you it was wrong, Cadence. I'm sorry."

"Then why'd you do it?" I'm surprised by my own tone. I'm angry. "You didn't ask me and you didn't tell me what you were doing."

"I'm an idiot. I wanted you, just like I want you now. I'm attracted to you. And I thought the magic would convince you to sign, like you did today. You're right. It was wrong. But I—"

"By fucking me in a bathtub with a witch spell?" I ask in a forced whisper. He smiles at my jab, and it makes me angrier.

"I never knew how aroused I'd get by hearing you cuss, Cadence."

I shake my hair out angrily. He touches my hand and I quickly pull away.

"Listen to me, please, Cadence, I wanted to show you our world. I figured the magic of that night would make you want to join."

"It was creepy. It's not how people show love."

"You're right. I was wrong. Very wrong. I'm sorry. I heard an earful already from Alondra."

"Who cares about Alondra, Bryce. This is about us."

"You'll care," he says, lifting his glass of wine and pointing at me. "Alondra is our leader."

"You're a pervert. It seems all you men are." And I stick my fork into a couple of pieces of broccoli over that conclusion.

"Yeah, probably. That's exactly what Alondra said. It was wrong." Then he touches my hand, but I pull away. "Look, I won't ever do anything like that again. I promise. Please forgive me, Cadence. I told you, I thought it was a way to introduce you to magic. I thought ... it was okay because it was magic. I never thought I was disregarding your wishes. You must believe, I would never want to deceive you. God, I'd never want to hurt you. Besides, the spell doesn't even work unless it's done by mutual consent."

He has this really sad look, but he still pisses me off. I look straight into his eyes, and I drawl very distinctly and slowly, "*F-u-c-k y-o-u.*"

I can't eat my steak. I feel too much pressure in my throat. And I can't look at him. Not even those to-die-for glorious blue eyes.

"Anyway, you didn't," I continue, "because nothing really happened. The whole thing was impossible."

Bryce puts his fork and knife gently down on his plate, leans back and closes his eyes. Then he says, "You chose a small bathroom. You covered the mirror with a large black drape. There were red rose petals along the sinks, and there was a small figurine of a goddess. The figurine was a white stone statue, covering her naked groin with one hand while holding her long hair with the other. You faced away from the door. There were two sinks, and the faucets were old-fashioned with long brass stems and bronze handles. There was a white carpet on the floor."

"You probably saw the figurine," I say with a shrug. "Or Maddie told you."

"I didn't see the carpet in the bathroom."

"A lot of houses have white carpets."

He exhales impatiently and then quips, "All right. You need more?" He talks more quietly. "First we held hands, then we kissed. You pulled at my shirt, yanking off the top button, then you took my shirt—"

"Enough," I say with my hand raised. I don't want to hear it played out. It creeps me out even more.

"I was there, Cadence. I was as much there as I am here before you. But it was a spell, an incubus spell."

"So I'm no longer a virgin?" I snap. He looks at me oddly; then he looks around the restaurant because I'm really loud. He laughs and covers his mouth.

"Really?" he asks.

"You took my virginity with a witch spell?"

"First off," he says, finally getting a little angry too but talking quietly, "I didn't know you were a virgin. That's adorable. Second of all, a virgin is someone who has not had intercourse. I did not have intercourse with you, Cadence. It was a spell. Any man would love to sleep with you, but that is totally up to you."

"I think you should take me home," I snap. I hit the table. "This is unreal."

"Jesus! Come on!" He runs his hand down his face.

"Yes, Jesus. Perhaps you and your coven should think more about him."

"*Our* coven! You know, Cadence ..." His face has reddened, and his lips are quivering in rage. "Cadence, you are the most difficult girl I've ever met. You're not just stubborn, you're completely impossible. I don't think you would believe in magic even if I pulled a rabbit out of my ass!"

He's really pissed. I just shrug.

I'm relieved. I've been wanting to talk about that night throughout our date. Now I feel like I've finally gotten everything off my chest. I don't even feel that angry at him anymore. In fact, even with his lingering rage, I'm studying his gorgeous features.

He gulps some wine and does everything possible to avoid my eyes.

"I'm enjoying dinner," I say, biting into more steak. "And my bath... It was lovely... Thank you. Are we having dessert?"

He cocks his head in amazement. "What would you like, Cadence?"

"Crème brûlée."

17

MANDRAKE

To say that I'm not nervous would be stupid. I'm sitting on one of Alondra's elegant white leather sofas, staring at the flat-screen TV on the wall. There's nothing on, but there's also no one to talk to at the moment. I'm by myself, tapping my knees and waiting. And that's making me more nervous. Meanwhile, every so often, one of the ladies from the coven walks by, gives me a nod, opens the sliding door, and takes something outside. They're preparing for some kind of outdoor event, and that's weird because it's cold and raining outside.

Every one of the girls is wearing a long black cape and short black dress. I'm not. I'm in a white sweater and jeans.

I cross one leg over another. Then I switch legs and stare at the elegant stone chimney. Then I cross the other leg back again, fidgeting with my fingers.

One of the members, Tammy—the pretty black girl with long hair like me—hands me a glass of red wine. I get up and smile. "I know it's a bit weird, Cadence, but we'll be done soon," she says with a wink. "Just sit tight, 'kay?"

"You sure there's nothing I can do to help?"

"Not unless you know how to brew cauldrons."

I laugh, but it's not really funny. Still, I like Tammy. She's a lot like me.

And I suppose she's prone to saying funny things at inopportune moments too.

The wine tastes good. It's very smooth.

Tammy rushes back to the kitchen. I can hear them murmuring. I wonder if they're talking about me. Probably.

I need to pee. But I'm tired of getting up and using the restroom. I have a bad habit of having to pee when I'm nervous.

Then Mira comes in. She's wearing exactly the same black dress and cape as the others. She seems friendlier than ever and reaches out to me with both hands, signaling that I should rise. I feel really weird but I get up.

"When it stops raining, we're going to go outside, Katie," Mira says. Her auburn eyes are staring at mine. "It's cold, but the cloak will warm you. And when we go to the service, the fire is warm enough. Why don't you finish your wine so you'll be more relaxed? The rain will stop soon, and then you'll know we're ready."

"It's going to stop raining?"

"Yes. In another fifteen minutes."

That's where all the magic starts, right? Now they can control the weather?

Maddie rescues me. She walks in holding a wineglass too. "I'm so excited for you, Kate!" she says. Mira backs away and sits on a furry chair beside the fireplace. "You nervous?"

"Nah." Of course I'm nervous. I'm terrified and Maddie knows it.

She sits beside me and pats my knee. "Things might get a little weird, Cadence. But you'll be fine. Trust me, right?"

"Yeah."

"She'll help you along."

"Just ignore Dr. Reardon," Mira chimes in.

"Why?" I ask.

"He's a sick fuck," Mira says. I'm shocked by her language, particularly since I saw Dr. Reardon a few minutes ago in his black cape, helping out in the kitchen with my to-die-for boyfriend. "His ideas are exactly what you're afraid of, Cadence."

"Even he will help you," says Maddie. She scowls at Mira.

"What about his ideas?" I ask Mira.

"Just forget it, Katie," Maddie says. She's warning Mira to shut up with a look of venom. "You nervous?" Maddie repeats, turning back to me. She looks into my eyes seriously.

"Should I be?"

"I was," Maddie says. "But things worked out."

"Sure did," quips Mira.

Maddie whirls back toward Mira, furious. "Why don't you go finish helping the others!"

Mira smiles slyly and sighs. "Okay." She gets up and leaves us, and I hear her laughing as she makes her way back to the kitchen.

Then Maddie turns to me and holds my hand again.

"Cadence," she says seriously, "Alondra is permitting me to tell you some things before we start. She thinks it might put you at ease."

"All right."

Maddie looks around and takes a deep breath. "Do you remember the July fourth party last year?"

"How can I forget?" I got more drunk at the Lambda Lambda Delta frat house than I had ever been in my life—I probably drank a full bottle of tequila. I vomited all night and wanted to die the next morning.

"Right, well," she says, looking nervous, "do you recall what we experimented with?"

"Ecstasy."

"Yeah."

"And three or four bottles of tequila."

"Yeah," Maddie says, laughing.

"And boys."

"Right." We both laugh stupidly.

"I promised I'd never go to their house again."

"Yeah," Maddie says.

"Just spit it out. Tell me, Maddie."

"Well," Maddie says, "you're gonna take something tonight. It's not ecstasy, but it's a drug and it'll make you feel weird. You're going to sweat, you may feel dizzy, and you might even vomit."

"If Alondra sent you to make me feel better, then—"

"I know," Maddie says, taking my hand. "But, Katie, it'll make you feel good too. And while you're doing it, all of us, even that bitch Mira, will be beside you helping you."

"What if I don't want to take anything?"

"You have to, Cadence. It's required for the initiation. You do want to join, right?"

"Not really. I joined to find out what the hell they're doing to *you*."

Maddie gives me a hug. Then she surprises me. She looks at me and she's fighting back tears. "I love you, Cadence. Really. You're so cute. Just...trust me, okay?"

"Yeah."

"All right. When Alondra hands you the elixir, drink it. It's required."

"I'd feel less nervous if you told me what else is required."

Maddie nods. "Nothing. Not for you. You're lucky." Then she jumps up. "When it stops raining, we'll walk through the mud to the fire. I'll be there, but I'll be under my cloak. We'll be chanting and dancing. Then we'll disrobe."

"Naked?"

"Yes."

"Do *I* have to be naked?" Alondra told me it was up to me. Would I ever want to? It's just so weird.

"No," Maddie says with a smile. "But you will have to be sworn in. The swearing in for the coven will involve blood. It isn't required, but it's how you make your vow. No one will force you, but out of respect for me, Alondra, Bryce, and the rest of us, I really would like it if you would let her initiate you with the knife."

I feel my bowels turn. I've been thinking about blood since Bryce mentioned it. I don't want to do it.

"Think about it," Maddie says with a smile as she helps me up from the couch. "It won't be so bad after the drink... And now, I told you just enough to prepare you. If I tell you more, I might just make you more nervous."

"You already have."

Maddie lifts my chin. "It'll be alright, 'kay? I promise, Katie."

"And I'll like it?"

Maddie laughs. It must be my expression. I'm completely disgusted and baffled by the whole thing. She nods.

"Excuse me for a moment," I say. "I have to pee."

$\sim$

After I finish relieving myself in Alondra's bathroom (which is very chic and cool, with marble countertops, a bidet, and a fancy tub and sink), I return to the living room. The lights are off, and lit candles are lying along the floor, beside the door. The rain has stopped. It's silent. Beside an end table near the sofa are my and Maddie's half-drunk glasses of wine.

Bryce is standing by the door in a black cloak. "Come, Cadence." He reaches out his hand. "Put on your cloak. And R-E-L-A-X. Try to. Don't let the ceremony scare you. I'll be with you the whole time."

Through the glass, I can see the coven. There's a bonfire, just as there was for the ceremony for my mother, only this time they're not sitting. Everyone is slowly circling the fire in their black cloaks. I can't make out any faces, but I count twelve.

I put on my cloak and step outside. It's damp but it's not raining anymore. The clouds are moving away quickly in the moonlit sky. It's a half-moon. I put my arms around myself because the cloak is really not warm enough. Bryce sees it and puts an arm around me. He's warm enough. I walk across the field to the fire, held by Tall, Dark, and Handsome.

The witches in the circle are chanting something not in English. When I'm close, I see a single plastic chair. Oddly, Bryce directs me to sit with my back turned to the flames as they continue to walk around the fire, and they walk behind me. The fire is warm, and the cold no longer bothers me.

Then I see faces circling me. I recognize Tammy, Hannah, Hope, Gilda, and Mira. Then I spot Dr. Reardon. There are other girls I don't know well. I remember seeing them in the kitchen when I walked in. They all look at me. They don't look drugged, nor are they particularly menacing. If anything, they're friendly. They all smile, even Mira, as they pass slowly by. They move fluidly; it's more like a dance than a march.

They circle very slowly for what seems like a long time. I'm tempted to check the time on my cell phone, in my pocket, but I recall Mira's séance and that stops my hand. They continue circling, but they turn so that none of them is facing me. I understand this to mean that I am not yet part of the group.

None of them makes me nervous. Except Reardon. He just creeps along, continually watching me. I don't like him.

When he passes me for the third time, he speaks. "Turn your back on me, I still am," he says in a commanding voice. They all say "Atman," and the head wizard continues to speak. "Be it virgin or harlot, I remain. From the seed of man art thou. That is all. Do not fall into trickery. To dust you go, to the depths of hell. In such abyss, nothingness shall pass. And there, you find me. When you close your eyes, I shall manifest in front, not behind. Hide no more. In nothingness lies peace. Know this. I offer your sacrifice, your death. Give me your virginity, I shall return my seed. This offering, this exchange, done in sanctum for centuries, will allow you to end your suffering. And so, let us chant, sisters and brother:

"*In sanctum e tenebris inferni, igne sacrificii unctus. Lux tenebris.*"

Everyone around me repeats, "*Lux tenebris. Lux tenebris. Lux tenebris.*"

"Here we all gather to partake in semen and…"

Okay, *semen*? I mean, *WTF*, right?

I'm totally spooked with all this weird old language shit. I never liked Professor Reardon, and now that he's gone from being a quiet, dull man to this freak, I feel serious heebie-jeebies every time he passes behind me. Then I have my fears confirmed after looking into his hungry old-man pervert eyes. It's like he wants to have sex with me, and that makes me want to throw up.

I jump as one of the witches circling me touches my shoulder. But it's Maddie. She's looking back at me with an encouraging smile. The bitch knows me too well. She knows I'm about to bolt.

"Lux tenebris."

After a few more rounds of "lux tenebris," they thankfully stop chanting, and they stop moving. Everyone turns and faces the house. They're all standing directly behind me, and a few have their hands on my white plastic chair.

A woman with a torch comes from the side of the house. I know it's Alondra. She's the only one who hasn't entered the circle yet. I'm relieved that it's her and I don't have to hear from this freak any longer. But then, my ease is shattered and my skin crawls as I look upon her. She's completely naked, with her long black hair flowing and her jade eyes glowing beside the flickering torch. She isn't even wearing a cloak. But there is no shame in her step. She sways her naked hips, her large breasts bobbing, as she treads straight over to me. Then she adds her torch to the fire and looks down upon me with the same smile she's always given me.

"A blessed day," she says, looking at me while addressing the coven. "A blessed day. We have a new initiate, someone I've waited to welcome since she first arrived in Hawthorne." She kneels on one knee, stark naked yet still comforting me with those eyes and that soothing smile. Then she says, "Don't be afraid, Cadence. Our ways seem odd to you now, but soon you will understand."

I can't say a thing.

"Do you still want to join?"

After the chanting, I'm not so sure. But then I look at Maddie. Her face is under the hood and she's nodding, trying to encourage me again. Then I turn to Bryce. They seem concerned—concerned for my welfare. They're all worried about me, and it gives me a warm feeling inside. I know that may seem corny to you, but it's a warm feeling in my chest. All these people care about me. And then I feel a little sad when I realize that these are my friends. Throughout all of Hawthorne, these are the people who are closest to me. This coven. This coven loves me. No matter how strange they are, they're my friends. And that is why I want to join.

"Yes," I say, and I mean it with all my heart.

"Glory be to the gods," Alondra says, looking up to the sky. Then she looks at Dr. Reardon. "Bathe your white witch with mandragora, Black Wizard."

Dr. Reardon takes an old wooden barrel, opens the lid, and carries it over to Alondra. I notice a bunch of similar barrels stacked near the pyre. He walks to Alondra, but she does not turn from my gaze. As she watches me, without moving or turning her eyes, Reardon pours the fluid from the barrel over her naked body. The reddish-brown liquid sticks to her long black hair and her breasts and back. She remains kneeling.

"Soon, Cadence, I will be in a trance," she says, staring intently at me. "Then I will no longer guide you with reason, only feelings. And so I warn you. No matter what transpires, know that you are free. If you wish to leave, go to the door. Run. No matter what I or anyone else in the coven says, this is my wish. It is my wish, and always has been, that you do what your heart tells you to do. Do you understand?"

The liquid is dripping from her hair to her cheeks and chin, but her face is serious and intense. I nod, but my body shakes a little.

"The herbs we offer you will change your perception. If you partake in the herbs ..." She pauses for a moment and signals to Mira to bring over a flask. Then she lifts it over my head and murmurs something under her breath, some sort of incantation. "If you partake in this drink, you will be bound to us and us to you. You will feel great joy. But you will also lose all reason. Do you understand?"

I nod again.

"Even now..." She closes her eyes in rapture. "I can feel the mandrake root inside me. Mandrake root, or mandragora, is a hallucinogen, Cadence. It is...powerful. It is said that when you pull mandragora from the ground, the herb screams. It has that great a power. The mandrake ..." She pauses for a moment, and one of the other witches helps her up. Alondra motions for her to return to her position in the circle. She opens her eyes, a little too wide, and then continues. "The mandrake is absorbed through the skin, Cadence. That is one reason, among many, that we witches hold ceremonies naked. Do you understand?" It's like she's giving a lecture again, only this time my professor is naked and drenched in a potion.

"Yes," I say, a little too sheepishly, I think.

"Cadence Hawthorne," Alondra says, taking a deep breath and raising her glass flask. The fluid in the flask is reddish-brown, just like the fluid that was spilled on her. "Do you wish to join our coven?" Alondra looks down, her eyes wide. I can tell she's fighting to control herself. Her hands and lips are twitching.

"Yes," I say.

"Take this flask." Alondra closes her eyes again and hands me the glass flask. "Take it to your lips. Sip slowly. But know—our secrets must remain in the circle. If you ever unveil our secrets, so you will be cursed and cast out from us forever. Do you understand?"

I simply nod.

"*Lux alba,*" she says.

Everyone in the coven repeats, "*Lux alba. Lux alba.*" They say it again and again, some even whispering it to themselves. Everyone repeats the incantation, except Reardon.

I look down at the reddish-brown elixir and, under the flickering fire, the fluid looks like blood. Bryce, Maddie, and the others nod encouragingly.

I sip. It's pungent and sharp. It's like the strongest alcohol, burning my mouth. It tastes like poison. I gag and spit some of it from my mouth. The act makes many of the other witches shout something while looking up to the sky.

Alondra touches my shoulder. "Drink it, Cadence. Drink all of it. Don't be afraid. It's diluted with wormwood and charcoal, but you must drink the entire flask."

I look at her like she's crazy. Then, judging from those jade eyes and that wet, dripping face, I think she may very well be insane. But the flask is already half-drunk, so I empty the rest into my mouth.

"Blessed are you, under the stars of the night sky, and in the cradle of Mother Earth!" cries Alondra, looking up with crazed eyes. She frightens me with her outburst, and I lean back in the white plastic chair. Then she makes it worse by looking down upon me with wild eyes. "Welcome! Here ye shall be known as Windstorm, for you are born anew upon the wind and rain. I am the High Priestess. As long as I shall lead, you shall follow. And when I depart, you shall carry on my order."

Everyone starts chanting the word *windstorm*.

"Turn toward the fire, Windstorm," Alondra says.

I face the fire now. Everyone does. But they're all looking at me.

Alondra turns to Mira. "Bring her the book."

Mira walks slowly over. She pulls off her hood and places a hand on my shoulder, smiling her stupid, geeky, uncomfortable grin. Then she hands me the book. "This is your Book of Shadows, Cadence," Mira says. "You will use this to record your spells. Keep it hidden. In time, as you advance in your wizardry, you may one day understand the secrets known by the High Priestess and the Eternal Wizard themselves."

I look down at the book and flip through the pages. It's just a simple diary. I even see a small price tag on the back.

"Welcome," Mira says and hugs me tightly.

Then the others come. Tammy. Hannah. Maddie and Bryce. Each of them hugs me as they circle around me.

"I'm Mandy," says a short blonde girl. "Welcome."

"I'm Frida," says another. "Welcome."

"Natasha. Welcome."

"Marilyn. Call me Mary. Welcome, Cadence. I'm so happy for you."

And that's all of them. The whole coven hugs me. Then Bryce walks over and takes my hand. He guides me slowly around the pyre. Everyone follows in single file.

"Follow me," Bryce says. "Try to match our rhythm and movement."

I nod and walk slowly behind him.

The music becomes heavier. I seem to see it, not just hear it. At first it was like birds chirping in the trees, but it changes its tempo and pounds into my whole body. I see it as color and flashes of light: red, blue, green, and white. The sounds light the grass of Alondra's backyard.

But there never was any music. Was there?

Alondra is no longer conscious. I catch a glimpse of her eyes, and she's completely lost in a trance, bobbing up and down. As she snaps her head back, showing the whites of her eyes, she appears more like an animal than a woman.

"Disrobe!" she commands.

Everyone begins taking their clothes off. In the recesses of my mind, this was the part I remember being most afraid of. This, and the knife. I watch as they remove their cloaks and cast them aside as they dance beside the pyre. They cast off their shoes. They pull their dresses over their heads. They came prepared, not wearing anything underneath. They're naked, bobbing and weaving, up and down, around the great fire pit. I remove my cloak and cast it aside with them, but I stop at my clothes.

Bryce stands in front of me as he pulls his shirt over his head and then pulls down his pants and underwear. He too dances naked beside the fire.

I'm aroused by him. I remember feeling this way in the bath with the incubus spell. I am so attracted to this guy—his strong back muscles, his tight ass. In another place, this would be a dream for me. And yet, at this ceremony and rite, it seems wrong to look upon him sexually. But I do.

I'm very aroused by his physique, and I can't stop glancing at his ass under the flickering flames.

I touch his shoulders. He doesn't stop dancing, but I walk behind him, feeling from his shoulders down to his back and back up again. He lets me.

Dr. Reardon steps out of the circle. As each naked body passes him, he splashes it with the fluid from the barrels. Each member of the circle shakes the fluid from their hair as if they're throwing off water from a pool. Many laugh and giggle. Some drops of the fluid from Bryce and the girl behind me, Frida, touch me. But I'm still fully clothed.

That's when it happens.

That's when I rise.

I feel like all the weight is being lifted from me, and my body rises into the air. The circle moves like a train, rising and falling on invisible tracks, up and down, around the flames. Alondra turns and her face is strangely altered. Her green eyes have enlarged and are now permanently fixed orbs like the eyes of an owl, her nose has extended into a beak, and her ears are pointed back along her flowing black hair. She laughs and gestures for us to follow.

We leave the flames and rise higher. And with our ascent, the clouds clear. I look down, seeing Alondra's house from above. For the first time, I see her mansion perched on a hill, and all the trees surrounding it seem to circle around it. The house is like the fire, directing the surrounding nature to follow her. We fly over a pond. I didn't know she had a pond. It's shadowed in the darkness.

I reach down to touch Bryce's buttocks, and I feel the crack of his ass. It arouses me uncontrollably as I run my finger along the plump tightness of his buttocks. Then I fondle him some more, running my palm along his tight abs. He's so muscular and my body tingles. He turns and I cradle him as we fly, as if we're spooning on a bed of air.

We fly over the dirt parking lot, and I can see my beat-up Honda and the rest of the witches' cars below. Alondra's sleek Jaguar is parked in the circular driveway in front of her mansion.

We pass into the hills and over the beautiful nearby lake. It's shadowed and everything is dark—except our bodies. The bodies of my companions seem to glow.

Bryce takes me in his arms as we fly together over campus. His hands glide along my body, and he presses his hand inside my sweater and under my bra. He fondles my breasts and then enters my mouth with his tongue. I close my eyes and feel only the rushing wind of air passing by us.

I look down and spot his classroom. I point. He nods with a smile. Again, I've never seen it from above, and it looks so lovely with the paths lit in the dark quad below.

We suddenly descend. We land softly on a plateau and I recognize it —it's the grassy plateau I found on my run in the center of Hawthorne. We circle over the ground again. The moon from the cloudless sky lights us from above.

I touch Bryce again, and I pull my sweater over my head, touching the lace of my bra.

Bryce looks back.

"Leave it on," he says. Bryce stops moving, but it's strange. I still feel like I'm moving around in the smoke, but Bryce is standing beside me, holding my arms. "Cadence," he says, "leave it on."

I shake my head.

"No, Cadence. Leave it."

"I don't want to."

"You have to. Just keep it on, okay?"

"But *your* clothes are off."

"No, they're not. It's the mandrake."

I look down and his pants are on, but he's shirtless. I feel panic and sudden embarrassment. To my left is the fire, and we're back in Alondra's yard.

"You okay?" he asks, running his hand along my cheek with a smile.

No.

The music is throbbing in my head. It's becoming too loud. But then I remember that there never was any music.

I'm feeling sick. I walk from the circle and lean over the grass. Sweat —is it sweat or is it the mandrake? I'm not sure—drips from my forehead. The field sways as if I'm on a boat. I stumble and fall to my knees. Then I throw up all over the grass.

"You okay, Cadence?"

I look up, but there's no one there. Everyone is still circling the fire. And they seem to be blurring and popping in and out of my vision. They're moving so slow. I'm feeling dizzy again.

"Windstorm, return to the circle," the High Priestess demands, so I will myself to come back. It seems to take forever for my feet to return to me.

I look around and suddenly everyone has gone. All that is left is a smoking pyre of logs surrounded by a white chalk circle. The coven is gone. There is no music. There is no chanting. There are no witches. Everything is gone. Only silence. And the wind.

It starts to rain. Then it begins to pour. I look up as the rain comes down furiously from a cloudless sky.

It's cold, but it cleanses me. It showers over me and seems to wipe away any fear and worry. I stand in the rain, closing my eyes, enjoying the drops of water over my cheeks and eyelids. Then I remove my sweater. I yank it off, resolved to stand naked under the pelting drops. I take off my bra, pants, and underwear. I reach out my arms and stand naked under the water as it washes over me. And I feel a strange mix of peace and exhilaration I've never felt before.

"I Yatu Raven," says the coven.

I repeat the words as if I've known them all my life.

"I Yatu Raven."

Alondra, wearing a cloak over her drenched naked body, is kneeling beside me. She looks exhausted. Then she looks over me gently with concern. She reaches into her cloak and brings out her metal pentagram and a dagger.

"With this blade, Windstorm, I consummate our union. Will you join us together forever as one?"

I nod.

She smiles, takes my outstretched arm, and cuts it. The cut stings, but it only lasts a second. Then the sting bites into my arm and I scream. I feel people holding me from behind. She takes the flask that I drank the mandrake root from and drips my blood into it, filling it to the top. The crimson blood is now indistinguishable from what was mandrake. Then the pain in my arm fades. Alondra hands the flask to each of the witches as they stand in a circle around me. Each one drinks from my blood. Then she hands the flask to me.

"Drink it," Alondra says, touching the pentagram to my forehead. "Finish the flask, my child, my daughter, my sacrifice, and be reborn. Let your own energy fill you as it fills each of us, your family."

I obey and drink the contents of the flask. It's salty and sharp.

The field turns and twists around me. Trees seem like obstacles flying toward my vision. I close my eyes and swoon, feeling as if I am falling.

I open my eyes and see myself naked on a large slab of granite, my wrists and ankles tied and my body lying in the shape of an X.

"You are the sacrifice," says a voice. It's harsh and low. It sounds like Reardon's.

My heart is racing, but it's not out of fear. It's desire.

I see Bryce. He stands before me, naked, holding Alondra's dagger and looking down upon me, unsure.

"Welcome," he says.

"Oh, Bryce, have sex with me," I say. I have never desired anything more. "Please! Fuck me. I'm here for you. Please, fuck me! Take me now. Fuck me now, Bryce!"

"Shh." He kisses my forehead. "It's the mandrake." He shakes his head and drops the knife. "Welcome to the coven, Cadence."

I'm lying in someone else's bedroom. The sun is shining through a window, and I block the light with my hand. The bedroom is elegant with a mahogany dresser, a white canopy over the large bed, and a small nightstand. The window looks out on the dirt parking lot, and I can see my beat-up Honda in the distance. I'm lying in bed in a white nightgown with lace. I recognize it. It's the one Maddie made me try on at Victoria's Secret the day I went home with my father.

I jump as something touches the bed. It's a black cat. I reach to pet it, but it jumps down near the nightstand.

On the nightstand is a book. I recognize it as the one presented to me during the ceremony. It's the same size, but this one appears old. It's open, with a pen, and handwritten on the first page is one word: *BROOMSTICK.*

18

———

CROWLEY

So we're walking into the university coffee shop, and Maddie is saying we're truly sisters now. *Actual* sisters. Like family. She's giddy and giggly over the whole thing. I'm having this weird sense of déjà vu and berating her for not talking about what the hell happened the other night, because I can't for the life of me remember all of it. But she says she can't remember everything either. All I recall is waking up in Alondra's house, grabbing an English muffin and orange juice, and being driven home by her. No one else was at her house.

I had assumed joining their stupid cult would give me all the answers I needed. It hasn't. I feel more confused than ever. Little does Maddie know that she's the main reason I joined. Well...and maybe that boy. Was I inappropriate with him last night? Under some weird spell? God, did I have sex with him? Again!

"I'm so happy," Maddie repeats with a flash of a wry smile, which is just as annoying.

That's when she reaches out and nonchalantly grabs a small drink off the coffee shop counter. Of course we haven't ordered anything yet. Then she signals for us to get out, and get out *fast*.

"You look good, Cadence," she says, giggling, a little out of breath as we dash down a paved path. "I'm so happy you joined."

"But you don't remember anything?" I ask.

"No. I don't." She sips some of her drink. Then she gives it a funny look. "This is really gross." She shoves it into my hand. "You have it."

I shake my head.

"Here, try it," Maddie insists.

"Why do you do that?" I ask.

"Just try it." Maddie giggles again. "The mystery is fun."

I sigh and sip it. "It's...coffee. With cream."

"Tastes like shit," she says.

"Well, maybe you should order something next time. You can tell them what you want."

"Yeah," she says with a giggle. Then Maddie hugs me real close and giggles again as we walk together. She's been in a good mood all day, since we came back to the dorm.

"So...when do I get warts?" I ask.

We make our way down the cement path. Unlike last time Maddie stole a drink, the grassy hill is vacant. Pretty soon, it will be icy. It's cold and I clutch my arms tightly inside my white sweater.

"You see a wart on me, Kate?" Hardly. Maddie's one of the hottest girls on campus. I've become used to seeing boys ogling her. She's cuter than me, anyway.

"Warts?" I ask again. "Cauldrons? Broomsticks?"

That makes me think of the book. Now it's on my bookshelf, back at the dormitory, as if it's another textbook. It looks a hundred years old, and half of it is written in someone's lovely calligraphy. Maddie said my job is to finish it.

"No warts, Katie," my friend finally answers as we walk under an ugly metal awning. She waves to an acquaintance named Bryan. Bryan's pretty cute.

I'm still in shock over last night. "Broomsticks, yeah. Remember flying? Did we fly?" I ask. I feel stupid again. Then I get mad. Why isn't she answering? Haven't I been initiated?

"Forget it, Cadence." She dumps the coffee into a trash can.

We open the double doors and, as usual, the lecture hall is packed. I can almost swear Alondra smiled at us as we walked in, although there are twenty aisles of students between us.

Alondra is wearing a sweater, gym pants, and glasses. There is such a contrast between her outfit and her witch clothes, or lack thereof, that I begin to doubt that the events of last night actually happened.

She's wearing plenty of eyeliner and lipstick, and her hair is tied in a bun. She looks pretty, almost alluring. If I were a boy I'd be too distracted by looking at her to pay attention.

"We're going to do things a little differently this morning," Alondra says through a microphone on her blouse.

Maddie and I grab seats along the long lecture desk in the fourth row.

"Open your book to page fifty-three."

I forgot my book. I look over Maddie's shoulder, and she pushes her book closer to me. There's a black-and-white picture depicting the beast: Satan. It's a classic image of a goat with a pentagram on his forehead. The goat has one hand up and the other down. He has horns and a tail, his head is hairy like an animal's, and he has breasts. And there are two snakes between his legs, of course—because Satan is a pervert, like all the witches in my coven.

"Many of you recognize this image," Alondra says, pacing along the stage. The lights dim and she presses a remote, projecting a very large image of the beast, now tinted red, on the screen above her. It's the same image as on page fifty-three of the textbook, but the dark red shade makes it look more menacing and evil. "The devil? Satan? Right?" Alondra says. "Who knows the origin? Where is the picture from?"

I raise my hand. Maddie tries to pull it down. Alondra looks over and smiles in encouragement. "Cadence?" Why I want to announce this in front of a hundred and fifty people is beyond me. But somehow, I want to.

"Baphomet," I say in a way-too-shy voice.

"Baphomet. Exactly right, Cadence." I love how she uses my name, and many students look jealous at the fact that she knows my name. "But do you know the origin?"

Now I might have the courage to call out a name, but there's no way I'm going to offer a monologue in front of all these students. NO WAY. So I squirm back into my plastic swivel chair and keep silent.

"Eliphas Levi's Sabbatic Goat," Alondra says. "Eliphas is thought to have adapted the tarot card of the devil to the goat that we now associate with the devil. This and this"—a picture of a red pentagram shines above

Alondra—"are usually associated with the devil by the Christian church." Then the image of Baphomet, this time in black and white, is projected. "The origin is thought to be much earlier. Hundreds of years earlier. The inquisition of the Knights Templar involved false accusations of worshipping Satan. You are responsible for reading about the inquisition, the Templars' desecration of the cross, and the subsequent torture and death of the knights.

"Note the black and white moons. These represent the two elements of nature, light and dark. Baphomet here is a hermaphrodite. His presence represents good and evil, man and woman. Some believe that Baphomet was a mistranslation of the word Mahomet or Muhammad. Others believe the Knight Templars to have been Gnostics. Of course Aleister Crowley, the well-known English occultist, believed this image had great power in magic. Satanic? Evil?"

Everyone is silent. The whole auditorium is as quiet as humanly possible with over a hundred and fifty students staring at my favorite history teacher with gaping mouths. Most students seem to adore her or be amused, but I can feel a negative tension about ready to burst. A few students have expressions of disgust.

"You will study the history," Alondra continues. "You will learn about this image, but more importantly, you will learn about yourselves. How does this image make you feel?" She points to the beast with an outstretched arm. "Does it make you uncomfortable?" *Yes.* "But is it possible, fellow students, that you have been told a lie? That perhaps, instead of magic or Satan, this is simply an image of idolatry? Like the worshipping of Baal by the Hebrews, condemned when Moses came down from the mount with the commandments?

"Well, I suppose even idolatry, worshipping other gods, is a sin in the Judeo-Christian world. But that could include any symbol from another religion, such as Buddha or Krishna. If I put up an image of this"—an image of a jade Buddha meditating is shown above her—"does it make you uncomfortable? Or ..." She presses on the remote again, and an image of a blue god with multiple arms among the clouds appears. "What about this one? Hmm? Do you feel at ease now?" She paces a little more, then turns her back on us and presses her remote again. The image of Baphomet is back up.

"And now back to this. Why does this bother you? Is it from years of Western Christian teachings? Does the goat here represent evil, an actual image of Satan that we so fear, or is it simply a goat, an idol, separate from the cross? Why does it stir up so much emotion in the twenty-first century? Your thoughts?"

Quite a lot of hands come up. She calls on one of them.

"It's the devil, Dr. Johansen," says a boy. "It's like putting up a picture of a vampire with blood. It's evil. Whether its historical source is evil or not...it's evil." The boy is a skinny young blond kid. I've never talked to him. He's kind of nerdy but seems nice enough. But he's very worked up at the moment.

"What makes it evil?" Alondra asks, more curious than challenging.

The kid doesn't say anything. Alondra points to another raised hand.

"I always see these things as the devil," says a boisterous girl named Claire. She's nice enough. I don't know her that well either. "The pentagram—"

"The pentagram is not always evil," Alondra interrupts, shaking her head. I'm suddenly remembering my private meeting with her. "If you turn it, it represents the five wounds of Christ."

"It's Satan, Dr. Johansen," the girl insists.

"Satan. The devil?" asks Alondra. Then she walks pensively with her head down. "Hmm. I posit there's quite a lot in this world we don't understand. And misunderstanding leads to fear. After all, it's the Buddha that teaches that ignorance is evil. Perhaps our ignorance drives our fear. Perhaps you fear this image because of a void in your knowledge."

I raise my hand. Maddie grabs it again and I tug it back up. I don't know what the hell's gotten into me, but it's like I want to save Alondra from the negative vibe in the lecture hall. I'm gonna say that it's just a stupid picture, that's all.

Alondra looks up and smiles again. "Yes, Madison."

Not her.

I watch my lovely friend turn pale. She shakes her head and mutters, "Huh?"

"What are your thoughts, Madison?"

No, me.

"Well, a lot of us are Christians, Dr. Johansen," Maddie says. "Some are taught in Sunday school to reject evil...to reject images like this."

Maddie is hardly defending Alondra. Alondra should have picked me.

"As schoolchildren," Alondra says, "you *should* hate representations of evil. But as adults, you should face them and try to understand them. Is this evil? Is it the devil? Satan?"

"Evil is evil," shouts another student. "The devil is the devil."

"Good," Alondra says with a nod. "I've gotten under your skin."

"I like it!" shouts another idiot.

The hall laughs.

"You will read the historical facts that are known about the above image and write an essay on it," says Alondra with a nod. "I want all of your honest opinions. Search within yourself. If evil is evil, as you just said, Monica, then tell me again. But read and incorporate facts into your essay. You have one week to write the essay—on Baphomet, the historical origins, and your thoughts on the subject. I want your honest opinion. Obviously, I will not judge your religious views on the matter. But I do want you to search within yourself."

"But you can't separate religion from it," says Monica.

"Then don't," Alondra says with a shrug. Then she switches off the image above her.

"But how are we supposed to be objective?" asks another.

Alondra just smiles. She's a master of getting our attention. That's why she always packs the lecture hall.

"And now for the more mundane," she says with a chuckle. The image above changes to a caricature of a man with a bird beak, goggles, and a long gown. That shocks us too, being hardly "mundane." "Turn your book to page sixty-five, and we'll start a discourse on the fourteenth-century Black Death. Soon you'll have to give me historical facts and thoughts about this too."

19

———

FRIDAY NIGHT

The coven meets at around eight o'clock at night. I prepare myself for another drug-filled hallucinogenic adventure but find instead an ordinary campfire experience, with the twelve of us sitting in a circle around the bonfire and just talking about the past week. In fact, the only thing particularly magical about the evening is a few introductory incantations spoken by Mira. And our clothes—we're all wearing long black robes with hoods, like ancient druids.

Mira, as creepy as always, stands up in a long velvet robe and throws colored smoke before the fire, saying things that aren't in English. I ask what she's saying, and Maddie tells me that it's a language Mira made up. She entered it in her Book of Spells. Then Tammy tells us about her new boyfriend. I feel Bryce's stare as she talks about this new student, who just arrived from Maine. I meet Bryce's eyes and he looks away, but he has a smirk on his face. And, of course, Maddie notices and nods at me with a gaping smile.

Then Alondra asks me about my Book of Spells, *Broomstick*, and how far along I am in writing it. I gulp nervously, hating to speak aloud, even to the small group in the coven, and tell her, feeling a little ashamed, that I haven't written anything yet. She surprises me with a nod and smile and asks if I read what was already written. I hesitantly shake my head. She raises an eyebrow at me and then moves on to Frida. Mira looks over and is seriously pissed at me. But before she can admonish me, Frida tells us about a sweater she's knitting. It's such a boring topic that I'm shocked at the interest everyone seems to have. Hannah's next, and she talks about her cat being sick.

I start looking around for a drink or something.

It's at this exact moment that Alondra makes me nervous again. She turns to me with her penetrating green eyes and says, "Windstorm, you're new to the coven. Tell us what you remember about your initiation."

Windstorm? I had forgotten that was my coven name.

I don't remember much of anything. Except everyone undressing. Was I undressed? I think so. And then flying.

"I remember seeing the school from above. I was flying like a bird."

She nods. "Do you remember what you felt in your chest? Do you recall an energy as you flew?"

"Uh...no."

"I flew with her," Bryce says. Then he looks at me with an encouraging smile. I suddenly remember holding his hands, soaring like a bird. But how could he possibly remember that? Was it not the drug, the mandrake root? "We flew twice over the school."

"Yeah, but not on a broomstick," I say.

"Do not joke about our sacred ceremony!" snaps Mira. "This isn't a joke, Cadence."

"I'm not trying to make fun of it. I'm just—"

"It's all right, Cadence," Alondra says. Then she turns to Mira. "Lighten up, Mira. You could learn from Cadence's sense of humor."

"Bullshit." Mira stands up. I'm surprised how angry she is. "Cadence should never have been let in. She doesn't believe."

"Sit down, Mira," Alondra says, cocking her head. "Stop it. She's a sister now."

"Fuck her, Alondra," says Mira.

Alondra stands up. "No, fuck you. Sit down," she snaps. I'm shocked by her reaction. Mira throws her hood off, shakes out her dark hair, and sits back down, folding her arms and glaring at me.

"Each of your sisters has no right to disrespect you, Windstorm," Alondra says to me, "but over the years since I started my coven, it's been common for it to take time for all of my sisters to get along. I trust you." Alondra's sharp eyes land on Mira. "And so will Mira."

"It's all right," I say.

"Since we're all pals, sister," Mira says, "why doesn't Dr. Reardon tell our new initiate about his views on religion? Then he can expound on his actions and how he helps the coven find true love."

"Really, Raven," Alondra says, shaking her head. "What are you doing?"

I learned from Maddie that Mira's coven name is Raven. And Maddie's name is Blackbird. The boys do not have coven names.

"I do not believe Windstorm will stay Windstorm, High Priestess," Mira replies. "I think she will desert us when she truly understands what we do and what happens in our ceremonies."

"What do you do?" I ask her.

Mira leans forward with a sly smile. "We sacrifice little children, drink blood, and fuck virgins."

"Get out, Raven!" shouts Alondra. "Enough of this."

"That's what the bitch thinks."

Maddie jumps up. "What is your problem, Mira?"

"I don't want Little Bo-Peep here. She's a Hawthorne. So what? Escoba's blood or not, High Priestess, she's still a goddamn Little Bo-Peep. And just because her mommy passed doesn't give her a ticket to our sacred club. The minute she gets over her mommy's death, she'll—"

"You bitch!" I shout, jumping up.

Alondra stands up. As she rises, she turns to Mira and I can swear there's a flicker of light in her eye. Maybe it's a reflection of the flames. I'm not sure. But then, under a cloudless sky, there's thunder. And Mira, of all people, looks at Alondra with sudden terror.

"*Get out! Leave now, Raven!*" cries Alondra.

Mira squints at me, but she rushes off into the house.

Alondra takes a deep breath and sits back down. Everyone else sits.

My heart is thumping hard in my chest. I want to fight Mira, I'm so mad. Maddie takes my hand and gently prompts me to sit back down.

"Raven's been through a lot, Windstorm," says Alondra.

"I don't understand," I reply. "I thought she wanted me to join?"

"That was what I asked her to say to you."

"Raven doesn't want anyone to join," Bryce says, looking over at me with a wink. "She's a witch—a real one."

"Anyway, Cadence," says Alondra, "you said you recall flying. Did you feel the chakra? The energy? The energy coursing through your chest and back?"

I look at her, confused.

"There are chakras within your body. The mandragora sometimes causes the chakras to become more focused. Not only might you feel as if you're flying, you can learn to control the energy along your spine, and great magic can come of it. This is why we share our experiences—so I can help you channel nature's energy. You can take the power that is grounded below and let it rise and flow through you. This is the point of our meeting tonight. Just as I told you when you first came to my house, we study our energies. Part of our coven's purpose, besides caring for each other, is to try to understand magic and our place on Earth. When you harness these energies, you will find great power."

"Like you just did with the weather, High Priestess?" Tammy asks Alondra.

"I didn't do a thing, Tammy. I was upset. Nature did what it did. Not me."

But no one believes her. Everyone thinks the thunder is a divine example of our coven leader's power.

"What else, Windstorm?" asks Alondra. "What else do you recall from your initiation? Or what other questions do you have for me? All is open now. You are one of us. You can ask anything you wish."

I look over at Dr. Reardon. He's been rubbing the whiskers on his chin in thought, even during the fight with Raven. He always seems stoic, unemotional, and pensive. He never says anything. He just watches.

"Okay," I say. "What did Raven mean about you, Dr. Reardon?"

Dr. Reardon looks over at Alondra, and she nods as if to allow him to share his secrets. It's the first time I've seen Alondra exert her leadership over him. Apparently, he defers to her just like everyone else.

"I believe in Satanism, Windstorm. I believe in the devil and worship him."

Well, Mira was right. I develop butterflies in my stomach and feel sick. Maddie turns to me, concerned.

"Do you all believe this?" I ask, turning to Maddie. Maddie shakes her head. "Are you Satan worshippers?"

"We've already had this discussion when you first came to my house, Cadence," Alondra answers. "You are an admitted atheist. Why should you fear a man who hates Jesus Christ?"

"Because he worships evil," I say. Dr. Reardon laughs. That doesn't make me feel any better. I turn to Alondra. "Is this why you mentioned this in class—because you worship the devil?"

"No, Cadence. I do not believe in Christianity; therefore, I hold no fear of someone who believes in an enemy of Christ."

"But Satan is evil."

"Not to Bill," Alondra says. "Is that not right, Bill?"

"In the Western world, Satan is evil." Dr. Reardon smiles at me. He's a socially awkward man, and his grin doesn't make me feel any better. "But I don't believe that, Windstorm. I worship the balance of nature."

"Dr. Reardon is the only one worshipping the devil in our coven," Alondra says. "And I let him. It's his right, just as any one of you has a right to worship anything you like. In fact, I believe that his left-hand energy balances mine. His dark magic and my white magic, my *lux alba* and his *lux tenebris*, create a very powerful magical combination. Just like Baphomet holds both the sun and the moon and represents a great dichotomy. As long as you follow the beliefs of the coven—that nature rules our lives—I allow our members to embrace other religious or cultist beliefs. In fact, I even allow Frida and Helen to continue their worship of the cross. But it is nature that rules the world. It is nature— the sun and the moon, the seasons, the stars—that ultimately rule us, Windstorm. We are animals, human animals, and when you accept this and discover the power that lies within, you will be a great witch. It is why we celebrate our nakedness in our rituals. It is why we do not eat meat until we sacrifice sacred lambs that we slaughter and eat together.

"We live in a world of plastic-wrapped foods and cold electronic devices. I consider it the height of hypocrisy when a Christian zealot argues with me about our beliefs when they happily live out their fake lives in a confused modern world. I will not force my beliefs or actions on anyone. I encourage you to eat vegetables and save consuming meat for the sacrifice. Just as I encourage you to remain celibate and only perform sexual acts during sacred ceremonies. If you follow this advice, your power will grow. But I do not force any of this on you. I do ask, however, that you allow for free thought and action from your sisters, our Great Wizard, and our Wizard Disciple."

There's a pause; everyone in the coven is silent and thoughtful. It's like they're all contemplating whether they're good witches. Not *good* as in heavenly, but *good* as in doing what the High Priestess is asking of them. Like only fucking during cult witch ceremonies.

Well, my thoughts are that I still don't trust them. In fact, she had my attention until she mentioned that celibacy and sex stuff. Maybe Mira's right. Maybe I am too skeptical of magic and the coven.

"Windstorm, Mira's doubt stems from knowing Bill's worship would disturb you," she continues, as if reading my mind. "She hoped it would drive you away from us. I hope, just as I said in class—as you mentioned —that being open about these fears will make you think. Make you stop fearing. That will make you stronger."

"I believe that worshipping Satan and the devil *is* evil, Alondra," I say.

I'm surprised at everyone's response to my statement. I turn to Maddie, but she just looks down pensively (and for her to be reflective about anything freaks me out a little). Then I look at Bryce and he looks down too. The rest of them avert their eyes. Reardon is glaring at me. It's almost as if I made a racist statement. Apparently, being a part of the coven trumps everything else. In fact, I think that if I express my distaste for Dr. Reardon's beliefs again, I'll be more of an outcast than Mira.

Alondra looks at me and smiles gently. "Let us hold hands," she says. Everyone does, gathered around the fire. "We have had two disturbances trying to disrupt our love tonight"—*Two? Am I one of them?*—"but our love is strong. The chain cannot be broken. We shall rejoice in our time together for the rest of the evening and stop dwelling on our differences."

And that's it.

My friends Maddie and Bryce stop looking down and seem to glow as they grasp the hands of those beside them. My hand is placed in Maddie's on one side and Hannah's on the other.

Then we sit basking before the warm fire.

By ten o'clock, our meeting is done. I'm relieved that I'm not taking any more drugs, but I'm not surprised. I'm guessing that even if they'd had another mandrake-infested party, no one would have forced it on me.

The coven isn't about drugs. It's not about nakedness or sex. It's not about devil worshipping. I realize now it's about friendship and love...I think.

Speaking of love, Bryce invites me to watch a movie at his place. I feel like it's a bit forward, but I'm still relieved over my boring coven meeting. So I accept.

But I'm underdressed. Beneath the black cloak—which I dispense with, on Alondra's couch, on my way out the door—I'm wearing a long-sleeved red T-shirt and gray pants. Of course I'd never tell Bryce, but the gray pants are workout clothes.

He drives me, in a beat-up gray BMW, to his apartment, on the south side of Hawthorne University. It's a small apartment in a building with only five flats. Bryce opens the door for me, foolishly chivalrous but cute, walks me up a few stone steps, and opens the door.

Bryce's place is simple. It's one large room, with a kitchen on one end and the bedroom on the other. In the center is a small "living room" with a large-screen TV. He points to the couch. "Have a seat." Then he rummages through cabinets in the kitchen. His apartment smells like fish or chicken or something. I can't quite make it out, but I'm guessing it's yesterday's meal.

"Want something to drink?" he asks.

"Sure."

"What's your taste? I've got beer." He opens the refrigerator. "And... beer."

I chuckle. "Beer's fine."

"Great. I got that."

He opens two and hands me one. He sits beside me and turns on the TV. The set is already turned to his game system. I see a flash of some gun shooting game. Then he switches to a TV channel.

"What were you playing?"

"Hmm?"

"I saw a game. What do you play?"

Does it really matter? No, but I really don't know what to talk about.

I'm lacking the courage I had at Alondra's, and I'm beginning to ask myself why I agreed to come to his house late at night.

"Nothing, Cadence." He turns on a random movie. A bunch of guys are running out of a bank, being chased by the police. I think it's a super-hero movie I've seen. He just sits near me and watches.

I sip some beer.

"Feeling better?" he asks.

Huh?

"You feeling better?" he repeats. Then he sits up straighter on his very cushiony brown corduroy sofa. "I mean, you know, when Gilda lost her brother, it was like we all did. We all felt for her. Of course Gilda was already an initiate. But your mother, I mean—"

"Forget it, Bryce." I haven't thought of her. The coven has been a big distraction. And now I don't want to.

"Okay, sorry." He falls back on the couch and watches TV.

I laugh. He looks at me with a smile.

"Thanks, Bryce, but...yeah, it hurts."

He loses his smile. "I'm sorry—"

"Forget it, Bryce." And I drink some more beer. It's an IPA, a little too sharp for my taste. I look at the screen. Then I look back, and Bryce is staring at me with a grin. "What?"

"I can't forget it, Cadence. I care about you."

That is *super sweeeet.*

He's wearing a button-down navy-blue shirt and slacks, and his curly hair is well combed. How does he do it? The minute he took that ridiculous robe off at Alondra's, he looked all formal again. This guy spends way too much time looking good—not that I mind.

I usually don't trust guys like this. But he's got stubble along his chin. And that imperfection is so like him. And he has this wise-guy look, you know, like, *Well, we all know why I invited you to my house, right?* And that's almost annoying enough to convince me to leave. But he's so sweet about it. And I feel safe with him. I like him. I really do.

"I'm fine," I say after taking a deep breath. "What about you? Have you ever had anyone close to you pass away?"

"No." Then he drinks some beer.

I laugh.

"Sorry, I really haven't, Cadence. And I don't particularly want to. But I told you, we're all affected by any loss in the coven."

I sigh again. Then I scoot up on his sinking cushions. "You know, I really wish you guys just stopped saying *coven*. It seems like you're just a bunch of people meeting together. Like a club. *Coven* sounds so weird."

"Okay. *Club*, then."

"Unless there's more to tell?"

"Nope." And he stares at the stupid movie on his screen, stretches out his arms, and yawns. "Look, why don't you sleep here with me tonight?"

"Jesus, Bryce. I mean, really?" I ask, sitting up straight.

"What? I don't mean anything by it, Cadence," he snaps, looking defensive. Then he laughs. "I can take the couch, Katie. You can take the bed."

"In your room? In this one room, *alone?* No, thanks."

"Suit yourself." But then he cracks another stupid grin and I giggle.

He sits a little closer to me.

"What do you want to watch?" he asks.

Does it really matter? I don't think either of us cares as long as we're next to each other.

At some point, I fall asleep in his arms, and I stay there the whole night.

I wake up in the morning, still in his arms on the couch. I slowly lift his arm, and he moves listlessly, snoring a little. I grab my coat by the door, deciding to walk back to my dorm. His apartment is only a block away from the university.

It's cold. There isn't a cloud in the sky, and my phone reads 6:32 a.m. There's ice along the foliage, and it snowed last night. But it's a temperate winter. Spring will be here soon enough.

I'll go to the library and study today. I have a big anthropology test Monday. And anyway, I need to work on Alondra's essay, which is due next week. Maybe I'll throw in something about psycho witches who harbor Satan-worshipping wizards in animal-sacrificing school cults.

20

MIRA APOLOGIZES

I'M READING *BROOMSTICK* ON THE THIRD FLOOR OF THE COLLEGE LIBRARY, AT a table not far from where I had my first date with Mr. Handsome. I know I'm supposed to be reading about the Kung tribe in Western Africa, or maybe the Black Death, but my curiosity over Alondra's gift is overwhelming. Actually, I hadn't thought much of it until our Friday Sabbath. I felt guilty over not even having looked at the book over the past week.

The library is packed; finals are in two weeks. But I've stopped studying. I don't know what's gotten into me, but I just can't study or go to class anymore. It couldn't be happening at a worse time. So I'm going to have to do what I've never done before—cram. Or fail.

So why am I reading *Broomstick?*

There are no chapters. Actually, the content really has no organization. Passages of beautiful calligraphy are mixed with chicken scratch. The topics are as diffuse as the handwriting. For example, on page twenty-two there is a lovely and inspiring excerpt from a poem regarding sunflowers and childhood training wheels—whereas the next chapter is on studying human feces and how one's diet can be ascertained from the color, texture, and scent. And the chapter after that is even worse, discussing preparations for copulating during menstruation. By page thirty, the narrator is back to calligraphy, describing prisms and the separation of light into rainbows. The book is an eclectic mixed bag of any and every topic one could discuss about life. There is an odd charm to that. And there are charms and spells too. A lot of them. Many pages of notes are on spells, usually derived by mixing herbs and potions. There are love spells, energy incantations, and even poisons. Sometimes I find my ancient book inspiring; at other times it's disgusting.

After an hour or two, I search for a book on Wicca and read about that too. Wiccans, a group of modern-day witches who are good, warn that any harmful spell cast on another will come back to the practitioner in a way that's many times worse. It makes me think of Escoba and her fate. Then I wonder if my coven believes the same thing. Are we "good"?

So I search *Broomstick* for any such warning. There's none I can find.

Maybe we're bad? Well, some of us are.

So I'm thinking about this, procrastinating on my real studies while staring at a browned, frayed page—at around page one hundred and seventy—when a shadow runs over the blank page. I look up and it's Mira.

"Hi, Cadence," she says with a wave. She's wearing all-black makeup and has her long black hair slicked back.

"Hi, Mira."

"Whatcha reading?" she asks, but her smile gives away any doubt that she already knows.

"Nothing. Just studying."

Mira puts her hand on my arm. It's very pale and feels cold. "Sorry," she says and forces a smile.

"Did Alondra make you say that?"

"Smart girl, aren't you?"

"If Alondra sent you to apologize, forget it."

"Does it matter?" she asks and throws her ugly hair back. "Look, can I talk to you, Cadence?" She points at another chair.

I shrug and she sits down.

"I really am sorry, Cadence. I was acting like a total bitch. And, yeah, Alondra told me to apologize. She was really pissed. And she was right to be. But...I just don't think you're gonna be what Alondra wants you to be."

"Yeah? And what's that?"

"You're just too vanilla, Bo-Peep."

"Stop calling me that!"

"Sorry... I—"

"I accepted the coven whether you like it or not, Mira. So you'll have to accept me as your sister."

"I know," she says. But she looks disgusted by it. "Why do you think I'm apologizing?"

"Apology accepted."

She smiles. It's not sweet. It seems wicked. Then she squints and looks down at the book. "So, what're you reading?"

My Book of Shadows.

"Well, Cadence, do you know what you're supposed to do with it?"

"Read it and write some spells, I guess."

"You're not supposed to read it," Mira says. "You're supposed to experiment with your energies. You're supposed to write experiments, your spells, in the book. It's like a lab book, but for magic. You have to ignore the other writings... You might want to start with your experience with Bryce. Talk about what it was like fucking him."

"You're such a bitch, Mira!" I hiss. A few people turn in the quiet library.

Mira laughs.

"Just go away."

"Sorry," she says, trying to get a hold of herself. "I couldn't resist. But that's—"

"Just go. Alondra's apology is accepted. Now go."

"Well, I'm not really good with people," she says, looking down.

That's for sure.

"I really did want to welcome you to the coven. Not because of Alondra. I mean it, Cadence. I'm sorry I challenged you... And I'll stop saying 'Bo-Peep.' Will that make things better between us?"

"Maybe."

But she still has this annoying smirk on her face.

She gets up and looks like she's going to leave, but she turns back. Her grimace becomes even more mischievous. "I stopped by to give you a present." She reaches into her pocket and takes out a handwritten note. She puts it on the table near my book. Then she takes out a few hairs from her other pocket. "Here. It's"—she smiles that infernal smile again —"a way to get even with your boyfriend. It's a lock of his hair and a love incantation. You can make him materialize whenever and wherever you want. You can get back at him for what he did to you. Be his succubus. He'll be yours."

I throw the stuff back at her. "Go away, Mira."

"I'll save it for you at Alondra's." And she winks at me, picks up the lock of hair and note, and gives me the stupid smile again. "I think you'll take it back after you think of what I'm giving you. You'll find there are advantages to accepting your powers. And what better way than to cast a spell and fuck Bryce again?"

Then she blows me a kiss and walks away giggling.

Fucking witch.

21

LACEY'S AGAIN

I'M HUFFING AND PUFFING, RUNNING AS HARD AS I POSSIBLY CAN ON THE treadmill, raising the ramp and sweating so much that my eyes are blurring from stingy, salty perspiration. And I have the distinct feeling that a lot of people in the gym are watching my madness. I don't know why I've decided to make this the most intense workout of my life. My heart rate's tracking at 125 to 130, my legs are aching, my back and neck hurt, and I'm about ready to collapse, but I'm running really hard, staring at the foggy mist and trees outside the floor-to-ceiling windows of the gym. It's early, but the sun's out in the clear sky and the gym is already very busy. It's busier during exam time; a lot of other people on campus are letting off steam too. But I can bet you no one's exercising like me.

I'm listening to new age music from Constance Demby. There's the sound of a Japanese koto. It's not the most aggressive music, and it hardly fits my exercise routine, but somehow the tranquility of Ms. Demby's mesmerizing voice provides a nice balance.

I'm thinking of Bryce. I'm remembering flying with him over the school. If my body wasn't shaking from the masochistic torture of my workout from hell, I'd feel a shiver run down my spine.

Bryce told Alondra that we had flown together over the school. How the fuck did he know that? Wasn't it all a hallucination? Then I'm thinking of the last Witch Sabbath and wondering why they didn't tell me anything more about the coven. Had I not been initiated? *Broomstick* is more a diary than a book; it isn't very informative.

There are so many other questions. Why did Maddie come home looking as if she'd been assaulted? She was bruised and looking shaken. Maddie is the most carefree girl in the world, but something happened to her that night. She never told me what, even after my "initiation." And what about the candle? When I came back to my dorm after sleeping over at Bryce's house, it was lit again, and Maddie insisted she'd never lit the candle. And what of Alondra's new fascination with evil and the devil? Is that what I am now—a devil worshipper? My father's Catholic. Mom wasn't very religious, so we rarely went to church, but Dad does. He would never let me anywhere near Alondra if he knew about her.

What about Mom? Maybe all of this weirdness is a way to keep away from my feelings about her. Like this exercise.

I stop the treadmill and do my cool-down walk. I hang my head and lean forward on the rails, breathing heavily. Then I turn to the right and jump. There's a little boy sitting about ten feet from me, leaning against the glass wall. He startles me because he's so creepy. So icy. He "feels" cold. I don't know how else to describe him. And what's he doing here? Children aren't permitted in the gym.

He's a black child, wearing old-fashioned clothes: suspenders with a raggedy beige button-down shirt and baggy pants. He's maybe ten or eleven. His hands and shoes are muddy, and his black hair's curled but a little disheveled. His eyes, open wide, reflect the light in the gym, like a cat's eyes.

He's staring at me, looking scared.

I lean down on the rail again and wipe the sweat from my head. I'm wearing a pink sweatband, but it's not doing anything. I look to my left and there's an older guy—probably a professor—riding an exercise bike. Then I look back at the boy. He's gone.

I hop off the treadmill and head to a water fountain to fill my bottle.

That's when I nearly drop the bottle. I see the boy again. He's at the door on the other side of the gym. He looks so afraid, which spooks me more. I stare at him because, for a second, it seems like I can see right through him.

I wave. His eyes turn big and I watch him fade. As he fades, the glass exit door reveals a tree behind him in the mist.

Now I'm not only completely winded and exhausted but totally freaked out. I turn to the bench press and see a young man sweating and lifting a lot of weights.

"Did you see him?" I ask the stranger.

The man looks at me funny, finishes his lift, and says. "Huh?"

"A boy? Did you see a boy? A black boy?"

The stranger shakes his head.

"How about you?" I ask the old guy on the exercise bike. He just looks at me like I'm crazy.

I walk over to a nearby weight-lifting bench and sit down. I lower my head again, still breathing hard, feeling exhausted. Then I stuff my earbuds in my pocket.

The stranger puts his barbell down and sits up and turns to me. He has that jock I'm-gonna-hit-on-you-now look. I'm really not in the mood for that, so I look away.

"Kids aren't allowed in the gym," he says.

"Oh," I say, finally catching my breath. "I thought I saw a boy."

I did see a boy. No, I saw a ghost.

It's seven o'clock, and I'm on my second dinner date at Lacey's. I'd told Bryce how much I'd liked the place last time, so he brought me here again. I wish he had thought of somewhere different.

"You're so mysterious, Cadence," he says. I'm feeling déjà vu.

"Oh, *I'm mysterious*? What about you and your cult?"

But then we're interrupted by a waitress in a suit. "Is your steak all right?"

"Everything's fine," says Bryce.

But everything's not fine. I'm unnerved by the gym incident. And I'm upset that, even though I've joined the coven, I still feel like everybody's keeping things from me.

The waitress nods and walks off. I look around the dark restaurant. Each table has a single small candle, and many couples are holding hands or leaning in close to one another. I recognize my sociology professor in the flickering light. His wife has long gray hair. She's pretty —she was probably gorgeous when she was younger. It's cute how the older couple's staring into each other's eyes.

"The coven is not a cult," Bryce says, a little miffed, cutting into his steak. "We're family."

"Hmm, well, if we're family, it'd sure be nice if my family told me all their secrets. I've been initiated, but I still don't know what the hell's going on."

"What do you want to know?" He's very sincere and that's sweet.

He also looks really handsome tonight. He's wearing a red sweater and green shirt. It looks like Christmas, and only someone as hot as Bryce could make it look good. And jeans—blue jeans. I'm wearing a simple black dress.

It's time, I think. Since he asked, there is something I've been wondering about for a long time. I push my steak and utensils to the side. Then I look into his gorgeous blues and force myself to ignore them.

"I want to know what happened to my friend. Maddie's initiation was a lot different than mine. After hers, she came home looking like she'd been in a fight. Every time I confront her, she says she can't remember everything."

He's surprised by this. He was probably thinking I was curious about another random historical fact about witchcraft. "And what makes you think it was so different?" he asks.

"Just tell me what happened, Bryce."

He nods and pushes his food to the side. He becomes very serious, which makes me more nervous. Then he pauses for a moment. "Believe it or not, Cadence, your friend had exactly the same initiation rites as you."

I don't believe that. I don't believe that at all. "Bryce, Maddie is why I joined. I'm worried about her."

"Maddie isn't why you joined," he says with a smug look.

"Well, something happened to her that night. She had scratches all over. And her clothes were torn. Were you with her?"

"Yes. I saw everything." He hesitates.

That means he's known all along. Well, of course he has. But then... why hasn't he told me?

He looks around. The other tables are far enough away that if he speaks softly, neighbors won't hear. "Madison took mandrake too." He takes a deep breath. "Only she didn't have someone with her to watch her. She got intoxicated on the drug, something happened, and we lost her in the woods. When we found her, she had fallen in the brush. That's what all the scrapes on her skin were from."

"No," I say, shaking my head, "there's more. Tell me what happened."

But I'm not sure I want to know. I feel like I'd be relieved if Bryce came up with more extraneous facts to block the real truth. In my gut, I know exactly what happened.

I look down at the candle and it starts to bother me. It reminds me of my mother's candle, the one that keeps lighting by itself. Before it seemed so quaint in the restaurant. Now it's almost spooky. And it seems to be flickering more brightly. I'm getting anxious and upset.

Bryce shakes his head and drinks some white wine. It seems he has difficulty swallowing.

"What happened, Bryce?" I insist.

"Nothing."

"What happened?" I repeat.

He shakes his head. "I know you've been initiated, Cadence, but I'm not sure you're ready for this."

"Ready for what?"

I can feel the warmth in my cheeks. The more evasive he is, the more pissed I'm getting. And it's because I know he's finally about to tell me.

"Do you remember your fight with Mira in the circle? Do recall Dr. Reardon and his beliefs?"

"In Satan. Yes. How can I forget?"

"Well, unlike Alondra, Dr. Reardon can be savage."

"Bryce, what happened!" I exclaim, hitting the table.

A few people at nearby tables turn during my outburst. I'm a little louder than I intended. Bryce looks embarrassed. He puts his hand up to calm me down, but I'm ready to take my glass of wine and throw the contents in his face.

"Bill," Bryce says very quietly. He searches my eyes and says slowly, "Bill had sex with Madison, Cadence. Under the influence of mandrake. They had sex naked, on the hilltop overlooking the university. There was another rite up there. Sometimes we worship there instead of at Alondra's house."

I feel sick. Bryce puts his hand up again, but now there's no point. I've lost all reason.

"Why the secrets? Why didn't you guys just tell me! Why wait until now, when I've already joined!"

"Because it was done during a ceremony," he insists, almost in a whisper. "It's our rule. If something like this happens, and it has been known to happen before, it is forgotten. Everyone, including Madison, intends to forget the whole thing. It is our law, in the coven, to forget anything that happens under the influence of our sacred root. It...it's why I stopped you, Katie. You were undressing in front of me, pulling me to you. You don't remember?"

My eyes are probably bulging out of my sockets. I can't believe this.

But I can. I've known all along. I could tell that Maddie had been raped. That was why she seemed changed. Now I'm furious that my friends, my boyfriend, and my mentor have all concealed it from me. And even Maddie—she seems to have hidden it from herself.

But by Dr. Reardon? That stiff dull old gray-bearded perverted prick!

"You think by stopping me from having sex with you, you're some kind of hero!" I rage. I can't believe my own mouth. The whole restaurant is looking over. I'm furious.

Then the candle on the table explodes. Everyone looks over. Bryce smothers the fire with his napkin.

"Cadence, calm down," he says anxiously.

I stand and shout at him. "How could you! How could all of you? How could you keep this"—my voice is cracking and I'm about to cry—"from me? And...I...I joined? You're disgusting. All of you are so disgusting!"

"You don't understand, Cadence. Please. Sit down. This is why we didn't tell you." He touches my arm, but I yank it away. "Please sit down, Cadence. Please. Let me explain."

"You guys raped my friend and you want to explain it to me!"

I feel tears run from my eyes. Then Bryce, my hero, my Prince Charming, does what he always does. In the midst of humiliation, in front of the whole restaurant, this guy swallows his pride and looks at me with concern. But this time his empathetic kindness pushes me over the edge.

"Please, Cadence, let me explain," he says desperately.

"Forget you!" I shout. "Forget all of you."

I run toward the exit. Bryce touches my arm again, but somebody stops him from following me. I think it's my sociology professor.

I run out the exit.

"Cadence, let me at least take you home!" I hear in the parking lot.

I run across the street to a gas station and call for a cab.

22

OFFICE HOURS

Wouldn't you know it, the very next day is Friday. And it's on Friday morning that Alondra has office hours, devoting two hours to answering questions. So after spending a sleepless night wandering around the school like a madwoman, in the freezing cold, I head to her office. Of course my BFF has been sending me texts all night. She's worried sick about me. But I take a sick pleasure in making her worry. It feels like payback for keeping such an awful thing from her best friend.

Of course there's a line of students waiting for Alondra. Finals are in a few days.

I promptly walk to the front and hammer rudely on her door. My mentor, my favorite professor—who, at the moment, I want to inflict bodily harm on—sticks her head out the door. She's wearing thin spectacles, an elegant blouse, and slacks. She sees me and looks surprised.

"Cadence? What is it?"

"I need to talk."

"Cadence, there's a line—"

"I need to talk *now*."

She looks at the line, then looks back at me and gives an impatient sigh. "All right. Fine. Just a moment."

A boy—I know the guy, he's a burly football player named Tyler—

comes out, giving me a grumpy look. The students in line are shouting objections at me in complete disbelief.

Alondra gestures for me to come in. I barge in and shut the door.

My teacher is leaning back, with her usual arrogance, in her leather swivel chair. She looks up at me inquisitively.

"What the fuck did you do to my best friend!" I shout. Alondra's eyes widen under her spectacles. "You could have told me before I was initiated. Now I'm initiated. I'm part of your sick sex cult. Now tell me what the hell you did to Maddie."

"Cadence, you need to keep your voice down," she says calmly.

"Why? So your little secret won't be out?" I yell, making sure the line of students hear me.

"Yes... Sit. Sit down and calm down... You look tired."

"I don't want to sit. I really don't want to do anything you ask of me."

"Sit down, Windstorm," she commands.

Oh, the audacity, using my mystic name. Is she trying to give me orders as if I'm some kind of cult slave?

"Answer me," I say, still standing.

"You already know the answer. You just don't want to hear it."

"So you raped Maddie?"

"I can't believe this," she says, removing her glasses and rubbing her eyes.

"You can't believe what?"

"Listen to me, Cadence," Alondra snaps. "You have the potential to be the leader of my coven. You have the power in your hands. You can do amazing things, but you don't believe. You suspect us, but you don't trust your heart. You think I'm evil, but you—"

"You asked us to write an essay about Satan."

"So that you could search your heart about what evil is. Is Satan evil?"

"Yes!"

"Then write that. Write the essay and tell me Satan is evil. Don't you think I know that Satan is evil, Cadence? Don't you think I believe that Baphomet and the pentagram are evil? Of course I do. But you have to know evil to know good. The coven is not evil. Our family is based on love. Love for ourselves and love for nature. Jesus teaches love. Is that not the same? Why don't you trust me? Why don't you trust us?"

"Because your associate fucked my friend!"

"Keep your voice down!" Alondra says, jumping up. I've never seen her so angry. "I know you're under stress with your mother, but—"

"No, you don't. You have no idea what it's like to lose a mother."

"I've lost my mother, Cadence," Alondra says, sitting back down. "And my father. I've lost both my parents. I know well what it's like to lose a loved one. That is why I am so focused on magic and religion. I would do anything in my power to stop death. But I don't have the power. I know of no one who does. I once thought Mira might, but no one has such power. Not even you."

"I don't have any power."

"You're a Hawthorne, Cadence. You hold more power than any of us. But you don't believe. You believe in evil, the devil, and Satan, but you don't believe in yourself. A witch can never be whole without believing in herself. Neither can a human being."

Alondra leans back in the chair and puts her glasses back on. Then she takes a book from a shelf. It's a Bible. She lays it before me on the desk.

"You think I can teach everything? Or you can read it from a book? Witches write a Book of Shadows as a book of discovery. You have yet to jot down a single word. You've experienced one of the spells with your boyfriend. You've experienced séances. And you've even seen ghosts. They're all real, Cadence. But you don't believe your own eyes. Well...at least read this book, then." She pushes the Bible closer to me. "If all you can do is read and not experience life, then at least read it. You think me and the coven evil? Would an evil, sinful witch hand you the Bible? Read it. Know it cover to cover for yourself. I have. Cadence, God gives you faculties with which to experience the world. Use them. But don't fear evil. Stare at it in the face." Then she recites the well-known prayer: "*As I walk through the shadow of death, I fear no evil.* Walk through it. Write down your fears. You will see evil in our coven. But the God who you don't even believe in asks you to walk through it. You won't even do that."

I sit down. As usual, she impresses me with her words. But I'm still furious.

"That was the point of the assignment," she continues. "Know yourself to be true and good, and then you can face darkness with the light of goodness that all religions aspire to."

"Bryce told me Maddie was raped." My teacher's eloquent words might calm me, but they can't sway the facts.

"I know," Alondra says quietly, looking down. "It was unfortunate. But it was consensual and under the influence of mandrake." She says it as if that makes everything all right. I can't believe it. And even with all her flowery words, she seems to be unsure of herself as she utters it.

"How could you?" I ask, having difficulty speaking. "How could you have let this happen?"

"The only thing stopping it from happening to you was Bryce. Bryce stopped you. You were willing to have sex too. Mandrake is a powerful aphrodisiac."

"So you've raped other students before?"

"Stop it. Cadence, don't be stupid."

"Isn't that what you're saying? You've had sex with students while they were under the influence of a drug?"

And finally, as those words come from my mouth, I understand the coven's secrecy. And I know why they haven't told me everything up until now.

"I've had sex with people under mandragora." Her bright green eyes look right into mine, unapologetic. "If you consider that rape, Cadence, I'm sorry you view it that way. It was consensual."

I want to cry, but that would be weak. I'm too upset. "This coven disgusts me," I say, standing up. "I can't believe what you did to my friend. You act like it's nothing. I don't want to be a part of it. I want out now."

"This coven is Mother Nature. It is what you truly are as an animal. It is the sun, the moon, the harvest, and the stars. We are all animals. It is what you truly are as a human being."

"No, I'm not."

"You are. And as Escoba Hawthorne's direct descendant, you're more a part of our coven than any of us. I have spent a lifetime studying this. You *are* it."

"How dare you!" I hiss. "Is that it, Alondra? Did you recruit me because of my family?"

"What do you think, Cadence? Why else would I have the patience to deal with you?"

And that is the last straw. I jump up, throw the door open, and slam it shut.

"I'm done!" I cry to the students in line. "You go talk to the witch!"

They stare at me as I take off down the hallway in no direction in particular. For I have nowhere to go.

23

ALONE

I HAVE NEVER FELT SO ALONE BEFORE IN MY LIFE. I CAN'T RETURN TO MY dorm because then I'll have to speak to my best friend. If I do that, I'll lose her. I know I'll yell and scream and only distance myself from her for good. I can't go to my other best friend, my "boyfriend," because I just screamed at him and humiliated him in a restaurant. I can't return home to my father because I'll think of my mother. I can't think of my mother because she's dead.

I'm alone.

I have no one.

Now I know why I worked out so hard at the gym.

So that's where I go. The gym. It's still open. It closes at ten, which is in half an hour.

But I don't want to be here either. So after I wander around the indoor swimming pool and weight room, I walk back outside into the gloomy night.

I walk a dirt path outside the school and into the woods. And the darkness only grows as I move away from the lights of the university. The woods are creepy at night. But I don't care anymore. I don't even care if I see that creepy kid. Hell, the creepy kid would be company.

So I'm walking alone through the woods in the pitch darkness, in the middle of the night, in a black dress and tennis shoes when my cell phone rings. It's Dad.

"Hello."

"Hi, squirt. How are you doing?"

I say nothing. Just silence on the line between me and my father.

"Hello? You there, Cadence?"

"Yes."

"You okay?"

"No. I'm leaving."

"Hmm? What do you mean?"

"Hawthorne University. I'm leaving." I start crying. It's finally the right moment to cry, you know. "I'm leaving."

"Why? What's the matter?" he asks.

"It's...it's really weird here. Everyone's so weird. I don't feel like I fit in. I want to go home."

There's a pause. Dad's thinking of what to say. I keep whimpering.

"You can come home anytime you like," he says, but he sounds really down.

"I'm sorry. I know how much—"

"Baby, I just want you to be all right," he says. "Can you tell me what's wrong?"

Then I lose it. I'm surrounded by trees and darkness—there's nothing out there. I can't even see the lights of the buildings any longer. I feel alone and afraid, even while speaking to my dad.

"Mom died," I say between sobs.

"I know," he says. But he sounds so fucking depressed about it.

"She's dead, Dad. And...if she were here, I would tell her."

"I'm sorry, baby."

"No... No, I'm sorry. It's hard enough on you. I should be there for you. I should—"

"Cadence, you're always trying to help everyone. Everyone but yourself."

I walk through bushes and trees and discover a reflective pool of water. It's our lake. A full moon is finally illuminating the clouds above and reflecting off the water, surrounded by the tall trees. It's strikingly beautiful.

"Are you still there, babe?" my father asks.

"Yes."

I stand over the dirt and moss beside the water and lean against a tree. I just sit there for a moment and collect my thoughts. My dad's still on the line. I like hearing him just breathing, but maybe I'm worrying him.

"I'm sorry, Dad. What...what did you want?"

"I didn't want anything. You called me."

I did?

I look out along the water; then I see something. It's on the other side of the lake. It's standing erect. A person. A short person. A child. I recognize the figure. It's the boy—that weird boy I saw this morning in the gym. This time he's standing still, just staring. His head is turned down, with his flickering eyes looking up at me. He's shaking, or shivering. He looks like he's being hunted.

Maverick. I hear the name whispered in the wind. Or perhaps it's in my mind. And the brown-skinned boy in dirty suspenders and baggy pants stares with his eyes wide open. He's terrified, and his fear is frightening me.

The child screams. But he doesn't move. I hear the boy's cry, but the apparition in front of me is just shaking and looking at me with a down-turned head and frightened eyes.

"Daddy?" I ask. My hand shakes, trying to hold the phone. The boy is grabbed from behind by what looks like a black shadow. It's as if the blackness of the surrounding trees swallowed him.

"Dad?" I repeat in a shaken whisper.

"Yeah, squirt?"

Dad is tired. He sounds worn out, not only by Mom's death but by worrying about me. And it makes me mad. Did I call him? I don't remember calling him. But I shouldn't have. I shouldn't even be talking to him.

"I'll just go."

"You're scaring me, Cadence. What's the matter? I can...I can drive over now. What's wrong, babe?"

"Nothing, Dad." Then I cry. He comforts me on the phone, but I just cry. I fall down by the tree trunk and cry. Because I don't want to talk to my dad, but my dad is all I have at the moment.

Then I think of my mom. If she hadn't passed, I'd be crying with Mom, and she would be comforting me. But it's not Mom, it's my dad.

I touch the cold, wet ground under me and muddy my free hand. My dress is now filthy. I just plopped myself down in a puddle of mud. While holding my cell phone between my shoulder and ear, I swirl my fingers in the mud, touching pine needles and leaves. It's really weird, because I've never liked dirt, but somehow the touch of the ground is comforting, because I know it will remain still. It won't talk. It won't get upset. It just is, soft like clay between my fingers as I grip clumps of wet soil with my bare hands.

"Are you still there, baby?" asks Dad.

The earth, the sound of birds, the wind, and the leaves—it's all there and won't change, regardless of my emotions. I yearn to be like that. To forget my ghosts and become one with the never-changing Earth.

But I don't forget my ghosts. My mother. And the real ghost I just saw across the lake.

I look out over the lake and, thank God, there is no boy standing there anymore. I whimper a little. Then I turn toward the path from whence I came.

That's when I drop the phone in the mud. There, standing only a few feet from me, is the boy. He's pointing at me, and this time he doesn't look afraid; he looks angry. He's accusing me as if all of his anguish is my fault. I'm frozen. This time, I feel like a hunted animal—a rabbit or squirrel—frozen, not daring to move. I can still hear my dad on the line, in the slushy mud, but I don't dare avert my eyes. And the boy is staring at me.

Then, in my mind, he screams. And disappears.

My heart is racing. I'm feeling sick. I'm having difficulty catching my breath. I'm breathing so hard, but I just can't breathe.

"Cadence? Cadence, are you okay?"

I pick up my drenched cell phone, now caked in mud.

"Cadence!" my father yells.

"Yeah, Dad," I say, out of breath.

"Baby, what the hell is the matter?"

"Dad ..." I try to catch my breath. I rub my muddy hands along my sleeves, wiping off the grime. Then I grip them tightly, trying to control my panic. I'm still holding the phone.

"It's all right, Dad."

"No, it's not. What the hell's the matter?"

"Dad ... You told me once that we had great-great-grandparents that settled and built this town. That we were related to Gweneth and..."

"Maverick."

Maverick appears once more, this time standing right over me. He's crying. He doesn't frighten me. I pity him.

"Mother," Maverick says. "Don't let Abigail hurt us."

I drop the cell phone on the ground. I raise my hands and he falls into my arms.

"I won't let her hurt you," I say. "I won't ever let her hurt you, my boy. I promise." And I kiss him on the forehead. His skin is dirty and muddied too.

"Stop scaring me," he whispers in my ear. His breath is foul.

"There, there," I say. "There, there, Maverick."

"Bairn, bairn, Escoba," he says. "Bairn, bairn. Bairn. Bairn."

I've had enough. I'm comforting a ghost. What am I doing?

My chest seems to explode. I can't breathe. Maverick fades from my arms. I fall and all grows dark.

24

MAKING UP

"WHERE HAVE YOU BEEN!" MADDIE DEMANDS AS I WALK IN MY DORM ROOM.

She looks terrible. She threw on a white T-shirt and sweatpants. It's early in the morning. Maddie's been known to sleep in occasionally. But she hasn't been sleeping. She has bags under her eyes and looks exhausted.

I ignore her, like a bitch, and walk to our bed. I take off my tennis shoes, which once were white but are now very brown from all the needless wandering I've been doing over the past few days. Then, without changing out of my filthy dress, I lie down in bed. I start to cry.

Maddie is looking down at me. She's obviously been up all night, worried—probably a few nights.

But it's Madison. My best friend. She stops yelling and sits down at the edge of the bed. Then she rubs my back as I cry.

"Jesus, Katie, what happened to you?"

It takes more rubbing and sobbing before I have the nerve to look into the eyes of my friend. She has a warm smile.

How do I put it? Does she even know I'm angry *for her*? I don't know what I'm going to do if she acts like Alondra and implies that having sex with that demonic freak bastard Professor Reardon was nothing.

"I know...I know why you didn't tell me what happened to you."

"Know? Know what? What do you mean?" Maddie asks. She doesn't seem evasive. She really seems not to know what I'm talking about.

"Your initiation."

Oh, that.

Her hands shake as she lets go of me. I can tell she doesn't want to talk about it. And her countenance changes so quickly from concern to anger. Her next words surprise me.

"I can take care of myself, Cadence."

That pisses me off, but it's not as bad as I'd feared. I think I would have run out of the room if she'd said it was no big deal.

I sit up in bed. "Why did you let me join?" I ask, rubbing my eyes with a dirty arm. "Why, knowing the bad things that happened?"

She takes a deep breath. Tears are starting to fill her eyes too. Then she shakes her head. "Cadence, you don't understand. I ... I'm not even sure exactly what happened."

"You know what happened."

"But I wouldn't ever let it happen to you," she says, giving me a pained look and shaking her head. "You don't understand that we all support each other. Even when terrible things happen ... I let you join because I wanted you to join. I trust the coven. I knew you would be safe. Had Bryce not made sure, I would have. But I needed you so much. I love you, Katie. You're my best friend. I ... I know what happened was wrong, but that wasn't what bothered me. What bothered me after the initiation was that I couldn't talk to you anymore, confide in you—you, Kate. That's why I wanted you to join. You're my BFF ... I'm just relieved I can open up to you now." She scoots onto the bed and holds me, her forehead leaning against the back of my head.

"Friends?" she asks after some silence.

"Yeah," I say, but I turn away from her.

She laughs and I chuckle a little too.

I drift off to sleep. I'm so tired. But after a few minutes, or maybe even an hour—I don't know—Maddie says to me, "Cadence, please, don't talk about it ever again. Okay?"

I don't answer her.

25

DADDY

I wake up to a knock. It's dark in my room, and Maddie's gone. I'm still lying in my filthy clothes on my bed. There's a note from my roommate: "Went to eat, Katesy." I know she's in the dining commons. And she wants me to join her—if I'm awake enough. I'm not.

There are more knocks. I sluggishly turn, try to get up, then sink back in bed.

Is everything supposed to be better now? Maddie and I made up. But I still picture that little black boy staring at me. And now, in my mind, I'm wandering again through the thick mist, smelling the moisture in the air, the dirt, and the thick foliage of the wilderness surrounding Hawthorne University. I'm remembering walking around in the forest like a madwoman. I can't recall all of it. I was so distraught. I just kept making my way through the trees, not looking for a path in particular, just walking over the leaves and mud. And playing...playing in the mud like a toddler.

What the fuck is the matter with me? I was careful enough with my steps, avoiding twisting my ankle. At least I didn't get hurt. I recall the moon lighting the darkness enough to see about five feet in front of me. And after a while, I just moved through the brush with no destination.

Like an animal. I remember a drizzle. But it felt warm. It was as warm as a sunny day.

I remember cupping my hands in murky water to drink. And I recall eating roots and sap from trees. I was an animal. I felt like I was drugged. Now...I'm scared. Because I wasn't drugged.

Never in my life had I given up, but last night I wanted to end everything. I wanted everything to be over. My life? I didn't care. I just wanted not to feel anymore. I wanted to feel numb. The wilderness gave this to me. And the weirdest thing about my mad break was the soothing feeling in the center of my body. I felt at ease. I even recall cutting my arm over a sharp twig and not feeling any pain. I looked down, but it was too dark. I felt the sticky trickle of blood, smeared it around, and tasted my arm, but I couldn't see the red. I felt nothing. No pain. Just curiosity. Curiosity about the metallic salty taste of my blood, mixed with the earthen taste of the caked mud-clay.

That was how I felt about everything. And it was good. No, it was wonderful. I recall walking, without direction, through the thick trees with my arms stretched out, as if I were in a dark cave, with only the shadows of the leaves of tall trees, under a white full moon and the clouds above. I even circled back to the lake a couple of times. The same place where I saw Maverick. Maybe if I saw the ghost again, it would snap me out of it. But the boy knew better. I probably looked more menacing in my madness than he did. He had asked me not to scare him. Because he wasn't the monster in the night—I was.

Someone knocks on the door again, this time really hard. BANG. BANG. BANG.

"Cadence," says a man's voice. Dad.

Shit. I look awful. Why didn't Maddie stop him!

I roll off the bed and nearly hit my head on the carpet. Then I rise to my knees, running my hand through my hair. I pull out some leaves—gross. Not good. Then I push myself up. I turn on the lights. It's so bright that I'm squinting. I run to the mirror ...

"Cadence! Open the door. Madison told me you were here."

"I'm coming, Dad."

My eyes look straight into the mirror and, for a moment, I think I see someone else. How can I explain the figure I see in the mirror? My reflection is horrid. My mascara has run down my cheeks. My lipstick is half-faded. My cheeks are smudged with a thin brown film of dirt. Small leaves are snarled in my long curly black hair. There are cuts along my arms and dried blood on my lower legs.

And Maddie slept in my arms. Gee, she must really love me.

Well, there is no way, no way, I'm going to let my dad see me like this.

"What do you want, Dad?" I ask, trying to stall him.

"Will you open the door so we can talk?"

"Not now. I...I...need to shower." Yeah. Maybe a *few* showers.

"I just drove two hours, squirt. I need you to open the door. Open it now."

"I'm not dressed, Dad. I was going to run to the bathroom and shower. Can you come back in thirty minutes?"

"Open it now, Cadence."

"I can't. Just...just thirty minutes. We can meet in thirty minutes."

I can practically feel his anger. His caring is actually kind of cute.

"All right... I'll wait out here."

"Dad."

"Hmm?"

"Dad, the shower is across the hall. And Maddie's still washing the towels."

"Fine," he snaps. "Thirty minutes, babe. But I swear, I'm going to stand by the exit to the dormitory. You don't know how worried I've been."

"'Kay. See you soon."

I spend the next few minutes pulling sticks, filth, and leaves out of my hair by the mirror. See, even though I know my dad will keep his word, I don't want my dorm mates to see me with this bird's nest on top of my head either. When I look passable as a human being, I open the door and run to the communal showers.

And people still stare. A lot of girls stare.

I think I smell. I clear out the shower pretty fast. The only girl left is a chubby girl with glasses, fixing her short hair beside the mirror. I know her. She's a nerdy, friendly girl named Veronica. She looks at me. Then she wrinkles her brow at the trail of muddy water meandering from my legs to the drain. "Hi, Cadence." She sounds confused.

"Hi."

I take a long shower—not too long because I know my dad was in such a state that he might run into the girls' shower and grab me if I don't meet him at the time I promised.

I run naked back to my room—see, I wasn't lying about Maddie not washing our towels.

Then I spend my remaining time fixing my hair and face. I throw on a short white skirt, tennis shoes, and a navy-blue blouse. It's a summer outfit. I don't know why, maybe it's intentional, but I'm not in the mood for gloomy winter clothes. When I'm done, I'm pretty impressed at my reflection in the mirror. I can look pretty good in a short amount of time. And it covers up the homeless-bum-whore look that I had when I woke up.

There's a knock at the door again. I straighten my skirt and open the door with the best smile I can manage.

"Cadence," he says. I've never seen him so worried. He quickly scoops me up in his arms. But then he steps back. I think I still smell a little.

"Hi, Daddy."

"What the hell's going on?" He walks in the bedroom and looks at my muddy clothes, lying in a hamper by the door. They're caked in dirt. I can't believe I was wearing them.

"Everything's fine, Dad."

"No—no, it isn't." He shakes his head. "What happened? Where have you been? Why haven't you answered my calls? Madison's calls? Why—"

"Dad." My voice chokes up.

He stops. I'm sitting in bed, which I now realize is dirty from my muddy clothes, and I throw a hand up toward him, warning him not to say another word. After a long silence, I turn and see him leaning against the closed door, staring at me. I notice huge bags under his eyes. Sweet. He hasn't been sleeping either.

"Don't worry about me," I say.

"Are you serious?"

"I'm fine. You're the one with Mom—"

"Katie, I told you on the phone that you worry too much about others. Try thinking about yourself. I'm worried about *you*. You scared the hell out of me..." He runs his hand through his short black hair. "You were yelling at someone. You kept yelling *Maverick*. I didn't understand. You kept saying, 'I'm a maverick.' You kept repeating that. Your voice sounded changed. It was really weird. Why?"

I did? I don't remember yelling "Maverick." I remember seeing Maverick.

That's when I feel it. Deep in my chest, I feel a weight that draws me deep into the cushion of my bed. I feel really sick. Dizzy. I put my head in my hands and start bawling. But I'm not sad. I'm scared. I'm horrified because I realize that I really must be losing my mind. I mean really going crazy. I spent the last few days wandering through the dark, cold forest alone. Now my dad says I told him things I can't even remember.

He sits beside me and holds me. I weep even harder in his arms.

"What's the matter, baby?" he whispers in my ear. "Oh, Cadence."

"I'm scared. I'm so scared, Daddy. I don't know what's happening."

"It's okay... It's all right, sweetheart. Tell me. You can tell me... Are you taking drugs?"

Uh, just a lot of beer. And mandrake root—yeah, there's mandrake. Maybe sometimes nightshade... And. Shit, yeah, I guess I am.

So I do something I never do with my father. I lie to him. Or is it a lie? I don't even know. "No," I answer.

"Then what's the matter? If it's school, you can just leave. I can take you home."

I pull away from him, angry. "I don't want to go home!" I snap. "The last thing I want to do is go home and see Mom. You made the whole house a fucking memorial for her."

"Cadence!"

"It's true. I can't go there. I don't want to ever go back home, thinking of her day in and day out like you. I...I can't—"

"Fine, Cadence. Fine. Then...what do you want to do? You told me on the phone you wanted to go home. You can come home for Christmas break."

"I don't know. I just don't want to go home. But I can't be here either. Everybody's so weird. I don't have any friends except Maddie, and they took her. Even she's been changed by them. They're everywhere in the school. It's like evil, you know. It's totally fucked up here."

"Watch your language, Katie."

"Whatever." I take a deep breath.

"Who took her?"

"Look, I just can't go home, 'kay?"

"You were fine here last year with Madison. Can you tell me what's going on?"

"No." And I clam up. I'm not going to tell him anything.

"I got a call from the provost," he says after a long silence.

Shit.

"You failed every class except metaphysical history, whatever the hell that subject is," he says. "And that was considered incomplete. You didn't take a single final exam this week. I don't understand. You're a straight-A student. I can't even remember a time you got a C." Then he rubs the thin whiskers on his chin. "No, I do understand it, baby. It's Mom. You're always so strong that I didn't realize how much her death affected you."

I shrug and force a smile.

I don't want to tell him what's really going on. Would he believe it? That I've joined a satanic witch sex cult? My father is neither a prude nor a zealot, but I know he wouldn't be happy about Alondra's coven. And there's something about his expression that tells me he knows—it's like he knows I'm hiding things. Just as I always knew the coven was hiding things from me.

"So, what do you want to do, squirt?" he asks. "Maybe...maybe you could stay at Jane's house if you don't want to come home. Then you could leave school for a little bit. How would that sound? I've already spoken with the provost. He's okay with you taking a break. He even offered to forget the semester, considering that you're grieving. He's attributing everything to what's happened."

I shrug.

"Whatever you want, Cadence. I just don't want to see you like this."

I look down and stare at the red-and-brown carpet. I've always found the dormitory carpet so fluffy and ugly. Now it's a comforting escape from my father's worried look. "I think I need to see a counselor, Dad."

"Yeah? Well there's Father Dayton. Why don't you talk to him about Mom?"

Mom. He has no idea it's not Mom driving me insane. Am I insane? Well, normal people don't live like animals for days.

"No." I shake my head. "No, I need to see a shrink, Dad. Serious. At least the school counselor."

His frightened expression makes me feel worse. Then I look at the window. The light peeking through the sides of the red drapes has darkened. Night is falling.

"Can we go out to dinner, Dad?" I ask, really wanting to change the subject. And, actually, I'm really hungry.

"Sure."

"I love you, Dad."

"I love you more, sweetheart."

He holds me and I almost fall apart again, crying. But I don't. I just sit there, looking back down at the carpet with my dad still holding me in his arms.

We go to a buffet restaurant. We talk. It's mostly about Dad and how he's holding up back home. He tells me he has no inclination to move, despite how much I hate the house now. I eat lots of servings of everything and wash it down with Coke. I do my best not to show dad how much I'm starving, but he gives me a weird look after the fourth plate. Then I'm sorry to see him leave. He offers to stay with me at a hotel, but I refuse.

Maddie comes back to our dorm room and acts like her jubilant self. She's so convincing that my dad and I seem to forget all about my breakdown, my need to seek a psychiatrist, and my failing out of school. Then Dad gives me a long hug, runs his hand through my hair, and kisses me on the cheek. I adore him. Then he hugs Maddie and goes home.

I log the whole thing in my Book of Shadows, called *Broomstick*.

26

———————

MIRA

So a month passes and I don't leave the school, I don't move out of the dorm, and I don't see a psychiatrist. I don't even give up on my studies. I work harder than ever. My classes were all fails, not only because I missed final exams, but because I didn't bother to attend any lectures over the last three weeks of the semester. I was too busy staring at ghosts or wandering around the school like a weirdo.

After I hang my head in shame—and add a little begging, mixed with some help from the provost because of my bereavement—my teachers are willing to give me a C if I retest and earn As on remedial tests. That means I'm studying harder than I've ever studied in my life, because I have to cover this semester *and* last semester at the same time. I know I can do it—except in Alondra's class. I don't ask her to remediate and, of course, I avoid Bryce like the plague (no incidental reference intended).

Right now, I'm in the dining commons, eating tacos. It's Taco Tuesday. I'm sitting with an old friend I met my freshman year. Her name's Catherine. We met in an English lit class because I walked up to her and said, "You know, my name's also Catherine, sort of." And wouldn't you know it, people call her Katie. Well, Katie is the most vanilla girl I've ever met. That is so refreshing. Her father's a preacher. But she's really nice.

I snicker inside as I crunch on a taco, imagining her expression if she visited Alondra's house during one of our ceremonies.

"Are you going to the dance?" Catherine asks.

What? Are we in high school again?

"There's a dance at the church," she explains. Catherine's an Asian girl, really cute with a big smile. I always liked her. Maddie can't stand her. "Oh, I forgot you don't go to my church."

"Yeah," I say, smiling back; then I sip some Coke from my straw.

On my right is *Wuthering Heights*, opened to page 132. I'm reading the novel for an English class. I'm glancing at it while she's speaking. Talk about multitasking.

"Well, I met a boy," Catherine says.

I'm reading about the Catherine who is the main character of *Wuthering Heights*, another nomenclature coincidence. So I'm completely ignoring the prissy Catherine across the table. Then I look up as I dip a chip in some beans and notice that my cute friend is staring at me. She looks a little upset. I think it's because I'm not listening to her.

"Huh?" I ask.

"I met a boy," Catherine says. "Kurt. He's really cute."

"Oh. Where? In class?"

"No. At church. You should come, Cadence. You should come to church with me."

"No, thanks." But I flash her a sweet smile. I'm trying to be nice. Honestly, I really like Catherine; it's just that I'm realizing I have to finish this novel and write an essay by eleven tomorrow morning to complete my English literature retest. I've never dealt with procrastination. The whole thing is new for me. I realize I don't even have time to talk to my friend.

But she looks hurt again.

"Sorry, Katie," I say. "I'm really busy with my studies."

"I know. But ..." Then she giggles. "He's really cute."

I sigh, close the book, and lean back in my plastic chair. "Tell me about him."

And can you guess who shows up and stands over me and my old friend? Mira. Mira with her black lipstick, her stupid superior smile, and her nasty penetrating eyes. She's looking at Catherine with disgust. I guess she can't recognize a girl who's innocent and pure.

"Is this seat taken?" Mira asks me. She puts a tray with a taco salad on the table beside Catherine. The table has four chairs. Catherine nods and scoots over. Mira completely ignores her and directs a sly grin at me.

"As a matter of fact, it is," I say.

Mira ignores me. "So, how are things?" she asks, holding a chip, turning her back on Catherine.

"I said the seat is taken, Mira," I say. "Maddie and one of her friends are coming to join us."

"Yeah, well," Mira says with a shrug, "I'm Maddie's friend."

Fucking bitch.

I look away from Mira and say to Catherine, "Kurt? Tell me about him."

"Well, he's really tall," Catherine says. She's giddy. "He's got a beard and he's like always smiling. I used to just look over at him on Sunday mornings during prayer. And we'd like"—Mira chuckles, and Catherine gives her a funny look—"meet each other's eyes. I know he likes me, Cadence. He's really nice."

"How cute," Mira comments. Then she eats more of her lettuce.

"This is Catherine, Mira," I say—mostly to get the bitch to finally recognize her existence.

"People call me Katie," Catherine says.

"How confusing," Mira says with a laugh. Then she lifts another chip, waving it in the air. "You know, *Katie*"—now she's talking to my friend—"I used to know a cute man in church too. His name was Jack. He was also tall with a beard."

"I'm sure Catherine doesn't want to know about your boyfriends, Mira."

"No, I do," Catherine says. "What about this Jack?"

"Well," Mira says, "see, Jack liked to drink. He used to drink so much that he'd sneak a couple of those small bottles—you know, the ones you can get at the gas station, pull out of your pants, and chug down. Vodka, bourbon, whatever."

Catherine giggles, and Mira waves her hand and winks like they're the best of friends.

"Of course," Mira continues, "he was only sixteen, but he had an older brother as a supplier... Well, Jack used to look over at me too. And I'd just kind of slip down my top a little, not enough to be noticed by others on the row, but enough for Jack to see. I'd dip down my top just enough to show my nipple. I used to laugh, 'cause the priest would look over in complete shock. Of course, I got Jack to notice. I mean, I might be big, but that has the added plus of giving me really big boobs. So as the priest is talking, I'm rubbing my cunt—"

"Shut up, Mira," I snap.

"She gets to tell her story, but I don't?" Mira asks, acting hurt.

"No one wants to hear your whore stories. Especially at church."

And this time, I was right. Catherine has her head in her hand, quietly scooping up some beans.

"Anyway," Mira adds. "I fucked him during confessional, Catherine. First, I sucked his dick real hard. Then I fucked him. He was the best fuck—"

"You would," I say, throwing my fork on my plate. "You're so cold, you'd have to be a whore in order to get any boy."

"Yeah, but Cadence, I didn't fuck the boy." Then Mira turns and winks at Catherine again. "I fucked the priest."

Catherine jumps up, disgusted. I do too.

"Where are you going?" Mira asks us.

"Tell Alondra she can talk to me herself!" I say. "I don't need her messenger."

"Who said Alondra sent me, Cadence?"

Catherine is already making a hasty exit from the dining hall. Mira sees her going too. "Sorry 'bout that," Mira says, snickering. "Some people just don't have a sense of humor."

"You're disgusting."

"Well, you're hanging out with Bo-Peeps," she says with a chuckle. "You asked me not to call you one, but if you're gonna hang with 'em, you might as well know what they are. That one's a closed-minded Barbie doll that thinks a date is a man and a woman slow dancing two feet apart."

"Catherine is one of the nicest girls I've ever known."

"Well," Mira says with a shrug and relaxes back into her plastic seat. "She's a sheep. A Little Bo-Peep, Cadence."

"What do you want?" I grudgingly sit back down.

"I want you to come back. Come back to us. *I* want this, not Alondra. Alondra's really pissed. She's tired of you. She couldn't care either way. And anyway, she's got other things to worry about at the moment."

"Well, I don't care for her anymore either."

"Right. But *I* want you back."

"Why? You asked me to leave."

Mira shrugs, twirling her chip around some salsa. Then she cracks the chip in her teeth and points at me, her finger covered in salsa. "You running away really fucked up the energy in our circle. Everyone, from your best friend to your boyfriend, is really down. It's not the same. I can't perform spells with everyone moping about. Even Alondra, who claims she doesn't care, is down about you. You need to come back to us. We're family."

Then she smiles and eats more salad. She's a pretty messy eater.

I look away from her. The flat-screen TV on the wall has a cartoon playing. I stare at it. I stare at anything but Goth Bitch. Then I think how amusing it is that doom-and-gloom girl is concerned with people in the coven being depressed.

"What'd you learn from your Wandering?" Mira asks. "Did you write it in your grimoire? Did you discover anything you can share with us?"

"What?"

"Your Book of Shadows. Did you write down your Wanderings? Your best friend told me you were in the forest for days."

I don't want to talk about it. I've tried to forget it. I've tried to bury my face in my books. In fact, it's because of that weird "Wandering" that I'm in this terrible predicament in school.

Then, thinking of books, I remember *Wuthering Heights*, so I move the book back where I can read it instead of listening to this witch.

"What was it like?"

"What, Mira?" I'm reading about Heathcliff.

"Your Wandering. Everybody has one after initiation. Usually it happens immediately after the trauma of intercourse and the loss of virginity. That's what happened to me. I wrote fifty pages after I was fucked. Dr. Reardon ceremonially fucked me too, and I kept trying to come to grips with it."

That's it. I grab my book and quickly make my way to the exit.

But she grabs my hand. "Wait, Cadence." Mira thinks she's being funny. The sick thing is she's also being completely truthful—probably about the priest story too.

"I already told the coven that I want to leave. Forget it, Mira."

"You're in way too deep, Cadence." She's holding my wrist tightly, actually hurting it. A couple of students look up from their tables.

"Let go of me!" I snap and yank my hand back.

I rush out of the Dining Commons and head straight to my dorm. It's not far, just two buildings down along a paved walkway.

It's humid outside—actually hot, even though it's around seven o'clock in the evening. It's early February and the hottest day we've had in a while. I look back and Mira is on my tail. I'm sure she intends to follow me wherever I go, so I reluctantly stop.

"Just leave me alone!" I yell.

Mira still has a big grin on her face and doesn't look deterred at all. In fact, she's a little spooky following me like this.

Then I see the real spook. The boy. The ghost in suspenders is standing still, in the shadow of one of the neighboring dormitories. It freaks me out to see a ghost staring at me. Then I shudder when I watch a student throw open a glass door and walk right through him.

I forget all about Mira, but when I turn, I see her behind me. She's staring at the boy too. There are ten to twenty students making their way to or from the dining hall. None of them see the specter. Only Mira and I do.

"Maverick," Mira mutters. For the first time, she isn't smiling. She seems afraid. Then her mouth and eyes open wide when the boy lets out an inhuman scream. No one turns; no one notices, except Mira and me. Then the boy vanishes.

"You saw him?" I ask Mira.

Mira nods slowly. But it doesn't seem like she's seen him before. Maybe it's the first ghost she's ever seen. I see the boy almost every day. But this is the first time he's yelled using his mouth. Usually I just hear it in the wind. I wish he hadn't. It reminded me of the scream from the animal sacrifice. I keep telling him not to scream.

Mira seems to forget what the chase was about. It's the perfect excuse for me to ditch her. I run across the lawn to the other building. I look back and, unfortunately, my pursuer is back to following me.

I open the glass door and head inside the dark hallway of my dorm. I hear the door close, then quickly open again. It stays locked, but it's not unusual for someone to let in a stranger. I'm pretty sure that's what just happened, and Mira's still following me.

I walk up the stairs, wave to an acquaintance of mine from last year's American history class, then rush into my hallway. It's even darker upstairs. I walk faster, remembering that Mira has never been to my room and probably won't know where to knock. But Mira's in better shape than I would have guessed, and she's huffing and puffing behind me. I cock my head back and see her familiar long trailing black dress, which fits more like a druid's cloak. I literally can't ditch this girl.

I'm mad. I'm angry that this coven is ruining my life, ruining my grades, and embarrassing sweet friends like Catherine and that now I can't shake the High Priestess's crazy noxious assistant. So I turn around, more furious than ever, ready to shout at her. And I see Maverick. For the first time, the ghost is not facing me; he's facing Mira. When Mira sees him, she falls right on her butt in horror. Again, Maverick lets out a bloodcurdling scream; this time he's staring at Mira and pointing at her. The whole floor shakes. The lights flicker and two of the ceiling lights go out.

Then the ghost disappears.

I have my keys in my hand and am about to open the door to my room, but I don't. As much as I hate Mira, she's not getting up. She looks terrified.

I sigh deeply and walk back to her. I reach out my hand and help her up.

"What's the matter?" I ask as I help her up. "Never seen a ghost?"

～

Mira stumbles into my dorm room. Maddie's lying on the top bunk, reading something. She jumps down as she sees me help Mira inside our room.

"What happened?" asks Maddie.

"She saw a ghost," I say.

Honestly, I'm feeling really happy about her suffering. I know it's wrong, but I can't help but be amused at our so-called paranormal expert being terrified of a ghost. I've been seeing Maverick every day, and I'm pretty used to him. It does surprise me that she saw him, though. No one has ever seen him when I've pointed him out.

We help Mira sit down by the desk near our window. The shades are open. The sun's down and many of the windows in Krunner Hall, the high-rise dormitory across the street, are already glowing in the bright yellow light.

Mira is drenched with sweat. She looks sick. Maddie hands her a bottle of water, but she pushes it away. Then Maddie sits beside me on the bottom bunk.

Mira looks up to me. Finally, the famous smugness I detest returns to her face.

"That's why I want you back," Mira says.

I roll my eyes.

"I couldn't shake her," I say to Maddie. "Bitch followed me to our room."

"Then you sent your little helper, didn't you, Cadence?" asks Mira. "Casper."

"Who?" asks Maddie.

"Apparently, our Little Bo-Peep is actually Wendy. You know, Wendy and her friendly ghost, Casper."

"Fuck you, Mira!" I snap. "When you feel less dizzy, go home."

"Shh." Maddie jumps up and puts an arm around her. I turn back to my window, brush my long hair back, and rest my head in my hands. Then I remember my studies. This fiasco is already costing me half an hour. I have to get back to *Wuthering Heights*. I need every second I can get.

"What're you gonna do?" asks Mira with a smile. Her color returns. "You gonna summon back your friend?"

"Mira saw your ghost?" Maddie is kneeling beside Mira, still trying to comfort her.

"Yep."

"She's been telling me about him for weeks," Maddie says to Mira as she annoyingly rubs the witch's back. "I keep telling her I don't see a thing."

"All true witches, when their emotion is high enough, can manifest magic," Mira says. "Apparently, Maddie, your friend's hatred of me is just enough to summon Maverick."

"I don't hate you," I say. But I know I'm saying it with a scowl and a look of disgust.

Mira just shrugs. Then she opens the bottle of water and drinks it. Her hand still shakes.

We're quiet for a moment. The excitement is waning, so I lie on my bed, pick up the paperback still in my hand, and start reading about Heathcliff again.

"I told you, Maddie, I need her back," the bitch finally says to my BFF. "She has great power. Alondra was right."

"Katie needs to work on her studies right now, Mira."

Yeah. So fuck off now, please.

They start laughing together over some secret séance shit they were involved in a few days ago. That takes me over the edge. I feel like they're keeping things from me again. So I whirl around and go crazy on Mira.

"You said Dr. Reardon had sex with you! Why'd you let him?"

"Cadence!" Maddie says.

Mira's staring at me in shock. She laughs nervously and says, "Careful, you might summon your ghost back."

"How could you remain in the coven after fucking him?"

"Cadence," Maddie says.

I look at my friend and my old sickness returns. I remember that Maddie "fucked him" too. God, I just want them both to leave me alone.

"Dr. Reardon has sex with me, Cadence, as part of our ceremony," Mira says, as if explaining the obvious. "In satanic witch rituals—"

"I don't want to hear it. Just leave me alone." And I turn to my friend. "You too. I...I need to study, Maddie."

"I know, Katie."

Then Mira drawls on, practically talking to herself. "The initiate is taken into the circle blindfolded, with her hands tied behind her with a rope. The coven then watches as the initiate copulates with the Great Wizard. In this case, Dr. Reardon. It's ritualistic—"

"It's disgusting! I don't—"

"Just calm down, Katie." Mira raises a hand. But the witch has a sly grin on her face. Then she cackles nervously. "I don't want Casper to come back."

"Get out!" I shout.

"Cadence," Maddie says again.

"What do you think, Cadence?" asks Mira. "You think I'm not ashamed? Why do you think I asked you to leave? Reardon's a sick fuck. I hate him."

"Then why do you want me back?"

"Let me finish," snaps Mira. She jumps up. "I hate him. But he's part of the coven. We have to allow him—"

"No, you don't."

"Yes, we do," says Maddie. I turn to my BFF, surprised. "Katie, I didn't want to talk to you about it, but I agree with Mira. I wasn't raped. I allowed what happened to happen."

"But why?" I ask my friend.

"We believe in nature," says Mira, now leaning against my desk. "Witches believe in eating and sleeping in the woods. That's why you had your Wandering. Your inner being, Cadence, is nature. That's who you are. You're wild. You're nature. And sex is also nature. But... Reardon's a major asshole. Sometimes I wonder if he's a part of the circle just to fuck virgins."

Maddie looks at Mira in irritation. My best friend is trying to convince me of something, and she doesn't seem to think Mira is helping. But what's she trying to say? That it's okay to let an old man have sex with us in the name of witchdom?

"Under mandragora," Mira further explains, "my joy was to be a part of nature. Cadence, that also involved sex. In fact, when you were deep under the influence, you asked Bryce to have sex with you too. I remember. Under normal circumstances, he would have. But we know Bryce. He's a Bo-Peep like you. And he knew you better than most of us. He knew that even with your vows, if he had taken you, he would have lost you."

So this sounds great to me and all, but I'm still picturing this old professor fucking my friend. I'm completely disgusted. And I still think it's rape under the influence of a drug.

The two girls know it. So they give up and look everywhere but at me.

"Let's get rid of him," I say.

Mira looks surprised, as if no one ever suggested this.

"He's the Great Wizard, Cadence," Maddie says.

"Then he needs to go."

"He's also Alondra's husband," Maddie adds.

Oh, God.

"I think that ghost is gonna be here any moment," Mira quips.

I'm going to be sick.

Then Mira chuckles nervously again.

Now I'm really sick. I feel dizzy and nauseous. So all I do is turn to the window and stare at the high-rise dormitory across the street. Then I say, "I need to read my book now. Please, please leave, guys."

Mira mutters, "Cadence, I really—"

"Stop it," interrupts Maddie. "Sure, Cadence. We're leaving."

And the two of them leave my dorm room.

Far across the parking lot—over a block away, barely visible—a translucent boy in suspenders stares at the ground. He has a grin on his face. I jump up and throw the drapes closed.

27

THE ESSAY

Another month passes. I stay home for spring break. Maddie gets really pissed over that, but all my energy is directed toward my books. I read and breathe history, English, and anthropology. I'm a history major. I never told you that, did I?

I actually manage to improve my grades. Then I complete all the extra work given to me by my professors during the break. I write three reports and two essays. I get very little sleep, and my eyes feel blurry and buggy.

I'm prepared to finally stop and rest for two days before the restart of the semester when I remember Alondra's class. I had an A at the start of her course; now I'm about to fail. I wonder if my final grade will be an F. Maybe Alondra will find satisfaction in doing that. Then I remember her essay on Satanism and evil. So before I'm done with everything, I decide to complete her class by finishing this one last assignment.

Dear Dr. Johansen,
You asked us to reach deeply within ourselves, within our souls, and write an essay on Satanism. You asked us what we thought of Baphomet, the pentagram, and the fallen angel. You asked us to discuss the Knights Templar. And to write about evil.

The Knights Templar urinated on the cross. That is the extent of my research on this topic. I won't dignify it by pursuing it further.

Jesus Christ died for our sins. His suffering was meant to reverse the fall of man. When Adam tasted the forbidden fruit with Eve, Adam was cast out of the Garden of Eden. The forbidden fruit could represent sex. Or it could represent Adam's awareness of sin.

The human condition causes suffering because we think. We are aware and we do bad things. We sin. The sins of our animal nature prevent us from seeing the glory of God. But Jesus was flagellated, tortured, and carried the cross, dying for those sins. And if you are Christian, you believe Jesus was God. So God was willing to suffer for us. For me. For you. There is nothing more beautiful than that.

This suffering, this willingness to kill oneself for another, is what I believe is good. Those that worship the taste of fruit and live simply to enjoy sin, caring nothing for anyone but themselves, are evil. Satan is evil. He is fallen. He represents the beast that offers fruits to blind us from the light. And so, if your assignment asks me to reach deep within my soul and tell you what I think of Satan —he is evil. So the disgust one feels when looking at Baphomet, the goat, and the pentagram is completely normal. Satan is an idol of evil. What is so confusing about that? Why are you asking me to write about it?

I posit that you, Dr. Johansen, obviously carry some hang-up about God and religion. You believe that Satan simply represents nature and its dichotomy of the sun and the moon? That witches and the like, dancing around a pyre, are merely worshipping humans as animals? You have so little faith in the human soul. Can we not transcend what lies in the forest for a better world? Can we not reach out to God? Will he not take our hand and help us out of our affliction?

Satan is evil. Witches and demons are evil. There are Wiccans who do not prac-tice evil, but your viewpoint as a witch is evil. If you cannot distinguish good from evil, then you are evil. I feel bad for you.

Honestly, at first I was really excited to have enrolled in your class. But now I think your teachings are the worst in the university. You entice students into listening to your twisted theories about God and religion. It's too bad, because you are really a talented lecturer.

Hellfire, the devil, pain, torture, and ritualistic sex with virgins (yes, RITUAL-ISTIC SEX) are evil.

You asked, that's my belief.
Sincerely,
Your disillusioned former student,
Cadence Hawthorne

There.

Fuck you, Alondra. I'll drop that in your lecture box tomorrow.

I've completed last semester and won't fail a single class—except, probably, Alondra's. I lean back in my bed and sleep for twelve hours straight.

28

BOYS

Winter is over and it's hot outside. I have fond memories of spending weekends over at Maddie's house last year in the summer on days like this, and today is no different. And that's precisely where Maddie and I are now: Maddie and her aunt Jane's house.

Aunt Jane has to be the coolest mom I've ever known. She's always cheery like Maddie. Well, she raised Maddie ever since Madison was a little girl.

Right now, I'm using the bathroom at their house and looking at the lewd white statute of Venus near the sink. That's making me think of that weird sex experience with Bryce. I still can't believe how real everything felt.

I miss him, I really do, but I know that if I speak to him, it will bring me back to Alondra. So I've been walking by him in school, completely ignoring him. I'm drawn to him, but I force myself to walk away.

I wash my hands and hear my friend bursting into laughter with her aunt.

Madison is reclining in an old super-cushioned recliner. Aunt Jane is leaning forward over an expensive white linen couch, covered with smudges and dirt. But that's Jane—there's nothing stopping this woman from being carefree. It also makes her house a bit of a pigsty.

"You're looking real good lately, Katie," says Jane as I walk in.

I'm wearing a white summer skirt. It's a scorcher outside, and I see a glass of lemonade with a lot of ice on the table between my friends. They're sipping from straws. Jane gestures for me to grab the free glass.

The lemonade is amazing. Jane knows just the right amount of sugar and ice to make it perfect.

"So, Kate," Jane says with a whimsical smile, "how's your love life?"

"Excuse me?" I ask with a giggle.

I sit down on the other side of the couch. We're near a sliding glass door, and Jane's beautiful outdoor garden is blooming like crazy. I sip more of the blissful lemonade looking outside.

"Boys?" Jane asks again.

Jane has very short gray hair and a long flowery dress. She reminds me of a 1960s hippie. She's got a strong, almost mannish chin and cheekbones but very pretty brown eyelashes and eyebrows. And she's always grinning.

"I don't have much time, with my books and all," I say.

"She's a bookworm," says Maddie.

"Well, don't forget to have fun," says Jane.

Maddie gives me an annoying wink.

Jane drinks some lemonade and looks thoughtfully at the glass for a moment. She says, "Weren't you going out with that boy? That...Bryce? I remember you meeting him for a date or something a few months ago."

No, I made love with him in your bathroom under a witch spell.

"He's like all men," I reply.

"Pricks, right?" asks Jane. We laugh.

"Yeah, my first husband," says Jane, still laughing, "was an accountant. He always wore shades and grabbed his cell phone on the pretense of doing business. Of course that never stopped him from taking me to bed with him."

"Really, Mom," says Maddie.

"Then my second was a bigger bastard." Jane raises a finger with a chuckle. "He was this burly guard from Jacksonville. He was really good in the sack. But he was more of a jerk than the accountant. And unlike the first, he didn't have any money. But he had something bigger in his pants."

"Ms. Taylor," I say, embarrassed. Maddie laughs at my expression.

"Well, I've had four, my dear," says Jane. "Four husbands, Cadence. And I wouldn't have had it any other way. They were all excellent in bed."

We all drink to that.

"My advice, Cadence, is when you find a sweet man, take him. Don't let him go. There are so many assholes in this world who will hurt you that if you find one who actually cares about you, never let him go."

"Sure."

"Well," Maddie says, "Cadence still likes Bryce."

"I don't."

"You do."

"I don't."

"You do, Katie."

"Whatever."

Of course I call him. I know what you're thinking: *how could you?* But despite all the witch stuff over the past few months, I really like Bryce. I do. And I miss him.

He was the person who turned me away from the cult in the first place. But he was also the one who got me to join.

Our conversation is short. He asks me out on a date by the second sentence. I laugh and say maybe we should talk a little longer. He says he'd rather not, for fear of making me run away again. I laugh again. I ask him if he's taking me to Lacey's. He says no. It's too risky. We'll just meet in the library.

29

OUR THIRD DATE

I'm wearing a jaw-dropping long, tight black dress. I've got fake pearls on my ears. And my curly hair is perfectly straightened and combed back. But I spare the makeup. It's the library, after all.

Bryce's mauve button-down shirt and black pants might look odd on someone else. But Bryce is too hot to look odd.

We're studying. The library is pretty empty right after spring break. I'm reading about Theodore Roosevelt and the Rough Boys for my nineteenth-century American history class. He's correcting papers.

I look up and his wandering eyes meet mine. He smiles. "It's good to see you again, Cadence," he says.

"I've missed you, Bryce."

"Me too." He looks up with those gorgeous blues.

"I've been meaning to ask," I say, "did you grade my last essay in Alondra's class?"

"Are you referring to the two you didn't do, or the one that Alondra personally graded?"

I bite my lip. "Yeah, well, I never got to the other two."

"Or her last test. You were the best student in her class until the last couple of weeks."

"I know."

"Well, you had an A going into it, so she probably won't fail you."

Probably won't fail. But he didn't read my last essay. I think she'll fail me after that. I wonder if it will hurt my relationship with my metaphysical history teaching assistant. No, he'll probably be more relaxed when we're not doing the teacher-student thing.

Bryce says, "I understand." Then he goes back to grading. "Don't worry so much. You're always worrying, and that's you. It's been hard for you. But I'm sure—"

And that's when it happens. I recognize my handwriting on a paper that plops down on the table between us. I was so pissed when I wrote my final essay that I didn't even type it. I handwrote it. I look up at the person dropping it on the table and couldn't be more surprised. Alondra, wearing her usual prim and proper button-down and slacks, is looking down at me. She looks pissed. Everyone in the library is staring and pointing, because everyone at Hawthorne University knows Alondra. She's infamous. And it's not often that she shows up in the library. Like never.

"Hi, Bryce," Alondra says, staring down at me. She gives us a tight smile. "Would you mind if I have a word with our *former student*?"

"Sure," Bryce says. He looks as confused as everyone else. "We were... having a date."

It sounds completely ridiculous. It's like an excuse. Or some way to explain the fact that he's with me. It's weird.

"Aha," Alondra says.

"What makes you think I want to talk to you?" I ask rudely.

"Well, it's not often that I personally meet with one of my students to give them their final grade." Yeah, she's pissed.

"I'm leaving," Bryce says. Then he walks over and gives me a peck on the cheek. Normally, I would swoon with ecstasy, but not now. I'm staring at the witch's green eyes.

Alondra and Bryce trade places. Alondra sits down and takes a deep breath. I look around and people begin to get back to their business, not visibly pointing but still gazing over from time to time.

"Take a look at it." Alondra gestures at my nasty letter to her.

I look down. There's a big red mark at the top of the page: *A–*.

"I would have given you an *A*," Alondra says, "but I thought the hostility was unnecessary."

"Was it?" I snap back.

Alondra scoots back in the uncomfortable plastic chair. "Of course you will not get an *A* in the class. You will get a *C*. You did not complete your final exam. I would allow you to remediate and change the grade, but I have a suspicion you aren't interested in anything from me anymore and more than likely wouldn't show up."

"Correct."

Alondra nods, looks around, and leans forward. "This isn't the ideal place to tell you more secrets, Cadence, but I have a sinking suspicion that I won't have another chance. So please humor me."

I don't say anything.

"I'm sorry," she says. "Your essay discusses sin. You talk about the human condition, good and evil. Surely you understand that we are fallible. We all make mistakes. I, as your teacher, was someone you looked up to. And I failed you. But I've made major mistakes in my past. My husband was one of them."

"So I've heard."

"You don't understand," she says, shaking her head. "Don't make the mistake of thinking that the problem was only him. I've done the same thing he's done—to boys. The ceremony sometimes works both ways."

"I really don't want to talk about this," I say.

"Right. Well, I came here to tell you that you were right about me. I suffer just like you, Cadence. Maybe more. And, unlike you, I'm way too far gone to be saved by any God."

"You know I'm not Christian, Alondra. You made sure about that when you schemed to add me to your cult when you first met me. I can't help you there."

"Well, you wrote the essay like a Christian."

Then something weird happens. She stops talking. And I don't dare say a word. A few students are still glancing over.

"I'm sorry I disappointed you, Cadence," she says.

Seriously? That's a fucking understatement.

"Now to the other matter," she says. "I didn't only come here to hand-deliver your grade. I also came because Mira told me about your visions. A witch, after initiation, can receive great power. I believe you are channeling energy, but it's moving in the wrong direction. I can help you. I can help channel it so that it no longer haunts you. So that you can control it."

"I don't want your help."

Alondra raises a hand. "I know. Think it over... You are still writing your grimoire, are you not?"

"How would you know that?"

"Natural witches are part telepathic, Cadence." Then she shrugs. "And it wouldn't be a hard guess. I wouldn't doubt you'd add entries to try to understand what's going on."

"Yeah? What's going on?"

"I think you can figure it out. You're channeling the ghost because of your family's heritage. Maverick is in your blood. According to the story, Abigail tortured Escoba and her child, Maverick, in revenge. Abigail so hurt Escoba and her son that it has left a mark, like a scar, in Hawthorne. I think you are tapping into this. Their pain has become your pain, and your mind has mixed it up with your own bereavement over your mother. And Maverick's ghost manifests to you as a boy because it was at that time that his psychic energy was at its strongest."

"How do you know Maverick is my great-great-grandfather?" I ask. I've always guessed, with my surname, that I was related to the Hawthornes. I've been remembering the Wandering and asking my father, confused, about our ancestry.

She doesn't answer me. Instead she pauses pensively for a moment. Then she adds, "Abigail went mad after murdering Escoba—so the tale goes. But we don't know if she murdered her. Maybe Escoba committed suicide from the stress Abigail had caused? But both were punished with a kind of madness. Both obviously had Wanderings of their own, just like you and me. But they never seemed to recover. I think *both* Abigail and Escoba were witches.

"The same madness could happen to others who aren't helped through their Book of Shadows... It is said that Abigail wandered through the forests around our campus, haunted by visions of Escoba's ghost, after Escoba died. Does all this sound familiar, Cadence?"

"What are you trying to say?"

"Nothing."

"Are you hinting that I'll go crazy unless I get rid of Maverick?"

"Well, it's gonna be hard for your sanity if you keep seeing visions of his ghost. Isn't it? I mean, Mira is pretty open to the paranormal, but she was severely shaken after seeing your spirit. She told me you were *used to* seeing him."

"I see him," I say, looking down.

But then I'm thinking Alondra is manipulating me. She's trying to get me back. And when I look up, she seems to guess my thoughts.

"I can help you, Cadence. Unlike Mira, I've seen ghosts and I've gotten rid of them. Ghosts thrive off energy. If you can't control your energy, you might start seeing them. It can get difficult."

"I don't want your help."

"You don't have a choice," Alondra snaps. People turn again. "Cadence," she says more quietly, "you're already too deeply into this."

And isn't that what Mira told me?

Now I am reminded of it. All the times Mira came to me, it was Alondra. Mira was her messenger. Probably the last time, too, even though Mira denied it. It's another secret that lowers my respect for her. I don't feel as if I am talking to a superior anymore; I feel as if I'm talking to someone like Mira.

"I don't want this," I say, shaking my head. Tears form in my eyes.

She surprises me by taking my hand. "Cadence, I'm sorry. I'm sorry our coven hurt you. I really am. I'm so sorry. But we knew we hurt Maddie. That was why Bryce and I made sure the same didn't happen to you. I've asked you to trust me. No longer do I come to you as a professor. I am here as the High Priestess of our coven. As your sister. I'm asking you to come back...to me. Please come back to me, Cadence."

I don't say anything. I put my arm up as if to push her away, as if I'm pushing away a demon. I shake my head and jump from my chair.

Alondra doesn't run after me. I don't look back, but I don't hear her.

I run for it.

As I make it quickly down the escalator, I see Bryce. He's near the library exit. He sees me and looks concerned.

I fall in his arms and weep. I don't care if anyone's watching. I cry. I feel so confused.

See, the thing is, I still like Alondra the Witch. I feel drawn to her. But I also hate her. I hate her for everything she's put me through. She's even admitted to being evil. Am I evil?

But I like her.

Bryce holds me and whispers into my ear, "Can I take you home?"

I nod.

We run out between the glass doors.

It's pouring outside even though it's eighty degrees. It's dark because of the fog, and a yellow glow radiates from the lights lining the sidewalk. As the water rushes down my long hair, it mixes with my tears. I'm still in Bryce's arms, crying. One hand is clutching me tightly while the other is hopelessly trying to shield me from the rain. Neither of us has an umbrella this time—there was barely a cloud in the sky before I came to the library. So we're rushing down the cement sidewalk to the parking lot. Even though Bryce grasps me tightly, he's letting me guide him. He seems willing to let me take him wherever I want. I don't know where he parked—I don't really care.

Then I trip and fall to the ground. I'm not sure if it was a crack in the pavement or if I'm just too distraught. It feels like my world is collapsing again. I thought I was done with her—with him. But I called Bryce. I brought him back. Why does Alondra surprise me so much? I should have known she would follow me.

Bryce helps me up. In the parking lot he points out his used gray BMW, parked only a handful of steps away. There aren't a lot of cars parked here—we're a long way from the next major exam. But I don't go to his car. He tries to guide me to his BMW, but I don't want to go.

I turn toward my dormitory and run down the grassy hill. Bryce takes my arm and follows me without saying anything.

Even the main drag of campus is empty tonight. I want to go home. Do I? No, not really. I don't know what I want to do. Or where I want to go.

So I do something weird. I walk off the path into the trees. And Bryce is still latched on to me, trying to comfort me. I hear him saying it's going to be okay. Is it? How? How can it be okay? But I just nod.

It doesn't take long to get lost in the woods. Bryce doesn't object, and he takes out his cell phone as a flashlight. I'm still crying.

I see Maverick. I see him on nearly every corner between the trees. Flashes of his glimmering eyes between the leaves, then through the branches. The tall trees surround me and comfort me. They're like Bryce's arms, embracing me. And for a moment, I forget that Bryce is even holding me.

There's no more path. We're walking through bushes. I'm wearing boots, but I think Bryce is wearing dress shoes. It's muddy. Sometimes I feel like I'm trudging through snow. Then I feel Bryce's arm. He's still holding me. Why? Why is he doing that?

I realize I don't need him. I have the forest. The forest is my comfort. I don't need anybody.

The moon shines through the clouds, lighting our way. Then we walk toward a clearing. The rain is pouring down now, drenching my long black hair and dress. Bryce has finally let go of me. He's standing in the shadows beside a tree—I can't see his expression. I'm guessing he thinks I'm mad. Am I?

I stretch out my arms and tilt my head back. The rain is now dripping straight into my mouth and over my chest. My mascara is running as the rain pelts my face, but I don't brush it off. I stretch, arching my back as I lean back. Then I laugh. I laugh and my laughter seems to spread throughout the field, as if echoing everywhere around the trees that circle the grass. The thick trunks of oak trees circle me. They hold me just like Bryce was holding me. I'm crying now, but I'm laughing too. And I recognize this place—it's the plateau I once ran to, the highest point around Hawthorne University.

It's a wild grassy knoll surrounded by tall trees. At the center is charred wood from past pyres built by my family of witches. I stand near the charred logs and stretch myself far back again, letting the water drip down my chest, stomach, and waist. My dress is now drenched.

Then I see the familiar brown-skinned boy in suspenders standing beside Escoba. It's the first time I see Escoba, but I recognize her immediately. She's wearing a bandana, a bright ornate necklace and a long dark dress. Her smile is welcoming.

Their ghosts are not frightening. Rather, the presence of my ancestors soothes me.

Then I see Bryce. He walks over cautiously. His short black hair is soaking wet. His formal button-down is as wet as a bathing suit. And the whole thing seems more like a dream than reality. Thunder strikes. Then lightning bursts forth, casting my shadow along the grass. Bryce seems scared. And I can finally see Maverick's face, and he looks frightened too. Frightened of what? Of me?

Bryce is beside me.

"Cadence, I'll take you home," he says to me. "We need to go home."

I shake my head. I run my hand through my hair, and it feels as wet as if I just left the shower. I suddenly feel stifled in my wet clothes.

Bryce has his hand stretched out to take me home. I grab it, and then I kiss it. Then I look into his eyes—those mesmerizing blue eyes. But he looks confused.

He tugs at me again, but I pull the other way. I just stand in the hot pouring rain. Then I pull him closer. I run my hand through his hair. Then I bring my lips to his. He gasps and shakes his head, but I refuse to let him go. I won't let him go.

"Cadence," he says, finally pulling away from me. But I bring him right back into a tight embrace. I unbutton his shirt. He stops me.

"You're wet," I say. "Take it off."

"It's raining. We have to go."

I yank on each button and one pops off his shirt. Then I pull the shirt off his back. His T-shirt is taken off even more quickly. I run my hand along the wet hairs of his chest as the rain falls. Then I grasp him close again, kissing him, moving my tongue into his mouth.

Next my dress goes over my head. He's now desperately tugging at my arm, telling me we have to leave. I shake my head. I am only in a black bra and matching panties. But the water is hot. He keeps pulling me to leave the field so we can go home. I keep laughing and pulling him closer.

The thunder cracks again. Then lightning illuminates my whole body. Bryce's eyes get large, looking at me, and that makes me hungrier.

I yank his pants down and he holds me tightly as we stand close together. Between kisses, he's still pleading to leave—I think. But the words coming from his mouth contradict his actions. I feel as if we're in a warm pool, the water crashing over our bodies. It's so soothing.

I take off my bra. My breasts fall, and I can feel the curves touching the hairs of his arms. Then I remove my panties. He leans his head against my forehead and runs his hand along those curves. The other hand is grasping the crack of my ass. My nipples are hard and he plays with them between two fingers.

He's naked now. I can feel his long cock against my naked hip.

I want it. I want it so badly. I want him to enter me.

I am a virgin. In high school, I was in a heated embrace like this in the back of a boy's car, but I never let him enter me. Now I want to be entered. I want to be fucked. I want the pouring rain to wash over me while Bryce fucks me. Just like when I was on mandrake. But now I want him to fuck me so hard that I forget about everything. I just want him to fuck me in the fields, under the moonlit trees, in the pouring rain— letting the water wash over me, washing away all my problems.

We fall to the grass, and we're sitting, naked, in an embrace. I'm laughing again. He's not. His eyes are very serious. He still looks frightened by my transformation and my desire. I straddle his lap. Then I run my hands over his hair and kiss him all over his face. I touch his hard cock. He has a condom. I don't know where it came from and when he got it on, but it's there. I guide him inside me. It hurts at first, but I don't care about pain. Soon it feels incredible and satisfies my hunger.

He's not asking to leave anymore. Oh no, he's not saying a damn thing. He's slowly bobbing my nude body up and down with his thick, strong arms. And it's careful and serene—it's Bryce. And as ravenous as I feel, his kindness and care drive me even more. But I'm too wild. I'm too untamed. I'm an animal in the woods. So I bounce up and down, riding him. It hurts again. I still don't care. Mud and water splash under his buttocks as the rain pours over us. I look down into his eyes. He looks as if he's worried he'll break me. It's so nice. So Bryce. It drives me even harder.

The lightning flashes again. I see a deer behind the trees. A flash of lightning lights up the animal's eyes. Is it a deer? A cougar? A wolf? The eyes shine white. The animal is staring at us and looks afraid.

Then I turn to my lover. He's staring at me too. I can see his eyes, flashing with the bursts of lightning. Bryce looks fearful too. But he mesmerizes me with his stare as we make love, naked, in the field. He caresses my breasts and runs his hands along my wet, dripping back. I move my hips up and down on his cock. He moans.

This is when I finally realize what we're doing. We're sitting together, entwined in each other's arms—naked and drenched—in the middle of a grassy knoll surrounded by oak trees—fucking. It's as if nature is our coven. The trees surround us like witches around a pyre. They seem to move in a circle around us.

The pleasure is beyond any imagination. I am fucking Bryce. He's not fucking me. I am fucking him in the rain in the forest. Why? Was it a spell? Did Alondra bewitch me? Or is it my spell? Did I conjure this? I don't know. But I relish holding and touching him and wish it would never end.

The rain pours harder and I push into him harder. I feel him deep inside me. I have his hair entwined in my hands, and I'm pulling it as he pushes into me. Our lips meet again, and we lick and taste each other's tongues as I bob up and down on him, again and again.

Do I love this man? He cares about me—that much is certain. I am so alone, but Bryce is here and he cares about me.

And I'm not alone. I have the grass, the trees, the breeze, the forest. I have the Earth. And I realize that when I walked through the forest in my Wandering, I wasn't alone then either. I feel like I'll never be alone again.

"Oh, Cadence."

There's an earthen smell mixed with his cologne and my perfume. I smell mud. Then I hear our naked bodies slapping against the water and dirt below him. I slam down harder. And I can feel the wind, oddly cold, under the pummeling drops of hot water.

I finally feel him climax inside me. It makes me jerk over him in a rush of pleasure. I cry out, moaning. We roll on our sides in the wild grass, my heart racing and the two of us breathing heavily. He's still holding me tightly in his warm embrace.

And then...I cry.

I'm as surprised as he is. I don't know why I'm crying. I don't feel sad. I feel confused.

"Cadence, what's the matter? Why are you crying?"

"Because it's raining."

He clutches me more tightly. On one side, I feel the sticks and mud against my naked body; on the other, I feel Bryce. He wants to get up, but I pull him back down. I want him to cover me. To stay with me.

It is sin. It's a baptism of sex under pouring rain. My virginity has been taken in this way because of who I am, because of what I am. I am a witch.

30

LATTES

It's Tuesday morning at eight thirty. Maddie and I are drinking together in the university coffeehouse. I tell her I want to drink inside so she doesn't steal anything. I have my laptop on the table. I was reading a passage on the construction of the Panama Canal before Maddie arrived. Maddie doesn't have anything in her hands. She's a known procrastinator. I've never known her to study until the night before a test. Except when she was in Alondra's class.

She's looking out the window at the lawn. There's something really morose and depressing about her. It's very unlike her. It's hot today. The coffeehouse is busy. I'm wearing a white lace summer skirt. Maddie has on shorts and a T-shirt. I see her looking at three boys at a nearby table. They're not looking at her. She could probably attract any of them if she tried, but I think she told me she's back with Nick. Is that what the doom and gloom is about? Nick?

"So..." I pause. I've been preparing how I'm going to broach the subject. Now I feel stupid about the whole thing. Of course my best friend has known me long enough to know something's on my mind.

"Do tell," Maddie says with a smile and a sip of her cup of Joe.

I look around as if it's a big secret. Of course no one can hear. The coffeehouse is packed. We were lucky to grab this small table after another couple left.

I lean forward. "I had sex last night."

Maddie giggles. She finally brightens up. "*And ...*"

"What do you mean?" I ask.

"*And ...*"

"And what?"

"Yeah," Maddie says. "*And what?*"

"What do you mean?"

"Oh, Cadence." Maddie is still laughing. I lose my smile. I feel like she's making fun of me.

"It ..." I bite my upper lip and shrug. "It was my first time."

Maddie gives me a funny look for a second. She stops laughing.

"That is *sooo* sweet, Kate." She's suddenly very thoughtful. She sips from her paper cup and touches my arm. "Sorry. I forgot. It was Bryce, right?"

"Of course."

"He's so hot. I'm happy for you, Cadence." But she doesn't look happy for me. "Really. You two make a really great couple. And anyway you've been yapping about screwing him since last year. It's about time. I'm kind of tired of hearing it. Where...where did you do it? You weren't home last night."

"I know. I didn't want to wake you."

Then she looks out the window again as if we aren't even talking.

"What's wrong?" I ask.

"Hmm?" Maddie asks.

"What's up?"

I'm a little disappointed. I thought my friend would want to know all about last night.

"It's..." Maddie hesitates. "Shit, Cadence, I guess I can tell you, technically, 'cause you're part of the coven, but then again...you're kinda not. You have nothing to do with us anymore. You don't really want to."

"Right."

"But you did just have sex with Bryce."

"Is something wrong with Bryce?" I lean forward. She laughs at my expression.

"No. I meant, you don't want to be a part of our family, but you just got really close to one of us. Now it's not just me, girl, it's me and Bryce."

"Yeah, I saw Alondra too—last night."

"I know." Maddie sips her coffee again. "She said she talked to you."

"Where did you see her? Your Sabbath is Friday, not yesterday."

"She came by our dorm," Maddie says.

"The dorm?"

I drink some of my green tea latte. I love green tea lattes—I'm a bit addicted, actually. I'm regretting choosing something hot, though. Even though it's air conditioned in the building, it's still humid and hot. Today's gonna be another scorcher. And it might rain. Like last night. Pouring rain like last night... *Pouring rain over Bryce's yummy hard body. Why aren't we talking about that?*

"Yeah, she came by our dorm," continues Maddie. "She thought you'd be back home."

"Our room? Is she chasing me now, like Mira?"

"Well, technically, Katie, Alondra is no longer our professor. Since she's not teaching us, she can come by as a friend. But our neighbors thought it was pretty weird when she visited."

"What'd she want?"

Why are we talking about Alondra? I thought Maddie'd be all over my consummated relationship story.

"Alondra's kind of down, Cadence. Haven't you noticed?"

"She seemed more pissed than down."

"Yeah," Maddie says with a chuckle; then she stares outside again. "She's really pissed at you. But she understands, Cadence. She understands everything." Maddie looks right into my eyes but seems to hesitate. Then she takes my hand in hers. "Kate...I...really."

She stops, lets go of my hand, and throws her long hair back.

"What?" I ask.

She shakes her head. Then she drinks more coffee.

"What?"

Maddie takes a deep breath. "Think about this: I need to ask something of you. I've never needed something from you so badly. Really think about it. For me. You don't have to do it, but it would mean so much to me."

"What?"

"I need you to come to our session Friday night."

"No."

"I wouldn't ask you if it weren't important."

"No."

"You know, girl, I never asked you to join."

"You coaxed me to come to her house to see Bryce," I remind her.

She's no longer sad. She's mad. She's seriously upset with me. But I'm upset too. I can't believe she's asking this of me.

"Yeah, but after that, Cadence, I let you stay away because I didn't want to hurt you. But now you're in too deep."

Not her too? What do they mean, I'm in too deep? Why do they keep saying that?

Maddie takes a deep breath, grabs my hand, and looks right into my eyes. "I'm asking you, as my best friend, to come to the session. You'll understand when Alondra tells you. You're still a part of our family. This is more important to me than you can imagine, Kate."

"Not you too," I snap. I'm surprised at how angry I feel. "I told Alondra I wanted out. I barged out of the library when she said the same shit. I don't want this."

"Babe, she came to our dorm. Do you know how weird that is? That's how important it is. It doesn't matter that she's a teacher anymore. What matters is us." She takes another deep breath. I pull my hand away, but Maddie doesn't want to let it go. "You ran away. You didn't let her tell you what she wanted to tell you."

"She told me enough. I'm a straight-A student," I remind her. I feel really nerdy saying it. "She almost destroyed my chances here."

"I know, Katie. I know. But you can study and still be with us."

"I am with you."

"No." Maddie takes another deep breath. "You're with me. But I need you with us. The coven. At least Friday night. For me. Just think about it. Everyone wants to see you again."

"Mira?"

"Especially that bitch."

I laugh at that. Then I test my BFF by being a little bit of a bitch myself. "What about Dr. Reardon?" I regret the words as soon as they come out of my mouth.

Maddie looks angrier than I've ever seen her. But then she snaps, "I don't want to fight. But...what happened, happened to me, not you, Katie. Get over it, 'kay?"

"You let that old—"

"Kate!" Maddie exclaims. Her eyes are wide and she has her hand up. "Goddamnit, Cadence, stop it."

"Sorry."

"Yeah," Maddie says, looking down at her cup. "Friday is very special. We really need you there. Friday night, that's all. As usual, you can leave if you wish. No one forces anything upon us. But everyone wants *you* there. And ..." She hesitates again. She gulps more of her coffee. "Alondra needs you."

"Alondra needs me? Why?"

"Can't tell you."

"Oh, come on."

"Just come, Katie. Please. I'm asking you to trust me. Just this one time. Please."

I run my hands through my hair and turn from my friend.

"For me?" she implores.

Then I take a deep breath and look out the window again. "Fine." I see her out of the corner of my eye, and she looks relieved. But I'm not looking forward to another meeting with them—not looking forward to it at all. I swore I'd never go again.

Alondra came to our dorm room? That's so weird.

Maddie leans forward with a huge grin. "So, how was it?"

"Hmm? How was what?"

"Your lover?" she asks with a shrug.

I giggle and she joins me. She pats me on the shoulder. Then she raises her cup of coffee to me in a toast.

31

—————

WINDSTORM

I DRIVE MY HONDA TO ALONDRA'S AND PARK AMONG THE FAMILIAR CARS driven by the rest of the witches in my coven. I'm late. I'm often late to things. And half of me doesn't want to be here. No, all of me doesn't want to be here. Maddie said she needed to get some things and would meet me.

It's dark, but the sky is clear under a full moon and it's warm out.

So I'm walking up the lovely walkway surrounded by Alondra's flowers. I see her Jaguar in the driveway and all the poorer cars, like mine, parked behind it.

I knock on her door and wait uncomfortably.

The door opens. It's Bryce. He embraces me, friendlier than ever.

Bryce and I have been talking by phone all week since *that night*. It's so easy to talk with him. I really like him, and as much as I really don't want to be here, he has this warm grin.

"Thanks for coming, Cadence."

"I came for Maddie."

"I know," he says. "But Alondra needs you more than she does tonight."

I walk into Alondra's chic home. Not all the lights are on, but her expensive vases, travertine floors, and lovely chandelier remind me of her wealth—however she gets all that money.

We walk down the hallway past the kitchen. I look over at the dining room, remembering that first evening party where I became acquainted with my witch professor. There's no one there. There are a few trays of snacks on the island, but nobody's in the kitchen. And no one's in the living room either.

"Mind telling me what this is all about?" I ask Bryce, holding his hand.

"You'll see."

But he doesn't look happy about it. He looks really sad and depressing.

There are two black cloaks on the couch. He hands me one, and I throw it over my clothes.

"You want me to strip down naked under this?" I ask with a silly smile. He doesn't answer. "It's nothing you haven't seen," I quip.

"Stop it, Cadence," he says. He's blushing a little and it's cute. He turns to me and holds me for a moment. "I don't know what I'm going to do with you."

"Love me," I say under his gaze.

He pecks me on the lips. "Come on."

I look out the sliding glass doors and see a pyre—of course. Then I squint and see people sitting around it in chairs.

"You still look nervous," he says as he walks slowly beside me to the fire.

"Because you guys never tell me what the fuck is going on."

He chuckles. But he doesn't tell me what the fuck is going on.

We walk toward the tower of flames. I recognize Maddie under her hood. And bitch Mira too. And asshole Reardon. In fact, Reardon begins talking as we sit.

I am told to sit near Alondra. She doesn't look at me, but she reaches out her hand. I hold her hand on one side and Bryce's on the other.

"Welcome," Reardon says. "Welcome to all who have come. Especially to Windstorm, who has once again brought her energy to the circle." *Yeah, fuck you, you pervert.* Then something really weird happens. Dr. Reardon, who is one of the most stoic, robotic guys I have ever seen, gets choked up. "We are protected, just as the darkness shades light. Through the darkness roams the hunter. The hunter brings the sacrifice. We follow truth and believe in shadows that shall guide us toward our salvation."

"Atman," says Alondra.

"Atman," say the others.

"And for Alondra, our High Priestess," continues Dr. Reardon. He looks right at me and I shudder. "Allow her to pass over to the Summerland and beyond. Let her not remain as a ghost or vapor. Let her move on to her next life."

"Atman," says Alondra.

"Atman," say the others.

"Thank you," Alondra says to Dr. Reardon.

Alondra lets go of my hand and rises. She lifts her hands to the sky and gazes at the stars.

"All things must pass," Alondra says, addressing all of us. She looks at me with a warm smile. "I have been fortunate to have been your leader for many years. It has been my honor to lead the coven... There was a recent rift in our family." Now she turns and looks right into my eyes, and I'm feeling uncomfortable. "The timing of one of our ladies' coming out could not be more difficult. With the recent loss of her mother, Emily, our sweet Cadence Hawthorne has been through more trials than many of us. So it is with heavy..." Alondra pauses, hanging her head down. The flames reveal tears in our leader's eyes. *Why is she talking about me? And all the witches are looking at* me *with pity.* "So recently, we have mourned the passing of Windstorm's mother. Now we must mourn the passing of another."

Mira loses complete control of herself. And she's not one to show much emotion either. Gilda, the girl beside her, grabs her and holds her. Alondra stands straight and gestures with an outstretched hand.

"We, here in the circle, are here for the pleasure given to us by the Earth," Alondra continues. "Your High Priestess suffers from an ailment of the womb. An invasive illness that promises to take my life in a matter of months... And so it is that we are challenged with a great test. I face the greatest test. We know that the greatest illusion of life—death— disturbs our circle once more." Mira is bawling and screaming in pain.

Alondra looks over but does not stop. "But do not allow it to shake our faith, girls. Death is the greatest illusion. So I face the Summerland with some trepidation, but knowing I have the support of all of you within the circle."

"Atman," says Professor Reardon coldly.

"Atman," say the others in unison.

"The coven needs a new leader." Alondra picks up a candle from the grass. It's the same type of candle as the one in my dormitory. A memorial candle. "Windstorm." She looks at me with a sweet smile, presenting the candle again. "You have the greatest power of the circle. I will my power and the leadership of our coven to you."

She gestures for me to stand. I rise from my seat and everyone looks at me.

It's supposed to be an honor. But it's not.

I'm getting angry. I mean, really, really angry. I'm feeling this mix of sadness and rage that I've never felt before, and somehow I know I'm not going to be able to control myself anymore. How dare she! How dare they all tell me this in such a contrived, weird way. It seems so cold. So cowardly. Why couldn't she just tell me like a normal person?

"Take this candle," she says. "Light it by the fire and—"

"What's wrong with you!" I shout. Alondra looks perplexed. "Why do you do this!" I yell, looking at the others. I see looks of bewilderment under their hoods. They seem amazed that anyone would dare interrupt their stupid ceremony. "Why tell me now! Like this, in your fucking freak ceremony! So you're dying, Alondra? Why didn't you tell me in the library? Why not tell me like a normal person!"

"Windstorm..." Alondra says.

"*My name is Cadence!*" I shout. I hear my voice oddly echo for miles around the forest.

"Cadence," Alondra says. "Please. Calm yourself. You must—"

"Bitch!" cries Mira, pointing at me. "You don't believe! Can't you see our High Priestess suffers? But you fight her. This is our belief. Our religion. If you don't believe in the coven, get out!" Then Mira screams, "Go away, for once!"

"She doesn't understand," says Maddie, weakly trying to come to my defense.

"You are no longer allowed to be in our sacred circle, Cadence Hawthorne," adds Reardon. It's my pleasure to ignore him.

"How long have you known?" I ask Alondra.

"A year," she says coldly. "But I didn't know it was terminal until this month."

"Why didn't you tell me?"

"Why would she tell *you* anything!" shouts Mira.

Gilda and Helen are holding Mira back. She wants to rush me. She wants to pummel me. Bryce stands before Mira to protect me.

"Everyone sit down!" Alondra orders. No one sits.

"You're so weird!" I say to Mira. Then I address all of them. "You're all so strange."

"Then leave, Cadence," Reardon repeats calmly.

"Bill is right," says Alondra with a nod. "Leave the circle if you must disturb our meeting."

"Bill is right?" I repeat incredulously. "Bill is right? And you want *me* to leave? The circle? The coven I couldn't give a shit about? You asked me to be here. You all begged. First you want me to be the leader of your sex cult, now you want me to go."

"You're obviously not ready, Windstorm," says Alondra.

"*My name is Cadence!*" My words echo once again. And this time there is a crack of thunder accompanying my words and everyone looks up, for there are no clouds. "Why didn't you tell me if you've known for so long? Why do you hide everything!"

Alondra doesn't say anything. She doesn't need to.

The flames do. The fire rises slowly over two stories high into the air. We're all stunned, staring at the pyre. Everyone is too afraid to move. I can feel the flames and smell them, and I'm wondering if it will crash down and kill us. But I can't move. I'm like a frozen animal just staring at the light. And it's real. I'm remembering that we haven't partaken in mandrake yet, which would normally creep me out even more.

But I'm not afraid. I am incensed. And thunder cracks through the valley once more, followed by a series of bursts of lightning. And some of the witches avert their eyes from me in fear.

Me? Why me? It's like my ghost. Why is everybody afraid of me?

I'm crying. My tears are flowing so hard that I can't see. Because I don't want to see. I don't want to see anything anymore. I want everything gone.

The flames blur through my tears. I feel someone holding me. Madison? Bryce? Alondra? I don't know. I don't care. I can't shake it. I can't shake them. Nor can I shake off my fury.

Alondra walks toward me, and her body is thrown back to the ground by some invisible force of air.

I look down.

Out of the corner of my eye, I see a vision of a boy in suspenders. He's out in the field, walking toward us, and there's someone beside him, holding his hand. A woman in a black cloak. The same black cloak that we all wear. They're walking over as if they're as real as we are. But I've been seeing that boy every day. I can see right through him as he fades in and out—he's Maverick, my ghost, and with him is the ghost of Escoba.

Some of the girls scream. For the first time, they can all see the ghosts too.

Then I look at Dr. Reardon. The man looks terrified. That's odd for him. His eyes are open wide, but he's not looking at the ghosts; he's staring at me.

Whoever's holding me is thrown off.

Then I face the transparent specters as they walk closer to us. I fall on my knees and my voice screams out, "Go away!"

They don't go away. They walk ever closer.

"Go away!" I yell again, between tears.

Another witch is trying to hold me back. I throw her off with ease.

"Go away!"

Maverick is only a few yards away now. I recognize his curly hair and his tattered suspenders and baggy pants. He's holding Escoba's hand. They both look as terrified as the witches surrounding the fire. Everyone is afraid. Of what? Of who?

Mira walks up to them, blocking the path leading to me. She seems to be trying to protect us. She says some incantation in a strange language, but she's thrown to the ground.

The two ghosts approach Dr. Reardon and push him toward the fire. Dr. Reardon is only a foot from the flames. He's lurching back, about to fall in. Alondra runs over to help him and tugs him away from the fire, but the specters are pulling him in.

Alondra turns to me in a panic. "Stop it, Windstorm!" she cries, looking at me. "Stop it! This is your doing. You must stop!"

"He should be killed!" I yell, but I'm surprised because my voice sounds guttural. "I sentence him. You should have thrown him in hellfire long ago for all he's done. Let him burn in the depths of the fire he so covets."

"Stop!" Alondra yells. "Or take me! If you push him in, I swear I'll go with him! Please, I love him! Please. Please, Windstorm! Stop!"

Dr. Reardon is so close to the fire that I think it singes him. In fact, he screams. And with his goatee and terrible expression, he actually looks like Satan. Like Baphomet. If he falls in, then Satan will fall into hellfire like he deserves. I want him to fall. I want him to return to hell and never bother us again. I want to be done with him and the evil he's let loose on the world. I want to burn him in hell.

"He's the devil!" I shout, pointing an outstretched finger at him. "The devil! The devil deserves to be burned!"

"No, Windstorm!" shouts Mira. She's still on the grass. She gets on her knees. "You're the devil! You're a witch! An evil black witch! It is *you* who should be burned!"

"*Currere, agnus, sacrificium!*" I shout. I wave my hand and Mira is thrown ten yards from the pyre. If everyone wasn't trying to help Doctor Reardon, they'd be staring in amazement at this act. Even I would be in awe, if it weren't for my rage.

"*Little Bo-Peep has lost her sheep,*" I yell mockingly, but then my voice changes again. What comes from my lips is a group of children taunting her as if we are in grade school. "*Little Bo-Peep has lost her sheep. Little Bo-Peep has lost her sheep. Little Bo-Peep has lost her sheep.*"

"Please, Cadence!" Alondra pleads, still holding her husband from the flames. The two ghosts are pulling Reardon into the fire, and she's fighting to keep him out. "Please! Stop!"

"How could you do this to my mother!" I ask Alondra, but I feel as if I've lost control of my own words. I feel as if someone else is speaking through me. "You cunt, how could you stab my mother through the heart! Take her from me and leave me to live alone! Why did you leave me alone, Abigail? Why!"

I feel an arm around me. No, two arms. I look around. It's Maddie and Bryce. They're holding me, trying to calm me.

"Stop it, Cadence," Maddie says.

"Please, Cadence," says Bryce.

There's smoke from Dr. Reardon. I look at Maddie. This man raped her. He raped my best friend. He took her when she was weak and vulnerable. How could he do that? And Alondra? She had sex with others too. Students? Unmarried men? How could she do this? They're both evil. They both deserve to be thrown to the flames.

Evil must burn. I send hellfire. The fire shall consume all to ash and cinders.

Flames are raging above us now. Dr. Reardon is shouting. It's not fear. I think it's pain. I believe he may be burning. Many of the witches are circling him, trying to pull him out. But for a second, it seems to me that they're walking around him like they walk around the pyre. They're walking around him as if he's their sacrifice. Not only him, but Alondra too. Meanwhile the two ghosts are pushing them in—all of them in. First they will burn Reardon, then Alondra, then the rest of the witches of Hawthorne. And all will be cleansed.

Escoba cocks her head back as she tugs Reardon into the fire, and the whites of her eyes stare at Alondra. Then I shout, "Why did you kill me, Abigail?"

Alondra is pulling Dr. Reardon with all her weight now. His body is completely horizontal, being pushed into the wall of fire.

"Cadence!" shouts Alondra, looking back as she pulls Reardon. "You can stop this. Maverick Hawthorne is your blood! Your ancestor!" She's frantic. "Josiah Billington is mine. You and I are family, Cadence! All of us are a part of the same family!"

I hear her words, but they incense me more.

Why tell me now? How many secrets does this woman hold? Is not deception the greatest sign of evil? That is the core of what this family, this coven, is all about. Slithering, deceptive, unblinking, dark magic vipers. They need to be killed. And I can kill them. I can rid Hawthorne of these snakes. The whole circle must burn.

All the witches in their black cloaks are thrown to the ground and dragged on the dirt, by an invisible force, toward the flames. They scream. Dr. Reardon is closest. He remains levitating over the grass, being pulled into the fire. Alondra grips him, leaning back desperately with all her might to pull him from the flames.

"You're burning him!" yells Alondra. "My God! Stop this, Cadence! You must! Stop it now! You're hurting Bill!"

I can't.

I hear voices in my ear. I hear Maddie and I hear Bryce. They're shouting in my ears to stop.

"I can't," I whisper. I shake my head. "I can't."

No one hears me. I shake my head again. Despite all of Alondra's will to save her husband, her eyes still look upon me. But she doesn't let Reardon go. If he falls, she'll fall with him. They will both die.

Only Maddie and Bryce are standing near me. The rest of the circle is being pulled into the flames. I look at Bryce. He's no longer enamored with me. There is no care or love. He's afraid.

I read his lips. "*Devil.*"

I wake up.

I'm lying in someone else's bedroom. The sun is shining in through a window. The bedroom is elegant with a mahogany dresser, a white canopy over the large bed, and a small nightstand. I've been here before. It's one of the rooms in Alondra's house. I'm wearing the white negligee I once wore when Maddie and I went shopping. On the nightstand is my book: *Broomstick.*

I stare at the white ceiling for ten minutes, maybe a half an hour. Then I remember the flames. In fact, there's a burning smell from my clothes—no, my body.

Someone knocks at the door. It's Bryce.

I sit up and I feel tears rush to my eyes. Bryce sits by the edge of the bed, smiles, and hugs me.

"Is everyone all right!" I exclaim. "Are you okay?"

"Everyone's fine, Cadence," Bryce says.

"I'm so sorry! I don't even know what happened."

"You proved your power," Bryce says, suddenly very serious. "You proved your worth"—he smiles—"as Alondra's replacement."

"It was real?"

Bryce nods. "Magic is very real, Cadence. I keep telling you that."

"Then I'm a witch?"

Bryce nods.

"Then I'm damned," I say, hanging my head.

Bryce chuckles. "You're human, Cadence. Alondra teaches us that it's up to you if you want to be good or not. Last night, you chose mercy." He pauses for a moment, looking out the window. "I think mercy is a sign of goodness. And Reardon...well, he's gone now. Finally. You helped Alondra and the rest of us get rid of him. He's packed his bags and left town for good."

"He deserved it for all the terrible things he did."

"We've all done things we regret, Cadence," Bryce says, looking down. He sighs. He shakes his head.

"I'm scared," I say. "And...ashamed." I feel stupid, but I remember last night. Everything. I feel like a frightened little girl because I wasn't in control. But, in some way, I feel like I *was* in control. Maybe that frightens me even more.

He doesn't say anything. Instead, he reaches over and hugs me again.

"Alondra's sick?" I ask.

"Uterine cancer, Cadence. It's terminal. She wanted to tell you. We all knew, but we hoped to lessen your pain with the ceremony. Seems it backfired."

"It's not fair. I can't take losing her. Not after my mother."

"I noticed, Windstorm," he says dryly.

"Has she seen a doctor?"

"Of course. But she doesn't believe in Western medicine. She's a witch. She's not about to take pills or radiation."

"That's stupid. She should take medicine."

"Oh, yeah? You've got such spirit, babe. I love it. I think that's why she calls you Windstorm. Your sign might be grounded, but you have a fire burning inside you, ready to be pushed out."

He runs his hand down my long hair. Then he kisses my cheek. I lean into his hand and enjoy the sound of his breath.

"I can make her take it," I say, sitting up straighter. "I'm our new leader, right? Isn't that also what last night's meeting was about? I can order Alondra to take medicine."

"I think you should just rest," he repeats, patting my leg. Then he rises. "Why don't you go back to sleep?"

"I'm scared, Bryce. I'm...scared I'm losing it. Am I?"

"No, Cadence," he says. "You're clairvoyant. You're a witch. Your initiation and Wandering made you one with nature. It strengthened your power. You'll learn to control it. Alondra can help you."

It's then that the candle Alondra tried to present me, like the memorial candle given to me for my mother, lights up beside *Broomstick*. I don't tell Bryce—I don't want to frighten him.

"Bryce, I love Alondra. I don't think I can handle seeing her die again."

Bryce doesn't have time to respond. The door creaks open wider, and I see Maddie and Mira, who have apparently been eavesdropping on Bryce. Maddie rushes over to me and hugs me.

"Are you okay, Katie?" asks Maddie. "We were so worried. After your little show, you fainted and fell asleep for hours."

They both hug me.

"I'm fine."

Then Mira walks in. But she's got a smug smile. She leans against the door and claps. "That was the most amazing shit I've ever seen, Windstorm. I guess Alondra was right about you."

I kiss Bryce on the lips. He leans against me, forehead to forehead, and closes his eyes.

"Get a room, guys," says Mira, shaking her head.

"I love you, Bryce," I say softly, staring into his blues.

"Love you too."

Maddie is giddy watching us. Mira rolls her eyes.

"Mira, can you hand me my grimoire?" I ask. "I've got some stuff to write in it."

"I'm sure you do. But it's not your grimoire, Cadence," Mira says. "It never was. *Broomstick* is Alondra's."

~

By nightfall, Bryce and I are alone at Alondra's. Everyone else went home, but Bryce stayed, watching over me. He tells me Alondra went to Atlanta for some private business. He says she'll be back, but she had to take care of some things. What? He wouldn't tell me. I can't even get all her secrets as her High Priestess.

I get dressed and he offers to take me back home. Then I turn off the light in the room, and we head down the dark hallway. I walk with him down the dimly lit hall, wrapped in his arms in an embrace. All the lights are off in her house.

He kisses me on the cheek as we walk. That's so sweet. But our romance is interrupted by two cats running across the hall. He laughs.

Bryce cocks his head. "Cadence, you forgot to turn off the light."

"No, I didn't. I just switched it off."

But I turn around and the guest room still has a yellow glow.

I walk back into the room.

That's not all I forgot. *Broomstick* is lying beside the memorial candle on the nightstand. I did switch off the light. The flickering light in the room is from the candle, which was never doused. So I grab my grimoire, and with a wave of my arm, I will the candle to blow out.

THE END

WINDSTORM

BOOK II

1

DARKNESS

Some people are afraid of the dark; others can't seem to turn away. It's so weird at Hawthorne University that my friends and I are actually having a back-to-school party just to watch it. And Maddie can't stop laughing. She keeps tapping my shoulder as we meander from a dirt parking lot, across the lawn, onto a lovely dirt path in Alondra's front garden. She taps me on my arm again. By the time we reach the white-columned deck at the entrance to Alondra's house, I finally turn. Maddie thinks it's soooo funny that she's wearing these cheap cardboard sunglasses I gave her. We're also wearing damp T-shirts and shorts—I say *damp* because it's hella hot outside.

Normally my friends and I meet at Alondra's house to gather around a witch bonfire on Friday Sabbath, but we're here Wednesday the week before the fall semester because this afternoon is very special. It's special for everyone in Hawthorne.

"Will you loosen up, Cadence?" Maddie says, still laughing.

"Take those off. You look dumb."

"Yeah, well, you don't look dumb. Because you're not having any fun."

"I'm just a little nervous, that's all," I say with a shrug.

"I know, babe." Maddie loses her smile and takes off the stupid cardboard things. "You'll be fine. Everybody wants to see you again."

Do they? I haven't spoken to most of my witch friends since the night I lost control. I haven't even had a chance to apologize. I feel so terrible about what happened.

The view at Alondra's place is to die for. Every time I come here, I feel like it takes me back to the nineteenth century. It's perched on a hilltop, surrounded by the forest and the flowing sound of a nearby brook. The perfectly manicured lawn is bordered by lilies and red and yellow roses, recently planted. In the center of it all is Alondra's white antebellum house. The place is quintessentially *antebellum* (I know what the word *antebellum* means, by the way, because I'm a history major at Hawthorne U). Only Alondra knows the right way to mix Neoclassical with chic, like her swanky dark gray Jaguar parked behind an antique red carriage in the driveway.

"I invited Rock, Katie," Maddie says. We're walking up the concrete steps onto Alondra's lovely outside deck.

"Why'd you do that?"

"Because he's cute." She cocks her head with a big smile. I laugh. Then Maddie raps on the door with this really big antique brass knocker. As we wait, she winks at me.

Wouldn't you know it but Alondra herself answers. She doesn't look at all like I expected. I was half expecting her in a dark witch cloak, but she's dressed in a loose saffron blouse over white shorts and sandals. She greets us with her familiar grin.

Alondra smiles a lot. She's always trying to be happy and nice. Sometimes it's really fake. Right now her expression gives me the feeling she's not dwelling on how I nearly killed her and her husband the last time I visited.

"Hey, Maddie. Cadence. Come in."

Her house is just as stunning inside as it is outside. I'm standing under a huge to-die-for diamond chandelier. Down the hall, I see her elegant dining room. This is my favorite room, with a window lining the wall looking out into the forest. It's next to her kitchen, with travertine floors, Viking stoves and a Sub-Zero refrigerator.

"Did you girls have a nice summer?" Alondra asks, pleasant as always.

"I had so much fun with Kate," Maddie says.

"Yes, you and Cadence stayed at your Aunt Jane's house, right?"

"Aha. How about you, Alondra?" asks Maddie. "Were you here in Hawthorne?"

Alondra is full of mysteries. I saw her practically every day last year, and I still feel like I don't know her.

"You girls excited?" Alondra says, avoiding Maddie's question.

"Yeah," I say.

"Did you bring protective shades? I don't think I have enough."

"You're talking about Katie, Alondra," Maddie replies. "My BFF has never failed to prepare for anything."

"How are you feeling, Alondra?" I ask solemnly.

Alondra has terminal cancer. You wouldn't think it, watching her agile step and cheerful demeanor, but I see bags under her eyes and a new habit of taking deep breaths. I'm guessing she's in pain. She told us the terrible news during our last ceremony. That's one of the reasons I lost control of myself. It drove me crazy that she'd been hiding that from me for so long, along with all the other horrible stuff last year. Then she made me their High Priestess, the leader of our coven. That's the thing about Alondra. See, even now, as she's walking with a quick step, she's being phony. I know she's unhappy. It's like my circle of witches. I love them so much, but I hate their secretiveness. And their deceptions. I mean, I love them all, but I hate them. Do you understand? ...If you do, please explain it to me.

"I hope everybody makes it on time." Alondra takes her cell phone from her pocket. She doesn't answer my question either.

We walk by her living room and Tammy, a cute bald black girl in our coven, is on her knees sorting through grocery bags on the coffee table. This room is just as I remembered, with the white leather sofa, fluffy white carpet, and elegant, modern stone fireplace and chimney. Through the sliding glass door is Alondra's backyard, where my coven held weekly Sabbaths last year.

Tammy jumps up and runs into Maddie's arms.

"Hey, girl!" Maddie says.

"Hey, guys!" says Tammy. She looks at me. "It's so good to see you! I missed you so much!" She hugs me.

Alondra's trying to pry open the glass door with all her weight. It's been stuck ever since I first stepped foot in her house. I walk over, lean against the bottom of the door, and pull it. It unlatches and opens. It's a trick Mira taught me last year.

"Oh, thank you, Cadence."

The door opens into her backyard. The yard is really the wilderness. It's the opposite of the front yard—no manicured lawn, tended flowers, or raked leaves—only wild grass surrounded by the dense forests of Hawthorne. In the center is a pile of logs. That's where we light our bonfires. But today Alondra has set up two picnic tables with yellow-and-red tablecloths. The tables are surrounded by the white plastic chairs we use during séances and rituals worshipping Selene, but now I see watermelons, a stack of soy patties, a few plastic bags of burger buns, red plastic cups, and a couple of glass pitchers of what looks like lemonade on one of the tables. I love lemonade. There's a Weber grill out too and a burly guy named Rocky, Maddie's boyfriend. Rocky is holding tongs, watching the soy burgers cook. Maddie runs into his arms.

"Katie," Maddie says after giving him a long embrace. "Look who's here. Can you believe it?"

He gives me a warm smile. "Hi, Cadence." I stick a palm up and wave.

"Babe," Rocky says to Maddie with a chuckle, "let me work."

"I love this guy," Maddie says.

Someone taps me on my back. I hear a quiet "hi" in a thick Brazilian accent. It's Frida. Frida is one of the shyest witches in our coven, shyer than I am. She's a petite, skinny girl with dark golden skin. Her family immigrated from Brazil fifteen years ago. She and I have always gotten along so well. As we hug, I spot Alondra walking back into her house. She just leaves us without a word.

"You stayed with Maddie in Hawthorne, right?" asks Frida. "I went home. It was hot and sweaty in New York." Frida lives in Jersey. "Awful," she says with a laugh. I'm swatting flies from my face. It's not cool in Georgia either. "Is Bryce here?"

I really wish he was.

"At least your man will be here in school," Frida adds after seeing my expression. "I'll be FaceTiming Greg every night."

We talk a little more, and Frida leaves, saying she's going to help Tammy and Mandy in the kitchen.

It's not too long before our whole coven is in Alondra's backyard. There are eleven of us (not counting my warlock boyfriend, who's still not here). Actually, twelve today as Gilda is visiting. Gilda graduated last semester.

I clam up. Large crowds turn me into a wallflower. So I sit near one of the tables in the yard, fold my arms over my lap, and do nothing. But I face the trees. The forest. I love the woods.

A butterfly lands on my finger. I'm not kidding, an actual butterfly just lands right on the back of my finger. I love that. I watch it slowly open and close its yellow-and-black wings. Then a shadow hovers over me. As I look up, I feel the butterfly fly off. The only witch actually wearing our black hooded cloak—in the hot humidity—is my over-weight goth friend, Mira. The sun shines along the red-and-black devil tattoos on her neck and glistens on her nose ring. Her face is coated in thick makeup. Her black lips curl in nasty smugness.

"Are you ready, Cadence?"

"Hi, Mira."

"I can't wait to see it." She smiles, looking around.

"Yeah."

"I'm sure your magic will come up too." I think she's the only one weird enough to actually want my magic to appear. "You know, Cadence, I did a lot of spell casting this summer. Learned a lot about tarot reading from Falconsong." Falconsong is Alondra's witch name. "The cards predict some interesting things on your horizon."

"We're going to eat burgers?"

"Falconsong is running the session. She said you wouldn't mind. You don't, right? We're gonna just talk."

As long as talking doesn't involve a two-story conflagration, ghosts, and possession. Or dancing around a pyre naked. Or taking drugs.

She surprises me by leaning over and gathering me in her arms. "I missed you, Cadence." And she means it.

"I missed you too, Mira."

"They're separated, you know," Mira says.

"Who?"

"Bill and Alondra. After your magic, Alondra kicked him out."

"I heard."

"And he's not a part of the coven anymore. I'd think that would make you happy."

"It does."

She sits down in a chair beside me. "You know..." Mira puts her hand on my leg. Then she runs her fingers over my bare knee. "I was in town two weeks ago. I texted you but you didn't answer."

The annoying thing about Mira is she knows why I didn't text her, and she's smirking about it. Yet she's not hurt, and she doesn't even look like she cares.

"I didn't get the text," I fib, biting my lip.

"Oh," Mira says with another wink. She touches my leg again. "I think it's gonna be a good year. Now that you're our leader. I can't wait for our first meeting. I'd love to try a summoning. I dealt the Magician card last night. That means great concentration and psychic powers are in our midst. There's a presence in Hawthorne and it's growing. But I also dealt the Devil card and the Death card. There's also black magic afoot." She looks around us as if searching for it. "I feel that too. Especially today. Left-sided magic."

What can I say to that? So I look at the trees again. From the corner of my eye, I see that Mira is also looking out into the forest, because she loves the trees too. She's a nature-loving witch like me.

"I also dealt the Lovers card," she continues, practically talking to herself. "But it was reversed. That means trouble in paradise. After meditating on it, I don't think it was for me." She chuckles. "I mean, I'm not much into lovers, you know. I much prefer raw sex. I think the card was for you. It came right after the High Priestess card. It was probably something about Bryce and you fucking."

"Mira!" I snap.

"What?" she asks innocently, laughing again. "I know you miss him. Is he gonna be here soon?"

She had to ask me that. But Maddie rescues me, handing paper plates with soy burgers to me and Mira. Then she gives Mira a hug.

"Hey, bitch," Maddie says to Mira. "You want to join me and Rock, Katesie?"

Yeah. But then Mira says, "I'll come too."

At Maddie's table, things go smoother. She has me talking with everyone. That's the kind of friend she is. She brings me out of my shell.

When everyone has had their fill of lemonade and soy burgers, Maddie starts clearing the plates. Mira and Gilda collect large wooden logs and throw them on the woodpile at the center of the yard. Other girls gather the plastic chairs from the tables and arrange them in a circle around the fire. Then Gilda takes a bag full of white chalk and carefully pours it around the perimeter of the chairs.

Maddie says goodbye to Rocky. She really doesn't want to, especially before the upcoming event, but she says our "club" has to meet in private.

Soon we're all sitting around a shallow fire, leaving a few chairs empty. Maddie sits on my right and Frida on my left. There's not much ceremony. It's more like a cozy campfire. But I prefer this. The only weird thing is it's the middle of the day. The sky is clear, and it's around three thirty in the afternoon. Our meetings are always at night.

Mira jumps up pointing when Alondra comes out of the house. It's like she's been waiting for her to appear all afternoon. Alondra is wearing our black cloak—the same one Mira's wearing—holding a fiery torch. Her face is covered by thick goth makeup like Mira's. By her side is another witch in a black cloak. I don't recognize this one. And following them are two other ladies in similar garb.

As the stranger walking beside Alondra pushes her hood back, I am struck by how beautiful she is. She looks like a model, with penetrating blue eyes, a perfectly tanned face, and long dark hair like mine. The stranger's skin is darker than Alondra's, like mine. She looks maybe five or six years older than I am. The two witches walking behind them are expressionless under their cloaks.

Alondra leans her torch into the fire. Then she says to us all with a big smile, "*Lux alba.*"

"*Lux tenebris,*" the stranger says.

"*Lux alba,*" we all echo almost in a chant.

Then, still standing, Alondra stretches her arms out wide with a big smile and says, "Blessed be the day that the circle is brought together again. Blessed be the coven under the gods Gaia, Selene, and Astraeus."

Her words and the chanting of the circle make my stomach turn. I'm haunted by the consequences of my magic at the last meeting. I might be a witch, but I don't like magic. Maybe it's the ghosts and throwing my friends into the fire thing.

"Atman," says Mira.

"Atman," the rest of us say.

Alondra sits down near Mira, across from me. The stranger sits on her other side with her two friends. Alondra looks at me. "The High Wizard couldn't come, Windstorm? I can't believe it." She's referring to my boyfriend, Bryce. As the only male in our coven, Bryce is the High Wizard.

"I hope he'll be here soon," I say.

"He will be," the stranger says to Alondra. "I've assigned him the job of being the apothecary for your illness, Falconsong. He'll be coming back after he collects the herbs."

How the hell does she know where my Bryce is?

"That's quite a sacrifice," Alondra says. "He should be here this afternoon. Especially this afternoon. Our circle is incomplete, Cadence." As if I want it to be incomplete. Believe me, the last thing I want right now is for Bryce not to be here.

"I don't think you realize how much your sisters care for you, Falconsong," the stranger says.

"So be it," Alondra says with a nod and a sigh. Then she turns and addresses all of us. "Allow me to introduce you all to Enora." She gestures to the witch sitting beside her. "Enora's mystic coven name is Panthera. Panthera is a guest from her coven in Albany, Georgia. Tonight, she is our sister and we welcome her. And she has brought Beatrix and Cordelia, witches from her coven. In Panthera's circle, their mystic names are Manthis and Adder. Please welcome our guests, sisters."

Beatrix looks so much younger than me. She's short and thin. Really puny. In fact, the girl seems to be high school age. Her youth seems indecent in our circle, but she's so serious and focused, like an adult. Cordelia looks wicked. Black tattoos cover her face, and she scowls at everything. Actually, both of them look like shifty, evil witches. Even Beatrix's expression isn't innocent, although she looks like a little girl. Not like the witches of my coven. My coven is full of students studying at Hawthorne University and casting witchery on the side. These two strangers literally look like they spend evenings drinking the blood of babies and eating little children. I don't like them.

"Yatu, Panthera," says Gilda. "Yatu, Manthis, Adder."

"Yatu," says Mandy.

"Yatu," says Mira.

We all greet them.

"And you visit us as well, Red Fox?" Alondra says to Gilda. Gilda's sitting near Frida, to my left. "Welcome to our circle again."

Everyone erupts, welcoming Gilda.

"Enora is the leader of her coven and a very good friend of mine," says Alondra. Then Alondra points to me across the shallow flames with an outstretched hand. "Cadence is our High Priestess, the leader of our coven, Enora. Her mystical name is Windstorm."

"Yatu, Windstorm," Enora says with a nod and a sly smile. Then she squints and glares at me. Even as Alondra introduces her to the rest of the circle, her bright blue eyes study mine. I don't like that.

Alondra looks up to the clear sky. She smiles again.

"Ah, it approaches. We have only a short time left, witches." Alondra looks to me. "High Priestess, what say you before I officiate?"

Me? Great. I'm supposed to talk now?

I never wanted to be their leader. I joined the coven because my best friend and boyfriend were part of the group last year. Alondra appointed me High Priestess after she announced she was dying. And then, like I told you, all hell broke loose. I'm a little surprised that they still want me to be their leader. I never even formally accepted the title.

"Well...I'm just happy we're together again," I say stupidly. My words fall flat. I turn quiet. Everyone looks disappointed, expecting me to say more. I clear my throat and add, "You're all my closest friends. It's so great to see you and I...I...think we should all go around and tell each other what we did this summer."

There's complete silence. I guess nobody wants to.

Beatrix whispers something in Cordelia's ear. It's so quiet I can almost hear the bad things she's saying about me. I'm sure it's bad because they glare derisively at me.

When it's obvious that no one intends on sharing, I decide to take the opportunity to bring up something that's been on my mind since summer break. "I...haven't seen a lot of you since that last meeting. It was terrible what happened, and I've been wanting to apologize. To all of you. I love you all so much, and I'm sorry if I scared you. It scared me. I'm so sorry for what happened. I've felt so bad about it."

There. I said it. I've been wanting to apologize for months. But I don't feel any better after seeing the reactions of my coven. They all look down or avert their eyes. The two witches from the other coven even laugh, but Enora puts her hand up and they quickly stop.

"That's sweet, Windstorm, but no one got hurt during the transfer of Selene last year," Alondra says. But she's not smiling anymore. She doesn't seem to like my mentioning it either.

"I frightened you. All my closest friends. I'm so sorry."

"You don't need to apologize," Alondra says. And there's an edge to her voice.

"What happened?" Enora asks.

How does she not know? That upsets me. I find it hard to believe that Alondra wouldn't have told her or one of the other witches. And she knew where Bryce was and I didn't. How? I really don't like her. I turn and look at Maddie. Maddie nods. Maddie and I are so close that we can read each other's minds. I know Maddie doesn't like her either.

"Windstorm had a little hissy fit after Falconsong announced that she's dying, Panthera," Mira says with a big grin. "Then Windstorm used her powers to manifest the ghosts of her ancient ancestors Maverick and Escoba to drag Professor William Reardon into our fire. She wanted to kill Bill for having sex with her best friend. She nearly threw Falconsong, me, and the rest of us in the fire too."

"Thank you, Mira, for being blunt as always." Alondra shakes her head. Mira laughs but Alondra remains very solemn. "It's difficult, Enora —very traumatic." Then she looks at me. "You did frighten us, Cadence. But of course we forgive you. You'll learn to control your powers."

There's silence. Like really uncomfortable loud nothingness, and everyone has her head down or is looking in any direction she can to avoid me. Boy was that a stupid thing for me to do. I so wish my Bryce was here.

"You guys know what I did last summer?" Tammy asks sweetly, trying to change the subject. "I met a boy."

"Ahh, do tell," says Maddie with a laugh.

"Yeah. My family and I traveled to California. I met him at Pier 39 watching the seals." She wrinkles her nose. "It stinks, but the seals are cute. And I forgot all about the stench when he came over to talk to me." She laughs and some of the other witches laugh too. "Before I knew it, he was taking me to the Golden Gate Bridge. It was so much fun. You know, you're so high up on that bridge. It's actually kinda scary walking the sidewalk and looking down. It's like you're on top of a high rise."

"What's the boy's name?" asks Helen.

"Davey."

"Is he cute?" asks Mira. A lot of the other girls giggle.

Alondra closes her eyes tightly and casts a stray glance at me. I think she's in pain. I don't think anyone else notices. Not even the new bitch, Enora. Enora is looking at Tammy, for the first time someone besides me. Alondra looks at me again and forces a smile, but she's not fooling me. She's hurting. And that hurts me. It makes me feel sorry for her.

"He's gorge," says Tammy. "An Asian guy, strong, like he can carry me with one hand. I probably weigh a third of what he weighs."

"Like Rocky," Maddie interjects.

Tammy laughs with a nod. "When we went to San Fran, I had gone with my folks. But after meeting Davey, the two of us left on our own and saw Alcatraz and that zigzaggy narrow street together. I can't recall the name of the street. And shopping. And walking in the parks near the Golden Gate... It was just so much fun."

"How were his lips?" Maddie asks.

She just laughs.

"How 'bout his bed?" asks Mira.

"Really, Mira," says Alondra, rolling her eyes.

"Just asking."

"What about you, Gilda?" asks Alondra. "You returned home to Savannah and got married, right?"

Gilda nods.

"Congratulations. The circle congratulates you and wishes you two well under Juno's blessing."

"It was a blending of Christianity and our handfasting," Gilda explains. "He was willing to incorporate both traditions."

"I wish I could have officiated," says Alondra. Then she looks at me. "Or Windstorm could have."

Gilda tells everyone about her new husband and their ceremony. The whole time the girls are talking about their summer, Enora is watching me again. It's creepy.

And I'm still squirming over mentioning our last meeting. I should never have said anything.

"You and Maddie stayed in town, right, Katie?" Marilyn asks me.

"What?" I ask.

"You were at her Aunt Jane's house?"

"Oh yeah."

"You guys just stayed near campus?" asks Tammy.

"We went to New Orleans." Maddie smiles and hugs me. "It was amazing. Bourbon Street. Gumbo. Crawfish. I love the food. There's so much history in New Orleans, you know. We took the carriage together, like Alondra's outside, only this one worked. We toured the French Quarter. I met a hot guy there too." The girls laugh. "Of course Cadence didn't. She kept talking about Bryce." We all laugh again. "We were there for a whole week. It wasn't long enough."

"Are you working here at school, Enora?" asks Gilda.

Enora tears her eyes from me and shakes her head. "I have an art studio in Albany. I'm a painter."

"Is your coven large?"

"Thirteen," she says with a nod. "Like yours." Then she looks right at me as if challenging me. About what? Why can't she look somewhere else?

"When I created the Hawthorne coven," Alondra says, "Enora was a part of our first circle. It was when we were just starting out. I had met her at Beltane."

"Too bad we missed Beltane last year because of Firestarter over there." Mira points at me.

"Mira, put a lid on it," warns Maddie.

"Windstorm brought it up," Mira says with a shrug.

"She apologized," Enora snaps. I'm surprised. It seems this stranger is defending me. "If your High Priestess lost control, you all have to respect her intentions. I can tell she loves all of you so much from her words. It was touching. I sense a great deal of energy from this witch." *Is that why you're staring at me?* "She has powerful chakras. Her anahata binds the circle, Falconsong."

"No doubt," Mira quips. "Well, I was impressed."

"So says the guest to our coven," Alondra says, smiling at me again. "Take heed of Panthera's wisdom, girls. She is very wise." Then Alondra looks up at the sky and her smile grows. "Blessed be the day. It is nearly time. Look up, girls. Everyone, put your cloaks on and grab your glasses."

The cloaks have been taken off the hooks in the outside patio and stacked in a pile not far from the bonfire. We all get up and grab a cloak. No one owns one; we just grab whichever one is available. They're all matching black druid-like cloaks with hoods.

"Do you have shades, Katie?" asks Hope. "I forgot mine."

"No, I don't, but if you want we can share."

"Don't be so nice," Mira says near me. Then she hands Hope a pair of plastic lenses. "I brought a few spare."

We all return to the circle and Alondra, who is once again across from me, raises her arms as high as she can toward the clear sky. She is ecstatic, almost as if in a trance, as she seems to speak to the sky itself.

"Today is a special day of magic, witches! Today we see a glimmer of Astraeus fighting Apollo and, for a moment, conquering the heavens. But do not forget that it is only due to the blessing of our revered Selene that such darkness manifests itself. It is like Yule, where the rain and snow manifest tenebris. Powerful Ceres and her daughter, Proserpina, who took the pomegranate, cycle every year from light to darkness and then to light again. Natural mysteries manifest themselves today. A blessed day. *Lux alba.*"

"*Lux alba,*" everyone repeats.

"Don your glasses," Alondra says. "Let us walk together, holding hands with love, facing the fire. But do not look at the fire today. Today, at this magic moment, look up to the stars and heavens. Walk now and wait for Selene to travel across the sky, causing day to turn to night. Nyx shall reign, witches."

And we walk.

As we walk, everything seems to slow. Just as Mira said, there is magic afoot. I can feel it. And I feel a trance coming on. I don't always look up.

Occasionally, I look at my sisters. But they are seemingly in rapture, staring up at the sky through their dark plastic glasses. I see shade forming over the sun above as it darkens before my eyes.

I feel a squeeze to my right arm and turn. It's Maddie. She looks funny with her shades, and she's smiling so widely, loving this.

Soon the sun is covered halfway, and Alondra's backyard and the surrounding woods have become darker. I don't feel my hands touching Frida and Maddie by my sides, but I know they're still there. And it seems we're walking more and more slowly around the fire.

A black bird with a streak of rainbow light soars off in the horizon. And oddly, there's color on the horizon, above the trees, like the red-orange of a sunrise. Rationally, I know that such a thing cannot be, for I see the eclipse above me; it's there. It's as if it is twilight or dawn out there while, up above, the moon is covering the sun.

When I look down, my heart skips. Alondra's face is changing. Her nose is stretching into a beak, and her cloak and outstretched arms have become large wings with dark feathers. Her fingers are turning into talons. Her bird eyes are still covered by the black shades. My right hand is holding a wing. My best friend has transformed as well—Blackbird is Maddie's mystic name. And Frida, known as Robin, looks like a bird with red splashed over her chest. My arm looks shiny, almost scaly. It's frightening what is happening, for we haven't partaken in any hallucinogens. In the past, I've taken mandrake with similar effects. But this is pure magic. It must be the effect of the eclipse on my coven.

The fire changes. Instead of a low flame, I see a pile of black snakes writhing on top of one another. It startles me and I jump. Maddie turns. Her face is still misshapen, with sunglasses. I point at the fire. She shakes her head. She must not see the snakes. I hate snakes. Then I hear a shriek and, instead of the joy of being part of our circle, I feel dread. I turn and there's a couple, only a few feet from the circle, lying naked in the grass in each other's arms.

"*Lux tenebris!*" Alondra shouts in ecstasy.

My dread is lifted. Alondra, though altered, is so joyous under the eclipse. It makes me feel good too.

All becomes dark. Completely dark. And still. I smell something rotting, like sulfur. Looking up, I can see the stars as clearly as in a night sky. That would normally fill me with joy, but instead I begin to feel cold. Only a minute ago, it was hot.

I feel something touching my feet. I look down and see a trail of black snakes slithering on the ground as I continue walking around the pyre of snakes. My fear is enough for me to want to break from the circle, but I feel locked in step with my friends.

"Nyx!" cries Alondra. "Holy of holies, bring your darkness on our coven! Shroud us in your protection under your loving arms!"

I force my eyes to look away from all the writhing snakes and gaze upon the couple on the wild grass, now covered by a purple fog. This must be an illusion.

The fog thins around the couple, and I watch them fornicating on the wild grass. A naked man with short dark hair uses his strong arms to support his naked body over his lover. Black snakes are slithering over their naked bodies too. The lovers' eyes are locked. The girl's tits are pressed against the man's body, and his butt squeezes tightly as he presses into her.

The circle stops. I feel like it's been dark for an hour. The conscious part of my mind, still dim, tells me this is impossible. I've never witnessed a complete solar eclipse, but I've read that they only last a moment. It seems like a moment passed long ago. And we're not circling; we're just standing. Even Alondra, who is ecstatic, is looking up to the stars, immobile, like a bird statue.

The purple mist beside the couple turns red as they continue to have sex. My friends don't even seem to notice. They're frozen, staring up at the sky like Alondra.

The woman on the grass is beautiful. Her breasts are perfect. Her long hair flows along the ground. She's pinned under the man, and I see her digging her black fingernails deep into his back. Her nails, along with the serpents, move under the thick red fog.

I feel sleepy. Drugged. But there was no nightshade or mandrake. This is real magic.

Then I hear laughter. The woman under the man turns and faces me. My heart jumps. Her eyes are piercing blue. I recognize her as the stranger I just met: Enora. She is Enora. In fact, Enora has left the circle. And then, in horror, I recognize the boy on top. When he recognizes me, his eyes open wide and he quickly averts them. He is my boyfriend, Bryce.

There's a scream.

The light grows, and I feel like we're moving around in a circle again, ever faster, swirling as if on a spinning ride in an amusement park. The terrible vision fades and I feel dizzy.

I sink. I feel like my whole body is weighing me down like a lead weight. Maddie tugs on me hard, still trying to circle the pyre. I feel like I don't have the strength to move anymore. But the snakes are gone. And the slowly crackling fire burns once more. Then the sun shines brilliantly forth, turning night to day. It's a bright, hot afternoon again. And Enora is standing with us in the circle without my boyfriend.

"Glory be the day!" Alondra drops her hands and takes a deep breath. "Ah, glory be the day for our circle. What a gift to see this vision, even if only once in one's lifetime. *Lux alba.*"

"*Lux alba!*" everyone cries joyously.

I don't. I've lost my will to move.

"Everyone sit," Alondra says, smiling joyfully as ever. She's taken off her shades. We all sit in the chairs behind us and face the fire. "Any of you, if you saw a vision, please share it with our circle."

Enora turns and looks at me with a wide grin.

2

CLASS

I awaken to Maddie hitting my shoulder, pulling my arm, touching my cheeks, and pulling at my feet. She's doing all kinds of things to get me out of bed. She could have just touched my shoulder, but I hate mornings. I can't function until, like, noon. And since our alarm didn't sound, I guess I'm skipping breakfast. Like I care. I've been moping around for days, since that vision during the eclipse. I hardly slept last night, not falling asleep until five in the morning. The last thing I want is to get up or get food. She's got that covered too. She's pushing a lightly toasted bagel toward my nose.

"Let's go! Come on! You're gonna miss class."

"It's not class," I mutter. "It's a study group."

And it's not our first day. It's Tuesday. Monday we had lecture, which, of course, Maddie didn't go to. And Bryce still hasn't gotten back yet.

"Up, up," she says, pulling me again. The bagel falls on the floor, and that ticks her off more. "Come on!"

I sit upright, stretch out my arms, and take a deep breath. She throws clothes on my lap.

"Just go without me."

"It's time for school. Now get up, Cadence!"

I lie back down.

"Get up!"

"Why? Why do you care?"

"Because you do. And we're both in the same class, so we can go together."

I force my eyes open, reach down, and pick up the bagel from the ugly red-and-brown carpet. I pull off my nightgown. Then I toss a white T-shirt over my bra, pull on some jeans, and reach for my backpack. She yanks me out the door before I can grab it.

There are a lot of students walking to and fro, among the brick buildings, to their classes. We rush off the cement path, across the quad of buildings, into a small room that reminds me of high school. I recognize it. It's the same classroom where my boyfriend taught my metaphysical history class last year. You know, the boyfriend who's not back yet and who I watched having sex with Enora during the solar eclipse. Well, there's no TA at the front of the classroom now. I suppose we're not that late.

The classroom's full and there are only three empty seats at the front. Both of us forgot our computers in the shuffle, but I did remember to grab my art textbook. It's the only class Maddie and I are taking together: art history.

"Why'd you have to rush me?" I ask as we sit down.

"Just eat your bagel." She turns and smiles at me.

"So," I say, "what's with you and Rocky?"

"What do you mean? We just met."

"Didn't seem like that at the party. You couldn't keep your hands off him."

She just smiles.

Our teacher walks in. I almost drop my bagel.

"See?" says Maddie, gesturing to the door. "I was hoping you guys could talk, dope. Why would *I* rush to class?"

I can't believe my eyes. It's my boyfriend. My to-die-for unshaven, broad-shouldered Adonis, wearing a gray polo shirt and black slacks. His short hair is perfectly trimmed. His eyes are gazing firmly at me, and he's smiling. At me. I have an urge to get up and throw my arms around him, but I resist. I'm not the only one staring at him. Bryce has most of the girls eyeing him. But as he lugs his leather bag onto the front desk and takes out a laptop, he flashes another smile right at me. Me.

"Did you know he was teaching this class?" I whisper.

"That's why I wanted to get here before class, dope! You ruined it." She's whispering—or trying to.

"Why didn't you tell me?"

"It was a surprise."

"You could have just told me."

"This is more fun."

"I can't believe you didn't tell me."

"Shush."

"Please, everyone…" Bryce looks right at us with a big grin. "Quiet."

But isn't this wrong? Am I going to have another class with him as my teacher?

"Everyone, please take a look at our lesson plan. You can access it on our website." He writes the web address on the whiteboard with a green marker. "You can follow along if you'd like. You all should have read about Leonardo da Vinci?" He presses a button on his computer, and *Virgin of the Rocks*, the one in the Louvre, shows up on a screen on the wall. I know it's in the Louvre because, yesterday after the lecture, I studied like I was supposed to, unlike Madison.

I'm munching on my bagel. I'm not sure if I'm allowed to, so I kinda eat it slowly and close to the desk.

"This is *Virgin of the Rocks*. There were two paintings. One is currently in the National Gallery of London, and the other is in the Louvre in France. For Dr. Riker's class, you're going to have to know that the first was painted in 1483, the second in 1509. There's some debate over whether Leonardo touched the second or if it was created by his assistants. It's not certain, but it's likely that Leonardo worked on both. Of course, the one in the Louvre is better. So if you're planning a trip to Europe to see Leonardo, you'll want to go to Paris, not London."

Some of the girls snicker. Especially a snooty Kappa Alpha Kappa. She's wearing school colors, a red sweater with gold Greek letters, and staring at *my* boyfriend.

I could light her hair on fire. I'm a witch, you know. I touch my black fingernails together, but before I can do anything naughty…

"What do you think, Cadence?"

Huh? I stopped listening. "What?"

Somebody laughs. It's probably the sorority snoot.

"Can you tell us what one-point perspective is?" Bryce asks.

Yes. I read it in the textbook last night, and I recall Dr. Riker discussing it in the lecture Maddie didn't go to yesterday.

"Uh, one-point perspective is how Renaissance artists created the sense of depth in their paintings."

"Exactly," Bryce says. "It's why I love Renaissance art."

You love Renaissance art? You never told me that.

"Dr. Riker is not only a great history prof," says my tall-dark-and-handsome TA, "he's a lover of art. What he wants to instill in you guys is the sophistication that comes out in this period. Leonardo da Vinci was a genius. He created a robotic lion that walks, he drew sketches of helicopters, and he sketched anatomical drawings based on actual human cadavers that he dissected." Grisly. That's something Alondra would have focused on last year in her metaphysical history class. "Do you know which painting of his really excelled in using the one-point perspective? It's a perfect example."

He's still looking at me, which is annoying. Last year I told him not to call on me. I don't like attention. Just because we're going out doesn't mean I want to be made an example of—especially 'cause we're going out.

After I don't say anything, he says, "The one-point perspective was key to *The Last Supper*. It placed Jesus Christ at the center of the painting and at the center of his disciples. Know this for your exam."

I daydream through the rest of the class. I'm less excited about seeing him, and I'm starting to get mad because Bryce didn't tell me he was in town today. So I stop taking notes and focus on finishing the half-eaten bagel on my desk.

I'm surprised when class ends.

Maddie drags me up to the front by my arm, and we wait in line while a couple of girls come up with "questions." I think they just want to talk to him. They're so stupid and giggly. But who can blame them? He's hot.

When it's finally our turn to talk to Bryce, Maddie says, "You have a knack for making her sound stupid."

I ignore her and jump into his arms, kissing him on the lips. Bryce laughs.

"Katie," he says, stroking my hair. Then he sees a couple of students still walking out of class, staring at us, and quickly pulls away.

"Why didn't you tell me you were back?" I snap. It's this weird mix of ecstasy and anger.

Bryce laughs. "I got in from Atlanta at four in the morning." He turns and stuffs his laptop back in his bag.

"I would have come by," I say.

"You need sleep."

"Don't tell me what I need. I told you to tell me when you arrive."

"I don't get it," Maddie says. "Are you guys fighting or happy to see each other?"

I embrace him again.

"Please, Cadence, we're still in class."

"I've got to run to sociology," Maddie says with a laugh. "And it looks like you two have some catching up to do. But, Bryce, I told you not to use my best friend as an example in class. 'Kay?"

We're not listening to her. We're looking into each other's eyes like stupid lovestruck schoolchildren.

"Toodles," Maddie says.

Bryce and I walk outside. He's holding my hand, rubbing my fingers. God, I missed him.

We head down the main drag of campus. There are so many students rushing back and forth now. It will thin out in another week when the school year isn't new anymore.

"You didn't pick Riker's class so you could teach me, I hope?" I ask.

"Of course not," Bryce says, still rubbing my fingers. "It was assigned to me yesterday."

"Well, it's not proper. How are you going to grade my exams?"

"I thought of that, but then I realized almost all his tests are based on multiple-choice questions. It's only extra credit when you show up to my study group. Actually, I was thrilled when Dr. Riker assigned me."

"Because I'm in the class?" I ask stupidly.

"No. He's the best teacher next to Alondra. I only wish Alondra were teaching this year."

We head over to a parking lot not far from Yorkshire Dorms, where Maddie and I are roommates again this year. I see his old gray BMW. He stops and turns to me. He runs his hand through my long black hair again, and I feel tingles down my spine.

"I think it'll be fine, Kate. If Riker assigns anything for me to grade, I can always tell him our situation and ask him to grade it."

I barely hear a word he says. You've got to understand it's been over a month since we've seen each other. We've been FaceTiming, but it's not the same. We hug each other again. For a long time. Tight.

"I missed you so much," he says.

I nod with my head still leaning on his chest, just listening to his breathing and feeling his heartbeat. He's breathing slowly, but his heart is thumping fast.

"I'm off to unpack," he says finally.

"Can I come?" I look up at him.

"Don't you have class?"

"Not till midafternoon."

3

UNPACKING

Bryce has a studio apartment right off the north side of campus, with a combined living room and kitchen separated from the bedroom by a wall. I practically lived there toward the end of last year. Then he had to go to his folks' farm in Missouri for the summer. Right now, I'm sitting on his bed, watching him unpack his shirts and jeans.

"I can help."

"That's okay, Katie. How's Alondra?"

"Fine."

He reaches down to his suitcase for more clothes, and I hand him a stack of socks. "Thanks," he says. As he stuffs more clothes into his cabinet, made of dark wood, he says, "What about Maddie? Is she okay?"

"You know Maddie. When isn't she?"

He laughs. "Her mom?"

"Everybody's fine, Bryce. Why don't you tell me about Enora?"

He closes a drawer and furrows his brow. "Whaddaya mean?"

"You know her?"

"I've known her for years. She's a powerful witch in her coven. She came to help Alondra. I told you that's why I was away."

"I know, but...how well do you know her? Like, were you two ever extra close?"

I don't like his expression. He averts his gaze. "She used to be a part of our coven. I think Alondra thought she was going to take over one day before she learned about you. Enora doesn't have your ancestry, but she has an innate understanding of witchcraft that's very rare. She picked up incantations and spells faster than anyone I've ever met. She even caught Bill's attention, and he shared things with her that he never shared with anyone else."

"That's not exactly what I meant."

"What did you mean?" He raises his eyebrows, leans against his dresser, and puts his hands in his pockets.

"Did you two have a romantic relationship?"

"Huh?"

"Did you have sex?" *God, do I have to spell it out for him?*

I figure he's being evasive. That upsets me more. Somehow, I think he had a very romantic relationship with her. No, I know he did... I don't know, maybe it's having seen him lying naked and having sex with her by our bonfire that makes me think that.

His eyes blink and he runs his hand through his short dark hair. He always does this when he's flustered. He also does it when he's trying to keep things from me. "It was a long time ago, Cadence." Yeah, they had sex.

I finally look away and say rather morosely, "It wasn't so long ago for me."

"What do you mean?"

He walks over. I look up into his mesmerizing eyes and smile in spite of myself. "During the eclipse, I saw you and her naked together."

He cocks his head and seems to ponder this. I'm not pondering it. I'm pissed.

"Really?" he asks. "During the eclipse?"

"Yeah. I saw snakes and other weird shit too."

"Then it was a vision. Cadence..." He takes my hand. Why is he doing that while talking about having sex with another woman? "It was a long time ago. I haven't dated her in years. I certainly haven't been close with her in a long time."

"I know. I figured that. And now, I suppose, I get why I saw it. I must have been seeing the past. But it bothers me."

He cups my chin with his hand and kisses me on the lips. His lips are so soft. And his breath smells like spearmint. That's so Bryce. This guy's always dressing right and smelling good.

"I missed you," he says quietly. And we kiss some more. But... *Hey... wait a minute, mister...*

"Enora told the circle that she sent you to some...somewhere to get something. Like you were her gofer. I was shocked that she knew where you were, because I thought you were still back in Missouri with your parents. That's what you told me. Why didn't you say you were in town? What were you doing, and what were you doing with Enora? Why did she know your whereabouts before I did?" I must be pouting. He smiles widely, which upsets me more. "Really, Bryce. Cut it out! Why?"

"Don't be jealous," he says, shaking his head. He sits beside me on the mattress. "I did it for Alondra. Alondra contacted Enora. Enora called me and asked if I could gather some things. I told you, I hadn't spoken to Enora in years."

"But why *you*?"

"Bill was cast out. Now I'm the High Wizard of our coven. The High Wizard is expected to get these things."

Hmm.

"You told me you'd be with your parents watching the eclipse," I persist.

He sighs. Then he takes my hand again. "Katie, it was for Alondra. When Enora told me she was here with Alondra, to make amends and help her with her cancer, I put our past aside and offered to do anything I could. For Alondra. I know Enora's magic is nearly as powerful as Alondra's. Enora gave me a list of herbs, many very rare and only found in the city. I gladly went to get them. The fact that it would mean I'd miss the eclipse with our coven was a huge sacrifice, and Enora said that would make the potion that much stronger for Alondra. But there's nothing between Enora and me anymore. I swear it."

"So you didn't get to see the eclipse?"

"I watched what I could in the city."

"It was pretty cool." I shake my hair back and take a deep breath. Then I look deeply into his eyes. "At least you didn't see what I saw."

"Oh, come on, babe." He holds my cheek and leans his forehead on mine. Then we kiss again. "There's nothing between Enora and me anymore."

"I know," I say. But I sound hurt. I reprimand myself for sounding stupid. I saw a vision, but I'm acting like I caught him cheating on me.

"I miss your perfume." He backs away and takes a deep breath.

"I just can't get over what I saw."

"Panthera is a tigress, Katie. Literally. The word *panthera* means wild-cat. A tiger. She's the last person I'd want to be with, trust me. Her magic is more powerful than Alondra's because she uses black magic. Alondra doesn't. You know Alondra uses white, right-handed, good magic. Black magic was taught to Enora by Bill. Enora still worships Satan with her coven. She's a devil worshipper. So much so that Alondra cast her out years ago." Now he takes another deep breath and turns to the window. Through a crack between the unopened drapes, he looks at the parking lot for a moment. "I think she heard what you did. I don't think she came only at Alondra's invitation. Stories about your power probably spread all over the state. Maybe the whole country. Now I wonder if she had something to do with your seeing us together..." Then he emphasizes, "*In the past*, Katie."

"She looked like a real arrogant bitch," I say. "Shifty. She reminded me of Bill Reardon. Now I know why."

"Bill trained her. Personally. And there's more." But he clams up all of a sudden. He just sits there, looking down, shaking his head. "I shouldn't say."

"Hey," I say, "no *secrets*, remember?"

"Alondra should tell you, not me."

This time, I take his chin in my hands. I'm not going to let him off so easily.

"You weren't the first one to cause a rift in Alondra and Reardon's marriage, Katie," he says with a nod. "About four years ago, Reardon took Enora as a mistress."

"That dick," I say, dropping his chin. "Why did you ever have anything to do with him?"

"Back then, I was a student of Alondra's like you, and I didn't know Professor Reardon that well. But I knew Alondra. Alondra introduced me to the Hawthorne coven. I watched Alondra suffer more from her marriage with Bill than she's suffering now from her cancer. You know, she used to be a lot cheerier, like your friend Maddie. The affair really brought her down. I think she separated from him, not in marriage, but emotionally and, well, she distanced herself from everyone after that."

"I didn't even know Alondra was married until late last year."

"Bill did that. She drifted apart from everyone. And here's the weirdest part—Bill sort of made up with Alondra. They became the couple you know. A shell of a husband and wife. Alondra never forgave him, but Bill made peace with her. He did that, I think, in order to ask for protection from Enora... Reardon was terrified that Enora would conjure something horrible against him. So Reardon had Alondra cast shield spells to protect him from her."

"Reardon asked Alondra to protect him from the girl he'd been having an affair with? You're kidding."

"Yes. That's Alondra. And she's such a bright white light that she helped him. She shut off Enora's magic, like you do with fire. But her shield cost her. Who knows, maybe Enora made Alondra fall ill with cancer."

"Then why the hell did you help her?"

Bryce takes a deep breath, seeming impatient. "I told you, Cadence. For Alondra. Alondra needs any possible help she can get. And I've learned enough about potions over the years that I'd have a hunch if Enora were tricking me. She wasn't. The stuff she asked for made sense."

"But why would Alondra invite her?"

"I really don't know," he replies, shaking his head. "Maybe she's desperate. Maybe for the same reason I'm helping her. For her health."

He grabs my hand. "How's the rest of the gang? Mira?"

"Creepy. You know Mira."

"Mira cares about Alondra more than any of us. And she likes you. She likes you more since your magic show last semester. She respects you now."

"She doesn't act like it."

"She's Mira," Bryce says with a chuckle. "And Gilda? She got married, right?"

"Aha."

"How's—"

I surprise him by pushing him onto his bed and running my hand along the short stubble on his cheek. I can't resist anymore. We lock lips again, kissing passionately.

"Frida?" he asks between kisses. "I hear her brother is studying to be a priest. How's—"

"Aha," I mutter and press my lips on his. I don't want to talk. I want to kiss. So I do. Again. And he laughs as we press our lips together harder. I enter his mouth with my tongue, and he tastes delicious. "Umm," I say. "You don't know how much I missed you. How dare you not tell me you were back!"

"Sorry." He closes his eyes tightly and nods. "But you might have stopped me from going."

"I wouldn't have stopped you from helping Alondra."

"Okay."

"I wouldn't have. You have to trust me."

"I do. I love your long hair, Katie. Your smell."

"I smell nice?"

"I'm addicted to your smell."

"It's a very expensive perfume." I throw my legs over him and straddle him. He laughs more.

"And your humor."

"Shh," I say. Our lips touch again. At first it's soft, but then I press hard.

"Your youthfulness..."

I press my lips hard against his again so he can't talk. But he manages. "Your innocence. But, behind it"—I start lifting up his gray shirt—"there's an inferno."

"An inferno, huh?" I laugh, pulling off his shirt.

"A windstorm."

I stroke the bristles of hair along his cheek again and then move down to his short chest hairs. He's so muscular and hard. I touch his pecs and can feel his heart racing. Mine is racing too.

"You should have let me come with you," I whisper near his ear. "Don't you dare ever do that again."

I pull off my T-shirt, leaving just my black bra while I gyrate a little up and down his waist.

"Cadence," he says, pulling back again. "Maybe we shouldn't..." He looks at the window. "It's the middle of the day."

"It's really hot in here," I say with a chuckle. "Isn't it? I think I should take this off."

I reach back while still straddling him and unclasp my black bra. Then I throw it to the side. He's staring at my naked chest. He's running his hands along my naked skin, the curves of my breasts, and my nipples. I'm so aroused.

We're committed now. And I want him. I want to fuck him. I've missed him sooo much.

"I saw how all the other girls were looking at you in class."

He answers by cupping his mouth over one of my hard nipples. He starts sucking. It sends tingles down my back and legs. I pull him toward me, with my hips pressed against the bulge in his pants, and lock my lips on his again.

"I love you, Cadence," he says. "I love you so much." He's breathing heavily now. And so am I.

"Show me," I say.

I jump off and put up a single finger with a sly smile. Then I yank off my jean shorts and panties. I'm naked. I had already removed my sandals by his door. To be honest, I knew what I wanted when I entered his apartment; I just wanted the right moment. I kneel down, unzip his pants, and yank down his black slacks and underwear. He's holding a condom in his hand, and I wait as he rolls it down his long shaft.

I sit on him again and grind slowly. He moans again. Then he finally does what I've wanted since I saw him in the classroom this morning. He enters me. It's electrifying.

"Oh God, Bryce. Make love to me."

I'm rocking slowly, forward and backward, sliding slowly up and down on him while he massages my boobs. His fingers press deep along my soft skin, sliding down like drips of water from the curves of my breasts, down my sides, until settling on my butt. There his hands remain, supporting me as I move up and down on him slowly.

"And I missed this too," I say with a chuckle.

"Oh, Cadence."

I reach down and our lips touch again. I enter with my tongue and taste his while continuing to move up and down on him. Our lips become wet from sucking and tasting each other. I run my fingers along the stubble on his cheeks once more and then over his short hair. Then I sit up and straighten my back, allowing my tits to protrude, as I feel him press even deeper inside me.

"Oh, God, Cadence."

The sex is better than I remembered. I think it's because we've been away from each other for so long. I've missed him so much.

Now I love the warmth of his skin. I love his bright blue eyes. I even love it when he closes them, enjoying me. Loving me.

It gets heavy. It feels so good. I lean down and run my hand along his chest and down to the ripples of his abs. He's so fit. The passion becomes hotter, and I start to move faster and faster. I bounce hard up and down on him while moaning loudly. There's a clapping sound as my pelvis rides up and down on him. I don't want it to stop, but I think I'm bouncing so hard that he's about to be spent. I'm groaning so loudly that it's almost a shout.

"Shh," he says, putting a finger over my lips.

But I can't. I kiss and lick his fingers and just moan louder. Over and over I land on him until I finally feel him collapse under me. I haven't climaxed yet, so my man, being Bryce, so nice, stays inside me until I come. After a few more thrusts, I climax too.

"Oh God, Bryce!" I kiss him hard on the lips, falling on top of him. "That was sooo good."

"I love you, Cadence," he says, out of breath, staring into my eyes again. Those baby blues are looking into my eyes so innocently, so sweet and kind. "I love you so much."

I lean over him in an embrace. We lie naked in each other's arms for the longest time. I don't think I could ever be happier.

4

———

PANTHERA

I'M HOLDING MY LOVER'S HAND AS WE WALK UNDER LEAVES AND THIN branches that darken the clear, starry night in patches. We tread over pine-needle paths, smelling the clean woodsy air, passing dirt trails, streams, and brooks, up into the hills that overlook our campus. It's so lovely out that I convinced Bryce to walk with me from his apartment. It's Friday night, and we're heading to Alondra's.

Somehow Bryce convinced me to go with him to our second Sabbath of the year. We're going to try a healing spell, he told me. But the closer I get to the house, the heavier my feet feel. Maddie's told me we're planning a summoning. That means it's not going to just be a meet-and-greet; it's going to be a full-fledged witch show. I don't know if I'm ready for that.

Bryce raps Alondra's large antique brass knocker. He turns to me because my hand is shaking.

"Relax, babe," he says.

"Why did I say yes?"

"Because I didn't want to go alone." He leans down and kisses me on the cheek. "And because you care about Alondra as much as I do."

"I guess."

The door creaks open, and Madison opens the door wearing a black hooded cloak, looking like an ancient druid, with her hood down and her black hair flowing behind her. She's got a gaping grin.

"We're out in the back, High Priestess," Maddie says with a tight hug. Then she puts her hands on my shoulders in the foyer. She knows I'm nervous. "You ready?"

"No."

"Mira's chanting," she says.

I roll my eyes. Mira does this thing where she makes up words and dances around the fire like a fool.

"It'll be fine," Maddie adds.

"Just don't call me High Priestess," I say, shrugging her hands off.

A gray cat scurries by my legs and I jump in fright. "Shit!"

"That's Pete," Bryce says.

"Come on, girlfriend," Maddie says, "everybody's waiting for you."

Everybody's waiting for me. Great.

We make our way down the hallway to the living room. The sliding glass door is wide open. I hear chanting from the yard. It sounds like gibberish. I lurch back at the sight of a tall bonfire; it's about the height of a person. I don't want to go out there. This isn't the campfire we had last week. It's a witch's bonfire, like the one I once stoked with my magic. But Bryce takes my hand, and my feet somehow carry me.

Large white rocks, instead of chalk, circle the white plastic chairs around the fire. The smell of smoke and fire permeates the backyard. I can see the witches, my friends, walking slowly around the bonfire in their black druid coats. At the front of the group is Mira, dancing like a fool, with my witches walking in single file behind her.

"*Yelee alterban exeet solimader infotado,*" cries Mira. Whatever that means.

"Does she have to do that?" I ask Bryce as we walk forward.

"She's got passion," he says, "you've gotta give her that."

"Yatu!" Mira shouts spotting me. "Yatu!" She stops dancing and everyone stops.

They all turn as we approach. I realize Alondra isn't here. And what's worse, Enora is standing beside her henchwomen, Beatrix and Cordelia. Cordelia scowls at me. Enora narrows her eyes. I wonder how she feels about me holding Bryce's hand?

Mira walks over and crouches on one knee as the other girls remain beside the fire. It feels ridiculous, like I'm some sort of queen or something. The flames are raging over Mira's head behind her welcoming grin. "Yatu, High Priestess, Windstorm," she says and looks deeply into my eyes.

"Windstorm is here, Raven," says Maddie, bowing her head.

"So I see, Blackbird. Falconsong wasn't feeling well." She looks back at the house. "But we have Panthera here tonight." *Great.*

Mira jerks up and reaches toward the sky. She moves so fast that I'm startled. Her cloak falls back a little. I notice her large breasts under the folds of her cloak. She's naked underneath.

"Blessed be the gods who bear witness to our coven! To the moon, the stars, the trees. Earth, water, wind, and fire. We all gather once more under your arms!" She looks at me. "Come join the circle, High Priestess. I told you of darkness. I believe it is afflicting our blessed Falconsong. Let us summon the demons, wraiths, and will-o'-the-wisps tonight to fight them back and heal her."

"Why do you think there's evil?" I ask.

For the first time, I notice how wild-eyed she looks, and I feel dumb asking her a question. I'm wondering if she's taken mandragora. Mandragora, or mandrake, is a drug we sometimes take during ceremonies. I told Maddie that if anybody does that shit again, I'm out. I think Mira snuck some. And I'm not sure she understands what I'm saying.

"I've sensed evil ever since my long journey back from shadows in the East," Mira says.

That's silly. Mira just got back from her parents' house in Orlando, Florida. She makes it sound like she just arrived from Transylvania.

"I don't feel anything," I say. Then I look at Enora. "Do you?"

"There's left-sided magic here," Enora says with a nod, looking around the yard. "Raven's right. That is why Falconsong summoned me."

"Why don't we all sit down?" I say.

And they do because I'm their High Priestess. We all sit around the fire. The flames tower above us, and my chest tightens because it reminds me of my conjuring again.

"May I begin the evocation?" Mira asks me.

I'd rather you not.

She's sitting on my right, with three girls between us. I'm sitting between my BFF and my boyfriend. After I don't answer, Mira says, "We will manifest the spirits that threaten us. Then we will banish them from Falconsong's home."

"Why bring them here?" Maddie asks.

"We're not bringing them. They're already here. We're manifesting them. Windstorm, may we begin?"

"Do your worst," I say with a sigh.

Anyway, it doesn't look like Mira can "evoke" anything. Enora, who's glaring at me, could probably summon some mean spirits. Every time she watches me, I squirm and hold Bryce's hand tighter.

"If we face the shadow that lurks among us," Mira says rapidly, "we free ourselves." She's definitely high, might be mandrake, could be a dash of nightshade. "Everyone rise and hold hands. Walk single file, but face the flames."

And we do, just like we did during the eclipse.

"Spirits of Nyx!" Mira exclaims as we walk, "Gaia commands you to reveal the wraiths that you shelter. Here before the fire..." Then she lets go of Hope's and Marilyn's hands, takes a small metal flask from her pocket, and sprinkles water on the flames. It reminds me of a priest performing a blessing with holy water. "Water, and the earth under our feet, and the air we breathe, come to light. We demand you show yourself. Come forth." And then she puts up a hand for us to stop. She searches the yard as if she lost something. "Come forth!" Mira shouts. "Reveal yourself. Show yourself now."

But we hear crickets and the crackling fire. The silence is loud. But that's okay, because I'd rather feel like an idiot than have some spirit come forth.

"Come forth!" Mira repeats, as if yelling will invoke her spirits. "Show yourself! Now!"

"Perhaps we should just sit down and talk," I suggest.

"What do you think?" Mira asks Enora. "Do you feel this presence? Can you help reveal it?"

"I do," Enora says, with her arrogant smile illuminated by the flames. "I can."

"From the power of our coven, can you manifest it?" asks Mira.

Cordelia likes that question. Her scowl changes to a wicked, sardonic smile. She leans over and whispers something in Enora's ear while looking over at me. Enora nods.

"I can manifest the evil among you," Enora says. "But I don't think you'll like it."

"Does the spirit harm our beloved Falconsong?" asks Mira.

"The spirits harm all of you."

Mira looks at me. "High Priestess, will you allow Panthera to assist us?"

No. I don't trust Enora. I turn to Bryce, but he gives me a tentative nod. Then I look at Maddie. Maddie nods too and says, "For Alondra, Katie."

"I guess," I mutter. "Do...your worst."

My words sound so uncertain. It's one thing to let Mira babble; it's quite another to let this creepy witch conjure a spell. Bryce is anxious too. He's gripping me so tight now that I have to pull my hand away.

"Follow me," Enora says with a faint grin and a nod. Then, with her finger, she gestures for all the witches to leave the fire. She leads us toward Alondra's house.

"Gather around," Enora says, "but away from the flames. The fire is too dangerous."

The fire is too dangerous?

Then she does something really weird. As we circle around her, she crouches down on the wild grass in her dark cloak, gathering herself into a black ball at the center of all of us. We sit around her and wait as she's motionless for a long time. Then she whispers *"Spiritus"* quietly with her head cradled in her arms. I hear her words as if they're a gust of wind in the woods. She repeats them like a mantra. *"Spiritus. Spiritus, venite foras. Spiritus. Spiritus venite foras. Spiritus."* She continues to repeat the words, ever louder. *"Spiritus. Spiritus, venite foras."* Then she looks up and locks her eyes right on me. I lurch back as if one of Alondra's cats grazed by my leg. I could swear Enora's eyes have changed from blue to white.

"Spiritus, venite foras," she repeats ever louder. I can feel the words. They're cold and seem to be blowing around us. It makes me want to return to the warmth of the fire. *"Spiritus, venite foras."*

But the fire is the last place I want to be near. There's a howling. The fire rises higher. That freaks me out because it reminds me of my own conjuring. Then a swarm of black birds, not snakes this time but birds, bursts straight up from the center of the flames. Some of my friends shriek. A hundred crows caw as they take off into the starry sky.

A body forms in the center of the fire. A human form. I see a face, contorted, melting. It opens its mouth and screams inaudible words. It's silent. Too quiet. Only the sound of Enora's chant can be heard. Other than her words, it's just as quiet as it was when Mira was leading us into the forest.

I look at Bryce. He's spooked too. He's squeezing my hand again. Does he see the body in the flames? I follow his gaze and it only gets worse. More bodies twist in the fire. An emaciated old man with a long thin beard and limbs like sticks stands beside a child—maybe his son or daughter? The child's eyes are sunken in. A line of men and women march toward them from behind, in single file, with their heads down. The fire seems to be a portal, and beyond these bodies are hills and valleys and a crimson lake with blood-like tributaries flowing into a river. And everything is seen through a dark red filter.

The fire rises higher. Enora's words are now a whirlwind, as if they're not words at all but a tempest surrounding us. Another man's form appears distinctly in the center of this red vortex. His body is emaciated as well, but he's young. He's entwined with the body of another. A woman. The woman's body melts in and out of the man and, though she is terribly thin, her naked breasts and belly are full. Among the red hills, a shadow, a figure wearing a dark cloak like mine, approaches the couple from behind carrying a curved knife.

I've had enough. I shout for Enora to stop and am horrified when I find my lips paralyzed. I can't utter a thing.

"*Spiritus, venite foras.*"

The mouths of the couple in the fire are now wide open, screaming in unison as they suffer in pain. I can hear their scream now, but it doesn't sound like the noise is coming from them. I look at the other witches standing in the circle with me. I realize that the scream is not coming from the couple but from my friends.

I see the torso of a man with a thin bone-like arm appear outside of the fire for a moment. Blood is dripping from melting flesh.

Enora points at the fire and, with her white eyes, cries, "*Ecce signum! Ecce diabolus vester! Ecce satanas vester. Ecce adversaries vester!*"

All the witches of my coven repeat her words as if reading them off a script. I don't know what they mean. Bryce is still holding my hands, and he's repeating her words too. His eyes are wide open, staring at the flames.

"Stop!" I say. The words explode from my chest, but my lips are still immobile. And yet Bryce and Maddie turn. The rest of my coven turns too. Somehow, they hear me.

Enora continues to chant. "*Spiritus, venite foras.*"

"Stop!" I repeat. This time the words echo throughout the forest. Oddly, my words seem to compete with Enora's. Enora rises from her crouched position and thrusts her hands toward me as if striking me.

There comes a terrible scream. At first I think it's one of my friends, but then I realize it's from the fire. All my friends stare at the flames. The fire rises, as it once did upon my command. It's two stories high, and the couple is now melting in the center.

"Stop!" I scream at Enora. My lips relax and I can move my mouth again. "Stop it, now!" I cry. "What are you doing? Stop!"

She turns and looks at the fire, as if curious about her own witchcraft. The flames are now spinning rapidly in a red vortex. And in the center of the fire is no longer a couple but bodies, hundreds of them, naked, melting, writhing, and circling ever higher in a fiery tornado. I know the fire is a doorway. Into hell? Occasionally, limbs appear outside the flames. The arms and legs are misshapen, with welts and open sores in their skin, and blood oozes. But most horrible are their faces. The faces are not of this world anymore. They are melted and contorted like wax on a candle. Some are missing eyes, ears, or noses. But they're alive, hollering in fear.

"Stop it!" I shout at Enora. "I command you! Stop this now!"

She turns to me and, in the midst of all the chaos, she smiles with those creepy pearl eyes. But the spell is breaking. The rest of the witches in my coven are stepping back toward the house, ready to make a run for it. No longer do their eyes appear glassy or in a trance. No longer are they blindly repeating her incantation. They're stepping back from the fire in horror.

"*Venite foras!*" Enora spits at me, as if challenging me with her words. Then she points at the fire. "Here is your evil!"

"What are you doing!" I scream back. "You're opening a door. Close it! Close it now!"

I rush to her and stare into those creepy white eyes. I feel an energy pierce the center of my chest. *Stop now!* I shout, but once more my lips don't move. It is a thought at the core of my very being. My soul. She shakes her head and closes her eyes tightly as if I've hurt her. She loses her smile and, for the first time, she doesn't look like she's in control.

You can stop this, Cadence. The words are not Enora's; they're felt by me. I don't know where they're coming from, but they sound familiar. Maybe my conscience? *You have the power to stop this. Stop it now. End the spell, Windstorm. End it now.*

Panic surges through my body. Then comes a flash of lightning from the sky. Enora looks up excitedly. A second bolt crashes down only a few yards from us, nearly striking her. She falls to the ground, covering her eyes as if blinded. When she opens them and turns to me, the creepy whiteness has left her gaze.

"*STOP!*" I shout. Not only the words but the thought springs from my body. Enora is thrown a few feet, rolling in the grass. A torrent of rain pours down. And then more lightning and thunder.

With the rain comes wind. A powerful gale strikes the ground, throwing my hood and hair back. Enora's hood flies off her head too, and her hair is blown horizontally. She slides across the grass, driven by a force as if a tornado has been summoned. A few witches stumble over, and for a moment the bonfire nearly burns out. Enora looks into my eyes, and her eyes are blue again. But she stubbornly yells once more, "*Venite foras!*"

"*Apage, diabole!*" I cry back, and my words are accompanied by more lightning. Each word is echoed by a crash from the sky. "*Vade retro!*"

I look over at the fire. It's spinning and bodies are still suffering in the flames. I run past Enora and land on my knees right before the flames. Then I raise my hands and repeat words never before uttered from my lips: "*Vade retro, diabolus!*"

A gust of wind knocks me over. It whirls around Alondra's yard and lands over the fire. A few wraiths nearly escape the flames, as if in a final effort to enter our world, but the wind crashes over them too.

The fire is snuffed out.

Then the wind leaves as quickly as it came. So too does the rain. So too does the thunder and lightning.

Everything falls silent.

I hear whimpering behind me. My friends are crying. They're in shock.

My breathing is fast and heavy. I cock my head back, and Enora's on her knees too. She looks exhausted as she stares at the pile of smoke, once our bonfire. She's in total shock.

"*Get out!*" I shout to Enora. "*Get out, now!*"

She looks at me and furrows her brow.

I despise this woman. She brought the same sort of magic that I've been trying so hard to forget. She's made my nightmare come true.

But she does nothing. She just stares at the smoldering flames. I think she's in too much shock to move.

I feel a hand on my back. I spin around. It's Mira. She's reaching out to help me up, but I bat her hand away.

"Leave our coven!" I shout at Enora. "Leave, now!"

"You asked me to manifest darkness and the spirits from hell. I warned you." She didn't warn me. She didn't say anything about "spirits from hell."

"I didn't," I object.

"You did."

"You did, Cadence," Mira says gently. But for the first time ever, Mira is completely serious. She's shaking leaves and water from her cloak. All my friends are slowly rising behind us.

I run right up to Enora, and the woman backs up, scared.

"How could you do this!"

"I did what you asked, Cadence." Enora raises her hand. "I summoned devils to show you what threatens your circle. You saw them. They are here. Close the door or not, they are always with us. I did not bring the devil to this coven. The past did. I only manifested it. Made it visible. This evil is among you. You just don't want to see it. This is the threat Mira feels. This portal is so close to being open. I simply brought it out from hiding. I manifested what is here, I didn't create it."

"You brought it here! You brought something that shouldn't be here."

"And you made it go away," Enora says, finally giving me her stupid smug smile.

I look around. No one is saying a thing. Some have sat back down on the wet wild grass with their heads in their hands.

Bryce comes up to me, helps me up, and embraces me. I start crying in his arms. Some of the other witches are still crying too.

"How'd you do that?" Mira asks Enora in wonder.

"I will show you." Enora seems excited. "I can teach all of you. It is powerful magic that—"

"You will show nothing!" I say, jumping out of Bryce's arms. "Go away!"

She doesn't go.

I stare at her for a moment. So...I go. I run away from everyone.

Bryce calls out my name, but I ignore him.

5

———

911

I run up to the sliding glass door leading to Alondra's living room, and I see very little light inside. All the lights have been turned off. Perhaps the lightning knocked out the electricity. I struggle to open her glass door, which is somehow now closed, and the fight to open it makes me cry even more. Tears are streaming down my face.

I didn't even want to be here. Everything is reminding me of last year, and last year was seriously fucked up. I just want a normal life. What happened is precisely what I feared would happen.

I finally throw the door wide open, pull off my dark cloak, and toss it on her fluffy carpet. Why did I come? I'm so mixed up. Since my wandering through the forests of Hawthorne last year, I've accepted that I'm a witch. Fine. I'm a witch. But I haven't accepted a witch's magic. Especially dark magic. I just want to have friends and be a normal person. I don't want a boyfriend who's a warlock. And I don't want a best friend who calls herself *Blackbird*. I want out of this coven.

But see, I'm so confused because I know in my heart that there is no way out. I'm a witch. And this is my coven. This is my family.

I rush down the hallway toward Alondra's large foyer. The lights are out everywhere, and it's dark and spooky. But I'm angry enough not to care. Of course, I could turn on a light, but I don't bother. I grab the brass knobs of Alondra's large mahogany doors to leave and am about to throw them open when I hear a groan. A sound of pain. It reminds me of the portal, but this is a solitary moan. It echoes through the dark, empty house.

I hear it again. It's coming from upstairs.

So? Why should I care? I should just go home.

But someone sounds hurt.

My feet disobey me, and I quickly make my way up Alondra's stairway. It only gets spookier as I ascend, in total darkness, away from the windows near the front door. And there's moaning again. A steady groan of pain.

I follow the moans down the hallway to an open door. I walk in and see a large window facing Alondra's backyard. If the window weren't there, I wouldn't be able to see a thing in this bedroom. The window overlooks the yard, where my sisters and Bryce are confronting Enora and her witches. It seems like a standoff, with the three of them shouting at the ten witches of my coven. Good. At least they're fighting her now.

There's a groan again. I turn and see someone in bed, in the shadows, clutching her stomach.

"Who's there?" I ask in the darkness.

The groaning stops. I don't think the person even knows I came into the room.

I find a light switch and flip it on, but the light doesn't work. The electricity is out.

I hear a soft, weak voice. "Cadence."

"Who's there?" I know who it is. Who else could it be?

"Cadence," the voice mutters again.

I kneel by the bed in the dark. Alondra slowly turns. She's wrapped in her sheets. She groans again, but more softly now knowing someone is listening.

"What's wrong?" I ask. "What's the matter?"

"Nothing...I...I saw everything."

"Enora?"

"Panthera," she says with a nod.

My eyes are adjusting.

Alondra looks awful. Her hair is disheveled, and she's wearing a simple T-shirt under the sheets. Her skin looks glassy and covered with sweat.

"Are you sick?" I ask. Of course she's sick.

"You've proven yourself once more. I knew your powers were great, but I've never seen anything like that."

"What's wrong, Alondra?"

"You are a powerful witch."

"So what?" I snap, shaking my head violently. This is so Alondra. One second wonderful, the next a complete bitch-witch. Who cares how good a witch I am? She's sick! I take a deep breath and say, "Are you hurting? I heard you from downstairs. What can I do?"

"I'm dying, Cadence."

There's silence after that. I feel a tightness in my chest, but I don't think I can cry anymore. My eyes are still wet from being so mad at Enora. The tightness in my chest rushes to my throat. She reaches out her hand and holds mine. Her hand is slimy. Her weak grasp makes me feel even worse. And her hand is shaking.

"You are our leader," Alondra says. "The embodiment of Escoba. And more. I shall give you my gift too. I will give you my power from Abigail. You will be the greatest witch that ever lived."

"Stop it, Alondra! I don't care." I reach into my pants pocket for my phone. "I'm going to call 911. You're sick."

"No doctors," she says. "I refuse any medicine."

"Bryce said you had an infection. Did you take your antibiotics?"

"A witch doesn't take antibiotics. Only herbs."

"You're so stubborn."

"This coming from you," Alondra says with a weak laugh. Then she shuts her eyes tightly. "I am close to the Summerland, Cadence. Let me go in peace."

I let go of her hand, jump up, and walk to the window. I'm surprised to see the fight is over. Enora's out there corralling my coven again. Somehow, she's organizing them around the smoldering fire once more, and my friends are following her. How does she do that? It is then I realize that this witch is sabotaging my circle. *My* friends.

Alondra groans. I think she's so sick she's forgotten I'm here.

"Why is Enora here still?"

"What?" Alondra asks weakly. She seems to have trouble even uttering a breath.

"Why is Enora in our coven? She's trying to take over."

Alondra laughs. I can't believe it. She actually laughs. But midway between a guffaw, she falls back, breathing heavily again.

"Wait. You brought her to take over, didn't you?" I ask in amazement. "You brought her here to lead the coven instead of me?"

Alondra takes a deep breath. Then she says, "Do you fight me even in my last days, Katie?"

"Am I right?"

"Of course, the Hawthorne coven must survive."

"Led by that witch!" I snap in disbelief.

"I can't...fight, Cadence...I can't..."

She has no energy. I rush over. Her eyes are wide open in the darkness, for a moment, as if she's truly about to die. She takes a deep breath and rolls to her side. But she's still breathing, thank God.

"You know what," I remark wickedly, "I know exactly how to get even with you." Even in her convalescence, she cocks her head curiously in the darkness. "No Western medicine, huh?"

I take out my phone and call 911.

6

THEY'RE SO WEIRD

I'M RUNNING.

Whenever I'm stressed, I exercise. I got so fit last year that I had well-developed abs, calves, and quadriceps. Then summer came and Maddie and I gained weight. Now, in the second week of school, I'm exercising again. I spent three hours in the gym this morning and slept the afternoon away, and now I'm running all night.

Maddie never returned to our dorm. I think she went with Bryce to the hospital, but I shut the phone off. I suppose since I didn't go to the hospital, I should have at least been studying. But I wasn't in the mood to study either.

I'm winding down a hill, and I turn, nearly hugging a tree trunk. My shoes are sticking between rocks in a thick, muddy stream, and I'm worried that I might sprain my ankle. I can barely see the ground. There's only a crescent moon.

I make my way up an incline from a dirt path, and the trees disperse. I can finally see the ground beneath my feet in the clearing. Then I'm paralleling a river. Soon the forest surrounds me again. I'm still making my way up, and I hear a lovely waterfall (I wish I could see it) flowing to my right. I'm pretty sure that if I were to climb the rocks up the waterfall,

I'd end up on a path that would lead me to Alondra's house. Her house is right by a tributary that flows into Hawthorne Lake.

I make it up to a hilltop and look out at a gorgeous view of the dark forest. Lights from campus are shining below me. There's no official name for this hillside view, but students are known to call it Hilltop Bluff.

I crouch down, breathing heavily, and lean my hands on my knees. I've been running for an hour. This is the third time I've been up here tonight. I must really be upset. It's a gorgeous view. There's not a cloud in the sky, and I can see the woods for miles. I can even make out the far-off mountains.

As dark as the night is, there's enough light in the clearing to see the field of wild grass at the summit. Last year, there were burnt logs in the center. This was where my coven did "ceremonies," sometimes the most wicked ones. Maddie was raped here. Well, Reardon and Alondra called it ceremonial sex, but I call it rape. They gave her mandrake, and the old fart had his way with her. It makes me nauseous thinking of it. I was never ceremonially raped and, thankfully, never witnessed it, but this is the other reason why I went berserko last semester and nearly killed all the witches in my coven. And that's why today I've weight-lifted, biked, run on the treadmill, and jogged over twelve miles. Do you understand? These are my friends. Now they're up to it again with hellfire. Why are these my friends?

There's a large boulder near the edge of a cliffside and, instead of returning to the trail, I take a small bottle of water from my belt and sit down on the rock, looking down at the lights from campus. I don't venture too far on the ledge, because the drop is treacherous and it looks like my weight could topple the whole thing down the sheer drop. I can make out the library in the woods. I suppose I should be studying there. That's the other thing my fucked-up friends did to me. I'm a straight-A student, and I nearly failed out of school the first semester of last year. I take the water to my lips and chug down three-quarters of the bottle.

And I sit here for the longest time. It's so peaceful—the beautiful wilderness under the stars. Stars shine brighter in Hawthorne. There's no smog to obscure the twinkling lights. I lean back on my hands and just stare up at the sky.

That's when I'm startled by the sound of something stepping on leaves in the bushes. I turn to my left and pull my phone from my pocket. I shine my cell phone flashlight in the direction of the noise. A deer's eyes shine white, reflecting the light. I don't like that. It reminds me of Enora's white eyes. Slowly, the animal approaches very close. I sit up and watch it as it timidly stands beside me near the cliffside. I shut off the light from my phone.

"Hey, girl," I say.

The deer walks right up to the rock, only a foot away from me. Then it turns its head and looks down at the view of the valley too. I reach out my palm and enjoy the touch of her hide. She seems to come closer under my palm. She closes her eyes as I pet her. Touching her fur not only soothes her, it comforts me too.

But then my hand jerks from the sudden vibration of my cell phone. The deer darts off, alarmed by the motion.

I had the phone off until now. My friends have been trying to reach me all day, and I've been ignoring their texts and voicemails. For some reason, I check it now and see my dad's number.

"Hey, Dad," I say.

I look at the side of the university furthest from Alondra's house. The oldest structure of Hawthorne, the Billington House, is barely visible among the trees.

"Hi, squirt." He sounds like he's in a good mood. "How are you doing?"

"Great," I lie.

"Hmm," he says. "You don't sound great."

I sigh. I lose myself for a moment looking down at the woods in the shadows directly below me. Then I wonder if my father would be happy to know that his daughter is running in the pitch dark of night, in the woods, by her lonesome. Probably not.

"I'm okay."

"What's wrong?"

"Why do you think something's wrong?"

"You know our deal, Katie. If things aren't going well, you're to come home. We'll make other arrangements at another school. Last year was too difficult. But...you were doing so well with Maddie this summer. I don't understand."

"What makes you think anything's the matter?" *Geesh, am I that obvious?*

"I got a call from Maddie. She's worried about you. She has no idea where you are."

"She's a bitch."

"Really?" He sounds shocked. No, she's not a bitch. But she is a witch. "You didn't think so this summer. You guys had such a great time."

"Well, she's a witch, I meant." I laugh. Dad doesn't understand. He doesn't know about my coven. He'd never understand. I barely do.

"Well, I'm glad to see you're all right."

"I'm okay."

"Katie...I know I'm not Mom. You know, when Mom passed last year I think you lost someone to confide in, but I can do the best I can."

"Don't worry about me, Daddy. I'm fine."

"Well, if there's anything going on, can you call me? Please? Can you let me know?"

"Sure, Dad."

There's silence. My deer is back. She dips her head down near my hand. I absentmindedly pet her hide again.

"There's one more thing, squirt. You know your brother is checking out colleges. I was hoping you could show Damie around campus. He really likes Hawthorne. I know it's more of a liberal arts school but, between you and me, I think he wants to do what you did. He looks up to you. And it's so close to home, you know." I'm letting him drawl on, but I'm squeezing my left hand really tight. I'm breathing fast and my chest is tightening. I'm about ready to scream. "So what do you think, Katie? Can he drive by the school and have you show him around with your friends?"

"No!" I shout. There's silence on the phone. I stop petting my deer and push myself off the boulder. "No! Don't let him come here. It's so weird here. Just have him go somewhere else. Somewhere where he can make normal friends."

"Kate...I...I thought you liked it there."

"I do. It's just...it's just a bad night, that's all."

"He really liked visiting you on campus last year. And he might have a few friends going there."

"Don't have him come here, okay? Please. Promise me. Just don't. Tell him… Let me talk to him. If he wants to be a doctor, he won't get anywhere with the science program here at Hawthorne. He won't get in. I'm a history major, for Christ's sake. This is not the place—"

"Okay," Dad says, disappointed. "Fine, Katie. Don't cuss. I don't want—"

"Please, Dad. I thought he was applying to Emory? And wasn't he thinking of Harvard? He's smart enough. Don't have him go here. Anywhere but here."

"Okay, okay. I shouldn't have mentioned it. It's just a nice town, Kate. He really likes how nice everyone is in the countryside."

"Have him go somewhere else."

"Sure. How about you tell him? I told you two I don't care where you go. If you can convince him, I'm fine with it. But I really don't understand. You two get along well, and Hawthorne has a fine track record for premed. It's a very good school… Well, you tell him. He wants to visit you."

"It's just weird here."

"I'm just glad you're okay. Turn your phone on so your friends and that boyfriend of yours don't freak out. Maddie said Bryce was worried too."

I walk to the end of the stone precipice beyond my boulder and look down at the shadows. If I were to jump, it'd be about a hundred-foot drop. Don't worry, I'm not stupid or suicidal. Never have been. But there's a weird rush when you're this high up. And I can feel the breeze brush pleasantly on my face. It's a cool wind. I shiver and grip my arms around my chest for a moment. It's getting cold. Running warmed me, but resting for too long makes me remember that winter is coming.

"How is Bryce, by the way?"

"Everything's fine, Dad." *Now please go. I can't talk anymore.*

"Okay, squirt. I love you."

"I love you too, Daddy. Bye."

My deer stands beside me and looks down into the abyss. I pet her soft fur. "All the witches are so weird here, aren't they, girl?"

7

———

THE VISITOR

Hawthorne Hospital is not really a hospital. It's more of a clinic. When people really have medical problems, they travel to Atlanta. This place is an ugly white two-story complex with concrete walls, a couple of bushes, and a silver metal overhang in front of the emergency room for their ambulance. The one thing that makes its ugliness bearable is the gorgeous surrounding trees of Hawthorne's forest.

After napping most of the day, I make my way through the electric glass doors into the lobby. It's Sunday. I should be studying, but the circle is fucking up my study habits once again. I know that sounds heartless, but that's the way I feel. Even Alondra seemed more interested in my magic jousting match with Enora than her fight with cancer.

The lobby just looks like a small clinic waiting room. A nice chubby nurse with curly brown hair takes my name and checks to see if I can come in as a visitor. She calls a room, probably Alondra's, and talks for a moment. She nods and asks me to sign a guest list. Then I'm off, down a really creepy dark hallway. There aren't many other people about, because the hospital closes in less than an hour.

As I get out of the elevator on the second floor and walk down another dismal, spooky hallway—even darker than the one downstairs—

wouldn't you know it? My favorite witch, Enora, wearing a black lace shirt barely covering her boobs, is strolling down the hall, staring at the white-tiled floor. She looks snooty. She passes right by a doctor and doesn't even give him the time of day. I have every intention of ignoring her, but she looks up and says, "Hi, Cadence."

"Don't talk to me."

"She's in room 214," Enora says. I don't stop walking. "Cadence, I'm sorry."

"You're not."

"I am. Truly. I'm sorry for what happened."

I force my feet to move, avoiding her gaze. I hear a faint grunt and the bitch is gone.

When I get to room 214, the door is slightly ajar. I knock. The door opens and, of all people, Mira is standing there in her usual long black dress and thick black goth makeup. Her mascara is smeared. She closes the door behind her gently and shocks me by falling into my arms.

"She's so sick, Katie," Mira says with a cracked voice. "I don't know what to do. It's terrible."

"It'll be okay," I say. But I'm not so sure.

Mira pulls away gently and shakes her head. "I don't think so. She's inside. Bryce and Alondra are asleep."

I haven't answered any of Bryce's texts in over a day. I don't think he's going to be happy to see me right now.

"You guys have been here since—"

"Yes." Mira nods. "Bryce and I went with her in the ambulance. What about Maddie? Did she come back with you to your dorm?"

I shake my head. I haven't answered Maddie's texts either.

"Maybe she went home to Aunt Jane's again."

Then we're silent. I kind of feel like Mira should be sleeping; she looks so worn out.

"I just saw Enora down the hall," I say.

"She was here casting healing spells."

I bet.

"Together we tried herbs," Mira says solemnly. "I prepared feverfew with honey. She added sandalwood and basil for pain." Mira chuckles.

It's the first time Mira has smiled, and for a moment she seems like her old sarcastic self. But then she gets morose again. "We had to sneak the stuff in under the nurses' noses. But Alondra's really suffering. I think the feverfew helped with the fever. Then we cast some spells. Enora chanted a healing incantation for hours. She's really powerful."

"I saw."

"She feels bad about what happened. Did she tell you?"

"Sort of."

Mira just shrugs. She looks so tired. Normally, she would really enjoy irritating me, but she's exhausted.

"Alondra's not very happy with you, Cadence," Mira says. "You know she didn't want this kind of help."

What? Doctors? Medicine? This is why they're all so weird.

"She was sick before we met for our Sabbath, you know," Mira adds. "She told us to still get together. She said..." Mira turns and wipes away tears with her black sleeve. "'If I die, Windstorm will lead the group and help me on my way to the Summerland.'" She looks at me and I have to turn away. I've never seen Mira so sad, and it depresses me. "She said that no matter what happens, the Sabbath must continue. So ...'"

"She invited Enora?"

I'm recalling my fight with Alondra. Why was I such a bitch? I mean, what do I care if Alondra appoints Enora instead of me?

"She called Enora in the event that you refused to go," Mira explains. "She knew you didn't want to perform ceremonies anymore after what happened."

"I was mean to her," I say, looking down. "I told Alondra that she should never have had Enora come. Why do I even care?"

"Because you're our High Priestess," Mira says with a shrug. "I understand."

I don't. Mira accepts me. Why don't I? "Maybe you should be our leader, Mira."

Mira smiles her old sly smile for a second. "Not after what I saw you do to Panthera's spell." Then she touches the latch on the door. "Come in. Alondra might hate you, but she's been asking for you all day."

We walk in quietly. It's a single bedroom and the drapes are open, but it's dark because it's nighttime and the lights are out. Through the window I can see the forest. The shadow of my boyfriend is lying on a recliner next to Alondra. Poor thing. Alondra wakes up. She's wincing in pain again. She smiles when she sees me.

"Turn on the light," Alondra says.

I do. The room has drab and ugly whitewashed walls like the rest of the hospital. It smells like chicken. There's a plate half covered by plastic on a nightstand next to Alondra's bed. Alondra has clear tubes stuck in her arms. One is hooked into a plastic bag thingy on wheels. Her hair's a mess. That's not like her. Alondra's like Bryce. She always takes care of herself. And her face still has that sick glassy look she had two days ago in her bedroom.

"Hi, Cadence."

I choke up and almost cry. But I can't cry. I won't cry. I might be sad, but I'm also mad. It's this weird relationship I have with her, you know.

"Are you feeling better?" I force myself to say. It sounds formal.

"A little," she says, scooting up in bed. "No thanks to you."

"You were sick. I had to do it."

"I know," she says with a chuckle. I look back and notice Mira left us alone. "Don't worry about it."

"I wasn't going to just let you die."

"You should." Then she turns to the window. "It would be better."

There's a small wooden chair next to the window. I grab it, glancing outside again. The forest extends for miles.

I sit down near her bed. "It's stupid for you not to seek help. If you know the doctors can help you, avoiding them because you're a witch is dumb."

"Is it? Not as dumb as you not believing in us after all you've seen."

"I do believe."

She nods irritatingly slowly.

"I know I have to accept who I am," I say. "I'm a witch. But I'm also a girl who just wants to study history and graduate Hawthorne."

Alondra looks out the window again. She can see the trees, but they look like shadows now that the light's on in the room.

"Can you promise me something?" she asks almost in a whisper. Then she reaches out for me. I hold her hand. It makes me almost tear up again. I nod. "When I die, let me die out there." She points to the window. "Not inside a house or in a hospital. No buildings. Out there. In nature. One with Gaia and Selene. Can you grant me that one wish, Windstorm? You know how much I love the woods." I don't answer. So she says, still holding my hand, "When I was a girl, I grew up in wide fields on a farm. The fields went on for as far as the eye could see. That was nature too, and beautiful, but there's something about the trees that reminds me of magic. Not magic like a magician, but magic with a *k*. Magik. Mystery. The occult. That is what's out there, Cadence. I hope that you not only see through the eyes of your sisters but, one day, see through the eyes of Bacchus. Or, as the Norse call him, Vidar. I've spent my whole life studying his mysteries. Funny how women, witches, are most in tune with him." She turns and looks at my eyes as if to see if I'm listening to her, and I have this strange sense that she's teaching me again. "Vidar, the god of the woods, I mean."

I nod. She's still holding my hand. She turns back to the window. "Turn the lights off again. I want to see the trees better... Will you see to it that I pass away in the forest?"

"Only if you allow the doctors to treat your cancer."

She stares at me in amazement. Then she chuckles and shakes her head. "You are the stubbornest witch I've ever known."

"Do we have a deal?" I ask. "I'll be a bona fide witch if you start seeing a doctor."

"You already are a bona fide witch. Especially after the magic I witnessed with Panthera."

"Why didn't you take the antibiotics the doctor told you to?"

She takes a deep breath and lets go of my hand. She says nothing.

"You are feeling better," I say.

She nods.

And I'm glad. You see, I care about her. I might have been stubborn and childish and refused to go with my friends in the ambulance—that was mean—but I had just fought with Enora. I wasn't in a normal state of mind. And I know I didn't visit her for two days. Okay, I guess I was a bitch. But I like Alondra. I know, it's really weird, but I do. And that's why I couldn't go with her to the hospital. Do you understand?

I take her hand again.

Bryce is snoring in the recliner. God, he must really be tired. Alondra looks at him too.

"I don't like Enora," I say out of the blue. I have to say it. I've been wanting to say it since Alondra was sick in her bedroom.

"Panthera is a fire element, Windstorm. She's competitive, brash, excitable, and quick-tempered. Like you. Also, like you, she is a very powerful witch. And stubborn. You two are actually a lot alike." I shake my head, and there's a hint of a smile from her. "But, unlike you, she's not grounded. She's unstable because she's afraid. You are stronger because you are afraid. I know this doesn't sound like it makes sense, but it's true. Your fear strengthens you. You're careful because of your fear. Enora is conceited. That weakens her. But both of you are natural witches. Your magic comes from within. Your atman is strong. If you learned casting like Mira, if you both did, you would be greater than any of us."

"I don't trust her."

"I trust her." She lets go of my hand again. "I think you and she will turn around. Just like you and Mira. You two seem like friends now."

"Enora's evil."

"I told you last year that there is no such thing as good and evil. The world is not a simple dichotomy of black and white. That is a puerile view from the kind of people who judge others by their black or white skin. Only fools see the world in that way. Evil is really an illusion."

"I disagree. I think there is such a thing as evil."

"So you've told me. Your disagreements have made you an apt pupil... And an annoying disciple." But she smiles.

"Enora opened a hellish world in our firepit. It was terrifying."

"She was testing you, Cadence."

"What if she couldn't close it?"

"She could close it," Alondra says, completely sure of herself. "And if not, you would." She looks out the window again. "And if not, I would... Please, please, Cadence, turn the light off again for me. I so wish to look outside at the lovely trees."

It's then that the doctor walks in. He's a thin, handsome man, clean-shaven, with dark-brown hair—almost in a crew cut—graying on the sides. He's wearing an open white lab coat with a button-down shirt and jeans underneath. He's got a big smile. I don't know what he's so happy about.

"How's my favorite patient?" he asks and sits by the bedside.

"I feel like shit."

I don't like it when Alondra cusses. She was my professor. It always feels wrong. Usually she's so prim and proper. She's an enigma. There's no explaining her mystery. Like our relationship. It's...

"Well," the doctor says, "your fevers have stopped, Ms. Johansen. And you're able to use the restroom again." He leans down and checks a tube beside the bed. It's full of yellow fluid that looks like pee. Gross. Then he stands up and examines the plastic bags full of fluids. He checks them and measures them with a pen in his hand. "You're doing better."

"I'm feeling a little better."

"What's wrong with her?" I ask.

"Urosepsis," he says. "A little bit longer and we would have shipped her to the ICU. Or worse. She was so sick she wasn't able to use the bathroom."

"Is it the cancer?"

"Are you her relative?" he asks.

"As good as one," Alondra says.

"How bad is it?" I ask.

"Cadence," Alondra snaps.

"She hasn't told you?" the doctor says, furrowing his brow. Then he looks at Alondra as if waiting for permission.

"Is it treatable?" I persist. This is my chance to finally get to the bottom of her illness. The doctor probably thinks I'm crazy, but I'll never get it out of her any other way.

"If she's willing to get surgery. But—"

"No surgery!" Alondra snaps. Then she looks right into my eyes and says sternly, "*No surgery... Never, Cadence.*"

Geesh.

The doctor takes out a pad and starts humming. He's so comfortable even though Alondra's dying that it's irritating.

"Will she stay another night?" asks another voice. It's Bryce. I think the doctor was finally loud enough to wake him.

"I think so. One more night and then she can go home. She'll have to take antibiotics after discharge. We have some running through the IV, but I'd like her to take the pills at home."

"She will," I say.

Alondra shakes her head at me.

"She'll take them if she can take them out in the woods," I add.

Alondra can't help but laugh at that. Bryce gives us a funny look, not getting it.

The doctor leaves.

I walk over to Bryce, reach down, and give him a hug. He hugs me, but it's like hugging a board. He's really mad. Why wouldn't he be? I haven't answered his texts.

"You could have at least answered your phone, Cadence," Bryce says.

"Sorry."

"I'm happy to see you together," Alondra says. "You make a good couple."

She's got that famous grin again and, for a second, it looks like the old Alondra.

"Why don't you go home with Cadence, Bryce? You need to rest in bed, not in a hospital chair."

Bryce stretches out his arms. Then he snarls at me. "Maddie's super mad at you too, Cadence. She kept calling me asking what your problem was."

"Where'd Maddie go?" I ask.

"She said she'd probably head to Aunt Jane's for the weekend."

"The light, Cadence," Alondra reminds me. "Please turn it off."

I get up and turn off the light. Only a crack of light from the hallway leaks in. But I figure our eyes will get accustomed. I see Alondra staring out the window again.

Bryce jumps up and grabs a pitcher. "You want some water?"

"No thanks, Bryce," she says with a chuckle. "Cadence, he's quite a man. He's been at my side every sleeping and waking hour."

The door opens wider, letting in more light from the hallway. I'm thinking it's Mira coming back, or the doctor, but it isn't. Another man walks through the door.

I jump back toward the window in shock. He's thin and bald, with a goatee and a black cape draped over a red-and-black button-down and slacks. Professor William Reardon. Alondra's estranged husband.

"What are you doing here?" asks Alondra.

"Go away, she's sick," I snap. But Alondra puts her hand up.

"I came to see my wife," Reardon says. "You don't mind, do you, Windstorm?" Then he looks at Bryce. "Disciple," he says with a nod.

"I thought you expelled him," I say.

"I did. I haven't seen him since, Cadence. I swear."

"She expelled me from the coven, not from our marriage, Ms. Cadence Hawthorne. And now, I would ask that you two leave. I'm taking her home." Reardon looks around with disgust. "As if anything in these plastic walls can help our beloved Falconsong."

"Why are you wearing that stupid outfit?" I say. His cape makes him look like a magician. It's so dumb and weird.

"Alondra," he says, ignoring me. "Let's go. This isn't a place for us." He looks around the room again. "Why come here? Why not stay home? Why would you ever agree to commit such a sacrilege?"

"I'm on medicine."

"I'll give you medicine. *Our* medicine." He sits down by her bedside, like the doctor just did, and I'm completely grossed out. I scowl at him again.

"I was sick, Bill," she says. Then she turns her head. She looks as disgusted to see him as I am.

"Was this her doing?" He points at me. I can swear I almost hear a snarl.

"Cadence did what she had to do," Bryce says.

"You agreed to her being taken by an ambulance, disciple?" he asks Bryce. "After everything I've taught you?"

"Stop calling him that!" I snap.

I hate him. He thinks I destroyed his comfortable little fuck-cult and stole his wife. It's times like this that I think I should have burnt him alive —sorry. It's just that he infuriates me. He gets up and walks over to me, just a foot away from my face, staring right into my eyes.

"Back off," I warn.

"Bill, stop," Alondra says weakly. "Both of you. Please."

"Get away from her," Bryce says, jumping up.

"Just leave, Bill," says Alondra, exhausted. "I didn't ask for you to be here. Leave the kids alone."

"*Kids?*" he says to her. "Maybe that's it. What you and I were never—"

"Bill!" she snaps. I'm surprised she has the energy. "That's enough!"

"You will pay for what you did," he says to me. Then he looks at Alondra. "I wasn't prepared for her inferno. I am now. Any magic she plans to throw at me and you, I can assure you, I'm prepared for."

"I never prepared for anything," I say. "I didn't need to. I just wanted you to drop dead for being such a perverted sick snake!"

"A snake, am I?"

That's when Mira walks in. She must have heard the yelling. Mira's in as much shock as I am at the visitor. She hates him too.

"What's he doing here?" asks Mira.

"Sister," he says, cocking his head back.

"I'm not your sister," Mira says.

"Get out," I yell. "Alondra doesn't want to go home. She needs to get well first."

"Are you going to stay in a hospital?" Reardon asks Alondra. "Are you serious? Let them poison you?"

"Bill, I..." Alondra's eyes close. It's too much for her.

"Girls, get out," Reardon says. He sits back down at Alondra's bedside and takes her hand. I want to throw up. "Leave my wife and me alone. Whatever fights we have, let's put it aside...for her. But ask her herself. She doesn't want to stay in a hospital. Do you?"

Alondra nods. Then she shakes her head. Weakly, she turns and looks out the window for a moment, then looks at me.

"Cadence," Alondra says, forcing her eyes open to look at me. I'm still looking at the satanic devil's hand clutching hers. I'm trying my best not to light it on fire. "It's all right. Thank you for your care. But this is between Bill and me."

I can't believe it. She's weak and sick, but she wants me to leave her with her nasty, perverted husband. This is why I can never like her. We have to endlessly fight, hating and loving each other.

"Let's go," Bryce says, touching my shoulder. I shrug him off. Bryce touches my back, trying again. "Let's go, Cadence."

"This is what you want?" I ask Alondra. "Are you sure? You need to get well."

"It's all right," Alondra says. "Now leave, please."

"Leave us," Reardon says, still holding Alondra's hand.

Alondra nods with her eyes closed. She says feebly, "Thank you, Cadence."

~

Why did we leave him with her!" I shout at Bryce after the elevator doors close. We're alone on our way down to the first floor. Mira's still back there in Alondra's room. As much as Mira drives me crazy, I get comfort in that. I know Mira always has Alondra's best interests in mind, and she'll fight fiercely for her. And she hates Bill Reardon more than I do.

Bryce doesn't answer. He scowls but looks down.

I'm so mad I grip my hands tightly. When the lights in the elevator flicker, Bryce looks at me in shock, because he knows I'm doing the flickering.

"Why didn't you answer your phone last night?" he snaps. "Alondra needed you."

"I didn't—"

"I needed you."

"I ..."

"You what, Kate? Why would you do that? What's gotten into you?"

We're silent as we leave the elevator and walk down the hallway. We're walking fast because we're both pissed. I don't think we've ever been this mad at each other before. But I'm still thinking of Alondra and that beast. And his hand on her. How dare he come back for her.

We walk outside through the automatic glass doors. Outside it's really dark and cold. There aren't any lights beyond the streetlights in the parking lot. The wilderness is pitch black.

Being outside is Bryce's excuse to unleash full throttle on me. "Leave me a note!" he snaps, a foot from my face. "Or voicemail. Something. Don't just walk away and not tell me where you are. Don't abandon me like that. I can't...I can't trust someone if they just close off and run away."

"It wasn't because of you, Bryce. It was—"

"What? You're always running. You run from our group. You run when Alondra's sick."

"I got her to the hospital."

"I know," Bryce says, finally simmering down. He runs his hand through his short hair. "But then you left."

"I'm sorry."

Bryce has his hands on his hips. He's staring at the hospital parking lot, shaking his head. "It's not enough. I can't trust you when I can't get a hold of you."

"I couldn't get a hold of you when you weren't at the eclipse." *Yeah. So there!*

"For the hundredth time, Cadence," he says with a sigh, "I was there to help Alondra. And I did answer your texts. But...I didn't tell you I was in town because I wanted you to go to the ceremony with the circle. Tell me, honestly, if you knew I was going to miss the eclipse and go to Atlanta, wouldn't you have gone with me?"

I don't want to fight. Bryce looks exhausted. I want to take him in my arms, but I can't. Now I've got him worked up.

"I'm sorry I didn't answer your texts," I say. "But it wasn't because of you."

Bryce shakes his head again. "I'm not so sure. I'm part of our coven. You turned your back on us. And so...you turned your back on me."

"I don't know what else to say. I'm sorry."

He shakes his head.

I force as wide a smile as I can muster and open my arms wide. "Still friends?" He hugs me, but not close.

I look back at the hospital. I'm still thinking of Alondra with that creep. "We should go back and get him away from her."

"He's her husband. It's up to her."

Outside surrounding the light of the hospital entrance is the dark forest. But the darkness isn't scary. It's inviting. I'm thinking of what Alondra said, and I'm enjoying the shadows of the trees too. I love the trees. And I like the darkness, even on a clear, moonless night like this one. I yearn to smell the leaves and touch the soil. I understand Alondra's wishes. I know that out there in the wilderness is peace. Gaia. The earth mother that we worship. And the moon and the stars. When I die, I want to die out there too.

"Just don't do it again, okay?" asks Bryce.

I nod, looking at the trees.

"Why didn't you answer me?" he asks.

"I just want to have a normal year, Bryce," I say with a shrug. And I look in his eyes. He runs his hand through his hair again, all flustered. I flash a slight grin.

"Oh, Cadence. What's *normal*?"

"No drugs, nakedness, and magic." He laughs, and I laugh in spite of myself. "Just a junior year in college. I just want to be a normal student."

"Alondra needed you." He shakes his head. I look outside at the shadowed trees again. "I needed you."

"Okay, Bryce," I say, turning back. "I'm sorry. I said I was sorry. You're right, I should have answered my phone. Okay? I'm sorry."

"You're going to have to make a choice. You have to accept who and what you are and help your friends. I saw what you just did to the lights in the elevator. You have more magic in your fingertip than Mira has after three weeks of ritual. I...I know what happened with Enora upsets you." That's an understatement. "It upset me too. I get it. But it's done. You stopped it. You have to help us and be the leader you are... Ceremonies again. Sabbaths. All of it. You have to accept this and lead us as our leader. As our witch."

I hang my head and nod like an admonished child.

"It's okay." Bryce raises my chin. "Let's go home, babe. I'll drive you back."

"No," I say. "I want to walk."

That's how I got to the hospital. I followed the sidewalks to a dirt path through the forest. It's about a mile walk from campus. Only about fifteen minutes. Of course now it's the middle of the night, so Bryce is squinting at me like I'm insane.

"I need to walk," I repeat.

"Katie, it's pitch black outside. Don't be ridiculous. I'll take you home."

"No, I need to walk. I'll meet you back at your apartment. It's not that far."

"You want to walk? Alone? In the dark? Are you sure?"

I'm absolutely sure. "I'll be fine."

He looks like he's about to object, but he nods while running his hand through his hair. He's completely exhausted, and I think he doesn't have the energy to put up a fight.

"Katie, I love you, but don't get mad when I tell you this."

"What?"

"You want a normal year but...you're not normal."

I laugh. "I'll see you back home, lover," I say and I kiss his cheek. "Go get some sleep."

8

WANDERING

Maybe Bryce is right about the dark night. I don't realize how bad it really is until I make my way deep into the forest. Then I lose the trail pretty fast. But the walk is such a joy to me. I can't see the ground, so I have to grope my way through the trunks and branches, but I know that if I keep walking in the direction I'm heading, I'll land in Hawthorne U. I think.

Crickets are everywhere. They're loud and soothing. I love their sounds.

I hear something in a bush to my right, and it sounds big. I'm guessing it's a deer. I don't really care. I like the sound of her, whatever she is.

The trees open into a large field of thick wild grass. I don't think I've ever been in this field. The grass is tall, up to my ankles, and muddy. For a moment, I realize I'm muddying up my white tennis shoes. That's okay, I don't really have a choice. I even walk through cold, shallow water. I can't see a thing. But I cup my hand and reach down into the water. I bring the water to my mouth and taste it. It's metallic and chalky. Cold. It's refreshing.

As I find myself under another canopy of trees, I realize that I am completely lost. There are no trails, only thousands of trees with thin, leafy branches hovering over me. But I move forward. It seems to only get darker. I think for a moment that perhaps I should reach into my pants pocket for my cell phone for a flashlight, but I decide against it. I'd rather just walk in the shade under Nyx—the arms of the night god. Alondra was so right. There is so much peace in the woods. I wonder if this is the direction she was looking from her window.

I take a deep breath. The fresh air is refreshing too.

In a different state of mind, I might be afraid. But I'm not afraid. I feel a rush of energy at the pit of my chest under the arms of the leafy branches. Such joy. Such blissful joy. I can't explain it. I am so happy to be among the trees, alone in the forest. I wish to never leave. My loneliness doesn't bother me, for I am not alone. I am one with the woods.

A bird flutters by me. Then another. A whole school of birds fly by me, touching my back and shoulders. That's okay. I can sense that they want me to leave because they have a nest nearby, but when I don't, one lands on my arm. It's a large, heavy black bird. A raven. I extend my arm and pet the bird slowly, marveling at the softness of its feathers. It turns its head. Its eyes flash white. Then it closes its eyes as I continue to stroke its back, as if I am soothing it.

"Amica," I say. Amica is her name. I don't know why, but I know her name.

The bird opens its white eyes and nods. "*Et nos unum sumus.*" The words are not uttered by the raven, but felt by me.

"Atman," I say. *Amen.* "Come with me, Amica," I say with a giggle.

And I walk, holding a large black bird on my outstretched arm.

The brush becomes thicker and more difficult to cross. Then I approach a slope leading down. It becomes treacherous, getting so steep that I cannot see the bottom. For all I know it's a sheer drop. All I can see are twigs and branches falling into nothingness below me. Above are leaves underneath a gorgeous starry sky.

I smell smoke. And a burning light appears far off in the distance. I turn away from the precipice and look to my left, where the light is coming from. It's a bright red flickering light, like fire. And it's growing. Is the forest burning?

It comes closer. Soon the red light is only a few feet away. Between three trees, it has become a burning pyre—I don't know who started it, but it's raging. It rises like Panthera's fire. Yes, exactly like that. And I smell sulfur. But this time I am not afraid. I look down at Amica and laugh. I think it's really funny. The raven doesn't seem to have any fear either. I pet her.

"To the door and away, turn my back from light, and into the night sky," I say, as if reading lines from a book. "Past flames that light the forest and trees, make sacred to my knees. Forgive and forget. As Gaia and I are one."

I kneel before the precipice and gently put my bird on the ground beside me. Then I pull my coat and T-shirt off my body. And my bra. I remove my dirty shoes. Then I pull down my pants and underwear. I stand naked before the precipice beneath me and stretch out my arms as wide as I can in the darkness.

As Gaia and I are one.

I look down at my bird. "Are you afraid, Amica?"

"You shall be my sacrifice." The words are not from my bird. I quickly turn and recognize it to be Reardon's voice. My eyes narrow. I search around me, ready to strike the man down in fury. I remember my anger in the hospital.

The fire and smoke have spread in the forest, forcing me to walk down the sheer precipice. Where else can I go? I understand that the villain is pulling me to meet him down there, in the darkness. Good. I shall greet him.

I grope my way down the hill. My feet guide me down the incline. I slide a few times, slipping along and slowing any fall with my hands, as I maneuver around twigs and undergrowth. Never would I normally descend such a dangerous cliff, but I am in a trance and at peace with Gaia, so I don't mind. My new friend, Amica, flutters close to me as I make my way down.

When I've descended twenty feet or so, I crouch on my knees and catch my breath for a moment. Amica lands on the ground and I pet her. Then I touch the soil and bring the dirt to my nose. I touch it with my tongue, enjoying the earthen fragrance.

I feel burning. And I see red smoke surrounding me. The flames have spread down the hillside. They warm me, but they appear to be transparent, like an illusion.

"You shall be my sacrifice," repeats Reardon.

"Fuck you, goddamn liar," I whisper. "I belong to no man. I am one with Nyx. No devil. How dare you bewitch me. In darkness, I am one with the inner shadows. Thanatos, Erebus." Then I shout out, "Wait! I'm coming, lover. Your sacrifice awaits to bring you pleasures."

"Come closer, Windstorm," says the air. The air sounds hungry.

"I'm coming!" I shout with laughter as I continue down the slope in darkness. Then I whisper ruefully, "I have the ground below, and Astraeus above that shall guide us, Amica. Gather around our poisons so that we may rub sumac leaves over his loins, stab him in the chest, or gouge out his eyes with the splinters of tree branches."

Clouds thicken—a red fog blocks the light. I can see nothing. My feet feel my way down to the bottom, stepping over bushes and through gaps between sticks and stones. Some branches cut the skin on my feet. I bleed. But I feel no pain. I will myself to feel no pain. I am spurred on by a feverish desire to hurt this man.

The incline ends and Amica returns to my shoulder. I reach down and touch a part of my leg that stings. It's sticky. Blood. I take the stickiness to my mouth and lick the saltiness with my tongue.

It is then that I see my foe. The darkness fades between two nearby trees to reveal the devil himself as he cometh clearly before me in the red mist. It is Bill Reardon, but he appears stronger, younger, and more virile than he did at the hospital. His goatee is perfectly manicured. His face is clean. He stands up straight, wearing his cape and red-and-black magician outfit, but everything is pressed and neat. He almost looks desirable, if I didn't know who he is and what a prick he is. He is leaning on a cane, waiting for me between the trees.

"Make love to me, Cadence Hawthorne, great-great-great-ancestor of Escoba and Maverick Hawthorne. Make love so I can impart my semen and together we can feel the power of your lineage."

I come close to Reardon and I embrace him. Amica darts off my hand and hits his face, making Reardon twist back for a second. I laugh and I place my lips on his. I cannot stop my laughter as our lips touch. I'm practically biting him, chewing on his lips. He breathes heavily. I rub my breasts against his body and watch as his wicked eyes stare down in rapture at my naked chest. He clutches me tighter, grabbing the crack of my ass. He's strong; his shoulders are as broad and his chest is as fit as Bryce's. This is not the aged Reardon but a conjured-up younger version of himself.

I place a finger on his lips and say quietly, "You call on family? I invoke them. I ask for Maverick and Escoba to appear by my side." I walk ten paces back from him and smile. Precisely ten. Ten paces are what is required for the spell. I don't know how I know that; I just do. He stares at my naked body ravenously, and I raise my hands high and move my fingers about through the fog as if touching the stars above. As if I'm dancing to Bacchus. "I ask that they devour you," I say with a giggle. "I, Windstorm, take you down into the shadows you so covet." And I drop my hands before him.

Two ghosts appear. Maverick, a boy, in his suspenders, and the voodoo witch Escoba, holding his hand. I look down and a snake brushes against my leg. Then another. For a flash, I lose my confidence and am afraid. Like the pile of snakes above the pyre, they swarm by my legs. It's as if they are a part of me, but they disgust me. For a moment, I fear that if I'm not careful, I could be consumed by them. Reardon stares with wild eyes at the slithering black serpents covering my feet.

"If you ever try even a taste of my skin again, these serpents shall devour you," I say, raising my arms again. "*Ishtar, Hecate, Amare.* I cast this spell, make it so, now and forevermore. I shield me from you. And I warn you—if you try to touch my skin with magic ever again, you shall feel poison from my fangs and choking from my skin that will draw you down to hell."

Amica falls on him like a stone. She pecks and claws wildly at his face. Then I drop my arms once more, as if officiating a race, and Maverick charges him from behind me. Maverick is a child in suspenders, a black boy, my ancestor, who lived two hundred years ago. His spirit transforms into a wraith with fangs that runs on all fours and jumps on him like a lion. And beside him is his mother, Escoba, the famous voodoo witch of New Orleans. She too transforms into an animal-like creature and leaps on him. They pull him to the ground. Reardon squints at me and cries out in rage. I raise and drop my arms again, to the darkness of night, and the serpents covering my feet fly at him and writhe all over his body, feasting upon him. He cries out in terror as I laugh joyously, cackling like the witch that I am.

In the recesses of my mind, I understand now. My wandering is my protection, and all this is a spell. I have been in a trance. I am unsure if it is from Alondra or myself, but the wandering was a shield protecting me against this demon. So was Amica.

Amica still sits perched on my shoulder, watching the old man being devoured by my spirits and snakes. I feel like it pleases her.

He intended to take me down, lie with me, or poison and kill me, but I resisted with my own magic and reversed his spell. Even the precipice could have meant the end of me if I hadn't used magic of my own. Without my trance, I could have rolled and plummeted down the cliff to my death. But his spell has backfired, and now I am shielded from him forever.

I turn and leave. But Amica tugs at me with her claws to go back.

"Finish him," my bird says. She doesn't talk. I *feel* her words. "Finish him."

I shake my head.

"Finish him, now. This is our chance. He will hurt you. Hurt him. Do it now!"

I laugh and pet my bird, shaking my head, and walk away from the man's screams. "This is enough."

But the bird doesn't stop tugging at me.

Somehow, I know if I return I will have no more control over myself. Indeed, I might kill him. My bird's claws begin to irk me, so I push Amica off my arm. The bird responds angrily by fluttering her wings at my neck and face and then flying off.

The fog lifts. I am still surrounded by trees, but I can see the forest more clearly now, even though it is dark. Reardon is gone. So is my bird. All that's left is the shadows and the forest. But as I gaze down, I realize that I am naked. I cover myself with my arms and feel ashamed. I search around me and realize that I don't even know where I left my clothes. I feel a rush of terror in the center of my chest. I am so confused.

～

When I knock on Bryce's door, I'm not sure what time it is. Not only have I lost my clothes, but I've lost my phone. When he opens the door to his apartment, I fall into his arms.

"He tried to kill me!" I say, crying in his arms.

"My God, Cadence, what happened?" Bryce pulls me quickly inside and shoves the door closed. The lights are dim in his apartment. I figure he was sleeping. "I've been calling you for hours! I knew I should have taken you home. You didn't answer me again. What happened?"

I'm crying.

He holds me. "What happened, baby?"

"Reardon tried to kill me. With his magic."

"Come inside. Where are your clothes? And..." He looks down at the floor. I'm tracking in blood. "God, Cadence, you're hurt."

He lets go of me and runs over to the kitchen, grabbing some paper towels. He wets them and pulls me over to his sofa. Then he kneels down and carefully washes my feet. He is so gentle. It's okay if he hurts me. The fact that he cares for me is so sweet. My heart is racing. My hands are jittery. I am so charged. So alive. It's like I'm on some kind of drug. I only wish I were still out among the trees. And I have lost my beloved new companion. My bird. Where is she? My new friend, Amica. Where did she go? She tried to protect me too.

After a few more trips to the kitchen, he's done washing my feet and legs. My cuts aren't deep, and he's managed to wash off all the blood. But he's still on his knees when he looks up at me.

I touch his hand and bring it to my upper leg. Slowly, I guide his hand over my skin and press it into my thigh. He looks at me funny. I feel so aroused. I bring his hand up higher. He jerks his hand back, but I catch it and press his fingers in and around my pussy. He stares into my eyes. I close them, enjoying his touch, pressing his hand up and down along my privates.

"Cadence, we should—"

I lift his finger to my lips and suck it. Then I move to another finger and slowly lick my tongue along that digit. Then another. I suck, gripping fingers between my lips with my eyes closed. When I open them and look down, Bryce looks bewildered.

My sex drive is so overwhelming. I don't feel like I can control it. It's the spell. It must be. I want Bryce so badly. His taste. His smell. His touch. I didn't want Reardon. I wanted to kill him. I wanted to lure him, even have sex with him, only if it meant I could destroy him. Bryce is different. But even with Bryce, I hold an irresistible desire to devour him.

I lean back against the couch cushion, take a deep breath, and guide his hand between my legs again, rubbing me once more. Slowly and carefully, I guide his fingers. He enters me with one of the fingers I was sucking. I moan, and he does too. I look down again. He gazes into my eyes, looking hungry. I groan and, for a moment, he closes his eyes in pleasure. But it's almost as if he's in a trance too. I don't like that. I want love, not magic. And so I snatch his hand from between my legs.

Holding his hand, as if I caught him stealing a cookie from a cookie jar, I shake it and ask earnestly, "Do you love me?" I search his eyes. He's taken aback and he laughs, looking at me like I'm crazy.

Well, I did just wander alone in the forest naked. Maybe I am crazy?

"Do you?" I persist.

"Yes," he says with an amused smile. "I love you, Cadence. I love you."

He's not wearing a shirt. He usually sleeps in just underwear during this time of year. I look at his rippled hard chest under the shadows, and I reach down and massage it. Then I massage his stomach and run a hand along his strong arms. He's so hot. I kneel down and violently yank down his underwear and shorts, staring at his long, erect penis. When I lift him up, he doesn't resist me, and I help lay him down on the couch. I lie on top of him.

"Wait. Cadence, I need to get something."

I kiss him on the lips ravenously. I don't want to let him go. It's like I want to eat him like an animal. I want him raw and inside me *now.*

He has to literally throw me off the couch. I land on the carpet and laugh. He's so nice, so Bryce, that he pauses while running to the bathroom and asks if I'm all right. I laugh again. It's not long before he returns. He lies on top of me, stroking the hair along my forehead, and I love his weight on me.

"Oh, Cadence, I think you are under a spell." He cocks his head, unsure.

"So," I say. "Fuck me, Bryce. Do it to me now." And I pull him close to me.

He shakes his head, but before he can object further, he's already inside. I'm pumping my pelvis slowly up and down and moaning. I love how he caresses me. He rubs my breasts and the sides of my hips. He moans too. I can just make out his face, and he looks right into my eyes again. We touch lips, and I taste him with my tongue as I continue to lift into him. But then he tries to pull away. I don't let him. He's stuck, tight in my grasp. I don't want him to ever let me go again.

"Cadence, I don't think we should," he repeats hesitantly. "I think you're under some kind of spell."

I answer by jerking up against him even harder. It feels so good. I feel his warm breath against my cheek. His breath near my ear. He finally gives in and presses up and down. I encourage him by moaning even more.

He's so deep now. It feels so good. It's like the forest. It's like we're a part of Gaia. We are one. *Et nos unum sumus.* In the wilderness, I derived comfort and safety from the trees. Now I find comfort in my lover's arms.

He stops and falls to his side on the couch, but I'm still in his grasp with him inside me. He's breathing heavily.

"Don't you love me?" I ask again.

"Yes," he says, furrowing his brow. "More than you can imagine. But this is wrong. You're under a spell."

Yet I hear hesitation in his voice. It makes me laugh—not to be mean, but because I know he's saying this more to convince himself than me. I feel like there's no stopping us anymore.

"I *am* under a spell, Bryce... My spell. Don't worry. Take me. Make... love to me. Do it now."

He gently rubs my cheek. I answer by pressing my whole body hard against him. I moan in pleasure as I thrust while we're facing each other. He touches my lips and I suck his fingers again, one after the other, as I continue to rock back and forth. Then he pushes into me, hard and fast, and I cry out in pleasure.

He's all in now, doing all the thrusting. He's moving faster and faster and I'm loving every push, every touch. Our lovemaking has become a spell of its own. And as I look at his face, he is in too much ecstasy to object to anything anymore. He digs deeper in me, loving me.

"Yes, I am your succubus," I say, breathless. "You...are under my spell, Bryce... But...it's okay. Because you love me. And I love you. I love you so fucking much."

"Oh, Cadence. I do love you. I do."

9

———

MADDIE AND THE DORM ROOM

"Where were you!" Maddie's pissed. I mean really pissed. She's clenching her fists and scowling, practically growling at me, by the door of our dorm room.

It's morning and time to get ready for school, but I've been at Bryce's all night. Luckily, I had a change of clothes in his room. It's not the first time I've stayed with my lover. It is the first time I came to his place naked, though.

"What?" I ask sleepily. That was the last thing I should have said.

"What do you mean, *what*? I was calling you all weekend."

"I was at Bryce's."

"Then why didn't you answer my call!"

I think the whole dormitory can hear her screaming. And it's not like Maddie. She's a carefree girl. She's really that mad.

"Sorry," I say with the cutest guilty expression I can muster. "Anyway, I thought you were at your house."

"It's Monday morning. I'm back because of, you know, *school*? We're in school, Cadence." Maddie shakes her head and sinks into my bottom bunk, burying her head in her hands. "I can't believe you just left her like that." I sit beside her and put my hand on her back. She looks up at me. "You left Alondra. I know you sent for help, but then you just vanished. I figured at least I'd catch up to you later that night."

"I know. I didn't call you and I forgot—"

"About me. You forgot about me. When I got back, I at least thought you'd be back in the dorm, Kate. When I called Mira and she said you weren't at the hospital or with Bryce, I thought you'd been kidnapped or something. So I called the police. I even filed a fucking police report. They searched all over campus for you. I should have known better. You don't like answering your phone anymore, apparently."

"I'm sorry," I say, rubbing her back. "I'm so sorry."

She starts crying. "I thought something terrible happened, like you were kidnapped or something."

"I kinda was."

"Huh?" That stops her tears and she looks up. "What?"

"I was under a spell. I had another wandering. But it was really weird. It was with Reardon. He cast a pervert spell on me."

But was it Reardon? As I relate the story to Maddie, I wonder. The problem with our wanderings is they're so mixed up with fantasy that some of it isn't real. Some of it is an illusion. She softens and I'm amused that talking about a witch's trance is enough to defuse her anger and make her calm down and not hate me so much. Only in Hawthorne.

"That fucker would cast a spell on you for sure, Kate. He blames you for everything."

"Then I lost my phone," I say, looking away, "and walked through the forest naked, ending up at Bryce's house."

"Wow, Katie. You walked all the way across campus, to his place, without clothes?" She's looking at me like I'm nuts now. I'm not sure that's much better than her being pissed.

"Sorry," I say again with a shrug and lean into her. "I'm so sorry I didn't call or text you, Maddie. I felt so bad after what Enora did. I just needed time to myself."

"You're really screwed up." She pushes me away, staring with wide-open eyes. I think she really believes I've lost my mind. "Next time, just text me. Tell me you're okay, at least, and I won't worry."

"Okay."

"We have to go."

We do? Where?

She jumps up and grabs a book from our desk. It's her art history textbook. Then she grabs her phone and starts texting.

She's smiling, back to her bubbly self. How does she do that? She's the only one I know that can be furious and then just let everything go as if nothing ever happened—the only one except her mom, Aunt Jane.

"The evil that Mira was talking about is Reardon," I say.

She nods absentmindedly as she types on her phone.

"He tried to touch me last night using his spell."

That gets her attention. "What a fucking creep," Maddie says.

I'm still sitting on my mattress. I just nod. Then I yawn. I came to Bryce's pretty late—it was probably three in the morning—and I didn't get much sleep.

"I'm just glad you're okay," Maddie says.

"Who are you texting?"

"Mira. She wanted to know you're safe."

Maddie shoves the book under her arm and grabs my copy, stuffing it in my black backpack for me. She doesn't have a backpack. She lost it. You know, she's the irresponsible one out of the two of us. At least she used to be.

"Time for lecture, okay, bitch?" Maddie asks with a rueful smile, handing me the backpack. God, it's already ten?

"Friends?" I ask, still sitting on my bed.

She rolls her eyes. "I'm mad because you didn't answer your phone, Katie. Not because I don't love you."

10

———

ART CLASS

Maddie and I arrive at our art history lecture. I'm in the front row in order to sit near Bryce. There aren't any seats left, so Maddie sits directly behind us. Bryce is leaning over the stage in front of us, rummaging through papers in his big brown leather bag, while the professor, Dr. Riker, is prepping his computer at the podium.

"Feeling better?" Bryce asks absentmindedly as he looks through some essays we wrote last week.

"Yeah. After seeing you last night."

He raises an eyebrow and smiles. Then he returns to rummaging through papers. "I don't see your essay in here."

"I was going to get it done but something distracted me." *Like running through the wilderness naked and then making love to you.* "Look at it this way," I say with a shrug, "now you don't have to worry about unfairly grading my work."

"Yeah," he says with a nod, flipping through another page. "I can just fail you, Ms. Hawthorne."

I shove his shoulder toward the aisle on his right and he laughs.

"Seriously, Cadence, ask Riker for an extension."

"Can I get an extension, Dr. Wallace?" I ask Bryce, stupidly blinking my eyes.

"No." He takes a deep breath and shakes his head. "Ask your professor."

I stick my tongue out.

Dr. Riker clears his throat. The noise is magnified by a microphone on the collar of his gray shirt. He's wearing an informal shirt with jeans, but Dr. Riker can pull that off because—with his spectacles and clean-cut hair, like my Adonis boyfriend, sitting to my right—somehow he always looks formal. The lecture hall's nearly full. And noisy. Class hasn't started yet. Dr. Riker's history class is really popular—the second most popular class, next to Alondra's last year. He picks up a laser pointer. The lights dim and everybody becomes quiet.

"We're going to discuss Leonardo da Vinci."

Again? We seem to always be talking about Leonardo da Vinci. I love his artwork, but I was hoping to cover a lot more artists this semester. A slide shows the *Mona Lisa*.

"Leonardo is the quintessential Renaissance man. His genius crossed so many fields, including art, anatomy, architecture, and physics." The slide changes to a drawing of water. "But most amazingly, he incorporated his studies of science with art. This is his drawing of flowing water."

"Are we going to Alondra's tonight?" I whisper to Bryce. Bryce told me that dickhead Reardon took her home. I want to check on her. And pay a visit to Professor Reardon.

Bryce leans over and whispers in my ear, "You want to?" His breath smells like spearmint. I turn and look dreamily into his baby blues.

"We can bring the coven."

He shakes his head. "Don't think they'll come. Everyone's mad at you for abandoning Alondra that night." *Oh yeah.* "They assume the circle's broken. Well, we can go, but I'm not sure Bill will let you in."

"Why?"

He shushes me. Dr. Riker is looking directly at us.

"Note that the drawing is similar to his drawing of flowing hair," continues Dr. Riker. There's a close-up of a woman's hair from a painting. "*La Scapigliata.* The flow of the lady's hair is striking, but so is Leonardo's love for the curves and his yearning to understand the flow of water."

"Water, one of the four elements, right, Katie?" Bryce whispers in my ear. "Like Alondra. I want to see her so much too... Of course... But—"

"But what?" I say a little too loudly.

"The point I'm trying to make," continues Dr. Riker, glancing at me, "is that Leonardo brought a combination of science and art."

This time I put my finger over my lips and shush Bryce before he answers me, but it's too late.

"Mr. Wallace," my professor says. "Will you be so kind as to accompany me on stage? I'm having some difficulty with my slides. I'd like to move on a hundred years to the Netherlands. We're going to discuss the Dutch artists, including my second favorite painter, Rembrandt."

Bryce runs up the steps to the podium. Dr. Riker turns off the mike on his collar and starts arguing with him. He gestures toward me. It takes them a long time to get the slides to come up on the screen. Of course an art class without slides is totally useless.

The murmuring behind me gets crazy. This would be the perfect time to check my phone. I touch my pocket but then remember I lost my phone. Dad's going to seriously kill me.

As I'm sitting, getting bored, Maddie taps my shoulder from behind.

"Going to Alondra's tonight?" She probably heard us.

"Yeah. Can you come?"

"I want to."

"The sisters are mad at me?"

"Yeah. But do you care? I mean, no one is expecting you to lead another session after what happened. Anyway, a lot of us want to skip this Friday. Too spooked."

When a painting of a group of guys in black hats and ruffled white collars—pilgrim clothes—appears on the large screen above, Bryce jumps back down the steps and sits next to me. Then he turns to me and Maddie and, this time, he's the one who puts a finger to his lips.

Maddie taps my shoulder again. "What time?"

"I'm not sure if we can," says Bryce. He's talking carefully while watching the professor. "Bill's not allowing any visitors."

"*Fuck Bill!*" Maddie is really loud.

"Please," Dr. Riker says, looking down at us from the podium, "please everyone be silent during lecture. If you have a question, you can come up after class."

If you have a question—that's so nice. Dr. Riker's such a nice professor.

He reminds me of Bryce. I feel bad for talking. I sink down in my chair, turn to Bryce, and cover my mouth. Bryce puts a finger to his lips again.

"Here's a self-portrait of Rembrandt. Notice the significant change in style from the Renaissance period. The dark brown and yellow tones."

"We should go anyway," Maddie says.

"Fuck yeah," I whisper to her. Maddie laughs.

Bryce leans his head on his hand, closes his eyes, and shakes his head.

11

PICKING LILIES

I grab my boyfriend's hand after getting out of his BMW in Alondra's dirt parking lot. There are no cars in her driveway. Even Alondra's swanky Jaguar has been moved. There's just her decorative antique red carriage.

I'm wearing a loose-fitting black dress. I'm regretting not bringing a sweater. It's cold. Mr. Handsome is in a button-down and slacks. The leaves are turning, and that reminds me that it's almost my favorite holiday: Halloween. As we walk onto a grassy field of weeds, an animal scurries along dead leaves and it makes me jump. I grab Bryce's arm and he laughs.

"What is it?" he asks.

"Nothing."

"Can you explain to me why you can wander through the forest naked and commune with the trees at night but you're afraid to walk in Alondra's front yard?"

Good point. Honestly, I don't know, but when I'm in a trance, things are different. I feel so confident and strong. Now I need a little help from my boyfriend.

Alondra's house is not usually creepy, but a fog rolled in this afternoon, causing a white cloud to cover everything. It's humid too and my cheeks are moist. There's light coming from one of the windows upstairs. The light spreads out in the fog like yellow smoke over her elegant mansion. The lawn is browning a little with the turn of the seasons, and under the fog at twilight, it's creepy.

"Hey, guys!" cries Maddie from behind.

I jump in the air. "Don't do that!"

"We didn't hear you," says Bryce, chuckling.

"I walked from the dorms," Maddie replies. Then she hugs me. "Hey, bitch."

We make our way up onto Alondra's elegant white columned deck. The lights that usually illuminate the steps are not on, and it's dark under the fog. Maddie knocks on the door, and who do you suppose answers?

Bill Reardon. He's dressed in ancient clothes. I've seen them before in ceremonies. They're baggy, wrinkled, and brown and held by a rope, making him resemble a Capuchin monk. He's glaring at us with the door half-open.

"I told you she can't have visitors, disciple," he says to Bryce, ignoring Maddie and me. "You have to leave."

He might be a little more cordial to my boyfriend, but I know Bryce hates him. Bryce told me that the two of them had an abusive relationship when Reardon was our High Wizard. He bullied Bryce into doing gruesome satanic work like some kind of ceremonial janitor: cleaning blood, pieces of tissue, and sinew from animals, cleaning up after sex, cleaning feces off instruments and planks, and a number of other unspeakable things that I stopped Bryce from elaborating on. Bryce said he tried to leave the circle a few times, and Bill threatened to curse his family. Since being "freed" when Alondra and I cast Reardon out, Bryce has recovered from his brainwashing and hates Reardon as much as I do.

"We just want to see Alondra," Bryce says.

"No."

"What of the Sabbath?" Maddie asks Reardon. He's just about to shut the door on us. "Can we hold it in the backyard this Friday? We can even go around to the side yard."

"No. No more meetings. Not now."

"Is this what Alondra wants?" asks Bryce, squinting.

"It's what my wife shall have," Reardon snaps. "You all nearly killed her with Western medicine." Then he looks at me. "And you nearly killed all of us."

"We saved her life," I say.

I'm ready for this. I think this man is taking advantage of Alondra because she's sick and weak. I also want to tell him off for what he did to me the other night. It gets rid of my fear of him. He disgusts me.

"Good day to you, Ms. Hawthorne." He sneers. "And the rest of your young friends."

"Have her come down," I say. "If she asks us to leave, we'll go."

"This is my house, young lady," he snaps. "I think sometimes you forget. I will care for my wife any way I see fit. She cannot be seen. Now go!"

"You probably hope she dies so you can claim her inheritance." My statement is so nasty that Bryce lets go of my hand and looks at me in shock.

"Cadence!" snaps Maddie.

"Go away!" Reardon says with wide-open eyes. "Now! Get out!"

I squint and he locks his eyes on mine.

He is about to shut the door, but I weaken him. I don't know how, but I stop him from closing the door. Then I raise my arms into the air.

I don't say anything. I don't need to. Instead, there's a flutter of wings behind me as if my arms are flapping like a bird. A chilly wind blows and clears some of the fog. My arms are not wings; the sky becomes a shade darker, not from fog, but from a torrent of black birds flying from behind me. Reardon unlocks his stare and looks around me in amazement. Then one bird—my companion, Amica—lands on my outstretched arm. Amica caws at Reardon. I distinctly hear her say, *"Back. Back."* I feel a trance coming on. Bryce grabs my shoulder and shakes his head, warning me, but it's too late. I feel elated with a sudden surge of power.

What a sense of peace and tranquility. Any sense of anxiety has faded, and I hope Reardon will try to do something stupid so I can hurt him. I dare him to. I challenge him with my glare.

"Cadence, calm down," warns Maddie.

Surrounding us are a hundred black birds, circling or walking around Alondra's front yard. Some are standing on the porch, others are fluttering and making noise above the deck, and still others are walking beside my feet.

"Get back, black witch!" cries Reardon in fear. "Stay away from me."

"I asked you to keep her in the hospital," I say. "You've hurt her. She needs medicine. Now I simply ask that you let us in so we can see her. If she wants us to go, we'll go. Open the door."

Bryce touches my shoulder again. His eyes are wide now. He looks afraid. Afraid of what? Me?

Amica repeats, "*Back, back.*"

"Leave me and my wife alone!" snaps Reardon. "She's too sick, I tell you! Leave her fate to the moon and stars."

I walk right up to Reardon and push him inside the house.

It's dark in there, with only a dim light upstairs. I could just walk upstairs and see her. But I don't. Because I know now she's not even there. It's been unveiled to me by the trees in the forest. I don't know how I know, but I know.

I approach Reardon the same way he approached me in the hospital and press a fingernail deep into his chest. Bryce touches my shoulder for a third time, but I bat him off.

"Watch yourself, liar," I say, "I know the spell you cast on me. Do something like that to me again and I will torment you a hundred times over. Got me?"

"I never cast a spell on you," he says, shaking his head.

I walk back out onto the deck. Amica is still with me, and I pet her as she perches on my arm. With my other arm, I gesture toward the door and say indifferently, "*Clausus.*" The black birds around us leap into flight and swarm the door, forcing Reardon to throw the door closed. A hundred black birds collide, one after the other, pounding against the closed wooden door.

My friends are speechless. They're looking at me the way they did when I conjured the bonfire spell and nearly burned the other witches alive last year.

"Let's go," I say.

Behind me the birds continue to throw themselves against the door. I look back and see a stack of the birds piling up, bloodied and shaking, as more and more birds crash down on them.

"He's a bad man, isn't he, Amica?" I ask my bird, petting her. "A bad, bad man."

"Cadence?" Bryce says.

I push the bird from my arm and she flies off. "Huh?"

"You all right?"

"Wonderful," I say with a furrowed brow. "Why?"

"You're scaring me."

Maddie doesn't say a thing. She's already down the hill, rushing back to our dorm.

"I'm just glad Alondra is feeling better," I say as Bryce turns on the ignition. He drives us out of the dirt parking lot.

I'm looking out the car window at the shadows in the wilderness. I can see her in my mind, gathering herself like a ball in her black cloak— the same way Enora did—meditating on feeling better. She's still sick, but she feels peace out there.

"How do you know she's better?" he asks.

"I can see her in the trees. She's telling me so." Bryce shakes his head in total confusion. I laugh and shrug. "I can *feel* her telling me, you know?"

12

____

ALL HALLOWS' EVE

Halloween at Hawthorne is more popular than Christmas. The whole university goes nuts with everybody wearing costumes all week, including the professors. Dr. Riker wore glasses with tape, carried an old 1980s calculator, and slicked his hair back. He was a total nerd. Well, people say costumes fit them. Bryce has been wearing an old person's mask with wrinkles and long thin white hair. I'm not wearing any costume—sort of. As of late, I've been using darker mascara and even wearing black lipstick. I've had black nail polish since last year, but the facial makeup is new. I look totally goth. My best friend, Maddie, does too. Like Mira, all the sisters of the coven wear black. Someone who's never seen us around campus might think we're wearing witch costumes. Or even guess what we actually are.

Every year there's a huge bash at the Psi Kappa Psi frat house. The Billington House. It's one of the oldest buildings in Georgia. It's perched on top of a hill surrounded by the shadows of the forest. It's haunted. People say Alondra's ancient relative, Abigail, stands alone by the window facing the hilltop, holding a candle by her chest, late at night. Escoba, *my* relative, roams the halls too.

The story of the haunting tells of the voodoo witch Escoba taking a fancy to Josiah, Abigail's husband. Escoba and Josiah had an illegitimate son, Maverick. Then Escoba cursed Abigail, killing her family. Well, Escoba was later found dead in her rocking chair in the Billington House with a knife in her chest. No one really knows if Abigail murdered her, but it's suspected. It's a really awful, grisly tale of revenge; that's why their spirits roam the halls. And that's probably also why Alondra, Abigail's distant relative, and I, Escoba's descendant, never completely got along.

I've never seen Escoba and Maverick in the haunted house. But I did see them roaming my dormitory and dining hall last semester.

Anyway, while we're walking up the hill to the house, I hear shouting and laughter. The party's already raging, but the raucousness is a good thing, because the paths between the woods and the house are rather spooky. Bryce is holding my hand.

"Why are you standing so close to me?" Bryce asks with a chuckle.

"I am?"

He nods.

"Must be love," I say stupidly.

"Or you're afraid again." He shakes his head.

"I don't like this place, especially at night," I say with a shrug.

"I'll try to keep you from hurting anybody."

He opens a creaky old wooden gate and we head up to the front door. I look at the window in the center of the three-story brick building and think about Abigail again. That's where legend says her ghost holds her candle. But now, rainbow-colored lights are flashing from the haunted window. And the noises inside the house aren't scary. I hear heavy metal music. I recognize Ozzy Osbourne's voice, which I love. We don't have to knock on the door. It's ajar; Bryce just pushes it open.

A guy dressed like an axe-murdering clown greets him by the entryway.

"Bryce!" shouts the clown. "How you doing, man?" He puts both hands on his shoulders. Then he reaches down into a barrel full of ice and hands us each a beer. A few other people shout, "Bryce!" He's very popular here. He was a member of the fraternity when he was a student. A few more people say hi, and I get lost in the shuffle. Bryce turns and looks back with concern, but I smile and gesture for him to go enjoy himself.

I enter a cramped living room. It's a big room, but it's full of bodies, shoulder to shoulder. A large wicker chair is occupied by someone in a purple dinosaur suit holding a bong. The dinosaur stands up and gestures for me to sit, then lifts off its head, with the ripping sound of Velcro, and takes a hit. It's Nick, Maddie's old boyfriend from last year. He offers the bong to me, but I shake my head.

"Enjoy the party, Katie," Nick says with a slur. He reeks of the musky weed and he walks like he's also tipsy. I sit in the large wicker chair. It's dizzying, and a bit surreal, watching so many costumed bodies dancing before me. Or maybe it's the marijuana in the air. I don't know. I sip some beer.

"Hey, Cadence," says a voice I recognize. Standing above me is Mira. She looks around but there's nowhere to sit, so she just kneels down next to me. She's holding a chocolate pastry that looks like an éclair. And she's not in a costume. She's wearing black like me.

"How's Alondra?" I ask. It's hard to hear my own voice over the blaring music. I recognize the song. It's "Sabbath Bloody Sabbath" by Black Sabbath—very appropriate, looking at her.

"She's okay. The infection is gone but she still has pain."

"How? If she's not sick?"

"The cancer."

"Is Reardon still keeping her prisoner?"

"He sure is scared of you," she says with a sly grin. She looks at me as if I'm some kind of rock star or something. I think that's stupid. "All the sisters heard about the birds. We talked about it at our last Sabbath. We're just so sorry you and Bryce couldn't make it."

"What last Sabbath? I thought Reardon forbade meetings in the house?"

"Enora ran it on Hilltop Bluff," she says, touching my hand. I can't help but think she's touching me with a handful of chocolate frosting and white custard. And as I think of it, she takes a big bite of her pastry. Then, with her mouth full, she says, "There's a bunch of cakes and candy in the kitchen. You should get some."

"I've already eaten."

"Your dress is pretty," she says with a lascivious smile.

I drink more beer from my bottle. It's an IPA. A bit too sharp for my taste.

I sway to the music. Mira doesn't. She remains on her knees, stiff as a board.

"I love this house, Cadence," Mira says. I recall last year when I watched her run a séance here. It's amusing how she hated me back then. Now I'm the only one she wants to talk to. "You can feel the haunting presence." Mira lights up as she looks around the room. "The ghosts. Your family, Katie."

I shrug and drink more beer.

On the floor is a vampire wrestling with someone in a white sheet, who is supposed to be a ghost, I think. A couple of other guys, sitting on the floor dressed in football uniforms, are cheering them on. But as the white sheet rolls off, I see a girl in a red bikini, and the wrestling seems more lewd than combative.

"Why is Enora still here?" I ask. "I thought she was just visiting."

"Do you care? I mean, I thought you wanted us to stop meeting anyway."

"Only because of Enora. I don't trust her."

"I don't trust her either. I wish you'd run our meetings. Your power is greater." Mira licks her fingers and stands up. "I'm gonna get something to drink. You want another beer?"

I shake my head.

"I'll be back."

Someone screams. A dinosaur nearly tackles Mira to the floor, shouting, "*Drink and stack!*" I jump. It's Nick acting like a complete idiot. "*Drink and stack!*" he shouts again. Mira nearly punches him in the face, but she pulls her punch and pushes him onto the wrestlers on the floor instead. "*Who wants to drink and stack?*" he shouts, trying to get up. He's so drunk that he falls on more people.

I've completely lost Bryce. I said it was okay for him to see his friends, but I meant for a few minutes, not the whole party.

I watch people clear a table on the other side of the room and decide I don't like sitting all by my lonesome anymore. I get up and make my way to the table. The music changes to something techno, and the lights swirl a bit. I chug down my beer. There's another bucketful of ice and beer bottles. (They're everywhere.) I grab another.

That's when someone throws her arms around me. A girl with a big fluffy velvet top hat and a brown suit with purple buttons and a purple collar—the Mad Hatter—squeezes me tightly. It's Maddie. Her breath reeks of alcohol. She came with Rock, but I don't see him.

"You want to play, Katie?" Maddie asks. The techno is only getting louder.

"Play what?"

"Drink and stack. We're gonna stack blocks. Come on, it'll be fun."

My friend Tammy, dressed in a white bunny suit, is arranging all of us in line. The line is zigzaggy and crazy, but by this time, half the people here are too inebriated for order. But it frustrates Tammy as she tries to gather people together. She waves excitedly when she sees me.

"Drink up, bitch," Maddie says, raising her beer in a toast to me as we get in line.

I do. I drink a lot of my beer. This one isn't a tangy IPA.

"Everyone," Tammy shouts. "Hey... Hey... Hey, *SHUT UP!*" Someone turns down the music. Tammy laughs. "Listen, this is gonna be so much fun! This is a block game. You're gonna build and then remove and you're gonna be timed. Okay? You each need to stack four rows of three blocks —for those who can't do math, four times three makes twelve. Stack them and then remove three blocks, one at a time. But you only have thirty seconds, so be quick about it. I'll keep time. If you can't set up four rows in time, you have to chug. If you pull out three blocks and the blocks fall, you have to chug. Got it? The person behind you goes and adds another four rows. You have to keep stacking the rows on top of each other until they come down ..." She takes a break, and by now I have no idea what the hell she's talking about. But this should be easy, because many people in line are a lot more drunk than me. "Technically, you can remove from the lower rows, but that would be riskier. Right? Whoever knocks down all the blocks has to chug beer. Then the next one stacks another four rows. And so on. And so on. Got it? 'Cause if you don't...guess what?"

"*Chug!*" shout a bunch of people stupidly.

"Right," Tammy says with a laugh.

I'm looking around the room. Where's my Bryce?

"Ready?" asks Tammy.

The table has a pile of blocks and a bunch of empty Jenga boxes.

I look around at all the costumed bodies dancing and swaying to the techno music. Then my eyes fall on something I can't believe. Near a corner of the room, I see Bryce. He's standing beside a woman with dark makeup, wearing a black dress similar to mine, who's leaning against a wall staring at me. It's Enora.

Mira stands beside me in line. She has no interest in playing; she just wants to watch. I grab her by the elbow and point at Bryce. But when I look back, my boyfriend and my archenemy are gone.

"What?" Mira asks, furrowing her brow.

"Did you see her?"

"Who?"

"Enora."

Mira looks at me funny. Then she gives me her stupid sly smile. "You casting a spell or something?" I think she's hoping I am.

"Maddie?" I turn around, but she's got her arms around Rocky and the two of them have stepped out of the line.

I look at the table. The first person is Nick. He places his blocks on top of each other without any order, turns, and bows to our line, and instead of removing three, he purposefully knocks his rows down. Everyone laughs and Tammy hands him his beer. Nick chugs down a beer; then a few people help carry the purple dinosaur away from the line.

I turn back and Enora's there again. Again, Bryce is talking, but she's ignoring him. She's glaring at me. She places a hand on his arm and runs her fingers down it—*while looking at me.* Then she closes her eyes with pleasure and laughs.

I practically shove Mira and point again.

"What?" Mira asks.

They're gone again. Replacing Bryce and Enora by the wall are a girl in a cheerleader outfit and a boy with torn clothes and zombie makeup. I reach into my pocket and take out my cell phone (I got my dad to buy me a new one) and text Bryce's number. "*Where are you? Come back. NOW.*"

"Was Enora coming to the party?" I ask Mira.

She shrugs.

"I just saw her with Bryce."

The next player in line is a short blond girl in a vampire costume.

Unlike Nick, she's actually playing for real, carefully but quickly aligning the four rows while Tammy stares at her stopwatch. This young girl's sober and easily stacks four columns and removes three central blocks.

Maddie comes over. "Hey, guys," she says. Rocky's holding her by the waist. "Looks like you're almost up, Kate. You playing, Mira?"

"No. Just watching Windstorm cast a spell."

"I'm not casting a spell," I say, shaking my head.

"I think she's going to," Mira says to Maddie, cupping her mouth as if whispering.

I turn to Maddie. "Did you know Enora's here?"

Maddie shakes her head.

"Who's Enora?" asks Rocky. With his free hand he drinks beer.

"A witch," I tell him. Well, it is Halloween. He doesn't think anything of it.

The next player is drunk. He's a senior named Nathan. I know him from my economics study group. A nice guy. Nathan stacks the blocks carefully. Everyone's amazed that he manages to add four rows. There are eight rows stacked and I'm next.

"Nervous, Kate?" asks Tammy with a chuckle. "It looks pretty high."

I shrug and drink more beer.

I almost spit out my beer. From the corner of my eye, I see Bryce and Enora again. This time Enora is standing close to him. Real close. She reaches up and kisses him passionately while running her hand along his chest and waist. Bryce gropes her ass. Then she brushes her long dark hair back, laughs, and looks right at me again.

All the colorful, swirling lights cut off for a second, and it turns dark. There's a scream in the darkness and people laugh. Then the lights turn back on.

"Just a circuit break," says Rock. "It's amazing this old building has any electricity at all."

"Where's Bryce?" Maddie asks me.

"That's what Cadence keeps seeing." Mira seems excited. "Did you shut the energy off just then, Windstorm?"

I did, but I shake my head. My heart is racing and I'm grinding my teeth, wanting to kill them. But when I'm about to do the deed, Bryce is gone. I quickly pull out my cell phone. No answer.

I'm next. I walk out of line to search for my boyfriend, so I can inflict bodily harm on him, and Tammy grabs my elbow. "You're next, Katie. Come on."

I shake my head hesitantly.

I'm surrounded by costumed boys and girls I don't know, staring at me, shouting for me to play. I'm dizzy. Sick. As if I am drunk, but I'm not. I look back at the corner of the room and, thankfully, my boyfriend's not there.

"Are you okay?" asks Maddie. As drunk as she is, she looks concerned.

"I saw Bryce."

Maddie looks in the direction I'm looking, squinting.

Mira has a really wide smile.

"Katie," says Tammy pleasantly, "come on, we're all waiting for you. You ready?" She raises her brow. "You okay?"

I look down at the stupid table. Then I look back one more time but don't see my boyfriend. It must be a vision. The past? That's probably it. It's probably a vision of the past, like seeing a ghost. Right? I'm not so sure. But everyone's waiting for me to play their stupid game. So I walk over to the table to get it over with.

On the table is the column of blocks. It reminds me of the white columns that stand along the wide patio before Alondra's house. It's like the light wood blocks are holding up her house. It's delicate. It could easily topple over and fall apart like a deck of cards. And now it's up to me. I have to keep it together. I finish the beer I'm drinking, and everybody cheers stupidly and wildly. It's like I'm already chugging before I lose. Then someone in a gladiator suit hands me another.

I haven't felt my phone buzz. Bryce hasn't answered me. Why? Is this payback or something? *Or is he really with her?*

A couple in black robes and white masks are holding hands behind me. Funny, I didn't see them before. Their get-up reminds me of a secret society. Beside them is a girl in a deer mask with antlers. She's in a tight red bikini. That looks weird. And behind the deer is a girl in a purple cloak. I've never seen this girl before. She has spooky red contacts and a black mark on her forehead that reminds me of Ash Wednesday, but it's in the shape of an upside-down cross. She's licking her lips. She lifts an open palm, and there's a red pentagram painted on it.

"Go ahead, Katie," says Tammy.

Get it together, Cadence. Just put the dumb blocks on top of each other and be done with it. Then go search for your boyfriend. If he's still your boyfriend.

My eyes stray toward the corner again. I'm not expecting to see them, but this time I do. My body shakes. Bryce is standing there in Enora's arms, and the two of them are kissing passionately. Enora only has on her bra and, as the lips of my lover touch Enora's, she's still looking at me, as if taunting me. Challenging me. Just like she did when we had our last Sabbath. Enora is slowly unbuttoning Bryce's shirt while he massages her tits underneath her bra.

"Are you ready?" asks Tammy again, confused.

Yeah, I'm ready. I'm going to fucking kill them!

I touch the pile of blocks. One of them rises an inch over the table. Tammy is staring at it.

"Here we go," says Tammy a little more cautiously. She presses a button on her watch.

I take a block from the middle, leaving only one block at the center holding up the tower. Physics dictates that the column should collapse, but it doesn't. People look in wonder. I set it vertically at the top.

"You can stack your rows first," Tammy says, trying to help me.

I turn back and watch Enora and Bryce making out. They are bare-chested and pressed close to one another, French kissing, sucking, and practically fucking right before my eyes.

I put a block vertically on top of the column without even looking.

"You only have to make rows," says Tammy. "Why are you laying them on top of each other?"

"They're gonna fall if you do that!" shouts someone behind me, laughing.

"She's already out! She hasn't stacked her rows!"

The column doesn't even teeter. I add a few more blocks standing vertically. Then I look at the tower. I start working quickly, stacking the blocks up in a single column on top while taking them out of the center of the tower. There are now about twelve standing on top of each other, up to my forehead, with large gaping spaces in the middle of the structure. There is no way, under normal dynamics, that the column would still be up.

"That's not what you were supposed to do," Tammy says, shaking her head. "Now how are you going to remove three more?"

"She wants to drink!" says someone.

"How is it still up?" asks another.

Bryce runs his fingers along Enora's naked back. He bends her down, still kissing her, and runs his other hand along her breast. Enora opens her eyes, throws her hair back, and glares at me once more.

All of a sudden, with mindless speed, I remove blocks from the bottom of the structure. I take them from the sides. The blocks should collapse, but they're not falling.

"I can't believe it's up," says Rocky behind me.

The blocks don't even sway. A couple of people who were ignoring our game are now surrounding me. In fact, most of the people at the party are staring at the table. It looks like the greatest feat of balance of all time.

I'm done with seconds to spare. I take my beer and start chugging it down anyway, because I really don't give a fuck anymore, and my crowd goes wild. Everyone is touching my back and congratulating me. As I drink, Mira looks at the corner that's been holding my attention and suddenly loses her amused smile. Her eyes open wider. But it seems she's the only one seeing what I'm seeing.

"What the hell?" Mira says.

I feel a rush of energy from my legs to my throat. Absolute raw fury.

"And thirty!" says Tammy. She looks at the blocks in shock. Not only is there a column of twelve stacked on top of each other, but there are three or four rows with gaping spaces on the sides. It is absolutely impossible that the structure is not teetering and collapsing onto the table.

"YOU BITCH!"

The words are screamed through the air, but nothing is coming from my mouth. They're uttered from my mind. But everyone hears the words and is searching the room. And then a whirlwind, like a gale, rushes through the Billington House. The blocks fly from the table all over the room as if from an explosion. A few of these projectiles hit my face and chest.

The lights shut off again. But this time, they don't turn back on.

I quickly make my way to the door, groping in the dark. A few people yell and scream, and this time it's not a joke.

Outside the Billington House, it's quiet. Cold. I'm running as fast as I can down the hill and onto the dirt path through the forest.

"Cadence!" cries Mira from behind.

"Leave me alone!"

"It's a trick!" yells Mira. "A spell. It can't be real!"

I don't believe her. It looked real. Very real. And I still haven't gotten a text from him. Bryce would never ignore my text or call. Unless...they were together. It was real. I know it was real. Because I'm a witch. It was not a hallucination or an illusion. It really happened. And Enora, that disgusting monster, wanted me to watch. She wanted me to see it. Did she bewitch him? Bryce told me he hated her. Maybe she cast a spell? Why would he touch her like that? Put his lips on her? Hold her tits! Naked and...

Mira runs close behind me, in her long black dress, gasping for air. I whirl around and she backs up, afraid. "Stay away! I'll hurt you!"

"Cadence," she says with her hand out.

"Keep away! I can't control myself!"

"It can't be Bryce," Mira says, shaking her head. "I'll talk to Enora."

That was the wrong thing to say.

"*Talk to her!*" I shout. My voice is guttural, inhuman. Rain starts to pour from the sky. "If you're my sister, you'll never even look at her again! Or Bryce! I hope they both...God." I start to cry. Mira steps forward, but I warn her again. "How could he! Why?"

"Cadence, it might not really have happened."

"You saw it, right?"

Mira nods.

"I want to kill him," I say, my eyes narrowing. My heart is bursting in my chest. My God, if Bryce were here now, I think I would. I would strike him down dead.

I'm afraid. I'm afraid I don't have control of myself.

"I'll tear him apart! ...I will."

Mira just nods.

Maddie runs over. She's out of breath too. I've run so far that I'm almost down the hill, near the lights that border the walkways on campus. It's pouring. Behind Maddie, far up the hill, I can see shadows leaving the Billington House. No electricity means no more party. Everyone's leaving. I ended their stupid party. Good.

"What's wrong with her?" Maddie asks Mira, out of breath. "What did she see?"

"Enora," says Mira, still catching her breath, "holding Bryce."

"Oh my God," Maddie says. "She'll kill him."

13

BUT I SEE FRACTALS

WELL, I DIDN'T KILL HIM.

I'm sitting alone in the back row of the one-hundred-seat auditorium where my Economics 101 class is held, sipping a latte—it's my second this morning—trying to keep my eyes open while I take notes. My economics professor, Dr. Garson, is really boring. His voice lulls you to sleep. I see a few students nodding their heads beside me. I'm doing that too. That's why I chose the back row, but that doesn't help prevent my professor from noticing me because there are only about thirty seats occupied in the entire room.

Prerequisites. What's one to do? I'm already halfway through my undergraduate major. I could have chosen a basic math or science class, but I figured that one day I'll have to make money. I'm not sure Dr. Garson's talking about money.

"We're going to take a look at comparative advantage." As boring as he is, he does love his subject. He gets excited. But it's over *comparative advantage*, for God's sake. He's a short, pudgy, bald man wearing glasses, a white T-shirt, and brown slacks. He's pacing like Dr. Riker's been known to do. He aims a remote toward the center screen on stage, but nothing happens. Then he starts fumbling with his remote.

I get a text. It's Bryce. Does he actually think I'm going to fucking talk to him? I think it's the twentieth message since last night. Funny, I didn't see him returning my text while he was fondling Panthera's tits. I ignore yet another message with the naughty pleasure of knowing how much he hates it when I don't answer his texts and calls.

"You must understand how comparative advantage calculates labor with units produced and can show favor of one agent over another in free trade."

What? Like *W-T-F*? This is why I came to the lecture. I have no idea what the hell he's saying.

"In the early nineteenth century..." Finally some history. "David Ricardo put the law to use, comparing two countries: England and Portugal." He walks up to the whiteboard and starts jotting down equations. *Isn't this math?* "If you take these two countries and observe their production of wine and cloth," he drawls on, "you can see that England can produce more cloth than wine and Portugal can produce more wine than cloth. The subsequent trade between the two countries allows for more goods to be available to both nations than autarky would. Right? Now let's move on to Harberler."

He is speaking English, right? And now he's moving on as I'm falling behind.

I can't stop seeing Bryce and Enora together in my head. It's like the vision is imprinted in my mind. Especially the bitch's sardonic smile. Oh, how I hate her. And I hate Bryce too.

My phone buzzes again. *Fuck off.*

Of course not all the calls and texts are from Bryce. A whole lot of them are from Maddie. And one, last night, was even from Mira. But I didn't call her back either.

I angrily throw my hair back and stare at Dr. Garson again. He's gesturing to a large graph on the center monitor. He's smiling and looks really excited about it. I take a deep breath and rub my eyes.

"Harberler's ideas were essential in creating a better understanding of the growing international market of the early twentieth century."

I look up. The lights are dimmed. I wish they weren't.

To my right, an exit door cracks open, letting in the early-morning sunshine.

A boy catches my eye. I know him. Kurt. Kurt's chewing gum and smiling at me. With his crew cut and well-built body, he's a total jock. His girlfriend, Veronica, is staring at Dr. Garson in confusion. I don't think Veronica knows what Garson's talking about either.

My phone buzzes again. I get it in order to finally answer him. My plan is to tell him off.

"I get it," Bryce texts. "U won't answer. But Alondra's sick. Call Maddie. Call her now."

Alondra's sick. So? I know she's sick. She's been sick for months. So what?

Maddie's calling now. *Oh, God.*

I take a deep breath. When I see Dr. Garson's remote get stuck again, it's enough reason for me to walk out. I mean, does it really matter that I miss the lecture? I think I can discern more from staring at my textbook than listening to him. I shove my book into my backpack and make my way out.

Outside the lecture hall, I answer my phone.

"What!" I snap.

"I've been trying to reach you all morning. Where were you? I'm sure it wasn't with Bryce."

"Yeah," I snap. "You guessed it. It wasn't with Bryce."

I make my way to the main drag of campus. Predictably, it's not busy. But give it another week or two and everybody will start studying for midterms.

"Well—"

"I'm never going to talk to him again."

"Whatever, Katie. I'm not calling you about that. You always think everything's about you."

"What? Just tell me. I'm heading back to our dorm now."

"Well, I'm not there. I'm at Alondra's. Didn't you at least answer Mira?"

"No."

"Come here now, Cadence. Please. It's not good."

I finally get it that she's worried. "What?" I ask, softening for the first time. "What is it?"

"Just come to Alondra's."

"Will Bill let me in?"

"I'm sitting across from Reardon right now."

~

I take my beat-up Honda to Alondra's. It's only eleven in the morning. When I get there, I'm surprised to see her dirt parking lot packed with cars. I jump out of mine and make my way to her door. Her grass has browned even more, and the leaves on the trees around the property, as elsewhere throughout the college, are orange and brown. I muse that if I weren't in such a state, I would enjoy it. Fall is my favorite season. But now, I'm thinking about Alondra.

I pound on the door with her large knocker, and Tammy opens it. She's wiping tears from her eyes. Inside it's noisy, almost like one of her parties, with the house packed with people. Many are my sisters of the coven.

Reardon walks to the foyer. He's wearing his stupid monk robe. He looks terrible and I fear the worst.

"Where is she?" I ask.

A bunch of the witches hear my voice and rush to the front of the house. No one's smiling. It's like they're holding a wake.

"She's very sick, I'm afraid," Reardon says.

"No thanks to you," I snap. I'm full throttle at this point, pissed at my "boyfriend" and in no mood to disguise my disgust at this sick, satanic creep. I look around the house. Then I nod toward the stairs. "Is she in her room?"

"We don't know where she is, Cadence," Mira says. "She disappeared."

"He knows where she is." I point a thumb in disbelief.

"I don't," he replies with seemingly equal hatred of me.

"Where's my disciple?" asks Reardon.

"You mean Bryce?" I ask. "Why don't you call people by the names given by their parents instead of your stupid cult names?" I walk up to him and he steps back, afraid. "No, I haven't seen him. Last I saw, he was with Panthera."

"He's not here," Maddie says. She's walking over from the kitchen.

She looks terrible. Not at all like her usual happy self. "Hi, Cadence. We were waiting for you."

"Why? For what?"

"We thought you'd know where she is," says Mira. "She kept telling me she wanted to talk to you. That was before she disappeared."

"You can't find her?" I ask Reardon. I don't want to talk to him, but there's just no choice. He shakes his head.

I make my way into the living room. Marilyn and Hope are crying on the sofa. I pull at Alondra's glass door. Of course it doesn't open, so I have to push on it hard. Outside, on a wooden rack on the outdoor patio, are our black cloaks. I put one on.

Mira and Gilda put on cloaks too. I didn't even notice Gilda. They must have called her from Savannah.

"If you want me to find her, I have to go alone," I say.

"How do you know where she is?" asks Gilda.

"She knows," says Mira.

I do. I don't know how I know, but I do.

I make my way into her backyard. Mira walks beside me.

"Mira, I said I have to go alone."

"She's really sick," Mira says. "Just bring her back to the house with you."

"Why?" I ask.

"Because ..." Mira's voice cracks and she turns away with tears. "I want to say goodbye."

And that's a terrible thing to say. I take a deep breath and embrace Mira, and she falls apart in my arms. I feel choked up too. As I look toward the house, I see all the witches of my coven have gathered outside, watching me.

"Katie, I don't know where the evil is," Mira whispers in my ear between tears. "Bring Alondra back. Please."

14

THE ONYX STONE

I'M WALKING THROUGH THE DENSE BRUSH OF THE FOREST, NOT FAR FROM Alondra's backyard. In fact, as I cock my head back, I can still make out her house through the dense trees and see my friends, still standing outside talking about me. Everyone wants me to find her. I acted so sure I could, but now I'm not sure.

After walking downhill for a while, I enter a clearing. The ground looks darker between the trees. I step in mud and water. There's about thirty feet of water in front of me—Alondra's water hole. I've never seen it, but I remember it. When I had my initiation last year, I saw it from above, in the air, under the influence of mandrake. At the time, I thought the drug had caused a hallucination. Later, I found that it was real. Bryce and I had flown. And, with a bird's-eye view, I had seen this water hole.

Something tells me she's across the water. There's a small tunnel made up of twigs and branches. And the only way to get through the tunnel is to walk across the water hole.

The water is about two feet deep at its center. It's not deep but it's cold. I tread slowly with my cloak and dress floating near my arms. It gets shallow again, and I crouch down and pass into the tunnel. It's only about three feet high.

I feel as if I enter a tunnel under a canopy. It is then I realize that this is a secret area. It's a natural tunnel and, maybe because it is so unique, I feel like it will lead me to her.

The tunnel is so beautiful. And as I walk, it feels like nighttime under so much yellow-and-red foliage. It's like a nest and, for a second, I wonder if it's man-made. Perhaps Alondra built this?

The end of the tunnel leads me to a field not all that different from Alondra's backyard. But this field has a ceiling of branches and leaves, making it like a natural amphitheater. In the center of the wild grass is a black figure crouched in a ball. This is the same stance Enora was in when she opened her hell portal. I take a deep breath and sigh. I found her.

I walk slowly to her. She doesn't stir. She remains crouched in a black ball, wearing the same cloak as me.

I remove my hood.

"Alondra," I say.

"You're a powerful witch." She sounds like she's amused, but she still barely stirs.

"What are you doing here?" I ask.

"Dying."

And that's horrible. I feel my breath leave me and my legs weaken. Now that I've found her, I don't want magic. I don't want any of it. I want to just run home to my dorm and study. Read. Try to discern Dr. Garson's *comparative advantage*. Anything but witchcraft.

"Please, come with me back home," I say. "Mira wants to see you. We all do." She doesn't move. She remains crouched like a black boulder, immobile. "Why are you sitting like this?"

"I am gathering my energy from the ground. I am grounded with Gaia. I feel peace in her arms. My only concern is you and your friends do not."

"Why did you ask to see me?"

"Because I'm dying," she says again. "Will you forgive me?"

"For what? For dying?"

"No. For what I did. I've asked you before, now I ask you one last time. Can you forgive me for what happened last year?"

"No." When I say that, my words sound as terrible to my ears as they probably do to hers. She says she's dying. Why can't I accept her last words? Or at least lie about it? She's talking about the "ceremonial initiation" of my friend. The deception of her circle, when the circle meant taking drugs and having sex ceremonies with Maddie and her sick husband.

"I'm sorry, Cadence," Alondra says. "I am fortunate to have talked to all those I love before I pass to the Summerland. You are my last."

"Don't say that." I choke up. "Just come back with me to the house."

"Don't be sad. I told you I wanted to leave under the trees."

"Just get up and walk back to the house."

"I don't have the strength."

There's silence. I don't know what to say.

"Do you believe that some things can never be forgiven?" she asks. It is so Alondra. She's acting like Socrates, trying to make me think at the last breaths of her life. I don't think she has an answer herself.

"I'm the one who's sorry," I say.

"For what?" she asks. There's a sense of amusement.

"Because you're dying."

"Ah. But I believe death is an illusion. It does not hurt the dead. It's one's loved ones who suffer. What do you think of that, Cadence?"

She's doing it again with a second question. It makes me almost angry. It seems like her teachings cover her real feelings.

"No, I can never forgive you for what you did to Maddie," I say, ignoring her philosophical questions. It's mean, but I feel like being honest is the right thing to do. Probably not to her. Probably not to someone who spent a lifetime avoiding the truth.

"All right, Cadence."

"You knew I'd say that. Is that why you wanted to see me?"

"No, Katie."

"Then why?"

"Because I love you. I feel like you are the daughter I never had."

That does it. I fall to my knees beside her in tears. But she's still sitting in a weird black ball, not even looking at me. Now she's calling herself my mother. It's so sad. And so upsetting. It's the confused relationship we've had ever since we met.

"Why do you do this, Alondra?" I rub my tear-filled eyes.

She lifts her head to me for the first time. Her hand unfolds and shakes as it touches my face. She runs her fingers along my long black hair. Her jade eyes are glassy. Her face is covered in leaves and dirt, as if she has been swimming in mud. She looks so weak. And yet she seems serene. She is dying.

"Don't worry."

"I...I thought you could help me," I say. "I'm so confused. I don't know how to use my powers. Every time I'm upset, crazy things happen."

"But you don't see ghosts anymore, do you?"

"No."

"At least that haunting has left you."

"But I see other things. I saw Reardon." I start talking fast. There's so much I want to tell her, and I need to tell her now. And quickly. Because... well, she's dying. "I was lost in the forest and I saw Reardon. He cast a spell on me. And then, last night, I saw Bryce kissing Enora. I wanted to take down the whole Billington House, and I know I could have if I wanted to. That scares me. I don't have control over myself." Tears stream down my face. "No ghosts, but I can't control my power. I'm a monster."

A tear runs down her cheek too, but she smiles. "Your power is greater than any of ours. Stop running from it. You can be Cadence. And you can be Windstorm. But whoever you choose, choose nothing anyone ever gives you. Just be yourself."

"But I saw evil. I saw visions of devils and Satan. And it was from *me*, Alondra. I'm evil."

"I told you there's no such thing as evil. It's easier to focus on what you think is evil, because evil is driven by fear. But your power isn't evil. You're not a monster."

"But I might be going crazy."

She closes her eyes and lowers her head. She's as still as a rock. I become panicked.

"Alondra! Alondra!"

But she's still breathing. So weakly.

"Bill isn't attacking you," she says, her head now buried in her chest. "And Bryce loves you more than anyone. I brought Enora back to the circle to make amends to her. I don't think you're seeing things right. Have you talked to Bryce about what happened? Or Enora?"

No.

She shudders like she did that night I called the paramedics. I think she's in pain.

"You told me last year you could help me control my magic," I say.

"I told you that to bring you back to the circle. And you came back—but not for your powers. You came back for me. Even when you almost hurt me and my husband, you did it all because you were upset about what was happening to me. Because you cared about me. So know that I forgive you." She pauses, as if to gain strength. "Windstorm, it doesn't matter if I show you magic. Tarot cards. Potions. Cauldrons. Spells. None of that makes you a witch. The earth does. Your power is from your heart. Give your heart to our mother. You keep manifesting your energy when you're upset. Learn to find it when you're good. A witch's wisdom is like that of a yogi. It's easy to practice black magic. It's much harder to practice white. It's harder to be good. Try to be good and you may find balance. A weak witch and a weak man only practice evil. You are not weak. Learn the harder path. Learn the balance and you will no longer feel unstable. Or crazy, as you said."

She takes a deep breath. It seems strained.

"I have to go. I don't believe there's an answer to my questions. Not here. Perhaps where I'm going. I love you. And I know you love me, whether I'm forgiven or not. Goodbye, Cadence. I wish you well. I've been so happy to have been your teacher. Yatu."

She slumps over into her chest. It is silent for a moment; then she says faintly, only to herself, "I'm afraid."

Her breathing stops. She's immobile.

I fall on her, sobbing. "Oh, God, Alondra, don't go! I forgive you! I do! I forgive you... Don't, don't go. Please. I forgive you!"

I touch her hand and her fingers move weakly. She squeezes my hand for a moment. But then—nothing.

When she lets go of my fingers, it's quiet. Birds chirp. Clouds move shadows over the grass. The woman I hated for so long is dead. But I loved her. She was right. She was not only my mentor; she was my mother. And now both my mothers are gone.

I stand and look down at this black orb on the grass. I realize that if it were up to Alondra, she would let the earth consume her body like this.

Her wishes would be for no funeral. She would be happy to just fade here in the forest. But I need to get back and tell the others. My witches need to mourn. And we will need to hold our Sabbath to help her spirit cross to the Summerland.

15

THE BILLINGTON CEMETERY

I DON'T LIKE FUNERALS. I DON'T CARE FOR CEMETERIES EITHER. I MEAN, I never visit my mother's grave. I'd rather honor her in my heart, you know?

Mom died around this time last year. That funeral was closer to Atlanta. This time, I only drove about forty miles from the university. It turned out that Alondra's family, the Billingtons, don't live very far from Hawthorne. So we all meet in Flintwood, a small farming town about thirty miles east of the college.

The funny thing about Alondra is that she was so mysterious I've learned more about her over the past hour, at their farm, than I did when I knew her. That is so irritating! I especially learned a lot from her garrulous uncle, Hanley. Uncle Hanley has been talking to me for the last half hour beside a large red barn close to the Billingtons' family cemetery. All the witches and a bunch of well-dressed strangers have convened here to shelter from the rain. My friends are wearing black dresses and actually look like witches today, but it doesn't seem inappropriate right now.

Uncle Hanley is giving me a history lesson on the Billingtons. He doesn't know yet how I knew Alondra. He just brightened up when I asked how Alondra had such an incredible house.

"Well, Alondra's relative was Abigail Billington, you know," he says.

"Figure she was living in high cotton, *literally*. She was born in a rich cotton plantation in Tallahassee, Florida. She had an arranged marriage to Josiah Billington and, well, Josiah cheated on Abigail, having an affair with a slave from Louisiana: Escoba Hawthorne. Escoba was a voodoo witch. And she was black. The Hawthornes weren't such a distinguished family." *Okay. That sounds a little racist. Not to mention Escoba happens to be my distant relative.* "So Escoba ended up on their farm and wooed poor Josiah. They had a mixed-race boy named Maverick. But the fact that he was illegitimate and that his mother was a slave was scandalous. And yet, you know, folks were so understanding in these parts back then that the town of Hawthorne grew under his family name just the same."

The fact that "folks are so understanding" probably has something to do with the Billington family. I'm struck by how nice Uncle Hanley is. Alondra always told me I had a great heart when, in fact, she did. I think her good-heartedness runs in the family.

I know all about my family tree, but he's talking so excitedly that I don't want to interrupt him. As Hanley's relating all this—and I find it amusing because, in suspenders and spectacles, he looks like he'd fit right in in nineteenth-century Georgia as a farmer—I just politely listen. But when he starts talking about how Maverick set up our university town, and he speaks with pride about it, I can't resist telling him my relationship to Maverick. He surprises me by scooping me up in his arms and calling me family. I laugh. It's really cute and it reminds me of Alondra.

Maddie catches the whole thing from the corner of her eye and smiles. But it's a sad smile, and her sadness reminds me of Alondra passing away.

As we're still waiting for the service, I ask Uncle Hanley a question Alondra never answered. "Why is her last name Johansen?" *Why not Reardon?*

"Well, that was her first husband's name. She got her teaching degree and figured she'd never change it."

Yeah, because then it would be Reardon and he's a total asshole.

Then I see the asshole walk into the barn. The bald devil is wearing a white shirt with a black vest and black slacks. Even though he knows my friends well, he stands alone near a snack table beside a stack of hay.

I pick up an hors d'oeuvre from another table. It's basically a cracker with cream cheese. Then I lean back against the table, by myself. Frida and Hope have drawn Uncle Hanley away. He's got quite a magnetic personality.

Then Bryce walks in alone wearing a navy-blue suit. That's a good thing, because I think my temper would have boiled over if he were with Enora. Sad or not, I would have lost my mind. I don't want to do that. Not at Alondra's funeral. He sees me but I don't walk over. I just remain leaning against the table. He doesn't approach me. Instead he walks over to comfort Mira. Mira leans into his arms, bawling.

"Katie," I hear beside me. I turn and see a thin guy with graying hair and matching gray eyes giving me a faint smile. It's Dad. I hug him tightly.

"Hi, Daddy."

"Hey, sis," says a broad-shouldered boy in a collared shirt and slacks. Damien. My brother. Damie is looking at my face funny. So is my dad. We've been talking on the phone, but they haven't seen me for a while. Not in witch attire, with all this black makeup. I look totally goth. But if they understood, they'd know that Alondra would have liked me dressing like this.

My brother hugs me. My dad and brother came because they know how important Alondra was to me, and their presence makes things a little easier.

"Hi, Mr. Hawthorne," says Maddie, coming over.

"Rocky couldn't make it?" I ask Maddie.

She shakes her head dismissively. "You must be Katie's little brother." Maddie reaches out to my brother.

"Damien."

"Damie," I correct him. "Damie for short."

"Well, he's not short, Katie," says Maddie with a chuckle. She checks him out from head to toe and, for a flash, she loses her frown and smiles. "And he's not little."

That's true. Damie's about six foot three.

"How're you holding up, squirt?" Dad asks me.

I can't say anything. I just shake my head.

"Kate and Alondra were probably closer than any of us, Mr.

Hawthorne," explains Maddie. She's somber again, which almost makes me tear up. "She loved her. And Alondra really loved her back."

"You guys were in an honors program, right?" asks Damie innocently.

"Yes."

"Sure," Maddie says with a smile to Damie. "Hey, you're graduating this year? Right?"

"Yep."

"You should come here. It's—"

"He's going to an Ivy League school," I interrupt.

"You're smart, huh?" Maddie asks my brother with interest.

Uncle Hanley comes over and starts talking up a storm. Apparently, I must look like my dad and brother, because he starts talking about our relationship to Maverick Hawthorne. I'm not sure he believed me.

Eventually we all gather outside with umbrellas on white wooden chairs in a wild grassy field. The service goes fast. Too fast. It's pouring rain and, from under a huge umbrella, I watch my teacher and mentor, my friend, lowered into the ground. That's awful. I think I should have just left her in peace in the woods.

The worst part about watching the casket being lowered is that Bryce is standing across from me. Twice he meets my gaze. I wipe my eyes pretending to cry but, really, I don't want to look at him. I'm furious. I know my "vision" at the Billington House was no vision. I know he was with her that night.

I don't cry. I don't shed a tear during the whole service. After Alondra died in my arms, I think I emptied all the water I had left in my eyes. I stayed there with her, alone, for at least a half hour before I went back to the house to tell my circle the horrible news.

When the ceremony ends, Maddie comes up to me and asks if it's okay if she stays at her house instead of the dorm for a little while. She says she needs some time alone with her mom to grieve. I nod. Her mom is the coolest mom I've ever known. If anyone can cheer Maddie up, it's her. But I really don't like it, because I'm fighting with Bryce. I'll be very alone.

Then I watch my cheating boyfriend walk across the grassy field and back to his BMW in the parking lot. He has a really small umbrella, and the rain just splashes on his short dark hair. For a moment, I have the urge to leave my dad and run to him with my umbrella, which is huge, but someone stops me.

Enora. I didn't see her during the whole service, but now she's walking across the grass toward me. She doesn't have an umbrella. She doesn't seem to care about getting wet. I really hate her. I hate her so much. She's even wearing a slutty black lacy dress. It's so inappropriate. And she doesn't look sad. Why is she even here? Did she really care about Alondra?

I turn to my brother. Damie's got his eyes on her too, but for very different reasons.

"You guys, I need to go. I'll meet you at Lacey's." Lacey's is a nice steak house my dad wants to take my brother and me to. "There's someone I have to talk to."

"Sure, Katie," says Damie. He hugs me.

"Thanks for coming."

My dad hugs me too and kisses me on the forehead. "I'll see you at six, okay, squirt?"

I nod.

My brother and dad leave with not a moment to spare. Enora walks right up to me. I'm ready to crack a hole in the ground and send the witch back to the hell where she belongs.

"Sorry for your loss," Enora lies with a sly smile.

I just give her a hard stare.

"I know this is difficult for you, Cadence. All the witches in your coven told me how much Alondra cared about you. And your mother died around this time last year, right? It must be hard for you."

I know all this. I'm living it. The last thing I need is for this bitch-witch to spell it out for me. She's only angering me more.

"I also heard from Mira about something you saw at the Halloween party," Enora says with a grin. "You realize that there's nothing between Bryce and me. Not anymore, anyway. He's yours." *Thanks. I appreciate your permission.*

"I know what I saw. What you *wanted* me to see."

My feet are about ready to turn and walk, but Enora puts her hand on my shoulder. I throw it off. Then, of all people to rescue me, Mira walks over. Mira, who's been crying her eyes out, who gave a speech and ruined it by crying too much, runs up to Enora and me. And she's not acting like Enora's friend. She's acting like mine.

"Is this really the time?" Mira asks her. "Why don't you leave her alone?"

"The time for two *real* witches to talk, you mean?" Enora says.

"You should be careful, Panthera. If you anger Windstorm, who knows what she's capable of?" Then Mira snatches my hand. "Come on. Let's go, Katie."

"Wait," Enora says to Mira. Then she turns to me. "You did see Bryce and me. I'm not saying you didn't. Bryce used to be my boyfriend, Cadence, when he lived at the Billington House. I think, for some reason, you conjured up a vision of our past."

"Boy, did she," Mira says.

"I don't believe you." I shake my head. "It wasn't the past." I turn, with Mira holding my hand, but Enora's not done.

"I have one request, Cadence. You are the leader of the Hawthorne coven. I ask permission to pay my respects to Falconsong at your next meeting." She looks around the cemetery in disgust. "Not in a Christian burial, but through the rites of a witch's funeral. I was Alondra's friend too. I—"

"That's not what she said," Mira interrupts.

"We had our differences," Enora says with a nod. "That's true. But we made up in the end." Enora nods to me. "Cadence, can I join your circle for her going-away ceremony? I too wish her a swift and pleasant journey to the Summerland."

"No."

Enora is shocked at my response. It's like I struck her across the face. She's not smug anymore. She's pissed. She frowns and her dark skin flushes enough to turn red.

"How dare you," Enora mutters. "You don't know what this means to a witch." Then she looks at Mira in contempt. "A *real* witch."

"I don't want you near our circle ever again," I say.

"Think it over. If you don't let me pay respects, you might as well call me her enemy. That will undo all the things Alondra did, at the end of her life, to make peace with me. And I know this is not what she would have wanted."

"I don't want you holding Sabbath with us again. You don't belong in my coven."

"I'm not asking to be a part of your weak coven, you stupid cunt," she snaps. "I'm asking you to permit me to pay my respects to the dead. A fellow witch who, although we had our differences, I admired."

"No."

Enora stares at me. Then she grunts like an animal and rushes off, seemingly humiliated.

Mira watches her with concern. I'm happy to have gotten rid of her, but just when I think she's gone, she turns once more.

"Oh, Katie," Enora says with a smile, cocking her head back. "I'd have a talk with your boyfriend about his college years. You seemed so upset when you saw him touching me that night. Perhaps you should ask him about all the other girls he touched while he was in the fraternity and when he was working with the High Wizard. Bryce was a very popular frat brother. And very useful to Alondra's husband." And with that, she spins around in her wet dress and leaves.

I can't stop staring in her direction. But I'm too sad and angry and in too much pain to do anything. I feel like just giving up and falling to the ground.

"Are you okay?" Mira asks.

I shake my head.

Mira surprises me by hugging me. Then she walks off alone.

It rains harder. I reach into my pocket and check my new cell phone. It's four thirty. I have a half hour to get back to campus and an hour to get ready for dinner.

I walk back to the freshly dug earth. Alondra's resting place.

By now, the cemetery is vacant. Down below lies Alondra, and I'm alone with her. I pick up some of the wet, muddy soil and let it run through my fingers under the rain. I bring it up to my nose. Touching the mud gives me pleasure.

I think of her two questions. One was her request for forgiveness. The other:

I believe death is an illusion. It does not hurt the dead. It's one's loved ones who suffer. What do you think of that, Cadence?

"You're so wise, Alondra," I say out loud, choked up. "You told me once the word *witch* means wisdom. You were a great witch. The answer to your final question, teacher, is...*yes.*"

I kneel in the mud before the mound and finally cry.

When I finally get control of myself, I stand up. I'm alone in the cemetery. The farm has fields for miles, which is a pretty break from the forest surrounding Hawthorne. I enjoy the beautiful view. In the distance, near my college, mountain ranges rise. But here the fields go on and on.

The clouds are clearing. I'm not sure how long I've been out here, but I don't want to leave. I even see the pastor who ran the service. He walks by, shakes my hand, and gives me condolences again.

I have to go or I'll be late for dinner with Dad and my brother, so I will my legs to move back to my car. The parking lot's now empty. As I unlock my door—by the handle, because my key fob doesn't work anymore—I see something in the fields. A figure in black. I whirl around to get a better look. She's a witch in our black cloak, walking the fields alone, about a hundred yards out. I can't make out her face because she is wearing a hood. I walk closer to see who it is. Enora? She seems to be walking toward me. Maybe she wants to curse me? I don't know. But then, as quickly as I saw the witch, she vanishes.

16

———

KINDA ALONE

I'M ALONE, BUT THAT'S OKAY BECAUSE I WANT TO BE. I'M READING A textbook on the Sumerians of ancient Mesopotamia on the cement stage in the center of campus. It snowed last night, and ice is still thawing in patches on the lawn. I'm wearing my red-and-gold sweater—school colors—over another sweater, a button-down undershirt, thick under-wear, and jeans. Yeah, it's cold. But I want to be outdoors. Especially since Maddie's still at Aunt Jane's. She told me she was just too depressed to return to campus.

It might be cold but it's also nice outside. The nearby trees are losing their leaves, and many branches are leafless. The gorgeous orange, red, and brown leaves that I love have fallen, but there's an early-morning dew that smells fresh.

I look down at the textbook on my lap. There's a picture of a statue and a guy with a beard. I take a deep breath and read.

Did you know that the Sumerians were thought to be the first great empire in the world? Some religious scholars think they were descendants of Abraham. *They lived around the Tigris River in modern-day Iraq.* Aha. It says that on page forty-two. Personally, I prefer learning about the Egyptians and their pyramids, but the Assyrians are neat because I don't know much about them. Well, no one knows a whole lot about them. They're an ancient, ancient civilization.

I sit straighter, stretch my arms, and take a deep breath. Down the lawn, I see another straight-A student at a bench, reading. He's a thin boy with glasses. He nods at me. Cute.

We had our Sabbath memorial a few days ago. Reardon was there. How could he not be? It's his house and his wife. Bryce wasn't. I'm such a bitch for not letting Bryce come. But hey, it was enough that I met with my sisters at all after the night Enora nearly brought hell into the backyard.

I gave Mira the memorial candle. In our tradition, whenever we mourn, we light the candle in memory of the deceased. I still have one for my mother's death. Mira was shocked at the honor. Everyone was. They all thought I should take the candle, since it's given to the witch closest to the deceased, but I argued that Mira had the greatest love for Alondra.

I look out at the trees. Beyond a few red brick buildings, I see a water tower, with the words "Hawthorne University" painted on it, beside a few rolling hills, and farther still is an old farmhouse. The buildings are old, but they'll be gone eventually. The buildings come and go, but the trees never change. If a tree falls, another takes its place. Just like their red and orange leaves. They haven't changed since I first came to Hawthorne two and a half years ago. They probably haven't changed since Maverick and Escoba walked here. There's a comfort in their permanence. Alondra was right. When I die, I want to die out in the wilderness too.

I thumb through some more pages and realize I have no interest in reading about Assyria. So I reach into my black backpack and replace it with another book: *Broomstick*. This is my Book of Shadows.

Alondra gave me *Broomstick* during my initiation ceremony last year. The first half was written by Alondra. That's why I take it out. This morning, I don't want to write an entry in it. I want to hear her words again. She's written so many entries in small writing or in the margins that I haven't read all the sections of her writings. Reading it now makes me feel like she's still here with me, you know.

I thumb through the pages, avoiding sections on feces and vomit—yeah, that stuff is really in there—and the equally ridiculous poetry on garden flowers, until I come across a page that intrigues me because it's about Sumerians, interestingly enough.

~

ASSYRIA, WITH PERSONAL DISCOVERY, ON THE SUBJECT OF GHOSTS

The spirit world is so close to our realm that it is easy for the dead to become trapped. As in life, most of these spirits are good and merely need to be nudged to find peace. They need you, witches, your friends and family, to show your love and guide them swiftly to the Summerland. Your help will ensure that one day, when your time has come, they might help you on the other side. And so our funeral rite is so important for a true witch.

Other ghosts remain in our plane for personal reasons. They are not trapped, they know the way, but they haunt the living for reasons that may not be apparent until a later time.

Finally, there are some that, as when they were living, delight in hurting others. Poltergeists. These spirits haunt the living. They have been spoken of ever since the most ancient of civilizations. In fact, it is the Sumerian sorcerers who wrote of the evil spirits we see today.

There are two main devil spirits referenced in ancient Akkadia: the Ekimmu and the Alu. The Ekimmu are the ghosts most commonly found haunting homes. These ghosts refuse passage from the spirit world, usually after dying a violent death. They are the most common, and potentially dangerous, poltergeists. Like modern vampires, they feed off the energy of the living. The Alu haunt victims at night, but usually during sleep. Doglike spirits, these ghosts are often erroneously thought, in modern times, to be simply nightmares experienced during sleep paralysis.

A witch can ward off these evil spirits with her usual remedies: salt and sage, burying small figurines of Lamassu, or speaking the words of Nineveh. Surely any witch knows this, but for true success, I tell you, there is no incantation of greater power than one's soul. Atman.

The failure of the mind is equal to the failure of a witch's spell. Our thoughts cannot fully comprehend the universe that surrounds us, so how can a witch do justice to the power of Selene? Practice with atman, sisters: no thought, one's heart. Approach with confidence in yourself and the power within will flow.

I had unique opportunities to rid my coven of poltergeists. One Ekimmu haunted Loraine, who joined the circle after my success. She had traveled from Wichita, Kansas, upon hearing of my reputation. The other was Winona, who

…

I hope my witch-ghost isn't an Ekimmu. Alondra never told me how to get rid of my ghost, Maverick. He just disappeared. But now I'm seeing a transparent witch around campus. I've seen her a couple more times since the funeral.

I stop reading for a moment and laugh out loud. Only Alondra would teach extra-credit Sumerian demonology right after her death. And, typical of her, she makes it sound so much more interesting than my early civilizations professor. I'm thinking maybe I should incorporate all this shit into my Sumerian essays for the final for extra credit.

And I really like reading Alondra's words. It's like she's here with me still.

But I yawn and close the book. I'm also really tired.

I lean back and look up at the cloudless sky. It's beautiful. The yellow sun blinds me, but I enjoy the hot rays hitting my face and warming me in the cold.

My eyes close. I haven't slept well for days, since the funeral. And before that, I wasn't sleeping after my fight with Bryce. And before that, I wasn't sleeping well because Alondra was sick.

I let myself lie on my side on the cement stage and drift off.

I hear footsteps that stir me. I think I hear my name.

I'm surprised when I see a young man walking across the grass carrying a big leather bag. I recognize his neatly pressed preppy clothes. Bryce? It is! And I think he sees me.

I catch him furrowing his brow, but he quickly turns his head. He's wearing a dark gray button-down and black slacks. He's sporting a beard now, or trying to, which is new. Usually he's just a little unshaven.

I shove my books in my black backpack and run to him.

"Hi, Bryce," I say. I'm surprised at how sheepish my voice sounds.

He stops, shuffles his heavy brown leather bag over to his other shoulder, and turns around under an ugly silver awning. His blue eyes look at mine over thick bags—he's not sleeping either—and, for a moment, I remember our old flame in those hypnotic blues.

"Cadence," he says professionally.

"I...I just feel bad because I didn't let you come to...our ceremony." I can't say sorry because I'm not. I mean, if I were sorry, I would have invited him. Right?

"I loved Alondra," he says. His voice is strained. "I asked Maddie because I just wanted to pay my respects."

"I know. I just couldn't see you there." That sounds really bad. And I'm wondering where I'm going with this.

"Okay," he says with a sigh. He pauses for a moment, but then he shakes his head and walks on.

"Wait," I say.

He stops again.

"I want you to know that I always liked you, you know, other than just as a date. You know. I like you as a friend. Because you're so nice. And I think you're really a good friend too, and—"

"Then why didn't you let me go to Alondra's memorial?"

Uh, yeah. Why? Shit.

"I didn't want to see you."

Is that supposed to make sense? He looks right into my eyes, baffled. My heart jumps because I'm still mesmerized by his baby blues, but that seems to disturb him more. It's like our old flame upsets him. His eyelids flutter and he quickly looks away.

"Okay, Cadence."

"Wait, I didn't want to see you," I stammer, "because I thought I'd hesitate. I like you, you know, but I...don't like you, you know. Because of what you did at the party. Ya know?"

"No, I don't know." He looks angrier than I've ever seen him. "I called you. I reached out and you ignored all my texts and calls. You just ran away. You abandoned me just like you abandoned Alondra. The moment something happens, you run away, Katie. You never let anyone explain. You just shut down."

"But you didn't answer your phone at the party." *Yeah. So there!*

"You accused me without letting me explain to you what happened."

"Okay, what happened?" I shake my head. "I saw you with Enora. And she told me about the other girls." I look down and bite my lip. "That disgusts me. You lied to me. You said you didn't do anything with the other—"

"Again, Cadence," he snaps. "You never let me explain."

He turns and walks off, and this time he's not about to turn back.

I don't know what to say. I can't apologize because I think I'm right. But I want to apologize. Just to be with him.

"Didn't you lie to me?" I holler. "Weren't you with all those girls?"

"Shut up!" He's never yelled at me like that. I'm shocked. Then, in a forced whisper, he snaps, "We're on campus. You don't know what happened, and now you're accusing me in public!"

But there's no one around us. I think the only student is that boy on the bench about fifty yards away.

"Well, were you?" I insist, searching his face.

"I already told you my activity is in the past. I don't owe you anything. How can I be with someone who doesn't listen and allow me to explain?" And that's it. Then he says, before turning from me a final time, "You need to grow up." I think he was going to say something far worse, but he hesitated when he glanced into my eyes again.

And he's gone.

I don't cry. I've done plenty of that. But I feel uneasy and a little sick to my stomach. And I don't believe it. Is he gone now?

I still feel I'm right to have done what I did about Alondra's memorial, but I guess he's right that I should have let him explain everything. But what he doesn't understand is that I knew if I let him talk I would accept whatever he said. I'm that attracted to him. That's also why I didn't let him go to Alondra's memorial. I knew I'd just get back together with him.

I watch him walk all the way down the long walkway and turn a corner. As he turns, I could swear he looks back for a moment. Maybe he's not gone from me?

I'm tired. My whole body feels like it has a two-ton truck on its shoulders. I just want to go home and sleep.

I reposition my backpack on my shoulder and head back to the dorm, alone, to take another nap. But I know I won't nap. I won't be able to sleep at all. Maddie's still away, so I can't talk to her. And I've lost Alondra. And now Bryce.

I'm so alone.

17

ICED COFFEE AND A LIGHTER

I'M NOT SLEEPING AND NEITHER IS MADDIE, SO, EVEN THOUGH WE SHOULD be having fun shopping in Atlanta, we decide to grab coffee on campus at seven in the morning. Maddie and I have a tradition of shopping over the weekend after our midterms are over, but neither of us wants to do anything. I'm just thrilled she's back. The university coffee shop is empty, with all the two-person tables along brown-painted walls and windows, and the four large tables in the center, being unoccupied. In fact, the whole campus is empty right now. People are still recovering from their exams.

Maddie didn't cry much during the ceremony, but she cried last night in bed. She tried to keep her whimpering quiet, but I heard her.

Right now, Maddie's staring into her cup as she absentmindedly stirs the cream, cradling her head in her hand. It's so depressing.

Maddie's been wearing black ever since the funeral, and this morning is no different. So I wore a black dress to match her. The clothes and our black lipstick, eyeliner, and nail polish make us look like real witches.

The grassy hill outside is not green. It's white. That's the other reason it's empty in the coffee shop. I hate snow and so does everyone else at Hawthorne University. It's icy cold. Slippery. Dangerous to drive on.

She's still stirring her coffee. I'm sipping a green tea latte, my absolute favorite.

I did well midsemester. It was the first time I'd gotten straight As since my first year. I think it's because I didn't have much to distract me. Enora ruining our Sabbath and Alondra's passing meant that I stayed away from our circle and studied. You know, my mother used to tell me to be positive and look at the cup as being half-full.

"I'm done with Rocky," Maddie says, finally looking up from her cup.

"You're kidding?"

Maddie shakes her hair out. I thought she was crying about Alondra last night, but maybe it was over her boyfriend. "He's a meathead. Do you know what a meathead is, Cadence?" She looks up with a flash of her famous whimsical smile, but it vanishes as quickly as it came. "It's an expression for jocks. You know, no-brain morons. All-muscle jocks. That's Rocky."

"He seemed nice."

"He's an asshole." She looks out the window pensively. "Like all men."

I nod.

"And he was cheating on me."

Oh.

"And..." She takes a deep breath, trying to smile again. "He's a loser. You told me that."

"I didn't." All I said was she should be going out with a doctor or something.

"Men are all the same. It really doesn't matter if they have brain cells or not. They're all goddamn assholes."

Two sorority snoots, wearing their letters on their red-and-gold sweaters, swing the glass door open and prance in, giggling stupidly. One has a long blond ponytail and is perfectly manicured, wearing a plaid skirt. (She must have been freezing outside). The other is a short dark-haired girl with flawless makeup. They both order something at the register. The blonde looks over. I could almost swear she's happy we look so miserable.

"How'd you do on your art exam?" Maddie asks.

"Ninety-four."

"Jesus, Cadence," she says, brushing her hair back. "How do you do that?" She lifts her cup, shakes her head, blows some mist, and sips some coffee.

"What'd you get?"

"Seventy-six. Guess I passed."

"It was a difficult exam," I say with a shrug.

"Stop being nice. It wasn't that hard."

"I hate this," I say and hit the table.

"What?" She furrows her brow.

"Everything's depressing. Why do we have to feel so down?"

"Alondra just died." Oh, yeah. She has to say it like that.

And that's when the two girls across the coffeehouse look at us and laugh some more. They think something's really funny.

"Excuse me, but aren't you two friends of Mira?" asks the blonde between giggles. She thinks that's really funny too.

I roll my eyes and look away. "Why do they have to be here?"

"Can't have the place all to ourselves." Maddie shrugs, sipping more coffee.

I take a deep breath. "What was I saying?"

"You asked why we were sad. I said it was because Alondra just died."

"Why do we have to dwell on that?"

The sorority girls laugh harder. I feel my face flushing. They're really pissing me off. Of course, the two strangers have no idea that this is the wrong time to mess with me.

"You're cute, Katie," Maddie says, touching my arm and distracting me from glaring at the snoots. "I don't know. Maybe you're right. Maybe we should have gone shopping. Alondra probably would have liked that."

"And now you broke up with Rocky? When?"

"He and I broke up before the funeral," she replies with a shrug. "I just didn't want to tell you. After the Billington House party, Rock asked if I wanted to go to another party off-campus. Being that you shut off all the lights..." I stick my tongue out at her and she laughs. "We went to Violetta's house. Violetta is Rocky's old girlfriend. I already had a bad feeling about that."

"Can I ask you two something?" interjects the blond-haired girl across the café. I really don't want her to. When we don't reply, she says, "Mira's so weird and she always dresses like you two dress now. Are you guys... what everyone says you are?"

"What?" asks Maddie.

"You know," the blonde says. Then she covers her mouth and looks at her short-haired friend. "Witches?" And that makes the two sorority sluts completely lose it. They're just laughing their heads off.

When they quiet down from whatever the fuck they think is so funny, I say, "I tell you what." They look at me. "If you keep bothering us, you'll find out."

The dark-haired girl loses her smile. See, we've developed a reputation through the gossiping channels around campus, and the press isn't very good. Usually, I just get a stray glance, but I suppose our black mourning clothes are just too much today. I knew I should have just put on a sweater and jeans.

The blond-haired girl chuckles again, but it sounds nervous.

"Don't do it, Kate," Maddie warns. She looks worried.

"What?"

"Whatever you're thinking about doing."

I roll my eyes. "So what else happened?"

"Well, Violetta..." Maddie continues after sipping more coffee. "She's not a meathead, she's a pothead. You know, she even wears a rainbow Rastafarian hat and braids her hair. But..." Maddie points at the girls sitting across the café. "She's like them. Hardly Rastafarian, ya know, more like a rich spoiled kid. The house is apparently hers, even though she's never worked a day in her life. She graduated Hawthorne three years ago.

"Anyway, Violetta has all her weed-smoking friends there, and they're nice but—it's not that I mind pot, but the whole house smells skunky. And no one's in costumes, unless you count Violetta's hat. So, I'm toking away with three of her girlfriends, and actually having a pretty good time. I mean, you know I had already drunk a lot. Everything's going swimmingly until I see Rock near the stairwell. And he's with Violetta, which I don't think much of, until I see her put an arm around him."

"Sorry," I say.

"I'm not finished, Cadence... I think everything's fine. I figure he's drunk." The bitches across the room are laughing again. "And the way she looks at him, she's lost in his eyes, you know. The way I've seen you and Bryce look at each other. So I begin to think we're there for very different reasons than to just get stoned with my boyfriend's friends."

"At least you didn't see him making out with her like Bryce."

"Right, Katie. I'm not done." Maddie pauses and sighs, staring outside at the white hillside for a moment. "An hour later, after I've gotten more fucked up, I have to run to pee. So I walk down a hallway, relieved that there's less smoke, and open a door, thinking it might be a bathroom. Well, it wasn't a bathroom, it was a bedroom. And there before my eyes... I don't have to give you the details. You can guess the rest. Needless to say, I didn't see him making out with her. They weren't wearing any clothes."

"Oh God, I'm so sorry."

"I wouldn't be surprised if Violetta planned the whole goddamn thing. You know, get me screwed up, distract me, and then have her way with him. The bitch. What do you think, Katie?"

I kinda register her words, but I kinda don't, because the sorority snoots are laughing really loud again, and I distinctly hear the word *witch*. Maddie touches my hand. "Whatcha think?"

"It's terrible, Maddie. What a jerk."

"It's okay. Honestly, I felt like we were moving too fast. It was, I don't know, too good. We never got to really know each other. I just loved doing stuff with him. He was fun. And he was a really good lover, you know." She giggles. "But it wasn't deep like you and Bryce."

"Bryce and I aren't deep."

"Hmm..." Maddie looks at her coffee. "You and he go really well together. I think you should give him another chance."

"Seriously?" I snap, hitting the table hard with my palm. The sorority snoots turn. Even the barista behind the counter, a large old woman with thin gray hair, who I've seen working the register since I first enrolled in Hawthorne, looks over too.

"Calm down," Maddie says.

"I tried to talk to Bryce, and he was just cold." I take a deep breath. "He's a player. Worse than Rocky, I think. I never thought he was, but he is. I should have guessed it, being that he was some kind of 'honoree' of Psi Kappa Psi. With all the girls there, imagine the supply he gave to Reardon. It all makes sense. I think he lied about that too. He told me he never had sex with the other girls in ceremonies, but Enora suggested he did. He fooled me. He fooled all of us, Maddie. He's not nice. And there's no way—"

"Don't get so upset. I like him. Why don't you ask him to explain himself? He told me you weren't answering his calls. Why don't you talk it out? You can't trust Enora. So they were making out. They weren't fucking like my asshole boyfriend. Maybe Bryce can explain himself."

"Ya think so, Madison?" I ask sarcastically, shaking my head.

"Yeah, I actually do, Cadence. What happened doesn't sound like Bryce. He told me he would explain himself, but now he's pissed that you didn't talk to him. And even more furious that you didn't let him go to Alondra's funeral."

"That was mean, I guess," I say with a nod.

"It was." She nods and lifts her eyebrows. "Very."

"Well, why didn't you tell me that when I didn't invite him?"

"I don't know, Katie. I've got a lot of shit I'm dealing with right now."

"I know." I touch her arm. "Sorry."

"It's okay," she says with a faint smile.

Then the two snoots are at it again. I'm angry at them, but part of me isn't. I get why they're laughing. Sometimes I think I should be at the other table, laughing at us. Why are we wearing these long black dresses and goth makeup? If I had seen us a year ago, I would have thought the same thing I thought when I first saw Mira: *freak.* If I hadn't joined the coven, maybe I would be over there laughing too.

I stare at the wall. The walls have murals. There are various drawings from an artist on campus. They're quite good. There's a sketch in white paint on a black canvas of a soccer player kicking a ball. We have a soccer team, not an American football team. We don't have a stadium large enough for American football. There are also drawings of two basketball players fielding a rebound and a swimmer swimming freestyle.

My eyes fall on the sorority girls. I can't believe they're still laughing. It's not that funny. I squeeze my hands. Maddie looks over too. They're like hyenas.

"Easy, Cadence," Maddie warns.

The blonde's cute red-and-black plaid skirt reminds me of a dress code skirt. It must be freezing outside with the snow. She looks like a whore. I'm sure her clothes were super uncomfortable out in the snow, but I doubt her ego cared.

So what I decide to do is help warm her up a little. Just a little kindling. Actually, I set her skirt on fire. A small flame, like a lighter, you know, but enough to make her jump up from her chair and brush the smoke from her heinie. Her friend jumps up too and starts slapping her ass to put out the smoke.

Then I laugh. I even cackle a little like a witch just for them.

"Cadence!" Maddie snaps.

The two girls are out of the café quicker than I can respond to my friend.

"What?" I ask, feigning innocence with a shrug. I drink some tea. "She looked cold."

"That was mean."

"I'm not in the mood to be nice, Maddie."

It looks so cold outside, and now that I've burned a hole in the sorority girl's skirt, she's going to be colder. But for now, her ass is hot. Her friend waves her hand over the smoke as they rush down a sidewalk paralleling the snowy hillside. I've really given them something to gossip about.

"Sometimes I don't know who you are anymore," Maddie says.

"A witch."

"Today you're being a bad witch."

As the two sorority girls rush around a corner and make their way to the main drag of campus, my jaw drops. There in the middle of campus, on the ice-patched asphalt walkway, stands a black figure. The same ghost I first saw at Alondra's funeral. The girls are rushing close to her, but it doesn't slow them down. She's a shadowy black hooded figure, wearing a black druid-like cloak just like we wear in my coven. I can't see her face.

"What's wrong?" asks Maddie.

"I see my ghost again."

"What?" Maddie jumps. She looks where I point but doesn't see anything. The two sorority girls walk right through her.

"Shit." I tear my eyes away and put my head in my hand. "You don't see her? Really?"

"No."

I used to see ghosts. I used to see Maverick and Escoba, but this figure seems different. Alondra said my haunting was over, and I was quite pleased she told me that. It had been torture going through months of seeing Maverick and Escoba. Am I going to be haunted by this new specter?

I look back out the window and the ghost is gone.

"I saw a witch. A witch...that ghost witch, I think. I don't know. Those girls walked right through her."

"Not good, Katie... Do you think it was Panthera?"

"I don't know."

"Maybe Alondra."

18

HIKING

I'm hiking. That's okay because I enjoy walking the paths around campus at night, only it's three in the morning and I'm alone in the dark forest. Well, I couldn't sleep. And staring up at Maddie's mattress from my bunk bed, I felt a trance coming on. Maddie was sound asleep, so I didn't wake her. She's finally sleeping again after a few weeks of mourning. Time always heals, right? Anyway, I just quietly threw on some clothes, a heavy coat, and boots and stepped out.

I'm ascending a path and it isn't too dark. There's a full moon. I hear running water to my right. My waterfall. My destination. I figured since I can't sleep, I might as well visit my favorite stream. It's so pretty with water flowing over stones and reflecting the moonlight. The sound is so tranquil. I reach down and touch the water. It's icy cold. I crouch down and cup some of the running water in my hands. It might be cold, but it's fresh and clean. As I gather more and pour it over my face, I hear a noise. I can't tell if it's a yell or even laughter, but I hear it coming from the top of Hilltop Bluff. There's a red fiery glow on the summit. I skim my fingers along the cold, flowing water one last time; then I walk back onto the path to see where the light's coming from. It couldn't be my coven. It's past the witching hour.

I feel drowsy as if in a dream. But the trees around me seem so vivid and real. My senses are heightened as I walk up the grassy hill. There isn't any breeze, but I feel the air brushing along my cheeks. There's a dampness too. I smell a pleasant odor of wet mud, dead leaves and blades of grass. My heart's beating fast. It's a weird mix of somnolence and excitement that I've only ever experienced when casting spells. I must have slipped into a trance... But why?

There's a flutter of wings and a black bird lands on a tree branch about a foot away from me.

"Amica!" I'm so happy to see her. I reach out my right hand, and the raven lands on my outstretched arm. I haven't seen Amica since before Alondra died. I pet her wings. The feathers are a little damp. Perhaps she's been in the lovely waterfall too. I walk towards the summit of the grassy hill as I pet Amica's wings. Up at the top is where I saw my deer. I wonder if she'll be there now.

The light gets brighter and I can smell fire. Then the light becomes redder. And I smell something like ceremonial incense. But then I smell something else that makes me stop. Something putrid and sulfur-like. I stand right below the summit, afraid to ascend to the top and approach the flames. Now it feels like I'm in a bad dream and, though I know I'm in a trance, I don't feel my usual sense of peace. I'm afraid. But Amica's tugging me forward with her claws.

"*Venite foras*," the raven croaks. "*Venite foras*."

"*Profecto*," I reply hesitantly.

Somehow, my feet follow my friend's claws. The burning of ash, frankincense, and myrrh fills my nostrils, but it fails to cover the stench of sulfur, which I associate with dark magic.

At the summit, girls are dancing naked. A group is circling around three witches on their knees. The circling witches' heads are snapping up and down as they dance, showing the whites of their eyes—they're quite drugged. I thought they would be from my coven. They're not. I don't recognize their faces. Except one. My skin crawls. Alondra. Alondra is standing close to a bonfire, naked and covered in camouflage paint. She is not worshipping. She is simply standing and watching a round wooden totem lying flat at a slight angle from the ground. Two men wearing black cloaks stand beside her.

I climb the last steps to the summit and walk behind the circle of nude dancing girls. They don't notice me. The totem in front of the fire is made of large wooden beams. Circling the wood is a thick burgundy velvet cloth. And on the wooden beams, facing the fire, lies a nude woman, strapped to the totem by ropes on her wrists. She is blindfolded with a strip of the burgundy cloth. When I back away from the fire and the witches, I notice that the beams and the circle of red cloth form an inverted pentagram, glowing in the firelight. I begin to tremble.

Then I recognize the men. I wish I didn't. Bill Reardon's devil face flickers in the red dancing light of the flames. Standing beside him is his "disciple," Bryce.

The woman on the pentagram squirms and pulls at her restraints. She's crying out in fear, but I can't hear her screams. I can't hear anything. In fact, the witches dance and chant, but I can't hear them either. I'm not sure if the captive is afraid because she's unsure where she is—for she's blindfolded—or if she knows where she is and fears what they're doing to her.

I run up to the pentagram and Amica darts from my arm. I pass Alondra and Reardon and run right up to Bryce. He just stares at the pentagram. His eyes are glassy—drugged.

"*Free her!*" I yell. But Bryce doesn't seem to hear me.

He looks different. His face is fully shaven, and he appears maybe five years younger. He walks right past me, ignoring me, and hands Reardon a curved knife from his cloak.

I move to the naked woman and tug at her ropes, but my hands pass right through them. I look at my hands. They're solid. I can feel warmth and smell the fire. But as the woman continues to clench her hands and fight against her restraints, my fingers can't even touch the ropes. My eyes drift down to my body, and I'm shocked to see that I'm not dressed either.

Is this a trance? A nightmare? It feels like both. I squeeze my hands, even pinch my hip, trying to snap out of it. I must be dreaming.

The witches are still circling a few yards away from the pentagram. I hear a steady drumbeat, but I don't see any drums. In the center, they continue to bow to the unholy totem.

Alondra walks over to the totem and pulls out a metal pentagram the size of her palm. She kneels and raises it to the moon. I run to her.

"Alondra! Please. Stop! What are you doing? Free her!"

She doesn't hear me. She just stares up at the moon.

I hear a scream. The woman is screaming and tugging on the boards, and I hear it this time. Reardon is gliding the curved blade along her bare skin.

"Stop!" I yell.

No one can hear me.

"Stop!"

But Alondra appears to be in a trance too. I've seen it before. Under the influence of mandrake, her eyes are wild. She is still staring up at the sky, drugged and unaware of everything. Then she looks toward the forest. I follow her gaze and see a shadow approach. It could be an animal. My deer?

I hear a scream again. I turn back to the pentagram.

"Alondra, help me!" I shout to her. "Is this a trance? Am I asleep? Help her!"

But she can't hear me.

There are more screams. This time it seems to come from the witches. They are all kneeling before the effigy. They've succumbed to madness, throwing their bodies on the ground, rising, and falling to the ground again. And now the totem is burning. No longer is the fire lighting the effigy from behind; it seems to be consuming the woman. And as she burns, the High Wizard runs his metal knife along her naked hips and breasts.

"Stop!" With all my might, I scream, "*Vade retro!*"

Lightning flashes from above and thunder quakes. The witches look to the sky for a moment and freeze. A shadow approaches from the trees, and I recognize it as the ghost I've seen on campus. She's a witch, transparent but wearing the same cloak as my coven. But as she moves closer to the fire, she vanishes.

Reardon removes the red cloth from the captive's eyes. Her eyes are a piercing blue. I recognize the face. Enora. But just like Bryce, her features are younger, much younger.

I run to Bryce. "Stop him!"

Reardon turns to Bryce, mouths words I cannot hear, and hands him the curved knife. Bryce nods, walks over to her, and runs the knife along her body. I see flashes of images, the same red images of a couple lying together that I saw at the eclipse. They surround me for seconds at a time as if transporting me back to Alondra's backyard. Every time Bryce runs the metal along the curves of Enora's body, flashes of their lovemaking reappear.

This is the sacrifice for my coven. This was their sick perverted way before I joined. They killed animals and "sacrificed" women by having sex with them. Images of Bryce having sex with Enora on the grass flash before me.

"End this incantation," says a very calm voice from the forest. I almost recognize the voice, but I can't quite place her. "End it now. Leave Cadence alone." I look to the woods, but I see no one.

Enora looks into my eyes as Bryce continues to run the knife along her body. She stops struggling and turns her lips toward his. They kiss passionately. Then she pulls away to look at me. "Witness what he did," Enora says with a smile. "I shall take my revenge on your Hawthorne coven. *Et nos unum sumus.*" And she bursts into laughter as Bryce continues to run the blade along her body.

I'm sick. The scene swirls in circles around me, and I am surrounded by Enora's laughter echoing on the hilltop. A chilly wind blows along the hilltop, and all the witches, the bonfire, and the effigy are scattered into the wind as if they were never there.

I'm left alone on top of the summit.

I fall to my knees, crying. But it's over. Hilltop Bluff is just a hilltop overlooking the university. It's dark. I'm naked. And cold. And alone.

I feel my raven land on my shoulder. That soothes me. Absentmindedly, I pet her.

"Oh, Amica," I say between tears. "What have they done?"

19

WHAT'S HAPPENING?

I'm knocking on Bryce's door once again without clothes. I'm well aware that I have now completely lost my mind. I'm a total fucking lunatic. I figure I either talk to my old lover or run through town and commit myself to the hospital. But I have to know. I have to know what this vision meant.

Bryce and Enora looked younger. It was my coven, but years ago, performing one of their "sacrifices." Yet the fact that Enora was struggling but then kissed Bryce, taunting me, made the whole thing feel like a message from her. Either Enora was showing me her past or the whole thing was her conjured-up illusion. It was just like the Billington House. Enora claimed the vision on Halloween of my boyfriend cheating on me was from the past too. I don't know. I have to know.

He opens the door in shock. I'm sobbing. He doesn't touch me.

"God, Cadence, what happened?"

"I saw you. I saw what you did."

"What? Do you have any idea what time it is?"

"I don't care!" I snap. "Look at me! I'm cursed! That bitch did this to me. She took off my clothes and made me watch her have sex. Have sex with you! Made me watch Reardon direct his disciple to fuck her. *How could you do that!*"

"My God. Just come inside."

But I don't want to. I'm so confused I don't even know what I want anymore.

So I curl up like a ball outside his door and sob more. If someone comes home in the middle of the night and sees me like this, they might very well call the cops. But I figure it's Bryce's fault. And Maddie's. Shit, I wouldn't be losing my goddamn mind if it weren't for my best friend and boyfriend.

Just when I think Bryce is going to close the door on me, he doesn't. Instead, in his pajamas, he just sits next to me by the threshold.

And I cry. I cry and cry. And the crying disgusts me.

I don't know for how long. Finally, when I stop, I look at him. He doesn't seem very nice. He looks angry.

"Come inside," he says impatiently.

I shake my head.

He just looks down.

"Enora threatened me," I say quietly. "And after what I saw, I don't blame her."

"What did you see?" It doesn't sound like he wants to know.

"I saw Reardon and you raping Enora."

"We never did that."

"Did you have ceremonial sex with her?" I can't believe I'm even asking that.

"Yes," he says. And that is far worse. I was hoping for a no.

"How is that not rape!"

"Calm down, Cadence." He puts his hand out.

"You said you never had sex with any of the girls in ceremony. You swore to me that it was only Reardon who did."

"I did swear and I meant it."

"Then what do you mean?"

Bryce takes a deep breath and runs his hand over his short hair. "If you really saw the past in a vision, you were watching the ceremony where I had sex with Enora."

"At Hilltop Bluff. Yes. *And* ..."

"At Hilltop Bluff," he repeats. But he hesitates and that almost makes me scream. He looks away, shaking his head. "It was years ago, Cadence. When I was dating her. I didn't have sex with anyone else in ceremony, ever, except her. At the time, I was having sex with her outside the ceremony too, because we were going out together. Reardon convinced me to do it and told me it was a requirement to join. He said since I was going out with her, it would be okay to do the public sex ceremony with her. She was also being initiated into the coven." He takes a deep breath again. "I know now it's wrong, Kate, and you've stopped our circle from doing this stuff."

"It's disgusting. Why did I have to be the one to put a stop to it?"

He nods with a sigh. "I'm not proud of it. I see that vision almost every day. You saw it just tonight... I wonder if I'm truly damned."

"Why didn't you tell me?"

"I did tell you. Just...not about my initiation."

"*Initiation?* Try rape. You had sex with Enora during a ceremony with her hands tied down with ropes!"

"She was never raped." He furrows his brow. Then he quickly shakes his head.

"With a curved blade and in front of the whole coven," I insist with a nod.

"Yes. There was that. But she was never tied down."

"You roped her to a pentagram with her screaming!"

"We never tied her." He shakes his head again. "And she never screamed. She never objected. She was fully able to get up and walk away at any time. You know that. That was always Alondra's code. She even told you the same thing on your initiation. She always told us that we could go if we became uncomfortable. Yes, she was on a pentagram—if that wasn't horrible enough. But she was never raped."

"That's not what I saw." I can't believe I'm even having this conversation. I don't want to and, looking at his forlorn face, he doesn't seem to want to either. "You said you never had sex in ceremonies. You said you just helped prepare and—"

"Preparing isn't a whole lot better, is it?"

I put my head in my hands.

"I didn't tell you because I was afraid I'd lose you, Cadence. That's it. I didn't want to lose you. I know how you felt, and you were right. I didn't want to disappoint you."

"So you lied to me. Just like you were afraid, last year, you'd lose me after telling me about Maddie, so you avoided telling me all winter? How many other virgins did you fuck ceremonially with Bill?"

That question makes him very angry. But he's too nice to lash out at me. He just doesn't look like he wants to fight. He wants to go to sleep. "Come inside, it's cold. Please."

It all fits Enora's story. It kinda absolves him...or does it? No, not really. So he had sex with Enora in a ceremony while going out with her. So? That's supposed to be okay? On a pentagram? Right. Oh, God.

He *claims* Enora wasn't tied down. That she wasn't suffering. That's not what I saw. But Bryce has never lied to me—he's hidden things but never lied to me. It's hard for me not to believe him. And I'm in a trance. Our witch trances are always mixed with illusion. How much of all this wasn't real? How much of it was Enora's spell? I mean, she was touching him while laughing at me again. But even still, he admits that the two of them did engage in public sex, and, as Bryce so disgustingly admits, it was on a satanic pentagram.

He doesn't look angry anymore; he looks awful. He probably hasn't been sleeping much either. How can he with Alondra's passing? And then I didn't let him go to the coven's Summerland service. That was mean.

I'm feeling bad for him.

"With no other girls, Katie," he insists, looking at me. "Not rape. Whatever you saw didn't happen that way. Enora consented and even wanted me to do it. Think about it. Alondra wouldn't have allowed Enora to suffer in ceremony...I told you, I did wrong. I've been struggling over this for years. Even before you joined. I've tried to apologize a million times. It was a long time ago. But there were no others in ceremonies with me. I swear it."

I get up and walk into his house. It's so warm and inviting. My raven, Amica, follows me in. Bryce would find that really weird if he weren't a warlock and member of our coven. It doesn't even faze him. I think he's too shocked at me being here.

I'm in my trance still. I can feel it. My heart is still racing. It's like I've drunk three cups of coffee. When in a trance, I feel a mix of sleepiness and power. But during tonight's vision, I was under a spell and felt weak. I must have been fighting Enora. Now that her conjuring is over, my power feels stronger. I feel confident. And all my senses are still in overdrive.

The smells in his apartment are overwhelming. I smell leftover pizza probably eaten by Bryce for dinner. I smell his cologne, which is odd because he usually applies it in the morning, but now it seems to permeate his entire apartment. It's irresistible. And even the mud and grime on my own body, from walking in the nude in the wilderness, is a pleasant earthy smell that reminds me of the lovely scent of fresh rain.

My anger fades, and as I walk around his kitchen naked, it's replaced by an odd feeling of arousal. I feel the warm air from a vent blow against my naked skin. And I feel his eyes watching me. I miss him. God, I miss him.

I open his refrigerator and grab a bottle of beer. I'm thinking he must be looking at me. I take out a bottle opener, snap off the cap, and drink it. It's cold. As I lift the bottle to my lips, I'm thinking he's checking out my silhouette, from the curves of my breasts down to my naked hips and ass. It's wrong, very wrong, especially with our fight, but somehow that makes it even more erotic.

I hear the door close. He must have kicked it shut because he's still sitting, leaning against a wall, watching me stroll around his kitchen in the nude.

"Enora?" I ask after drinking more beer. "Were you with her when I was at the Billington House? Feeling her up? That's what I saw." I'm being a bitch. But I want to be. Somehow, it's not anger anymore. It's almost playful. I smile at him lasciviously. He seems to squirm from my gaze.

"Yes."

I almost drop the beer bottle. I convinced myself that I was watching a scene from the past. This is not turning out to be a good night.

He quickly puts a hand up. "She tricked me, Cadence. She took me into a private room in the house." I'm not sure I want to hear this. "We talked. She apologized for things not working out. She said she missed me. Wickedly, she even congratulated me on finding you."

I walk over and crouch down beside him near the door. I drink some beer and then offer him the bottle, but he refuses. I catch him staring at my breasts for a moment, but he quickly looks up at my face. I smile and gaze into his eyes. That seems to make him more uncomfortable.

"Go on."

"Then she closed the door and pinned me against a wall," he says with a nod. "She used a love spell. She almost had me." He shakes his head. "I was so confused." He sighs and looks horrible. I feel bad for him. "I pushed her away. I thought of you. I was so upset. Then I heard she used magic to show you the whole thing. I was mortified hearing that. I felt so bad that I hurt you. I was so worried that I'd lost you, Cadence. Then I couldn't talk to you. I...can't lose you. I love you, Cadence... Enora's doing this. Panthera. I told you, she's not to be trusted. She wants us to break up so she can have me again. Or she just wants to make us miserable."

I jump on top of him. The beer rolls somewhere on the carpet, probably spilling, but I don't care. I want him so badly. I'm naked and I want to feel his warmth beside me. And there's nothing that's going to stop me from fucking him *RIGHT NOW*.

I'm in a trance. I must be. There's no way I'd ever do something crazy like this. I'm dirty—literally. There's mud on my feet and leaves and dust on my body. My hair is probably a complete mess. But I'm so aroused. I'm pushing my thoughts of the disgusting rites in his past and everything that happened during the Halloween party to the side. I don't care. The desire to touch him again is irresistible. And he's said enough to make me want to make up and be near him again. I believe him. I'm sorry for fighting. I want to touch him. To feel him touching me. Smell his cologne. It's everywhere. I want to feel his perfectly kempt hair. And...feel him inside me again.

I'm alone. I'm so unhappy. So sad. I have no one. I feel cold. And he's here. I'm in his house, touching him.

I run my hand along his new beard as my naked groin glides along his leg. The dark whiskers are thin, but cute. He neatly manicured it— that's so Bryce-like. I admire his hard cheek and his ever-so-slight dimple. And, of course, his blue eyes. Well, they may not glow like Enora's but, while hers are haunting, his are adorable.

I roll with him on the ground until I land on top of him again with a laugh. His blues look into my eyes with a mixed look of confusion and hunger. He wants me too. He looks shocked, but he doesn't push me off. I roll once more, roaring with laughter, until we hit a wall. I straddle him and my laughter stops. We look at each other, deadly serious. I close my eyes and move my hands along the curves of my breasts and circle my erect nipples. Then I bring one of his fingers up to my lips and suck it while slowly gyrating my naked pelvis up and down on the bulge under his soft pajama bottoms. He moans. I run the other hand through his short hair and down one of his arms. I clasp his fingers and lean down and kiss him passionately.

"Katie," he says between kisses. "Wait. You're still in a trance, baby, fighting Enora. And ... we...were just fighting too."

I open my eyes and look at his beautiful blues again. Even though his brow is furrowed, his pupils are dilated. I shake my head. I run my hand under his nightshirt, over his thin chest hairs and hard pecs. Then I lock my lips on his again, kissing him hard. I let go of his hand while he squeezes my tits.

I giggle and pull up his nightshirt; then I run circles on his hard chest. As my skin grazes his, I feel his breath, and I can feel his heart beating fast. I want to be close, so close. God, I miss him so much. I want to feel someone close to me again. I move up and down along the bulge in his pants, nearly orgasming on his cock.

"Cadence, wait," he says again. It's a weak objection, but because he's repeating it, it makes me pause. I don't want to. I know what I want. He answers the silence by reaching up and touching his lips to me again.

Quickly, though we're still at the threshold of the doorway, I yank down his pants and underwear. I'm so violent that I might hurt him. I don't think he cares. Then I grab his cock and rub it with my palm, up and down. I jerk him fast while he closes his eyes and moans. But I don't let him orgasm. Quickly, I mount him and take him inside me.

I'm riding him. Everything is happening so fast, but that's arousing me even more. We've never had sex like this before. It feels so good having him inside me again. We don't lock eyes. I just keep moving up and down, with one hand against the wall and the other on top of his chest. All my angst is gone. I feel alive being with my man. I'm not even sure what all the fuss was about. My senses make me feel more than I ever had before—a glimpse of his gaze, or the touch of his skin. Each thrust drives me to press harder into him. I grip his cheeks with both hands and rub his hair as I bounce up and down. Then my head dips down and we lock lips passionately once more. When I release his lips, I shout out his name. I love him so much. I press my fingers in between his. I think he objects again, but I'm in a trance and it only spurs me on harder. Nothing can stop me. Fucking and being in a trance have removed all concerns. It feels wonderful.

He groans. That makes me grind harder. I moan too.

I don't think either of us is even aware of what's going on until my raven, Amica, flutters right between us. This awakens Bryce and he shouts, "*Stop!*" and throws me off him. I fall and bang my head against the wall.

"Ow."

"What are you doing!" he shouts. "I said stop! What's gotten into you? Jesus, you're putting a spell on me too, Cadence!"

"I'm not," I say. *I think I am.*

"Get out! I don't want this! You haven't talked to me in weeks, and now you want to have sex with me?"

I snap out of my trance. I feel ashamed. I've never done anything like this before with Bryce. All my confidence, all my joy, all our love collapses like those blocks in the Billington House. I feel like I can barely move. And then I remember that we were fighting. I feel awful.

I lean against the wall naked. Bryce has already pulled up his pants and is standing over me. He's never looked so angry. Amica is still fluttering around Bryce, hitting him, but Bryce is too focused on shouting and hating me.

"Get off him, Amica," I say to my raven. "Stop it!"

I crawl over to the door and open it. Amica flies outside. Then I jump up. I have every intention of running away in shame, but Bryce snatches my wrist.

"Christ, Cadence, wait! Let me get you some clothes!"

"I'm...sorry," I say, shaking my head at him. I yank my hand back.

"I'm...really sorry. I don't know what I was doing. I'm so sorry. It was a trance. I'm—"

"Just come back in," Bryce says, shaking his head. His voice is calmer. "Please. It's so cold outside. It's okay."

I shake my head, running out of his apartment in tears.

What was I doing? Having sex with him? What the hell's the matter with me?

20

———

AS IF IT COULDN'T GET ANY BETTER

I DON'T KNOW WHAT TIME IT IS WHEN I REACH MY DORMITORY. FOUR? FIVE? Six in the morning? I don't know. All I know is it's foggy and dark outside. And I'm freezing. I touch my naked hip to the dormitory entrance and realize that, obviously, I am not carrying a card key. I should have remembered.

When I reached campus, I was running from tree to tree to avoid prying eyes. But no one was out there. Just the streetlights, shining down yellow curtains of mist. The touch of my wet, cold hip reminds me more of a toad's skin than anything human. I'm muddy, wet, and cold. I wrap my arms around my naked breasts and shiver like crazy before the glass door to the dorm. I sorely miss being in a trance. Being awake makes me aware of my horrible predicament.

I hesitate, look back at the trees lining the walkway, and look through the glass. The lights are on, but they're very dim. This is the one time when I'm not too keen on one of my neighbors opening the door for me.

Of course, there's only one thing for me to do. I stand on the walkway. The large high-rise, Krunner Hall, is across the road, and I'm wondering if any boys are gazing out their windows, seeing me naked in the shadows of the trees. Then, as if things could get much worse, I notice someone across the street, beside the entrance to the neighboring dorm. At first I think it's a guard or a student. Then I wish it were. It's a shadowy figure in a dark cloak staring down at the ground. Well, honestly, this is the one time I don't mind seeing my new witch-ghost.

I get to my dorm room window, squeeze myself into a bush, and rap hard on the glass. The lights are off, and I assume Maddie is sleeping. She turns on the light. I crouch down, doing the naked dance, moving about trying to cover my breasts and privates. I whirl around to Krunner Hall again, realizing that if no one could see me before, in the wee hours of the morning, they can now. My black figure's gone. Of course.

"Jesus, Cadence!" Maddie is looking out our window. Well, if people couldn't see me, now they can hear my indiscreet roommate. I gesture, telling her to run across the hallway and open the fucking door.

You can't imagine the relief I feel walking into the dormitory. The heater is like heaven. So is Maddie's hug.

I don't cry. I walk into her embrace, wearing her long coat. I think one or two people walk out, attracted by the commotion, but I don't turn to look. When they see me cradled in my BFF's arms, with mascara running down my face, probably, and mud on my arms and naked legs, they quickly run back inside their rooms.

I'm shaking. Freezing.

Maddie gets me inside our room. She turns off the light. Our drapes are open, and she gets that we shouldn't be showing all of campus our business. She pulls up the wooden desk chair—she probably doesn't want my dirty body on the bedsheets. Then she turns on a small lamp by the desk, along with our Keurig to brew something hot. I stare outside. My witch is back, facing our direction.

"I don't think he's going to talk to me ever again," I say finally.

Maddie sits on my mattress, facing me. All I hear is the percolating Keurig cup. She can't say a thing. We're silent until the drink is ready; then she jumps up, fills her Donald Duck mug, and hands it to me. I just blow the mist from it, enjoying the warmth. I still have her coat over my arms.

"I saw a vision," I say. I drink from the cup, still shaking. "Just now, out the window." I point at the witch across the street, near the entrance to Krunner Hall. Maddie opens her eyes wide, jumps up, and throws the curtains closed.

I chuckle. Maddie doesn't think it's funny.

"I had another vision earlier tonight. It was Enora," I say. "She was being ceremonially raped. And my boyfriend was in line. You know, Maddie, it was in the past. But it was as real as you are now."

"If it was in the past, Bryce already told you he was involved in those things."

"I know. But it was so horrible watching it. And then Enora looked at me. It was like a dream. I was in a trance, and I think she was too. She wanted me to see it. It was her conjuring. Then she threatened us because this happened to her."

We pause and I drink more tea. It's good. It's Earl Grey. Maddie knows I like Earl Grey.

"Then I came to Bryce's house. At his house, it was my turn. Naked, I jumped him and had sex with him. It was...I wanted so bad to get close to him again, you know. It felt good. But then I felt awful. Well, I don't think he's ever going to talk to me again."

Maddie's looking at me like I'm completely insane, and that doesn't make me feel any better. I sip more tea.

"Did you hurt him?" she asks.

I laugh. That makes her squirm. "No, I said I had sex with him. It happened so fast, I wasn't even sure how I got on top of him. I was in a trance. He threw me off. Then I ran."

Maddie gets up and walks over to the window. She's wearing a very cute blue lace robe. I recall buying it last year.

"What's outside the window, Cadence?" Maddie pulls back the drapes and peers out across the street.

I don't like the way she asks me that. I know Maddie, and she sounds really scared.

"The ghost I was telling you about."

"Are you all right?" she asks, looking back at me.

I chuckle. Because I'm thinking, *Sure, I'm fine. I just got transported to the past to watch a satanic witch ceremony, attempted to make up with my boyfriend by fucking him, and then ran across campus naked. No, I'm not fine, Madison.*

That's when someone knocks on our door. The noise makes us jump. I'm thinking it's the campus police.

Maddie walks to our peephole and looks out. "Shit," she says.

"What?"

"Reardon." She looks back at me, and now I'm the one with eyes bulging. "Did he follow you?" Maddie asks.

"No. Of course not."

She puts her hand on the door and locks it.

"Answer it," I say.

"What? Why?" She shakes her head. "No."

I jump up.

"Katie, you're barely dressed."

I wrap the long coat more tightly around me and walk up to the door. "What do you want?" I say.

"I have to talk to you two."

"It's..." I turn to Maddie. "What time is it?"

"Four thirty."

"It's four thirty," I say.

"Ms. Hawthorne, I need to talk to you now. It's very important. Even at this time. I must talk to you as High Priestess."

"At four thirty?"

"Yes. You probably won't sleep anyway."

As I open the door, Maddie pushes against it to stop him from coming in.

The former High Wizard is dressed in a blue-and-white checkered button-down, black slacks, spectacles, and loafers. He looks like a college professor, not the ringleader of a satanic cult. He nods as he walks in. I'm wondering if any of our neighbors saw him. Professors don't visit dormitories often—like never. Certainly not at four thirty in the morning. I clutch my coat a lot tighter, remembering he's a total pervert. Also because I'm still shivering. But I'm not scared of him. I remember the shield spell that I cast on him.

"I'll be brief," he says. I shut the door behind him. All we have is the dim light of the lamp. He faces me and says, "Ms. Hawthorne, I need your help. All of us are in trouble. The whole circle. And, as proof, I will tell you that I saw you tonight. I saw you in my dreams. We were at the hilltop reliving Enora's and Bryce's initiation. I saw you standing by my wife. And I know you weren't there a few years ago. You were there because of a spell. It happened in your sleep too. Tonight. Right?"

"I wasn't sleeping. I was wide awake on Hilltop Bluff."

He furrows his brow and looks at me as if that's impossible. Then he looks down at my naked legs. I don't like that. I snap, "What do you want?"

"Panthera entered my dreams," he explains. "Her hunt has begun. I knew this would happen. My hope was that my wife's efforts to make peace would stop her lust for revenge. My wife and I were able to keep her under control while Alondra lived, but now that she has passed, Panthera is free to torment us again."

"Alondra made peace with her before she died."

He shakes his head. "Enora is an evil witch." He leans against the wall and shakes his head. "Wicked. A twisted woman. She tormented me for months. She has great power and is well versed in witchcraft. She probably knows more of the arts than I do, maybe even more than Alondra. Not only that, but her energy is similar to yours. The combination is powerful. Her greatest talent is to work dreams. We need the witches in our coven to fight her."

He runs his hand along his goatee. Then he sits in our wooden desk chair. It sickens me to think that Professor Reardon is sitting in my bedroom on my chair.

I look at Maddie. Her pretty blue robe. Then I look down at my naked legs again. It reminds me of what this creep really is.

"Just get out," I snap, shaking my head. "I can't help you."

He furrows his brow. I admit, my anger seems random, but remembering his perversions disgusts me. He puts his hand up. "Wait. I need your help. You've proven your powers. I can help you channel it. I can cast a spell with you. You're stronger than Panthera, but you don't know how to use the craft. I can show you the craft through ceremony. I can—"

"Like you showed Bryce? No. I don't blame Enora. For all the sick—"

"She wants us to fight. She wants to break me. And to break the circle. She showed you everything tonight to align with you. She wants you to help her destroy me. That's why she had us share the vision." Reardon finally looks at Maddie. "I need you. Both of you. We can join the coven and fight her." He turns back to me, looking stern again. "If not, she won't stop. She'll slowly wear you down. I know. She did it to me for months until Alondra helped shield me from her. Now I'm asking you to help me."

"You came to me in a trance too. I had to cast a spell to ward you off."

He shook his head. "I dreamt that. That was her again, Ms. Hawthorne. She brought me to you in my sleep. She's trying to get you to hate me."

I already hate you.

"Why should we help you?" Maddie asks.

"She would never think I'd approach you. But I know we can only defeat her together. She means to break the circle. Joining together is our only hope to fight her. If we can't, she'll finish me, then she'll go after your boyfriend and then the rest of you. I warn you. She was once a part of our coven. Alondra had to expel her."

"Like she expelled you," Maddie says.

He nods impatiently. "Look ..." He stands up and focuses his eyes on me. "I heard about your vision at the party. Do you think I conjured *that*, Cadence? Isn't that proof enough?"

"Then why did Alondra make amends to her?" I ask.

"My wife was kind to a fault. She told me many times over the past year that her biggest wish was to befriend everyone she had slighted before she died...even you, Ms. Cadence Hawthorne."

I look away from his gaze. I hate him so much.

I walk over to the window and open the drapes, just like Maddie did earlier. Outside is my ghost witch. Immobile. More like a dark statue. Somehow, I knew she'd be standing across the street, facing me. I just knew it.

"Please leave," I say with my back to him. "But...I'll think about it. For my friends. Honestly, I don't like either of you."

"You don't have much time, Windstorm," he says. I hear the door open. "Come to my home when you two come to your senses. We will hold a ceremonial rite of protection. Our shield spell. But be quick. If you don't, none of us will be sleeping anymore. Goodnight, witches."

The door shuts behind me.

I hear whimpering. I whirl around, and it's my best friend with her head in her hands, crying on my bed. I run over and crouch beside her. I'm still filthy, but she doesn't seem to care. She falls into my arms.

"What's the matter, Maddie?"

"I'm scared, Cadence."

"I thought you thought I was crazy?"

"No, Katie," she says, shaking her head between tears. "I'm scared because I know now you're *not* crazy."

21

THE LOVERS

It's Tuesday morning and Reardon was absolutely right—neither Maddie nor I can sleep. Maybe his threat was just enough to keep us up the rest of the night. At least we don't have bad dreams.

So the two of us decide to go to our art history study group, being taught by you-know-who. It's the only way I can think of how to make up with Bryce. Well, I can't very well call him. Can I? That would be weird, right? I don't know. I'm so ashamed of what I did.

We arrive early, take two seats in the front—that's Maddie's idea—and wait for Bryce to arrive. There are only four desks at the front and three are taken, so I sit in the front and Maddie sits right behind me. It's cold and smells wet in the classroom from the rain outside.

I don't know why I want to see him teaching. It's a weird way to apologize. But I do want to see him. Besides, Maddie thinks it's a good idea to talk to him about Reardon. But we haven't been to Bryce's class in weeks. So I feel odd and a little nervous about the whole thing. But I suppose I have Maddie pulling up the rear behind me for support. My best friend's always there for me. I don't know, the whole thing is fucked up. It's screwy. But I don't know what else to do. I think I want to see him again. But then again...

"You look good," Maddie says, tapping my shoulder with a smile.

"So?"

"You look good. That helps."

Helps what?

I do look good. I cleaned myself up. I'm not wearing anything spectacular, just a light blue sweater and pants, but I took the time to apply some makeup and fix my hair in a ponytail. And I'm not wearing black makeup today. I'm even wearing red lipstick. I went with the normal-girl look because I want to feel normal. Like a normal college junior.

The three people sitting near me in the front row are looking me over too, but not in a nice way. These girls remind me of those snoots in the coffeehouse. They're talking about me. I'm not dressed like a witch, so it's not that. Maybe they heard gossip about me coming home in the dead of night, naked, in my best friend's arms?

Half the room fills up, which is impressive being that it's a study group. Bryce might not be as exciting as the professors, but he always gives away the most important stuff to know for the final exam.

Maddie taps my shoulder. I cock my head back, and she's pointing to the door, grimacing. Bryce walks in with his short hair soaking wet. He has a habit of not bringing an umbrella. He lugs his heavy brown bag up to the desk and looks out at the twenty or so of us. He has bags under his eyes. His gaze falls on me for a second, and his expression becomes hard to describe—like he was looking forward to seeing me, but also dreading it. He runs his hand through his short hair and sighs. Then he pulls out his computer and textbook, acting like he didn't see me.

"Open your textbook to page one hundred and thirty," he says. "If you don't have it, just log on to the website. I've highlighted what we're covering this morning. Surrealism." He presses a few buttons on his keyboard. "I was going to talk about Salvador Dalí first, perhaps the most famous surrealist artist, but this morning..." He looks right at me. "Suddenly I feel inspired." He puts a painting on the screen of a couple with white shrouds over their heads, embracing and kissing. "This one is from René Magritte. Magritte is my favorite surrealist. Actually, Dalí and Magritte met each other in 1929. They were contemporaries.

"What does this painting mean to you? It could mean that the couple is anyone you know who's in love. Perhaps your own wife or husband, girlfriend or boyfriend. Or the white clothes could represent shrouds.

The death of love." He glances at me. "But this is a history class. I'll leave your artistic interpretation to you." He pauses and looks down at his computer.

Maddie taps my shoulder. I look back, and she's got a big smile on her face. She thinks he's being funny.

"The surrealists came out of the Dada movement. Know about the Dada movement for your exam. The Dada movement strove to break down all the rules in society following the horrors of World War I. A famous example is the urinal by Marcel Duchamp. It's literally a urinal signed by the artist." A picture of a urinal comes up on the screen, and students laugh. "You all know how silly modern art can be. This is one of the earliest examples.

"Out of the chaos of the Dada movement came surrealism. Remember, this period was a time of great turmoil. We had the 'war to end all wars,' World War I. Estimations vary from twenty to eighty million deaths in the world. Some of the deaths, of course, can be attributed to the Spanish Flu epidemic of 1918. Then there was the Great Depression, starting in 1929, followed closely by World War II. Obviously, World War I was not the 'war to end all wars.'

"World War II introduced us to Nazi gas chambers and fears of complete domination by the new racist-fascist world order of the Third Reich. And, of course, the H-bomb. Nuclear fission. I postulate that all these horrible things made society ripe for escapism, to transport people away from the world's troubles. In film, the fantasy *The Wizard of Oz*, in 1939, is another great example of this. Many of you are history majors. Knock yourselves out citing examples like this in your final essay." He pauses for a moment, types something on his keyboard, and looks back at the screen. "Here's my absolute favorite."

On the screen behind him is a painting of a nude woman, blue at the level of her chest and skin-colored below. "This is Magritte again. This is called *Black Magic*. I love how Magritte blends the woman's profile into the surrounding clouds and nearby rocks. This is one of my all-time favorite paintings. Magritte is mixing her body into nature. It's magnificent. Many different adaptations of this were painted during World War II. This one, the greatest in my opinion, was painted in 1945. Obviously, Magritte was trying to deflect the stresses of war."

He stops for a moment. Then he rubs his chin, walks pensively around the desk, leans back, and looks at us. His eyes fall on me and he says, "Why do you think he called it *Black Magic*?"

No one answers.

"Cadence?" he asks, infernally looking right at me.

"She didn't raise her hand," Maddie snaps behind me.

"I just want to know her thoughts, Maddie," he says with a shrug. A few girls snicker behind us. I think by now it's a foregone conclusion that he and I are dating—or were dating. Everyone knows the three of us know each other, and there's plenty of gossip about our weird goth cult. But, as I told you, I don't like it when he picks on me in class, and he knows it. So does Maddie. We've told him a thousand times.

"It's a lovely painting of a naked girl's body," I reply with as much smugness as I can muster.

The class laughs. Bryce, who's trying to act cool, blushes a little.

"But the title's interesting, isn't it? I did some research." He jumps up, paces a little, and walks behind the desk again. Then he looks down at his computer screen. "Magritte never explained why he called it *Black Magic*. It almost makes you wonder if he had knowledge of the occult. For those of you in last year's metaphysical history class with Dr. Johansen, you might recall that the occult deals with how nature affects the human condition. Certainly, this painting broaches this subject. The woman is blending in with nature, and practitioners of the occult, particularly witchcraft, worship nature. This is why I adore this painting so much— not just because the model is naked"—the class laughs again—"but because Magritte has blended his model into nature. The lower half of her body is flesh-toned and part of the rock. The upper torso is a part of the clouds. This also hints at the dichotomy of our very existence, doesn't it? Some parts being of the earth, our animalistic primal nature, others being a part of the heavens. It is the dichotomy of the human condition. I love this one."

I raise my hand.

"Yes, Cadence?"

"I think I prefer the painting of the couple kissing behind white shrouds." I challenge him with the bitchiest look I can muster. If everyone weren't looking at me, I would have stuck my tongue out at him.

The class laughs again.

"You can fancy whatever painting you want. This is a history class." *Yes, I know. So why don't you stop making it a talk about US?* "*Black Magic* became a theme for Magritte in the mid-1940s," he continues, "in the same year as the Battle of the Bulge, the last German offensive. And, of course, the same year as the dropping of the bomb on Hiroshima and Nagasaki. Once again, I suggest that Magritte was taking us away from the horrors of his time. And by showing the dichotomy of the heavenly and the earthly, I believe he made the figure in the painting more human. Fallible in a way." He checks his computer screen again. "Well, there I go interpreting again. Know the dates of the Battle of the Bulge and the bombs dropped on Imperial Japan. Delve into the details, like how many soldiers, tanks, and bombers were used in the last German offensive. When the atomic bombs were dropped. Etcetera. These two events were critical in ending World War II. Magritte provided us a refreshing respite during this terror."

I do like the painting *Black Magic*. And I like *The Lovers*. I even like Dalí's stuff. Bryce and I have similar taste in art, you know. I even fancy Dalí's weird mustache, because I like weird stuff too. But I kind of think that my boyfriend is extrapolating his feelings into the artwork. And I don't like how he was looking at me while talking about *Black Magic*. Like I represent the half-earth, half-heavens girl to him.

I jot down the dates and yawn. Then I zone out for the rest of the class. This is a bad idea because, unlike the last time I came to Bryce's class, I haven't gone to lecture this week, so I haven't seen the paintings he's showing on the screen.

Class ends.

Maddie and I join the line to talk to Bryce as the classroom empties.

"Are we supposed to be *The Lovers*?" I quip when it's my turn to talk. Maddie and I were the last people in line, so I don't think he'll mind my bluntness.

"So we're talking, Cadence?" He shoves his computer back into his bag. "That was a really strange night last night."

"She saw Enora," Maddie says.

"I know," he says with a slight smile at Maddie. He throws the bag over his shoulder. Then he says, "I know you were having a hard time,

Katie. But running from my house naked—did it make you feel any better? Because I thought it was reckless and stupid."

Then he looks at Maddie, probably wondering why she hasn't left us alone. Maddie's holding my hand. This is my best friend's opportunity to get to the point. But instead, she's defending me. "She's having a real hard time, Bryce. We all are."

"You two," he says, looking down at Maddie's hand. "You're inseparable." He leans against the desk. The classroom has emptied out. Then he looks at Maddie. "Can you give us a second alone?"

"As long as you tell him," Maddie says, looking at me.

I nod.

Maddie's gone. Now it's just me and my "boyfriend."

It's pouring outside. I have an umbrella in my backpack. I walk over to my chair, pull it out, and hand it to him. That's my unspoken attempt to sort of apologize. It's weird, but sometimes I just can't be direct when I'm upset.

"I told you everything, Cadence." He stares down at my umbrella in his hands. "I've never lied to you. Enora was an old flame, but it's over. I'm sorry you saw what you saw—both times. But you hurt me." He looks into my eyes. "I loved you, Cadence. But I can't love someone who doesn't trust me."

It's silent except for the rain. Bryce looks out, still holding my umbrella.

"I need some time," I say.

He furrows his brow. "It didn't seem like you needed time last night."

"I was under a trance. I don't know what came over me. I'm sorry."

He nods.

"I just need time to think. On Halloween...Halloween, that night, I do think you were under Enora's spell. But I'm not sure that—"

"Okay, Cadence." He walks to the door.

"Wait."

He stops and turns.

"Reardon came to my dorm last night. He saw me watching you and the circle in my vision. Enora had him reliving the past in his dreams. It was Enora. Just like it was Enora who flipped me into a trance. He thinks Enora is conjuring spells to hurt us. She threatened us last night in my vision. Reardon thinks she's going to do worse in our dreams if we don't do something."

"She is. She's messing with us, Katie. And she's done it before. I told you she's a wicked, evil witch."

"Then I need your help. That's why I came here this morning."

"That's why you came here this morning?" he repeats, finally permitting a smile.

"Well..." I bite my lip. "I'm also a little rusty on studying. You know, I didn't go to lecture this week."

"I won't tell Professor Riker."

"Maddie and I talked things over. In order for the circle to be complete, we need you. You. You know the last thing I want to do is hold a Witch Sabbath, but after last night and Halloween, I believe Reardon. I know Enora is casting spells to hurt me. To...hurt us. I'm scared for us. Reardon can preside, but he's still technically expelled by Alondra. We need you there."

"You didn't let me preside over Alondra's funeral."

"I know. God, I'm sorry, okay? How many times do I have to tell you that?"

"How many times do I have to tell you?" he asks, and he takes a deep breath. "I've apologized about my past. I don't want to go over it anymore. When are you going to just forgive me?"

And that reminds me of Alondra. It was so hard for me to accept her apology. Only in the final moments, when she touched my hand, did she hear me accept her apology. I felt she heard it. I just know she did. Now Bryce is asking the same thing.

But the things they did. Is it forgivable? Alondra asked that too.

"I accept your apology, Cadence," he says formally. But he looks a little angry.

"Oh, Bryce," I say, tearing up. But we don't embrace. And I'm thinking of last night. I wanted so desperately to hold him. It wasn't just a trance. Or lust. I wanted desperately to be near him again. And that makes me choke up even more. I force my words. "Just meet us this Friday. Mira's already preparing. We're going to see if we can invoke a shield spell. The same one Alondra cast to protect Reardon. He's the last old fart I'd ever want to protect, but if it will protect our sisters, I'll do it. I'll meet with our coven this last time."

"I don't like this." He shakes his head. "I don't trust Reardon anymore either." But he takes a deep breath. He walks a little closer. In the past he would have gathered me in his arms, but he's still hurt. I suppose I could grab him... but I already tried that last night. I'm so conflicted.

"If you do this," he says, "you can bet Panthera will fight. Are you ready for that, Katie? She'll use her powers again. If she can get you to channel your power with the High Wizard, she could turn it against us. Then there's Reardon himself. You'll empower him too. This is so risky."

"I don't think she'd ever expect me to try to help Reardon. I can't believe I want to do it myself. But she's got to be stopped. I know she's messing with us, Bryce. I don't think Reardon is. And it's for a shield spell."

"All right. Name the time."

"Friday, of course. At ten."

He looks down at the umbrella in his hands, shakes his head, and hands it back to me, but I don't take it.

"We'll walk together," I say.

"Are you sure?" he asks.

"Yes." I nod. "Friends?"

"Always, Katie."

22

TACO TUESDAY

Taco Tuesday is my absolute favorite meal at the dining commons. It's like you can mix just the perfect amount of shredded beef, cheese, lettuce, and salsa with either their crunchy shells or tortillas. I don't know. I mean, it's not *that* amazing, but I look forward to it every week. I always fix up a couple of tacos with a couple of cookies. They usually bake fresh cookies on the same day. You'd think they'd spread out their cuisine and leave the really good stuff for Meatloaf Monday but, apparently, they want Taco Tuesday to be perfect.

So I'm sitting with Maddie at a table, in these blood-orange plastic chairs, watching cartoons on the TV screen on the wall and waiting for Mira. And since when have I ever waited for Mira? She doesn't even go to the dining commons anymore, being that she's living in an apartment off-campus her senior year. So she'll have to pay. But Maddie and I invited her.

Now I'm throwing some extra shredded cheese on my taco.

It's really busy. The semester is coming to an end, and finals will be here soon. Christmas will be here soon too, but you'd never guess it at Hawthorne. There's no celebrating Christmas at Hawthorne U. From what I heard, the college felt that celebrating Christmas would be prejudicial to all the other holidays. This is why Halloween is so big.

Anyway, I'm enjoying my stuffed soft taco when Maddie, who hasn't touched her food, says, "How are you and Bryce doing?"

"Good, I guess." I shrug.

"That bad, huh?"

"I don't know. I told you after class we walked through campus, but I used my umbrella more to keep us dry than to keep us together, you know?"

"He likes you."

"He said he loves me, but it's just distant right now."

There's a stupid cartoon on with a cat. It's like a take on Tom and Jerry. There are so many cartoons like that about cats. Of course, half the students are staring at their phones anyway. I think the TV show is really old, like from the '90s.

"The two of you will come along." Maddie finally picks up her taco. She picked a hard shell this time, and it crunches as she eats. She's in such a sour mood that it looks like the crunching bothers her.

"What about you and Rock?"

"I told you it was over, Katie. You know that."

"Too bad," I say with a shrug.

"He's an asshole. Not like Bryce." Then she looks at the shadow cast on our white plastic dining table.

"Hey, guys." Mira waves.

"I paid for you already," Maddie says with a smile, standing up and giving Mira a hug. "Did they tell you up front?"

"No. But it doesn't break my bank."

"Fucking fuckers." Maddie hits the table.

"It's okay."

Everyone in the room is staring at Mira. She's wearing a really long black dress that's trailing from her back. She's got on the same black lipstick and mascara we're wearing tonight, but it's thicker. Mira takes one of two open chairs. Then she looks at me and smiles lasciviously. "Hi, Windstorm," she says with a wink.

"Hi, Mira."

"Shall we get down to business?" Maddie asks.

"If we must." Mira tries to make herself more comfortable in the plastic chair.

"You should get some tacos," I say. "They're to die for."

"I already ate," Mira says. "So, what did that jerk tell you?"

I put my taco down, wipe my face, and nod. "He says the circle's in trouble. He says we need to perform magic to shield the coven from Panthera."

"More like shield her from him. Alondra protected him. Panthera hates Reardon more than anyone. I don't like either of them."

"Bryce told me that. But—"

"How are you and Bryce?" Mira asks, renewing her grin. She's leaning back in the chair with her head on her hand, staring at me. I look around the room again. Some of the eyes have left us, but I still feel like we're being watched. Because of Mira. The funny thing about Mira, with her large glistening nose ring and red-and-black demon tattoos along her neck, is that she doesn't really care.

"Fine," I say. "So what do we do?"

"You two still copulating? I told him that sex weakens magic."

"Shut up. That's none of your business."

She laughs. "Don't you love it how Cadence gets flustered, Maddie, when I tease her about sex? She gets so worked up." Her black-lace-gloved hand touches my hand. "Sorry, you're still a Bo-Peep at heart. No longer a Bo-Peep, no offense, but just a Bo-Peep at heart. It's really cute."

"My sex life is none of your business."

"Aha."

"Can you prepare a shield spell with Reardon or not?" asks Maddie.

"Of course I can," Mira says, turning stern. "But why would you want one? The things he did to our circle. He deserves anything coming to him from Panthera. Let her torment him. And as for the rest of us, I'm not sure she cares. I think she might just leave us alone." But then she looks at me pensively for a moment and wags a finger. "But maybe not you and Bryce. You and Bryce... Cadence, Bryce was Reardon's *special* assistant. Perhaps he's not safe either. Maybe she's not just trying to make you jealous. Maybe she's tormenting him."

More like tormenting me.

"Did he ..." How can I say this? My stomach turns. I've never asked Mira this. "Did he partake in the sex ceremonies with Reardon?"

Mira laughs. I don't think it's very funny. "He had his way with Enora in ceremonies, Katie. That made him powerful in the circle's eyes. But that was their initiation. Bryce didn't screw other girls in the circle—as far as I know. He helped arrange things for the High Wizard, though. So did I. He even helped him with—" She looks really uncomfortable for the first time. "Me." Then Mira falls quiet. She narrows her eyes and looks angrily at the table. "Are Windstorm and Bryce still having romantic problems? I told her—"

"I said it's none of your business," I interrupt.

Mira laughs again. "You just asked me if he had sex with other women in our ceremonial rites." Mira looks up at the TV cartoon. She rolls her eyes and shakes her head. Then she looks back at me. "I told you the tarot cards showed a disturbance in love. I told you it would probably be you and him."

"What do we need to prepare?" Maddie asks impatiently.

"She doesn't want to know," Mira says, pointing a thumb at me.

"Tell us," I say. "That's why you're here."

"No, that's not why I'm here," Mira snaps, wrinkling her nose angrily at me. "I'm here because your friend invited me."

And that's when a familiar voice says, "Hi." I've heard this voice all my life but, here and now, I just can't place it. So when I see a tall guy with long light-brown hair thrown to the side, wearing a T-shirt and jeans, I'm dumbfounded. It's Damien, my kid brother.

"Hi, sis," he says with the same smile he used to give me when he wore Mom's frosting on his lips and cheeks. It's cute. But under the current circumstances, it's not. I'm in complete shock. He nearly loses his smile, probably because I don't jump into his arms. The absolute last thing I want is for him to be a part of our special witch meeting.

"Why are you here?" I ask rudely. That seems to confuse him even more.

Maddie gets up and shakes his hand. "Hi, Damien."

"Hey, Madison." He puts an arm around her. Then he looks at Mira, who is looking at Maddie, waiting to be introduced.

"This is our friend Mira," Maddie says.

"Charmed," Mira replies, shaking his hand. When Mira does her famous wicked grin, it's too much. I jump up, take Damie's arm, and pull him from our table.

"It's hard right now," I say, dragging him away, "'cause finals are coming up and everything. And, you know, Alondra and all."

He gives me a hug. I think he's shocked I still haven't hugged him.

"Don't worry, sis, I'm here with Harvey and some friends. I just wanted to say hi. Harvey's probably coming here next year. Isn't that great? You know, Katie, that Harvey's like my best friend. It's going to be so much fun. And being that it will be your senior year, you can show a measly little freshman around town. Right?"

"Sure, Damie."

We're near the table and I'm, like, physically pulling him away, but he's resisting. Mira and Maddie are all smiles, and that's upsetting me more.

"Wait a second," I say. "Did you say *coming here*?" *No way. Nuh-uh.* "No!"

Damien steps back. It's like I struck him in the face. You have to understand that I love my brother to death, but I can't stand the idea of him coming to school here.

"I thought you'd be excited," he says, furrowing his brow. He looks bewildered. But then he recovers his usual kid-brother energy and says, "Harvey's premed too, you know... Katie, I just wanted to say hi. Forget it. I can see you're busy. I'll see you 'round later. I'm going back home tonight."

"Okay, fine. Hi," I say derisively. And that seems really mean.

"It's sure good to see you again, Damie," Maddie hollers from our table, being a bitch.

"Nice meeting you, Mira," he says.

"You too," Mira says with a wink.

Damien leaves.

I sit down and stare at my tall brother as he walks back to a table full of boys. He glances back, still looking confused. I feel really awful for being so mean. I really love him. I feel like he should be joining us or something. But if he knew the weird stuff we were talking about, he would probably be happy to stay away.

When I turn back and see Maddie staring at him, I hit the table. "Cut it out!"

"What?" Maddie asks.

"What do we need to do, Mira!" I snap. "Stop beating around the bush and just say it."

"What a nice brother," Maddie says.

"Shut up, Maddie," I say.

"Just saying." Maddie shrugs. "I was a lonely child. I think you're pretty lucky, Cadence, to have a brother like that."

"What do we need to do to prepare, Mira?" I ask for like the fifth time.

"Windstorm," Mira says.

"Yes, what do we need?"

"No." Mira shakes her head. "We need Windstorm. Windstorm is what we need, Cadence. *You* have to prepare Windstorm. You haven't let us hold a true Sabbath for months—with the exception of the time you let Panthera cast her spell in Alondra's backyard. You haven't let us perform sacrifices, which"—she narrows her eyes and shakes her head at my taco—"would excuse you for eating meat. You don't abstain from sex outside ceremonies." She infuriatingly chuckles. "All that weakens a witch. No doubt you hold the strongest magic in the coven, but your lack of belief, your disregard for Selene, for our circle, even for your lover's power, might lead us to peril." Mira pauses and looks around the room. She frowns. "So...are you two witches or are you losers like all these stupid kids enjoying cartoons and tacos?"

"I like tacos," I say.

"Serves my point." Mira opens her hands in an irritating gesture of mockery.

"But what do we do?" Maddie asks. "What do we need for the ceremony? Just tell us."

"I've prepared things at Alondra's house. The stones have been placed around the logs, our unused cloaks remain on the wall, and I do not foresee any clouds to upset our ceremony." Mira glances at me with a grin. "Unless Katie plays with the weather. We have to cast a spell around us. We can use the normal circle with our stones, but we need to amplify our power. Specifically, we will need to name the witch that threatens us: Panthera. Reardon will have to be present but, of course, he's been banished—and I don't think, Katie, you're about to reinstate him. So your boyfriend Bryce will preside as our High Wizard. I hope you're not fighting so much that Bryce is refusing to come. Are you?"

"No, he'll be there."

"Then it's all set. Everyone just come to our Sabbath on Friday."

"Do we have to hurt Enora?" I ask.

"How sweet." But Mira looks down in thought, as if I just asked her about a difficult scientific theorem. "She will fight back. She's not one to back down. When she sees what we're casting, she will want to shatter our magic shell. She might get very aggressive." Mira's auburn eyes stare into mine. "You'll have to be ready. You are our High Priestess. She's already fought and tested you. She now knows your weaknesses. But she's also likely to be afraid of you. No one doubts your power. You're going to have to be ready for a tough fight."

I don't want to fight. Especially with magic. I hate witchcraft. I don't mind being a witch and feeling one with nature, but I hate spells.

"Cadence doesn't know how to conjure spells like you do," my best friend interjects. "Do you plan on running the incantation?"

"No, Bill will."

"No." My eyes open wide and I shake my head. "No way."

"You're kidding," says Maddie.

"He's cast out," Mira explains, raising her hand, "but he's the only one who can recast the same protective spell Alondra used. He knows the spell. I can help, but we'll need his grimoire. We could cast a different spell, but we know this one worked. As long as we conjure a protection spell and name the excluded party, Panthera, Reardon should stay in line."

"I trust him even less than I trust Enora," I say.

"Yeah, but without Reardon's help, you won't be able to shield us from Enora with the same spell Alondra cast. Again, Bill will come as our guest, not the head warlock of our coven. That's why we need Bryce there."

"So that's it?" asks Maddie. "We all meet and just cast the old shield spell?"

"Aha," says Mira.

"No nudity," I warn. "And no drugs."

"You're no fun," Mira says with a grin.

"Alcohol's all right, Katie?" asks Maddie with a grimace.

"Nothing, guys. You promise?"

Mira shrugs but nods. Maddie nods too.

I finally bite into my taco. Somehow it seems to have lost its taste. Maybe it's the butterflies swarming in my stomach. I'm so scared. This is why I never go to meetings with the witches in my circle anymore. I love them, but I don't want to face magic.

"Don't worry, it's gonna be fun." Mira touches my arm with a wink.

23

THE BLACK SABBATH

The three days from our meeting with our Sabbath planner in the dining commons to Friday were painful, sleepless nights. Almost every couple of hours, Maddie woke me up, asking if I was sleeping. She was scared too. Not only were we worried about today, but we were afraid Enora was going to attack us in our dreams.

Now we're together in Alondra's backyard, and there's relief in that. All my friends grab their black cloaks from the wall. We're somber. Few laugh or even talk, which is not normal for my friends, but not only are they anxious, but coming to her house reminds them of Alondra's passing. We haven't gathered since the funeral.

Bryce is here. He grabs his cloak next to me, nodding coldly. That bothers me too. It makes me wonder if we will ever be close again.

I see Reardon. He takes his cloak off the metal hook just like the rest of us. His bald head reflects the patio lights. He even smiles at me, the weirdo. I don't smile back. I just wish he weren't here.

Mira has already arranged all the white plastic chairs around a low simmering flame. It's dark out without a moon and a little cloudy, and the flame is so low that we can barely see the yard, aside from three lights on a backyard overhang. When the fire rises and we're more accustomed to the night, we'll shut the unnatural lights off.

It's cold, but it's not raining or snowing. Mira was right about that, as usual. That's one of her quirky powers—forecasting weather. I've got on a sweater and two shirts under the cloak, but it's not warm enough to stop me from shaking a little—unless I'm shivering from nervousness.

As we make our way to the large white stones and chairs, the ceremony has kind of already started. Even walking together makes me feel like we're worshipping. Some of us carry lit candles by our sides, and others carry incense in their palms. Mira is walking in front of us, carrying an old book with a crescent moon on the cover. She's chanting something in gibberish in front of me. Usually it's funny, but somehow tonight it's not. It's creepy.

All of us except Reardon sit down on the white plastic chairs, which have been arranged around the fire. Reardon stands and faces us, with his bald head glistening in the red light from the flames behind him. The fire is about three feet high, and it's difficult to see the girls behind him. Maddie and Frida are sitting beside me. I've lost Bryce. Mira hands Reardon his small grimoire before sitting down a few chairs to my right.

"Close your eyes, girls," Reardon says. "I am honored to have been asked by Windstorm to perform this shield spell with the Hawthorne coven one last time. A disturbance has entered our circle since the passing of my wife. We are here to stop it." Sounds sensible enough. I just want him to get it over with. "By shadow and darkness, we focus. Hold hands." He closes his eyes. I don't. Just as in the past, this bald figure with a pointed beard, wearing a black witch cloak with flames behind him, looks like the very manifestation of Satan. He opens his eyes and starts reading from his small wizard book. "All hail the dark lord. Come to us. We beckon you. We stand before you. We call on your names, prince of darkness. Mephistopheles. Beelzebub. Lucifer. Baphomet. We are safe within your arms inside this sacred circle. The white stones defend us against all who attempt to penetrate the circle. Neither scourge, nor dagger, nor sword shall pass. *Lux tenebris*."

We all say "*lux tenebris*." And the magic has begun. Because the words come from my lips, but my mouth is not fully under my control.

"Sacrifice yourself in meditation and allow atman to flow, girls. With virginity cometh my seed, sacred semen, to enter your very being. My offering." Here we go. I'm squirming. And I feel Maddie's hand tighten. She knows I'm super uncomfortable.

"*Lux alba*," Mira says meekly, not at all like her normal self.

"Bring me the mandragora, disciple."

I didn't see it prepared. Bryce walks between Maddie and Hope, carrying a heavy barrel. He sets it next to Reardon. Then he lifts the lid and stands beside the High Wizard, placing his hands behind his back, and closes his eyes. In my trance, it takes me a moment to register what's going on. This is mandrake, or mandragora. Mandrake is a drug. A powerful hallucinogen. And I forbade all drugs for tonight's meeting.

"Wait. No." Everyone opens their eyes and awakens from their trance. "We had an agreement. I said no drugs."

"You asked Raven and me to protect the circle," the High Wizard says. "The only way is with potions. This is what Falconsong used when she protected us. If you want protection for the whole circle, there's no other way. I can't cast this spell without it."

"No drugs," I repeat.

"There can't be a shield spell, then. You must consent."

Am I to stop everything now? Maddie looks at me, knowing I'm capable of canceling the whole thing, and shakes her head. And certainly, Bryce didn't object. He just brought the barrel over. I'm trapped.

"I don't consent," I say. "I am the circle's leader."

"No doubt you are, Windstorm. But I tell you that the spell is worthless without mandragora. This is the only way. If you permit me, I can sprinkle but a small amount on our sisters."

I look at Bryce. He hesitates, but then he nods somberly. I turn to Maddie, sitting beside me, and she nods too. Then Mira. Mira doesn't move. She's just staring into the fire.

Using mandragora is not that strange to us. In fact, we had countless Sabbath ceremonies with mandrake last year without sacrificing virgins or worshipping the devil. But I don't like it.

"It is clearly written in this grimoire," the High Wizard continues. "In fact, Falconsong herself officiated with it many years ago. Your own initiation involved it. This comes from the ancient rites as far back as Eliphas Levi. It is a secret rite used by Falconsong and the Hawthorne coven and the only way for the magic to fully manifest itself. I assure you"—he addresses everyone in the circle, even the witches behind the flames—"this will shield us from the coven's threat. Once and forever. Do you not want me to do this, witches?"

And this is what everybody wants. Everyone's afraid of Enora. In fact, I was not the only one with visions. Hope, Frida, and Marilyn came to Mira and told her of their own terrible nightmares. The whole coven has been affected by this evil witch. And then I think of Halloween and her casting a spell showing me my boyfriend and nearly tearing our relationship apart. And the eclipse and Panthera's nasty smile.

"Raven?" I ask Mira. "Do we have to use mandrake? Is there no other way?"

Mira looks away from the fire and finally meets my gaze. She is already in a trance. "If he must use such powerful black magic, there is only one other way under Baphomet." She shakes her head and looks fearful. "But you won't consent to that, Katie. I'm absolutely sure. And even he"—she points to the High Wizard—"has never performed it."

"What?"

Mira hesitates.

"Blood," the High Wizard says with a nod. "A disturbance with blood would be enough to throw you all into a trance. Human blood. My wife always chose mandragora. There are other witches practicing under Baphomet who perform human sacrifice. Injury, murder, or even sacrificial abortions."

"Disgusting," I cry.

"It'll be quick, Katie." Maddie squeezes my hand. "Let him use mandrake to protect the group." Maddie looks into my eyes in the flickering light. She nods. "Please. Panthera's hurting us."

I hesitate. I look around the circle.

"Are you all willing to do this?" All of them nod. "Do you all consent to this?" I look at every one of my sisters. They all nod.

I reluctantly give a quick nod to the beast.

"Everyone circle the fire slowly," the High Wizard says with the hint of a smile. I sense triumph in his grin. "I shall stand here and anoint you with the holy magic of mandragora. I will sprinkle it on your skin."

I return to my place and begin walking behind Maddie. Frida, one of my other favorite friends, walks behind me.

"Walk sideways," the High Wizard instructs. "Hold hands as you walk, facing the fire. We weave this shield."

We walk facing the flames with craggy old Bill Reardon waiting for Bryce to hand him the flask beside the fire. Bryce dips the flask in the barrel. Surely, I figure, Bryce is already getting a dose of the drug by scooping his hand in. Mandrake is potent through skin contact. This is the reason witches dance naked around the fire. Naked, the full potential of the drug is felt as it permeates the skin. But as Bryce hands the High Wizard the flask, Reardon takes it a step further. He tilts his head back and empties the entire flask of reddish-brown fluid into his mouth. This is a powerful dose, one that once made me very sick. Indeed, Reardon's eyes become wide, and he looks at us with madness. It's as if he's been given great power.

I'm already ashamed. I should have stopped him. I feel weak. Alondra trusted me with her coven. She handed me responsibility. Now I'm handing it to a pervert to shield us. Why? Why should I trust him? I don't trust him.

Reardon hands the flask back to Bryce, and Bryce refills it. I glance at Bryce as I circle the fire. Judging from his blank stare, he is already getting high off the mandrake too.

As we circle around like schoolchildren, holding hands, Reardon begins sprinkling the liquid on each of us. Each witch, as we slowly pass, gets a few spritzes and then a few more. He sprays it on their faces and, after a few slow circles around the fire, I catch some of the witches licking it off their lips, bobbing their heads up and down, loving the blood-colored liquid. He does not spray me. But some of the liquid meant for the others hits me anyway. How can it not?

"The purification is almost complete," says Reardon with wild eyes. "I can feel the power, witches! We purify our circle once more. We anoint you with our dark magic. *Lux tenebris!*" He starts laughing like a madman. "*Lux tenebris!*" he shouts. "Say it."

"*Lux tenebris!*" the witches repeat, laughing.

"*Lux tenebris!*" Reardon shouts again, as if trying to rile up a crowd.

"*Lux tenebris!*" the witches shout. Frida and Maddie are beside me, yelling the words.

"*Lux tenebris!*"

The witches shout and I feel a warm wind circle around us. It becomes hotter. Purple smoke, like fog, circles the white stones around the fire. It reminds me of the fog I saw during the eclipse. My palms feel wet holding my friends' hands. That's mandragora. Did I get a dose even though the High Wizard avoided sprinkling it on me? Or is it their hands? I look at Maddie, and she's bobbing her head up and down, dancing hysterically. She's very high.

But Maddie's also becoming blurry. My God, the drug *is* affecting me.

"Bring forth dark light," Reardon says. He's reading from the book again with wide-open eyes. "Close thy soul and turn your back on me, and within feel the great presence of Baphomet through the shadows of darkness." He closes his eyes tightly. Many of the witches are closing their eyes too. "Adramelch. Marduk. Proserpine. Beelzebub. Lucifer." He stops for a moment, opens his eyes, and takes a deep breath.

The fire behind him rises like it did the night I lost control. But this time it's not sucking him in. It's like he's using the bonfire. He's still spraying the mandrake on each witch as we circle the flames. And he spills some on me this time by accident.

"*Hoc circulo, Satana.* With your great wisdom, I ask for protection. Bring us protection. *Hoc circulo.*" His words echo through the yard. "*Lucifer Lucifer. Lucifer. Satanas!*"

"*Lucifer!*" the witches in the circle repeat in rapture. "*Lucifer!*"

"And now, as I feel the power of mandragora course through my veins, I invoke the spirit of Selene," the High Wizard shouts. "Hecate, in this protected circle, I shall name the accused who shall be cast out from our Hawthorne circle. They shall remain behind the walls of the Hawthorne coven."

The High Wizard's skin changes to a darker hue. His ears elongate and he grows a tail and horns. As I walk by him, still locked in Frida's and Maddie's hands—now feeling as if my friends' hands are no longer comforting me but chaining my wrists to the circle—he picks up the entire barrel and lifts it above my head.

The circle stops. I look up at the barrel above me and feel frozen. A third of the barrel has to be full of mandrake. I can't move. I'm so sleepy. All the witches are frozen, staring at me with excitement. He pours the remaining fluid in the barrel over my head.

NO! I cry in my soul. And there is lightning and thunder from above. For a moment, the circle's spell is nearly broken. Some awaken and gasp. Maddie looks over in horror. But most of the witches giggle. The sticky red-brown liquid drips down my face and neck after soaking my hair. I feel humiliated, too weak to even move.

Then everyone, even those who objected before, bursts into an uncontrollable laughter, pointing at me in derision and mockery. Even sweet, shy Frida, who is the nicest girl I've ever known, is pointing at me. She removes her cloak, sweater, shirt, and bra. Maddie completely ignores me, staring at the flames. But she, too, removes her cloak and unbuttons her jacket, kicking off her boots. It's not long before they're all laughing, rolling their eyes back, and dancing naked around the flames. They have let go of my hands and are dancing in circles around me as I stand paralyzed, surrounded by purple smoke, before the bonfire.

"Panthera," the High Wizard says. "*Venite foras! Venite foras!*"

I hear another scream. It frightens me. As I use all my strength to blink the warm, sticky liquid out of my eyes, I see the totem from my vision on Hilltop Bluff appear beside the High Wizard. Yet in the back of my mind, I know we're still in Alondra's backyard. Enora is tied to that same horizontal wooden X with a red ribbon circling the totem and forming a pentagram. Enora is struggling with her restraints again, but this time she is not young like she was in my vision, and she is not blindfolded. She glances at me in fear.

Reardon removes a curved dagger from under his cloak. The purple fog circling us alters to crimson.

"How dare you!" Enora hisses to the High Wizard. But her eyes look everywhere in panic.

"I am the High Wizard of the Falconsong coven," says Reardon.

"Windstorm is High Priestess." Enora shakes her head and looks at me desperately. "She can cast you out. Do it, Windstorm. Please! Use your power and stop him. Stop him now! It's your coven."

"*You* are the accused, and *you* shall be cast out," says the High Wizard.

"Let her go!" I yell. But I can't move. And it took every ounce of energy I had left to utter my words. I feel so dizzy. Everything is beginning to sway as if I'm on a boat. I'm so nauseous.

He responds by stabbing her in the chest with the knife as if she were an animal sacrifice. Blood sprays from her torso. Then—I can't believe my eyes—my friends turn, like rabid wild dogs, rush to Enora's bloody body, and lick and suck the blood squirting from her chest and stomach. I am the only one not engaging in this hideous act. Even Maddie and Frida are leaning over and partaking in this sick meal. They're cannibalizing her. Hope and Marilyn have grown fangs. Then I remember that the High Priest spilled mandragora on me. This must be a hallucination.

The High Wizard Reardon turns to Bryce, who still stands beside him. Bryce is staring at the fire.

"Expel Maverick's seed from the circle now, disciple. She aligns herself with Panthera. She has hurt you with evil magic. You heard her objections to our acts against the black witch. The two witches conspire to do the coven harm. No longer is Falconsong here to protect us from these wicked witches. Change Windstorm so that she can never hurt us again."

Bryce nods, in a trance. As the witches continue to feast on Enora, Bryce walks to me. His eyes are glassy and I spontaneously step back.

"I expel you from the coven," Bryce says to me like a zombie.

I cannot form words from my lips to even object.

"Disciple, help turn her," the High Wizard says. "Help her transform. She needs your assistance. Change her. *Muta. Serpentus. Mutatio.* Turn her. Then she can no longer harm you."

"*Fiat voluntas tua.*" Bryce bows his head toward Reardon. Then he turns back to me, glassy-eyed.

"She is cast out," the High Wizard shouts. "Rid our order of the evil witch. Begone. Cast her out and shield us from her harm."

As Bryce turns to me, there is an explosion by the fire. Even in his trance, Bryce turns. A thousand black birds launch into the air, and Enora is no longer on the totem. All the witches of my coven circle around the totem, looking everywhere in confusion as their meal has left them.

Bryce pushes me, with an index finger, outside of the surrounding red smoke. His single finger feels like a hundred people shoving me out of the red fog into the wild grass. I feel so weak. So sick. I stumble. I still cannot utter a word. I try to shake my head or raise my hand to stop him, but it takes all the strength left in me to keep my eyes open. I fall.

Tears flow from my face and Bryce blurs before me. I think he recognizes me for a second, but then he shakes his head as if shaking off poison. Not only is he under the influence of mandrake, he's under the High Wizard's spell. Bryce points a finger at me. "*Proditrix.*" I have no strength. I close my eyes as I hear Bryce speaking these strange foreign words. I close my eyes, hoping that everything around me will stop spinning. "*Proditrix. Muta. Serpentus.*"

I feel cold, freezing cold. Whereas before our ceremonies always warmed me, now I feel frigid. I force my eyes open and see Bryce become larger. He fills my view as I seem to fall under the ground. The colors change as if through a prism. The central bonfire becomes almost too bright, and I avert my eyes. I feel like I'm descending, in an elevator, under the earth.

I finally utter something from my lips. I scream with all my might, but it's inhuman, guttural, low-pitched. It sounds like a drum.

I feel pain in my throat and a tearing sensation in the center of my tongue. I no longer see Bryce's cloak, only a huge blurry red blob with yellow and blue around it. And, even stranger, when I blink my eyes, the color fades into black and white. I move to clutch my neck with my hands, but I don't have hands. Then I try to run, but I don't have feet. I'm bound like Enora was to the pentagram, only I'm not bound by ropes. I'm bound because my arms have been consumed into my body.

My cloak and all my clothes cover my eyes. I wiggle, shake free of them, and make my way along the ground. I'm surprised at how fast I can move. I turn to my side and look back. The fire is blinding my eyes, but I like the heat emanating from it. Yet I fear their feet as they dance around the fire. The witchgrass is taller than my head. I have shrunk, I think?

My ability to think is fading. I'm confused. I can't recall what is happening.

Why am I here? I have to get warm. Somewhere, but not near that fire. No, not the fire. I dread their feet.

I'm so cold. I have to find warmth.

I can't hear well. In the background, there is a low drum-like sound. I quickly wiggle my body away from the flames. But out here, in the night, it is cold. So cold. I need to find shelter.

I smell something. Gamey. It reminds me of barbeque meat, and for a flash I recall the smell of an animal once sacrificed by Alondra in this very yard. But this smell isn't coming from a cooked animal.

I see something in a bush. I change my vision from black and white to a weird blend of yellow, red, and green. I can do that easily. I don't know why. Now I see something clearly in the leaves. It's a towering beast two times taller and fatter than I am. It's so big and soft. I can see its heart racing. And it's shaking. I'm so hungry. Why is it shaking? Why is it hiding when I can so clearly see it? I reach closer and its odor is overwhelming. I stick my tongue out—don't know why—but when I do it smells wonderful. But I don't feel wonderful. My heart races again in a panic because, you see, my tongue is forked and as large as my head.

24

———

I DECEIVE YOU NO MORE

person slips away. Now I am remembering her. I must gather my thoughts before I fade.

I've gone through many sunrises without knowing who or what I am. At times, I just recognize light and the glorious warmth of the sun. I don't want to live like this, so I fight. I must retain my identity. I'm thinking of this, not only for you, but for my very existence. For when it fades, my identity fades, and I go with it.

Another day passes and I am awake again. I will try once more.

I'm under a white structure. Rather, I'm under white boards, hiding from the tower sticks. That is what I call these creatures. I have seen many tower sticks walk on their two long branches and make their way across my garden. I don't know what they're looking for, but they have no business being here.

There's one close to me now. The sticks are dangerous, but they move slowly. I fear they will trample me. They are the only things I fear. Tall and smelly.

One of them is searching the danger road, full of tall blades of grass, crouching and looking around the flowers. What is it doing? I love my flowers and bushes. They aren't theirs! They're mine!

I have had my fill of the large, furry animals under my shelter. They are so easy to catch and drag down here. So easy to eat.

One of the tower sticks approaches. I hear it walking above me now. I am under it, hiding, like the furry animals hide from me. And just as the furry things quake under me, I quake under the tower sticks. They are so tall. But they emit such strange sounds.

Two more approach. One is looking right at me. I laugh.

You're so dumb! Can't you smell me? Can't you see me?

I flick my tongue at it.

Right here. Right here. Don't you see me? Idiot!

They never see me.

It gives me a sense of confidence, you know. So I quickly slither out of my hiding place and let them chase me. It's a daring game, but I'm much faster than they are. I've done this a few times now, and this time I decide to let them have my home for a while. They chase me. One even throws a net. But they're far too stupid. I consider biting one, but that would slow me down, and then I might as well be shaking for good.

～

I like the morning light because it warms my garden. Sometimes, I'll come out just to feel the warmth when it's not too cold.

～

I'm alone. When I don't think, I don't care. But right now, I'm thinking. It makes me angry. Why am I angry? I am so alone. I am so mad.

～

I hunt. I'm not hungry now, but I want to kill. In my rage, I want another creature to suffer. So I wiggle my way around the trees, looking for something to strike dead. I'll kill it and leave it for some other animal to devour. As long as I can make it feel pain like I do.

It's dark—which I love—but cold—which I hate.

There is no friend of mine. I am utterly alone.

I can't cry. I learned that on my first night. Then, I wanted to cry. My greatest wish was the power to cry. What would I cry about? Why would I cry?

～

I'm caught. I don't know how, but one of the tower sticks snared me. I'm wiggling terribly with my armless torso, trying to escape, but I cannot. I hiss. And I spin wildly. But I cannot bite and get out of this cloth net.

I squeeze through a hole. *Ha!*

～

"*Hominis, venite foras.* Transform back, Cadence. *Muta.* Find peace within your heart. *Mutatio.* Follow. I free you of this curse. I demand you transform now. *Muta. Hominis. Hominis, venite foras.* Come out, Cadence Hawthorne."

My eyes open. I run, actually I wiggle, shifting my body back and forth very fast across the field. Circling above, I see a black bird chasing me. It must want to eat me. So I scurry as fast as I can to the bushes. But I fear that I cannot escape it like I can the tower sticks. The tower sticks are slow, but this bird is quick.

It must want to eat me. It is my comeuppance for going after the shaking furry things under the bushes. This is my fate. Now it's my turn to be eaten.

I stop by a bush, but I don't go under it. I turn and face my adversary. It swoops down but does not grab me. Instead, in lines of perfect black and white, the black bird stands over me. I don't know why, but I feel as if it has no interest in eating me at all. In fact, I feel as if I recognize this bird.

Words come from its beak. "*Et nos unum sumus*, I deceive you no more. *Et nos unum sumus.*"

"*Amica?*" I say. I'm shocked to hear the word from my mouth and to understand it. My word is like a low growl, but it can still be heard. I have said this word before. The bird dips its head down and touches mine softly, and for the first time in such a long time, I do not feel alone.

"*Mutatio*, Cadence," Amica says. "*Mutatio.*"

I answer by flipping my forked tongue at it. I am still beside the bush and, although I feel safe with this bird, I am still apprehensive.

I shake my head.

I can swear I see a smile from the black bird's beak. "*Mutatio.*"

The bird shakes and crouches along the grass. Already, the bird was twice my size; now it becomes even larger, rising toward the clear sky. It forms into a tower stick. An unclothed one. I look at its face, and it is strangely familiar.

"Change back, Cadence. Now. It's okay. Change."

I shake my head.

The tower person reaches out a hand larger than my head. For a moment, I consider biting it. "*Et nos unum sumus. Hominis, venite foras,*" the tower person says. And she repeats it again and again. Her hand remains stretched out. "*Et nos unum sumus. Hominis, venite foras. Et nos unum sumus. Hominis, venite foras.*"

I feel like I'm rising. I feel pain in my throat. I'm shaking. The leaves around me move as I get bigger and bigger. Everything becomes vibrant. Beautiful. I am in a clearing of grass surrounded by trees.

I recognize the woman in front of me. Enora.

I grab her hands and burst into tears. The ability to cry makes me cry more than I've ever cried in my life. My tears are so sad, but being able to shed them makes me so happy.

Enora takes me in her arms.

"I'm sorry," I say, shaking my head in her arms. "I'm so sorry."

But when she gently releases me and those familiar bright blue eyes stare back at me, my old distrust returns. She's smiling, but I feel like I'm being deceived.

"But you were being eaten by my coven," I say, shaking my head.

She laughs. Then she narrows her eyes toward the trees and looks dangerous. "He has the power of illusion. Like a stupid magician. But the feasting of the witches was incomplete. And not real. I believe he had every intention of killing me that night, but he did not know of my power to turn into a bird and transform back." Then she looks down at me in pity. "But you, you don't, you poor thing. He had hoped to fog your brain so you would be trapped as an animal forever. He did not know, as you didn't, that I could turn into a bird at will. And I don't think he predicted that I would help you."

I look down and my naked body is covered with dirt and filth. It's like I rolled in mud. Enora isn't totally clean either, but at least she resembles a woman. I can't even see my skin under all the dust and muck.

Her blue eyes look deeply into my eyes. "You know, Cadence, I didn't do this as a friend. I know you hate me after what I did to you and Bryce. But I need your help. Witch to witch. Coven to coven. Woman to woman. For revenge. I help you, you help me. Understand?"

She reaches down and helps me stand. Standing on two legs is so weird, and I have to lean on her to straighten my body. But when we walk, it's even weirder. I don't know how long I was gone, but walking feels like I am pressing on cushions instead of feet. My legs are so weak.

To my amazement, I realize that I'm still in Alondra's backyard. We pass logs in the center of a wild grassy field. In all my slithering, I wonder if I ever left.

My stomach aches. God knows what's in there. Believe me, I don't want to know.

"It will take you at least a day to recover, Cadence," she says, cocking her head, as we walk.

"Thank you, Amica." She looks at me slyly. "I mean, thanks if you helped me. And...I guess we are kind of friends if you're my bird."

"I am not your friend," Enora says. "And I am not *your* bird. But I'm surprised you remember my transformation. It's rare to remember anything unless you're practiced like me."

I'm blinking as my eyes adjust to the sunlight. It is so bright. And all the colors are so vibrant. I feel good. Wonderful. The warmth outside feels glorious against my skin even though I'm not wearing clothes. Then I notice my bare feet squishing into the leaves. We're walking through mud. Even though the sky is clear, it must have rained. Or snowed? In my other form, I never noticed. It was cold, but it was always cold outside my shelter.

When we make it to the backyard patio and I see all our witch cloaks hung on the wall, I lurch back and start shaking violently. But I'm not shivering from cold.

"What?" Enora asks.

I shake my head, opening my eyes wide as I look toward the house.

"He's not there. The asshole leaves every Sunday morning. I bet you it's not to worship in church. All I know is I've been watching him from the trees for the past week, waiting for the right time to bring you back."

We enter Alondra's house, and the warmth of the living room feels like heaven. It must be cold outside, but I've felt so cold that just being human again warms me. Here, it feels like a warm toasty fire. I'm alive. Not dead. But I shiver.

"Go shower." Enora looks at the hallway. "I'll watch for him. If he dares return, you and I will face him alone, but this time he won't be prepared."

"What if he changes me again?"

"He needs the circle to do that." She looks down at my filth with disgust. "Go shower, Cadence."

I still don't trust her. And I think she knows it. The way she looks at me when she talks.

So, she saved me? So what? And Reardon hates her? And she's Amica? So? Does that make us suddenly friends? Isn't this the same Enora who opened a portal to hell? And who paraded her sex with my boyfriend?

"Now that you're human, you have the human curse of thought," she says as if reading my mind. "Stop thinking, Cadence. Just go take a warm shower."

But I don't mind thinking. In fact, I like it. Even the shivering. I like all of it.

When I turn on the shower in the guest bathroom and close the white curtain, I feel fear again. It's like I expect that creep to throw open the shower curtain, like in *Psycho*, and kill me. And then, even worse, I wonder if Enora is tricking me. Maybe the curtain will fly open to reveal not a psycho killer dressed in drag, but a witch holding a curved dagger. So I wash myself with both eyes open.

The warm water feels soooo good against my skin. And washing off the clumps of dirt and leaves makes me feel as if I'm washing off scales from reptilian skin. It's like I'm shedding a terrible costume. I run the water down my long dark hair for the longest time. It starts to fog up in the bathroom. Enora's probably pissed it's taking me so long, but I'm glad I'm taking my time to get all the mud off. And there's a *lot* of it.

"Cadence, we have to go," Enora says with a knock.

On the counter is a change of clothes. I didn't see Enora bring it in—I was probably too enthralled with my wondrous warm water. I look at the clothes, and they're a little large. I recognize them. It's a white button-down and black slacks. On the floor are gray tennis shoes. I've seen the clothes before. They're Alondra's.

When I get out of the bathroom, Enora's not there.

"Come upstairs, Cadence," Enora shouts from upstairs. "I want to show you something before we go."

I walk upstairs, and it fills me with dread. I've only been up here a couple of times, and the last time was when Alondra was sick and I called the paramedics.

"Come on," Enora says again.

I turn left to the master bedroom, but Enora's not in there. I enter the hallway again and go into a small room across from the master bedroom. It is a library with books on shelves. But Enora's not here studying books. She's standing by the window, pulling back a white lace curtain, staring outside. She points.

I look down and see a bunch of people walking around the front yard, searching under rocks and bushes. And I recognize them. There's Maddie, Bryce, Mira, and a handful of my other friends in my coven. They don't look like witches. They look like students gathering trash or collecting butterflies in Alondra's garden.

"What are they doing?" I ask.

She chuckles but, when I turn, I am surprised at Enora's expression. She's not amused. She looks angry.

"Idiots," she replies. "They'll be surprised to finally find you."

I turn and look out again. Maddie's in tears as she crouches down, pulling back the only yellow flowers in the garden. All the other bushes are just branches. Bryce is focused too, looking under the wooden deck.

I rush out of the room and run down the stairs.

When I open the door, the fresh smell of the bushes, trees, and grass overwhelms me. It's winter but it might as well be spring. I remember my black-and-white vision when I was my former disgusting self. Color only came in blurry blotches. Here, everything is so brilliant, in all the colors of the rainbow. It is so beautiful. The lilies and roses. The yellow sun as it warms my face. I feel so good. Then my eyes fall on Bryce, who's only a few steps away from me, looking under the patio with a stick. As the wood creaks under my shoes, he looks up. When he recognizes me, he rushes into my arms.

"Oh, God, Katie, I thought I lost you forever!" he says. His voice cracks. He clutches me tightly. "God, never leave me again. Don't ever do that again! Never!" And he draws me even more tightly in his arms and kisses me repeatedly on the face. I would never let go if it weren't for the others. I hear shouts as they run to me. They too embrace me. Mira, Frida, Hope, Helen, and Tammy. They all run into my arms. Last comes Maddie. She's too distraught to say a word. She just stands by the porch looking at me. She starts to cry. I do too.

The strangest thing, as if anything could be stranger than all this, is that they all keep looking at my body. From head to toe. It's like they want to make sure I'm really human again. Then I remember running, or scurrying, from the "tower sticks." They were so tall, like buildings. For me it was just a stupid game, like hide-and-seek. For them, it was desperation to catch me and make me whole again. They must have been looking for me all this time.

Our exuberance is dampened by the opening of the front door. All my friends in my coven step back in fright. I think they fear it's the High Wizard. When they see it's Enora, they look relieved.

In the excitement, I didn't even realize that Enora is now wearing one of our black cloaks. She puts the hood over her head and stands beside me on the deck, looking straight ahead.

"Meet me with your coven on Hilltop Bluff," she says, still facing forward. Then, almost in a whisper, "The very same hilltop where the wizard unveiled my ravishment to you. Meet at midnight on the Witch's Sabbath this week. Both High Priestesses, you and I, Panthera and Windstorm, shall have our vengeance. That is my price for restoring you."

And she proceeds down the walkway, ignoring anyone else who greets her, down the dirt path, and into the forest alone.

25

THE WITCHING HOUR

And so we meet, my whole coven, beside the Jonathan Brewster Taylor Library, at the appointed time set by Enora: the witching hour. Midnight. I'm seriously conflicted because half of me never wants to come near any magic again. But the other half wants to conjure up a serious windstorm, a goddamn tempest, that will bury that old bald-headed creep in the hell where he belongs. He destroyed my dignity. Then he buried my grades. (I'm gonna fail another fall semester at Hawthorne University, by the way. I wonder if that was his contingency plan in case I was changed back to a human. He's a professor, you know).

My friends are pretty intense too. They're all gathered under a dim floodlight, silently changing into black hooded cloaks behind a trash dumpster. I welcome my cloak because it's cold outside. Gilda brought the clothes all the way from Savannah because you-know-who isn't about to lend our cloaks from Alondra's backyard. How Gilda got enough of them for all of us is beyond me. Well, she's highly resourceful. Anyway, it's good that it's late and we're hidden beside the building because, even though it's after midnight, there are still students walking to the library to study. The school keeps the library open during the wee hours of the morning for finals. Of course, that reminds me of how I'm going to fail again.

I straighten my cloak and throw my hood over my hair. Bryce takes my hand. "Are you sure you're up to this, Katie? Maybe we can meet another time?"

"Yeah, babe?" Maddie asks. She's beside me too. "Are you? After everything that happened?"

"Especially after what happened," I reply. "Let's just say that if I have the chance to throw the dick in the fire this time, I will."

"Hell yeah," Mira says behind me.

"Hey, Mira," Maddie says. "What's the plan?"

"Yoozh. Gather around a pyre, dance, and let Windstorm throw the dickhead in the fire." She chuckles and winks at me. "Didya bring your Book of Shadows?"

"Yeah. Why does she want it?"

Mira shrugs.

"I'm not here to hurt him, Katie," Frida says in her thick Brazilian accent. "I...I want him to just leave us alone."

"Me too," says Helen.

"Yeah," echoes Tammy. "What is she planning up there?"

"Don't know," I reply with a sigh. "But he tricked us." I look at Bryce and nod. "Yeah, I'm ready. I agree with Enora. We have to do something."

"Enora tricked us too, Cadence," Bryce says uncertainly, forcing a smile. "Nearly broke us apart. I don't trust her either."

I just nod.

"Let's go," I say to all of them with as much confidence I can muster.

Tucked under my right arm is my old book *Broomstick*, my Book of Shadows, and Bryce is holding my left hand as we wind our way down into the thick dark woods. The rest of my friends trail behind. When I look back at them, their eyes are fixed forward under the moonlight, ready for a fight.

We wind our way through more dirt paths under the trees, soon nearing the sound of my beloved waterfall. Then I smell smoke and see red flickering flames. The red fog looks like it's over the hill on Hilltop Bluff. That slows me down for a moment, because it reminds me of the vision Enora gave me.

"You okay?" Bryce asks me. He can sense my hesitation, I think.

I just nod. We head up the grassy hill.

When we make it up to the summit, Enora is the only one there. She's sitting cross-legged, in a black lace dress, with a tall bonfire burning behind her, in the center of the grass field. Her black-gloved hands are folded over her lap, and her face is covered with thick witch makeup. None of this is surprising. What is surprising is what's behind her—another wooden totem between her and the fire. It's the same totem that was in my vision and the same one that materialized in Alondra's backyard before I was transformed into a snake. A burgundy velvet cloth is wrapped in a circle over the large wooden beams, forming a pentagram. Fortunately, there's no one bound to it this time.

"Yatu, Windstorm," Enora says pleasantly. "Happy Yule."

Happy Yule? Who cares about Yule right now?

Yule is the Witch's Christmas. Shows how much I'm paying attention to time. Of course, Christmas falls near finals, which reminds me yet again of how I'm going to fail my exams.

"Sit, Hawthorne coven," Enora says. "Let us gather around the warm fire, witches, and celebrate the upcoming sacred night of darkness."

All of my coven sit on their knees or cross-legged on the grass, but only after they look at me. They wait for my permission. Enora sits beside Mira and Bryce. I sit on the grass opposite her, beside Maddie and Frida.

"Raven, can you say some blessed words to our witches about the change of seasons?" Enora asks Mira.

"We're here to celebrate Yule?" I interject, glancing at the pentagram behind her.

I mean...really?

"What do you mean?" Enora asks. "Revenge or not, Cadence, we're still witches. Don't you want to celebrate our Winter Solstice? I want to." Then she turns to Mira. "Can you recite some of the words of the turn of seasons? Do you remember some of them?"

"Yes," Mira says.

Mira's hesitant, and for her to be hesitant about anything is really something. I think she's spooked by the pentagram too. Not that she's never seen it. She's accustomed to practicing ceremonies, but she's probably wondering why this is happening *now*.

"Yule is a special time when energy has left our world," Mira begins.

"Like fire, it extinguishes only to be relit once more in the turning of the wheel." She casts a stray glance at the pentagram. "Yule. A powerful turn of seasons. The world changes from wetness and ice to warmth again. Just as Ceres mourns the loss of her daughter Proserpine and waits for her return above in Ostara, so does warmth become reborn. Remember with joy, fellow witches, that even under your cold feet, the warmth of the earth remains. All things pass. But together, in the comfort of our touch, may we never thirst."

"Yes," Enora says, closing her eyes and nodding. "Yes. Blessed be your words. So well said, Raven. I knew it would be from you. Indeed, shall we hold hands, witches?"

I catch Enora looking at me with that same determination I saw in my friends when we walked across campus to the bluff. She's in for a fight too. I just know it. But I don't trust her.

Enora closes her eyes again and looks down. "*Sacrificium consecratum.*" She quietly says the words repeatedly like a chant. Mira repeats it too.

"Wait a minute," I say. They open their eyes. "What are you planning, Enora? After everything that's happened, you can't expect us to blindly follow you. I mean, I owe you for changing me back, but with everything we've been through, you need to tell us your plan."

"I know what you've been through more than anyone here, Cadence. Of course I'm not here just to celebrate the solstice. I'm here to hurt the devil who hurt you. Who hurt me. But you need to be patient."

"How are you going to do it?" Bryce asks.

"With patience," Enora replies with a fake smile. Then she turns to me with a more genuine smile. "Did you bring your book?"

"Yes."

"Bring it to me. We should chant using your book. I will use it to summon him."

"Tell us the plan first," I insist.

I agree with Bryce. What's going on? I recognize her words. That is the same incantation we used to sacrifice animals that we would eat during gatherings. But why now? There's no animal here. There's just that infernal pentagram Enora forced me to see in my vision.

"The book." Enora gestures to me. "Bring it to me and I'll show you."

Bryce shakes his head. "Your plan."

For a moment, Enora loses her smiles and looks dangerous. "I intend to use the power of your circle to sacrifice the High Wizard. We will summon him, bind him, and prevent him from ever fucking with you or the Hawthorne coven again. The fool thought he could get rid of Cadence and me. He knows our power, and he wanted to expel us—for good. Now I will help you get rid of him instead. Is that simple enough, Bryce?"

"But why the pentagram?" Bryce points to the wooden totem.

"We're witches," she says to him with a laugh. "That's our symbol. My sisters helped me put up the decoration for Yule. Why does it disturb you?"

"It's inverted with two points projecting up. That's not the symbol for witches, it's the symbol for Satan."

"It never stopped you before."

"I have told my coven never to practice under Baphomet again," I say.

"Are we fighting?" she asks all of us. "This is exactly what your demon wizard wants. He wants us to fight, to keep the circle broken. Just as he wanted to imprison Cadence in the body of a snake." But none of my witches seems to be on her side. They keep looking at me, and that seems to make Enora more upset. "Come on. How can a pentagram disturb *him*? Bryce of all people? He consummated our love using one before your coven."

"Maybe we should go," I say, getting up. "Look, I owe you, Enora, but I don't feel like you're being straight with us. My coven's been through so much already. We don't worship the devil anymore."

"Wait," Enora insists. "Sit. Please." She takes a deep breath and raises her hand. "Sit. You used to worship the devil, but I'm not asking for that. I simply need the symbol to stop your High Wizard. You all brought this upon yourselves when he tricked you into protecting him." She addresses all of us. "Please, sit." She laughs. "Come on. We're all witches under Selene."

But Bryce and I are still standing. So is Maddie. And Mira. And Tammy. And a few other witches are getting up too.

"Katie, bring me your book," Enora says. "Give it to me so I can summon him and stop him from disturbing you. That's the plan. The book will help summon Alondra's husband here. I can't reach him through your protective spell without it."

I look at Mira and she hesitantly nods. Bryce folds his arms and shakes his head, refusing to sit down.

"Bring me your book, Katie," Enora says.

"Is this why she wants it?" I ask Mira.

"Yes." Mira nods. "I think so. It's Alondra's Book of Shadows too. A Book of Shadows is representative of a witch's inner being. Her soul. We've used these books to evoke witches who have passed on before. She can probably use it to bring forth Reardon."

"Yes, I can. So can we get on with it?" Enora asks, lifting her eyebrows. "Or would you prefer to fight? May I remind you all that he turned Cadence into a snake? I changed her back." She looks right into my eyes. "Remember?"

My friends look to me again. I answer by walking over to Enora. She's still sitting cross-legged in front of the bonfire, looking up at me.

"Here, get it over with," I say, handing her my book, "so we can go home. We want to be free from harm, and I owe you for making me human. But...I don't want to be a part of all this." I look at the fire and the pentagram with disgust. "I just want to go to school. Away from magic and hexes. Okay?"

Enora nods with her infamous smugness. She takes my book and jumps up. Then her black-gloved fingers glide over the frayed old cover and open it beside the fire. It's like she's using the light of the bonfire to help her read it.

I walk beside Bryce and hold his hand. His palm is wet and his hand is shaking.

Enora throws her hand up without turning to us. "Sit down. Please, witches." She cocks her head toward me. "You've logged everything. *Broomstick*, huh? It's become a bit of a witch's almanac, hasn't it? A diary. You even wrote about this year's Halloween party and me and Bryce. Sweet. And here is last year's party at the Billington House."

"It's my Book of Shadows.".

"But not the beginning," she says, shaking her head and raising a finger. "Alondra jotted down her experiences too."

Everyone's watching her read my book. Why? She has so much charisma. She is a natural leader. Unlike me. How does she do that?

"This is your past too, Bryce," Enora says. He's sitting near her again. "Don't you want it to be over?"

He furrows his brow. Before he can answer, she turns her back to us once more, facing the fire. She closes the book, presses it against her forehead, and quickly bows three times. Then she says, "In this time of renewal, I sacrifice the past. As the book turns to ash, let it burn the sins of the Hawthorne coven." And then she tosses my book into the flames. She throws it so casually, as if she's simply adding more wood to the fire.

Everyone leaps up. There's so much noise and pandemonium that I can barely hear my own screams. Then lightning strikes from above. Then thunder. That's my rage.

Enora looks up at the sky with a grimace. A shiver runs down my spine when she glances at me, her eyes flickering pearly white.

Bryce and I run to the fire. She threw it dead center in the flames, and it ignited by some sort of magic. I can't even make out the border of the cover anymore. I reach in, but Bryce snatches my hand so I don't get burned. The book is already unsalvageable.

Mira answers my rage by walking up to Enora and decking her in the face. The violence is so strong that it throws Enora to the ground.

"That was her book!" Mira yells. "How dare you. No one has the right to burn a witch's book."

"How could you do that?" Bryce adds. "You had no right to destroy Katie's book!"

"Are you all stupid?" Enora shakes her head. "Reardon's shielded from me otherwise. The book must be burned so that the coven's sins can burn. Like the solstice, the wheel must turn."

"Windstorm is our High Priestess, not you!" snaps Mira. I've never seen Mira so mad. "You had no right!" Then she turns to me, and I get the feeling she's about to spit something nasty at me too.

"It's my past too!" Enora snaps. She's still on the ground. We're all crowding her, hating her. "All of you are guilty if you accept it. Don't you see, burning it represents the wish that it never was. I cleansed you. Now you all need to calm the hell down and—"

"Yatu!" cries a young voice from down the hillside. "Yatu!" cries another.

We all turn. Two bright torches are making their way up the hillside. "Yatu!"

"Ah, they're here." Enora rubs her cheek. She's lying on her side. "Watch the change now, witches. Yatu, Manthis! Yatu, Adder!"

As they arrive, there are more gasps. It's Enora's two witches from her coven, Beatrix and Cordelia. They're pulling a man by thick ropes. The man is blindfolded in red burgundy velvet cloth, like the one used on the pentagram. He's dressed in a brown Capuchin robe. He's bald with a goatee. Professor William Reardon. The High Wizard. He can't speak. His mouth is covered in gray duct tape.

We panic. This is not a vision. None of us has ever seen anything like this before. No one has partaken in mandrake. They literally kidnapped a professor.

"My God, Enora, what have you done!" cries Bryce.

Enora answers him by jumping up and brandishing a long curved dagger from inside her dress. Bryce steps back. Enora smiles at us playfully. We all back up.

Beatrix and Cordelia pass us, pulling their prisoner to the fire. Reardon's head is jerking all over the place. Enora walks over and tears the duct tape from his mouth.

"Help!" Reardon shouts. He's still blindfolded, turning his head all around. "Help! My God! Please!"

"What?" Enora asks, bursting into laughter. "Something the matter?"

"Let me go! How dare you! Take off this blindfold now!"

"What? No one can hear you. Because nobody cares! Go on. Shout! Do it. I want you to try, devil." Enora runs the dagger along Reardon's neck. "Cry to the heavens! Yell to your god in hell. No one will help you. What did you think? You thought you could humiliate me again? Then turn the leader of your coven into a snake? And nothing would happen to you? Scream until you don't have a voice! Come on, warlock, let me hear your impotent cries. To the High Priestess. To all your witches. None of them care!"

But I care. I can't believe my eyes.

"Let him go, Enora!" I yell. But my shout is one of many. I don't even know if she hears me. She runs her tongue along his beard and cheek. Then she laughs heartily and stabs him in the arm.

A few of my witches rush to her, but she raises the bloody knife back to his throat. "Uh, uh, uh. Step back, Hawthorne witches! Return to your seats and watch the spectacle, or I'll slice his throat and then you'll be to blame."

Beatrix and Cordelia laugh. Then Beatrix, the blond teenager, kneels before Enora. Enora looks down at her, still holding the blade to Reardon's neck. Beatrix touches Enora's free hand and bows her head. Enora nods. Beatrix leans down near Reardon's arm, still on her knees, and sucks the flowing blood from his wound.

"*Sacrificium consecratum,*" Enora says in Reardon's ear. Her two witches repeat the words. "*Sacrificium consecratum. Sacrificium consecratum.*"

Enora stabs his other arm. This time it's Cordelia who licks the blood dripping down to his fingers.

"Black witch!" cries the High Wizard. "Step back! I warn you!"

"Get away from him," I cry.

Enora laughs harder.

"Stop!" I yell. I look to my friends. "Stop her!" I shout again. I feel so helpless. I feel like I did when witnessing the past under Enora's spell. Most of my witches are in too much shock to lift a finger. But we can't let her keep hurting him.

"There's no magic here, Cadence." Enora turns her head back toward me with those creepy white eyes. "That's what you wanted, isn't it? You asked to just go back to school, away from spells and hexes. Right? See, I can't cast a spell because you stupidly shielded him from my magic. So I have to do it the old-fashioned way. Blame yourself. Either way, believe me, I shall have my sacrifice this Winter Solstice."

She yanks off Reardon's blindfold. His eyes are bulging. He sees me and pleads, "She's going to kill me!" Then he sees Bryce. "Please, disciple! Help untie me. Stop her!"

Meanwhile Enora's two witches are repeating the mantra, licking, sucking, and biting at his wounds. Enora draws a little blood from his neck and runs the dagger along her tongue. Then she thrusts the knife into his stomach.

I'm horrified. Sick. I'm remembering Enora being stabbed, but that stabbing was an illusion under mandrake. This is real.

Mira rushes to Enora. But, yet again, Enora brings the knife to Reardon's neck, and Mira backs up. "Uh, uh, uh, Raven," she says mockingly. "Why you? This man turned your leader into a snake. And the things he did to you and me. You actually want to save him?"

"Let him go," Mira says.

"We didn't want to hurt him!" I shout. I'm only about a foot away from her, reaching out to her. "We just wanted him to stop hurting us."

"Step back, fools," Enora warns me. She's still holding him with the blade near his throat. "Step back. There is no other way for him to stop hurting you."

Then she smiles widely, joining her two witches again as they continue their chant and lick his bloody arms:

Sacrificium consecratum. Sacrificium consecratum. Sacrificium consecratum.

I look at Bryce. He seems helpless. All my witches do. Every time we rush them, Enora threatens to slice Reardon's throat with her dagger.

Reardon's in too much pain now to object. He's crouching near the ground, hanging by the ropes. "Help me," he groans quietly.

I feel so sick. The hilltop is spinning. I close my eyes for a moment, but my dizziness remains. This can't be happening. This is not a trance. Enora has literally kidnapped a professor from our school and is torturing him in front of our eyes. I can't stand him, but I hate her too. She's right, this isn't magic. It's far worse.

I rush Enora. I have every intention of tackling her, whether she stabs him or me. I don't see any other way. Cordelia stops me. She's bigger than I am. She grabs me and throws me to the ground.

"Why don't you try a little magic?" Enora taunts me, laughing. She's terrifying, with pearl-white eyes. "Now I shall sacrifice him like he sacrificed me." Then, as if she's too impatient, she shrieks, "I sacrifice you, Satanas! Beast. Lucifer. Baphomet. Come take this warlock, Satan from hell, and drag him to your pits! Bring him down to the depths he so covets! *Sacrificium consecratum!*"

Enora runs the blade across his neck. Reardon falls lifeless, still held by the rope like a puppet, hanging a foot from the ground. Cordelia releases me, but it's too late.

Everyone's quiet. Stunned. The only sound is from Beatrix as she gets up and unties the ropes from the totem, releasing his body. Reardon's limp body slams onto the ground.

Enora laughs, walking in circles, twirling her bloody dagger. She seems drunk with her kill, as if she really did take mandrake.

I charge Enora again, but Bryce snatches my arm, trying to protect me.

"How could you do that?" I shout.

"We trusted you," Bryce yells.

Enora looks at Bryce and me and then stares, with her pearly-white eyes, at his hand holding my arm. She loses her smile.

"Traitor," she says. "Of course, you would complain and take his side. You betrayed me too, Bryce. So, you see, this season shall not only turn with Bill Reardon's death. No. You wanted to know my plan? You. *You* are my plan. You and that devil who now lies dead. Any High Wizard of your coven needs to be cleansed. And as you, Bryce Wallace, are now the Hawthorne coven's High Wizard again, in order to cleanse all the coven's past sins, I will sacrifice you too."

"Stay away from him!" I warn.

Enora laughs. "You have no magic, Katie. You let me burn your book. That's like inviting a vampire through your front door. You let me in, and I stripped you of your powers. All of you shall witness my sacrifice. But then I will let your broken circle go home in peace."

She takes off her left glove and pushes her palm right up to Bryce's nose. I see a red pentagram painted on her hand, like that girl in the Billington House on Halloween.

"Sleep," she says to Bryce. "*Prohibe.*"

Bryce falls to the ground like a stone.

"What are you doing!" I cry.

Then she lifts her left palm before me too. "*Prohibe*," she says, almost in a whisper.

I fall. I feel numb. So weak. I have no control over my arms or legs. I can only move my eyes. I see Enora face Mira and Maddie, who are beside me. "*Prohibe.*" She repeats the incantation to every witch of my coven. We all fall frozen before her.

Enora looks at her two witches over Reardon's dead body and snaps, "Manthis! Adder! Leave him. It is time. Take little Katie's concubine and strap him to the pentagram. We might not have been able to burn Reardon in sacrifice, but we can burn Bryce."

I can't say anything because my lips won't move. I'm trying. I'm desperately moving my face, but I can't say a thing.

I'm facing the fire. I'm lying on my side, totally helpless. I watch Beatrix and Cordelia drag Bryce's limp body over to the pentagram. Enora looks at me and walks over. Then she kneels in front of me with those creepy white eyes.

"As they prepare, I shall explain, Katie," Enora says. "This is a blood sacrifice, High Priestess..." Her goons have stripped Bryce, who is still paralyzed, and they turn his naked body upside down on the wooden planks, laying him on the pentagram. "A witch's magic derives from emotion. You saw that when you cast your famous bonfire spell. But unlike me, you failed to kill the devil. It was anger that fed your power. Rage. What I do tonight comes from blood. Human blood. That provides just as much punch as mandrake. In fact, more. That, mixed with my burning your book, makes you too weak to object. What amazes me"—she turns and points to Mira, who is lying frozen and immobile—"is that Raven didn't warn you. She should have known.

"What I suggest is you just lie back and relax. Just watch. It will only take me a moment to burn your sinful boyfriend alive. And when I'm done, you can gather his ashes in an urn, along with your book, and go home and study. See? I never really wanted him back. I just messed with you two to hurt him. Understand? I didn't mean to hurt you. I just wanted him to feel pain. Like the pain he made me feel... Why I'm your friend Amica, right?" Then she roars with laughter, twirling the dagger in her hand, thinking she's being so funny. "Right, *Windstorm?*"

I'm panicking, doing everything I can to say an incantation. To say anything. To do something! But she's right. Normally, with so much rage and anxiety, I could send a whole tempest down onto the bluff. But I can't cast a thing. I can't even move.

That's when I see black boots and a witch's cloak pass by my immobile head. I see Beatrix, Cordelia, and Panthera hanging over Bryce, so I figure it can't be one of them. Maybe it's one of my witch friends? But then I see that this witch is transparent. I can see Bryce and the fire through her cloak. No. This is not a witch, it's my ghost. And for the first time, the ghost turns her face toward me. I'd recognize those bright jade eyes anywhere. Alondra.

The ghost stops over Bill Reardon's dead body. Neither Panthera nor her henchwomen even notice her. Panthera—that bitch—is running her bloody curved blade along Bryce's naked chest. I'm screaming inside.

"*Sacrificium consecratum.*" Enora kneels beside Bryce's face and nods. She runs her hand along his cheek. "I loved you once. I think it was that night when you used me in the ceremony that you destroyed my love. And now you can feel the way I felt that night." Enora watches her witches struggling to tie his wrist on the other side. "Hurry up!" Enora snaps. "Then bring me the torches. Let's light this up so his fucking girl-friend can go study."

I'm screaming in my brain, but I can't say a word. Can the ghost hear me? And can Alondra's ghost even help me?

Alondra kneels before her husband, still staring at his dead body. Enora turns back to me with her stupid grimace, probably to gloat more, and finally notices my ghost. She looks at Alondra and quickly looks back at me. She steps back and trips on a stone. Her witches, still having difficulty tying the ropes, are oblivious, but when Beatrix follows her master's gaze, she screams in fright.

"Why do you disturb my rest, Panthera?" Alondra's ghost asks. Her voice is so calm.

Enora can't say a word. Her face pales, and her eyes change from white to blue. She starts shaking.

"I approached you in friendship, pupil," Alondra's ghost says. "We finally made our peace. Why do this to my husband? Why are you doing this to his disciple?"

"You're not real." Enora looks at me and points. "You're from her."

Alondra turns to me once more. It is eerie how real her facial features appear. She smiles. "And you torment my students. This is how you repay our friendship? Release them from your spell."

"This said by a ghost?" Enora laughs nervously.

Alondra loses her smile. *"Resurrectio,"* she says, facing me and twirling the fingers of one hand. She utters the spell as if it's a bother for her.

I'm free. I can move. I don't know what's more shocking—the fact that Alondra's ghost just helped me or that her ghost can cast a spell. Like I care at the moment.

I sprint to Bryce, shoving the witches away from him. They're still in too much shock at seeing Alondra to resist me. Bryce is still paralyzed, but I see him follow me with his eyes.

"Why did you kill my husband?" Alondra asks.

It's taking me forever to untie the ropes. It drives me crazy.

"And now you attack my coven?"

Enora shouts at Beatrix and Cordelia. "Why are you letting her untie him! She's tricking you! This ghost is her magic. It isn't real!"

But they can't stop staring. Alondra walks right up to Enora, who slashes her with her curved dagger. The knife passes through Alondra. Then Alondra grabs Enora's wrist and violently shakes the dagger from her hand. Enora stares wide-eyed at her wrist, in Alondra's grip. "Impossible!" Enora says.

"You summoned me," Alondra says, shaking her head. "Your blood sacrifice ends now."

"I didn't summon you."

"You burned my book."

And with that, Alondra throws Enora to the ground. Then Alondra crouches down, once again grabbing Enora's wrist, and drags her across the grass. The whole time Enora's hollering in surprise and terror, twisting and turning, trying to break free. Beatrix and Cordelia run to help their master.

My coven starts getting up. They appear drugged. I loosen the last rope on Bryce's wrist and throw my arms around him.

"Oh, Bryce."

"I'm...okay...Katie."

Enora isn't. She's screaming.

Mira and Maddie rush over to help us. Then Mira grabs my shoulder and turns me toward Enora.

Alondra's spirit is dragging Enora to a boulder at the highest point on the bluff. It's that same boulder where I once stood petting a wild deer while talking to my dad. The steepest, most treacherous drop from Hilltop Bluff.

"She's going to throw me off the cliff!" shrieks Enora. "God, Cadence, send her away! I freed you. You owe me!"

"Let her go, Alondra." I approach. I can't believe I'm addressing a ghost.

"Revenge for revenge, Cadence," Enora cries. "Life for a life. Save me. Save me and I won't hurt Bryce. I promise. Just rid me of this vision, sister. Stop it, Cadence. Stop it before she throws me over!"

"Leave her, Alondra," I repeat.

"No." Alondra shakes her head.

I can't believe this. Whereas before I was yelling at Enora to release Reardon, now I'm yelling at Alondra to let go of Enora. I'm trying to protect the people I hate. Why? But I don't want Enora to fall and die. I walk past Reardon's dead body. I didn't want him to die either.

This is so like Alondra. She saved Bryce, but now she's going to kill Enora? I loved Alondra when she was alive. She would do anything for me. But that included evil. And she was evil, because she let her husband and the coven do all those terrible things to my boyfriend and my best friend. Things I could never forgive. I love and hate her so much!

When I realize Alondra won't listen to me, I follow them onto the boulder. Her two witches, Beatrix and Cordelia, are reaching out, but they don't follow me. They're too afraid of the height. This rock overlooks a hundred-foot drop, and there's nothing to hold on to on either side. When I petted my deer, I was never crazy enough to venture this far. My knees are shaking as I crouch down and approach the two of them at the edge. I'm less than a foot away from death on all three sides.

"I ..." I sputter beside them. "I demand that you let her go, Alondra!"

"She burned your book, killed my husband, and tried to kill Bryce," the ghost says, holding Enora over the ledge. It's so eerie how calm Alondra is as Enora fights desperately to break out of her grasp. "Why don't you want her to fall?"

"Why would I want you to kill her? I want your protection, not another murder. You're as bad as she is."

Alondra turns from me and moves Enora closer to the ledge.

"You said you gave me Abigail's magic once!" I cry desperately. "By both her and Escoba's power, I demand that you leave her alone. I command you as the High Priestess of the Hawthorne coven."

"Then where's my book, Cadence?"

I can't believe this.

All the witches are now near the edge of the bluff. I'm closest. Alondra is standing upright now, holding Enora effortlessly with one hand. All it would take is just a small push to throw her off the cliff. I creep closer to Enora on my knees and grab her leg. I can see pitch darkness on three sides of me. I'm so close to the edge that I feel I'm balancing on one side. I even wonder if the weight of Enora and me alone could cause the rock to break and send us hurdling down the bluff. My friends are yelling for me to come back.

"Take my hand." I reach for Enora. "Come on."

Enora kneels down and reaches.

Alondra squints down at me. Then she yanks Enora's body upright, holding her right over the drop. I think Enora's too terrified to say anything.

"Why don't you want this, Cadence?" Alondra asks.

"I am Windstorm!" I say. Lightning strikes with a roar of thunder. I feel magic returning to me. The lightning and thunder are from me. A gust forms, blowing my hair to one side and swaying the trees far below. This is *my* gust. "Go away! Leave her alone!"

But Alondra turns her back once more, looking ready to drop Enora.

"I don't forgive you!" I yell at Alondra's ghost. "Okay? This is why. You're as evil as she is. You want her to die? God, I will never forgive you, Alondra! Just go away! I will never forgive you for what you did!"

Alondra stares back at me for a moment. Her face is so vivid with her bright green eyes. She's here. Somehow. And she actually looks hurt. She shakes her head, but then she nods. She finally starts to fade. As she disappears, she says, "All right, Cadence. Forgive *her*, then."

Nothing is left to hold Enora. She teeters on the edge, but I'm close enough to fall to my knees, scoop up her waist and legs, and pull her to safety just in time. Then I feel my friends grabbing for my feet and ankles. I'm holding on to Enora with as much strength as I can as my witches pull us from behind. We make it to the center of the boulder. Then, slowly, we're dragged further from the ledge.

Enora stares down into the abyss on both sides of us when we're finally safe. The wind stops blowing. It becomes very quiet.

"Get out!" I shout at her. She jumps. "Leave! Take your witches and go. You killed him. How could you do that? You're a murderer!"

Cordelia and Beatrix help Enora up. It is so nauseating how the two witches' lips and cheeks are stained with blood. Enora turns to me. She stares as if trying to think of words to say. It reminds me of when she watched me during the eclipse. It's like I'm such a mystery to her. But this time, it's not only confusion that I see in her bright blue eyes; it's fear.

"Get out!" I repeat. "Stay away from us."

Bryce and Maddie help me up. Then all my witches stand behind me. They have that determined look again, as if it's a standoff between our two covens.

Most of Enora's power is gone. She's no longer drunk on a trance. She's seems almost somber.

She finally flashes an infernal smile at me. She just mutters, "*Et nos unum sumus, amica.*"

Then she turns and walks with her witches to the bonfire and collects three torches.

"What about him?" Cordelia says to Enora, pointing down at Reardon's dead body.

Enora dips her fiery torch onto his body and waves her other arm in the air. "*Lux.*" Her words stoke the fire, and his body bursts into flames. Then she turns to the pentagram, throws her torch on it, and says yet again, "*Lux.*" Now there are three bonfires burning in the night.

"Never come anywhere near Hawthorne again," I repeat.

She nods with her back turned to me. Then the three of them make their way down the grassy hill as if nothing happened. We watch them, not wanting to drop our guard, as their torches move down the hillside and onto the trails in the wilderness below.

When I finally lose sight of them, I turn to Bryce. He takes me in his arms. All my friends hug me together. Some of them cry. Others just stand holding one another. We're in shock. No one can believe what just happened.

When things are calmer, quieter, Maddie touches my shoulder and points to the conflagration. The flames surrounding the pentagram and Reardon's body are brighter than the bonfire. Apparently, the wicked witch still had a little bit of magic left in her after all.

"What about Enora, Katie? Should we report her to campus security?"

It seems like such a weird suggestion. A very normal weird suggestion. But even if we do, what the hell are we going to tell them? I nod anyway.

"And of Reardon? Should we call the cops?"

"It's too late for that, Maddie," I say with disgust. "Much too late."

26

CANDLES

Maddie and Mira are standing in the foyer of Alondra's house wearing long black dresses and black goth makeup. Bryce and I just walked through the front door and saw them next to Uncle Hanley near the stairway. My friends look like witches. Bryce and I don't. I'm wearing a sweater and jeans. It's fairly warm outside today, even though it's December. And anyway, witch clothes are the last thing I want to wear at the moment. Of course Uncle Hanley has on his suspenders, a white cap, and his huge smile.

"Hey, guys!" says Maddie. "Wait till you hear what Uncle Hanley's got to say."

"You guys can come here anytime you want," Uncle Hanley says with a nod. Then he tips his cap to me. "Especially a Hawthorne. And if you'll agree to care for the place, why, it's yours. See, I've got the farm, but I don't want to sell this place. It's been in the family for generations. And, well, Madison told me you guys love to hold parties in the back. So why not? If you guys agree to care for the house, you can come here to stay. I think Alondra would have wanted it that way. I'll give you the keys."

"Seriously?" asks Bryce.

"Yeah."

"How do you like that, Katie?" Maddie asks with a wink.

"Thanks, Mr. Hanley," I say.

He surprises me by hugging me. "Call me Uncle Hanley, Cadence. And don't mention it. I know how much Alondra liked you."

"We were planning on throwing a barbeque out back next Friday, Uncle Hanley," says Mira with a sly grin.

"Suit yourself. Just tidy up when you're done. I saw you out in the garden in the morning, a couple weeks ago. If you guys keep working the garden like that, I'd be eternally grateful." And he walks to the door.

"You're leaving already?" I ask.

"Yep. Got to go back home and arrange the rest of the estate." He looks down in thought for a moment, holding the door. "You know, it's a common thing for a husband or wife to die right after their loved one, but I didn't expect this from Bill. He was so healthy. It's so damn peculiar, him being struck on that hill. I mean what're the chances? Lightning? The authorities said the energy to do what happened to his body had to come from a bolt of lightning, and there was some lightning that evening. But come to think of it, there was a fire that night, like the fires he and Alondra used to light in the backyard. A bonfire right next to his body. I don't know. I'm thinking the damn fool probably was doing some unorthodox shit by the fire again, excuse my language."

We look at each other, but no one says a thing.

I don't think Uncle Hanley cares what really happened, but he's such a sweet man that he removes his cap for a moment, out of respect for Bill Reardon, and shakes his head with a sigh.

"Well, goodbye," he says.

Mira and Maddie walk beside him to the door. I'm surprised because the plan was for the two of them to join us.

"You guys leaving too?" I ask.

"We'll leave you lovebirds alone," says Maddie chuckling. "Anyway, I've got a final tomorrow and we have to study."

She had to say *that*. I bite my lip.

Finals. *Shit.* Bryce reads my mind. He squeezes my hand more tightly and nods as if to say, *It's all right*, but it's not all right. I'm certainly going to fail this semester again like last year. Bryce said it's okay because I was "sick." He said I can make up for it and that, as he's my TA and "close friend," he can vouch for me. Still, he can't very well tell the provost I was a snake. Daddy's going to kill me.

Before I can explain my anxiety, my two friends are out the door.

"Come on," Bryce says, tugging my hand.

We walk down the hall to the guest room. It's a familiar room that I used to sleep in from time to time last year. It's a simple room with a mahogany dresser, a white canopy over a large single bed, a draped window, and a small nightstand.

I pick up two candles from their candleholders on the dresser. They're yellow memorial candles. One is from last year, for my mom. I left it here. The other is for Alondra. Mira left it here. Now Bryce is holding both of them.

I pick up the lighter on the dresser. Then I light the candles. I gaze into his eyes. The flickering light is reflecting in his to-die-for baby blues. "So, what are you going to say, Bryce?"

"Do you really think she was evil, Cadence?" Bryce asks. The question surprises me.

"Who? Enora?"

"No," he says, shaking his head. "Alondra."

He looks like the question is of such great importance. But knowing him as well as I do, I kind of think he's referring to himself.

"Oh, Bryce." I run my hand over his short hair. "I don't think anyone is pure evil. Alondra said that herself. I think there's evil in all of us. But we should be judged by our love. Who we love. What we love. And not just in the past, but in our future, you know... Don't you think? Right?"

"I love you, Cadence."

I touch my lips to his and then, after we've kissed for a few seconds, I say, "I love you more, lover. Now... what are you gonna say?"

"You go first," he says and hands me a candle. "Talk to your mom."

"Okay." I take a deep breath and close my eyes. "But you know I hate this stuff." I really do. I'm so bad at it. It's like how I can never think of the right thing to say on a card. I can write a whole essay, but I can never think of a few words. But I try.

"Mom, I love you so much and miss you more than you can imagine. I miss...your smile. Your voice. I miss going to see you and Dad and seeing you stand by the window, just watching me until you can't see my car anymore. I miss talking to you about all my troubles. And how, well, everything about me was so important to you. I...miss you... And, well, so much more.

"I'm with Bryce now, Mom. I wish you could see him. He's such a wonderful man, and I'm so lucky to have fallen in love with him... We both hope that wherever you are, you're happy and at peace."

Simple, right?

"Your turn," I say, opening my eyes with a thin smile.

He leans down and kisses me on the lips again. I guess it's romantic with just the candlelight. But I push him away. "Cut it out," I say with a laugh. "Just say something."

"Couldn't resist," he says with a shrug. He clears his throat and closes his eyes with a smile still on his face. But his smile fades. "Alondra, I...I can't believe you're gone. You know, Katie here always says you were like a mother to her, but you were my mother, Gilda's mother, Mira's mother, Maddie's, everyone's mother in the circle. The whole group was under your bright white light. You were so wise. The coven hopes you are in peace now. That you have crossed into the Summerland. We love you and will miss you so very much. Goodbye, Falconsong."

A tear falls from his eye and he brushes it back. I nod as he hands me the two lit candles, and I put them in their candleholders on the dresser.

"Thanks, Katie," he says.

"Oh, Bryce, I should have let you say all that at Alondra's ceremony," I say, feeling really guilty. "That was so stupid and selfish. It was so wrong."

"I wasn't thanking you for that. I meant, thanks for mentioning me to your mom."

And that is soooo sweet. I turn and look deeply into his eyes again. We touch hands. Our fingers entwine.

"I love you, Bryce. But I'm done with the past. Let's just move on. Together. Okay? You know, have a 'normal' rest of the year."

He grasps me in his arms and we kiss. "Let's go home, baby," Bryce says, running his hand through my long hair.

I nod.

Before we walk to the door, I turn once more to snuff out the candles. I wave my hand because I can't resist just a little magic but, before I do, I gasp. Bryce pulls back and lets go of my hand.

"What is it?" he asks.

Sitting on the nightstand by the bed is my book *Broomstick*. I point at it.

"Spooky," he says, but he's not trying to be funny. His eyes are wide open.

"I hate her, Bryce. She's such a witch."

I wave my hand and will both candles to blow out.

THE END

THE HAWTHORNE WITCH

BOOK III

1

ADDER

I'm worried. One reason is real dumb. I've prepared for this service all week, and even though these are my closest friends, I hate talking in front of people. I should never have become their leader. But there's a far greater reason for my troubles. A witch showed up at my doorstep last night and ruined what was supposed to be a romantic evening with my boyfriend, Bryce. As all my friends hug each other, with their hoods back, revealing smiling faces by flickering firelight, they're oblivious to my uninvited guest, hiding somewhere behind me in Alondra's dark nineteenth-century home.

Outside, I enjoy the smell of the burning embers of our bonfire as everyone sits in the circle of white plastic chairs. The crescent moon and stars shine brightly in the center of Alondra's backyard and I still can't get over how lovely the night sky is away from the city. The stars are so vivid and bright. You can even make out the river of light across the Milky Way.

After everyone sits, all smiles, we hold hands. My best friend, Maddie, sits on my left and the love of my life, Bryce, is on my right. I clear my throat and prepare to recite the words I rehearsed.

"Yatu," I say.

"Yatu," they all repeat with a nod. Yatu means "hello."

"We celebrate Lammas. Lammas recognizes hard times ahead. It is a turn of the season, like all holidays on the wheel. This afternoon was hot. Soon it will turn cold. Lammas is the first harvest. Mabon comes next, and finally, my favorite, Samhain." I face two new recruits across from me and smile. "Samhain is Halloween."

The newbies look nervous and out of place. I mean, they're the only ones not wearing black cloaks and thick witchy makeup.

I pause and gather my thoughts. It's quiet. The crickets chirp more loudly. The fire crackles.

"Lammas is a special harvest, as it represents the time when Apollo radiates his energy down upon Gaia, growing our first grain. As such, we celebrate the reaping by partaking in bread. And as we share the grain, we consume the Earth. Gaia is a part of you. You consume the Earth, and as you pass into the Summerland, you shed her. So as you partake, I ask that you reflect, deep inside, about your place among Earth and..." I raise my arms and feel the sleeves of my black cloak slide below my wrists. "The moon and the stars. One soul. Atman. Blessed be my coven under the gods Gaia, Selene, and Astraeus."

"Atman," says Bryce, nodding and closing his eyes with a smile.

"Atman," says everyone else.

"Blackbird, please hand me the bread."

Blackbird is the mystic name for my best friend, Maddie. Maddie jumps up and walks over to a white linen cloth behind us on the grass, where there's a chalice and a loaf of bread. She seems so happy. Everyone is. We're all loving the festival and seeing each other again.

"It's buttermilk bread, Katie," Frida explains in her beautiful Brazilian accent, reaching over and touching my hand. She's next to Bryce. I can't wait to taste it; she always bakes the most amazing stuff. "And I brought pomegranate wine."

Maddie hands me the loaf. I tear off a piece and lay it on my lap. It smells fresh and sweet. I hand the loaf to Bryce, on my right. Bryce nods to me, breaks off a piece, and passes the rest to the witch beside him.

"Happy Lammas," I say with a big smile.

They all burst forth with "Happy Lammas!"

Then my friends jump up, saying the words over and over in greetings to one another. Hope hugs Mandy, and Helen leans down and kisses

Maddie on the cheek. Tammy leans over and lays a white flower wreath around my neck. As I'm still technically officiating, I'm seated in the middle. I sit quietly, readjusting the sleeves of my cloak, just enjoying the warm, clear starry night in the company of my best friends.

"May you never thirst," Maddie says on my left.

May you never thirst.

Usually those words make me happy, but tonight I'm a little sad. I first heard the saying from my friend and mentor, Alondra, the owner of this house, who passed away last year. These words have many meanings, but to me, the most personal is love. A wish that the togetherness between me and my twelve closest friends, who are in this circle, will never dry up. That's sweet...but bitter. See, this is my last year at Hawthorne University, and my friends are leaving. Every event, starting with this one, takes me closer to the end.

"May you never thirst," I echo, feeling the bitterness. I try to hide my thoughts.

Hope, the only one still standing, walks behind me and grabs a fancy-looking gold chalice from the white lace cloth behind me. (Shh, don't tell anybody, but the cup's a brass trinket I bought with Maddie in Atlanta.) Hope hands it to me, and I hold the cup with both hands, drinking some of the tart pomegranate wine.

"Umm. This is really good, Frida."

"Thanks, Katie." We laugh.

I wait for Bryce to pass the cup to all the other witches in the circle. When everyone has sipped, I nod to Maddie.

"Thanks, Windstorm," Maddie says. "Hey, guys, have a nice summer? I want everybody to meet our two new recruits, Josie and Debra. They're considering joining us. Can you believe it? Crazy, right? Try not to scare them. They're terrified."

"We're not!" cries Josie.

"Yatu, Josie," says Bryce. "Debra."

"Yeah," Maddie continues with a chuckle. "Josie likes hiking. Not your enjoying-the-fresh-air type of hiking but mountain climbing. Like risking her life hiking in the mountains at Zion State Park. She's also a physics major, and that marks the first witch we've ever had in our coven that's a scientist. What is the world coming to, right, Katie?" I just nod. "And—my best of friends—Debra is a local girl, living close to Flintwood. I knew Debra in high school, guys. She's quiet but has more of a love for magic than anyone I know—except maybe Mira. In fact, she was practicing witchcraft even before I joined. She's also real scared."

"Yatu, Debra," says Tammy, who is sitting close to them. Tammy's a super-sweet bald black girl. "Relax, girls. The only one to be afraid of is Cadence over there."

"Stop," I say.

We laugh some more. It's fun. This is the part I love about our coven, just turning to friends and talking, you know.

"Thank you, Madison," I say. "Welcome, girls. This is just an introduction. If you're still interested, let us know and we can initiate you."

"Thank you, Windstorm," says Josie. Then Debra nods.

"Thank you for introducing them to the group, Madison."

"Don't mention it, Cadence Hawthorne." There's more laughter.

"Let us eat," I say. "And as we eat, be thankful for the food that the gods have gifted us."

And that's it for the ceremony, thank God. Like I said, I don't like talking in front of people. Alondra made me their leader last year, but I never asked to be.

"Are we going to make puppets tonight, Cadence?" asks Frida innocently.

"I've gathered the cornhusks in the kitchen," replies Maddie. "The newbies have already made some. If you guys want, later tonight we can do it with popcorn."

"And I brought beer," says my boyfriend.

"Hey, Bryce, how was last night at the house all alone with Cadence?" Tammy asks. But we weren't alone, and Bryce loses his smile.

"It was fun," he says after swallowing some bread. "We just got back from Atlanta, where Katie introduced me to her dad and brother."

"Oooh," says Tammy with a big smile. "Getting serious, guys."

"They're as amazing as she is," says Bryce, hugging me.

"Ah," I say, leaning into his arms.

Everyone's happy. But, you know, the minute I talk about the visitor, things will sour.

I glance back at Alondra's house. I left her in the bedroom upstairs, where a floor-to-ceiling window looks out into the backyard. But it's dark inside. Well, I don't want to do what I did last year. Last year I opened my mouth at our reunion gathering, and it was a total downer. But Bryce keeps looking at me. I'm guessing he expects me to say something. As Tammy talks about a date she had with a pilot in Savannah, Bryce grabs me by the arm and leans close to my ear. "You want me to tell them?" I shake my head. I think Maddie overhears, but she's busy stuffing her face with bread.

We go around the circle, and everyone talks about their summer, enjoying the freshly baked bread.

"Did you guys hear about Greg and me?" Frida asks, showing off a big diamond on her finger.

"Congratulations," I say. "I'm so happy for you. Maddie said he's cute."

"Duh," Maddie says. "Look at Frida."

"He asked me in Hawaii, Katie," Frida explains. "I'd just been having fun in the sand, and I was lying on a towel when I felt a hand on my belly. I tipped my shades and my Greg was on his knee." She laughs again. "He's so romantic. I said I dreamt once that I'd be asked for my hand in marriage on the beach. Greg had planned the whole Hawaii thing just for that moment, I think. He's wonderful."

"Cute," shy Helen says. Frida nods.

"Greg is really cute," Maddie says with a nod. "Wait till you guys meet him. But then why wouldn't such a swell guy be hanging with Frida?"

"I can't wait to introduce you," Frida says.

We talk about clothes. Then shopping. It's times like these that I feel like Bryce is left out. He's the only boy in our group. But that's tradition. One male High Wizard and twelve witches always make up a coven.

"I went with Don to Europe, guys," Tammy says. She's just as boisterous as Maddie. "England. The traditional home of witches, you know. Mother Shifton's Cave in Yorkshire and the Petrifying Well. It was cool. You know, maybe it was Mother Shifton's famous ugliness that made everybody think that we witches are ugly." We laugh and she tells us about all these petrified teddy bears and hats.

I feel more at ease. As my friends keep yapping, I glance over at the tall, thin trees in the shadows of Alondra's yard. The trees surround Alondra's backyard field. I love the woods.

I've wandered alone there many times. It's so peaceful. If you venture down the hill from here, along some dirt paths, you'll be at my college. Hawthorne University is surrounded by trees too. And looking over the trees, if you gaze far enough, you can see the nearby mountains. But everything else is shadowed by the woods.

I have an urge to leave and wander right now. Besides the sound of crackling wood and my friends' laughter, there's a calmness in the air. The crickets are still chirping. Air brushes gently against my cheek. A squirrel darts up a tree trunk, running away from a deer whose hooves are crunching leaves. The deer looks right at me, but I know she can't see me. The deer is standing near a ditch, in a clearing in the forest, about a fifteen-minute walk from the backyard. I know because I've walked along the path many times before.

Then I feel something in my chest. Magic. I feel myself slipping into a trance, and that puts me on edge. It's bad because usually when I've slipped into a trance unknowingly, it's been for protection, with a spell.

Someone shrieks. Tammy stops midsentence with her mouth wide open. There's another gasp. Then another. Everyone is looking at the house behind me. I turn.

Beatrix—you know, the unwanted guest I still haven't told anyone about—walks slowly from the back porch to our bonfire. She's wearing the same brown leather jacket, jeans, and shirt she wore last night, with her long blond hair flowing around her pale face. But her makeup isn't running down her face from crying like it was last night. She's an uneasy young girl, only seventeen. And she's close enough for my friends to recognize her. How could they forget her? Last year she helped murder a professor and tried to hurt Bryce.

Maybe I should have told them?

Everyone except Bryce and the two new recruits jumps from their chair. The newbies have no idea who she is. My friends do. They remember her licking and sucking the blood off our murdered professor's arms last year.

"Yatu," Beatrix says with a shy wave.

No one's "Yatu-ing" anyone.

Bryce gets up and tries to shush everyone, but they're in a panic. I remain seated, but I turn my chair toward her and the house. I wait for everyone to calm the hell down. When they're quiet enough—

"Guys, I invited her," I say. "And if you all knew what she's going through, you would too."

That makes them go nuts again.

"Everyone, quiet!" shouts Bryce. "Let Katie explain."

"I didn't come for your service," Beatrix says to them. Then she looks down at me. "I'm here to warn you. Adder is coming. She'll be here any minute. She's coming for me, so...I have to go." But she pauses, looking very unsure about it. "I don't want any trouble for you. Thanks for everything, Cadence. All of you are so lucky to have Windstorm as your High Priestess. Remember what I told you about Raven. Adder's not only coming for me, she's coming for you. All of you. Don't trust her. She only wishes bad things for you."

"Go back to the house, Beatrix." I finally rise from my chair. "I won't let her touch you."

"You can't do that," Bryce says to me. "You need to let her go."

I stare at my boyfriend, dumbfounded. You have to understand that this is Bryce. Nice Bryce, the nicest guy in the world.

"She told us Enora has it in for us, Bryce," I say. "We're in danger whatever we do. Why wouldn't you want to protect her? Enora will kill her if I let her go."

"What's going on?" asks Josie.

"They're forbidden to come anywhere near us," Mandy says to the new recruit, pointing with hatred at Beatrix. "Everyone from the Abaddon coven has no right to step foot in Hawthorne. That was your own order last Christmas, Katie."

"Her life is threatened."

"So?" Mandy replies. "Ours is too if you let her in the circle."

The recruits look scared again, but now they have good reason to be. For them, this was just another visitor to our holiday festival. An excuse to meet new friends to help them make corn dollies.

"Maddie, please take Josie and Debra into the house," I say. Maddie nods and quickly corrals the two girls in her arms and rushes them back to the house.

I turn to Mandy, a witch with long blond hair who's in a perpetually bad mood. Well, she doesn't like me, anyway—especially as the coven's leader. She and Natasha have never accepted me. "I'm not letting her in our circle," I say.

"You're involving us if you let her stay," Mandy replies. "Weren't you here when Reardon was killed? Or what about Bryce? Weren't you there when she tied up your boyfriend? Tried to burn him alive?"

"Of course I was!"

The two recruits look back as they walk to the house. They heard that.

And now Beatrix is walking away. It looks like she's heading into the woods.

"Wait, Beatrix."

"Let her go!" Mandy snaps.

"If you heard what Enora asked her to do, you'd protect her too."

"What? What's so bad that you're willing to risk our lives for her?"

Beatrix stops. She begged me not to tell anyone. She made me swear. She turns and looks right into my eyes, reminding me.

"She was asked to have ceremonial sex with a stranger."

"So? They're a black witch cult."

"That's not all."

"No, Cadence!" Beatrix runs back, shaking her head desperately. "No!"

"She was to have sex until bearing a child," I continue. "Then in six months, the fetus was to be removed through ceremonial abortion and—"

"Cadence! You swore!" Beatrix violently shakes her head.

"They planned to drink her baby's blood."

"*I told you not to tell them!*" Beatrix is right up in my face, practically spitting on me. "*I told you!* How could you tell them? How could you do that!"

Everyone turns quiet. Some sit back down in the white chairs and stare at the fire.

"Why'd you tell them!" Beatrix shouts again in my face. "Why? You swore, Cadence! How could you do that!"

"They have to know why I'm protecting you."

"I don't need your protection!"

I laugh. Yeah, I actually laugh in the poor girl's face because, honestly, right now I hate her. I spent all night talking her down from killing herself when she threatened to slice her wrists in front of Bryce and me. I've lost all patience, and now she's destroyed our holiday. She's exhausting me. I don't want to protect her. I wish she had never come here.

"She's not a part of our circle," I explain to my friends, "but that doesn't mean she doesn't have a right to stay at Alondra's house. Alondra would have wanted us to help her."

"Keeping her here is the same thing," Mandy says quietly, shaking her head. But she doesn't seem to be in the mood to fight with me anymore. She doesn't say another word.

Beatrix turns to the house hesitantly, looking like she's going to leave again. It's too late. She screams instead.

Another witch, carrying a torch, is slowly walking toward us from the side of the house. Her cloak is similar to ours, but it's scarlet. Under the fire, I recognize a face completely covered in black tattoos. Cordelia. Her mystic name is Adder. Last year, Cordelia and Beatrix were Enora's henchwomen—her favorite witches. Yeah, Cordelia tried to kill my boyfriend too.

Behind Cordelia, candles are flickering through the living room sliding glass door near the outdoor patio. The electricity doesn't work in the house. At least Maddie has the new recruits inside the house, hopefully trying to do something nice like make more corn dollies or prepare popcorn by the fireplace.

"Sit down," I say to my witches, staring at Cordelia as she makes her way over. The bitch has a large smile. "Do as I say." From my periphery, I see my friends obey.

"Yatu, Windstorm," Cordelia says with a fake smile. Then she lifts her left palm and shows us a red pentagram painted on her hand. She looks at Beatrix. "Yatu, Manthis. Sister. What are you doing here? Do you think witches you tried to kill can help you?"

"They have nothing to do with this." Beatrix shakes her head. "Just leave them alone."

"Then come back with me."

"If she wants to," I say.

Cordelia walks right up to me. Her black-tattooed face is right up against my nose, and I can feel the warmth from her torch on my chest. Bryce grabs Cordelia's arm, but she yanks it off, still staring at me.

"Happy Lammas," Cordelia says smugly, gazing down into my eyes.

"I told you to never come here."

Cordelia laughs. "Then why is she here?"

"I'm leaving," Beatrix says.

"It's sweet that you honor your teacher by holding your holiday parties on her sacred grounds," says Cordelia, finally backing away and looking around. "I hope her spirit won't come here to disturb your gathering again."

"She only comes when you and your friends are here."

"That was a neat trick. The power to summon a ghost is impressive. But I told Enora that you never really saved her life. I said you summoned your teacher and that all you did was not finish your kill. Enora understands. Ghosts don't have the power to throw people off cliffs, only people do. Only you did. Enora doesn't owe you a thing." Cordelia sighs. Then she looks at Bryce and smiles smugly. "Yatu, Bryce. Enora sends you a special greeting."

"Go to hell."

"My pleasure."

"I'll say it one more time," I say. "Get out."

But Cordelia nods and walks over to the bonfire. She touches the fire from her torch into the flames and then plants the torch firmly in the grass. With a fake smile, she sits down cross-legged in front of the fire. We're all standing over her.

"Tradition allows a witch from another coven to visit freely during Lammas," Cordelia says. "I send you greetings from Panthera and her Abaddon coven, as a representative of her circle. My master would love for me to join with you in partaking of bread."

"Get the hell out of here," I repeat.

"How rude. Enora warned me you'd be like this. She said you sent the same regards for Alondra's memorial." Then the bitch looks at Beatrix with contempt. "And how are you doing, Beatrix? Didn't you help me bind Bryce's wrists and try to burn him alive? I think it was you. It was you, wasn't it? I think Katie remembers."

I grab Cordelia by the arm. She's much bigger than I am and could normally bend me over her knee and break my back. She jumps up, flaunting her size. But I'm angry, and when I'm angry, I feel magic. I feel my trance growing and giving me confidence and power. And when she moves to grab Beatrix, I throw her to the ground.

"*Get out!*" I yell.

She laughs, lying on her side on the wild grass.

"Okay." She puts her hand up because I'm about to grab her and throw her again. "I'll leave. But I come with another message. My master told me that I better not find you actually helping our little harlot. For a year, she respected your wishes for saving her, but if you dare help Beatrix, you are threatening to break the peace."

"Where's Mira? Beatrix said you've taken her. You're the one who's breaking the peace."

"We didn't take her," Cordelia says. "She was bored. She wanted to practice real magic."

"I don't believe you."

"Ask her yourself."

"I can't reach her by phone."

"Raven is a real witch now." Cordelia laughs again. "She doesn't need a cell phone."

Beatrix starts wailing on her knees by the fire. We all look at her. This is what she did all last night. She just cried and cried and cried. She's a complete mess. It's really annoying. Cordelia looks at her with disgust, and I'm thinking she's probably spent hours consoling the witch too.

"You won't let me return with her?" Cordelia asks, still leaning on an elbow in the grass. "I told you the risk. I warned you, Windstorm."

My silence is my answer.

"Very well." Cordelia gets up with a nod. "I'll tell my master. But I don't think you're going to be happy with Enora's response."

"Wait, I'll go!" Beatrix yells, jumping up, still in tears. "I'll go! Please! Please leave them alone."

Of all people, Mandy grabs Beatrix's arm and pulls her close. Mandy looks at me and shakes her head.

Cordelia lets out what sounds almost like a growl. For a moment, I could almost swear her eyes flicker red. I reach for her torch, leaning beside the fire. The torch flies about twenty feet through the air and lands in my hand. Cordelia stares and shakes her head, and she looks afraid for the first time. I shove the torch against her chest.

"*Go!*" I shout. "*Get out of here! Get out!*"

Cordelia steps back from me, nearly falling over. "Talk...to Mira," she mutters. Then she forces a fake smile but steps far away from me. "We'd love to recruit you too."

2

THINGS ON MY MIND AND, OH, SCHOOL

TODAY I'M NOT GOTH. THAT'S UNUSUAL FOR ME, BUT THIS MORNING'S different. My usual look on campus is thick black lipstick and mascara, a black dress, and black boots, matching my long wavy black hair. Instead, today I'm dressed like a *normal* girl, with a sharply pressed navy-blue dress, my hair in a ponytail, and red lipstick. And I'm sitting stiffly in a black leather chair across from the dean of the history department, Dr. Bainer. Dr. Bainer's a short baldheaded man who's holding spectacles while staring at papers behind his large dark-mahogany desk. He's been doing that since I walked into his office five minutes ago. Behind him, through the window, is a gorgeous view of Hawthorne Forest.

I already waited thirty minutes in the history department's administration office, and now I'm waiting again. That gives me time to think. I really don't want to think.

I've got so much stuff on my mind. My friends. Mira. And...Beatrix. I left Beatrix alone at Alondra's house. What if she burns the house down? And Damien. I'm supposed to meet my brother, Damie, by ten to help him move into his dorm room at Krunner Hall. Yeah, my brother's going to Hawthorne this year. Can you believe that? That's after I warned him and Dad against it like a zillion times.

Dr. Bainer sighs and sifts through more papers. I pull out my cell phone to look at the time. I bite my lip. My brother's waiting for me. It's ten thirty.

I take a deep breath, hoping it will elicit a response from my interviewer. It doesn't.

Mira. I thought Mira was still in Florida with her folks, looking for work after she graduated. She wanted to land a teaching job. But Beatrix told me she'd moved to Atlanta with Enora's sick satanic sex cult. I entertained the idea of driving downtown last night to visit her, but Bryce convinced me not to. Apparently, I have an interview I'm not having.

I wiggle loose a nail jutting under the armrest of my chair. Dr. Bainer's oblivious, still staring at whatever the hell he's staring at. I wiggle and wiggle until the nail comes out and falls into my right palm. I put the nail on the leather armrest. Then I play with it a little more, looking down and rubbing the silver metal thingy between my black-polished fingernails. It moves very easily. It spins like a top.

Bryce. I just have to get into graduate school at Hawthorne next year. If I do well in this interview, my boyfriend and I are set. Bryce is finishing his dissertation and plans to teach history here next year. But...what if I don't? What if I go somewhere else, like another state? You've heard about what happens in long-distance relationships, right?

That was the wrong thing to think about. My heart races and I suddenly feel sick—like I have to move my bowels or throw up. But I'm supposed to be nervous, right? I am in an interview, aren't I?

"Hmm," Dr. Bainer finally says. But then he's back to staring at the paperwork.

Fuck.

It smells like books in here. Or is it old musty carpet?

My metal nail is spinning by itself now, but the dean doesn't notice. He doesn't notice me either. I hold my hand about three inches over the nail and jerk my palm every few seconds to keep it turning.

Maddie calls him Dr. *Brainer*. I know that's real corny, but it's also funny. He really doesn't talk much to students. Bryce says he's a little rough around the edges.

His office is a mess. I'm surrounded by boxes, books, and papers. The dean's Indian, which is cool. I see a book from ancient India, the *Bhagavad Gita*, that I've always admired on his bookshelf. The *Bhagavad*

Gita says that we should just act and not worry about consequences. I wish I could do that. Especially now. Then he's got books I don't care for as much—modern history books on the Cold War, the space race, and the Vietnam War. I don't really like modern history. There's a very nice old picture of a wedding on a matching mahogany bookcase. He had hair back then, and he and his wife were wearing lovely multicolored robes. It looks like a traditional Indian wedding. It sits beside a picture of two kids next to a roller coaster. The boy is carrying messy vanilla ice cream, and the girl has cotton candy.

"Is that Disney World?" I ask, just to say anything.

He glances at me in irritation, leans back in his reclining leather office chair, and thumbs through more papers on his desk.

Fuck!

I look behind Dr. Bainer at the gorgeous view of the dense forest. It's so lovely. I wonder if he appreciates just how lovely his view of Hawthorne Forest is.

"You've had a tough time," he finally says, wrinkling his brow and staring at one particular page. "What happened?"

"What do you mean?"

He looks up at me and raises his eyebrows. "What happened, Ms. Hawthorne, to the fall semesters in your sophomore and junior years?"

"Well, my mother—"

"Died. That was in your sophomore year."

"And last year, Alondra—"

"Dr. Johansen died last year." He puts one stem of his glasses in his mouth and squints his eyes. "So? Ms. Hawthorne, this is Hawthorne University."

I'm kind of hoping he notices what he just said. Like maybe the fact that my family founded the city could help me get in? No, I don't think so. This interview is not going so—

"Hawthorne University's history program has the top reputation of all the liberal arts colleges in the United States. I can't accept slips every time something bad happens. We've all lost loved ones. You can't fail your semester because of it."

"I didn't fail. I passed after making everything up."

"Well, I'm not sure why the provost allowed you to remediate. You remediated twice. And you passed, you didn't excel." He chuckles, but I don't think it's very funny. "You did do well on testing. Every test was nearly a hundred percent—or a complete fail due to absence. A peculiar record. Then there are notes by your teachers. Everyone liked you. Especially Dr. Alondra Johansen. Dr. Johansen recommended you with high marks in her honors program, even though you only received a C in her class."

Yeah, Alondra's "honors" program was supposed to ensure that I could get into the graduate program here—or anywhere in the country, for that matter. And if Alondra were still alive, I know she would have vouched for me and I'd be in. Maybe even Maddie, with her miserable grades, could have gotten in.

"Then there was Dr. Riker." He raises a finger. "He's the only teacher who failed you." He looks down at the note he was studying before and laughs. "You had Mr. Wallace teaching you then, right?"

I'm getting angry. This guy seems mean. First, he makes me wait half an hour; then he says nothing for what feels like another. Now he's belligerent over my grades. Why even interview me? I've got so much shit on my mind right now. I don't think this guy could even imagine my stress.

But I have to calm down. Maybe he's just testing my nerves. You know, I have an anger problem.

My "top" is spinning like crazy, on its own, under my palm.

"Mr. Wallace actually had good things to say," he continues. That's *Bryce* Wallace, my scrumptious boyfriend and TA for two of my classes. "He wrote a note in your file. Would you care for me to read it?"

No. Not really.

He reads:

Dr. Riker does not believe in remediation. Therefore, unfortunately, Cadence Hawthorne must fail her art history class. But we want it to be noted on record that she is an outstanding student. Dr. Riker believes that her final essay was one of the best student essays he's read in his twenty years of teaching. As for my observations as her teaching assistant, for the second time, I can vouch for Cadence's outstanding work. It also should be noted that she fell ill during the month of December of her junior year. She approached the provost, who allowed her to remediate. I hope her illness will be considered when looking at her fall semester grades in her junior year.

Signed, Bryce Wallace.

"Everyone likes you," he says with a very long sigh and an open-armed gesture. "Especially your boyfriend."

Why, you patronizing fuck!

"Look ..." I stammer because my word sounds like a shout. "I...I don't like what happened. I really don't. If I could go back and change it, I would. But I know I can give it my all. I love history. And I love this school. I love studying here. Near the forest and the trees. There isn't a better school in the world than Hawthorne. And everybody, all the teachers, are so nice. It's the perfect place. I really like studying history and—"

"What do you like about history?"

"It's like a story, you know."

"It is a story. It's the most important of stories, because it allows us to learn from our past. But why do you want to study here?"

Because my boyfriend is going to be a professor here next year. Instead I stupidly repeat, "Everyone's just so nice and friendly and it's so beautiful, you know."

My "top" is spinning super-fast on the armrest now. It's as desperate as I am to get his attention.

"Dr. Brainer...I mean—" *Idiot, Cadence!* "Dr. Bainer, I had so much trouble because I love it here. Alondra was family. So when she died, I lost it. It was like my mom died all over again. Because when my mom died, Alondra was there for me."

"I thought you were sick," he says, lifting his eyebrows suspiciously.

"I was. I know it doesn't excuse my actions. I know I should have done better."

"What are you going to do if something like that happens during our doctoral program?"

"I don't plan on anyone dying."

And that does it. It sounds really sarcastic. He squints and looks angry. But it's so unfair. If anyone should be angry, it's me. I think this guy's really mean.

He shakes his head and jumps up.

"Well, good day, Ms. Hawthorne. This program is very selective. The problem is your GPA dropped because of the fall semesters in your sophomore and junior years. You're a good student, but your grades are not typically acceptable for our graduate program. I agreed to the interview because of how well liked you are and because you went here for undergrad. I will notify you of my decision in a few weeks."

I think you just did.

He sticks his hand out for me to shake.

"But, Dr. Bainer," I say, standing up and handing him a limp handshake. "Isn't there anything I can do to bring up my GPA? If that's all that you're concerned with, can't I do something to make up my grades? You saw how well I did other than those two semesters. And on testing—I ranked at the top in the country. And you said everybody likes me."

"I read you that note because I found it inappropriate," he replies, shaking his head, "I don't approve of favoritism, Ms. Hawthorne."

"Then just ignore it."

"Good day. I can't change your past. I'd love to erase it, but I can't change what happened to you."

And that hits a nerve. *Erase?* That's what Enora tried to do last Christmas when she tried to burn my Book of Shadows along with my boyfriend.

"No one can erase the past!" I snap.

Shit. Apparently, my thoughts are directly connected to my lips because I'm so angry. Now he knows I don't like him. His eyes open wide, and he moves back a little. Or is it a sudden gust of air that I feel rushing through the room? I'm not sure. Boy, I really hate him.

"I...I...I..." I do everything in my power to force a smile. "I'd be willing to do any extra projects or any testing that could raise—"

He shakes his head.

"Isn't there anything I can do?"

"No."

"But—"

"I'm sorry."

"There must be something I can do to—"

"No. Good day, Ms. Hawthorne."

FUCK YOU!

The nail flies from my armrest into the window. There's a loud crack. Dr. Bainer whirls around in surprise to see a crack at the side of his window. He jumps up to look outside, thinking someone hit it with a ball or something.

I'm running out the door. I might have nodded a goodbye to him, or maybe I didn't. I don't know. I don't care. All I know is it was a horrible interview—the worst interview of my life. Of course, the office assistant gives me a really big smile as I rush out of the room.

In my high heels, enduring blistering summer heat, I rush to the dorms to catch up with my brother. I'm late. I'm going to help him move into the school I begged him not to go to. At least *he* will be coming to Hawthorne University next year.

3

———

THE BILLINGTON HOUSE

I'M SUNK IN A VERY UNCOMFORTABLE BROWN LEATHER BEANBAG CHAIR, staring toward a big central window in the Billington House, as a bunch of freshman kids are getting drunk and talking up a storm around me. I don't mind their noise. I like that others are happy.

The Billington House is a large haunted house, the oldest house in Georgia. Even older than Alondra's. It's a brick building with sash windows and a broken-down white fence, sitting on a grassy hill surrounded by the woods. The large central window—the one I'm staring at now—is where a ghost is sometimes spotted after midnight, holding a candle or knife and facing our campus below. Meanwhile, the inside of the mansion has been transformed into the Psi Kappa Psi Greek frat house with the usual cheap, ratty furniture, holes in the walls, pool and ping-pong tables, paper murals announcing events, and bikini-clad, beer-holding girl posters.

Maddie's leaning on the wall beside a door, holding a red plastic cup, talking to my brother. She tosses her hair back a few times between guffaws. She's having a great time with him. Damie brushes back his long hair, which is longer on one side with this surfer look. They're happy together. That's nice. But I'm still pissed that my brother's even going here.

Bryce is only a few feet from me, laughing with a bunch of his old friends. Bryce loves the Billington parties. He used to live here, you know.

My phone vibrates in my jeans pocket. With my free hand—the other is holding a beer bottle—I answer it.

"Hi, Cadence," says a real depressing voice. It's Beatrix. I have to press the phone close to my ear since country music is blaring.

"How you holding up?"

"All right." She doesn't sound all right. "I wanted to ask if I can keep a cat here?"

"Sure. Alondra used to love cats. As long as you take care of it."

"Oh, great. And I want you to know, I've been cleaning up the place. It's the least I can do. But the AC keeps turning on around sundown. It gets really cold at night."

That's super weird. Bryce had an electrician come by to take a look at the place after our weekend stay. The man looked at my boyfriend like he was nuts when Bryce told him about the air conditioner turning on by itself. He said that there was no way it had turned on because he had removed the power grid last month, to prevent fires, after our complaints of flickering lights. When I heard that, I became convinced that Alondra's house is haunted. So now there are two haunted houses in Hawthorne.

Bryce reaches down and touches my knee and winks at me. He's in such a good mood. Of course I haven't told him about Dr. Fucker yet. I just nod and point to the cell phone. Then I make a gesture circling my finger around my ear. He nods. I'm sure he can guess who I'm talking to.

"It's the least I can do," Beatrix says in my ear. "You've been so nice, Cadence."

"Are you feeling any better?"

"I guess."

She's so odd, you know. She keeps telling me how she misses everyone in her coven terribly, even though they all want to kill her.

"So the cat's okay, right? Are you sure?"

"Yes, Beatrix."

Bryce nods when he hears her name. He sips his beer. A short, overweight, dark-skinned guy with a beard is standing beside him, looking around the room, drinking. I think Bryce wants to introduce me to him.

"Thanks," Beatrix says. And she sounds happier. "Talk to you later, Cadence."

"Bye, Beatrix."

I hang up the phone.

Bryce leans on a knee beside me. There are no more chairs or bean-bags to sit on.

"Katie, this is Mason. Remember Mason? You guys said hello on the phone a while ago. He's down for the weekend. We used to be roommates."

"Hi, Cadence." Mason takes my hand. "Great to finally see you. Bryce said so much about you."

"Oh, yeah? Good stuff, I hope?"

"Very. You're a grad student too?"

"I'm a senior."

"Oh. So you didn't know Bryce back in the days when he used to live here?" And he has this really big smirk. Well, I know the crazy things he did in my coven. I can just imagine the "normal" party animal things Bryce did. Not to mention he used to go out with Enora back then. Yeah, really. His girlfriend was Enora. Can you believe that?

Then Mason adds, "He was *quite* the roommate."

"Oh, really?"

The sweetest thing is Bryce's reaction. He blushes. "Mason was quite the frat boy himself," Bryce quickly says.

"*Oh no*," I say with a big grin. "You don't get off that easy, babe. Don't try to put the blame on him. Tell me more, Mason. Please. Tell me. I want to know all the specifics."

"Cadence," says Bryce.

Mason smiles again, but he just shakes his head and says, "They were great times. I remember lots of beer."

"And girls?" I ask.

He nods. Bryce sighs and I laugh.

"Boys will be boys," I say, reciting the old adage. "As long as he doesn't go back to being *quite the roommate* now."

"I wouldn't dream of it, Katie."

"Where are you living, Mason?" I ask. I want to get up, but I'm sunk in the beanbag and he's standing in my way.

"I'm a gamer," Mason says. "I work near Columbus. I couldn't resist coming to the back-to-school party." Bryce is still leaning on a knee, and Mason puts a hand on his shoulder. "And I had to see my old buddy."

"What sort of games?"

"Mainly role-playing and adventure games. I love it. It's fun programming the details of characters. A lot of fun. Bryce and I used to play a lot on the computer back then."

"Among other things," I say with a sly smile.

Bryce puts an arm around me and says, "Just lots of gaming, Katie."

"Aha." I laugh.

"Listen, I've gotta catch up with some of the others," says Mason. "Fantastic meeting you, Cadence. You're as attractive as he said you were." I try to get up to hug him, but he's still standing right in front of me and I'm deep in the beanbag.

Bryce jumps up and grabs his hand. "Come by later, man. We have to go out while you're in town."

He nods.

Then Bryce kneels beside me.

"*Quite a roommate*, huh?" I ask, running my fingers through his short, feathery hair.

"Stop, Katie," he says with a laugh. "Listen…I was hoping we could go on one of our dates this Monday?"

I look at him funny because he looks nervous. That's super weird being that we're living together.

"Love to."

Then he furrows his brow and examines me. "What's wrong, babe? Why are you so blue?"

"Just got a lot on my mind."

"That was Beatrix on the phone, right? She's okay?"

"She sounded okay, but I'm not sure."

"She's lucky to have you. You've been so nice to take her in."

"That's not what you said when she first came to the house."

"I know. She's disturbing." But he winks again. He's being cute. I smile in spite of my sour self. He's in such a good mood. "It was such a nice thing to do," he says.

"Must be learning from you."

He reaches over and kisses me on the lips.

When I unlock my lips from his and stare into his blues, I say, "Is this what being *quite the roommate* is?"

"Stop it, Katie."

"Hey, guys, get a room," says a young boy's voice. I'd recognize that voice anywhere. It's my tall brother, Damie. Maddie's trailing right behind him. Maddie looks funny standing next to my surfer brother. She's got on a black skirt and dark makeup, but nothing would stop her from looking beautiful.

"Showing my kid brother around, Maddie?" I ask.

"Sure am. He loves this house. He's freaky and weird like you."

"I don't like being freaky."

"Any drinking games 'round here, guys?" asks Damie.

"Not after what happened last year," Bryce says, lifting his eyebrows.

I elbow Bryce hard in the shoulder and look at him crossly. Last year, I nearly tore down the house on Halloween during a drinking game. Enora was using a spell to show me her and Bryce together. I got so mad that I nearly took the house down. But I don't want him telling Damie. I don't want Damie involved in any of our witch stuff.

"Hey, man!" says another tall dark-haired boy. It's Harvey, Damie's best friend. He hugs my brother and they clink beer bottles together. Damie looks like a surfer, but Harvey's more preppy looking, like my boyfriend.

"I heard this place is haunted by your family." Harvey smiles at Damien. "Escoba and Maverick Hawthorne." Then Harvey turns to us. "Hi, Cadence. Bryce. Maddie."

"You see that window over there?" Maddie says to Harvey—pointing, with her red cup in her hand, at the window I've been staring at. "The ghost of Abigail supposedly haunts the window, looking down at Hawthorne every night. Abigail knifed Escoba, a voodoo witch..." She points at me with a wink. "Katie and Damie's relative. Or people think Escoba was knifed by Abigail. It was never proven. Abigail's killing was revenge for Escoba's curse. Abigail's ghost appears by that window every night holding a knife."

It's an awful tale, but it's told to all the freshmen who come to

Hawthorne, especially during the orientation party. When Maddie finishes, Damie looks at me and says, "Witches, huh. Interesting."

The little shit. He's said other things, over the past two weeks, hinting that he knows I'm a witch. I hate that. I mean, my makeup is suspicious, but I keep telling him I just like looking goth.

"Babe," Maddie says to me, touching my hand, "how'd your interview go?"

Shit.

"Yeah, sis?" asks Damie. "How'd it go?"

Bryce looks at me but doesn't say anything. I think he's tired of prodding.

"Excuse me," I say to all of them, finally climbing out of my sunken beanbag. "I have to use the little ladies' room."

I don't, of course, but you know I don't want to talk about my interview. I haven't talked about it in days. And as I walk away from my friends, dodging more bodies, I could swear I see Maddie and Bryce talking behind my back, looking concerned. They're on to my failure. I just know it.

When I return to my beanbag a few minutes later, all my friends are off to the side, enjoying getting inebriated together. I don't mind. Like I said, I like that everyone's having a good time.

Then I recognize my dear, sweet friend Frida. I'm so happy to see her, but she startles me with her expression. She runs over, so scared.

"Katie!" Frida says. "Katie! She's here. Did you see her? She's here."

"Who? Who's here?"

"Enora."

I open my eyes wide. "Here?"

Frida nods.

That's when two girls wearing tight pitch-black dresses and thick, dark makeup walk into the living room. Accompanying them is a tall, blond man; he's shirtless, flaunting his buff physique. They get a lot of attention. A crowd forms around them. It's Enora and Cordelia. I don't know the bare-chested man.

Many older students say hi to Enora because she used to visit the fraternity house when she was Bryce's girlfriend. She's also very pretty. Like model pretty. Everyone's looking at her face and tight black lace dress. She's got tanned skin and a perfect figure, but her dress is indecent —it's just nasty. She keeps staring over at me with her bright blue eyes. She's always done that. She's so fascinated by me. I hate her. They're socializing as if they're just visiting the orientation party, but Enora keeps glaring at me.

The guy standing with them is really odd looking. He's got pale skin, a goatee, and a rippling muscular chest, and he stands like two feet taller than the girls. Actually, he towers over everyone. He also snarls and glares at everybody. He reminds me more of an animal than a human. Enora pulls at his elbow as if it's a leash for a pet dog.

Bryce approaches them, and that lures me out of my beanbag. I swear if Enora or that meathead even lays a fingernail on him, I'm gonna go berserko.

"Bryce," Enora says, all fake and cheery. "How are you?" Like she cares. Last time they saw each other, the witch tried to burn him alive.

Then Damie walks over with Harvey. Enora sees my brother. My hands grip into tight fists, and for a moment the lights in the room flicker. Most people don't notice, because it's not that uncommon for the lights to do weird stuff in this old house. But Cordelia does. She flashes an infuriating sly grin at me.

"Aren't you?" Enora asks, wagging a finger at Damie. The bitch giggles. "Why, aren't you? You even look like her. You're little Katie's younger brother, aren't you? I can see the resemblance."

Don't you dare touch him!

Damie nods. He seems enchanted. Like I said, Enora's strikingly beautiful. But when she talks to Damie, I've had enough. I rush over.

"What are you doing here?" I snap.

"Katie?" Enora says in fake surprise. "Oh, hi, Katie. I didn't know you were here." Then she lifts her left hand, flashing me a red painted pentagram. "I should have guessed after seeing Bryce. So very nice to see you again."

"She's rude, master," says Cordelia, looking at me with disgust.

Her tall dog-man snarls at me. I lurch back when he opens his mouth. His teeth are filed down and he has two fangs. (Seriously, I'm not making this up.)

"Adder," says Enora, "this is our reunion, dear. It's so great to see little

Katie with her boyfriend and family." Then she looks around the room in wonder and seems to address the crowd. "Family." Enora gestures at the living room with open arms. She rubs her black-lace-gloved hands together. "Ah, why, you can just feel the paranormal energy run through the walls." Then she looks at me with full-on bitch-smugness. "Even the lights flicker. Almost, one could guess, a witch's magic? Your ancestors still roam here, Cadence? How are they? You been talking to them lately?"

"Where's Mira?"

"Nuh, uh, uh. You first, Cadence. Where's Beatrix?"

"Who is this ape?" I ask.

"Gus," he says, turning to me. "My name's Gus. And you better watch your mouth, girl."

There are some oohs and aahs from bystanders. I reason that this must be a lot of entertainment for the party. Even though few know what the hell's going on, it must be obvious that there's some kind of commotion. In fact, all my witches who attended this party are now standing behind me.

Enora runs her hand lasciviously along Gus's naked arm. "Careful, Gus. Little Katie might look like you can squash her, but looks can be deceiving."

"She seems like an ordinary little girl," Gus says, looking me up and down.

"Yeah?" asks Bryce. "Well, Katie's right. You look like a gorilla."

But then he freaks Bryce out by opening his mouth, showing his fangs.

"Shut your mouth, Gus," Enora says, waving an arm at him with a chuckle. Then she turns to me. "Adder and I want to know where my sister Beatrix is. Can you please tell us?"

"She's with me."

"Where? I don't see her. You know, it's a real long, boring drive from Atlanta." Then Enora looks around at all the students swarming us. She puts a hand up. "No offense, everyone. The forests at your school are very pretty. I miss the trees. But the drive's shit. I was hoping you'd be more welcoming, Cadence."

"How can you expect anything else from us!" snaps Frida in her

Brazilian accent. I've never seen Frida look so angry. Those who know her are shocked. Frida's the sweetest, shyest girl in the world.

"Shh," Enora says to Frida. She runs a lace-gloved finger over Frida's lips, and Frida knocks her hand off. "This is a talk between *real* witches, señorita."

When she touches Frida, the witches in my coven go crazy. No one touches our dear Frida. There's Tammy, Hope, Helen, and Mandy. They shout profanities and yell at Enora and Cordelia. The other students at the party have no idea what the hell's going on, but everybody in the house is now gathered in the living room. I glance at my brother. He and Harvey are completely dumbfounded. I gesture for Bryce to do something, anything, to get my brother the hell out of here.

"Let's talk away from the party," I say to Enora when it's quiet enough to get a word in.

"But I always liked the Billington House back-to-school party. I miss it here. Bryce and I had really good times together. Remember, Bryce?"

"Outside," I repeat.

Gus grabs my arm and I angrily shrug it off. I think if he touches me again, I might light his hand on fire.

"Suit yourself, Windstorm. *Et nos unum sumus.*" Enora chuckles. Then she turns to her crowd. "Don't fret, dears, I'll be right back. Apparently, Katie Hawthorne and I have some catching up to do."

She laughs at her own words, which aren't funny. Then she gestures with a black-gloved finger for us to walk outside all snooty, as if I'm deigning to be in her presence.

All my friends and Enora's two companions walk together into the front yard. There are still partygoers watching us. Bryce doesn't accompany us. At first, out of curiosity, Harvey and my brother were going to join, but Bryce grabbed them to keep them inside. I signal to my other witches to stay in the house also. Everyone but Maddie. I need some support. Anyway, Cordelia's by Enora's side and has always been like Enora's best friend, so why can't I have mine? Gus remains by the front of the house, leaning against a wall with folded arms, staring at us.

We walk down the hill to a dirt path near the forest, where Enora finally stops and turns. She's not smiling anymore. She looks dangerous.

"Enough playing around," I say.

"Agreed. You have Beatrix. I want her back. She will accompany me and Cordelia back to my Abaddon coven. *Now.* Either have her leave Alondra's house or have her accompany us. I wasn't joking about not enjoying the drive here."

"What are you going to do to her?"

"That's none of your fucking business," Cordelia snaps.

"I told you to never return here," I warn.

"I had to come to take back what's mine," Enora says. "I respected your wishes, but then one of my witches left and came to you. She's *my* witch. From *my* coven. *My* circle. Give her back to me and I'll leave." Then she looks around at the forest. "Honestly, I don't really care for Hawthorne. I lied about the trees. They're really boring."

"Beatrix told us what you were planning to do to her," Maddie says.

"Why are *you* here?" Enora asks.

"She said that you were planning on getting her pregnant," Maddie continues, ignoring the insult, "so that you could drink blood from her dead aborted baby."

Cordelia bursts out laughing. I don't think it's very funny. Enora develops a big grin. Then she shuts Cordelia up by showing her hand— the hand with the pentagram.

"Beatrix is mentally ill, Madison," says Enora. "I already visited her before I came here. I knocked on Alondra's door but, of course, the little whore didn't answer. She's hiding. And lying. And you're helping her. She did the same to us, but we still love her. She's a part of my coven, crazy or not. Release her from your house, Cadence."

"She can go if she wants," I say. "But if she's unsafe, I'm allowing her to stay."

"Then you're minding my business," Enora says, infuriatingly wagging a finger at me. She raises her eyebrows. "You know a witch that harbors another witch is calling her one of her own. You're taking one of my sisters. Or must I teach you again about our arts?"

"How do we know you didn't send her?" asks Maddie.

"Why would I do that?" Then she looks up and down at Maddie as if amazed that she's daring to speak again. "You're an interesting witch. Are you one? What exactly do you do? I've never heard of you casting a single spell. Do you just follow your High Priestess around like a dog?"

"Like her?" Maddie points at Cordelia.

Cordelia's eyes open wide, and I could swear there's a flash of red circling the whites of her eyes.

"Uh, uh, uh," says Enora. But she chuckles, amused. "Careful. Adder is a powerful witch, Madison. Unlike yourself."

"Maddie's a lot better witch than any of you," I say.

"Fine," Enora says, rolling her eyes. "Whatever. Look, you saved me, Cadence. I haven't forgotten that. I respected your wishes and kept away. But taking one of my sisters from my coven is not acceptable. All I ask is that you let me take her home."

"Why do you have Mira?"

"I already told you," Cordelia answers.

"I want her to tell me."

"She loves our spell casting," Enora says with a shrug. "It's her life. I offered her an opportunity to practice magic. You never did. She was willing to move to Atlanta with me. As you know, our coven just moved, so I invited her. She enjoyed it so much that she wants to stay."

"I don't believe that. Mira never liked you. Maybe if you release Mira, I'll give you Beatrix."

"I don't have Mira to release, you fuck!" snaps Enora, suddenly enraged. Then she looks down and shakes. But she tries to laugh it off. "She's free to go if she pleases. That's more than I can say about that harlot you're harboring."

"I'll talk to Beatrix. If she feels safe, I don't care if she leaves."

"No." Enora walks right up to my nose. Then she shakes her head. "I didn't travel to the middle of nowhere for nothing. You will release her now, whether she wants to or not. You will tell her to leave, or I will take her. I warn you. The choice is yours. Do not test me. I was very happy to leave you and Bryce alone after I killed the High Wizard, but if you get in the way of my coven's business, I will have to move into yours. And if you don't release her, I'll take her my way—very possibly in a fashion you won't like. Mind your own business, or I'll mind yours. Like that of your boyfriend or...your brother."

"Don't you dare touch him!"

A wind develops from clear skies. Clouds cover the moon and it becomes dark. Cordelia looks around nervously as our long hair blows in the wind.

"Always a pleasure, Cadence." Enora looks at the sky and feigns a smile. "You don't have to conjure a windstorm to remind me who you are. This is about you trespassing on me, not the other way around. Tell Beatrix to leave. Tell her I'm giving her a week. After a week, if she doesn't return, I'll take her. My way."

And that's enough. The bitch twirls her dress and walks away with Cordelia.

"Forget the party," Enora says to Cordelia. "We've seen all we wanted." Then she signals toward the house, claps her hands together, and hollers, "Come, come, Gus. We're going home now. I have a special treat for you."

And all three of them briskly walk down a side path to an adjoining road, away from the Billington House.

"You have to get rid of Beatrix, Katie," says Maddie, watching them.

I turn and look at my friend. Maddie forces a smile, but she looks really scared.

"I hate her," I say.

"Let's just go back to the party," Maddie says with a nod and takes my hand.

4

DARKNESS

"Beatrix?" I shout.

I'm in the foyer, yelling up the stairs to Alondra's bedroom. That's where Beatrix usually is. Standing in the entryway of Alondra's house is terrible because the house is super creepy at night without electricity. Bryce drove me here from the Billington House after the back-to-school party. He wanted us to go home and go to bed, but after seeing Enora, I had to check on Beatrix. He was going to join me in the house, but his old car was vibrating on our way over. Right now, he's checking his engine.

I wish I weren't here. It's so dark. Well, at least the AC isn't on. That would be too creepy. But it's warm inside after another hot summer day.

"Beatrix?" I holler again. "Are you up there?" She wouldn't answer her phone either.

So I do what I really don't want to do. I light a candle from the small table by the front door and walk up the shadowy stairway.

"Beatrix?"

Damn it. Where is she?

At the top of the stairs, I turn left down the hall to the main bedroom. I hate going in there. I still see images in my mind of a sick Alondra groaning in bed. But her ghost isn't here. At least I've never seen her ghost here.

The main bedroom is brighter. The drapes on the large window are open. This view looks over the grassy field behind the house; in the center is a pile of logs where we light our bonfires. Shadows of trees in the distance surround the yard.

The master bed is a complete mess. There's trash strewn all over the floor—paper bags from fast-food restaurants with leftover food, magazines, books. I take out my cell phone and call her again. I jump when the phone rings under the bedsheets. Then I jump again when my phone vibrates in my hand. Bryce is calling.

"Hey, babe," he says. "Did the ghost get you?"

"Shit. You really scared me. Not funny. What's the matter with the car?"

"I don't know. Maybe the spark plugs or engine mounts."

"Wow. Sounds like you really know your stuff."

"I just looked it up on my phone."

I laugh.

"The car can wait till tomorrow. I'll take it to a mechanic. Look, can we go? Is she okay?"

"I don't know where the hell she is. The room's a complete mess. And I can see why she's not answering her calls. Her phone's on the bed. I'll look around the house."

"You need me there?"

"No. No. I'm okay. I'll be outside soon."

I hang up my phone and make my way down the stairs with my candle.

"Beatrix?"

I pass my favorite dining room. It's really dark. It's brighter outside, and I can make out the lovely forest through the floor-to-ceiling window. Then I check the living room. It looks chic when it's brightly lit, but in the shadows, it's just another dark, creepy room. I walk back to the entrance to the house and head down another hall toward the guest room.

That's when I really get the heebie-jeebies. A light flickers near the end of the hall—right where Bryce and I slept a few weeks ago. The guest room.

I walk down the hall. By the door, I gasp. There's a black cloak curled up in a ball in the center of the room. The cloak is circled by flickering candles, which are surrounded by a pile of white chalk. And in front of the cloak is a book. My book. *Broomstick*. I'm thinking maybe it's Alondra's ghost. With a hood over the witch's head, I can't tell. But then—

"Hi, Cadence."

"Shit!" I exclaim. "You scared the hell out of me, Beatrix."

Why she's curled into a ball in the middle of my guest room, with candles and my book, is beyond me. Last year, Alondra sat like this when she was dying. It's similar to a yoga pose.

Beatrix breaks all the spookiness when she lifts her head, revealing her girlish features, long blond hair, and chubby cheeks. But her makeup is smeared. She's been crying again.

"What are you doing?" I snap.

"Meditating on death. I'm trying to cast a protective shield spell with your book. I'm drawing power from Gaia by our feet and energy from Alondra and your Book of Shadows."

"Well, can you stop and answer me next time I call out your name? You're really freaking me out."

"Sure, Katie," she says with a sweet smile. "Sorry." For a second, it makes me let go of my anger.

"You okay?" I ask.

"Sure. How come you're here so late?"

"I saw Enora at the party."

"She came by here too." Beatrix nods. "But I didn't let her in."

"She told me that. She's asking for you back."

Beatrix turns her head, fighting back tears.

"You can stay here," I say. "You don't have to return to her if you don't want to. I told you, you have a home here."

Beatrix nods again. But then she starts to cry.

"What's the matter? I said you can stay."

"That's not it." She shook her head. "The cat died."

"What?"

"The cat I asked you for. She died."

"You asked for her only a couple hours ago. What are you talking about?"

Beatrix wipes her arm across her nose and flashes a fake grin. She shrugs. "I took her in from outside. She was wandering the woods. She didn't look good. Her back had hairless patches and she limped. I could tell she was sick. That's why I wanted to help her. I felt so bad for her. Alondra used to love cats, you said, right? You think it was one of hers?"

I shake my head. I personally gave Alondra's cats away a year ago.

"Then…" Beatrix shrugs again. "She just died in my arms. God, it was so terrible, Cadence." And Beatrix starts crying again. She's so depressing.

"It's okay, Beatrix. We can get you another cat that's not a stray."

Beatrix shakes her head and her eyes bulge. "It's a sign, Windstorm. It means I'm going to die. I just know it. And you know what else, Cadence? I'm going to hell. Damnation for all my sins. For all the sins Enora had me do. I just know that too. See, the cat is me. One of Panthera's cats. It's like a prophecy. It was sent by Panthera. I saw the cat in the forest and it ran right into my arms, but it was hurt. It was so hungry. Just like me. And, I don't know, maybe I overfed it, but it just wasn't going to make it. So I took it into my arms. And then…and then you were nice enough to let me keep her. So I got her some milk and fed her. But she drank so weakly. Its fur was shedding all over the patio. And its nose was full of mucus. I tried desperately to care for it, rocking it in my arms." She looks right into my eyes. She's so awfully sad. It's horrible. "She just died in my arms. On the patio. She's gone! She's dead!"

She loses it and starts bawling again.

I sigh and put a hand on her shoulder, but she shakes her head and jerks from me.

"Stay away from me! I'm cursed. Damned! Stay outside the circle." She points at the chalk surrounding her. "Enora is Panthera, right? Think about it. She sent her animal totem. A cat. To send me the message. She warned me that I'd die if I didn't return, but if I go back, I'm going to die anyway. So I set this magic circle to prepare my passing into the Summerland. To meditate on death. But I don't want the curse to spread to you. No, not you of all people. You're so nice."

"Oh, come on, Beatrix. You're being ridiculous."

"It's a sign," she says, nodding, her eyes bulging again. "It's a sign that I don't have much longer to live. Enora is coming for me. I even…saw a flock of crows overhead right after the cat died!"

They probably smelled the dead animal, but I don't tell Beatrix that. I don't think logic will make her feel any better right now.

Beatrix is scared because Enora's mystical name, Panthera, represents cats, although all last year she used her magic to shapeshift into a blackbird. In fact, last year Enora deceived me by becoming my "friend" after transforming into a raven. I have to admit, when you put all these signs together, it certainly looks like Enora could be behind it. But it could just be a coincidence.

"I'll get you another cat," I say.

"And then you can get yourself a new Beatrix."

"Oh, Beatrix, stop. You've got to get a hold of yourself."

"Did you know, Katie, that my father is a Catholic priest? Did I tell you that? I ran from him too. I will never have a home again. Last time I came by his house, he said, 'Get back, devil.' He said that to his own daughter. He knows I'm a witch. A satanic witch. He doesn't want my sins to rub off on him. He doesn't want to be damned like me. Same thing happened when I went into a church a few months ago. I went to ask for forgiveness. The priest chased me out of there too. I will never have a home under God, because I'm damned. All because of what I've done. Do you understand?"

She completely loses it again.

"*Fallen like God's fallen angel!*" she screams. "*To the depths of hell under Lucifer's wing! When I die, I join Satan down in the depths of the Earth to suffer from pain and burn for an eternity in hellfire!*"

And she weeps again.

My phone buzzes in my pants pocket, and it's a welcome distraction. It's Bryce again. I don't have to look. I know he's asking me if I'm almost done. Done with what? No professional psychiatrist could help this girl.

"I just came by to make sure you're safe," I say with a sigh. "And to make sure you're not doing something stupid."

"Like kill myself? I wouldn't do that. You...you know why, Cadence?" She looks at me with watery, bloodshot eyes. I just shake my head. "Because that's a sin." She chuckles. "That would be proof to the Lord above of my evil. It would seal my fate and bring me down even faster to damnation. But...I suppose it doesn't really matter anyway." Then she bursts into laughter.

"Look, I have to go. Bryce is waiting for me in the car. I told you, I'll get you a new cat. Okay? I think Alondra would like a cat roaming these halls again."

"I wish Alondra were here. Falconsong was such a powerful witch." Then she puts her hand out to me and shakes her head. "But, of course, you are too, Windstorm. I need all the protection I can get."

"You're safe, Beatrix. But it's really late. I'm going to go."

She nods.

"Can you get up off the floor?"

"I won't leave this circle tonight. Can you say an incantation to protect me? I set up the candles, Windstorm. And I poured white dust around the light to make a sacred shield. I thought of painting a pentagram in the center of the carpet, but then I thought it would make you mad. Enora used to give me a spell to protect me when I felt like this. I tried to use your book, but I'm not sure it has enough energy alone. Can you utter a quick incantation to protect me?"

Enora used to give her a spell when she felt like this? So she's felt like this before?

Her request for an incantation sends shivers down my spine. It reminds me of a child asking their mother for a bedtime story. I'm beginning to be more creeped out by Beatrix than by Enora.

"I have to go," I say with a sigh. "Just go upstairs and go to bed."

I walk to the door, but before I can leave, she begs, "Please? Oh, please, Cadence! Please, say an incantation for me. I know it will protect me tonight."

"An incantation?"

She gestures to the circle of candles around her and nods.

I roll my eyes. "What do you want...?" I look at her. She's so scared. So I take a deep breath and cross the room to stand beside her, flick my fingers over her head, and say the first words that come to my mind: "May the witch inside this holy circle be protected."

"Oh, thank you, Windstorm! Thank you! I just know any magic from you will work."

I nod. Then I head to the door again.

"Wait. Before you go, I have to tell you something else."

"What?" I snap. I don't mean to sound mad, but she's so difficult!

"I lied to you."

"What?"

She sits up straighter and looks really guilty. She fights back tears again and averts her eyes. "Enora sent me. She sent me on purpose to break the peace."

"What?"

"You've been so nice. I wasn't going to tell you. I wasn't ever going to tell you, but I owe you. I like you and your friends so much. I owed you the truth. Enora said that if you took me in, she'd have an excuse to go after the Hawthorne coven again. I told you, she still hates you. She just needed an excuse. Right after we came to Atlanta, she said she had to cleanse the lands under Hecate and take care of Hawthorne."

"Beatrix, explain quick. I'm getting mad. What exactly do you mean?"

"I told you Enora gave me two choices, right? It wasn't two, it was three. There were the two terrible blood sacrifices—the blood of my unborn child or the death of me. But there was a third choice involving you. Of course I didn't know you well enough, so I didn't really care. But you've been so nice, and I don't think there's much hope for me now anyway, so I wish I had chosen one of the two blood sacrifices instead. I'm doomed anyway. I don't really want anything bad to happen to you. The thing is, maybe I should have just accepted the blood sacrifice of my unborn baby. I think then she would have rejected Mira and kept me. I could have gotten pregnant again and then, you know, we usually get a doctor to do the procedure. Enora makes sure we're safe. I did it once before."

You did it before!

"The thing I was worried about was that she could ask me to do it again. And again. And again. I just thought it was the height of sin to do it again. Maybe it's because my father is an ordained Catholic priest? I don't know. But maybe I should have accepted her—"

"Beatrix!" I put my head in my hands. I take a deep breath. Why am I helping her? How can I help her? I don't think anyone can help her. And now she's endangered me and my friends.

"Look, the stuff you're saying is horrible," I say. "You've done it before? What do you mean you've done it before? Are you serious?"

She almost starts crying again and, for a flash, the lights in the room turn on. This is, of course, impossible as the house has been disconnected from city power. But my hands are clenched tightly. It's me. I'm furious. Beatrix opens her eyes wide. Then she quickly crouches into her ball again, terrified of me. She is shaking and whimpering again.

Shit.

"Stop crying!" I shout.

She nods with her head still buried.

"Beatrix...you lied? You weren't in danger of being forced to do something you hadn't done before?"

"*But I didn't want to do it again!*" she yells, shaking her head. "Don't you see? *I didn't want to do it again!*" She's screaming between sobs. "I didn't want to do it again, because I knew she would keep having me do it over and over and over. *Again and again and again!* It would never end, Cadence! That's another reason why I came here. I couldn't do it anymore! I thought following her and coming to see you would get her off my back."

"All right," I say as calmly as I can. "Okay. Just calm down. Stop crying. It's okay."

She shakes her head. And then...she laughs. That sends another shiver down my spine. I think laughter is the last thing I'm feeling right now.

"You don't know us," she says, shaking her head. "You don't know our ways. There are many secret witch gatherings like ours all over the world. There isn't just Wicca. Many other witches worship evil. The devil. Under Baphomet. Against the Christians and any god you would consider good and holy. What you're so disgusted by isn't as bad as other things I've seen. Or done." She shakes her head and leans over the carpet outside the circle. She dry heaves for a moment. I'm expecting her to throw up, but she doesn't. "I've partaken in eating flesh too."

What monster did I let into Alondra's house?

I step back. She's still crouched like a black onyx stone, wearing her black cloak, curled up in a ball. That angers me because it reminds me of my teacher. How dare this girl pretend to be anything like Alondra. I reach down in front of her and snatch my book. It seems random, but suddenly I really don't like her being anywhere near my book.

She laughs again with her head still buried. That only makes me hate her more.

"I'm damned. But so are you, Cadence. Alondra's husband worshipped Baphomet to increase the power of Hawthorne, and whether you're a devil worshipper or not, Cadence, you were initiated into the Hawthorne coven under Baphomet's rule. Your power stems from Satan. And Enora hates Hawthorne more than anything in the world. Last year, she tried to take control of your coven, but you stopped her. So now—"

"Beatrix, stop for a second. What do you mean, you ate flesh? You mean like human flesh? Like cannibalism?" I mean, can we step back and revisit this for a moment? I can't believe this.

"Well," she says, lifting her head and finally looking at me with her bloodshot eyes. "I mean, I didn't kill them. It was fed to me."

Ah. That makes it much better.

Beatrix looks down and practically talks to herself. "My hope was that if I did what Enora asked, she'd take me back. I could come back home, and things would be the way they were before Mira joined. And then Enora wouldn't hurt me anymore. But any love she once had for me is gone. I could tell when I talked to her today. She just wants to finish you. You and Mira. And Hawthorne. And Bryce. She wants you all gone. But Mira's too lovestruck to see it."

"I'm going to go."

"There are no more lies," she says, raising her head. "I'm sorry. I know how much you value the truth. I won't lie to you anymore. I promise."

"Okay." But how can I trust anything she says after she told me all those things? Then again, I don't think I ever really trusted her.

"I see the way you're looking at me," she says with a nod. "I get it. Now you know I'm a monster."

No, I think you're insane.

"Well, so is my master. So is my coven. But after I leave tomorrow, I won't blame you. I will only feel grateful to you for letting me stay here when you did."

"You're not leaving tomorrow."

She looks at me like I'm nuts. In another circumstance, perhaps that would be funny.

"You don't want me to leave tomorrow? After I lied to you? After

Enora threatened you? I..." She looks at her candlelit circle and trembles. "I understand. I'll leave tonight if that's what you want, Windstorm. That's okay. I will."

"No." But half of me is thinking, *yes.* "You're in danger, whether she sent you here or not. And even with all those things she made you do, you need protection. Right?"

She nods.

"Then it's up to you. My invitation stands. You can stay here as long as you have to."

"You're such a white light!" she says with a big grin, almost breathless. "Such a bright white light! You remind me of your teacher, Alondra. No, better. I... thank you so much, Cadence. Thank you!"

"You'll be all right, Beatrix," I say. "I'm going to get you a cat, okay? A healthy one."

"You're so nice," she says with a chuckle. Then she looks down and shakes her head. "But you know, Katie, I really think we're damned and going to go to hell anyway."

5

BY CANDLELIGHT, MY DREAM

Lacey's is always a romantic dining experience, with candles, large comfy booths, and darkness. You can't see much except your date. I think that's why Bryce loves it so much. It's really romantic. And in Hawthorne, it's the only fancy romantic steak house for a hundred miles. Bryce and I come here now and then. Our first real "date" was here. I signed a confidentiality agreement to join the coven. Back then, unlike now, there were good reasons to be secretive. Even now, my witches are still secretive, and we don't talk about our coven in school, but we don't do anything crazy that warrants confidentiality agreements anymore.

Anyway, we're here again and Bryce is looking through a menu, even though he probably already knows what he wants. I'm not. I'm sipping water, staring at an empty table across the room, thinking about Beatrix. And that makes me think of Mira. And then...my interview.

"They have a new special for lobster bisque tonight, babe," Bryce says.

"Sure," I say with a slight grin.

"We could order something different?"

"No. No. I don't mind either way. Just happy to be here with you." I force a smile.

Bryce puts the menu down. He's about to say something when our waitress comes to the table.

"Welcome," the waitress says, lighting a candle in the center of our table. She's an older woman, with her curly dark hair in a bun, wearing a bow tie and a black-and-white suit. "Is this a special occasion?"

"Just celebrating the new school year," Bryce says. "We'd like a bottle of wine. Your house merlot." Then he looks at me. "Merlot's okay, Katie?"

Sure. But a whole bottle?

"Can I see your IDs?"

Why do they always ask that? I don't look that young. And Bryce, he has a beard, for goodness' sake. Then again, his beard is pretty thin.

When she leaves, Bryce turns back to me and says, "What's the matter? Still upset about Beatrix?"

"Of course. Sorry. She's so odd. She asks me if she can keep a cat, and then three hours later the cat's dead. For all I know she killed it. We've been helping a total wacko."

"Well, how about I take your mind off of it and we talk about something else?"

"Okay, like what?"

"Us."

I lift my eyebrows. *Sure.* And he scoots closer to me on the booth. *Cute.* We're sitting side by side.

"How's your classes?" He's close enough for me to smell his lovely spearmint-laden breath and Bryce-cologne.

"I thought we were going to talk about *us*?" I ask, blinking my eyes stupidly.

He kisses my lips. Then he shrugs. "What's there to talk about? I'm madly in love with you."

I laugh, but then I feel a little sour. "Classes aren't great."

"Jesus, Katie, what's the matter? I can't believe how down you are."

I brush my fingers along his short hair and then his cheek, over his thin beard. "You're not. I like that. You're in a good mood."

"I'm not happy if you're not. What's wrong with your classes?"

"You're not teaching them," I say with a shrug. "And Maddie's not in them."

He laughs again and puts an arm around me.

"I like my Eastern religion history class, I guess. We're studying Buddha."

"Dr. Grange kinda looks like the Buddha."

"Aha. He's the sweetest guy in the world. Everybody loves him, and the class is always packed. I mean, sometimes I feel like I'm meditating just listening to him. And it's neat, Bryce, 'cause the religion reminds me of ours in a way."

"Ours? We don't have a religion, Katie."

I shake my head. I'm about to reply, but we're interrupted by the waitress again. I love the wineglasses she places in front of us. They're giant, like twice the size of normal wineglasses. She serves the wine and leaves us again.

"To us, Bryce," I toast and we clink glasses.

"It is a religion," I say after swallowing some wine. The wine's good. Smooth. "All of our witches believe in the magic and power of nature. Nature is our religion. Buddhism isn't all that different. Dr. Grange teaches us that the goal of Buddhism is thoughtlessness. This is so similar to what Alondra talked about with meditation. She always told us to center ourselves, concentrating on our oneness with nature. And it's not that different from Hinduism either, with the belief in one thought, one soul, or Atman. I mean, Alondra even adopted the word Atman, meaning *the soul*, for our circle."

"You seem to really like this stuff."

"It's interesting," I say with a shrug. "Yeah, I really do."

"But it's not really history."

"Well, you taught art last year. Dr. Riker's class was more like an art class than history. And I've got to tell you, I don't think Riker was as nice as I thought."

"Why?"

I don't want to answer that. If I answer that, I'm going to talk about my interview. And if I talk about my interview, I'm going to bring up how I may never see my gorge boyfriend, who's peering at me right now with his irresistible bright blue eyes. And if I do that, it's going to be another thing, along with my schizophrenic houseguest and magical witch-bitch archenemy, to be concerned with instead of focusing on this lovely candlelit dinner date and smooth, yummy wine. So I fall silent.

"Dr. Riker liked you," Bryce says after some silence.

"He failed me."

"I know, but that's his way. He doesn't believe in remediation. It wasn't personal."

"You know, Satanism is a religion too."

Bryce lifts his eyebrows.

"Christianity is a religion of dichotomy, right? Good versus evil. A religion, like Judaism and Islam, against sin. Well, Satanism takes the evil side and just mimics these three religions, worshipping everything antithetical to them. But that's still worship. It's still a religion, Bryce."

"This is coming from someone who hates Satanism more than anyone I know."

"I didn't say I like it. I said it was a religion. They worship the opposite of Jesus's teachings. They worship the body because Jesus worshipped the spirit. They worship sin, arguing that there is no afterlife, no heaven. And they worship ceremonial sex because the Bible tells us to refrain until marriage."

Bryce raises his eyebrows. Yeah, well, we've kind of failed that one.

"Satanism worships everything antithetical to the church. But see, they worship. William Reardon worshipped the devil. It is a religion."

"You're smart, babe," Bryce quips, sipping more wine.

"Shut up," I say with a smile. "Anyway..." I sip more wine; it is really good. "That's why I took a religious history class. I like this stuff."

"So that's your favorite class?"

"Yeah. I guess. How 'bout you?"

"I like teaching Dr. Riker's class. I like art."

"But how boring. I don't get why they made you teach the same class this year."

"They didn't make me, I chose to," he says with a shrug. "You know, I'm so busy working on my dissertation. Of course, Alondra was supposed to have been my dissertation advisor. Now, who knows. I'm not even sure they'll graduate me this year."

"Come on. The department loves you."

"Hmm."

The waitress walks over. "You guys decide on what you want?"

We already talked it over during lunch today. It's kind of silly, in a way.

Bryce and I have our "date" tonight, but I'm living with him. But coming here, making it a date, makes us concentrate on us. And that's nice. But we're talking about school instead. Maybe that's what Bryce is doing? Maybe his plan was to join me in a romantic dinner to sneakily bring up my failed interview?

We order and then Bryce looks nervous. Why? That's weird. He's looking all over the candlelit room. He's in a good mood, but he's nervous.

Well, I'm nervous too. I want to talk about the interview so badly, but I don't. He takes my hand and smiles, and I bring his hand up to my lips and kiss it. Then we just hold hands and fall silent. I scoot as close to him as I can and just enjoy his warmth, sipping wine.

"Speaking of religion," I finally say, "you know, when I visited Beatrix, she really affected me. I haven't been sleeping well."

"She's creepy."

"She said I was damned."

"Is that it?" He looks right at me, searching my eyes. Then he shakes his head. "She's the one damned, Katie. Not you."

"But Reardon was practicing Satanism when you initiated me. She's right about that. Doesn't that mean that I became a witch under the devil? Doesn't that—"

"Oh, Cadence," he says, shaking his head again, "are you joking? You pulled me through crazy talk like this last year. And you know, if anyone is damned, it's me. So you took mandrake? You didn't do a blood sacrifice."

"She cut my arm."

"You never bowed under a pentagram," he says, getting angry. "Or... Jesus, had sex on one." He runs his hand through his short hair. "If there's anybody going to hell, it's me."

"So? So we can go to hell together."

"Is this why you're so unhappy?"

No.

He shakes his head vigorously as if trying to shake off these thoughts. "Don't you remember what you said to me when we lit candles for Alondra and your mother? You said there's no such thing as pure evil. Just like there's no such thing as pure good. Alondra believed that. Your love saved me. Don't you think if there's a God, he or she judges us by all the good we do? You said yourself we're judged by who and what we love. Even if a rite damned you—and it didn't—don't you think God will forgive you? I mean, you're an angel for taking Beatrix into your home in the first place."

"She needed me."

"But you risked so much for her. And after she lied to you and told you all the crazy stuff she's been involved with, you still want to keep her safe. That's goodness. That's angelic. That's love. If it's not, I don't know what is." He snatches up his wine and swallows a little. "I don't like Beatrix. She's messing with your head, and that makes me really mad. Especially after everything we're doing for her."

"Sorry, Bryce. Now I'm bringing you down."

"It's okay. I just don't like you saying stuff like this. If there's anyone in the world who's going to heaven, it's you, Cadence."

"Well, anyway, that's not the reason I'm down. There's something I need to tell you."

"What, babe?"

Yeah, what?

"I...I..." I want to tell him so badly about my interview, but I just can't.

"What?"

Shit, I don't want to tell him. But now, with the "date," I feel like I have to. Because it's about us and...about us never seeing each other again!

I clam up and my chest feels tight. He squeezes my hand more tightly.

"Bryce, I didn't just *feel* like the interview went badly, it did go badly. I, sort of, lied to you. The interview...he told me. I don't know, I—"

"It's okay, Katie. Forget it."

"Hmm?"

"I get it about the interview, Cadence."

I furrow my brow and look right into his eyes, and he gives me that lovely reassuring Bryce smile.

"What do you get?"

"That it went badly. It's obvious."

"It was horrible," I say, shaking my head. "Dr. Bainer's a total jerk."

"He is," Bryce says with a nod. "No one likes him."

"You hinted that."

"I didn't want you to worry." Then he forces a smile and brushes the bangs from my eyes. "I think you're unhappy because you're worrying too much. Stop worrying, babe. Whatever happens, things will work out. I know they will."

"But how? He said he's not accepting me, Bryce. That's what I didn't tell you. What does that mean for us? I want to stay with you next year. I can't if I have to go to some other school. God, some other state? Can you imagine? Dad's going to want me to go wherever I can to study history. He's not going to settle for me not moving on in school. What am I going to do? I've got to go here next year. I just have to. But now I feel like I blew it."

He shakes his head. "Everything will be okay."

"No, it won't."

He loses his smile and becomes very serious all of a sudden. For a moment, I feel this sinking feeling that he agrees with me. But then he lifts a single finger to gesture *just a minute*. He lets go of my hand and digs into his pocket. I'm looking at him like he's crazy.

He takes out a small jewelry box and puts it on the table, sliding it over to me. The box is teal and velvety. I pick it up. It looks like a ring box.

Can this be what I think it is?

"What's going on, Bryce?" I ask suspiciously with a smile.

"You asked why I wanted to take you out to dinner tonight."

I open the box. Inside is a sparkly diamond ring that glistens in the candlelight. I carefully take it out of the box and lift it toward the flickering light. It's a large single diamond on a silvery ring. Exquisite.

"Well, what do you say?" he asks.

"What...what do you mean?"

"Will you marry me, Cadence Hawthorne?"

What...? "Are you serious?"

He's looking at me with a smile, but he looks nervous. I put out my left hand to try it on, and he grabs my hand to help me. But I still haven't said yes. Should I say yes? Do I love this man?

Yes, I love him. I adore him more than anyone. But I don't feel ready for this. There's so much going on. How can I get married *now*?

I look into his eyes. And I feel his fingers putting an engagement ring on my hand. He's putting it on whether I say yes or no. Wait, did I nod? Did I say yes?

Of course it's yes. I mean, God, I love him. I love Bryce so much. But I'm scared. I'm so frightened by everything that's happening.

"Is this a yes?" he asks as he's about to slide it all the way onto my ring finger.

I feel a tear fall from my eye, and that is definitely not the response my boyfriend was expecting. It makes me feel stupid, like I'm a crybaby like Beatrix.

"Now?" I mutter, almost to myself. "Oh...Bryce. I..."

"Babe," he says, looking into my eyes. He gently puts the ring back in the box. From the corner of my eye, I see our waitress coming over with bread, but I think she sees the ring and me rubbing my eyes, and she quickly walks the other way. "Don't you see? I love you. I want to spend my life with you. And, well, you've been so worked up with your interview this week, but I felt like it wasn't because you wanted to study at Hawthorne. I'm thinking it was for me. Us. I don't think it's Hawthorne. Sometimes I think you hate it here. I think it's because you were so worried you'd never get in and be with me. But, Katie, I'm telling you now that whatever happens to us, if you don't get into Hawthorne and get in somewhere else, it's okay, because I want to be with you. I'll leave the state if I have to. And if I land a teaching job somewhere else and you can arrange to do a graduate program there, I hope you'll follow me. Because we have to make it work for us. Together. We need to stay together, no matter what happens."

He pauses and smiles, but he looks really worried. I'm looking at his thin beard and perfectly groomed hair, his bright blue eyes, and his perfect smile. He's so gorgeous. Like, *too* gorgeous. Why does he want me? Then I'm thinking of his heart. Bryce is the nicest man I've ever known. Maybe my dad comes close, but Bryce is definitely at the tippy-top. And he's asking *me* if I'll marry him? Seriously? I don't deserve him.

"I love you," he says, looking into my eyes. "I want to spend the rest of my life with you. The interview, your last year, my last year in graduate school, made me think of all this, Cadence. So I decided to get you this ring to tell you that... but what about you? Do you want to be with me too?"

"Oh God, Bryce. Yes. Yes, I do!"

And I fall into his arms, sobbing like a baby. But my tears aren't tears of sadness; they're tears of joy.

"You make me so happy," he whispers in my ear, rubbing my back.

After Bryce finally puts the ring on my finger, the waitress comes over with our basket of bread.

"We're getting married," I say to her. It seems so weird to say it, but it feels wonderful.

6

ENLIGHTENMENT

I'm flying among the clouds. And it's not only that I'm marrying a man I'm madly in love with. That helps, of course. I realize the source of most of my anxiety has been leaving school after this year. Bryce being Bryce, once again, is helping me through it all. Will I marry him? He really needs to ask me that?

I'm surprised when I get up at seven in the morning for my lecture that isn't until ten. I'm never an early riser. On the other side of the bed, Bryce is facing me with his eyelashes delicately closed over his chiseled cheeks and with those soft lips. He's so cute. He's fast asleep and I don't want to wake him.

I grab a green tea latte, my favorite, from the university coffee shop and ramble along cement walkways, people watching, for an hour. So many students are making their way around campus right now. Even the grassy hill by the campus coffee shop is full of students, sitting on the grass, studying. The temperature fits my mood. It's a perfect seventy-two degrees without a cloud in the sky.

I decide to sit down on the lawn. I take out my black backpack and thumb through some folders I got last week, at the start of classes. But then I put my work down, lean back on my hands, and just look around. Down the grassy hill is the wide walkway that crosses the main campus, and behind me is the library. The main drag is full of students walking to and fro, in and out of the many brick buildings, heading to class. Some are riding bikes. Bikes are only allowed on certain paths, not near the lecture halls, but the riders are probably freshmen that don't know any better. Everything finally feels right. Perfect.

My phone rings.

"Hello?"

"Hey, sis." It's Damien. He sounds like he's in a great mood too.

"How are you doing, Damie?"

"Great! Orientation's been a blast. Maddie was right. I went around with Harvey and, just like Maddie said, it was so fun with him. Having my best friend with me made it awesome—like it was for you and Maddie. Did you hear that Dad might want to meet us down here for Thanksgiving instead of us heading back home? He figures since we're both down here, he can just come to us."

"I can head up."

"I know, but Dad thought it'd be better for me to settle in."

"Whatever, Damie. That's still a ways away. How are your classes?"

"Tough. It's not that the classes themselves are hard. It's just that I have to get As to get into med school. Physics and general chemistry are boring. I already had most of these classes in high school. I never liked physics. I love my biology class, though. It's with Dr. Rogers. You know him?"

"No, Damie. I've never taken a science class here."

"He's a lot of fun. Maddie recommended him at the Billington House party. Hey, what was with you and that older graduate...Enora? It looked like the two of you went outside to fist-fight or something."

Yeah, something like that.

"She used to go out with Bryce. I was suspicious when she came over."

"Maddie said something about that." *Maddie better not have told him anything else.* "You two caused quite a stir."

"Yeah, well, don't worry about it, Damie. So, Maddie recommended a science teacher? She's a history major. How does she know?"

"She said she used to have a friend who attended his lectures. She recommended choosing him instead of another teacher and, boy, was she right. You know I have that scholarship where I get first pick of classes. But how are yours?"

"I love my religious history class. I'm heading there in another two hours."

A girl wearing sunglasses and a large backpack nearly steps on my backpack. "Sorry," she says. It's so busy today.

"Must suck that Bryce isn't teaching you this year," he says with a snicker.

"Yeah, well... look, Damie, can you keep a secret?"

"Sure."

"Like a major secret? Like something you can't tell anyone."

"What?"

"You won't tell? You promise? This is a really, really big secret."

He pauses. Probably because he thinks I'm crazy. But why am I about to tell him when I haven't told anyone yet? Well, why not? I am crazy.

"I promise, sis. What is it?"

"Bryce proposed to me."

"Are you fucking kidding me! Really?"

"Yeah," I say, laughing. "I'm so happy. But..." I bite my lip. "I'm a little nervous about Dad."

"Dad loves Bryce. I think he'll like the news."

"I hope so. Look, just don't tell him yet, okay? You promised."

"Of course."

"Don't tell anybody. Word spreads fast around here. You'll find that out soon."

"Okay, I won't. I just—"

I have to move my backpack closer to me. It's so crowded that another student nearly tripped over it. "Huh?"

"I'm just congratulating you, Katie."

"I'm so excited." I giggle stupidly again.

"When are you getting married?"

"Huh? Oh, I don't know. Who cares? I just know he's going to marry me."

"Okay, sis," he says, laughing.

"We haven't planned anything yet."

"I won't tell Dad. Just like I won't tell Dad that you've been sleeping over at Bryce's."

"Hey, how did you know I've been sleeping over at Bryce's?"

Sleeping over? Well, I'm not just sleeping over—I'm *staying* over. But he doesn't know that, and I'm not about to tell him.

"Maddie told me."

"That snitch!"

"Or I kinda guessed when I visited her. Your bed was made, and a lot of your stuff wasn't there."

"Oh... hey, what were you doing in my dorm room?"

"Maddie had an American history book I'm borrowing."

Maddie and I took that class together in our freshman year. American History 101. There were non–history majors in the class too—people who needed to take the class as a general college requirement.

"She still has the book?"

"Yeah. It's one of her favorites. I'm just borrowing it."

"Damie, how is it—"

"Got to go, sis. I'll call you later. Love you."

"Love you."

"Oh, and congratulations again, Katie."

Yeah. I put my phone back in my shorts pocket and lean back on my hands, looking up at the sky. Cloud nine. Like I'm up there. I told you. I'm in love.

Dr. Grange holds his Eastern religious history class in the same lecture hall where Dr. Riker teaches his art history class. It's a large lecture hall, big enough to hold up to two hundred students. Both teachers pack the room, even at unusual times like midsemester. I loved Dr. Riker's class, even though I got my only F at Hawthorne University in it. And I love Dr. Grange's class too.

Dr. Grange is a tiny man with short hair, always wearing colorful clothes. Today he's in an orange turtleneck and brown pants. And, just as Bryce said, it makes me think the Buddha himself is visiting. He's Indian and has an Indian accent I love.

"No one knows for sure, it was such a long time ago," he says with a cough, talking into the microphone on his shirt collar, "but the dates and facts our history majors will be eating up this morning are about Buddha's life. Siddhartha Gautama lived until the age of around eighty years old, dying in around 500 BC. He lived in the northern regions of India, growing up in the city of Kapilavastu." A map of India pops up behind him. "That's *Kap-il-av-astu* and, no, you do not have to know that word for the test." Everyone laughs. "He was born into a rich royal family, and legend says that he was sheltered because it had been foreseen that he would achieve enlightenment if exposed to the world. *That* you need to know for the test." More people laugh and he chuckles. "One day Gautama ventured out of the royal palace and saw old age. Then he saw poverty. It pained him so much that he left his home and family, even his wife and child, and set out on a journey to find enlightenment."

Everyone is listening carefully to Dr. Grange because he's just that entertaining. I'm sitting in the middle of the lecture hall, near an aisle, feeling more content than I have in a long time. The cherry on top of my absolute bliss is my best friend, Maddie, is here. She's sitting beside me. You see, last week I complained to her about how bored I was in all my classes because none of my friends were in them this year. She picked this lecture to pay me a surprise visit, even though she's not enrolled. She just came to keep me company. She loves me, you know.

But having her here is a mistake. She won't stop yapping.

"I'm really worried, Katie," she whispers in my ear. "Do you think Enora's gonna do something crazy? We should meet and talk about it on the Sabbath. Maybe you should have just let her take Beatrix and—"

"Shh," I say. A few of the students in the row in front of us turn around, annoyed.

"Oh, sorry."

But I can't resist asking a question I've been wondering about. "What happened to Josie and Debra?" I whisper. "Are they totally freaked out about our coven? I feel like we ruined their night."

"No." Maddie shakes her head with a large grimace. "They're dying in anticipation to see what you're gonna do next. They saw that little trick with the torch. There's no stopping them from joining our coven now."

"Maddie!" I exclaim in a hushed whisper. She laughs.

"We were watching from the window. Sorry. But they're in for sure now."

This large guy to my left pokes my shoulder. He smiles sweetly. "Can you two keep it down, please?"

"Sorry." I turn to Maddie with a finger to my lips and look back at the stage. There's a large picture of a tree behind Dr. Grange.

"It's significant," Dr. Grange continues, "that Gautama believed in the middle path. At his time, there were many who believed in starvation, even bodily torture, in order to achieve a different state of consciousness. And the Buddha tried these techniques too before his enlightenment. He sat under the Bodhi tree and starved himself. It wasn't until a girl came to him and offered him food and drink that he had enough strength to prepare for his enlightenment. And that was what he discovered. After years of following harsh techniques, he realized that it was only through strength, the middle path, that enlightenment could be achieved."

I turn to Maddie and whisper in her ear, "Why did you lend my brother your history book?"

She was listening to Dr. Grange. She turns and furrows her brow. Then she leans into my ear. "He told me he was taking American History 101. I told him I took that course and that I still had my book."

"Yeah, but how did he get to talking to you about all that?"

"We had time waiting in line at administration on his first day. Remember? When you fucked up your interview."

"Thanks, Maddie."

Maddie chuckles. Then she sees the guy to my left. She puts a finger on her lips to shush me.

"So what did Gautama discover under the Bodhi tree?" asks Dr. Grange. "This." He points to the screen behind him, and there are four sentences. "The four noble truths. Know this. It is fundamental to the Buddhist religion. The first noble truth is the realization that life is suffering."

"Maddie," I whisper really quietly in her ear. She nods, still staring at Dr. Grange with interest. "The interview doesn't matter anymore."

"What?" She furrows her brow. "Why not?"

"The second noble truth is that suffering is caused by desire," says Dr. Grange.

I point to my ring finger. I had been covering it with my book since she arrived.

"And the way to end suffering," Dr. Grange says, "is to end desire."

"*No fucking way!*" Maddie shouts and like half the class turns.

I sink in my chair with my head in my hand, completely humiliated. She has her hand over her mouth, apologizing profusely to everyone. Dr. Grange is squinting, searching the room and looking toward us, trying to see what all the fuss is about. It's like she just performed a sacrilege or something. I mean, I know we're in a lecture hall, but Dr. Grange's lectures are so good that they feel like something sacred. I feel ashamed. Like Maddie's insulting the Buddhist religion. So does Maddie. She feels awful. But as everyone in the room is shouting at her, she keeps looking down at my ring with a huge smile.

We get out of there. And I'm really mad. But when we're outside in the sunlight and I turn to my best friend, I just can't yell at her. I'm so happy that she came to see me that I can't reprimand her. I'm in too good a mood.

"Sorry," she says.

"I really like that class, Maddie. Why couldn't you just keep it down?"

"Keep centered, Cadence," she jokes. She's trying not to smile, but she can't help it.

"Are you making fun of—"

"Yeah. It's a history class, Kate. That guy runs it like a temple. But I am really sorry. And..." She looks at my left hand again and jumps into my arms. "Whatever, I'm so happy for you, babe!" Her voice is cracking, and she's trying not to cry. "Anyway, you're the one who flashed your ring. I was finally starting to enjoy the lecture. How did he ask you? I'm so happy for you."

"He asked me at Lacey's."

"Lacey's?" She puts her hands on her hips and frowns. "Lacey's! You're joking. Couldn't he have announced it to everybody at a Braves game or something? Jeez. Like, are you kidding me?"

"I don't care, Maddie. It's Bryce. He's vanilla, we know that, but he's... delicious, you know. I'm just so happy he asked at all."

She hugs me again.

"He said he saw how worried I was that we might be apart. He said he never wants to be apart. He said this was his way of telling me. To relax me, you know. To tell me that no matter what happens we'll be together."

She nods and rubs my shoulder. "I'm so happy for you, Cadence."

I nod.

She looks back at the lecture hall, worried. "Sorry I screwed up your class, babe."

"That's okay. I'm just happy you came."

"He's really good," she says with a nod. "Just like everybody says. He makes you want to convert."

"I've thought about converting."

Maddie laughs. I don't know what's so funny. I think it's because I said that really seriously.

"I've thought of moving to Sri Lanka to a Buddhist temple. It would put me at ease. I need that. I worry so much here in Hawthorne, Maddie."

"Just stop." She won't stop laughing. "Really."

"What? I'm serious."

"I know," Maddie says with a laugh. "You're the only girl I know crazy enough to do it."

"Yeah." I look up pensively. "A Theravada Buddhist temple. Like the original temple. To reach Nirvana."

"Just please stop, okay."

"I'm serious," I say with a shrug.

I stop. But I am serious. And why not? If there's one thing I need in my life, it's peace. Dr. Grange told us that he's had students that have done it before.

We're both silent at the moment. But I'm happy, despite my friend humiliating me. And Maddie has a grin splashed over her face. She's so excited.

"Maddie, you want to go to lunch?"

"Thought you'd never ask."

"And...tonight, I was hoping you could help me with something."

"What's up, Mrs. Wallace?"

"Stop."

"What?" she asks snickering.

"Can you come with me to Alondra's? I'm checking up on Beatrix, but

Alondra's house is still creepy as hell at night. Bryce is pulling an all-nighter working on his dissertation. He usually checks on her with me."

"Sure. I'd love to." Then she smiles ruefully. "Oh, Kate, I miss you so much. I'm so happy you found Bryce, but I'm so lonely, you know."

"I'm right here," I say, hugging her. "Let's go do lunch."

"You're not mad about class?"

"I am," I say, but I can't hold back a smile. "But I'm so happy you came."

7
______

LIGHT

By nightfall, I'm walking with my best friend up the familiar creepy weed path, once a lovely garden, into Alondra's house. I used to adore her front yard. The flowers and freshly cut grass, surrounded by the tall, thin trees of Georgia, make the mansion look iconic, like some kind of Civil War historical landmark. Now the flowers are withered, the grass is brown, the one-hundred-year-old red carriage in the driveway—that used to be such a cute decoration—looks more like a creepy gateway into the supernatural. With Beatrix staying over, Bryce hasn't gotten much gardening done. I was supposed to help him, but Beatrix foiled that too, because I was busy consoling her. Now I'm dreading visiting her, because she's probably going to bawl her eyes out. Well, at least I have Maddie beside me.

Maddie's carrying a fat gray cat in her arms. I can't wait to give Beatrix the present. I think she'll love it.

Even though the grounds are creepy, what's really strange is all the outside lights are on. Everywhere, along the driveway and in front of the house. So much light makes it even creepier. And I thought the electricity wasn't working.

"Ah, can't we keep him, Kates?" asks Maddie, bringing the cat up to her lips for a kiss. "He's so cute."

"No. He's for Beatrix."

"What should we name him?"

"I was thinking we can name him Pete, Whiskers, or George. We should never have gotten rid of her cats."

"Well, who was going to take care of them—you?"

"Sure, why not?"

"You're not good with pets, Cadence."

That's true. Maddie and I once had a pet fish, and I was supposed to take care of it but I forgot to feed it. Then I bought another. That one died too. I like dogs and cats, though.

Maddie pets him. She's in a great mood as always. "I think Whiskers sounds good."

"We'll leave it up to her. Listen, why are all the lights on? Did the electrician come back to fix the place?"

"Sure seems so. You'll have to ask Bryce."

We make it to the door and I turn the key in the lock, but before I can open it, a blackbird lands on the patio a couple of feet from us. That freaks me out because Enora has power over these birds. I freeze by the door.

"It's okay," Maddie says with a chuckle. She kisses the cat again and puts him down on the floor, letting him roam freely around the house.

It's so bright inside. Too bright.

"Maybe Uncle Hanley called the electrician?" Maddie suggests, reading my mind. But no, not just some lights but *all* the lights are on inside. "It turns on sometimes by itself for a couple hours," Maddie adds with a shrug. "AC too. Even when it's impossible. The whole house is screwy, you know. Haunted."

"Well, why are *all* the lights on?" I ask.

Right?

The lovely crystal chandelier above glows, reflecting light throughout the room. It's so bright, but pitch black upstairs. It's always creepy up there in Alondra's bedroom.

Maddie shivers and presses her hands together, blowing on them. "Fuck, it's cold. The AC must have been left on again too."

"Beatrix should have turned it off," I say, furrowing my brow. Then I yell, "Beatrix? Beatrix?"

Maddie looks around. "Hey, Beatrix. Yoo-hoo. Where are you?"

"Beatrix," I shout again. "I'll go upstairs, Maddie, and take a look."

"Well, I ain't going up there," Maddie says with a big grin.

"Check the rest of the house, then."

"Make it quick, Katesy," she says, touching my arm. "I want to catch that movie." Maddie heads down the hallway, humming. I slowly make my way up the pitch-black stairway. It's so cold that I wrap my arms around my red coat. But it smells nice. Beatrix must have been burning incense.

"Beatrix? You up there? Beatrix?"

She's doing it again. She's not responding.

When I make it to the top, I notice the bedroom door is wide open, but no light is shining inside. Not even a candle. I have to take out my cell phone and use its dim flashlight.

I'm worried. Every time I've visited her, she's been holed up in the bedroom sulking—except that one time in the guest room.

I take a deep breath and force myself to step inside. I can see the yard through the floor-to-ceiling window, its light emanating from the windows downstairs. I glance at the bathroom. Nobody's there. I have to be careful where I walk, because there are bags of food and papers all over the floor. When it's clear, I quickly head out and see Maddie beside the banister downstairs.

"Beatrix?" shouts Maddie, facing the kitchen. "Beatrix? Where the fuck are you?"

"She's not in the bedroom," I say. "I'll check the study and side room."

"Okay. But I don't get why she won't respond."

"Not in the guestroom?" I ask.

"No." Then the cat jumps into Maddie's arms. "Whiskers! Aww, boy. You're so cute. Let me take him home? Please? I mean, Crazy isn't even here."

She walks down the adjacent hallway, by the banister, petting him.

I walk into the study, still using the flashlight of my cell phone. I run the light along tons of books on the bookshelf. They're Alondra's. History books and witchcraft grimoires. We never packed them away.

Then I jump like thirty feet in the air. I *feel* a scream in my chest and then I hear it. It's Maddie's voice from downstairs. And she won't stop screaming.

"Katie! Oh my God! Come quick. Katie. Come here!"

I rush down the stairs, nearly skipping a few steps; I could have sprained my ankle. When I get to the living room, Maddie's standing by an open sliding glass door with both hands over her mouth. She spins around and her eyes are bulging. In the center of the brightly lit patio is one of our black cloaks, shifting ever so slightly as it hangs from a wooden rafter.

"Look, Katie! Look!"

I run outside. Bare feet dangle underneath the black cloak, and I get a glimpse of a girl's pale naked body. I recognize Beatrix's long golden hair inside the hood. Her head droops over a rope, her eyes are open, and her face looks ghastly white.

"Look at her hand!" Maddie screams, in tears. "Jesus, Katie! Look! Look at her hand! Look at it!"

Red fluid drips from her palm. I grab her limp arm and turn it, thinking it's blood from a cut. But the red isn't blood. It's paint. A red pentagram has been painted on her palm. I look up, doing everything I can to avert my eyes from her face. I can't. I can't stop looking at Beatrix's lifeless blood-red eyes staring down at me.

8

UNCLE HANLEY

Within a few minutes, the house is packed with my friends. Alondra's house is only a short walk up a hill from campus. Maddie's still in the living room being comforted by some of my friends. She's in shock. I'm with Tammy and Frida in an adjacent hallway.

Uncle Hanley arrives. We call him "uncle" because he's Alondra's uncle. He owns the place since she passed and has been letting us use the house. He lives in Flintwood, but he told me he was in Hawthorne when I called. He walks into the hallway with his farmer suspenders, thin glasses and sparse gray hair. Usually the guy is boisterous, talkative, and in great spirits, but now he walks slowly in a morose silence. He pats me on the shoulder.

"Cadence," he says with a nod. Then he nods at Tammy and Frida beside me. He gazes hesitantly toward the living room. He knows Beatrix is hanging from a rope outside the sliding glass door there. "Wish we were meetin' under better circumstances."

"It's terrible," I say.

"None of you girls were home when it happened, I hope?"

I shake my head. "Just saw it after."

"Called the police?"

I nod.

"Still not here, huh? You do know it's a suicide, you reckon?"

That's the question that's been haunting all of us. Maddie's convinced it wasn't, and I know Beatrix was afraid of death. Sure, she threatened to slice her wrists, but I never felt like she was actually going to do it. It wouldn't surprise me if Cordelia had come back and killed her. Enora's involvement makes me feel caught between anger and feelings of sadness and fear. Beatrix was such a young girl. I feel like maybe she could have straightened herself out and lived a normal life had this not happened.

Uncle Hanley takes a deep breath and says, "Well, it's my house, I suppose. If you'd excuse me, Cadence, I'm gonna take a quick look."

He gestures above his head with a finger, as if tipping an invisible hat, and makes his way slowly into the living room. Most of my friends soon head out the front door. I think only Uncle Hanley has the guts to walk into the living room. I hear Maddie talking to him. I remain in the hallway doing nothing. I don't know whether I should get out of the house with my friends or wander into the living room and see Maddie. But I don't want to go back there. I can't.

It's still so bright. And that's weird and irritating. That night Bryce and I spent together, we would have given anything to have the lights on. Now I'd do anything to turn them off. I switched a few lights off, but they just turned themselves back on again.

"Katie?" It's Bryce behind me. I'd recognize that comforting voice anywhere. I spin around. "I came as quickly as I could."

"Oh, Bryce..." I fall into his arms. "It's horrible. I...I'm so upset."

"It's okay, babe," he says, rubbing my back.

Someone shouts and I jump. It's Uncle Hanley's voice, which is really weird because I've never even seen him scowl, much less shout. I squeeze Bryce tighter, looking down the hall.

"It's okay, Kate," Bryce says.

I nod. Then I gently push him back and gaze at my man. He's wearing a light-blue button-down with brown slacks. Handsome as always.

"How was your meeting?" I ask.

"Unfinished. That's okay. We'll meet again later. When I told him I had to go to a student suicide, he wasn't about to stop me. Anyway, it was going about as well as your interview." He puts his hand up, smiling ruefully. "Don't worry, babe. Maybe it's not that bad. But he wants to reorganize my whole project. It's crazy. I should have asked someone else. I really like Dr. Riker a lot, but I don't have time to compulsively go over every detail with him. You know how he is. And my topic is the plague. It's like he's more interested in the architecture of medieval Europe than illness. But he's the best I could get to be my advisor now."

Maddie walks into the hallway wiping her eyes. Her change in mood is incredible. She was humming and practically dancing when we entered the house, but now she looks like she can barely walk.

"Poor Mr. Hanley," Maddie says. "He got so furious. I've never heard him so mad. He started cursing up a storm at Bill Reardon. He thinks it all has something to do with him. When he came back inside, he apologized to me for the outburst but told me that seeing that palm made him crazy ... I can't believe Enora did this."

"You really think Enora did it?" I ask.

"I *know* she did it, Katie."

"You saw how desperate Beatrix was," Bryce says, shaking his head. "Her coven..." He stops for a moment and looks over his shoulder at the living room, probably worried he's too loud. "They might have driven her to do this, but it was *her* suicide."

"Then how do you explain her hand?" Maddie asks. "Why would someone paint a pentagram on their hand before killing themselves? She wanted a faster way to go to hell? And the cloak? Why would she dress up in *our* coven's cloak? She never associated herself with Hawthorne. That was a message too."

"Maybe," I say.

"It could have been a spell preparing herself for the Summerland before taking her own life," Bryce says, turning back to Maddie and me. "Katie said she dressed up in our cloak when she drew up a protective circle."

"And she decided to draw a pentagram on her hand?" Maddie asks, raising her eyebrows. "Katie also said she was terrified of being damned. So...she decides to kill herself while worshipping Satan with a red pentagram, Bryce?"

"Why are you protecting Enora, Bryce?" I say. "I think Maddie might be right."

"Come on, Kate, I'm not. I'm just saying we don't know."

"I know it was Panthera," Maddie says.

"Look, even if it was, so what? It's not our business."

"No. It's mine." I hang my head. All of a sudden, I feel horrible. "I kept visiting her all week. You heard her. She wanted to die, but she was more afraid of damnation. And ..." I take a deep breath and lean against the wall. "I think it's my fault, guys."

Shit. It is totally my fault.

"It's not your fault, Cadence," Maddie says. "Don't be ridiculous."

Beatrix came to me for protection and I failed her. Maybe Enora cast a spell that drove her to do this. Or maybe Cordelia returned and tied a noose around her neck. Who cares? It doesn't change the fact that it happened. It happened in Alondra's house, essentially my coven's house, and I'm sure I could have stopped it if I'd stayed here to protect her. How is that not my fault?

I feel a tightening in my chest. I'm thinking of Beatrix's beautiful blond hair and large eyes. She was so young and vulnerable. She could have become a normal girl. Enora ruined her life.

I start crying. Bryce takes me in his arms and comforts me. And now, so does Maddie.

That's when Uncle Hanley walks out of the living room. He approaches the three of us, shaking his head.

"I ..." His hands are shaking too. "I'll talk to the police when they get here. They're going to inspect everywhere around the house and probably block off the backyard. I'll talk to them ... poor girl. She's so young. It's so horrible. And she was into that weird devil stuff Bill used to get involved with." He looks at Bryce. "Did you see her hand?"

Bryce nods.

"Yeah," Uncle Hanley says, nodding back. "Look, I appreciate the cleaning you guys have been doing, but maybe for a little while, you kids should stay away from the house."

That's how nice Uncle Hanley is. The house is a complete mess. We hardly cleaned anything.

"I saw a pile of burned wood at the center of the backyard again," Uncle Hanley adds, scratching his head. "That's suspicious for Satan worshipping. You guys know if there's been any of Bill's stupid devil worship still going on outside?"

He looks at me. Damn, he has to ask me? I hate lying. Maddie is standing behind him, and she quickly shakes her head, worried I'm going to mess up our favorite gathering spot.

"No devil worshipping here, Mr. Hanley," I reply, wiping my tears with my arm.

He examines me, and for the first time, there's distrust in his eyes. But then he nods.

"Okay. But that doesn't mean it's not going on outside of you guys' control... that poor girl. Poor girl. Maybe I should put up security cameras? Yeah, I think I should... I'm just so happy to find you're all okay."

We hear sirens from outside.

"We shouldn't have had her stay at the house without asking you, Mr. Hanley," Bryce says. "I'm really sorry about that."

"No. No, I reckon with everything that happened, that girl needed all the love she could get. Alondra would have wanted you to help her. She would have supported that. Don't blame yourself. Just hope Jesus can forgive her tormented soul, the poor, poor girl." Then he looks down, shaking his head.

"Sorry we had to bother you, Uncle Hanley," I say with a nod.

"No bother." He forces a smile. "No bother at all."

We all walk slowly out to the front of the house to greet the police.

9

STROLL WITH A FRIEND

MADDIE'S HUFFING AND PUFFING BESIDE ME AS WE MAKE OUR WAY DOWN A leafy, muddy path beside a stream. The trickling water running over stones under the foliage of leaning trees is simply gorgeous, and the outside temperature is perfect. Birds are chirping and there's a light, pleasant breeze. The leaves on the ground and above us, on the sheltering trees, have turned my absolute favorite fall colors: various shades of red, yellow, and orange. It's so beautiful that you'd think we were in the middle of a national park or something, but we're not. We're about thirty minutes from campus.

"We need to hold a Sabbath, Cadence," Maddie says between breaths.

I adjust the water bottle attached to my belt for a firmer grip, grabbing her hand to help her climb over a large tree branch.

"This is serious," she says. "You know as well as I do that Beatrix was murdered."

"I don't."

"Come on. You saw her hand."

"That was the symbol of her coven and she was suicidal."

I told Dr. Bainer that I loved the woods around our school. I do. And I love hiking. But I could never get Maddie to go with me before. Well, unlike me, Maddie is very out of shape. She doesn't exercise. But the walk was her idea for some reason. I told her this morning, on the phone, that I had to study because midterms are coming up, but the silence on the other end was enough to tell me how important it was for me to meet with her.

"We have to meet. You told me you felt …" She doesn't complete her sentence. We reach a steep hill full of brush, which covers the dirt path, and Maddie shakes her head. I take her hand again and we maneuver around more bushes on our climb up the hillside. She's really hating me over this hike, but I keep telling her it's worth it. She takes a deep breath and finally says, "Beatrix never really wanted to kill herself. Come on, Kate, that was Enora. We need another Sabbath this week. This Friday. Stop avoiding it."

We get back on a straight path under the trees, and Maddie looks relieved. The trees are so dense above that it's a little dark, but at least it's flat. But even though it's a straightaway, Maddie stops and rests. She leans over with her hands on her knees.

"Fuck, how do you do this? You're barely even sweating... Katie, Enora planted Beatrix. Beatrix told you. It was all to fight us again. I don't know what the bitch is planning, but it's trouble. We should meet with our sisters to plan what we're going to do next. If we don't, she's gonna do something first. She planted Beatrix and then killed her. It isn't just a warning. She's in our business just like Reardon was last year."

"I've got midterms Monday. Maybe we can meet next week."

"Goddammit," Maddie snaps. She quickly turns away. "Okay. I know. I know—"

"Maddie, I screwed up my grades last fall, I'm not going to do it again. Dr. Brainer made it very clear. If I mess it up again, I won't make it into any graduate school."

"You're the leader of our coven. It's your job, babe, to do something."

"Isn't it enough to just meet with Mira?"

"It will help. I want to know her thoughts too."

We start walking again. This part of the trail is easy. You know, it's the climbing that's the killer, but because it's a tough hike, no one's around and it's peaceful.

"This is the easier part," I reassure her.

"Better be, bitch," Maddie says, but she smiles at me. "Damn, the things I do for my bestie."

"We could meet Wednesday. I can do that. Instead of me seeing Mira, I could have the gang meet—"

"Don't talk to me like you're not a witch. It has to be Friday, if at all, and you know that. There's no magic on Wednesday. At least meet with Mira." Maddie takes my hand and holds it, which is cute. "I'm really spooked, babe. Please, just talk to her. At least do that for me. But not on the phone. Go see her and ask her about their coven. I'm really worried something else is going to happen. Mira will tell us. I don't think she'd ever mean to hurt us."

"You want to go with me?"

"I really do, but I can't. You know Aunt Jane's going into surgery."

Aunt Jane has been having stomach pain all month. I visited her at her house last week, and she couldn't stop throwing up. She has gall-bladder surgery scheduled. That's another reason Maddie has been so glum.

"Maybe you can convince Mira to come down and join us for a gathering next week, Katie. We've got to hold a Sabbath. With Mira, the wait could be worth it."

"Okay, Maddie, got it. I don't want to talk about it anymore."

"Okay," she says. "But...there's something else I need to tell you, Kates."

"Yeah, what?"

But she stops in her tracks when we pass some bushes and see another steep, grassy hill above us. She puts her hands on her waist and stares. Then she looks at me. I try not to laugh. She looks really pissed. There's finally a clearing in the woods about fifty yards up. She looks down at another stream, meandering around the trees, that we have to cross.

"How much further?" she asks, shaking her head.

"Right over the top."

"You're such a bitch. Don't ever forget the..." She carefully jumps on a few rocks, trying not to fall in the water. "Things I do for you."

"It's gonna be hard with Bryce this week too. He's busy with his dissertation."

"Then go alone. But do it. At least talk to Mira. Mira will tell you what's going on. Brainwashed or not, she'll be honest. Mira's always been honest."

"For sure."

That makes the old Maddie I know come out. She smiles. "Are we almost there? I don't think my out-of-shape bones can take much more of this, babe."

"It's right over this last hill. I promise."

We finally get to the top. It's breathtaking. Maddie nods at me, still out of breath, and seems to forget her complaining. Below us are miles upon miles of yellow, red, and orange trees in the valley below. It is truly gorgeous. In the far corner, we can just make out Hawthorne Lake near campus. Then straight out, about thirty miles from the cliff, is a mountain range. But below are miles and miles of trees.

It's a long drop down there. Maddie takes a rock and throws it down. She chuckles. Then she pulls out her cell phone from her shorts pocket.

"Come here," she says, putting her arm around me. She holds the phone in front of us, with an extended arm, for a selfie. Behind us is the sheer drop and a gorgeous view. "That's a keeper."

After staring for a little longer, she sits down on the wild grass and smiles up at me. "You were right. I should have taken you up on this a long time ago. It's amazing."

"Beautiful, isn't it?"

"Incredible. Just like you said it would be. We should do this stuff more often."

"I'm just so busy."

"I know." She loses her smile and looks away. "With you and Bryce."

"I'll go see Mira, 'kay? I'll see what she says."

But Maddie keeps looking down. She picks up some of the grass and brings it to her nose. Then she tastes it. We're witches, you know. We can tell what's edible. She even offers me some.

"What's wrong?" I ask. "Why so down? I told you I'll go see her, okay?"

"We need the Sabbath this week," she says with a shrug, still staring at the grass. "But I knew you'd say no."

"Then what's the matter, Maddie? I've never seen you so blue."

She nods her head, throws her dark hair back, and focuses on me. I look into her eyes, behind her witch makeup, which looks a little smudged from sweat. I could swear her eyes are tearing up.

"You know, Katesie, honestly, I knew this would be a tough hike. I never wanted to do it. But I thought suggesting it would be enough to finally see you again."

I furrow my brow.

"I miss you so much. That's all. I miss you. And I'm so worried about next year. I'm worried I won't see you after we graduate."

"Oh, Maddie, stop it. You will."

"Unlike Bryce, I don't have a ring to lasso you in."

"Come on," I say, plopping down on the grass and putting my arm tightly around her. I lean my head against hers. "We're best friends forever. BFFs. Remember?"

"The very best. Absolute best."

10

MIRA

I take Maddie up on her suggestion to meet Mira, at Piedmont Park in Atlanta, at noon on Wednesday. Bryce isn't too happy about it, but that's why I love him to death. He has so much work to do on his dissertation, but he still drops everything to take me there. He drives me, parks his car under a tree, leans his seat back, and closes his eyes. He hasn't been sleeping well, and I told him I'd rather speak with Mira alone anyway. As long as he can sleep in the parking lot, he's content enough.

Piedmont Park was actually my idea. I've loved the park since I was a kid. My dad and I used to walk on the grass and feed the ducks in the lake when I was a little girl. I still have fond memories of my brother running after the ducks in this silly sailor outfit and hat mom used to dress him in when he was little. I must have been only nine. He would have been, like, six. It was fun times back then.

I couldn't have chosen a more perfect day. The sky is clear and it's, like, a perfect seventy-two degrees again.

After Bryce drops me off, I walk alone in my saffron T-shirt, black shorts, and white tennis shoes. I realize that Mira and I didn't agree on a particular meeting place. I take out my phone but remember that she never answers her phone. But I don't worry. The park is huge, of course, being Atlanta's "Central Park," but I feel like Mira or I will *feel* our way to one another. I know, that's weird. But somehow, I just know. So I amble along the cement walkway beside the grass, constantly moving to the side so as not to be run over by bicyclists. There are a lot of families out. We started the semester early, and early October is still warm. A lot of kids are running around on the grass, playing ball or picnicking with their families. In the not-so-far distance beyond the fields, I see the Atlanta skyline.

I'm right about Mira. She isn't hard to spot. She's the only one wearing a long black dress trailing along the ground. I think she's gained weight. She's always been overweight. And I can spot the black paint on her face from a mile away—she's wearing much thicker eyeliner than I am. I try to be discreet with my goth look, but she's never cared. She never cared at all what other people think.

It seems to take forever for us to catch up to one another and get close enough to hug. "Yatu, Windstorm," she says. Then she backs up and looks at me quizzically. "How's Hawthorne?"

"How are you?"

"Fine. Maddie and Bryce? You and Bryce still sharing the same bed?" She gives me a sly smile, the bitch. Then she laughs. "Where is he? I'd have guessed he would come with you."

"He's in the car sleeping. What about Derek?"

"Split."

"Oh, that's too bad."

She just shrugs.

"Well, all Bryce cares about is rest. He's working so hard on his dissertation that he's not sleeping. Anyway, I thought you and I would talk alone first."

"Alone?" She squints and nods slowly. "Hmm. Must be very important."

"Bryce and I are doing fine. Real fine." And I put up my left hand and show her my ring. It doesn't take much for me to parade my ring around.

She just nods dismissively. "About fucking time. I see little Katie's growing up."

"It's so lovely here," I say, throwing my hair back and trying to deflect her usual sarcasm. She's already annoying me. Somehow I had forgotten her prickly ways. It's funny that distance and time can do that to people.

"I don't like it," Mira says with a deep breath, annoying me more. "I hate this park. I'm not interested in seeing large man-made buildings over lots of fake manicured grass. But I guess it's a lot like you, isn't it?"

"That's insulting."

"I've really missed riling you up." Mira laughs. "I like watching you get all flustered. Your lovely tanned skin flushes, and you get all hot and bothered. It's hilarious."

"Shall we?" I ask, gesturing to the walkway.

She nods, walking with her arms folded.

We fall silent. I've lost the nerve to raise the question I'm dying to ask her.

It doesn't take long for Mira to veer off the walkway onto the grass. I follow her across a bridge over the lake. The water reflects like glass the surrounding fall leaves on one side and skyscrapers on the other. Two dogs rush by, and Mira dips down and pets one. We both do. We love dogs. But we still don't say anything to one another. We just enjoy the view of the fake manicured grass and buildings.

"You want to know why I joined the Abaddon coven?" Mira finally says, cocking her head, with her arms folded again, as we make our way across the beautiful bridge. "Is that it?"

"You always knew how to get to the point."

"So did you," Mira says with a chuckle. "That's why we became friends."

I stop and turn. She puts her hand on a rail on the bridge. She smiles a wily grin, waiting. Then I just spit out what I've been dying to say.

"Why would you?" I ask. "I mean, I don't get it. After everything that happened? Last I heard, you were looking for a job back in Jacksonville. What happened? I asked you on the phone, and you just laughed it off. What did Enora do to you? Hypnotize you or something?"

"Enora's my friend."

"Seriously?"

"What's wrong with her?"

"She's evil. You told me that last year."

"Alondra was never good, Katie, but you joined us. Alondra taught us that there's no such thing as good and evil. You're the only one who's insisted on being good. You've limited your freedom. If you allowed

Hawthorne to be free, like Enora, I probably would never have left. Why are you so worried?"

"Are you for real? Do you really have to ask me that?" I'm staring at her. Then I say more quietly, "You were there when she stabbed Professor Reardon to death."

"She had the courage to do what I'd always wanted to do." Mira looks down, serious. "What I didn't have the nerve to do. I hated Bill Reardon more than anyone. Bill lusted after me, along with most of the other girls in Hawthorne. He was a pervert and after he raped me, I wanted him to die."

"Not to be murdered."

She annoyingly shrugs again.

"What about Bryce?" I remind her.

"Katie," Mira says and takes a deep breath. She turns and gazes at the lake. She gestures to the water. "You know, this water is a little like you. Gorgeous. Pretty... but fake."

"Don't be mean," I snap. "I didn't come here to fight. I'm worried about—"

"I know," she says, smiling. "But you *are* fighting. If you're asking me if I'm okay, I am. But if you're here to convince me to leave the Abaddon coven, I won't." She looks around the park she hates again. "Bryce was the one thing that almost stopped me from joining. But Enora explained that she had to erase all the men who had humiliated her publicly from our coven. As much as she once loved Bryce, she assured me it wasn't personal. She wanted him gone because she blamed him—"

"It wasn't personal that she tried to burn him alive? I don't believe this."

But she doesn't join in my anger. She smiles. "And this is the reason you're here. Not to see me, or to check on me, but to get information?"

"I told you, I'm worried about you."

"No, you're not." Mira shakes her head. "You would have visited before. You're worried about your coven."

"Well, I care about our friends. And my fiancé." I lift my eyebrows, sounding really condescending. I can't help it. She's really pissing me off. She's acting like she's being logical, but it's all crap.

"You know, Alondra loved you more than any of us, but she and I always marveled at the conflicts in your head."

"What conflicts?"

"Your not accepting being a witch." Her dark eyes just stare at mine as if we're in a showdown. Like she's daring me to disagree. I don't.

"I accept being a witch, I just wish I weren't one."

"That's funny, Katie, because, you know, I would do anything to have your power. You were given a gift, but you don't accept it. I've pored over books about the occult. I studied and pestered Alondra, sucking out every morsel of information I could from her before she died. Now I'm learning from Panthera. But I don't have your gift. I'd give everything for it."

"You can have it."

She laughs. "You asked me why I joined. Enora accepts who I am. She practices the occult. She doesn't care if she is "good" or "bad." Those are Western concepts. She asked for my help, and we work together in order to work magic. She sought me out because of my knowledge of spells and incantations. Of divination. Where else can I practice what I love? Not with you. Not in Hawthorne. Do you see what I mean? Why is it so hard for you to understand?"

"Your leader is a murderer."

"Katie, I would have stayed with you in a second if you had asked me. You're not thinking this through. If Enora had killed Bryce, I'd agree with you. Bryce didn't do what Reardon did. But Bryce wasn't killed, and Enora agrees that what she did to him was wrong. But Reardon? Why are you upset that that prick died?"

"She really did brainwash you," I say, staring at Mira in amazement. "You didn't trust Enora last year. Why do you now?"

"Enora explained to me everything I told you," she says with a shrug. Then she gazes into my eyes, challenging me again, and she gives me her infamous smug smile, very much like the old Mira.

"Beatrix hanged herself."

Mira loses her smile. Her eyes examine mine and she shakes her head.

"And I think your Abaddon coven was behind it," I continue. "Maddie's convinced Enora is. Isn't that enough evil for you to turn from Enora? What other crimes do you have to see from that bitch?"

But Mira loses her infuriating smugness, along with all the color in her face. Then she turns from me and leans her head in her hands over the rail of the bridge. I hear whimpering.

"Oh, God... you didn't know?" I can't believe it. "How? Your coven knows. Gilda knows. How can you—"

She shakes her head.

"Mira ..."

"I've been wandering," she explains with her head in her hands. "My first. I haven't been there... I've been away all week. I... I think I'm going to be sick..."

"Mira, I thought you knew."

"I heard Beatrix had run away to you. Cordelia said you were protecting her. Enora was furious. I know she visited you to bring her back. But...I can't believe this."

"Mira, she was hanging by a rope, with a red pentagram painted on her left palm. You know that's Enora's symbol. Your satanic coven. Beatrix told me Enora had sent her. And she wasn't wearing any clothes except—"

"I don't want to hear this!" Mira snaps, staring wide-eyed at me. She shrugs my hand off her back and walks fast, not seeming to care whether I follow her. She rushes over to the shade of a tree, puts her head in her hands again, and cries.

"Mira, I'm sorry! I'm sorry. I thought you knew."

"God," Mira says, wiping her now smeary mascara on her sleeves. "I loved her. We loved her so much. It's...it's like hearing something happened to you or Maddie."

"She was young."

"Very." Mira nods. "And she was sweet like you. She was just mentally ill."

"Mira, she said Enora sent her. She said Enora sent her to start a fight between our covens again."

"Stop worrying about Enora, Cadence!" she snaps, wiping her eyes with her long black lace sleeve. "Enora's left you alone like you demanded. I know she didn't do anything to Beatrix. That girl did it to herself. She's been attempting to kill herself for years."

Mira's never lied to me. She's irritating as hell, but she has never lied. Even Maddie and Bryce have lied to me. Not Mira. In a weird way, I trust Mira even more than my best friend and my fiancé. Obviously, she really didn't know. And she really believes that her coven had nothing to do with it.

"Mira ..." I hesitate. Then I just say, "I'm sorry."

"Forget it." Mira shrugs, wiping her eyes again. "I understand. It's okay. It's...good seeing you, Cadence."

Is it? All we've done is fight. But, come to think of it, all we ever did was fight.

"We should have lunch," Mira says, trying to change the subject. "Bryce too. I'd love to see him again."

"Sure."

But I'm not done. I have to ask her more. Now. Now, when she's upset. I don't want to bring this up later and upset her again.

"Mira, Beatrix told me she was running away from a blood sacrifice. That's why she wanted to stay with me."

"We do blood sacrifices," Mira says. "You allowed Alondra to cut you at your initiation, if you remember."

"She said sex ceremonies."

Mira nods again.

"And she said Enora threatened her life."

Mira shakes her head.

"She said she was given a choice...it's disgusting." I look at Mira and I'm hoping that she gets what I'm saying so I don't have to say it. But Mira just wipes her nose and eyes. "She told me that she could either birth a fetus and drink its blood or be sacrificed and killed in a ceremony."

Mira chuckles. That's definitely not the reaction I was expecting.

"She was manipulating you. That's Beatrix. That's what she does. She needed a home. We love her, but she's very sick."

I turn and gaze at the Atlanta skyline. The *fake* concrete buildings Mira hates. Well, I think the view is pretty. I believe Mira. At least I believe this is her understanding of the situation.

"Okay, Mira. But ..." I'm remembering that Beatrix also said Mira was doing sex ceremonies with a girl in the coven. "Mira, are *you* doing sex ceremonies again? After hating Reardon for—"

"I'm not going to talk about that," Mira says quickly, shaking her head.

"Okay, sorry...and I'm sorry I had to be the first to tell you about Beatrix."

Mira nods. Then she looks down at my ring finger and forces a thin smile.

"You know, Beatrix and I were so close...because of her friend. Congratulations, Katie. I'm so happy for you and Bryce. I'm finally going out with someone I love too. Her name's Courtney. I wish you were here longer so I could introduce you. She was Beatrix's best friend. I don't know how Courtney is going to get through this."

11

BACK TO THE DORM

I'm rushing down the main stretch of campus on my way to Maddie's place, because I can't wait to give her the 411 on Mira. I feel better. Now I think Beatrix just committed suicide. Mira was sure of it, anyway. Our lunch went so much more smoothly than our first meeting at the park. That could be because of Bryce. He gets along with everyone. And, you know, Mira and I always had a rough relationship, but we still love each other. And I'm so happy that she found someone and is happy in Atlanta.

It's late, about eight in the evening, as I make my way to "our" place. Bryce is being a bookworm, working late in the library. Since it took us all day to drive to Atlanta and back, the poor guy is exhausted. The plan was to get a hotel, but Bryce convinced me to come back tonight. He said he's got a ton of work to do in the library. I suspect he's probably not working. He's probably sleeping in a cubbyhole—he was so tired.

Anyway, I walk down memory lane and use my extra key to get through the glass door to the Yorkshire Dormitory. I feel a little guilty when I unlock the door, since it reminds me of how Dad's paying for my room with Maddie. That's when an old neighbor of mine, Sophia, waves at me in the hallway.

"You back here, Katie?"

"No. Just visiting."

"Everyone misses you so much." She gives me a hug.

"You going to the outdoor concert next week?"

"No. I have to study." Like really study. Like, if I don't get it together, I'm gonna mess up another semester.

"It's gonna be fun. You should go."

"I'll try."

Then she smiles goodbye, and I mosey down the dimly lit hallway. I head around the bend to the other side of the hall. Here everybody's got their door open, welcoming me. I miss them. If it weren't for Bryce, I'd love staying here my last year.

Finally, I'm in front of Maddie's room. I take out my keys, but when I check the doorknob, it's unlocked. I open the door. The room is dimly lit by a single lamp, but I can see well enough.

The key falls from my hand. First, I hear what I don't want to see, then I see it. On my bottom bunk, Maddie is naked, straddling a boy and moving up and down on him. She's moaning, which is super gross because she's my best friend. And her tits are moving up and down while the boy is breathing heavily under her. That's grosser. I am so embarrassed. I'm about to throw the door closed, but as Maddie's naked body rolls off him in surprise, and she sees me and shrieks, the man she was fucking falls off the bed. Damien. My little brother.

"Oh my God!" I yell.

"It's not what you think, Kate," Maddie says.

Ewww! How is this not what I think it is?

Damie jumps over to the desk and grabs his clothes off a wooden chair. Unfortunately, my eyes see his bare ass, and I can't stop staring. In my eyes, his naked body seems childlike. Maddie has a white sheet over her chest with her hand extended. My heart is bursting in my chest.

"Sis, it's not what you think," my brother says, pulling up his pants.

Not what I think? I think it's exactly what I think. And did he call me SIS?

"How is this not what I think!" I yell. A few people in the hallway probably hear me screaming.

"I know you're not staying in the dorm with Maddie," Damie says. "You're living with Bryce."

Is he accusing me? Seriously? Is he going to go tell Daddy after I tell him he's fucking my best friend! REALLY?

"What ... huh?" I don't know what to say. I look at my best friend. Her eyes are filling with tears. So are mine. She's still stupidly clutching the bedsheets over her chest. "Why...why would you—"

"Gotta run," Damie says. And that's exactly what he does. He runs out of the room so fast that I can't stop him.

"I'm sorry, Kate, but—"

"My brother?"

"Kate..." Tears are streaming down her face. "We really like each other. I've tried to tell you, but you won't listen. You just ignore me when I mention him. Your brother is so nice. He's like the first boy I've ever been with who's got it together."

She had to say *been with*. She could have said *dating*. She could have said *going out with*. But she said *been with*. Like *fucked*!

"I hate you!" I say, wiping my tears. "How could you do this?"

"Oh, Cadence," she says, squinting.

"He's...he's just a boy."

"He's not," she says. "He's an adult. More of a man than anyone I've ever been with."

"Been with! Stop fucking saying *been with*!"

"Katie," Maddie says, putting her hand up again.

"Just don't talk to me. God, Maddie. Just...don't talk to me ever again!"

And I slam the door.

I feel horrible. There's a pit in my stomach. I can't believe this. I feel alone.

I could go to the library. See Bryce. But he's finally studying—and a little mad at me. I coerced him into leaving in the middle of the day to go to Atlanta when he's got so much work to do. I can't go to him after all I've done. So what can I do?

Maddie said she couldn't go see Mira because of her mom's surgery. *Aunt Jane*, even though no one understands why the hell Maddie tells everyone to call her mom "Aunt Jane." She's her mom, right? Does it matter if she's not biologically her mom? A mom is a mom, right? And now her mom's sick. She just had surgery. But, apparently, Maddie had some spare time to go fuck my brother instead of visiting Mira or taking care of her *aunt*. What a bitch!

I run out on the one-lane road near our dorm. I look at Krunner Hall, the tall building where Damie stays, across the street. Then I look back at our room. It's too dark to see inside. The drapes are closed and all the lights are off now. Maddie probably has her head in her hands, bawling on my mattress—you know, the one she was fucking my brother on.

Some of me, the really small, gentle part that's buried, wants to go back into Maddie's room and hug her. But most of me wants to go back and slap her across her face! I keep seeing her having sex with my little brother. It's imprinted on my mind. I don't think I'll ever forget that nasty image.

I walk into the woods.

Mira's right. Piedmont Park is fake. So is the lake and the ducks. I want to live in the woods. In nature. Away from people. Because I'm a witch. I don't love people. I don't think I like people. I love the forest. I love nature. Fuck people. They're too busy fucking themselves.

12

TEATIME AND TRYING

I don't really want to meet with my former best friend. I'm so angry with her that I'd rather just not talk to her ever again. But there's something I learned from my tall, dark, and handsome fiancé—when you're angry, sometimes it's better to communicate than to shut down. You need to talk things out.

When I get mad, I withdraw. Last year I fought with Bryce for months. Enora had showed me images of her and Bryce having sex, making me jealous as hell, and I got so angry that I refused to talk to him. Well, I'm not going to do that again.

Sort of. Okay, Bryce convinced me to meet with Maddie. I had every intention of ignoring the bitch until she graduates, but Bryce said it's been long enough. It's time to "talk things out."

I told Madison to meet me in the morning at the university coffee shop. It's our favorite hangout. Unfortunately, since we're still in midterms, it's so crowded that the four large wooden tables at the center of the place are packed with students. But I'm early enough to find one of the nicer two-person tables by the window.

I gaze at the decorative murals on the brown walls of the coffee-house. A runner is crossing the finish line, and a soccer player is kicking a ball. Then I bury my head in my textbook on the Industrial Revolution, but it doesn't take long for me to look out the window. It's a cloudy day, and the wet main walkway on campus is packed with students carrying books, laptops, and backpacks. A few people are sitting along the grassy hill. It's not too cold, but the lawn is wet from the morning rain. That's where the two of us once loved to study—on the grass beside the library.

The Industrial Revolution is not my favorite part of history, but it fulfills one of my requirements. This chapter talks about the flying shuttle and spinning jenny. It's boring stuff, really. If I'm going to study the eighteenth or nineteenth century, I'd much rather study Gettysburg or the French Revolution.

I decide to suffer and read on.

This section is about calcium hypochlorite. Like, what does calcium have to do with history? Bleach. Calcium hypochlorite is bleach, apparently. Bleach for clothing.

Madison comes through the glass doors, carrying a forest-green backpack over her shoulder, with jeans and a matching green T-shirt. Her makeup is black, giving her a goth look, just like mine, but her expression is very un-Maddie-like. She looks depressing as hell. She's looking down or to the side, doing whatever she can to avoid my eyes.

When she arrives at our table, she plops her backpack by the chair across from me, runs her hand through her long hair, and sighs. She puts her heavy red coat—which is just like mine, we got them together—on the chair and sits down.

I gesture to the white cup in front of her. It's a no-foam vanilla soy milk double espresso latte. (Her favorite, when she's not stealing other people's drinks. She's a bit of a kleptomaniac.)

"Hi, Cadence," she says, forcing a grin.

"I want you to stop seeing Damie." There. Blunt enough? I figure it balances the peace offering. Might as well get to the point and "talk things out."

She sips her drink and looks out the window at the gloomy day, ignoring me.

"Out of everyone I know, maybe even more than Bryce, you know I don't want my brother mixed up in our stuff. You dating him means he'll get close to our coven. I can't have that. I don't want him anywhere near our witchcraft. Jesus, Maddie, you know that. I can't believe you want to be with him. Unless...you are dating him, right? You're not just—"

"Bitch," Maddie snaps with her eyes wide. "How dare you. What do you think I'm doing? I told you, I like him."

"Okay," I say, putting a hand up.

She turns to the window again. I'm a little surprised she doesn't jump up and leave, but what did she expect? I mean, the whole thing is gross. My brother. Maddie. I mean, what the hell—

"You're so selfish, Cadence. You always think everything's about you. I'm falling in love with Damien, okay? Your brother. So? Why is it so hard for you to understand? No, I can get how it's hard. But what am I supposed to do? I really like him."

"Do you? Really?"

"What else do you think I'm doing?" she asks, hitting the table.

This isn't going well. I told Bryce. I should have done it my way. Maybe this is why I'm withdrawing. I don't have much patience when I'm mad. And talking to my former friend is like dealing with Beatrix, but instead of "crazy," I'm dealing with someone who—

"What do you want me to do?" Maddie stares into my eyes. "Is this really important enough to break up our friendship? What do you want me to say to make this better?"

I put my head in my hands, running my fingers through my long hair. Then I rub my eyes and shake my head. I feel her touch my wrist.

"God, Katie, you know I love you," she says with her voice cracking. "I'm so sorry I hurt you. I love you more than anyone in the world."

I feel tears coming to my eyes. I shake my head. "You're not hurting me, Madison. You're hurting my brother. He needs to stay away from us. That includes you."

"I can't do that."

I look at the wet grassy hill. The two of us have had so many lovely afternoons out there together. I miss it. And I miss those times. What happened?

"This is your way of being with me, is that it?" I ask. "You told me on our hike how much you missed me. You figure you can just hang with my brother and screw—"

"Damn it, Cadence! Shut up! I told you I love him."

"You don't love him."

"I love him. And, yeah, I miss you. But think about what you're saying —you've got Bryce. Who do I have? Yeah, I've been lonely. But your brother is really cool. He's the sweetest guy I know. I can trust him, which is more than I can say about anyone else I've ever gone out with. I'm sorry he's your brother, but that's the way I feel about him. I really like him, babe."

"I'm also your High Priestess," I say, staring at the hillside again. "I'm ordering you to stop seeing him."

She gets up and stands over me, putting her wet coat back on and shaking her head.

"You don't understand what's happening. This is real love, Cadence. Love. It's like what's between you and Bryce. You don't know how close we are because I kept it from you. I've been seeing him since school started. I didn't tell you because I was scared that what just happened would happen. I can't do what you're asking, High Priestess or not. I remember when we started and you were outside our group. Then I didn't want you in the coven at first. But...but, if you can't open your heart to me and your brother the same way and accept this, I don't know what we're going—"

"I'm ordering you, Blackbird. You're a witch in my coven. You have to do what I ask. You have to stop seeing him."

"*No! I don't!*" she shouts, shaking her head violently, and grabs her backpack. People all over the room stare at us.

She's gone.

Our meeting went exactly the way I thought it would go. Now I suppose I can take my anger out on Bryce when I get home because it was his idea to "talk things out."

Shit.

I sip some of my favorite drink. A green tea latte. It tastes really bland.

Shit.

I lean on my hands again and think about crying. But I'm not going to cry.

How dare she. She's the one messing with my brother. She can just stop seeing him.

I look out at the field once more, and this time I wish I hadn't. Maddie is rushing by, on a cement walkway, holding her head in her hands, crying. I feel a lump in my throat.

Maybe I'm being unreasonable? Maybe I need to accept the two of them? How can I not? I love Maddie so much.

My phone rings. I really don't want to answer it.

"What!" I snap.

"Katie." It's Dad. He sounds awful. "Did you hear?"

"What? What's the matter? I'm not really in a good mood right now, Dad."

"It's Damie. He's at the hospital. I'm rushing down now."

"Oh my God!" I say, jumping up. "What happened?"

"A car accident. He's going into surgery for his leg. I talked to him right before he went in. At least he's all right now."

"I'll...I'll come right away."

"I'll meet you there, Cadence."

I look out the window again. It's pouring rain now. Out in the center of the grassy hill, using her red coat to shield her from the pouring rain, Maddie is on her cell phone. I run out to catch up to her.

13

HAWTHORNE HOSPITAL

We take my car. It's awful because we have to walk through pouring rain to the apartment I share with Bryce, where my old Honda jalopy is sitting in the parking lot. Maddie's a bit irresponsible, and she doesn't have a working car at the moment. We walk really fast, practically running through puddles, while we do our best to shield our heads from the deluge with our arms or backpacks. Throughout the long walk, neither of us says a word.

Before we know it, I'm driving into the hospital parking lot. It's still pouring and the rain clouds are so dark that it feels like nighttime. Maddie still hasn't said anything. Actually, I think she's only said one or two words since I met up with her outside the coffeehouse. It's really weird: we're both so worried but still so furious with each other. When I stop the car, she jumps out and runs without me.

Hawthorne Hospital is a really ugly small hospital, more of a clinic really. It's a two-story building with drab white concrete walls and a hideous silver overhang in front of the emergency room. That's it. The only thing making the eyesore bearable is the lovely Hawthorne Forest surrounding it.

When I catch up to Maddie, she's asking the receptionist at the front desk what room Damien's in. A gray-haired black lady smiles and hands us a visitor board to sign. She looks up something on her computer and tells us that Damien is still in the operating room.

"What's wrong with him?" Maddie asks.

The receptionist just looks at her monitor, bewildered.

"Can we meet him at the room he'll be staying in?" I ask.

She nods and tells us it's Room 174, on the first floor.

Maddie and I practically run again, which is really silly because she just told us that Damien is still in surgery, but we're just that worried. When we make it, the white room is empty. In fact, newly folded sheets are laid out on the bed. The drapes are open, showing rain splashing over a walkway and the surrounding dense thin trees of the forest. The room smells very fake and sterile, like Lysol. There are two chairs near the window, and Maddie removes her coat and takes one. She looks out the window for a moment; then she grabs her cell phone and calls somebody.

"Who are you calling?" I ask, sitting down on the bed.

"Oh, we're talking now, Cadence?"

"Actually, you're the one who ran from me."

She laughs derisively, leans on the armrest of the chair, and puts her ear closer to her cell phone. "Hey, Mom. Yeah. Fine. Look, can you come to the hospital and bring me some of my stuff from home in a suitcase? Clothes. Makeup. My travel purse. You know, my vacation stuff. I'm probably going to stay here overnight. Yeah. A car accident. I know. It's...terrible. I'm all right. No, I'm just worried about Damie. I don't know. I just don't know yet. Yeah, I really need stuff from home. Yeah. No. No, I'm okay. Great. Thanks. Love you. Bye."

She sighs and shoves the phone in her pants pocket. Then she stares out the window, acting as if I'm not in the room. She sighs again.

"I can get you your clothes from the dorm," I say.

She looks over as if saying "are you for real?" and turns back to the window.

I like the view of the forest even when it's raining. But right now, I don't like it so much. Not when we hate each other.

We sit like this, not talking, for about half an hour. I can't remember a tougher time between me and my former friend. But, like I told you, I'm used to ignoring people when I'm angry. Maddie's not. She's always bubbly. And right now, neither of us wants to be in the room together, but we're forced to wait.

I'm so worried. Why does Damie need to be in surgery after an accident?

My mind wanders as it always does. I'm fantasizing images of my little brother being a paraplegic or something. Maddie looks just as worried. She keeps going through multiple sticks of gum. The sound of her chewing is driving me crazy. First it was constant sighing, now it's chewing gum. These sounds mix with the incessant pounding of water on the ground outside and against the window. Normally, in our old world, the two of us would be comforting each other. At least she'd offer me a piece of gum. Instead, she keeps staring out at the trees, and I keep looking at the ugly plastic tile floor and whitewashed walls.

Finally, a nurse wheels Damie into the room in a wheelchair.

He looks fine. I jump up to gather my little brother in my arms, but Maddie beats me to it. They kiss on the lips, and I remember again why we're fighting.

"Hey, Maddie," Damie says. "It was compartment syndrome. Can you believe that? That's so rare. The dashboard in Dad's old Toyota fell on my leg."

"Oh God, babe, your face," Maddie says, brushing gently over it.

"Yeah, just a few scrapes. It's nothing."

"But they sewed some," she adds.

"Sutured a little," he says with a chuckle. "Nothing that will scar badly. It's mainly my forehead." Damie looks at me and smiles. "Hi, sis."

"I'm so relieved you're okay," I say. I can't believe how formal and fake I sound. I feel totally out of place, which is really weird because he's my brother.

"Yeah." Then he turns to Maddie and smiles again. She annoyingly strokes his hair. "Maddie, compartment syndrome. I can't believe it. They had to cut into the flesh to relieve the pressure. Isn't that cool? Fasciotomy. I asked if they could let me watch. Normally, they'd put a patient out, but the doctor was really awesome and let me watch the whole procedure."

"You need to rest," comments the nurse with a smile. She's staring at a plastic bag on a tray. "You want me to help you get back into bed?"

"I'd rather sit for a while."

"At least let's get you into the chair, then."

We all help him into one of the wooden chairs: the nurse, me, and my ex-friend. We also move the large tray with a tube hooked into his arm, placing it beside him.

When the nurse finally leaves, Maddie takes my place on the bed beside Damien, holding his hand. I'm now standing, uncomfortably alone, near an empty wooden table.

"Dad's coming," I say.

"I know," Damien says. "I talked to him before surgery. He was just glad I was okay. I did black out for a second, but I didn't injure my head. Nothing serious."

"What happened?" I ask. "You're a really good driver. I don't get it."

"It was raining. The roads were slick. I was just driving to the grocery store. I needed to restock some things, and Harvey had gone home for the weekend. I didn't think of the rain. And you know, Kate, the rain is like ice this time of year."

"So you slipped?"

"No. Not exactly. It was weird. I—" He hesitates and I can almost swear he shakes for a second. "I saw something in the middle of the road. I'm not sure what it was. I thought it was a deer. It flashed red before me under the pouring rain. Almost like fire. It just appeared suddenly in the middle of the road. This red object. I quickly swerved to miss it, and that's when the car slid on the black ice and hit a tree. I was still moving fast, probably like thirty miles per hour. And, of course, it's Dad's beat-up pickup truck."

"God, Damie," Maddie says, reaching down and hugging him again. "You could have been killed."

"I'm all right." He smiles, looking up. Maddie looks at the bandaging on his right leg as if noticing it for the first time. Damie follows her eyes. "The doctors said I probably would have just been casted if I hadn't lost blood flow to the whole leg. They had to operate."

I turn and stare out at the now very familiar view of the forest. It's still pouring rain outside. I rub my temples.

"Thanks for coming, sis. I know how it's been."

"Of course."

"She's still mad," says Maddie. "She's a bitch." In the old world, Maddie would have laughed or winked saying that. She's very serious right now.

"The strangest thing was after the accident," he adds. "I got out of the car. Smoke was coming from the hood. Of course half the engine was wrapped around a tree trunk, but when the ambulance came, I noticed two cops hovering around the center of the street. At first, I didn't really care. The paramedics were loading me into the ambulance. But then I looked more carefully. In the middle of the pouring rain was a round wooden statue. In the center was a figure shaped like a person made of leaves and straw. And it was tilted on this large, round wooden wheel. It was really weird."

I look at Maddie. She meets my stare as if challenging me to care. But then she leans toward Damie and touches his arm. "A wheel? Was it shaped like a symbol? Like the pentagram I showed you?"

He thinks for a moment and nods. "Yes, I think so. I thought it was somehow related to that witch stuff you guys do. The same symbol. A pentagram, but huge and painted red with a strawman on it. The strawman was on fire."

Maddie buries her head in her hands for a moment. Damie furrows his brow, looking at her funny. Then she jumps up and walks to the window.

"God, Cadence, Enora could have killed him," Maddie says.

"You don't know—"

"Don't you see?" she asks, whirling around at me. "I told you. I told you after Beatrix died we had to stop her. That we had to cast a spell against her on a Sabbath. Seeing Mira wasn't enough. Mira's brainwashed. First Beatrix and now... why haven't you done anything? You're our leader. You've done nothing."

"What are you guys talking about?" Damien asks.

"This isn't the time," I warn.

"Not the time?" Maddie asks. I've never seen her so angry. "When's the time? Would you have preferred talking about it in a fucking morgue? Your brother almost died! Are you and Mira going to tell me it's a fucking coincidence?"

"Maddie, stop. What are you trying to say?"

"It's Enora. It's obvious. Our coven needs to get rid of her. Just like we met to get rid of Reardon, we need to meet again and get rid of her. We should have done it after she sent a message with Beatrix. She knew exactly when and who to strike. Don't tell me you don't agree. Don't tell me you think someone else got in the way of his car." She turns to Damien again. "You said you swerved to avoid a wooden pentagram? Red? And it just appeared out of nowhere? A pentagram? You're sure?"

"Yes."

"It's like how you almost killed Bryce last year," Maddie says, squinting at me with hatred. "It's all your fault. Alondra should never have made you our leader. You aren't one. Had you been, Beatrix would never have been murdered. Mira would never have been taken from us. Damien would never have gotten hurt. Your brother could have died, and that would have been your fault too. It's all because of you."

I don't say anything. I don't bother. I just rush out of the room.

14

HAWTHORNE LAKE

I'M WALKING AROUND AND AROUND AND AROUND HAWTHORNE LAKE. Moonlight and shadows of the trees reflect off the ripples of waves with the thick woods surrounding me. The rain has stopped, the air smells fresh, and the view is beautiful, but even this lovely place isn't enough to still my mind. Maddie laughed when I told her I was thinking of going to Sri Lanka to study Buddhism. Boy, could I do with some meditation right now. Or maybe Hinduism? A little action without thought, like in the *Bhagavad Gita*?

It's my fault?

That's what I keep asking myself.

So, it's my fault?

Maddie's right. She must be. Right?

This is my former best friend, who used to laugh off every problem we had. Now she's acting like she'd rather I not exist. Like any problems of hers are because of me.

Maybe she's right? Last year was nearly a disaster for Bryce. He almost died. I am a terrible leader. I'd be the first to admit that. And Maddie urged me to run a Sabbath. She wanted me to see Mira even more than I did. She would have gone with me had she not had to take care of her mom—or rendezvous to fuck my brother, which I learned later as you well know. Hmm...if screwing my brother was more important than the Abaddon coven and Enora, maybe she's to blame. Right? Fuck her!

My fault! You've gotta be kidding me!

I don't know... maybe it is. I'm so confused.

I'm walking my fifth lap, I think. I don't know. I keep walking around and around the water's edge, staring at the small waves lapping up against pebbles and mud. It's like I have a purpose, but I don't know what it is. I threw off my shoes and socks a long time ago—I have no idea where I threw them—and I occasionally dip my bare feet into the cold water. I feel the pebbles; most are soft, massage my feet in the muddy, shallow water. It's after midnight. I think I've been walking for hours.

Why did I let Beatrix die? She was my responsibility. She was so young. I failed her. She died because of me.

I see a vision of a pale body in a black cloak ever so slightly swaying over Alondra's patio.

About halfway through another lap, I stop and walk a little closer to the edge. I dip my hand into the water and touch the rocks. Most of the stones are rounded and feel smooth against my fingers. Then I gather some mud underwater and let it drip down my hand. The water's cold, but it soothes my skin. I dip my fingers through the opening of my shirt, probing under my bra and enjoying the feel over my breasts and along my nipples. It's a warm night.

Something startles me from behind, in the bushes. I jump and squint, searching the blackness through the trees. I hear it again. Then I'm breathless as an animal bursts forth from the thicket, its eyes shining an eerie white, reflecting the moonlight. It's a deer. She stops close to the shore beside me, slowing down to a trot, and gently dips her head in the water to drink. I walk closer to the water and pet its fur. It steps closer. Then I get on my knees beside the deer, soaking my pants, and run my hands in the cold water again. At first it's to wash off the mud and grime, but then I bring the water up to my mouth to taste. It's dirty, earthy, and bitter, but cool and refreshing. I get why the deer likes it. The deer nudges me a couple of times with her head. I giggle and oblige, petting her again.

I stand up and remove my red coat and throw it by the water's edge.

Then I bring more water up to my bare arms, bathing my skin. It feels good. It cleanses me.

Why did I hurt my brother? I'd rather die than let that bitch lay a finger on him. She knew that. She taunted me at the Billington House. Maddie's right. There's no way it's a coincidence that he crashed because of a burning pentagram.

I should have confronted Enora. I should have fought her long ago. I'm such a coward.

The deer walks deeper into the water and turns as if waiting for me to join her, as if beckoning me. Perhaps the water can splash away my thoughts? I could walk in and swim? But...wait, that's crazy. It's the middle of the night.

When Mira was lost, I told Bryce a thousand times I should visit her. But, to be honest, it wasn't hard for him to convince me not to. I didn't want to mess up my grades. That sounds stupid, but I just wanted a normal fall semester. Every year, all I wanted was to be a normal student.

No, that's not honest. I was afraid. Very afraid. I'm scared of Enora.

I need to cleanse more. I have to clear my body of these thoughts. Usually walking helps me forget my troubles, but tonight it's not working. Earlier I considered just walking in circles until dawn. But now I feel a pain in my chest. I feel horrible. I'm so sad. It's all my fault.

I start crying.

I feel so alone.

Perhaps I should go to Bryce. Bryce. He's so nice. He kept calling but I didn't answer my phone. I'm not sure where my phone is now.

I need thoughtlessness. My thoughts are painful. I need to find a way to ignore them.

I pull up my T-shirt and unclasp my bra. I pull down my pants and underwear and pile my clothes by the side of the lake. Slowly, I wade ankle-deep, in the nude, following the deer, but it's really cold. I bring the cold water along my arms and belly. Then I splash the water on my face. The deer is beside me again. I bathe with her. I crouch down and run the cold water along my legs and up to my sides and waist. I walk in deeper, knee-deep. I throw cold water along my stomach and breasts. Then I feel the cold along my groin and butt. For a moment, I shiver. But I'm committed now. I enter deeper. I sink until the water is at the level of my belly button.

I smell and feel charred, rotting flesh and chalky talc powder. There's a flash of red and an upside-down pentagram. Then my skin is soothingly warmed as if I'm standing near the jets of a whirlpool sauna.

The deer swims beside me as if trying to grab my attention. I laugh. I think she's beckoning me to join her. That's crazy. The water's so black. And...wasn't there a reason I shouldn't be in the water?

Soon my whole body is dog-paddling. I enjoy the icy water as it touches my skin. It feels like it outlines my body. I feel it against my face, hands, belly, back, and arms, just like before, when I ran water along my body. It's as if I've summoned Vidar, the forest god, and he is touching me. Caressing my skin. I feel him along my chest, then running his hands over my pussy and ass. Being this bare in the middle of the night in the water is pleasurable and incredibly erotic. I feel as if I am giving myself to the forest god. I want to. I want to let go and have no thought or care anymore.

I'm a good swimmer. In the furthest reaches of my mind, I think that. Beyond the black water, I can see lights from campus between the trees in the forest. The deer and I swim toward the artificial lights of Hawthorne University.

Then I rest. I lie on my back and float on the lake, naked, staring up at the gorgeous bright stars. It's so serene. It's as beautiful as the empty, quiet forest. At my side, I catch my deer's eyes open wide while it treads water.

I roll and dip my head under the water. I open my eyes and can't see a thing, just a little light dancing in blurred lines under me. The bottom is blackness. For a moment, as I look down into complete darkness, not able to see under my feet, I'm afraid. There's this fear that some sea monster will come barreling up to the surface and consume me. I always have this fear when I swim in lakes. Sea monsters, alligators, and snakes. The fear's greater now because it's dark. But it's a small lake. It was safe during the day; why wouldn't it be at night? So I tell myself not to be stupid and scared.

When I get to the surface of the water, I realize I've lost my deer. I'm close to the center of the water now, about fifty yards from either side of the shore.

Feeling a little crazy, perhaps as if I have nothing to lose, I dive. I'm shocked by how long it takes to touch the ground at the bottom of the lake. I swim deep in the pitch darkness. My ears pop. It's much deeper than I could have imagined. I touch some sort of plant or branch near the bottom, and I quickly push myself back up to the surface for air. As dark as it is, I actually see moonlight on the surface as I emerge from the water. I spit out some of the water and rub my eyes. I'm treading water and, at the center of my chest, I feel elation. I feel happy. Wasn't there something wonderful happening in my life right now? Or was it tragic and sad?

There's a flash of Beatrix staring at me with her bloodshot eyes wide open, hanging from a rope. My neck tightens. I can't breathe.

I splash the water, shake my head, brush my wet hair from my eyes, and swim toward the light at the other end of the lake.

When I'm close enough to the other shore, I wade until I feel rocks and boulders jut out. Then I slowly walk to the water's edge. The water laps up against my tits, and I feel aroused again. I enjoy the tingle of the dripping water falling from my neck down to my breasts. Then the water laps up against my butt and privates again. It's as if the lake is making love to my naked body. My water-lover touches me with drips of water as I emerge on the shore.

I turn from a noise in the bushes toward the faraway lights of campus, on the other side of the thick trees of the forest. It's dark, but my eyes have adjusted. On this side, there's a dirt path that leads right to campus. People are laughing and murmuring behind thick trees. Two people run out from the trees to the shoreline, about twenty yards from the water, where I'm standing. They stop in their tracks. Two boys—I think I recognize one of them from one of my classes—and they're staring at me with mouths wide open. Then comes a girl's voice. She appears right next to them. One of the boys points at me, and the girl gasps. Of course, I've completely forgotten that I'm stark naked until now. I don't think my mind is all here right now, to tell you the truth.

I'm mad. I have no interest in "talking" to anyone. Why am I angry? They're disturbing my peace. That's why. I love my lake. My joy comes from swimming and walking along its shore. I don't want to talk to anybody. People bother me.

"Cadence?" asks a girl, unsure. She's so far away, but I recognize her voice. She's standing over rocks by the river's edge.

I see a vivid vision of a witch falling from the rafters of Alondra's porch with a noose around her neck. I feel tightening along my neck again, but I cut the cord when I utter, "*Lux mortis. Ariadne. Hecate. Astraea. Gaia. Limnades.* Summon me, Nyx. Welcome. Not far from man's curse. Hecate, know my own. Blind me in darkness so that I feel Vidar's pleasure. Not pain. Fuck you. *Lacus. Aqua. Lacus. Aqua.* Fuck me. Fuck me now."

"Katie, is that you?" she asks again, squinting.

"*Somnus,*" I say, waving a hand before the girl. She collapses on the rocks. Her two friends run down the rocks from the woods and grab her, trying to revive her.

I walk up, swaying my naked hips. When I'm beside them, I look down at the two boys. They're so worried about their fallen comrade that they didn't even hear me approach. They're pushing and tugging at the girl. I know her. Her name is Kendra. She's an Asian girl who was in my economics class last year.

I don't know the boys well. One is a nerdy-looking boy with glasses, a button-down, and slacks. The other's cute, wearing just a T-shirt and jeans. I smell alcohol. The boys reek of it. The moonlight shines on their faces. The cute one has short hair and a thick beard, which I like. He's broad-chested and really muscular. He looks up at me. I smile, remembering that I'm not wearing clothes. I have a strong urge to fall to the ground and fuck him. I want to hit the ground right now, run my hand along his short hair and all the strands of that bushy beard, yank down his pants, and have at it. And with his gaze, I think he wants it too. It wouldn't be hard. He'd have no way to stop me. Not in my current state. I could easily *make him* love me.

The other boy's staring now. In fact, both of them have stopped even caring about their fallen comrade. What a surprise if I fucked the nerdy one too. Just grabbed those glasses, licked his face and cock, and squeezed my body against his thin girlish figure—like I really fucking care about his figure at the moment—and screwed the virgin until the sun rose. Or I could fuck both boys together. Why not? It would be fun.

I kneel down and touch the fluffy beard of the buff one. He just stares like a frozen rabbit playing dead, allowing my dripping wet fingers to run along his hairy cheek. I see him stare at my tits. I smile. I look at his T-shirt. Both boys are staring at my tits. They're on their knees, looking blankly at my breasts.

"Take your clothes off," I order.

The strong guy removes his shirt first. I lick my lips, looking at the ripples of his muscular chest. His perfectly developed triceps, deltoids, and pecs. His abs. The nerd undresses too. Even his run-of-the-mill body attracts me. I rub the muscles on their arms and shoulders and then down along their chests.

"You shall be my sacrifice. *Lacus. Delactatio, delectatio, fructus.*" I gently lay the two naked men down on the dirt. "*Coitus, fructus. Fructus... coitus. Fructus.*"

They nod, obeying me, and lie still beside the passed-out girl. As I crouch beside them, running my fingers over the thin, lanky boy's hair, I use my left hand to reach down to his hard cock. As my gaze hungrily follows my hand down to his groin, I see a twinkle in the moonlight on my finger. My ring finger.

I feel a sharp pain in my head. It becomes crushing. And fear. My confidence leaves me, and I'm feeling as if something terrible is happening. I squeeze my hands and quickly shake my head. I can't breathe for a moment. Then I jump to my feet and look at the two naked boys.

My God, what am I doing?

"*Somnus! Somnus!*" I shout, almost screaming, throwing my arm out toward both of them. They both turn their heads, close their eyes, and fall asleep.

"You are alone," says an echoing voice behind me. The voice laughs. "Only in magic are you free. Let go of your power and you are nothing. Blind."

I search the trees and the lake. I don't see where the voice is coming from.

"Why not join them? Take these men as they lie here as your sacrifice.

You have that great a power. Take them. They're yours with magic. Don't you want to? You can have any man with your power. Afterward, you can even wipe away his memory. Take whomever you want, whenever you want. You are a witch. You can do whatever you want to men under the rays of Selene's blessed darkness. No longer be a part of God's deception and guilt, descendant of Escoba. Roam free, descendant of Hawthorne. Rise up in this baptism. Join me. Your friend. Once you have a taste, you will never go back. You won't want to. Join me. Be free. Within the water or upon the walls of the forest, you can be reborn and finally be happy. You can finally feel free."

"Who are you?"

"*Amica.*"

Dread deepens. My blackbird, my majestic raven, who I haven't seen in a year, stands beside the shore of the lake. I hate her. But...part of me misses her. Part of me feels free before my bird. Cleansed. And the raven nods its head, as if reading my thoughts.

I see my brother sitting in a wheelchair with his leg bandaged.

"What did you do to Beatrix!" I shout, and the bird flutters its wings. Then I jerk my head in every direction, looking around the lake. "What did you do to my brother! How dare you bewitch me! How dare you put a spell on me!"

"*Et nos unum sumus,*" says the voice, bursting into laughter. "*Et nos unum sumus.*"

Laughter echoes from a thousand trees, surrounding me.

I wake up naked in a bush beside the lake. It is still dark.

LOVE ME

IT TAKES ME ALL OF EARLY DAWN TO FIND MY CLOTHES. I CIRCLE LIKE THIRTY times to find where I placed them. It doesn't help that the sun hasn't risen above the trees on the horizon, so it's still dark. But at least it's still summer, so I'm not too cold.

I run barefoot to my apartment. By the time I get to the door, the sun's rising. And the minute my key is in the lock, the door swings open.

"What the hell happened!" Bryce exclaims. "Oh my God, I've been so worried! Maddie called and told me about Damie. She's been desperately trying to reach you. She said she was mean to you. She said she thought you went crazy when you left them. You haven't answered your phone!" He's hysterical. He won't stop talking. "I've told you a million times to answer your phone. Damn it, Cadence, I've been pacing all night!" But he lets go of his rage, looking at my head and touching my hair. "Your hair's wet and dirty." His tone becomes gentler. "Why? Are you okay, baby?"

"I went walking," I say with a shrug, entering the apartment. "It was a warm night. I walked to the lake to take my mind off things."

"What?"

"It was a spell. Enora's, I think."

He closes the door and I sit down on the couch and stare across the living room for a moment. Then I start crying.

"It's all my fault," I say when he puts an arm around me. "Beatrix and now Damie. They're all being poisoned by Hawthorne. Beatrix thought I could protect her. And now Enora's after my brother. God, Bryce! You know how much I didn't want him to come here."

"Damie's fine, Katie. That's what I was trying to tell you. He's fine. Everyone is fine. And Beatrix wasn't your fault. She was going to kill herself sooner or later, with your help or not. I've told you this a million times. Hell, you even said she probably killed that cat she told you about."

"She was murdered." I shake my head violently. "It wasn't suicide. Maddie's right. And now Panthera is going after us. My brother."

"It's so late. Just stop worrying." He holds my hand. "Why don't you go shower and rest? I'm just relieved you're okay."

"Fuck you!" I toss his hand back to him. "We could have saved her! Maddie's right. We could have watched her and stayed at the house and stopped it from happening. Seeing Enora in the Billington House should have been enough to convince us to never leave that little girl alone at Alondra's house. I should have stayed with her. What sort of protection did I give her? I made it worse. It's all my fault. And Damie could have been okay if I had just told him. I should have just said to stay away from Hawthorne. I should have just told Dad about us. That would have done it. Daddy would never have let him come here. But I'm a coward. I'm such a coward. If I had told Dad that I'm a witch, he would have done everything he could to keep Damie from becoming one too."

"Calm down, Cadence. Please. That's not true. None of this is your fault."

"What do you mean!" I yell, standing up. He falls back on the couch, furrowing his brow, looking at me like I'm insane. "How the hell can you say that! Beatrix was just an innocent, confused little girl."

I'm looking down at Bryce like I hate him, but his blue eyes look up at me with this mix of confusion and sweet concern. He looks worried. About me. I don't think anyone else cares about me. Nobody in the whole world. Only he cares.

His care finally disarms me. I fall back on the couch and put my head in my hands. But I don't cry. Crying reminds me of Beatrix.

"I'm sorry. I...I'm so sorry, Bryce. I'm really confused right now."

"You're not being yourself. You were in a wandering tonight, right? A trance... was it triggered because of what happened to Damien, or do you really think it was Enora?"

"I don't know. I heard her. I saw Amica. It...was her."

I am in a witch trance. Even now. A witch's trance is set off by extreme emotion. Seeing Beatrix hanging from a rope certainly provided the first impetus. Then seeing my sweet baby brother having sex with my best friend spurred me on. His surgery probably threw me over the edge. No, my fight with Maddie did.

But I think I would have gone swimming in the middle of the night whether influenced by Enora or not. So, in a really weird way, I'm not so sure whether the trance was because of her or because of me. Maybe she came to take advantage of it?

My heart is racing. My senses are heightened. Even though Bryce's door is closed, I can hear a student throw her keys and purse in her car and start her engine outside. That's beyond the wall and around the corner in the parking lot. The scent of my body overwhelms me—it's of the ground and the fresh water of the lake. I love that smell. The earthen scent soothes my anger. It makes me long to be back in the lake again. It's funny because Bryce wants me to shower and stay home, but I would be happy right now just sleeping in mud under a tree.

"I am in a trance," I admit with a nod.

I look at Bryce. He's sitting beside me, running a hand through my hair. He's probably been worried about me all night. I run my hand along his forehead, touching his feathery hair. Then I lean over and kiss him on the lips. I love him so much.

"I'm sorry I worried you," I say. "I lost track of the time."

"It doesn't sound like you had a choice," he says with a nod.

He's breathing more heavily. I think he is. Or maybe I'm noticing his breathing? I'm not sure. I know I'm breathing more heavily.

I reach closer and press my lips to his, harder, entering with my tongue. And we make out. It's nice. I run my hand over the curves of his biceps and along the muscles of his neck and back. Bryce doesn't wear a shirt to bed until we're deeper into winter. It's too hot. With my other hand, I make my way down his pecs and along the ripples of his abs to his boxer shorts. I sneak a hand in and start rubbing his cock.

"Cadence, stop," he says, pulling my hand out of his pants. "What are you doing? We were just talking about Beatrix and your brother. Let's not do this again. You're in a trance."

I laugh.

"Go shower, baby," he repeats. But his words seem almost sultry to my ears, like a whisper.

"Why, do I smell?"

He chuckles despite himself. That brings my lips back on his.

Ooh, I want him so badly. I don't think I've ever wanted anything so badly before. Trances do increase sexual drive but...so? I really love this man.

"I probably do smell," I say between kisses. "I swam in the lake."

"What! You swam in the lake!" he exclaims with eyes wide, pushing me back again.

"Aha."

"Jesus, Cadence."

The apartment doesn't feel like my home. I can't explain it. It feels like Bryce's. Sure, I've been living here. My stuff is here, and I've slept here for many months, but it doesn't feel like home. The forest is my home.

He takes my hand and pulls me to my feet. He helps me take off my red coat. Next is my shirt. I just stand there and stare at his naked chest. He undresses me. He's taking care of me. It reminds me he's the only one in the world who cares about me. Why? Why should he? I hurt everyone I love.

He removes my bra. I feel the circulating cool air brush over my nipples, and that arouses me more. They feel hard. The air conditioner is like the lake. Like when Vidar caressed me in the water. Now the air touches me. I want Bryce to do that now. I feel every stroke of his fingers as they graze the curves of my breasts and belly and massage my soft skin. I feel it in slow motion. He is probably moving quickly, but it all seems slow. It feels so good. This is part of a spell too. My spell. I look at his wide eyes, and they're staring at my body. I think I'm confusing his mind. He thinks he needs to undress me to help me, but really he's undressing me to touch me. I feel his fingers as they slowly pull my pants and underwear down from my hips. Then he strokes my skin, brushing lightly along my legs and ass while breathing more heavily. He touches my inner thighs and the hair between my legs. Purposefully? I don't know. I catch his eyes and he quickly averts them. I'm naked.

"Where's your phone, Kate?" he asks.

"Huh?"

"Your phone?"

"What?"

"Where's your phone?" he asks sternly.

Oops. I laugh. He doesn't.

"That explains why you didn't answer our calls," he says with a sigh, shaking his head.

"Aha." I'm staring at him, thinking of his stern tone of voice. "Did you want to punish me?"

The question makes him really nervous, and he blinks his eyes and turns from me.

He takes my hand to lead me to the bathroom, but I don't move. That's one thing I'm not going to let him do. I'm not going anywhere. I'm staying put right here by the couch. I told you, it doesn't feel like my apartment. It feels like his. I love that. It's like I'm visiting his place. His things. His body. I can smell him. His scent permeates the whole place. His smell. Not just his cologne. His body scent. It's irresistible.

"What's the matter?" he asks, looking at my dirty feet. "You need to go shower."

"I want to fuck you."

"Katie," he says, closing his eyes and shaking his head. He looks angry. "You're in a trance. Let's not do this now. And...you're bewitching me. Stop it. Go shower."

"I want to fuck you, Bryce," I repeat, and I run my hand along his short hair. He freezes. It reminds me of the students. He is under my spell. Really, I could do whatever I want with him. I could make him fuck me. Enora was right about that. With Bryce, it...wouldn't be so wrong. Would it?

I look at my ring. I don't want him to fuck me. I want him to love me.

He's wearing his pajama pants. I remember having sex with him one night last year, practically attacking him and yanking them down. That was after a trance too. I don't want to do that tonight. I won't do that. I want to make love *with* him. I know the trance is spurring us on, but is that so wrong? When we love each other? I slowly run my hands along his chest, over all the ripples of his muscles. He's so cut. I make my way with my hands down to his boxers once more. Then inside. His penis is large. He may be telling me to stop, but his body isn't.

"I'm sorry I worried you," I say almost in a whisper, stroking his cock.

"Cadence," he says, closing his eyes. "I said you were in a trance. We should stop."

"You don't want to?" I ask, pouting like a child. He regains his smile.

"I do ... of course, I do. But I'm worried. It's Enora? You're sure?"

"I think so. She was trying to hurt us. Separate us. But I stopped her." I'm still rubbing his cock.

I look into his gorgeous blues. God, I almost had sex with those boys by the lake! That's almost enough to break my arousal with Bryce. To think that I could have done that. It would have destroyed me. I would have been lost forever. Was that Enora's plan? It must have been.

"How? How...did you stop her?" he stammers. He closes his eyes in pleasure.

"You. You stopped me."

"What do you mean?"

I shrug. Then I drop to my knees and pull down his pants and shorts. I hold his large cock in my hands and bring my mouth next to it, but he pushes me away. I move close again and take it inside.

"Cadence! You're in a trance."

"So?" I ask, looking up at him.

I drop to my knees again. That drives him mad. I never have oral sex with him. It just feels too dirty. Nothing's too dirty at the moment. I still smell the grime from the lake on me. And dirty is something I yearn for right now. In fact, it makes me even more wet. I take him inside again.

"Stand up," he says. But he doesn't push my face away. "Please... Cadence...just stand up and go shower."

"Okay," I say, obeying him with a laugh. I'm guessing he's disappointed. "I'll go shower."

But I'm not done. Not even close.

I stand up and touch his beard, staring into his eyes again. Then I press my lips hard against his, tasting him. I kiss him passionately, entering his mouth slowly, rolling my tongue along his.

"God, Cadence, what are you doing to me?" he asks, breathless.

"Loving you. Would you prefer I stop?"

"No. I mean, yes, if it's a spell."

"This isn't a spell, husband."

That word does it. *Husband.* It drives me wild. The word *husband* drives me absolutely over the edge. It's like throwing open a jammed door between our true love and our passion, now mixed with my witchery. I have never felt such strong attraction before.

Somehow, we land on the carpet. We roll from the couch to the center of the room.

"What are you going to do to your wife?" I ask, with a sly smile, in his embrace.

"Make you shower."

I giggle. "Can I tell you a secret?" I whisper in his ear.

He nods.

"After," I whisper.

I roll him on his back and straddle him on the carpet. Our lips touch again. Then, slowly, I gyrate my pelvis up and down along his shaft while running my fingers through his hair. Already, I'm feeling what I've wanted in my pussy since jumping into the lake. I suppose if I didn't have Bryce, I would have the lake. And the trees. But I do have Bryce. And that makes me forget all my troubles.

He runs his hands along my breasts, tracing around my curves and touching my erect nipples. I run my hand along his beard again and his short, feathery hair. I grind around him, teasing him, only making him crazier. I want him. I want him inside me so bad.

"I love you, Cadence," he says. He enters me. "You're... you're unbelievable, Cadence. You're—"

"Love me."

He's so slow and gentle, moving up and down inside me, just holding me by the hips. Then he runs his hand along my back, and his other hand squeezes my boobs. He brings his fingers up and traces my areolas and erect nipples. Then he brings me really close, his hands rubbing lower, down over the crack in my ass. My face is an inch away from his. I smile and suck his lips hard. My heart is racing. I feel his race too. But he doesn't smile. He's determined.

It's quiet otherwise. The door's locked. The lights are dim, only coming from the kitchen. There's nothing to disturb us. No distractions. Nothing. I don't hear anything outside our apartment anymore, because I don't want to. There's just us.

He jerks faster, moaning. I bounce on him harder, and I can hear the sound of me riding up and down on him. It feels so good. All the while, I'm sucking and kissing his lips hard. I even bite him. That stops him for a second. He answers by lifting himself deep into me, even harder, lifting my entire body as if punishing me.

"Oh, Bryce," I say quietly in his ear. "Yes. Fuck me. Fuck me hard. Fuck me. Do it. Do it to me now. Fuck..."

"Is this...a spell?"

"No. Not a witch's spell. It's me. Love. I love you so much. Don't...stop. Please. Please just don't stop."

I feel him climax inside me. That puts me over the edge and I come with him, falling into his arms. It's only then that I realize I'm still covered with muck and grime from the lake. *Gross!* I realize that he wasn't asking me to shower just to stop himself from making love to me. I'm filthy. I get off of him.

"Come here," he says, laughing, gesturing for me to fall back into his arms. Hesitantly, I do. I lie back down on the carpet with him and close my eyes in his embrace.

We lie quietly for a little while. Then—

"Bryce."

"Yeah?"

"The thing that stopped me from losing it, you know, from giving up everything, from being lost, was your ring. Your love. Otherwise, I think I would have been lost forever. I love you so much, Bryce. Do you love me?"

"Oh, Katie," he says, squeezing me tighter, kissing my cheek. "I love you. What am I going to do with you?"

"Love me."

16

FAMILY DINNER

AUNT JANE'S HOUSE IS ALWAYS A COMPLETE MESS, AND IT'S AMUSING HOW she's hidden all her junk behind unhung paintings and rugs. I know better. I've stayed over at her house many times and attempted to clean it. She usually just leaves stuff all over the carpet, but tonight, in order to entertain us, she's cleared out the whole dining room. She's also set fancy silverware along the long light-oak table with elegant white tablecloths and candles. The room is dimly lit with lamps.

Jane's also not a great cook. There's turkey, mashed potatoes, and cranberries on the table, but I know that she microwaved it or took it out of cans. But that's okay. Who cares? Because, like Maddie, Jane's one of the most fun, smiley women I've ever met.

Well, Maddie used to be. I haven't talked to her since the hospital. She's still blaming me for Damie's car accident, so we're back to ignoring each other. In fact, she's even been intervening with my other witch friends. I actually listened to her and finally scheduled a rendezvous with the coven to talk about Enora, but we didn't meet because only a couple of girls showed up. Frida told me Maddie had convinced the rest of the gang not to go. That's how crazy she is. Maddie was the one who originally told them we needed to gather. Now she's sabotaging our Sabbaths. It doesn't make sense, right? I'm telling you, she's gone cuckoo.

Anyway, Aunt Jane is wearing a bunch of fake gold necklaces, these large red-jeweled gold earrings, and a long trailing multicolored dress. No makeup. And she has her hair short and gray. I really like her. I think she's the coolest mom in the world. I never can understand why Maddie fights with her (but again, she's crazy). My dad is sitting beside Aunt Jane, and the two look like polar opposites. It's funny. Dad's wearing a formal button-down and slacks. His hair's getting grayer, and the wrinkles are deeper around his gentle gray eyes. He's smiling and laughing a lot. And my fiancé and brother are dressed really sharp too.

My brother is sitting across from Bryce and me, with his cane leaning on the wall behind him. I'm sort of talking to him. I mean, if he talks to me, I talk back, but we're not really communicating with each other anymore.

"Bryce," Damie says after another minute of silence, "can you pass the mashed potatoes?" Bryce pushes the bowl over.

"Your leg's feeling better, man?" asks Bryce.

"Yeah. I can't run, but I'm doing physical therapy. I should be able to be back to exercising in a few weeks. I'm working my arms with rowing now. I want to join the rowing team."

"That's a fun sport," Bryce says with a nod. "And a good team."

"You guys were discouraging me so much from fraternities that I thought I'd give it a try. You know we have a great lake. And the upper-body work is fantastic."

"If I were to join a team, I'd join rowing." Bryce smiles at him and I love that. He always gets along well with my brother, even when we're fighting. But I mess up that niceness by turning to my brother and saying, "Where is she, Damie? When did she say she'd be here?"

"Now," he says with a shrug. "I don't know what's keeping her."

"Maybe we should just start eating," I say to Bryce.

My brother's already eating, but that's Damie. He doesn't really care if he's rude. Somehow, he can get away with it. He's always gotten away with stuff like that in my family, and Dad and I just expect it. Aunt Jane watches him eat with a big smile. I don't think she minds either. I don't know how he does it. Honestly, Damie seems so happy about rudely eating that I don't really care either.

I hear a key jostle in the front door. Then my former friend Madison walks into the room. She's wearing a long black dress and dark makeup. It's ridiculously goth and witchy for a family dinner. I'm in a similar black dress but "normal" makeup, including red lipstick.

"Sorry I'm late," she blurts out.

Yeah, sure.

"We've been waiting for you," Aunt Jane says, losing her smile for the first time.

"Sorry."

She walks over to the chair beside Damie, leans down, and kisses his lips. My dad watches the kiss and doesn't seem to mind. I mind.

"Hi, Maddie," Bryce says.

"Bryce."

"Maddie," I say. The bitch doesn't even look at me.

"Hi, Madison," says my dad.

"Hi, Mr. Hawthorne."

"Well, now we can eat," Aunt Jane says.

"Wait," says my dad. "We should give thanks." Damie finally looks guilty, puts his fork down, and pushes his plate away. We all look at my dad, and he looks at each of us and smiles. "It's times like these"—he turns to my brother and Maddie—"with family, that all of us, together, can be thankful for what we have. I am always so grateful for what I have. To be with you two."

"Now we can eat?" asks Damie.

Dad smiles again, but before he nods, he says, "Things are happening so fast. I see my two favorite people in the world with partners now. People who really care about them. Who love them. It makes me so happy." He stops for a moment and looks at the table thoughtfully. He suddenly looks sad. "It's so special to find someone…someone who loves you." He's probably thinking of my mom. "This is what family is about."

"That's so sweet, Rick," says Aunt Jane, touching his arm.

Dad turns to Damie with a grin. "Now we can eat."

"Rick" talks to Aunt Jane for the next few minutes. The two hit it off. They always have. Aunt Jane is constantly laughing. She's in great spirits.

Bryce holds my hand while we eat and, for a moment, I feel good. I forget all my worries. Maybe everything is all right now? I wasn't so hot about meeting with Maddie for dinner, but perhaps it will all work out okay.

But then Maddie kisses Damien again in front of all of us. And I could swear—no, I know—that she's making sure I see it.

"How are classes, Maddie?" Bryce asks.

"All right," Maddie says with a shrug. "European and African history. It's really interesting but I'm burning out. I just want to graduate."

"Then what?" Bryce asks.

"I don't know. I've thought of helping out in the history department at Hawthorne. Maybe I'll end up helping you if you're a professor next year."

"How's that dissertation coming along, Bryce?" asks my dad.

"Nearly finished, Mr. Hawthorne."

"It would be great if you teach here," Dad says. "You want to teach at Hawthorne, right?"

"Of course. I love Hawthorne."

"Why wouldn't he want to stay here?" asks Jane with a smile. "It's so lovely. The woods and the hills. I wouldn't want to live anywhere else."

"Maybe you and Katie can work here together if Katie gets in," Dad says.

Bryce looks at me. I know what he's thinking. That's not going to happen. But then I feel his hand pressing the finger wearing my engagement ring. I get it. He's so cute.

"Where else have you applied, Katie?" asks Aunt Jane.

I try to swallow some cranberries and sip some white wine. The wine is really good. Jane may not know how to cook, but she knows wine. I lie, "All the big ones."

"Like where?" my dad persists.

You want to know the truth? None. I haven't applied to a single school except Hawthorne. I know, that's super dumb. But Jane's right—where else would I want to go? And I'm sure Bryce is going to work here. But if I tell my dad the truth, it's going to ruin the rest of dinner. So I lie a little more.

"You know, Harvard and Yale."

"Wow, sis, nice schools," says Damie. He smiles a little too wide, probably suspecting that I'm full of cranberries.

"This is why I didn't apply," says Maddie to my dad. "It's so stressful. I'd rather just complete my time at Hawthorne and figure that stuff out later."

"Well, you lovebirds will have to decide soon," says Aunt Jane.

At first Maddie and my brother irritatingly look at each other, thinking she's referring to them. She's not. She's looking at Bryce and me. That gives me a wicked sense of justice. Maddie doesn't have a ring from my brother keeping them together. *Haw!* Nor does the bitch deserve one. *So there!*

"Have you decided where and when the wedding will be?" Jane asks. "I'm so thrilled for you two."

Leave it to her to talk about something pleasant. I laugh and raise Bryce's hand over the table and kiss it. "We don't know yet, Ms. Taylor."

"How about Alondra's house?" Bryce asks me. It makes my heart jump, because he looks into my eyes so seriously. I never even thought about that.

"Yeah, maybe."

"Damie and I will probably get an apartment together off campus next year," Maddie says. "I just need a break from everything, but Mom's right. I don't want to leave here."

I laugh and that's super mean. Living together before marriage is forbidden by my dad. It's one of his biggest rules. Bryce and I still haven't even told Dad.

Damie coughs and says, "Well, I'll probably do the dorms again with Harvey next year. But I'm hoping Maddie doesn't go anywhere."

Maddie puts a hand over her mouth, realizing how stupid she's being.

"I don't think two people should live together until they're married," my dad says.

"Really?" asks Aunt Jane, amused. "That's kind of old-fashioned, don't you think, Rick?" She's not trying to be mean. She's being Aunt Jane. She really looks sincerely surprised.

My dad tries to manage a smile. I know he likes her. "Two people who love each other should have their love recognized under God. That's my belief. I think cohabitation is a sin. Marriage under God is special."

I force some turkey down my throat.

"I didn't know you were so religious, Rick," says Aunt Jane. "I didn't know." She puts a hand up. "I don't mean any offense."

"Can you pass the gravy?" Maddie asks Bryce. She doesn't dare ask me, even though I'm closer to the dish.

"I'm not that religious," my dad says. "But I believe that things are just too relaxed these days. You lose how special love is between a man and a woman if you don't sanctify it under God."

"Interesting," Jane replies.

Now Damien laughs, and it's really bad timing because it looks like he's making fun of Dad. In a weird way, I suppose he is. And even though he can get away with eating before we do, making fun of my father during dinner goes too far.

"What's so funny, Damie?" asks Dad.

I glare at my brother, ready to jump over the table if he fesses up to what he's thinking.

"Nothing, Dad. I'm sorry. You're just...a bit quaint in your beliefs sometimes."

"We're Catholic," he responds. Then he turns to Aunt Jane and she just nods and smiles.

"I think times have changed a lot, Mr. Hawthorne," Maddie says. "You know, nowadays people are getting together younger and marriage is an important thing for commitment, but look at how many people divorce. Love is what's important, not marriage. Just like you said, giving thanks. It's not about God, it's about love."

"I don't agree with that," my dad says.

I really don't like Madison right now. Who gives a shit what she thinks? It's as if she's getting upset with my dad. My dad is the sweetest man I know, next to my Bryce. Just because she hates me, that doesn't mean she should hate him. But, luckily, Jane talks before I do.

"Everyone's entitled to their own opinion, Maddie," says her mom. "I agree, but we must respect his beliefs."

"I do. But some opinions hurt people."

"What?" I snap. "How do my dad's opinions hurt people?"

"Are you serious?" Maddie says, laughing. "This coming from you?"

Bryce squeezes my hand, telling me to shut it. I look at him and see the unspoken warning on his face.

"What do you think about the subject, Bryce?" Maddie asks with a wry grin.

I squeeze Bryce's hand tighter. I feel blood rush to my face. How is it that my very best friend is my archenemy now? What happened? I really hate her.

"Alondra taught us to respect each other's beliefs, Maddie," Bryce says. "Even if they're different. You know that."

"Sure. But what do *you* think? Do you think two people in love should live with one another before marriage?" And then she leans on her hands with a really nasty grin, anticipating his response.

What are you doing?

She looks at me but quickly turns back to Bryce. She's playing us. Is she purposefully trying to get me in trouble? She must be.

"I ..." He looks at my dad, unsure. "I think if two people really love each other, truly, then it's okay for them to live with each other before marriage. True love's bond doesn't break even before the ceremony. But... I totally get Katie's dad's point too."

Dad shakes his head and goes back to eating turkey. He doesn't look up. He eats some more, pours some gravy, and takes more bites without looking at anyone.

Everyone eats in silence. Even Aunt Jane just picks up a roll and munches on it, staring at the wall. Any semblance of a pleasant dinner seems over. All because of my fucking bitch former friend Maddie.

"Do you know why Katie and I like to wear black makeup, Mr. Hawthorne?" Maddie asks.

I drop my utensils on my plate and stare at her. Then I shake my head, warning her. Everyone stops eating.

"What are you doing?" Damie asks her. "Stop it." But she's looking at my dad with this evil smile. I feel like Maddie left the house and bitch Enora's taken her place. Like my former friend is possessed or something. What's gotten into her? My dad furrows his brow.

"You can hate me, but you don't have a right to go after my dad," I say.

"Who says I'm going after your dad? I like your dad."

"Why did you even invite me?"

"I didn't invite you, Cadence. My mother did."

"I invited your friends, Madison," says Jane, furrowing her brow. "So be nice to our guests."

"Cadence isn't my friend."

"You're being a baby," I say.

"Am I? And you're being a liar. And it's because of your lies that Damie got hurt. Mom, do you know why we wear dark makeup? Being truthful was once very important to Katie."

Jane looks at Madison and loses her famous smile. "Yes, I do, Madison."

She does?

"No, you don't. We're not a part of the latest vampire fashion craze. Ours is a tradition passed on—"

"Just shut up!" I snap, pounding my fists on the table. "What are you trying to do?"

"This is why Damie got into a car accident. Because of your family's lies." *My lies?* "You need to be out in the open about what's going on. And I need to be open with my mom. People shouldn't be kept in the dark. If something's bad, it should be brought into the light, right out into the open."

"What's going on here?" asks my dad.

"Well, you see, Mr. Hawthorne," Maddie says, "your daughter is a witch. So is her boyfriend, Bryce. Except in our coven, we call Bryce a *High Wizard*."

The lights flicker in the dining room. Everyone looks around the room in surprise. Bryce squeezes my hand so tightly that it hurts. Maddie's rage dissolves for a moment, along with the color in her face, but then she regains her bitchiness and frowns.

"Damie's been suffering for weeks, ya know, Windstorm. You'd think if you can mess with the lights, you could have used magic to help him with his broken leg."

"He didn't want me to come over. He told me to stay away."

"We could have held a gathering to stop Enora. Could have—"

"Shut up, Maddie!"

I stare at my dad. He doesn't understand what's going on. Jane's looking at the wall.

"Why not be open? Why not—"

"You're such a bitch. If you really wanted to do something about my brother, you guys wouldn't have been so evasive. You would have let me through the door—"

"Of *our* dorm room?" Maddie asks with a nasty grin.

"You guys, we shouldn't be talking about all this right now," warns Bryce.

"Instead of sleeping with your fiancé, Cadence," Maddie continues, "you could have met with the coven and planned your revenge."

"You didn't let us meet!" I jump up from the table and slam my fists down. Bryce jumps up to pull me back. "You didn't let me anywhere near you!"

"You never answered your phone."

"Why are you even here? With my family? On Thanksgiving? Haven't you had enough of me? You thought being with my brother would bring me back after I left you? I don't want to be anywhere near you. I never want to see you again. Ever! I hate you!"

Maddie jumps up and scowls at me. No one else dares say a word. Then she looks at my dad, pointing. "She's a witch, Mr. Hawthorne. Your Christian daughter is a witch. So is your future son-in-law. Not only that, but they've been living together for months. Two witches cohabitating before marriage. How does that fit in with your moral Catholic beliefs?"

"*Get out!*" I scream.

The lights shut off for a second, and I hear banging against the window and the pounding of a rush of wind.

"Where?" Madison says, looking all over the room, when the lights turn on again. "Where do you want me to go? You want me to leave my own *fucking house*! Why don't you go?"

"Maddie!" Aunt Jane stands up too. "These are our guests."

"So? Isn't that what I am to you? Aren't I just your guest too, *Aunt Jane*?"

"You're my daughter."

"Well, you're not my mother."

Jane looks stunned. She puts her hand to her mouth.

It's clear to Bryce and me, and probably to my brother, that Madison has completely flipped her lid. She's beyond nuts and she's hurting everyone in the room. If there weren't a shred of love from our past, I think I would blow open one of the windows and have her sucked out of it.

"I don't want to ever see you again, Cadence!" Madison yells in tears. "I hate you too!" Madison rushes out of the room. My brother hobbles after her with his cane. We hear the front door fly open and slam shut.

They're gone. Everything falls silent. We just stare at the ceiling or look away from one another, but nobody picks up a fork or says a word. Then Aunt Jane runs into the kitchen with her head in her hands.

"We'll talk about this later, Cadence." My dad throws his utensils on the table and joins Aunt Jane.

I sit down in shock. Bryce and I are alone in the dining room. I lean my head on Bryce's chest, but I don't cry. I just sink into his arms. "God, Bryce. I told you we shouldn't have come. She's flipped."

He doesn't reply, but he holds me. Maybe he thinks I have too?

In the other room, Aunt Jane is crying. "I'm so sorry, Rick," she says. "She's so difficult. She's never accepted me. Now it's the accident. The car accident with your son made her even crazier. She keeps telling me it's Cadence's fault. I adore your daughter. I told her that's just crazy. I can't control Maddie anymore. I guess I never could... that accident must remind her of the death of her parents. Your son said something about the occult. He saw a pentagram. There was witchcraft involved in Maddie's parents' car crash too. I think I should never have told her about that. This town has been into witchcraft ever since I was in grade school... I'm sorry, Rick. I'm so sorry. I'm so sorry we spoiled your Thanksgiving."

"It's all right. You didn't spoil it."

No, she didn't. Maddie did. I hope I never see her again.

17

FORGIVE ME

It's dark. Not because it's dark outside—it's not, it's morning and cold—but all the lights have been turned off and the drapes are closed in a white-walled hall with a vaulted ceiling. A heavyset pastor is up on stage in an umber suit. His words echo throughout the room as he covers a candle with a golden snuffer. He has lovely dark golden skin, short dark hair, a mustache, and black eyes. Every time he discusses a sin, he douses the flame of one of the candles. There are seven candles. Right now, he's about to snuff out the last candle: pride.

Frida's sitting beside me on a wooden bench near the central aisle. I look over and she's all smiles. She loves it. We're both wearing formal black dresses, but our makeup is light and not too witchy. A lot of people are dressed up. It's church, you know. She's so happy I came. This is the last day her brother, Liam, will be here from New York. It's Liam who's preaching. I think the service is almost over.

"Take a look at Proverbs 11:2," the priest says, dousing the candle. "Pride is our greatest sin." He has a thick Brazilian accent like Frida. He smiles like her too. "Get rid of pride, reach out your hand to the Lord and savior, and allow the light of Christ to fill your heart." It's really dark as the last candle goes out. "Pride leads to anger. If you care so much for yourself that you darken your soul towards others, you live in darkness like the devil."

I bite my lip. I think I have a lot of pride. And you know I have an anger problem.

Liam turns to a young boy sitting on a piano bench by the side of the stage. "Open the front drapes, please, and let in some light." The boy jumps up to help. As he opens the drapes, light shines forth over the large cross behind the altar. "Now let us light the seven heavenly virtues. Humility. I will light a candle for each virtue to represent God's grace." He smiles. Again, his smile reminds me of Frida's. I look over and Frida gives me the same look.

But then I see someone I didn't notice before, sitting behind her. My brother. I haven't spoken to Damie in weeks. I'm not speaking to Dad either. Well, Maddie did that. My dad isn't very happy I'm a witch. Nor is he very happy I'm living with Bryce. He really loved Bryce, but not anymore. Maddie was right in thinking that unveiling our coven to him would hurt me. She knows me too well. She knew exactly where to strike.

Frida turns because I'm staring at my brother and she sees him too. It's the first time she's lost her smile.

"She's loco, Katie," Frida whispers in my ear. "You know, crazy. She started screaming and crying one night on the phone. Then she told me how we need to protect each other from *you*. Maddie blames you for everything. Like you're worse than Enora or something."

I nod. I'm not arguing about Maddie flipping her lid. I don't need to hear it; I saw enough on Thanksgiving. But Damie doesn't look happy. Something else is wrong. Damie's like Frida, always smiling. This morning he seems disturbed.

"How can God lead us to the light?" asks Liam.

The church is now bright, with all the drapes open. I look at a window and see reflections off the snow outside. It's warm in the church but really cold outside. Winter is not my favorite time of the year, but this week is winter break. That's nice. And I actually did exceptionally well with my grades for the first fall semester since my freshman year. All As. This year I—

"Loco, Katie," Frida whispers again. "She blames you for Damie's accident, as if Enora's better. As if you're hurting her and our circle. But you know, I reminded her what Enora did to us."

"Give your heart to Jesus Christ and allow his light to fill your soul," says Liam, moving his hands over the seven lit candles. "Now, please stand."

"She went totally loco and I had to hang up on her," whispers Frida quietly, getting up. "I took your side and told her she's totally crazy, Katie."

I nod while looking at Liam. Liam looks down, closes his eyes, and clasps his hands in prayer.

"Let us pray. Lord, thank you for this church, which allows us to gather together under your grace. I ask for your blessings. To the Father, Jesus Christ, and the Holy Ghost, thank you for this congregation this morning. Amen."

"Amen."

"This concludes our service," says Liam with a smile. "Blessed be our Lord, Jesus Christ, our savior. Remember that through God's forgiveness, you can all see the light. Thank you for coming."

Everyone gets their things and prepares to leave. The church is pretty full. Frida takes my hand and, after we wait for a line of people to move down the aisle, she rushes me to the front of the church to meet her brother. She's so excited about it, and I love that.

Liam's shy. That's surprising to me after watching him lead the congregation, but when Frida brings me up to the altar, he seems to avoid my gaze. But he smiles the family's famous smile as he gathers his Bible under his arm and the candles in his hands.

"Hi," I say with a wave.

"You must be Cadence. My sister has talked a lot about you."

"Frida says you're heading back to New York. We should get together today for lunch or something."

"I wish I could, but my plane leaves from Atlanta this afternoon."

"Shit, I should have come to watch you sooner." Then I cover my mouth. "Pardon my French. Damn. I mean, too bad. I've just been so busy with studying, you know."

"Katie's a bit of a bookworm," Frida says with a chuckle.

"Nothing wrong with studying a book," Liam says with a wink, lifting his arm to show us his Bible.

"So ..." I put my finger to my lips in thought. "You just became a priest, or something?"

"Yes. Just ordained."

Frida laughs. "Cadence isn't Christian, Liam. You don't know what it took to get her to come to church this morning. I told her it was your last sermon in Hawthorne."

"Honored to introduce you to the Lord's teachings, Cadence. To *my* favorite book."

"Yeah," I say. "Uh...about that. Can I ask you a question?"

He looks at me with his kind eyes. So does Frida. With those same sweet brown eyes. "You said forgiveness helps fight pride. Do you...do you think some things are unforgivable?"

He furrows his brow. "What sort of things?"

"Sins and stuff. Damnation."

"The Lord, our God, was crucified for our sins. Sin is a part of our existence ever since the fall in the garden. You can't live without sinning. But you can ask for forgiveness."

"From *all* sins?"

"You like books, huh?"

I nod.

"Take a look at Isaiah 55:7, Cadence. In the Bible, you'll find your God forgives you if you accept his love. Where I think people err is when they give up trying. Let God light your heart, and do not fear darkness. Your trespasses through the seven deadly sins can be forgiven if you accept Jesus. If you accept him in your heart, your soul, you will find the seven heavenly virtues feel natural. Goodness is the natural way of things that leads us to the light. That was the point of my sermon this morning."

Interesting. Christianity is so much more based on a book than Buddhism. I like this forgiveness stuff. It reminds me of my teacher, Alondra. At the time of her death, I told her I'd never forgive her. I've felt so guilty about that. I feel like, in my heart, I can't forgive her, and I feel like she can't forgive me for not forgiving her. Does that make sense? Do you see what I'm saying?

Am I damned? Beatrix said I was. Is there hope for me through Liam and Frida's God?

"I don't know if I can believe in God's light, Liam," I say. "I've seen evil in light sometimes too." Like Beatrix hanging from a rope in the brightest light. I wake up seeing her like that in nightmares almost every night.

"Find a quiet place, then, Cadence. In darkness or light. It doesn't matter. I am talking about lighting your heart, not physical light. The physical light is only symbolic. Sometimes, God reveals himself in darkness when you're alone. Pray. Accept the love of God. But you have to find God within your soul. The Holy Spirit. I can only preach. Only within can you find your true faith. But when you do, I promise you will find great joy. We all have the potential to find the Holy Spirit within. I have, and I've never been happier."

He touches my chest with a finger and smiles gently.

Frida laughs. "You'll never convert her, Liam. You can try, but she's the stubbornest girl in the world."

I nod.

That's when I feel someone else's finger tap me. I turn and it's my brother.

"Cadence, can we talk?" Damie asks.

I turn back to the pastor and reach out my hand, but his hands are holding candles. Frida helps him, and with a free hand he shakes mine. "It was a lovely service, Liam. And so nice to meet you."

"Thanks for coming. I will have to take you up on lunch next time, Cadence."

And we shake hands again. He's definitely Frida's brother. He's so nice. Frida helps him move the candles from the altar.

"What is it, Damie?" I follow him down the aisle. The church has emptied out. "Are we talking now?" But he doesn't say anything until we're about halfway to the exit, then he turns. He looks so nervous.

"Maddie and I had a fight." He shakes his head and puts a hand up. "That's not what I want to talk about... after the fight, she left for Atlanta. I know because I got in contact with one of her friends. She told me she never wants to speak to me again." He pauses and shakes his head. "That's also not what I'm trying to tell you. Katie, Maddie didn't leave for Atlanta during winter break. She left before finals. She didn't complete her classes. Not only that, I got a few calls from Aunt Jane. Her mom's so upset that she called the police to look for her. Unlike you, her mom has been in touch with her—until she went to Atlanta. Now Maddie's nowhere to be found. And her friend doesn't even know where she is. You said you're not talking to her. But do you know where she is?"

"No, I don't."

He takes a deep breath and runs his hand through the long side of his hair.

"Why didn't you tell me before?" I ask.

"You haven't been answering my calls."

Oops. I'm doing that anger thing again. You know, the thing where I don't speak to the person I don't like for weeks. I block calls too.

"Jane never called me," I lie. But I think I might have blocked calls from her too.

"It's only been a couple of days that her mom's been worried," he says. "It's been a week for me."

"Who's the friend you were talking to?"

"Gilda. Gilda said something about how Maddie was going to go see this girl named Mira. There's some weird witch thing going on in downtown Atlanta, but Maddie didn't tell me what it is. She never told me anything about your witch stuff. She said that was the only thing she agreed with you about.

"But Maddie's been acting so strange since last time you saw her. She never sleeps. She spends the whole night lighting candles around her. She curls up in a ball and just cries all night. She shuts down and stops talking. She doesn't talk to anyone. When I couldn't take any more, we fought and I stopped seeing her. But the last night before she left the dorm, I came back for one more attempt to make up with her. The door was unlocked, and she was curled up in a weird dark cloak in her dorm room. She had spray-painted a red pentagram on the carpet and placed candles all around it. And she was whispering this weird chant. I tried to rouse her, but she wouldn't lift her head. All she did was flash her left hand up at me. She had a red pentagram painted on her palm. It really creeped me out. So I gave up. I stopped visiting. I wish I hadn't. It was after that night that she went missing."

He wipes his eyes.

Now I'm the one freaking out. I have this sudden mix of fear and anger building in my chest. I'm having flashbacks of Beatrix sitting in the center of the guest room just like that. And to think Maddie's doing that now? And she painted a pentagram on her hand? I'm scared. All my anger at Maddie has left me. Now I'm only scared for her.

I look toward the altar and blurt out, "Frida! Frida, come here! Come over here. Quick!"

She touches Liam's shoulder and rushes over.

"What is it, Katie?"

"It's Maddie. Damie's saying she's been taken. She's in Atlanta. Panthera took her."

"Oh my God!" Frida says.

"What's happening?" asks my brother. "What do you mean? Who's Panthera?"

I jump into Damie's arms. He's so surprised. I start crying and hugging him so tight.

"I'm so sorry, Damie. Forgive me. I've been so mean. I should have accepted you two. Now I'm scared for Maddie. I'm so worried something's going to happen to her. I just hope I'm not too late to help her. I love you both so much."

"I love you too, sis," he says, sounding confused. "It's...okay. But what's happening?"

"It's a spell," I say, shaking my head. "Maddie's under a witch's spell. She must be. That might even be why she did what she did on Thanksgiving. That wasn't the Maddie I knew."

Liam runs over. He looks concerned.

"And, God..." I feel so heavy. I feel like the ceiling and walls of the church are falling on me. "It's my fault. Again. Maddie was right. I've done nothing with our coven, and this is my punishment. And now...I did this to Maddie. My friend."

"It's not your fault, Katie," Frida says. "Don't say that."

I search around the church. Then I look into Liam's caring eyes. And I think, *Can your God really forgive all sins?*

18

RED

I'm descending narrow, muddy concrete steps, and I'm smelling red.
It's a burning smell of cinnamon mixed with sandalwood and rotting
meat. Red smoke rises from below. Cold concrete walls enclose me as I
crouch down to avoid hitting the ceiling. After a few steps, I stop and look
back. There's bright yellow light along the sides of a metal door above
me. I'm guessing it's sunny outside. There's a slow drumbeat. And voices
—whispering, repeating themselves over and over, as I slowly descend.

At the bottom, the thick red smoke surrounds me, but it clears
enough for me to see a large room with a central bonfire, similar to what
I've seen in our witch gatherings. The flames rise to about the height of a
person. This must be a conjuring, for I doubt a fire like this could be
coming from the concrete floor. In front of the fire is a circle of witches in
crimson cloaks. Dancing around the women, jumping up and down like
a bucking bronco, is a naked man, the man I saw with Enora at the party.
Gus, the creepy, freakishly tall guy with fangs. He's nude with a tail and
long beard, reminding me of a Greek satyr. Like Pan. He's even playing a
flute. And in the center, near the pyre, a nude couple is fucking on a red
pentagram painted on the dirty concrete floor. The woman has short hair
with antlers and very thick black makeup. She is sitting on a man, riding
him up and down with her tits bobbing. The witches around the couple

are bowing. Each bow, each thrust, follows the beat of a drum. So does the satyr, who is synchronously jumping up and down. A circle of white candles illuminates the walls of the room. And along the walls I see red painted pentagrams and upside-down crosses in the flickering light.

"Blessed be thy servants," says one of the cloaked witches, the central one. "O holy Baphomet, we unite under the number six hundred and sixty-six, your servants under your power. Let our offering hang by your feet so that you may feast on the virgin under the stars. Hail Astraeus. Hail Selene. Hail Satanas. *Lucifer. Lucifer. Lucifer.*"

Everyone falls prostrate before the copulating couple. They all freeze, repeating the word *Lucifer* in whispers.

"Fire from the pit of hell!" the central cloaked witch yells. I finally recognize her voice: it's Enora. "Enlighten us so that you may reveal secrets to your beloved servant!"

"Did you kill Beatrix?" I ask. It takes all my energy to form the words. I'm so sleepy. I don't even know how I'm here. Is this a trance? A dream? How did I get here? I feel so disoriented.

The witches turn and start shouting at me. Then I see a face I recognize under one of the hoods—Maddie. She looks back at me, emotionless and curious, as if she's as confused as I am. Enora turns and faces me with creepy white eyes and an evil grin.

"Maddie," I say to my friend, "come back with me. Please. Please come with me. I'm so sorry."

"She's here, Cadence," says Enora. "Come here and get her if you care."

But Maddie turns back to the couple having sex.

Then everything freezes. All the prostrate women, even the couple having sex, freeze as if being paused in a movie. Only the third witch in a cloak turns. It's Mira. She has bright white eyes, like pearls, just like Enora. Mira stands and points at me.

"*Serpentus,*" Mira says.

Enora laughs. Mira rushes to me with those creepy eyes. Then she wags her finger by my face.

"*Serpentus. Serpentus. Serpentus.*"

All the witches cackle in derisive laughter.

"*Muta! Serpentus! Serpentus! Serpentus! Muta! Muta!*"

I fall to the ground, shaking. Then I watch Mira and Enora grow as I fall closer to the cold concrete. My arms and legs merge with my body. I feel frigid. I shiver. I'm so cold.

I twist and slither, desperately trying to escape up the stairway. But the steps are too steep. They laugh harder behind me, but I can't get up the stairs. I can't run. I'm trapped. And they will come and get me. They will tread on me. They will finish me.

I awake with a start. I'm in bed and it's dark aside from the light from a streetlamp in the parking lot shining through a crack in Bryce's curtains. He stirs.

"You okay, babe?" he asks sleepily.

"No."

I sit up in bed, throw my long hair back, and hold my head in my hands. I'm breathing so heavily and I'm covered in sweat. My heart is pounding. The white sheets fall from my breasts, making me realize I'm not dressed.

"What's wrong?" asks Bryce.

"I'm naked."

"You fell asleep after we made love."

"Bryce ..."

He lies on his side and just looks at me. I can barely make out his eyes in the shadows. He nods. "It's just a dream, babe."

I take a deep breath. Then I touch his hand, and he plays with my fingers. I'm so grateful to have hands. I know that sounds weird but, you know, I really was turned into a snake last year. Yeah, that's what Bryce meant, in his letter to the dean, when he said I was "sick." I was an actual snake. I'm not kidding. For two weeks, I was a slithering serpent. And you'd never guess who made me a person again. Enora. But she wasn't being nice. She needed my coven so she could use me and my magic.

I touch Bryce's face, but I'm not doing it to be loving, I'm doing it to make sure he actually has one. I make sure he's not another figment of my demented imagination.

"Tell me this isn't a dream. Oh God, please, Bryce."

He loses his smile, takes a deep breath, and shakes his head. "Not a dream. I heard you talking in your sleep. But you're awake now."

"I was underground. With Enora. I think she wanted me there to witness one of her Sabbaths. To show me that Mira and Maddie have become a part of her coven now."

The white covers fall from my naked body as I push myself to the edge of the bed. He rubs my back. I throw my hair back and turn with a smile.

"I'm scared, Bryce. She knows how to upset me. She knows we're going to try to get Maddie back. And I think she wants me to come. It was like she was taunting me."

"She used to haunt my sleep at night after our breakup. She did it for weeks. But they're just dreams. She has no power to do anything to you in them."

"She could drive me crazy. Make me keep having nightmares during the day. Or turn me insane like Maddie."

"She'll try, but you know they're just dreams."

"What does she want? At the lake, I thought it was to join her. Then I realized she wanted me to cheat on you. To hurt you. To hurt us."

I stand up with my back to him. The moonlight casts my shadow on the wall. I have arms and legs, a human form, thank God.

"Maddie was right, I did do nothing. We had enough of a warning with Mira. Then Beatrix. My brother. I've endangered all of us. I don't think she's going to stop. And now that wicked witch has Maddie. Who's to say she won't take us all away?"

I hear the sheets shift, and he stands up and touches me from behind again. I cradle my head in his arms.

"Everything's okay," he says, kissing my shoulder. "They're just dreams."

"We need to face her," I say with a nod. "To get back our friends."

"We're going to. I already spoke with the others. We're meeting this Sabbath."

I turn. The dim light is so dreamy that I almost fear for a moment that Bryce will change into a monster or something. He doesn't. He just shows me his lovely, warm smile.

"Oh, Bryce. I'm so scared. We can't wait till Friday. We need to do it now. Today. It can't wait. I need our coven to meet tonight."

"School starts today," he says, sitting back on the bed.

"I don't care. We have to meet tonight."

"All right," he says. "We'll meet tonight, then."

I walk over and turn the lights on.

"What are you doing?" he asks, squinting.

"Not sleeping. Not after my dream. I'm getting dressed." I walk over to the dresser. I smile, catching him staring at me. I turn to him. "And no funny business. I am sooo creeped out, babe."

"I'll try to resist."

I crack a slight grin. But then I turn serious again. "She's taking everyone from me," I say, grabbing clothes from the second drawer. I get dressed. "If I don't do anything, there'll be no one left. She'll even take you."

"I'm never leaving you, Cadence."

19

———————

THE MEETING

MY FRIENDS AND I SIT AROUND OUR FIRE, HOLDING HANDS. WE ARE ALL ON white chairs in the center of Alondra's backyard. White chalk has been poured in a circle around us. I'm shaking a little because it's really cold, but thankfully it's not snowing or raining. The flames are the height of a person, but not warm enough on this winter night. We're all wearing sweaters or jackets under our black cloaks. Bryce is sitting closest to me, and I feel like if it weren't for the ceremony, he'd have his arm around me. Tammy and Frida, the other witches closest to me, are on my other side; they're shivering a little too.

"We should get started," Bryce says to me.

"Let us begin," I say with a nod. Then I turn to the circle. All my friends, with hoods over their shoulders, look over. "*Lux alba.*"

"*Lux alba,*" they all repeat.

"Blessed be the day that our circle is brought together once more. Blessed be the coven under the gods Gaia, Selene, *et* Astraeus."

"Atman," says Bryce.

"Atman." We all nod.

My good friends Tammy, Helen, Frida, and Bryce are all smiles. Mandy, Natasha, and Hannah aren't. They're across from me, behind the flames, and I think they chose to sit there on purpose to avoid my gaze.

Maddie had convinced them, for the past few weeks, not to come to our Sabbath. It was only when Maddie went missing that they agreed to come. The new recruits, Josie and Debra, are wearing black cloaks and sitting to my left, near Frida. They look really nervous. To my right, sitting beside Bryce, is Damie. Yeah, my brother is here. I know, that's really weird, but at this point there is no reason to lie to my brother, pretending that we're not witches. And he's more concerned than anyone else that Madison is missing. He doesn't have his leg bandaged anymore, but he still walks with a limp. The weirdest thing is seeing him wearing a black cloak.

"You all know why we're here," I say earnestly. I might as well get to the point. "Maddie has been taken by the Abaddon coven."

"Was she taken or did she go 'cause she wanted to?" asks Mandy.

"We're here to find out," Bryce replies.

"It sounds like she's been in a trance," I reply. "I can't help but think it's a spell cast by Enora. She's also been messing with my dreams."

"Mine too, Katie," says Frida.

"Me too," says Hope. And a few others nod.

"Damie, tell the group the changes you saw in Maddie."

My brother tells them what he told me in church. He talks about how she stopped leaving her dorm room and sat on the floor, catatonic, staring at the wall and murmuring incantations. She stopped going to class. She didn't take her final exams. She withdrew and disappeared.

"Like Beatrix," says Tammy.

"Maybe Beatrix wasn't crazy, Katie," says Frida. "Maybe she was under a spell too."

"I've felt like Enora has been up to something since she threw me into a spell a couple of months ago," I say. "I had a wandering at Hawthorne Lake...no, I felt it even before that. You guys know. Beatrix. Maddie said Beatrix was killed and she didn't commit suicide. I believe that now. So if Maddie truly believed that Beatrix had been killed by Enora, why would she go join her coven and blame me? It all just doesn't make sense. She's not herself."

"Why wouldn't she blame you?" asks Mandy, acting like a total bitch. "We're in this mess because of your fight over your brother. It doesn't sound like you were very welcoming to her. I've spoken with Gilda. Mira's fine in Atlanta. She said Maddie ran to Mira. She probably accepted Enora after that."

"Enora's been conjuring nightmares, Mandy," I remind her.

"Katie's right," objects Tammy. "I spoke to Maddie too. She's totally nuts. Not our lovable Maddie, but transformed into a person I don't even recognize anymore."

"She's not herself," says Frida. "That's for sure." Mandy's scowl fades a little.

"I'm not sure you're right about this either, Cadence," Natasha says.

"Guys, we have to stick together," Bryce says. "This is what Enora wants. She wants us to be divided."

"Because Cadence never should have been our leader," snaps Mandy. "She never even wanted to be."

"I didn't," I snap back, opening my eyes wide. "But I do want my friend back." Then I look at all my witches under the flickering firelight. "We all do. This isn't just about dreams. This is about Maddie." I put a hand up because Mandy's about to say something, and I can already predict her nastiness. "When Mira left, it was assumed she left because she wanted to. Now I doubt that too. But Maddie kept asking us to meet. *To stop* Panthera. Why would she join her? Come on, guys. It doesn't make sense."

Everyone pensively stares at the flames. Mandy just turns from me in disgust.

"Last year we gathered to get rid of Reardon," I say. "I thought I could trust Enora because she helped me. But you know what happened. And then she threatened Bryce. I feel like she's been finding a way to get back at us since Lammas. Beatrix told me she was sent to disturb the peace. The bitch is scheming. And now she has two of our sisters."

"Maddie hasn't even spoken to her mom," interrupts my brother. "I'm so worried."

"It's okay, Damie," says Frida.

"I think we should—"

"Are we going to hurt Enora?" Helen asks. Helen rarely says anything in our coven. She's a shy, bald, dark-skinned girl who joined our coven when Tammy, Maddie, and I joined. "What are we planning, guys?"

Then Tammy and Bryce make suggestions again. And then there's more arguing.

I stop paying attention. This isn't a Sabbath. We might all be wearing witch cloaks, but it's really just a meeting. In some ways, that's better, because it means I'm avoiding magic. But in another, it means that we're wasting time.

I look up at the moon and stars. There are a few wisps of white clouds, but it's really clear and beautiful. Alondra's backyard really is peaceful. Everything is peaceful here, even though my mind isn't. And though we've still neglected caring for her place, the backyard was, and remains, wild and the best reflection of Mother Nature—a witch's paradise.

I hear howling in the distance. And a full moon. And there are sounds of scurrying animals among the bushes and trees. But it doesn't bother me. I'm a witch. Wolves, full moons, and creepy-crawly things in bushes are my thing.

I hold Bryce's hand. I feel like it's a beautiful night, if only it weren't so cold.

It's our first week back, but I didn't go to class today. I'm too worried about Maddie.

In the background, witches are still arguing. One subject that finally perks my attention involves an ancient summoning that Bryce, now the oldest member of our group, remembers Reardon conjuring once as High Wizard. The idea is to enter a trance by the fire and summon spirits who can provide us protection from the netherworld. We can cast a shield spell. But the last time we tried this against Enora, I was transformed into a snake. And even if we protect ourselves from Enora, how is that going to bring back my best friend?

"No," I interrupt, shaking my head. "No way, Bryce. I'm not going through that again."

"Then what can we do, Kate?" Tammy asks. "What do you propose? You're the only one not saying anything."

"We should go to Atlanta and demand that they give Maddie back."

"That's her territory," Tammy reminds me, shaking her head. "Her hallowed ground. You might be a powerful witch, but we'd be on her turf."

"Why not?" suggests my brother. "I'll go tonight. What are we waiting for?"

"Bryce and I are going," I say. "I met with you all to try to convince you to go with us. The only way to confront this evil is to face it. I've been avoiding it, hoping Enora would stop, but she's slowly destroying our circle. She'll take all of you, and there'll be nothing left of our coven if I don't do something."

"It's just not safe, Katie," says Frida, shaking her head. "We're not sure what we're getting into there."

"I'll join Bryce in a conjuring," Mandy says, frustrated and in a huff. "Or I'll go with you to Atlanta...but we need to do something. Seems Katie's already made up her mind."

But before I can say another word, cries of "*Yatu!*" erupt. The interruption is jarring. I turn. The sound's coming from Alondra's house. Two witches with hoods over their heads are wearing cloaks similar to our own, only crimson. The tallest is carrying a fiery torch. The other one is much shorter. When they're close enough, I recognize their faces: Cordelia and...Mira.

"Yatu, witches," Cordelia repeats, bringing up her left palm to show her red painted pentagram. Mira lifts her left hand, flashing the same symbol.

"Mira!" A few witches are happy to see her. Mira looks over but doesn't smile.

"Celebrating Thoth and Diana, Cadence?" asks Cordelia. "On a Monday? What a strange coven. You don't gather on the Sabbath, you choose Monday. No doubt Selene holds power, but this is very unorthodox. I can see why Raven and Blackbird left you."

"We come on behalf of the Abaddon coven," Mira says. She's deadpan. Morose. I squint at her. Typically, she's infamously smug and derisive, but tonight she looks depressing as hell. I'd rather she made fun of me. She doesn't seem like herself.

"This is our business!" snaps Tammy to Cordelia. "Your circle is evil."

Mira looks at me. "You invited me, Cadence."

"Yeah, I did. But I didn't expect you to come after you hung up the phone. Nor did I expect you to bring her."

"Sorry," Mira says. And for a second, I do see her old sly smile. "I brought a friend."

Adder is your friend?

There's an uncomfortable silence.

Do they really think we're just going to let down our guard and let them sit with us? Let them hear us discuss our plans to take back my best friend after they kidnapped her? So no one says a thing. They just stand over us staring as we stare back.

When they finally walk to our bonfire and add the flames of their torches to the fire, I say to Mira, "I need to talk to you alone."

"Fine." Mira nods.

The two of us leave the circle and walk across the backyard. From the corner of my eye, I watch a very uncomfortable coven squaring off against Cordelia.

Mira and I walk away from the house toward the forest. Alondra's backyard is large, and when we're beyond earshot and I'm about to say something, she beats me to it.

"Why are you threatening Enora?" She stops by a tree trunk and turns. It's dark but the full moon is bright enough for me to see her face. With her red hood and thick, dark goth makeup, she looks evil. But her expression is pained, as if I hurt her, which is ridiculous being that I fully believe Enora is attacking me. "I belong to Panthera now, Katie. You know that."

"Yeah. I know. Mira, Enora's messing with my dreams again. A month ago, she cast a spell on me and made me nearly cheat on Bryce. She hurt my brother, then she possessed my friend. Our friend. I want Maddie back. And I'll do anything to get her."

"It just isn't true, Kate," Mira says, shaking her head. "It's not true."

"Bring Maddie back to me."

"Maddie came to us," Mira says. "She's having a hard time. She said she had a fight with you. Then her boyfriend and her mom." Mira cracks a smile for the first time. "I heard about her and your brother." She gestures toward my friends. "Cadence, you're playing with fire. It's very dangerous to provoke her. I'm a powerful enough witch now to know you were considering a conjuring. You best be careful. Enora has a bad temper."

"No. We were talking about coming to see you. And it's Enora who's been provoking me."

"You took Beatrix into your home. You refused to give her back. Then you rejected your best friend. Enora gave her a home. What's the problem here?"

"Mira," I snap, quickly shaking my head. "I've had enough of this. Why do you think everything's all right? You hated Enora more than anyone last year. And Maddie was convinced that Enora killed Beatrix. Either you two are brainwashed, or something's up with your memory. Be straight with me. Deny to my face that Enora has been entering my dreams and casting spells."

"I can't deny it. I don't know. But you're not listening. I came to warn you. She views you as a threat because you're minding her business. My master's coven is her coven. Yours is yours. You're all meeting here to hurt us. Now deny *that*."

"You're calling her *master* now?" I ask in disbelief.

"So?"

"*Master?* Alondra never had us call her master. Certainly never me. We wouldn't have allowed it."

"This is what you do," Mira says with a sigh. "You judge people. You should just leave her alone. Maddie told me how you stopped speaking to her over your brother. Do you think that you're guiltless over everything—"

"He's my brother!" That makes me furious. "Fuck! Mira, your bitch 'master' knows exactly how to get under my skin. The fact that you don't see what's going on is incredible. You're either bullshitting me or you're under her spell. I'm sure Maddie is." I see Damie turn in the distance. I wasn't being discreet. All the witches are staring at us now. "Did she tell you about the car accident?"

She shakes her head. "Lies. These are lies. You have no proof that Enora did that. Of course Maddie told me, but there's more witchery in Georgia than just our two covens, Katie. I explained to Maddie that there are many satanic covens. Maddie doesn't blame Enora anymore. Why would you guys blame Enora for that? You have no proof. Cadence, if you knew my master better, you'd know that if it was her, she would have killed your brother, not hurt him."

I shake my head. "She's playing games. Why are you protecting her?"

"You're paranoid. You're as delusional as Beatrix."

Clouds develop over us, covering the clear sky. That's my anger. Mira looks up but she doesn't become afraid, she gets angrier.

"You violated our peace!" Mira closes her eyes and shakes her head. "I warn you. If you attack Enora, I'm on her side now. You're attacking me. We all know your powers, but with my help and my knowledge of spell-casting, I can make her equally strong. Be warned. If Enora entered your dreams, that was a warning too. Stay away. Stay away, or I can't tell you the harm that'll come of it."

Her eyes are ablaze in rage. I search them. I don't get it. What's she doing? Has she been hypnotized?

Then I think about that girl Mira talked about. When I told Mira about Beatrix's suicide, she seemed so concerned about her friend's welfare.

"It's the girl, isn't it?"

"What?"

"It's Beatrix's friend. That's why you're doing this. Beatrix told me Enora's dangling a carrot. Your new girlfriend. That's why you've betrayed us."

"I haven't betrayed you!" she says, shaking her head. Her rage leaves her, and she looks terribly depressed again. "I loved you," she says in a broken voice. "I would have stayed with you had you practiced real magic. Now it seems like the only way for your gang to assemble is to hurt us over fantasy."

"Fantasy?" I snap. "What do you mean, fantasy? She took you. Then she took Maddie. She'll destroy everything. She hates Bryce and she hates me. If you don't help us, she'll kill us."

"I just said I'm on her side. I'm a part of the Abaddon coven now. I'm not one of your sisters anymore."

"Then go! Get the fuck out! If you're not a part of my circle, Alondra wouldn't want you in her yard. Go love your girlfriend in ceremonies under your new master, the master who hanged your other friend by a rope."

I point and when I turn back, Mira looks like she's about ready to deck me. But she doesn't. Instead she quickly turns her back on me and rushes back to the fire.

There's a crack of thunder in the skies. It starts to rain. "*I want my friend!*" I shout. "Damn you, Mira! You hear me? I don't care about you! I want Maddie! Bring her back and I won't do anything to Enora. Just bring back my friend!"

"She's with us now."

Oh, no, she isn't! "Your master can have you! I don't care about you. But she can't have Maddie! Tell her that, Mira. She can't have Maddie. And stay away from this house! Don't ever come back! Alondra wouldn't want someone like you here anymore."

"We're leaving." Mira nods with her back still turned to me, but her voice cracks again.

My friends rush over to me.

"*You're not my friend anymore!*" I'm still screaming like crazy in the pouring rain.

Cordelia grabs their torches and runs to Mira. She puts an arm around Mira as if comforting her. That makes me even angrier. She's acting like I'm hurting her. As if Mira hasn't hurt me.

My friends catch up to me, turning to watch the two red-cloaked bitches quickly leave Alondra's side yard. They don't look back. The whole time, my friends stand behind me in silence. They just stare with me under the pouring rain.

"I'm going to Atlanta," I say to my witches. "With or without you."

Meeting adjourned.

20

———

ABADDON

I'm standing in the dark on a sidewalk, staring at the plain, boring white house, across a one-lane street, at the address that Gilda gave me. This is supposed to be Enora's new home in Atlanta. It's not what I expected. In my imagination, her house was a gothic fifteenth-century tower, all in black and white, sitting by its lonesome at the summit of a hill. Instead, her two-story house is wholly unremarkable, no different from any other house on the street. She's not far from downtown. I can see the windows of the skyscrapers a few miles away. There's a train of cars beside the road with windows open and heads hanging out, staring at the boring house too. These are my friends from my coven. Bryce is standing beside me. We're wearing heavy coats because it's really cold.

I look back and see my brother sitting in Bryce's BMW, waiting impatiently. He keeps asking in a hushed voice what we're doing.

I'm tired. It's early in the morning, around one o'clock. The drive from Hawthorne to downtown Atlanta takes two to three hours.

"Let's just knock," Bryce says. I finally turn and Bryce is smiling, with his hands in his pockets.

"Maybe I should have driven here alone. I'm putting you all in danger."

I hear a car door and see Gilda jumping out of her white SUV. She met us here from Savannah. She's worried about Mira and Maddie too.

"What the fuck's the matter?" Gilda asks, rushing to us. "Why are you guys just standing here?"

"Katie's getting cold feet," says Bryce.

"I'm not." *Okay, maybe I am.* I feel uneasy and a little queasy.

Gilda shakes her head and runs across the street, up a concrete path, and to the door. Bryce and I follow her. Then I hear another car door. It's my brother, standing impatiently on the sidewalk, eagerly watching us. Bryce signals for him to stay back.

Gilda knocks on the door.

The door swings open with laughter. A young girl with long blond hair and dark makeup, goth like ours, opens it. She's wearing a tight violet lace cami and gray sweatpants. She's attractive. She squints at us and laughs again. "What? Huh?"

"We're looking for Maddie," I say. "Is she here?"

"Who are you guys? It's really late."

"I'm Gilda. Is Madison here? We came a long way to see her."

The young girl just shrugs.

"What about Mira?" asks Gilda.

"Mira went someplace down to nowhereland," the girl says. "Some really boring college town in the woods or something."

But she should be back. We left a couple of hours after they did. For all I know, we were traveling together on the freeway.

"Is she here?" I ask, raising my eyebrows.

The teenager just shrugs annoyingly again.

"What about Maddie?" Bryce asks impatiently.

The girl turns and calls out Maddie's name. I look over her shoulder, hoping to see her. Directly behind her is the kitchen, lit by a dim yellow light. A girl with a protruding belly is standing by the kitchen entryway, wearing dark goth makeup and a black nightgown. She's smoking a cigarette and staring at us.

The room smells like incense mixed with perfume attempting to cover sweat, rotting food, and weed. Plastic chip bags, banana peels, and magazines are strewn all over the floor. A couple lying in each other's arms are asleep on a beat-up couch close to the door. The woman has only a thin T-shirt and underwear rising up her butt crack. The boy is in his underwear.

"Who are you?" I ask the girl who greeted us at the door.

"Courtney," says the girl. "How you guys know Blackbird and Raven? You close or something?"

"Friends from school," I say. "Can we come in?"

"Oh." Courtney puts her hand to her mouth and chuckles again. "Oops. Sorry. You guys must be from that place from nowhere."

Gus appears beside Courtney at the door. You know, the really tall, thin, deathly pale monster with long blond hair and a rippling shirtless chest, wearing only jeans. What a creep. I think he came from an adjoining room. He looks at Gilda and then Bryce. When he sees Bryce, I could almost swear Bryce stands on his tippy-toes.

"What's up, Courtney?" asks Gus. "These guys bugging you?"

"Nothing I can't handle," she says, running her fingers along his naked chest. She stumbles a little and Gus quickly hunches over to catch her.

"What do you want?" Gus snaps, looking at us.

"We want to—"

"They want to see Blackbird and Raven," Courtney says with a laugh, rubbing her hands along Gus's hard pecs again.

It finally dawns on me who this girl is. She must be Mira's lover, Courtney. The one I yelled at Mira about but couldn't recall her name. Mira said her lover's name was Courtney. Beatrix told me Courtney was her close friend. She looks young enough. So why is this girl, who's supposedly Mira's girlfriend, fondling Gus's chest?

"Do you have any idea what time it is?" asks Gus.

"It's important," I say. "We drove really far. If you can't show us Maddie, at least let me talk to Enora, the owner of this house."

"Enora's not the fucking owner of my house," Gus says with a laugh. He slaps his chest. "I am. And I'm not letting in people in the wee hours of the morning. Goddammit..." He looks at the couple sleeping on the couch. "Are you crazy? People are sleeping 'round here." Then Gus looks out at the five cars across the street. Some of my friends have their heads stuck out the windows again. "Hey, what the fuck's going on?" And he walks right up to Bryce.

"We told you," Bryce says, looking up to meet his gaze. "We're just here to see our friend Madison."

"Get the hell out of here," he says, sticking his finger in Bryce's chest. Bryce slaps his hand away. Then Gus raises his fist, ready to strike him.

"Stop it!" I snap. "We'll go, but not until—"

"I'm here, Cadence," says Mira. She is walking down a very dark stairway to our right. She looks solemn, like she did at Alondra's—no, even more depressed. She's wearing a thick turquoise robe and her hair's wet. All her makeup is off. It looks like she just showered.

By now the couple on the couch have woken up, and another three girls have rushed over from another room, standing near the girl smoking by the kitchen, staring at us.

"Get away from them, Gus," Mira says. Gus steps back. "Why did you come here? You guys crazy? You demanded Cordelia and I leave. I think, Cadence, you yelled that you never wanted to see me again. Now you're here? That was only a few hours ago, wasn't it? And now you're on Enora's hallowed ground. Are you nuts? After I came to warn you. And you think Maddie's crazy? Get out of here."

"Where is Maddie?"

"Get out of here, guys," Mira repeats. Then she sees the cars outside. She slowly shakes her head. "What the hell are you doing? Get out now."

"I'm not here for you. I'm here for Maddie."

"You made that plain enough." Mira looks at me and shakes her head again. "You have to be the most infuriating witch in the world, Cadence."

"Is she here?"

Mira rolls her eyes. "Yes."

"Can we see her?"

"Will you leave? If we prove she's safe, will you go?"

I nod.

Mira rolls her eyes again and walks over to Courtney, hugging her and kissing her passionately on the lips. Gus narrows his eyes. I have a feeling there's some sort of love triangle going on between the "vampire" and these two witches.

"This is Courtney, Cadence," Mira says with a big grin, still holding her in her arms. "On better terms, I would have loved to introduce you guys. But you hate me now, right? And anyway, Courtney's totally fucked up and baked."

"I'm not baked, Meer!" Courtney snaps.

"You are," she says with her old grin. "You're also drunk." Mira turns to Gus. "High Wizard, meet Cadence, the leader of the Hawthorne coven."

"We've met."

"She wants to see Maddie. Show her. I think Blackbird is in ceremony. Do you know if she's with Panthera underground?"

"She should be."

"But not you, Gus?"

"Not yet. I was told to wait until after the witching hour."

"Why don't you go take the three of them downstairs. Show them Maddie's safe. Then they'll leave."

"Okay, Raven," he says.

"She won't want to go back with you," Mira adds with a shrug. Then she pecks Courtney on the cheek one more time. She turns from us and heads sleepily back up the stairs.

As Mira walks upstairs, she cocks her head back. "Oh, and by the way, Cadence, fuck off. I don't care about you either."

"Goodbye, Mira," says Gilda. Gilda looks confused. I think she thought it was really weird Mira didn't even say hello.

"Bye." But Mira doesn't look back.

"Shall we?" Gus asks, showing his filed teeth and fangs. He gestures to the door.

Gus walks out into the night shirtless. Of course, Gilda, Bryce, and I are still wearing coats. I think Gus goes out without a shirt to be tough. He even scowls at the other members of my coven in their cars. Damie jumps out of the car again, and Bryce and I shout and gesture once more for him to stay back.

We walk around the house to a side metal gate. This dark iron gate creaks open into the backyard beside a wall separating the yard from the neighbors'.

The backyard is just a small dirt lot. Tall trees surround the cement walls of the house. By the far end of the yard is a small wooden shedlike structure. It's wide but very short, looking too shallow for anyone to stand in. On the shed, in the dim moonlight, there's a painted red lion. And surrounding the caricature of the lion, in the same red paint, are small backward pentagrams and crosses.

Gus lifts a heavy metal door. Warm air rushes from inside. Steep concrete steps are lit by red smoke at the bottom. That makes me lurch back. Bryce tugs on my hand, but I don't want to go down there. This is exactly what I saw in my dream.

"One of the perks when I bought this house was this old nuclear fallout shelter," says Gus with a chuckle. "Wait till you see the space. It's huge. It's ready for Armageddon. You know, when the nations of this world finally lob bombs, this will be the safest place in Atlanta. I think it's the only shelter for miles. It's really cool, but the steps are muddy as hell, so watch your step. Guests have been known to slip and get hurt. Wouldn't want that. Watch your step. And head."

I smell incense trying to cover the smell of sulfur and burning meat. The same smells from in my nightmare. But it's brighter than it was in my dream. The red is almost blinding. And there are no drumbeats or whispering chants. I feel unsettled. Usually with this much stress, I'd feel magic. I don't. I just feel fear.

When we make it to the bottom, another metal door opens into a very large chamber. It's warmer, almost hot, here. Once again, like in my dream, there is a thick red fog, but this time no central bonfire. But the walls and ceilings of the chamber are the same gray concrete with backward pentagrams and crosses scrawled in red paint. The room is very large. It could fit three rooms of a house, I think. But there's a drab, dirty carpet and sparse raggedy furniture lying around. At the farthest end of the room is a circle of witches wearing the crimson cloaks of the Abaddon coven. They're kneeling with their hoods over their heads, and in the middle of the circle is a couple. The couple is naked, a man on top of a woman, on what appears to be a very large brown cowhide rug. The woman has small antlers tied to her head. Unlike in my dream, the witches surrounding the couple are calm. They're just observing instead of bowing and worshipping. It's almost as if they're studying the act. Other than the couple, the room is quiet.

"We buy the men," explains Gus, talking softly to Gilda. "We advertise it as a modeling job. Of course the witches in our coven like handsome ones. So when I'm not fucking the girls, like tonight, we hire models. They take mandrake and become disoriented. If they have moral problems when they wake, Enora threatens to kill them. Of course few of the models have ever dared challenge us." Then he shines his fangs at Bryce and me. "Those that do become a different sort of sacrifice, if you know what I mean? It's one of the advantages of living near downtown. You guys use models in your coven?" Gus is not asking for a response; he's trying to intimidate us. He's a real asshole.

"You're disgusting," I say.

That makes him smile, showing his carved animal teeth. My disgust satisfies him.

A few witches hear us talking and turn. One rises. As she walks over, I can just make out the infernal face under the red hood. I'd recognize those pretty features anywhere. Enora.

"Welcome," Enora whispers. "It's been a long time, Red Fox. Welcome. And Bryce."

"Mira asked me to bring them," Gus says quietly. "They want to see one of their friends, Blackbird."

"Well, you saw Mira, didn't you, Windstorm? Wasn't Mira once one of your friends?"

Oooh, I hate her!

Enora walks over to Gus and kisses him passionately on the lips in front of us. She makes out with him while rubbing his chest. Gus runs his hands inside her cloak and fondles her breasts. Enora's completely naked underneath her cloak. He runs his hand slowly down, opening the cloak more, so we can see her silhouette, caressing her chest and down over her butt.

"Well done," Enora says, releasing her lips. "Well done. Return to the house. Guard it from the rest of them. Make sure none of the others step out of their cars. If they do, put them back in, would you?"

"I don't like them," Gus says, shaking his head. "I don't like the way they look."

She takes his hand and pats it. "Just don't touch them unless they leave their cars. 'Kay?"

He nods.

"Prepare my room for later," she says, reaching up and kissing him again.

"Tonight?" he asks, suddenly opening his eyes wide. He breathes more heavily in rapture. "Oh, tonight, my love?"

"Your reward, my dear," Enora says, patting his hand again. "Your reward."

The beast leaves. Enora turns to me and loses her smile.

"I need not ask what you think of us. I can already see it in your eyes."

"You're disgusting."

Enora laughs. A couple of witches turn toward us. Others continue to watch the sex show.

"Perhaps you three would like to partake in our sacrifice?" Enora asks with a laugh. "There's vital energy when it comes to lovemaking, especially with confused men. This one's quite handsome, don't you think, Cadence? Did you see his penis?"

"Where's Maddie?" I ask.

Enora looks at me, confused, and turns to Bryce. "I would be willing to consider you two as replacements." She runs her hand along Bryce's arm. "But not you. No, not you. You know, Gus may be well endowed and a good caretaker, but he's not smart. Oh, how I missed jousting with your mind, Bryce. And you were bright enough to keep up with me, weren't you? No, I'm not going to let you into our fucking ceremony. I would much rather hurt you."

"Where's Maddie!" I snap. "We came for her. We'll take her and leave."

The witches who were watching the couple suddenly whirl around and hiss like snakes at my outburst. The couple having sex seem disturbed too. They stop moving.

"Shh, Cadence," Enora says, putting a finger to her lips. "Your tantrum is messing up my ceremony."

"Where is she?" I repeat. "Where's my friend?"

"Blackbird," Enora says, turning to the witches in the circle. "Sister Madison Taylor. Please exit the circle and come here."

One of the witches in red cloaks slowly gets up and walks over. When she takes her hood down, I nearly fall apart, fighting back tears.

"Maddie," I say, "come back with us."

"Please, Maddie," Bryce says.

Maddie says nothing. Then she looks at Enora. At first, I don't know why, but then I surmise it's to ask permission to speak. Apparently, this is how much control the bitch holds over them. Enora nods.

"Why are you here?" Maddie asks me. Tears form in her eyes, and she violently shakes her head. "Go. Get out of here, Cadence. Hurry. Leave. It's not safe. This is Enora's coven."

"Maddie, come back to us," says Gilda. "We're so worried about you."

"*Come back to us,*" a few red-cloaked witches repeat quietly. "*We're so worried about you.*" And as they mock us, many of the witches in red cloaks rise and stand behind Enora. The man who was having sex falls on his knees with his head in his hands. He seems sick. The nude woman with antlers gets up and walks over to a bunch of red cloaks hanging on the wall, nonchalantly throwing one over her naked body. Then she joins the other Abaddon witches surrounding us.

"Master, you told me you'd leave them alone," Maddie says to Enora. She shakes her head as if trying to shake off Enora. "You promised. You lied to me. I was right about you. I shouldn't have trusted you. Now Katie's here? What are you planning to do to her?"

"Well," Enora says, walking right up to Maddie. "I wasn't expecting this tonight. She's early. See, Friday you were going to give yourself to Gus. If little Katie had seen you then, that might have been enough to make her lose her senses."

"Let's go, Maddie," I say. "She's crazy."

"You swore!" Maddie cries to Enora. "You swore you'd leave them alone if I joined!"

Enora nods to Gus, who's standing behind Maddie. The man lifts Maddie from behind and pins her arms behind her.

"Let her go!" I shout.

"*Sopor,*" Enora says, displaying the painted pentagram on her left palm to me. "*Sopor.*" It makes me so drowsy. Enora signals to some of her witches, and they walk over and grab me, pinning my arms behind my back. For some reason, I can't fight. I'm so weak.

"Madison, I didn't lie to you," Enora says, turning back to her. "You're still a Hawthorne witch. You can't join us. I didn't lie because you can't live up to your end of the bargain."

"What are you doing?" I ask. It's strange, but it takes all my effort to just ask the question. I feel as if I'm in a dream again. I barely have enough energy to open my eyes.

"I don't need her, Windstorm," Enora replies, cocking her head back. "I have you. Now I have my true sacrifice." Enora addresses the witches who are now standing around us. "Take Bryce and chain him to the wall. He won't give up his seed, so instead I will hurt him."

My eyes open wide. I cry out with all my energy, "*Ad infernum! Exite! Ad infernum! Exite! Exite!*" From my chest to my head, I focus my energy and imagine Enora being thrown back. But nothing happens. There's silence. Enora and her witches stare at me. Then... Enora chuckles nervously.

"No incantation can hurt me here," Enora says. "You're too weak."

Three witches who I don't recognize grab Bryce. Bryce struggles, but he seems too weak. They drag him over to the wall, where there are handcuffs on chains.

"Bryce!" I cry out.

"*Bryce*," repeat some of the witches. "*Bryce.*"

"What's going on!" Gilda asks. She seems to be the only one able to move now. "What are you doing? We just came to take Maddie home."

"Oh, you're free to go, Red Fox," Enora says, waving a hand dismissively. "You're not a part of the Hawthorne coven anymore."

"Let them go," Gilda mutters desperately. Gilda looks at me and Bryce and shakes her head.

When Gilda doesn't move, Enora's eyes open wide. "Go! Get the fuck out of here. Go before I change my mind. *Run!*"

Gilda runs. I hear her rush up the cement steps.

Enora walks right up to Bryce as they chain him to the wall. I try with all my might to fight her, but I can't even move my legs. I'm standing, but completely immobile. Then my heart pounds as I watch her run her fingers along Bryce's beard, over his face, his chest and down to his legs. But he's as immobile as I am.

"Bryce, you're as gullible as little Katie. Why didn't you stay away from here? You knew it wasn't safe. You've changed. You were always so responsible...except that night." She licks his ear and says, "Oh, for that night, I loathe you. I shall never forgive you."

"Don't touch him!" I yell.

"Pity you didn't get to marry him, Cadence," Enora says, looking back at me. Then she walks up to me and raises her left palm, showing the pentagram again. "*Sopor. Sopor.* Sleep. Shh. Sleep, Windstorm. Sleep. Don't fight it." I'm standing, but I can't move. I can barely open my eyes. "You're not dumb. You just do dumb things. It took me a year to plan this. You thought you could just walk in?"

I can't open my mouth.

"I thought that it'd be enough to take Mira." She taps her black nail on the center of my chest. "I thought she'd send you running over, but I was wrong. Your friendship with her was weak. In your snobbish mind, she wasn't good enough. Well, no matter, I used that too. I gave her Courtney so I could get her to work magic against you." She looks down for a moment, and when her eyes look back at me, they're solid pearly-white. She wags her stupid finger at my nose. "You see, Mira likes you, only she likes Courtney more."

Behind her, her witches slowly surround me whispering: "*Sacrificium consecratum. Sacrificium consecratum. Sacrificium consecratum.*"

"I can't get myself to forgive Bryce," Enora says, shaking her head. "Sorry, I never will. I wanted to kill him in Hawthorne, but Alondra's ghost stopped me. Or...you stopped me. But now that he's here, he's mine."

I can't respond.

"I will bleed you," she says with a nod, staring at me with solid pearly-white eyes. "If I can't destroy your book, I will destroy Windstorm. Not you, but the High Priestess. Every day until Friday, I will bleed you, undoing the magic given to you in your initiation. With the magic of the Abaddon coven, Windstorm will be no more. Then, though you'll feel sicker than now, I'll enjoy watching your expression as I slice Bryce's throat."

"Don't...touch...him!" I blurt, my tongue slurring each word.

"What are you gonna do?" she asks with a sly smile.

My eyes fall on Maddie. With all the strength I can muster, I stammer, "I'm soorry...I...loovve you." Tears run down her face and she nods.

"Oh, stop," Enora says, closing her eyes and shaking her head. "Just stop. Don't feign kindness. You're an evil witch. The only reason it took so long for me to trap you is because of your selfishness. I don't think you care about anyone. You certainly don't care about Mira.

"The last days will be unpleasant. I will bleed you. Slowly. Other covens will hear. They'll judge me, but I think they'll be on my side when they hear how you stole one of my witches and she killed herself. I will bleed you. Your blood, the blood of Escoba and Maverick, will be the most powerful of sacrifices. With it, I will finally destroy Hawthorne."

She comes up to me and runs her disgusting fingers along my cheek. Her eyes are still solid white. I feel no control of my head. I can't even turn away from her.

"You will suffer. But don't worry. After all is done and you're just a normal little girl again, I'll let you go back and study."

She smiles, but then she narrows her eyes.

"*Sacrificium consecratum!*" All her other witches join her, echoing her words. "*Let the first drop fall now, Windstorm!*" She pulls out a curved dagger from her robe and slices my arm. Bryce cries out from the wall.

I'm dizzy. There's so much pain. I fall backward and witches behind me grab me. Everything blurs. The pain is unbearable. Enora laughs and licks my blood from the end of her blade. My arm stings. When I open my eyes and look down, some of her red-cloaked witches are on their knees, feasting on the blood dripping from my fingers. When I try to say something, only a grunting sound comes forth.

"Our real Sabbath is in four days, blasphemer. Four days. This will be the end of the Hawthorne High Priestess. Perhaps that will teach you the importance of a witch's traditions. Friday. Sabbath. Never have a gathering on another day, unless it is one of our holidays. And never come to a witch's coven uninvited." Then Enora looks at the witches surrounding my feet. "Take her into the supply room. Let her and her best friend spend their last days together, since little Katie wants to talk to her friend so badly. That is why you came, right?"

21

THE SUPPLY ROOM

"KATIE, WAKE UP. COME ON. WAKE UP, CADENCE! WAKE UP."

I blink my eyes. I'm lying on my side. I'm so weak. My hand, pressing against the floor, feels like ice. The air is cold too. Maddie's standing over me, shaking me.

"What... what's happening?"

I look up at the gray concrete ceiling. There are three recessed lights and a fire alarm above me. I wince. There's an unbearable sharp pain along my arm.

"Cadence, you collapsed when they threw us in the room. Then I blacked out too. It must be Enora's spell."

I can't move. Maddie carries me and props me against the wall. The wall is concrete and as cold as the floor. It smells. It smells of feces and urine. And a metallic putrid smell. Blood. Behind all the unpleasant smells is a background scent of food. I see the source—there are wooden shelves along one wall filled with stored food: canned foods, cereal, bags of rice, soda, and water. We can survive here for a long time, even if they keep us locked up. I don't see any candles. If they turn off the ceiling lights, it will be pitch black.

I see a flash of Enora's pearl-white eyes in my mind. That reminds me of why Maddie and I are alone in the concrete room.

"How... how long have we been here?"

"I don't know." Maddie shakes her head, looking around the room.

Her black makeup is smeared on her face, and she's still naked under her red witch cloak. I'm not. I'm still wearing my red coat and blue jeans.

I think of Bryce chained to the wall. That's enough for me to stumble to my knees. I tip over and Maddie catches me. I see blood dripping on the gray floor from a large gash in my left arm.

"You have it worse than me," Maddie says. "That bitch cut you. She cut you real bad."

I look up into her eyes. She looks pained. So sad. She forces a smile.

"I'm sorry, Maddie. God, I'm so sorry. Can you forgive me?"

She nods. "I know." She tears up and looks around the room. "I know. I am too, babe. And now it's my fault that we're in this mess. I'm always getting us into trouble."

"I thought you were blaming me?" I ask, actually managing a faint grin.

She shakes her head hard. "I know you came for me. I love you more than anything in the world, Katie. Even with our fight, I never stopped loving you."

"Did you know Enora was going to attack?"

"Of course not." Maddie shakes her head. "I saw bad things happening here, but she was always nice on the surface. She used me. I should have seen through it. But I've been in a trance. I've been so upset that it flipped me into a trance, like you. At first, I was proud of myself, thinking I was finally feeling my power as a witch. My wandering, you know, from the initiation was never very—"

"You went out again," Maddie says.

I feel myself being propped up against a wall. I touch the wall. It's cold.

"The supply room?" She looks at me with an empty expression. "We have to get out of here and help Bryce."

I struggle to rise, but then I feel so dizzy. She helps me lean back against the wall. "Outside are the rest of our friends. They're waiting by the street. God knows what that creepy Gus is doing to them."

"He's a vampire."

"What?"

"He lives off blood," Maddie says with a nod. "I've seen it. At first, we just saw the fangs, but he really does everything he can to live like a vampire. He never eats real food. He gets most of the blood from the hospital. And Enora uses magic to strengthen him. He's like her dog, but he's inhumanly strong. He's the strongest man I've ever seen, Kate. But he's part of the sick stuff I've seen here too. I've watched him beat up strangers on the streets. He does it just to make them bleed. Then he drinks their blood."

"Gross."

Maddie nods.

"Well, this *vampire* is outside with my brother. Our Damie."

"*Our* Damie, Cadence?" Maddie smiles faintly.

I roll my eyes. "We'll figure that out later."

The metal door swings open. Maddie gasps when Mira, still wearing her blue night robe, is thrown into the room by two witches wearing red cloaks. The door is slammed behind her.

"You fuckers!" cries Mira, jumping up and spinning back toward the door. "For everything I did! All my sacrifice! Damn you all!" She slowly turns to us as if noticing us for the first time. She throws her dark hair back, takes a deep breath, and straightens her blue night robe. Then she gives us a big wave. "Hi, guys."

"You bitch!" I run to tackle her, but I don't have the strength. I fall on the ground right in front of her. She actually reaches down to help me up. "We're in this mess because of you!"

"Sorry," Mira says, looking down at me. "I warned you at Alondra's. I warned you to stay away."

"Why did you trust her?"

"Katie," Maddie says, grabbing me and helping me up. "We can't fight now."

"I should be fighting with you too," I snap, snatching my arm back. But I feel woozy again, ready to faint. I put my head in my hand. The room spins. I say more quietly, "God, what happened to you two? If you wanted to be stupid, leave Bryce and me out of it. She's gonna kill him."

"She's gonna kill all of us," Mira says. She seems surprisingly contemplative.

We stop talking. We just sit in the center of the room, feeling hopeless. I wait for my nausea to pass. Then Mira starts crying.

The room smells disgusting. That's not helping my nausea. I glance at the pile of towels at the corner of the room and finally realize that's the source. It's a "bathroom." No doubt there's human excrement on those towels. Where else do prisoners go to the bathroom?

"What can we do?" I ask, looking at Maddie. She doesn't look at me. She just shakes her head. I stand up slowly. I'm grateful for enough energy to do that. Mira's still bawling on the floor.

I dawdle over to the shelves and start looking for things that can be used to open the door. A crowbar would be nice. I'd even settle for a hammer and chisel. But I'm so weak that I'm leaning against the cabinet in order to stand.

"Mira, shut up and help me find a way out."

Mira just shakes her head and cries.

"Have others been thrown in here?" I ask.

"Yes, prisoners," Mira says.

"Why would you join this coven knowing they kept prisoners!" I say.

"They were criminals. And she let them go free after our ceremonies. That's what she told me, anyway."

"You hated Reardon for sex ceremonies. So did Enora. Why would you guys do them again?"

"I don't want to talk about it."

"Yeah," I say, putting my hands on my hips and glaring at her. "Well, you have to. Start talking. You got us in this mess. You've been here longer than anyone. Get up and help me find a way out so I can help Bryce."

But Mira keeps shaking her head, staring at the ground.

"You're still bleeding, Katie." Maddie touches my arm. It's dripping with blood. "You're not only dizzy from a spell, you're losing blood. The first thing we should do is find a bandage or something to stop the bleeding."

"No. Don't worry about me."

"You need to be strong," Maddie says, shaking her head.

I turn my back to her and start searching the shelves. I throw cracker and cereal boxes on the ground, desperately searching for something to use to get out of this pantry from hell.

Mira cries again. That takes me over the edge.

"Why did you join her!"

"For the magic!" Mira snaps between tears. "Okay! I told you."

"No, you did it for Courtney. For sex with her. You'd been hitting on me since we met. You did it to have sex with her." Then I turn to Maddie. "And as for you, I don't understand you either."

"I told you I fell into a trance," Maddie says, putting up a hand. "But we can't fight now, Cadence."

"I helped Enora put a spell on her," Mira explains miserably between tears. "Enora lied to me and told me it was to bring Maddie to us. I...I was fooled into thinking Maddie wanted to come here. I thought I was just helping Enora communicate with her."

"Just shut up," I say, shaking my head. "I don't want to hear any more."

Mira doesn't object. She just cries. But Mira's not a crybaby, crying all the time, like Beatrix. It's just that once she starts, she can't stop. During Alondra's funeral, she bawled through the whole service.

Maddie finds bandages. She takes two out of a box, rolls up the sleeves of my red coat and shirt, and sticks them on my gaping wound. It doesn't stop the bleeding. I ignore my arm and keep searching the cabinets. I don't care about me. But I do have to pause a few times and close my eyes to fight off the spinning sensation.

"They won't open the door until Friday," Maddie says. "It's no use. They figure we can survive until then. Then they'll gather us and ceremonially sacrifice us. Probably kill us."

"There must be something we can do?" I look up at the ceiling. There's the small fire alarm near the recessed lights. Hmm... "What about the fire alarm? Can we set it off?"

"Even if you could start a fire, what are you going to do?" asks Maddie. "We'll die of asphyxiation or smoke. They won't open the door."

"I think they will. They won't let their shelter burn. If they hear the alarm coming from the room, they'll open the door and we can fight our way out."

"They'll let us burn to death," interjects Mira miserably. She's sitting on the ground, leaning on her hands now. At least she stopped crying.

"Mira, Enora needs us Friday," Maddie says. "Why? Why on the Sabbath?"

"If Enora bleeds Cadence in ceremony," Mira says, wiping her nose with the sleeve of her robe, "she'll get rid of her power. Just as Cadence got her power from blood, Enora can take it away by bleeding her in a ceremony with her coven. Once she does that, it's like burning her book. She can destroy the coven. She hates Hawthorne. Alondra. Bill. And Bryce." Mira rises slowly. Then she throws her long hair back and straightens her robe. "She hates me, I suppose. I see that now. She lured you here for the right time to strike. It was all to get you here."

"But why?"

"She'll never forgive Hawthorne. She told me she felt publicly humiliated. She only let Bryce go because you stopped her on Hilltop Bluff, but she intends to kill him. She's told me otherwise, but I can see through her lies now. She's been scheming since. When she recruited me, I thought it was just plain jealousy over Katie's power. That's what she told me. She said she needed me to make the Abaddon coven greater than Hawthorne's. But now I see she just wants to destroy the coven."

"If she's so upset about rape, why would you guys hold sex ceremonies again?" I ask. Mira doesn't like that. For a second, she clams up.

"Our ceremonies are different," Mira says, staring at the ground. "Here, it's men who are drugged, not women. Strangers. Criminals. For the women, it's voluntary. Not so for the men. Except...for rare punishment."

"And that makes it better?"

"For Enora, yes. You know a sex sacrifice is powerful magic. In a way, for Enora, using men is part of her revenge. But I, I don't want to talk about it anymore, Cadence."

"Because you're guilty with Courtney."

"Guys, stop!" cries Maddie. "Please. We have to work together."

"Why?" Mira asks. "I don't give a fuck what Katie says. We're as good as dead anyway."

Well, I don't want to talk to her. I've had enough of her.

I return to looking frantically along the shelves. Maddie watches over my shoulder, but I can't find a single lighter or match in all the boxes on the shelves.

"It won't work, Katie," Maddie says. "I've seen terrible things here. They'll let us die if you set the alarm off. They're animals."

"What else can we do?"

I have some hope when I find cleaning materials. One section of the cabinet is storage for household bleach and toilet bowl cleaner. Beside them are combustible things like paper towels and plates, but nothing to light them on fire. That's when Mira surprises me by walking up from behind and handing me a piece of steel wool. I look at her like she's nuts.

"Here," Mira says, "if you want to start a fire and kill us, this will do. Maybe I deserve it."

"What's this?"

"There's some batteries stored on the second shelf over there." Mira points. "Take a nine-volt and rub it against the wool. It will cause sparks and start a fire. All we have to do is place it near the alarm."

"How do you know that?"

"Mom and Dad loved camping," Mira says with a shrug. "It was the first time I started to like the outdoors. They were the only vacations my sister and I ever had as kids."

"You have a sister?"

"I told you that a long time ago," Mira says condescendingly.

"This will work?" I ask again, holding the silvery piece of metal in front of her. "You're sure?"

"With a battery, yeah. It'll start a fire that will burn us alive in the supply room, Cadence, if that's what you want. I suppose you're my High Priestess again. Upon your command, we can die together."

"I want to see Bryce," I say, holding the piece of metal as if it's a lifeline. "I want to make sure he's okay. And my brother. And the rest of our gang."

"You're still bleeding," Mira says, looking at my arm.

"So?"

"No," Mira says. Then she points to the line of blood following me from the center of the room. "You need to be strong. Maddie's right." She takes my arm. I look at her funny and snatch my arm back.

"Not now."

"Stop being stubborn, Cadence. Give me your arm."

I hand it back. Mira closes her eyes. *"Claude,"* she says. Then she repeats it again and again, hovering her palm over my bloody arm. *Claude. Claude. Claude.*

Before my eyes, the gash running down my forearm closes and the blood stops dripping. Mira looks down and smiles at her work.

"How'd you do that?"

"Magic," Mira says. Then she touches my chest and closes her eyes. At first, I'm not sure what she's doing. Then I feel energy. Some of the weakness I've felt since seeing Enora is lifted from my chest. "I'm getting better," Mira says to me, opening her eyes. "I told you I had my first wandering a couple months ago. You might not agree with left-sided magic, but it's made me very powerful."

"Mira, how can you have magic when Katie doesn't?" asks Maddie.

"I'm an Abaddon witch," she says with a shrug. "I renounced your circle. This is my hallowed ground."

"Then Katie can," says Maddie excitedly.

"No. I was initiated into Enora's coven. My magic still works here, hers doesn't."

"Then get us the fuck out!" I cry. I can't believe this. I mean—*really?* If she can do this, why are we yapping? Why doesn't she just open the goddamn door!

"I don't have your power, Cadence. I can't break open the door. And I can't start a fire out of thin air like you can."

"What can you do?"

"Simple things. Healing spells, like that one. I can kindle a fire, I suppose. But I'm not..." And she really annoys me with this smug grin. "Not a Firestarter like you."

I turn from her stupid grin because I'm about to slug her. I stare at the metal wire and battery again. "So how does this work with the battery?"

"You just rub it. If we do it under the fire alarm, it should go off. But it could also light up the cabinets. And if they don't open the door, the smoke could kill us."

"Show me, Mira. Start the fire."

We look up at the fire alarm. The problem is the cell has a high ceiling. Mira tries to climb the cabinet, but she's nowhere near the fire alarm at the center of the ceiling.

"We could just light it down here."

"No," I say. "I'll carry you up."

"I'm too heavy. And you and Maddie are too weak. We can light it and carry it up there. I'll rub the battery along the coils. But ..." She grabs a broomstick near the cleaning items. "I'll attach it to this with some paper towels."

"What do we do when they run in?" asks Maddie. "We don't have any magic."

"We just fight," I say.

"I have a little magic left in me," Mira says while tying the metal coils to the broom. "I can conjure up an illusion of smoke. I can make the fire appear much worse than it is. Hopefully, you two won't have to fight at all. They'll run."

I nod. So does Maddie.

"Okay," Mira says, "but even if we get out of here, how are we going to stop them? We're outnumbered. And if Gus is there, forget it. I've seen that man pin down five people."

"We have to," I say. "God knows what he's doing to Bryce."

Mira gets to work on her homemade broomstick torch. Then, after she inspects it, she says, "Okay. I can light it when you're ready."

"The fire alarm is our diversion," I say to both of them. "They'll be in a panic. Do what you can to make them think the cell is burning completely, Mira. Build up the smoke with your spell. Can you do that?"

"Of course. Not sure I can unlock the chains on your boyfriend's wrists though. But usually in ceremonies, we leave keys along the altar."

"Well, if the cell really does catch fire and Bryce is trapped, he'll die. Then I'll die with him. I'm not going to leave him down here. If he goes, I go."

"Wish Courtney loved me that much," Mira says with a shrug.

"When, Katie?" asks Maddie.

"Now. But, Mira, what if they're not outside the door? How will they hear the alarm?"

"Gus rigged the alarms to sound in the house. You might be right about this, Cadence. I think he cares more about his chamber than the house. So does Enora."

"If all works well," I say with a nod, "we'll race up the stairs, free Bryce, and make a run for it."

Mira nods. But she looks worried. I'm really worried too.

"It could work," Mira says.

"Best friends forever?" Maddie asks with a wry grin.

I hug her tightly. "Forever." Then I reach for Mira. She looks surprised and slowly joins our embrace.

"I love you guys," I say. "When we get out of here, *forever and ever.* Okay?"

Maddie smiles. Mira just nods.

22

MIRA'S CAMPFIRE

It surprises me how fast the fire alarm sounds. It seems like all Mira had to do was wave her burning broomstick on the ground to set it off. The shrill sound irritates my ears. Then Mira makes it worse. She places her hands together, as if in prayer, and dips her head down while standing in concentration. Gray smoke starts covering the whole cell. And it's weird because I expect to cough, but I don't. The smoke is an illusion. It's her conjuring.

I hear noise from outside the door. There's banging and people are shouting. We all stand to the right side of the door, waiting for it to open.

The door swings open. A woman with black tattoos on her face rushes in: Cordelia. But the minute she enters, she's covered in smoke. She starts screaming. All three of us duck around her. More witches circle the exit—most are wearing red cloaks—and we have to shove our way out.

Bryce is still chained to the wall, staring at the growing cloud of smoke.

"Katie," he says with a big grin.

I yank at his wrists, but they're chained. I pull as hard as I can, but they won't budge. Of course they won't; they're chained to the wall.

"By the altar," Mira reminds me, running there.

I look at the altar and see what I don't want to see. Enora. She's walking over to us with her head down and those creepy white eyes raised. The smoke is surrounding her, but she doesn't care. I feel weak as she approaches. She's casting a spell again. Bryce says something to me in a panic, but I can barely hear his words. I collapse. By my side, Enora stands over me. She crouches down to touch me, but then someone comes behind her and tackles her. I see a turquoise robe. It's Mira. Mira throws me the keys then rolls with Enora on the ground.

"*Vade retro!*" cries Mira. "Black witch! *Vade retro! Vade retro!*"

"Traitor!" cries Enora. "Me? Black witch? What the fuck do you think you are!"

With all the energy I have left, I pull myself up. For Bryce. The room is rocking as if I'm on a boat. I am so sick.

I see a red cloak. I jerk away, thinking it's a witch from the Abaddon coven, but then I see her face. It's Maddie. Maddie grabs the keys from my hand and jumps up to unlock Bryce's restraints. Enora and Mira continue to wrestle on the ground. The rest of the witches are running to the stairs, away from the smoke, as we planned, thinking the chamber is on fire.

Everything blurs.

There are glimpses of houses and a road as I blink. Streetlights. Cars. I recognize Bryce's dark gray BMW. It's cold. It feels so cold. I'm outside on the street. Bryce's bright blue eyes are looking down at me with sweet concern, and for a moment, I feel peace. I can't remember how I got here, but I don't really care.

I sit up with his help. Then I try to focus. I see Enora's house. That's when I remember. My sickness returns.

An orange hue forms above the houses. The sun is rising.

"Take it easy, Cadence," says Bryce, holding me.

Others crouch down and touch me. My friends. My coven. All of them are hovering over me. They never left. Maddie's recovering too. I see her under a streetlamp near Bryce's car, still wearing a red cloak, being held by Damie.

"Where's Mira?" I ask Bryce. Bryce loses his smile. That's enough to prompt me to sit up.

"Katie," Bryce says, "take it easy." But I don't want to take it easy.

I stand up facing the Abaddon witch house. My friends look at me really oddly, probably because I was struggling to open my eyes a second ago. Now I'm standing up straight, full of energy. In fact, I feel really strong. I understand. I'm slipping into a trance again. *My* magic is growing now that I'm away from that devilish house.

"We need to get Mira," I say to Bryce. "She saved us."

"We can't," Bryce says, shaking his head. "We have to go."

"We have to go," Tammy echoes, touching my shoulder. "Every time we go anywhere near there, we're thrown back. Sometimes it's an illusion, other times it's Gus. There's no way in. We already tried to get you guys out."

I look at Frida, who nods sadly.

"We have to try," I insist.

I walk over to Maddie and Damie. Maddie appears to be asleep in his arms. I reach down and touch her shoulder. She looks up at me and smiles sweetly.

"Better?" I ask.

"Yeah," she says sleepily.

Then Maddie furrows her brow, looking at me. She opens her eyes wide, staring at my arm. "Look, Cadence." I follow her eyes to my arm. There's no cut. Not even a healed cut. Even the sleeve of my red coat, which had been sliced open, is whole again.

"You're better," she says. I am better.

But then I hear my friends gasp. Maddie's eyes bulge out of their sockets over something across the street behind my shoulder. I hear an odd growl. I turn.

Gus, still shirtless and baring his fangs, charges berserko at us like a bull. He leaps over the hood of a car across the street, growls, and runs toward Maddie and me. Bryce jumps in front of the car to protect us. I yell to my friends, "Get behind me." They obey, but it's too late for Bryce.

The vampire leaps on my boyfriend and slams him against the car. The impact is so violent that it dents the side of his BMW and cracks the back passenger-side window. They struggle on the car, and in horror, I catch the beast trying to bite my boyfriend's neck.

"Cadas!"

Gus falls like a stone before Bryce. I stand over Gus, wanting to hurt him more, but then I hear my name being called from the house. Enora is in the front yard with all her witches in red cloaks. Then I see Mira. Still in a blue-green robe, she's being led by two of them with her hands tied behind her back.

"Nuh, uh, uh, Cadence," Enora yells. "Play nice or your friend gets it."

"Let Mira go!" I cry.

"Come get her. You never cared about her before."

"Let her go!" I grab Gus by the arm and drag the huge beast across the street. "I have him. I'll hurt him."

"Keep him," she says. "I've had enough of him. I'd much rather punish Raven. If you'd like, Katie, you can stay and watch."

"Let Mira go, Enora," cries Bryce. He's wincing and holding his right arm. It looks like Gus might have dislocated his shoulder.

"I get Mira and you keep Gus," I say, still dragging the huge man. "And then we call it even. Okay?"

All the red witches walk to the edge of the lawn and stop by the sidewalk. I drag Gus all the way up to the line of red-cloaked women and toss him at them. They help him up onto the grass.

"There," I say, standing on the sidewalk facing Enora. "Now give me Mira."

"No," Enora says, walking right up to me. Her mouth is bleeding. Good. It appears Mira hit her before she was subdued. "You took Beatrix. I get Mira."

"You killed Beatrix!"

It's weird. She's about a foot from the sidewalk, but she doesn't dare cross. Even with those beastly empty white eyes. Neither do her witches. And, as much confidence as I have while I'm in a trance, I'm remembering my sickness in her house. I'm afraid to cross her property line too. Just the thought of walking over there makes me sick.

"What a cruel accusation," Enora says. "Manthis was my sister. Don't worry, this isn't over. You might have stopped the Sabbath, but there'll be others."

Then she wags a finger, about to say something else, but the minute her digit crosses the line of the sidewalk, her hand bursts into flame. My anger is so strong that just the thought of burning her is enough to start a fire. Enora steps back, wailing. She covers the fire with her other hand, but her finger keeps burning.

She can't douse the flame. She falls to the ground, trying to put out the fire in the grass. Cordelia runs over to help, hissing at me.

"*Bitch!*" Enora screams, looking at me. "*You bitch!*"

"I'll leave!" I shout. "But the minute you step out, I'll be waiting for you. For what you did to Beatrix! And for anything you dare do to Mira!"

One of the witches runs to Enora with a cup and tosses the liquid over her hand, but the fire won't burn out. Enora starts screaming. She can't put the fire out. The rest of my coven is beside me, staring.

"Mira!" I yell. "Come here. Come home with us."

"I can't, Cadence," Mira says with teary eyes. "I'm sorry. I can't leave."

"*Prohibe!*" Enora screams, staring at her burning hand. "*Prohibe! Prohibe! Prohibe!*"

The flame finally stops. Enora screams some more, staring at her smoking, blackened hand. She spins around and yells something unintelligible at me.

"Mira, please," I yell. "Come with us."

"It's too late for me, Cadence. This is my home. This is my family now."

Enora scowls at me, holding her smoking hand. Then, with a mischievous smile, she whirls around to Mira and screams, "*Lux!*" Mira's hair lights on fire.

"*Mira!*"

"I'm not the only witch who can burn!" Enora exclaims.

I run to help Mira. Some of the witches who were circling Enora run to the sidewalk to stop me, but something grabs me from behind before I cross into the front yard. I turn and Bryce has his arm around me. I could easily shrug him off, but he's shaking his head desperately. "Stay back, Katie! Stay away from them! Please! Don't cross the line!"

One of the witches in red grabs Mira and throws her to the ground, trying to douse the flames.

"*Prohibe!*" cries the Abaddon witch over Mira. "*Prohibe! Prohibe!*"

The hood falls from the witch's cloak as the two roll on the grass, revealing blond hair. I recognize this witch. She's the drugged, inebriated girl who greeted us at the door. Courtney. She's desperately trying to douse the flames on her lover. Thank God, her incantation works. But then Enora approaches them.

"*Stay away from her!*" I shout. "*Leave her alone!*"

Bryce is still holding me back. His hands are so weak I could easily throw him off, but I know he's right. If I walk onto the grass, I'm as good as dead. I feel weak just leaning toward it.

"Are you a traitor too!" screams Enora at Courtney. "You? How dare you help her! You actually care about her? I don't believe it."

"Leave her alone!" cries Courtney, in tears, holding Mira on the ground.

The fire's stopped, but I can tell Mira's hurt. I'm sure some of the flames burned her scalp. Enora looks down at her hand. She waves her smoking hand back and forth to ease her pain. Then she turns back to me.

"Come over!" Enora cries. "Come on. Fight me! Come here, you coward! Try to stop me from killing Mira, Cadence! I will. I'm going to hurt her. Believe me. If I can't hurt you, I'll hurt her. I swear it!"

Damie grabs me, and I'm between him and Bryce. Then Maddie grabs my shoulder. All three are holding me back, begging me to leave.

"Did you kill her!" I cry.

"She's okay," Courtney shouts at me, still crouching beside Mira. "She's okay, Windstorm. Go. Please go. Take your coven and leave before more people get hurt."

Mira looks over. She's not okay. She looks like she's in so much pain. But Mira says weakly, "Cadence...please go. Leave."

The way back home is the most unpleasant drive I've ever had. I sit in the passenger seat, staring at the illuminated windows of the skyscrapers of

Atlanta. There's something about early morning that always feels like a waking dream to me. Though I'm not a morning person, I have fond memories of this feeling, like waking up during a family trip. Not today. This morning I'm filled with dread. I got Maddie back, but I left Mira again. I can't imagine Enora's doing anything less than killing her.

Soon we pass the high rises and enter the suburbs. All the while, Maddie is in the back seat, crouched against my brother, crying. Their closeness is exactly what started all this horror in the first place. I know I apologized to her, but between you and me, I'm still a little mad.

Bryce touches my hand. I hold his as he drives, but I don't look at him. I just stare out at the fields and the yellow-orange sun rising over the horizon as we make our way back to Hawthorne.

The trees get denser. I tear my eyes from the scenery, dig in my pants pocket, and check the time. Six thirty. But we're still not over the hills into Hawthorne Forest. At least Maddie stops crying. Now the two of them are sleeping.

"Nothing's changed," I say to Bryce. They're the first words I've said since Enora's house.

"What?" I think he thought I was sleeping.

"It was all for nothing."

"That's not true, Katie."

"Why?"

"You got your best friend and brother back."

I squeeze his hand tighter. He's right. He's always right.

I take a deep breath. Then I finally take my hand from his and curl up against the door. I close my eyes, but I know it's for nothing. There's no way I'm going to sleep.

"Will Mira be okay, Bryce?" I ask almost in a whisper.

"She hasn't been since she left for Atlanta. But it was her choice. Maddie's wasn't."

"We shouldn't have left her."

"There was nothing else we could do."

My trance is over. I'm so drowsy. So tired. My eyes close. I feel Bryce's hand run along my hair. I know he's trying to be nice, but that bothers me because it reminds me of Mira's hair. Mira's not feeling any pleasure on her head right now. She must be in so much pain. She probably can't even see a doctor under that wicked witch. And that might not be all Enora's done to hurt her.

"Katie," I hear quietly from behind me. My brother's snoring.

"Yeah, Maddie?"

"Thank you for coming back for me, babe."

23

THE BURNING

I'm sitting discreetly in the middle of Connor Sill Hall, with a notepad and pen, listening to my new teacher, Dr. Stoferson. Connor Sill Hall is one of the smallest lecture halls in Hawthorne University, with rows of ugly orange swivel chairs along cream-colored walls, all dipping down an incline over a large black stage and podium. Dr. Stoferson is probably the oldest professor in school. He is way beyond retirement age, but he still teaches because he loves it so much. He even walks with a shuffle across the stage, hunching over as he talks. He's got a short beard and he's always wearing a sharp navy-blue suit. Most around campus know him from orientation. He's a smiley man who loves attending every orientation and graduation and meeting everyone. I was lucky to get him for American history.

Anyway, he's discussing the impeachment of Andrew Johnson, which is not that thrilling, but his enthusiasm gets me into it.

"Could Abraham Lincoln have been impeached had he not been assassinated?" asks Doctor Stoferson, shifting his legs slowly and staring at the ground. "Couldn't he have gone through the same process as President Johnson?"

Just as Dr. Stoferson looks up at us, my phone vibrates. I don't dare look at it, as my professor's staring right at me. There are only around thirty of us scattered throughout the auditorium. That's because it's the beginning of the second semester and the lecture is at night. As good as Dr. Stoferson is, few people attend evening lectures.

I'm really lucky to have Tammy sitting beside me. She got into his prized class too. And, as you know, unlike shy me, Tammy's boisterous and fun. So Tammy hollers out, "There's no way Abe would have done that, Professor. Lincoln could have gotten away with anything."

"True, Tammy," the professor says. (I marvel that he knows her name). "Lincoln was a wily politician. But it was troubled times. Certainly, he'd have faced tremendous challenges just as he had during the Civil War. Of course, Andrew Johnson was no Lincoln. In March of 1865, during Lincoln's second inauguration, Johnson was drunk. He was inaugurated as president a month later. Some believe he was thrown out of the Petersens' house by Mrs. Lincoln for drinking again when Lincoln was on his deathbed. But it wasn't only whiskey...he was strongly disliked by his own political party for his disregard of the South's discrimination against black Americans."

Dr. Stoferson is so into his subject that he looks up pensively for a moment as if he were talking about the most important subject in the world. I just love that. But it's hard for me to pay attention.

I'm so worried. After I missed my morning Crusades lecture and got up after noon, Bryce had to stop me, in our apartment parking lot, from running to my beat-up old Honda and heading back to Atlanta, alone, to try to spring Mira. I'm so upset. I feel like it's my responsibility as High Priestess. It's my fault. All over again. The gang's probably going to meet again on Friday, but that's too late. I shudder to think what that wicked witch will have done to Mira by then.

"And in this turbulent time in America," continues Dr. Stoferson, "the challenge of rebuilding a decimated South, our South, whose economy was based on agriculture, did not really end on April 9, 1865. I think, had Lincoln lived, this healing could have been done so much better. The Civil War was a big turning point for our country. Know all the dates. But most importantly, go beyond what you've been told in school. The Civil War was a war representing a struggle of old against new in addition to being about slavery. Industrialization versus agriculture. It was industrialization's time to win. Technology had evolved, bringing our race into a new era. So the question I pose to all of you tonight is, what do you all think will happen with the next change in humanity's evolution? I don't know. But whatever it is, sadly, I don't think it will end racial prejudice."

I can't care. I mean, of course I care, but I can't stop thinking about Mira. I keep seeing Mira's hair burning in my mind. Bryce shouldn't have stopped me. But he didn't stop me, you know. I stopped me. I don't want to go anywhere near that house ever again.

I feel a vibration from my cell phone again. Then Tammy's phone rings. Following that, the lecture hall goes crazy with phones ringing all over the place. Everybody digs into their pockets or purses to see what's going on. The noise from all the phones disturbs Dr. Stoferson. Then his own phone buzzes.

A boy bursts through a side door in the auditorium. "The Billington House is on fire! It's on fire! Fire!"

Tammy's eyes open wide. We jump from our seats.

"The Billington House," says another. "It's on fire!"

Dr. Stoferson's squinting at his phone. "Oh my," he says.

Tammy and I run outside. It's dark. We're at the edge of campus and not far from the Billington House, perched up on the forest hillside. When I follow everyone's gaze, I don't like what I see. There are clouds of gray smoke and a bright yellow-red glow on the hill.

"My God, Katie!" cries Tammy.

My phone buzzes again. It's Bryce.

"Katie, are you all right?" he asks.

"I'm fine, Bryce. Did you hear?"

"Of course I heard. I'm here, remember? Remember the reunion with Mason?"

"Oh my God, Bryce, you were inside! I totally forgot. Are you okay?"

"I'm fine. But are you, Kate? I'm checking on you."

"I'm fine."

"Bryce was in the house?" asks Tammy in a panic.

"He's fine," I say, turning to her.

"Thank God you're okay," Bryce says. "We were on the first floor. Those on the second and third...aren't doing so well."

"I can be up there in a minute."

"It's all ablaze, Cadence. The fire trucks are here, but I'm not sure there's much that they can do. I don't think there's going to be much left for you to see. First it was smoke, but in a few minutes, it exploded into flames. I heard screams. It was terrible."

"I'll be right there."

"We can drive up there, Katie," Tammy says. "My car's outside the lecture hall."

"Okay."

"Bye, Bryce. I'm coming up now."

I hang up the phone, and we run to the parking lot and jump into Tammy's SUV.

When we get on the road, we regret it. We're not the only ones who are curious. There's traffic. Can you believe that? Traffic in Hawthorne. That's something I never see. There's a line of cars heading up the hill, and we're not moving.

"Tams, I'm gonna jump out and run. Okay?"

"Yeah," Tammy says, still staring at the car in front of her. "Just go."

I sprint over to the walkway, dodging more bodies, on my way through the woods and up to the Billington House.

The smoke gets heavier, and white ash falls between branches and leaves. Many students are talking on their phones as they're rushing up the hill. Others are smiling or laughing, thinking the whole thing is funny. I don't think it's funny. I want to slap them in the face. How can this be funny? I mean, I'm a history major. The Billington House is the oldest house in Georgia. It has so much history. And it's burning. Then I think about how Bryce was in there when it caught on fire.

My phone rings again. It's Maddie.

"Did you hear?" asks Maddie.

"Of course I heard."

"Bryce told me he was trying to reach you. You were in class with Tammy, right?" I hear my brother. Maddie says in a hushed voice, "Yeah, she's fine. She's fine." Then Maddie's voice is loud again. "You coming? You gotta see this, Katie. It's so sad. The whole place is burning down."

"I'll be there in a minute. Tammy's stuck with her car still on the road."

"Well, the police blocked it off." Maddie coughs. "And they're starting to push everyone back. I think the whole school is up here. And...my

God, Katie, it's horrible. I saw a few students limping out of the building. One was being carried. I think it was Nathan. I'm not sure. And one...his face was covered with blood. Then there was...I don't even know how to say it. I don't even know how to say it."

"What?"

"There were bodies wrapped in white cloths. People died."

I hang up the phone. I don't want to hear anymore. I also don't need to. I can see the house up the hill now through smoke and tree branches. I wrap my arms around myself tightly. Even though I'm wearing my red coat, it's frigid.

At the top of the hill, the smoke is thick. People are coughing and it's raining white ash. There are sirens, and red and blue are reflected off the smoke. I can't walk fast anymore because too many students are in line, heading up the path. Maddie's right, everyone from campus is here. I see many trees and grass around the house on fire too. The brick building is covered in more smoke than flame. A black-and-red cloud billows through the shattered glass of Abigail's famous haunted window. The only actual flames burn in the upstairs windows and on top of the roof. There are gaps in the structure where the wall or roof has caved in, and bricks and cement are strewn along the ground. Maddie's right, I don't think there's any hope of salvaging anything from the rubble. Firefighters are spraying hoses, but it doesn't look like it's going to save the house. I'm thinking they're trying to keep the fire from spreading into Hawthorne Forest.

I stand about fifty yards from the front door, staring, with a hundred other students. Someone touches my shoulder and I whirl around. It's Bryce. I jump in his arms.

"It's terrible."

"I don't think Nancy and Nick made it," Bryce says with a nod. "They were upstairs. And there's...so many injured. If you happened to be on the first floor with me, you were safe. God, I'm so glad you were in class. Can you imagine if you had decided to join me? One girl jumped from a window on the top floor and broke her leg. I saw another tumble down the stairs running from all the smoke. It was horrific, Cadence."

"I'm just glad you're okay," I say, clutching him tightly.

"You too."

Maddie and Damie run up to us. Maddie's face is streaming with tears. I brush my eyes and am surprised my eyes are wet too. Everything is so crazy I didn't even know I was crying. Or is it a reaction to the smoke?

We're all coughing and I'm beginning to wheeze, and the fire and smoke from the Billington House actually warms me. The police start signaling for us to back up. I think the entire police department from Hawthorne is here.

"You okay, man?" Damie asks Bryce, touching his shoulder. Bryce nods.

"That's over two hundred years burning," I say, shaking my head at my brother.

The police are signaling for us to move back. We walk backward toward the path and trees down the hill.

"Do you know what happened, Bryce?" asks Maddie.

"I thought it was the kitchen. Mason and I ran in there, but nothing was on fire. It was coming from one of the side bedrooms on the second floor, we think. It smoked the entire house. Mason told me Jill heard a window smash before the smoke started. Mason thinks someone started the fire from outside."

"Where's Mason?" I ask.

"He went in an ambulance with Jared. Jared broke a leg climbing down from a window upstairs. He's burned too, but I think he's all right."

"It was a reunion, Bryce?" asks Maddie.

"Katie was invited," he replies. "Mason was visiting from out of town. God, I'm so glad for her class. Seems being a bookworm saved her life this time."

"Guys!" We turn. It's Tammy. She's pushing through people to get to us. I'm surprised she made it through the crowds and traffic. Maddie hugs her. We all do.

"I can't believe it," Tammy says, staring at the fire. "It's so sad. The Billington House."

"Bryce," I say, "you said your friend Mason told you the fire was started from outside? Was he sure?"

His open-mouthed look of shock changes to anger. His eyes narrow and he slowly nods. He knows my implication.

"She did it, Katie?" asks Maddie.

"I think she did." Bryce nods.

"You guys don't know," says my brother.

My brother's objection bothers me. I still don't even like that he's here. Or that he even knows what we're talking about. Damie saw that "vampire" at the house. And then he saw my magic. I still can't get used to him being a part of all this craziness.

"She's the only one with a motive." Bryce looks back at the house, frowning. "She knew I'd be in there. Maybe she thought you'd be there too, Cadence."

"She burned the house down just to get Bryce?" asks Tammy.

"No," I say. "I think she burned it to burn the town. Just like my book. She wants Hawthorne destroyed. The fact that Bryce was there was an extra bonus."

"Fire for fire, Katie," Maddie says, nodding. "For what you did to her. She's gone on the offensive."

"Alondra's house!" Bryce turns toward the opposite side of town. "Shit, guys! We've got to go to Alondra's! If she did this to the Billington House, Alondra's is next."

"Tell everybody to meet there," Bryce says, turning to Maddie and Tammy. "That house is as much a part of Hawthorne as the Billington House. More so. It's our coven's home."

"Guys, are you all right!" We hear a Brazilian accent rushing through the crowd. It's Frida.

"We've got to get over to Alondra's, Frida," Bryce repeats. But I hug her first. Poor Frida's crying.

The police sirens start blaring again. Then I hear a megaphone:

"Everyone move back. Move back down the hill. For safety, we need all of you to..."

24

THE OWL

When we finally arrive at Alondra's house, it's super creepy. It's chilling that all the lights are on again in the house. *All of them.* Lights illuminate the driveway, surround the lone red carriage and weed garden, and shine through all the windows of the first floor of the house. I can still smell the fire from the opposite side of town, but here the stars are out on a clear night.

"I don't like this, Katie," Frida says. "All the lights were on when you saw Beatrix, right?"

Ah ... yeah.

We check the house. There are no ghosts or witches hanging out. But there's still the outside to investigate.

We enter the backyard by the side yard, because there's no way I'm going to go through the living room to the patio after what happened to Beatrix. In the side yard, Natasha, Mandy, Hope, Josie, and Debra meet up with us after piling out of Natasha's pink VW Bug. Our whole coven is here tonight, summoned by Bryce, and we all walk together onto the wild grass of Alondra's backyard.

The backyard's spooky too. All the lights coming from the house glow on the grass and cast shadows of the leafless branches and bushes in the forest. When I get closer to the middle of the field, I finally muster the courage to look back at the house. The patio's bright, but there's no hanging witch, thank God. But then Maddie gasps. She points at two red figures, running behind the trees, holding fiery torches and laughing.

"Our arsonists?" suggests Tammy.

"Doesn't look like they finished their job," says Damie.

"Should we go after them, Katie?" asks Frida.

I don't know. I stare at their torches, hidden behind the leaves and branches, wondering about the two witches' intentions. Bryce, Mandy, and Frida sprint after them.

"Wait!" I yell. "Let them go!"

It's like they want us to follow them. It feels like a trap. Thankfully, Bryce and the girls listen to me. Frida runs back to me in a panic but sweetly asks, "Why not go after them?"

I don't know. It doesn't feel right.

Alondra would know what to do. She was our true leader. It's times like these I wish Alondra were here.

"Why don't you want us to chase after them?" Bryce repeats.

"What are you gonna do if you catch them?"

"They're Abaddon witches," snaps Mandy. "It must be them. We have to stop them."

"And do what?" I shake my head. "They were taunting us to follow them. It felt like a trap. Stay here. Let's talk first."

"*Talk?*" snaps Mandy. "*Talk? Talk about what?*"

"We came here to protect the house, not chase after witches."

They don't agree. I can see it on their faces. They want to run after them. Even Bryce. Even my brother. But they follow my orders, not because they believe in me, but because I'm their High Priestess. I watch the torches and hear the laughter of the retreating witches moving deeper and deeper into the woods until they disappear.

"Is this your order?" quips Mandy. "You want us to just let them go and *talk*?"

"What if they burn down the school, Windstorm!" demands Natasha. "You're just gonna let them do that?"

That really pisses me off. No, I was planning on sitting down as a group and talking things over with my coven in order to plan our next step, but everyone's so crazy and in such a panic that I doubt I can even get a word in. I don't answer.

Instead, I turn my back on all of them and walk toward our pile of wood alone. And then...I feel peace. And that's super weird because all my friends are still shouting at my back. The trees feel like arms hugging me, comforting me, while the gentle breeze brushes against my hair. I just wish they'd stop yelling.

I stand before the burned logs. Then I sit down facing the house and creepy patio. I think of Alondra again. In my teacher's last days, before she passed, she chose to leave our friends for the woods. She decided to spend her last days alone. Now I understand. People can be so agitating.

I look down at the floor and feel energy flow from my belly to my neck. I become oblivious to my friends' words. Then I completely stop hearing their chatter.

It's cold. So I will the bonfire to light by itself behind me. I feel the pleasure of its heat warming my back. The breeze against my cheek is cold, but comfortable with my newly lit fire behind me. I hear animals. Then, from the corner of my eye, I see them. A red fox walks behind the bushes to my right, and a large black snake curls along in the leaves beside a tree trunk to my left. But my attention focuses beyond. Something's drawing me to look down the hill through the trees. Far in the distance, miles from the yard, an owl perched high up on a leafless black tree branch has its head dug deep in its chest. I stop noticing everything else and stare at this owl.

A few of my friends are now standing over me with their eyes bulging, their nostrils flaring, and their mouths soundlessly yapping. They're so crazy. I laugh and turn back to the owl perched on the branch.

At first, I'm not sure why this owl fascinates me so much, but then I realize that the bird looks exactly like a witch in a meditative pose. Just like when I saw Alondra and Beatrix crouched in black cloaks.

The only sounds I hear are the breeze rustling through the trees and deer and coyotes walking over leaves in the forest. And as I look down, I see that I'm wearing a black cloak and holding my book, *Broomstick*. I don't recall changing into a cloak. Nor do I know how I came into possession of the book. Did I grab it when searching the house?

Bryce appears over me, pushing my shoulder and saying something, but I can't hear his words. He looks concerned. I laugh, grab his hand, and kiss the back of it. He keeps talking frantically. All my friends stand over me now, looking at me weirdly, but I don't hear what they're saying. I don't care. I laugh again. They look funny.

I position my Book of Shadows, *Broomstick,* in front of me. Then—I've never done this before, but it seems like the right thing to do now—I crouch, just like the owl, dipping my head down into my chest and leaning my body toward the ground. I whisper, though my words seem to echo throughout the yard:

Ut videam. Ut videam. Ut videam. Lux alba. Lux Nyx.

Everything blurs.

My eyes open in a dark room with a vaulted ceiling. I'm sitting on a wooden bench in a church. There's a large cross above the altar, and standing on the stage is Frida's brother, Liam, lighting candles. He doesn't look at me. It's almost as if he doesn't see me. It's dark and all the drapes are closed. This is Hawthorne Church.

When I turn toward the windows to my left, I jump. There's a witch sitting next to me. With a black cloak, this figure appears sinister, like the grim reaper or something. But I'm wearing a black cloak too. The hood is drawn over the stranger's head, so I can't make out her face.

"Who are you?"

"You know who I am."

I recognize her voice. "Alondra?"

The figure nods but doesn't turn.

"Oh, Alondra, Hawthorne's in trouble. The Billington House was destroyed. The town's in danger. What can I do? I felt like I had to do something, so I thought of magic. I felt like I had to speak to you. Then I saw an owl bury its head on a tree, and it reminded me of you and what you did at the time of your death."

I'm distracted by singing from a choir. I turn and face the stage, but there's no one except Liam, straightening white cloths on a table under the candles.

"I am here, Windstorm," Alondra says, "calm yourself."

"Why are we in a church?"

"This is the Summerland. You summoned me here because your father is Christian and you feel at peace with the cross."

I do feel at peace. But I don't think it's because we're in a church. If anything, being in black cloaks here feels almost sinful. But I feel at peace sitting beside my teacher again. I miss her. And, come to think of it, I was wishing that I'd see her as I crouched in meditation. Maybe I did summon her?

"Alondra, Enora's destroying the town. What can I do?" I ask again. My voice sounds desperate.

"Do you accept that you are the leader of the Hawthorne coven?"

"Yes. Of course."

Her hand pats the book on my lap. I look down and am surprised. In this house of God, I had thought I was holding a Bible. It's my Book of Shadows, *Broomstick.*

"You gave it to me after it burned in the fire?" I ask.

"No, you did. Have you accepted that you are the leader of the Hawthorne coven?"

"I said yes, but what does that have to do with anything? Alondra, you have to help me stop Enora."

"If Enora chooses to fight, your fate will depend on whether you have accepted your rightful place as leader of our coven."

Liam opens the drapes and it becomes very bright. I can't see outside. All I see is a bright white light through the windows. It makes me uneasy. It reminds me of the bright light in Alondra's house when Beatrix died.

"Who turns the lights on in your house?" I ask Alondra. "There's no electricity. Is it you? Your ghost?"

"No. It's you."

I finally see a glimpse of her profile under the hood. I can just barely see Alondra's face, but I recognize her features and her infamous smile, and that makes me feel more at peace. I was scared that this was some other witch tricking me. But this is Alondra.

"You're a powerful witch," Alondra adds. "You brought me back from the other side during Yule, just like you are doing now. And when Beatrix died, you brought me back as a warning to Adder. Just as you lit up your house now, as a warning, after the Billington House was burned."

"You know about the Billington House?"

She nods.

"It's terrible."

There's the sound of footsteps. I look, but I don't see anyone walking up the aisle.

"Well, it's not my house, Alondra. It's yours."

"Maverick built the house when he built the town," she says, shaking her head. "I moved in with my first husband, but Maverick built it. That house is more a part of Hawthorne than Josiah's. The house is Hawthorne. And Hawthorne is our covenstead. Do you understand?"

I nod.

"I don't think you do. When I first brought Enora into my coven, I thought she would take my place as our leader. Like you, she was powerful. But she cannot feel the peace you feel. She cannot…" She touches my hand. At first I jerk, ready to move away, thinking that her hand will be ice-cold. It isn't. Her hand is warm. "She can't feel this, Katie. Do you understand? This is Enora's evil. When I realized this, I expelled her from the coven. In Hawthorne, she is an outsider now. Do you know what that means?"

"Alondra, you're never straight with me." I shake my head.

"I'm being very straight with you," Alondra insists with a laugh. "I'm answering your question. You asked how you can stop Enora. Now you answer me. Do you accept your position as the leader of our coven?"

I hesitate. Then she turns and faces me. I physically draw back. She doesn't look scary; her facial features are vivid and real. Indeed, Alondra is sitting in front of me. It's her. I don't know how to explain it to you, but she is not a vision and she is not a ghost. Alondra Johansen is sitting right here beside me. And she is smiling, trying to comfort me.

"Yes," I reply.

"Take what is yours." She nods and turns back to the altar. "Do it now. Don't delay. If this outsider is so blinded by her rage that she foolishly fights you on your hallowed grounds, she will not only fight Hawthorne, she will fight the Hawthorne Witch. When she realizes they are one and the same, it will put you in great danger. She will find that the only way to fulfill her revenge and destroy our coven will be to destroy you. But when *you* finally realize who you are, it will make you very powerful. The struggle is no different than it was over the fate of your book, *Broomstick*. Let the book burn to ash, and you will burn. Fail to burn you, and neither the book nor the town will burn. Cast the outsider out, Cadence Hawthorne. And do it now."

I don't understand everything she's saying, but I feel it. I feel it in the pit of my chest, and I feel determined now. I mean, I was determined before, but now I feel confident. And my newfound conviction is all because of Alondra.

But I also feel sad. As the two of us sit in the quiet church alone, I really feel like I'm sitting by my old teacher. Maybe my stress made this magic happen. Or maybe Alondra did. I don't know. Whatever the case, I feel like I won't ever see her again.

"I miss you, Alondra. And I do forgive you."

I touch her hand again. I hold it. Its warmth is pleasant. It reminds me of holding her in my arms in the woods at the time of her death. I even see an image of darkness in the center of this bright church. I'm wearing a black cloak, and my teacher is wearing the same. And I'm holding her, desperately trying to tell her those words after she died in my arms.

"I forgive you."

Alondra shakes her head. She points to the cross at the front of the church. "I'm not damned, Cadence. Whatever you believe, have faith that there is a mercy and love far greater than anything anyone can imagine."

Everything fades.

I wake up crying. I feel an arm around me and lift my head. Bryce is looking at me with concern.

"What happened, babe?" asks Bryce. "We sat and watched you after you seemed to drift off to sleep."

"I just love her so much, Bryce," I say in tears.

I'm back in Alondra's yard. My friends are all sitting around me and staring at me. They look sad for me, but I don't think they understand why I'm crying. I'm not sad. I'm crying tears of joy over being able to see Alondra again. No, not see her, *be* with her one final time.

"Who was it, Cadence?" asks Bryce.

I shake my head. Then I pick up the book in front of me and get up before my friends.

"What did you see?" asks Hope.

"Yeah, Katie?" asks Frida. "Who?"

"Who?" they all ask. "What?"

I feel this weird sense of longing. The peace I felt with Alondra, in that gateway between life and death, was so much more comforting than this moment. My friends are so worried, and I feel stress again due to all their fears.

My phone rings. I dig through my jeans pocket. The phone reads *Mira*.

"Cadence." Mira's voice is expressionless. "She wants to speak to you."

"Mira, where are you?"

"Hello?" asks another voice. "Hello?" It's Enora's voice. "Cadence, is that you?" The hand not holding the phone clenches into a tight fist. Then my friends jump up from the grass and back away from me. "Am I speaking with—"

"What!"

"You'll be happy to know I haven't killed Mira yet." She laughs. "*Yet.*"

"You better not—"

"Shh. Quiet your piehole, I warn you...don't say a word. I have her. I offer a trade. I'll hand Mira back to your friends in exchange for you. You'll turn yourself in and go back with me to Atlanta, where I'll complete our Sabbath and dissolve your coven. And your magic. This Friday, I'll finally dissolve the Hawthorne coven by sacrificing you..." She takes a deep breath and screams, "*For my charred finger, you motherfucker!*"

I look at my friends, staring up at me, and the fire behind me. They're staring wide-eyed, as if afraid.

"Just don't touch her."

"Shut up! Shh. Quiet. Shh, Cadence. Quiet yourself. If you upset me, your friend might just die while you're on the phone. If you want her to live, you'll allow us to take you back. I tried to trap you, now I see I just have to take you. If you don't give yourself up, I'll destroy the rest of your stupid school. First the library, then the halls, then Alondra's house. Mira will be killed, of course. Either way, I will have the dissolution of the

Hawthorne coven. But don't worry, I'm willing to spare your life. You can choose to survive under my circle just like Maddie and Mira did. Letting you live and watching you kneel before us is worth more than your life. It's the least you can do..." Then she screams in my ear, "*For my finger, you fucking cunt-sucking motherfucking bitch!*"

"Where are you? If you want—"

"*Shut up!*" she screams. "*Just be quiet!*" She takes a deep breath and then says unnaturally calmly, "Shh, shut...just shut the fuck up. Do we have a deal? Huh? Huh?"

"Fine. Where's Mira?"

"Why, we're where Maddie told me you two used to steal coffee. There's nobody else here at the moment, since I've got the whole school watching their stupid frat house burn down. Come share a cup of joe by the library with Amica. Hurry before the next building falls. And Raven." And she hangs up the phone.

I look behind me and the bonfire is like an inferno, rising higher than ever before. I figure that's why my friends are all staring wide-eyed at me.

"Katie," Bryce says. "Katie."

"Yeah, what?" I snap.

"Look."

He points at my feet. I realize he's under me. They're all under me. My black boots are hovering about twelve feet above the ground.

25

———

MY RIGHT

I'M SCARED. I MEAN REALLY, REALLY SCARED. I TRY NOT TO SHOW IT WHEN I run with my friends, but my bowels are turning and my heart's racing. And yet, since I saw Alondra, I also feel confident. I didn't feel that when I was in Atlanta—at least not until I was out of Enora's house. Maybe it was my teacher's words. Or maybe I'm entering a trance.

Did Alondra mean that I could beat Enora with magic tonight? Or did she just mean that I had to confront her here? I don't know.

We make it to the base of the grassy hill under the library. The Abaddon coven looks super weird in their crimson cloaks, standing in the center of the field amidst the shadows. There's mist on the ground. I think it's smoke from the fire. In fact, behind the clan, I see smoke and flames over the horizon, at the Billington House.

The field is well lit. This is one of the brightest areas on campus at night. The library's open late, so most of the light comes from the summit to my left. A little yellow light also shines from path lights along the main drag, to my right. Enora's coven have their hoods over their heads, but there's enough light to make out Enora's nasty face.

Mira's the only one with her hood back. Her hands are tied behind her back. She looks gloomy as hell, but she doesn't seem to have been hurt, though there are a few bare patches on her head. The only other one not wearing a hood is the beast, Gus. As usual, he's bare-chested, baring his stupid fangs.

We stop about twenty yards from them, coven to coven. It's a full-fledged witch showdown, only they're wearing their red cloaks and we're in regular clothes.

"I'm here," I say to Enora. "Let Mira go."

"That simple, huh?" asks Enora, shaking her head. "Nuh-uh. I doubt that, Cadence."

"Take me and let Mira go. You have my word. I'll go with you. Just let her go."

Bryce grabs my arm. "No, Katie. I told you, I won't let you go with them."

"It's okay," I reply, still glaring at Enora.

On the periphery, a few students with backpacks over their shoulders stop on the surrounding pathways to watch us. A boy even kicks up his skateboard and stares. Two couples by the library are looking down from the top of the hill.

"Katie," Bryce says, gently turning me. He lifts my chin. "You can't go back there."

I know. Does he think I want to? But what am I to do? I trusted Alondra's words, but now I feel doubt. I don't know what to do to make things right. She said, "Cast the outsider out." And she said, "Do it now."

"It's okay," I say.

"No, it isn't." Bryce opens his eyes wide and shakes his head. He looks so stern. So worried. I run my hand along his gorgeous thin beard and force a smile. Then I reach up and kiss him on his lips.

"I love you," I whisper.

He closes his eyes and shakes his head, clenching his teeth. He embraces me tightly. We kiss some more.

"Come on!" Enora snarls. "Fuck! Do we have to watch this? Are you done? Gus, go get her. Bind her so that she can't cast any tricks."

Gus nods and comes over carrying a thick rope. But when he yanks me around to bind my hands, Bryce grabs his wrist to stop him. Gus easily pushes him to the ground. My friends and all the witches of the Abaddon coven shout at each other, threatening to charge.

"Katie, let us help you!" cries Tammy desperately.

"Please, Katie," says Frida.

I shake my head and let the beast tie my hands behind my back. Then Gus leads me up to Enora, who smiles her stupid wicked grin. Enora removes her glove from her right hand. She shows me her palm. Her right hand doesn't have a red painted pentagram. It's charred and blackened. With a fake smile, she lifts the hand and strikes me hard in the face. My friends scream. I fall to the ground. I hear stupid Gus laugh.

"Katie!" yells Bryce.

"Give us Mira now," I say on the ground.

"Sit up first," Enora is still smiling and looking down at me. "Come on. Sit." She loves that I'm under her feet on the ground, I think. As I try to get up by leaning on my knees, she kicks me really hard in the stomach. I fall again, losing my breath, gasping for air. She drives her charred hand practically up my nose. "Do you see this? Huh? Do you see my hand! You bitch! You call yourself a witch? You don't know spells. You barely know our traditions. You were initiated by a hypocrite who was bullied by a pervert. That is your coven. That is your magic. It must be taken. I am the true witch. I will remove you."

"Fine...just...give me Mira," I say, trying to take in air. I'm watching her boot for another strike. "I don't care. Give me back my friend."

"Sure." Enora walks where I can't see her. "You know, I'd rather have you." And she wraps her arm around my neck and hoists me to my knees in front of my friends. My friends are ready to charge. But then—

"Stand back!" Enora brandishes a curved knife from her inside her cloak. I feel the cold metal slide along my neck. "Everyone get back or I'll cut the little bitch's neck! I swear, I'll cut little Katie's fucking throat."

"Okay," Bryce says, putting a hand out. "Just don't hurt her."

"You're really willing to sacrifice yourself for Mira?" Enora asks, lowering her head to stare at me with her flickering white eyes. "Really? I don't believe it. You have another trick up your sleeve? Is Alondra going to walk up behind me and grab me?" She chuckles and pulls me real close to the metal blade. "Huh?" I gasp. "How 'bout I kill her now?" she asks my friends. "I can just slice her throat, and that will be the end of the coven. Why bother with the Sabbath? She sure doesn't honor it." Then she lowers her face to mine again. "I am the only witch in Atlanta. I rejected Alondra and your coven because Alondra didn't have the courage to fight a man. A man who hurt us. So I gladly killed him. But you didn't let me finish."

"You never left our coven," I say. "Alondra expelled you."

She furrows her brow above those creepy white eyes, seeming surprised that I'd say anything with a knife to my throat. But, I...I don't care if she cuts me. I can't. I hate her so much.

I feel magic. There is a trance coming on, and I look up and see clouds swirling above us. A wind picks up.

"Let her go," pleads Bryce. "Please." Gus throws him on the ground again.

It starts to rain. Then there is a strike of lightning and thunder.

"More tricks?" Enora says in my ear, looking up toward the clouds. "Careful, one slice of your neck and the windstorm's over."

"Enora, please," Bryce says. Gus is now sitting over him, pinning him with one knee. "Let her go. She said she'll go with you."

"You'll really go back with me, Cadence?" asks Enora, holding the blade closer to my throat. I feel the sharpness cut. "You'll really let us bleed you for Mira?"

"Yes."

Enora squints. Then she lifts the blade from my neck. I hear Bryce's sigh of relief.

"Bullshit." Enora lets go of my neck and throws me down on the grass. "Anyway, for what you did to my hand, there should be punishment. You can come join us Friday, if you want, but someone still needs to pay tonight. So, I tell you what, Katie. How 'bout I let you decide?"

Enora nods to Gus, and Gus chokeholds Bryce. Then Enora walks behind Mira and grabs her from behind, just like she did to me. But unlike me, Mira's so lifeless, as if she doesn't care. It's like she's given up. Enora presses the knife to Mira's neck. "After all, I think my hand was more Mira's fault than yours."

"Stop!" I cry. "Just stop it!"

Enora jerks Mira's neck closer to the knife and Mira winces, but Mira doesn't speak.

"What will it be, Katie?" asks Enora. "I've got my arm around Raven, and Gus has his around your lover. Which one dies tonight for my hand?"

"Please. Just let them go. I'll go with you."

"No, you won't go willingly. I know you won't. I'll have to take you, so stop the bullshit and choose tonight's sacrifice before I haul you back to Atlanta."

"Allow me to teach you witchcraft, *witch*," she says. "Both Bryce and Gus are High Wizards. But there can only be one *real* coven in Atlanta. Only one High Priestess and one High Wizard. I think I'll throw the knife to Gus. Bryce should go tonight. Sorry."

"Let them go, you bitch!" screams Maddie. "Katie's offering to go with you! What more do you want!" Then a bunch of others in my circle cry out with Maddie.

"Yeah?" Enora asks them.

"Just let her go," I say. I'm desperate because I know Enora is crazy enough to kill them. "Please, Enora. You have me. Take me on the Sabbath. We have a deal."

"It's okay, Cadence," Mira finally says, looking down at me. She looks awful. "Choose me and save Bryce. I follow my master's will."

"Why not choose the Wizard?" suggests another red-cloaked witch. It's Courtney. "Won't his death weaken the Hawthorne coven the most, master?"

"Shut up, Courtney," says Enora dismissively.

"You fucking better not lay a hand on them!" Maddie shouts.

Enora glares at Maddie, narrowing her white eyes, and her smile quickly vanishes. "And which hand would you like me not to use, Blackbird? The left one or the *charred* one?"

She draws a dark line of red on Mira's neck with her knife. It's dark, but not too dark to see the blood drip from her neck.

"Stop, please!" I cry.

"On my master's will," Mira says closing her eyes and taking a deep breath.

"Mira!" I say, shaking my head and putting my hand out. "She's not your master. You're our friend—"

"No!" shouts Enora. "You fucking liar! More lies! Mira is not your friend. She has no friends. And you don't give a shit about her. Her life is shit. Just like Beatrix. And I will have my vengeance tonight for my hand! If it wasn't for her, it wouldn't have happened!"

"All right," I say. Enora's pearl-white eyes are bulging with rage. "Please just, calm down. Let her go. I'll—"

"*For my hand! For my honor! For my circle, this is the first sacrifice before you. Sacrificium consecratum. This time, for your lies. The lies of Hawthorne shall never be forgiven! Sacrificium consecratum!*"

And Enora runs the blade across Mira's throat.

Lightning strikes overhead and clouds cover the stars and moon. The wind becomes fierce, spinning along the grass like a tornado, forcing people to tumble or crouch down. It starts to pour. But the rain is not water. It is dripping white ash. Could it be from the fire at the Billington House? This far?

Mira falls lifeless to the ground. A bolt of lightning strikes near Enora, and she's thrown on the ground.

"Oh, am I upsetting you?" Enora asks, getting up. "Huh? How 'bout my hand, Windstorm! Don't you think what you did to my hand—"

Another bolt from the sky lights up the grounds. It doesn't strike her, but Enora looks up, scared. Enora forces herself up and turns to Gus. "Here, cut the bitch's fiancé next. Do it quick before her next tantrum."

She throws the dagger to Gus, but in midair the knife stops its trajectory and veers straight down into the grass. I crawl as fast as I can to Mira with my hands still shackled.

Mira's eyes are closed, dead. It's dark, but just bright enough to see a dark red trickle of blood bubble over her neck. The white ash starts covering her like snowflakes.

It's my fault. Again. All my fault. Mira was *my* witch. From *my* coven. I failed her. I feel so heavy in my chest. The rain and ash hail on me as tears run down my face. It's my fault. Again. And I failed Alondra. She seemed so sure that I could defeat Enora. She gave me such confidence. If I'm so powerful, such a great witch, why does my friend lie dead?

Thunder and lightning crack again.

I look up at Enora. She's staring down at me with those creepy white eyes. I rise to my feet effortlessly. It's surprising, for my hands were bound, but the ropes fall from my wrists as if they were made of paper. Those from my circle not crouching over Mira are now glaring at the red-cloaked witches in fury. When Enora gives one last nervous cackle, we lose all reason. Helen, Mandy, and Natasha charge first. Then come Hope, Frida and Tammy. They have every intention of pummeling the Abaddon coven, but when my witches are within striking distance, they freeze. Everything freezes, even Enora. It's as if time stopped. At first, I'm as surprised as they are, but then I realize that I willed it.

I walk around all the witches with my right hand raised. Everyone stands like a statue under the falling white ash. Slowly, they regain head movement. A few turn and stare at me. Gus, the beast that he is, finally breaks the spell. He lets go of Bryce, and he charges me, like an animal, on all fours. Effortlessly, I throw him. Then I turn back to Enora.

"*Vos invoco Escoba et Abigail. Relinquo. Deleo Panthera, deleo Panthera. Relinquo.*"

A bolt of lightning falls only a few feet from Enora. She's thrown, stunned by the bolt. When she regains her strength for a moment, her eyes lose their white glow. But then she shakes her head and flashes me the painted pentagram on her left palm.

"*Muta! Muta! Muta Panthera!*"

Her back elongates, her arms lengthen, and she falls on all fours. Yellow fur and a large mane appear along her neck, and she growls. She is a lion, like the lion I saw at the entrance to her cave.

The animal jumps on me with solid white eyes, snapping its teeth, trying to tear my face. The distraction is enough to stop the freezing of the witches. The moment I start rolling with the lion on the grass, I see in my periphery that the two covens are finally charging each other.

But my magic is strong. I grab Panthera and toss her across the lawn. Then I raise my hands once more. Rain falls. Torrential rain, washing the ash from the grass. Panthera, still a lion, recovers from my throw and jumps on the victim closest to her—my brother. Of course, the bitch knows this will upset me the most. Damie fights for his life, trying to push the lion's teeth away from his face and torso. I flick both wrists out.

"*Veni foras, Panthera. Veni, veni, veni foras.*"

The lion drops my brother, sliding up the muddy hill across the wet grass, pulled by an invisible force. At first, Panthera resists, but then she turns and uses the force to leap on me.

"*Hawthorne Witch*," the lion says in a guttural male voice. "*Lux. Lux.*" Panthera's blackened right paw is aflame, and I feel burning pain as I try to hold her once more and throw her.

I will another flash of lightning. This time it's so close and bright that I have to shield my eyes. It cracks across the field. There's a yelp. Panthera falls from me. My eyes burn and I blink repeatedly, struggling to see, after the lightning strike. When my vision clears, Panthera's lying by my side, shaking. I pull myself up and grab the lion's legs. Then I toss her once more, this time nearly fifty yards, across the entire field to a group of trees. Stunned, the animal jumps back on all fours, shaking its head.

"*Hawthorne relinquo! Decipula Panthera! Decipula!*"

The tree trunks swoop down, with branches and leaves entwining and gathering up the lion, stretching Panthera until her arms dangle from the sides and her head hangs limply. While inside the tree branches, the lion changes back to Enora, but Enora remains ensnared. The trees trap her, almost like a medieval pillory.

Meanwhile, the witches still fight. I see Cordelia's ugly tattooed face under a red hood. She waves a hand and lights Mandy's jacket on fire. Even sweet Frida is rolling on the ground with one of the red-cloaked witches. Maddie's shoving and punching another. And Bryce is back to swinging his fists and kneeing Gus.

I raise my arms.

"*PROHIBE!*"

For a flash, the witches freeze again. The rain stops. The wind dies. Everything stops.

After a silence, many collapse on the grass. Some clutch their heads. Others start crying. I kneel, panting, as the rain washes down my now-drenched black hair.

That's when I notice the onlookers. Whereas before it was a handful, now there are tons of onlookers on campus and up the hill by the library.

"Windstorm! Windstorm!" I turn and one of the witches in red is kneeling over Mira. "Windstorm! Come here! Quick!" It's Courtney—you know, the witch who suggested Enora kill Bryce. Well, now she's holding Mira in her arms.

Mira's squinting and wincing in pain. I run over on the muddy grass. Mira's moving but with her eyes closed. Dark blood is collecting over her neck in the shadows.

"She's alive?" Bryce asks excitedly, sliding beside me. Mira can't speak. She just keeps wincing in pain.

"Oh, Meer!" says Courtney, shaking her head. "Meer, I'm so sorry. Can you hear me? I'm so sorry. I was afraid. I didn't dare help because I was afraid. Will you forgive me? ...Meer. Meer, can you hear us? Please wake. I love you."

"We have to stop the bleeding," Bryce says.

"She can do it," I say. Then I touch Courtney's shoulder. "You can do it. Stop the bleeding."

Courtney looks up at me, confused.

"Stop the bleeding," I repeat, touching her arm gently. "You can do it."

"Why? Why me?"

"Do you love her?" I ask.

She nods.

"If you love her, you can heal her. Use your love. Right-handed magic. Good magic. I will help you."

She looks at me funny. Then she shakes her head. "I can't. You do it. You're more powerful, Windstorm. I'm not."

"Try," I say. "Feel your love for her and touch her neck. I will try to help."

She hesitates but I don't falter. For some reason, I'm sure she can do it.

"You do love her?" I ask again.

She nods, wiping her tears with her red sleeve.

"I do too. We can do it together."

Courtney closes her eyes and presses her palms along Mira's neck. I touch Courtney's arm, and a white glow appears around her hands. Then, before our eyes, the wound closes and the bleeding stops.

"We've got to get her to the hospital," Bryce says to me.

"And call the police," I add with a nod.

"No need for that," Bryce says, shaking his head and gesturing toward campus.

I didn't see it before, but apparently the police that gathered at the

Billington House have finally arrived from another disturbance in town. Red and blue lights and a bunch of police cars are blocking the main drag of campus from a large crowd of students. "We didn't do this in secret this time, Cadence."

I stand up. All my friends, even some of the red witches, are standing around us. But then I hear a scuffle. Tammy and Mandy are grabbed from behind, and I hear metal clasped. That's when someone grabs my arms and pulls my wrists behind my back. This time my wrists are trapped in metal, not rope. Fortunately, I'm myself now, so I don't do something stupid and resist. Then I see the same thing happen to Bryce and Courtney. They're arresting all of us. I don't care. As long as they help Mira, I don't care anymore.

We walk with the police, under bright lights, from two squad cars, which are now parked along the grass. A hundred students stare. There have been suspicions on campus for two years about my witchcraft. Well, if they saw the lion flying across the lawn, their suspicions have been confirmed. I wonder if they saw the fight? They must have.

The police did. One of the cops asks Bryce if he saw where the lion went.

I pass Queen Bitch herself. Her eyes are blue. She's still imprisoned in the branches of the trees.

"How'd you do it, Cadence?" asks Enora feebly. She looks so weak.

I stop with Bryce for a second. "Hawthorne is my hallowed ground."

"But we weren't at Alondra's."

"*All* of Hawthorne is my hallowed ground."

Enora nods with a slight glimmer of a grin. Then she looks down, forlorn, and says—more to herself—"Till we meet again, Hawthorne Witch."

"Should I kill her?" I say, cocking my head to Bryce. You know, like will the branches to squeeze her chest until she can't breathe?

"You students are in a lot of trouble," says the cop beside me, grabbing my arm and pulling me away. "Come on."

As we wait, handcuffed, against the police cars, my friends mingle with our red-cloaked archenemies. We don't fight. We don't even yell at each other. We're too exhausted. And in a strange way, the people in Enora's coven look relieved. Even Gus, in handcuffs, is staring peacefully at the ground. I think they're relieved I locked their beast in the trees. I think they were afraid of her too.

Then two men run across the lawn to Mira with a stretcher.

"Thank God," I say to Bryce, gesturing to the paramedics. "I hope she's all right."

"If she is, it'll be thanks to you, Cadence."

I shake my head.

26

EXIT INTERVIEW

I'M SITTING STIFFLY IN A BLACK LEATHER CHAIR, FACING THE PROVOST OF Hawthorne University. I am holding her cell phone, watching a video of my friends and me fighting the red-cloaked witches of the Abaddon coven. Doctor Kenosha Trent is a black woman with really short black curls. She's wearing a shiny violet dress jacket and slacks and is sitting behind a mahogany desk—similar to Dr. Bainer's desk. She even has a lovely view of the outside forest behind her too.

It's a cold day and snow is falling behind her. I met the provost last year when I was sent to her office regarding my failing junior year. She's a really nice lady, unlike the history dean. But she's not looking nice now. She has her arms folded and is staring at me.

Seeing what happened is stranger than being part of it. As I watch, occasionally I see students stopping their bikes or pointing at us. I was too busy fighting to notice them. It seemed quiet outside, but a lot of people were watching us. The video was made with night vision, so everything's black-and-white and there's no sound.

Then comes the part where I'm walking in front of everybody, sticking my right hand out. Everyone's frozen. It's almost as if the video is paused, but I'm still walking with my outstretched right hand. And then the security footage reminds me of a horror movie, or some supernatural thriller, when Panthera shapeshifts into a lion and lunges at me. It's too unreal to be real, you know. The lion attacks me, throwing its claws at my face and snapping its teeth at me.

I don't really want to watch this again. I'm tired. I got no sleep last night. After a trance, sometimes releasing all that extra energy drains me. Not to mention I spent the night in a jail cell smelling of pee. Well, the police let me out after they made me review the same security footage. Apparently, although people got hurt, I didn't do anything wrong. I mean, were they going to prosecute me for sticking my hand out and fending off a lion?

I take a deep breath.

"Keep watching."

"Why? I've already gone through the footage with the police, Dr. Trent," I say, shaking my head.

"Do it," she insists, folding her arms again.

I sigh and look back at her phone.

It's at the part where my friends are staring at something outside my field of vision. This is the part where Enora's tied up in tree branches. You know, when I threw her across the grass and trapped her body between the trees. Well, you can't see Enora at this angle, but all the bystanders around us are staring in her direction.

"Rewind it," she says, leaning forward. "Go back before Enora gets trapped in the tree."

"Why? I don't understand. I...I mean, why do you—"

"Just do it, Cadence."

There's no arguing. Dr. Trent looks really pissed.

I press the screen and find a rewind button. I don't know why she wants me to see it, but I go back to where I left off—you know, the part where everyone's freezing while I raise my right hand. Gus charges me, then the lion, Panthera—and I easily throw them off. And then I get her off Damie. The speed at which the lion is hurled seems unnatural. The lion smears along the black-and-white video as if the camera can't track the throw.

"Enora's been thrown?" Dr. Trent asks.

As a lion...yeah.

Dr. Trent nods and then sighs. She sifts through some papers on her desk. With her head in her hand, she starts writing something. This reminds me of Dr. Bainer. I just sit there and watch her. This time, I don't even have a loose nail to play with. Instead, I run my hand across my hair. God, it's so shaggy and ugly. I haven't showered for two nights. I'm just wearing a simple T-shirt and jeans, with my red coat on the chair.

I fiddle with my fingers, staring for a moment at my black nail polish.

"Am I getting expelled?" I ask, not looking at her.

"Do you know how many people witnessed this, Cadence?"

"No."

She finally drops her pen. "The security footage I showed you is only coming from the library. But on campus, over two hundred students were watching you guys as the police kept them back until it was safe. We had to confiscate everyone's phone. They videotaped you. One caught a lightning strike near your body. Another showed Enora's transformation into a lion. That part where you threw her, fortunately, looks almost like a glitch or a trick of lighting. The lion moves too fast. But..." She folds her hands and leans toward me. "Three students managed to record the trees that bent down and trapped her. Those videos were quite remarkable, and one of them was leaked on social media."

What does this have to do with me getting expelled?

"You and your friends have created quite a mess. One of the biggest messes this town has seen in over a century."

I bite my lip. What am I supposed to say to that?

"I will interview your fiancé. Then I will interview your best friend, Madison. Your brother, Damien. Then all the others. The police will deal with the non-students, the guests from Atlanta. And, of course, Enora will be behind bars. But it's not the first time she's been in prison."

"What do you want from me, Dr. Trent?" I don't like the edge in my voice, but I can't help it. I'm so tired. I just want to go home. I'm getting angry. She forces a smile and finally stops folding her arms. She leans back in her chair. Then she does something really weird. She smiles—a real smile.

"Cadence, do you still want to attend Hawthorne as a graduate student next year?"

What?

"I need to know so I can make plans."

"I... I..." *I mean, what the hell?*

"You've been through so much," Dr. Trent says, almost sadly, with a nod. "I'm sorry. I've tried to do what I can to help. And on your part, you've worked so hard to clear your name. I have to say that, unfortunately, it's affected your school record. You know, in Hawthorne, we can forgive certain things because we have an understanding, but I'm concerned for you if you apply to other schools. If you do, your record is tainted because of the things you've done. I don't feel like that's fair. I'd be willing to write you a letter of recommendation to try to clear things up, but your record stands with Cs in the fall of your sophomore and junior years. Here, as the head of the university, certain things can be, shall we say, put aside. But with the other schools, it will be hard to clear your record. If you still insist on going elsewhere, I understand. I'll do what I can."

I'm squinting at her and wondering if this is the start of my true psychotic break.

"The dean sent me his report, Cadence. But you know, Dr. Bainer can be an asshole."

Did the provost just call Dr. Bainer an asshole?

"It's up to you."

"What? What's going on here?" I snap. I'm surprised at my outburst, but I'm getting really angry. This is just too weird. I'm so tired and I just want to go home. "You made me watch a witch fight on campus. With a lion. And now you're talking about graduate school. I don't understand. What's happening, Dr. Trent?"

She nods and opens a drawer in her desk. She takes out a shiny silvery metal object the size of her palm and pushes it toward me across the desk. It's a small metal pentagram. The same pentagram, I think, that Alondra once showed me on her desk before I joined her "honors program."

"You're a witch!"

"There are many of us," she says with a nod. "Hawthorne has become the center. Escoba brought witchcraft from the Caribbean. After she hurt Abigail's family, Abigail studied witchcraft, for revenge, from the ancient Celtic sources."

Dr. Trent pauses and looks down for a moment. She reaches forward and grabs the pentagram back and places it in her desk.

"I showed you the footage to prove that I am aware of your powers, Cadence. Although there have been many witches in Hawthorne, no one has ever shown the power you hold. Maybe Enora. And Alondra once thought she could train Enora, but her heart is blackened. She is wicked." *No arguing with that.* "If the tables were turned, I don't think Enora would have trapped you in a tree. She would have killed you."

"Who are you? I mean …"

"I'm a witch. Just like you said I am. And, yes, there are others. Many others. We are occult. But we've been shaping the world since the beginning of time. Stonehenge. Africa. The Caribbean. Do you really think that with all the magic you've seen, there aren't others who know about our magic?"

She stops talking for me to digest all the crazy things she's saying.

"I'm not only offering you a position as a graduate student. I'm offering you a leadership position as a witch." And she's no longer scowling; she's grinning and looking friendly. This is the Dr. Trent I remember from last year.

"What do I have to do?"

"Simple channeling spells. Hold Sabbaths. Divination. Perform incantations. Conjurings. Be a witch."

"I don't worship the devil."

"Alondra delved into the workings of Satan because of her husband," Dr. Trent says with a slow nod. "That was her choice. You can choose to do or not do this. The basic nature of what we are is powerful, but I leave the direction of the pentacle up to you. I'm asking you to practice, I'm not telling you how. If you agree, you can meet with your sisters and take in new recruits, just as Alondra did for me. We will set up a new *honors program* run by you and your fiancé. Hawthorne is a hub for us, Cadence. You can be the leader Alondra wanted you to be. She believed in you. You can even continue to use her house."

"She told me it was my house."

"I see no other claim." After a pause, she adds with a smile, "So...do you want to come here as a graduate student in our history program?"

With Bryce? Are you kidding me?

27

OSTARA

"So, before I begin, do you guys all know how Bo Peep and I met?" asks Mira.

I'm cringing. Bryce is too. I feel his palm twitch as I hold it.

The two of us are facing Mira. Mira's got on this really long draping black dress that drags on the grass behind her. She looks like a total witch. She's got thick witch makeup on. The red-and-black demon tattoos along her neck don't cover up her new long, thick horizontal scar. Well, she told me she likes the scar and thinks it looks really cool. I'm wearing a lovely draping white dress. My hubby, or future hubby, is wearing white too. I have discreet red lipstick and natural makeup and have curled my hair so that it's flowing like a goddess's. (I look really good.) The only witchlike thing I'm wearing is a crown of yellow and white flowers.

Anyway, Mira's making everyone real uncomfortable, because she's got this big grin and she's pausing before her microphone, waiting for us to laugh after she called me *Bo Peep*. No one's laughing. All my friends are sitting uncomfortably in the lovely white wooden chairs we rented and set up on the wild grass. Red roses are strewn in the central aisle. And the forest, of course, is its normal loveliness, surrounding Alondra's yard. My yard, I suppose.

"Well," Mira says with her famous smile, "Katie here used to be the most innocent little girl in school. Like, she just didn't get the world. I thought it was really cute, so I teased her. I used to call her Little Bo Peep. Know why?"

The funny thing about Mira is that people who don't know her think she's shy like me, because she doesn't talk much. But she doesn't talk much, not because she's shy but because she doesn't care about anybody. Just like I don't think she cares what people think about what she's saying right now.

I turn to my left and Maddie has her eyes wide open. She shakes her head at me. She's scared about what else Mira's going to spew out of her mouth. So is my brother. He's beside Maddie in his sharp navy-blue suit, furrowing his brow. He's staring at Mira too.

"I first met Cadence at this house. She could barely say a word, she was so quiet. Then at the Billington House, Maddie invited her to summon spirits for fun. Cadence drank a lot of beer back then. Lots. Remember, Katie?"

Okay, I might have been drinking, but I didn't drink *lots*. I'll never forget that day at the Billington House. That was the night I found out my mom had passed away. Through magic.

I look around and no one is laughing or smiling. And though the spring weather is absolutely perfect, with birds chirping and not a cloud in the lovely blue sky, I'm feeling impatient and a bit claustrophobic in my heavy draping white dress.

"I really didn't like you back then," Mira says to me. *Oh, God.* "You were more focused on your looks than on the spirit world. It seemed you were always fixing your hair or looking in a goddamn mirror. Sometimes I think you still are."

Okay, now people are laughing.

"We went through tough times, you know. Katie and our friends. And Katie was so innocent. But things have changed us." She pauses and nods. "She once asked our circle what *sodomy* means..." More laughter. It's turning into a roast, sort of. The thing is, I'm not sure Mira intended it to be. "It was weird that she didn't know, because she loves studying, but some things are just not taught in school. You know Cadence used to squirm when our friends talked about sex. I mean, she was a Little Bo

Peep." She looks right in my eyes with her infamous sly grin. "You didn't think I'd say all this stuff, did you?"

No, I didn't. And I really, really hope you're finished.

"Ghosts, witches, vampires." *She's not finished.* "You know Hawthorne's really different, but since I left, I really miss it. For those of you just visiting, I don't think you know how close our friendships were." She gestures around the yard. "This place, these grounds, have been so special to me. That's what I miss. Well, Katie isn't a Bo Peep anymore. I mean, look at Bryce. Damn."

If she were drunk, maybe the guests would understand. But I see people just shaking their heads.

"And then there's Bryce."

Bryce smiles nervously.

"You know everyone in school wanted Bryce. I mean, *everyone*. I knew him before Cadence. But when he met you—damn, girl—he only had eyes for you, Katie. Why, I'll never understand."

Yes, it is a roast. And people are laughing. That was *sort of* funny.

"Okay, I'm only kidding. I'm just saying all this stuff to... I mean, what I'm trying to say is...I love you guys. I really love you. Not only as friends, but because..." She starts choking up. "Well, I can't say. All I can say is that, Cadence, you saved me. And...I'm in love too, you know. I love the girl down there on the third row. Cadence saved her too."

"I love you too, Meer!" yells Courtney.

"Sure, Courtney, anyway—"

"Can we get on with it, Mira?" Maddie says, lifting her eyebrows impatiently.

Mira nods. She brushes tears from her eyes.

I look behind me at the crowd again. There are about forty people. Most are from our coven. Frida is holding hands with her new husband, Greg. Gilda came down from Savannah with her husband and baby. And Aunt Jane is here. Everyone looks so formal, and they're all smiling. And they look "normal." Mira and Courtney are the only ones crazy enough to be dressed in black, wearing thick goth makeup.

Then I see someone in the back row. I can't believe it. It's my dad! My dad, who vowed never to come to my wedding. Well, we've been talking again. He's talking to Bryce again too. I mean, how can he not love Bryce?

But he's still disturbed by the whole witch thing. He said he couldn't come to our handfasting today because he's Christian. But...he's here.

I wasn't tearing up until now.

"Ready, guys?" Mira asks with a genuine smile.

"The first symbol is the eternity symbol," Mira says. And she reaches down and grabs white ropes on a small wooden table beside her. "Can Cadence's dad please come up to the front row?"

I turn again and my dad looks as surprised as I am. I don't think anyone told him he'd be a part of the ceremony, certainly not me. He walks up the aisle, and I start crying really hard. They're not tears of sadness; they're tears of joy. And many of my witches start crying too. Bryce puts his hand on my back.

My dad faces me, looking at me with his gray eyes. He's wearing a tan suit and, although he's obviously made his decision to respect our wishes, he has a very conspicuous silver cross pinned on his coat.

"Are you okay with this, Cadence?" Dad asks.

"Of course, Daddy," I say, wiping tears on my sleeve and nodding. "Yes."

Dad looks at Bryce and smiles.

"Please face each other, Cadence and Bryce. Hold each other's right hand. One ribbon represents each family. A final ribbon represents the new joining the two of you are creating with this marriage."

Mira does this weird knot, which only she can create, on our right hands. (This is why I asked her to officiate, not for her to yap nasty things about me). Then she shows my dad the correct movements to knot the ropes around our wrists.

"Now the couple will say some words," Mira says. She puts the microphone right up to our faces.

I bite my lip. I don't want to talk. You know how I feel about that. Bryce goes first. He looks deep into my eyes and smiles sweetly.

"Katie, I'm so lucky to have met you. All I think of are the qualities of Venus when I am with you. Beauty. Not only beauty in looks, but in your heart. Your soul. I once told you your energy is of the Earth. You're an Earther. A pragmatist. I think, somehow, we've been tested. And you've grounded us. All of us. With your leadership and your heart. It's funny because—I hope you don't mind me sharing this—you said to me recently that you don't know why I fell in love with you. Cadence, truly, I don't know why you fell in love with me. I am so lucky to have found you. I love you. Will you be my wife? In sickness and in health?"

"I will." My brother walks up and helps put my diamond ring on my left hand.

Then he smiles, and for a moment, Bryce and I feel like kissing. But we can't, because it's my turn.

"Bryce ..." I'm kind of falling apart. I look over at everyone, and I try really hard to stop crying. "I don't know what to say." I look over at everyone. "I planned a bunch of stuff but I can't remember a word of it." Everyone laughs. "It's not funny."

"We should have written it down," Bryce says.

"I told you that... yeah, well... I don't know why you'd take me, either," I say, shaking my head. "I'm so lucky to have you. And I am so in love with you, Bryce."

There. I stop and he's just looking at me with a smile.

What?

Then he furrows his brow. "*Will you...*" Bryce hints.

"Oh yeah...will you be my husband?" Everyone laughs again.

"Yes, Cadence. I will." Damie helps put the ring on Bryce's left ring finger.

"The knot is tied," says Mira, tying the literal knot from our hands. Then she hands the tied rope to my dad and raises her arms. "Blessed be the two of you under Astraeus, Selene, and Gaia." She looks up. "Hecate, witness this bond. May it never break." She looks back down at us. "Now just go kiss each other already."

And we do. And everyone in the crowd jumps up and claps. I embrace my lover. Then I turn to my dad and hug him tightly.

"Congratulations, Katie," Dad says in my ear. "I love you."

Mira hugs me. She congratulates us too.

Everyone comes up. Everyone hugs. The attention is off of me and I relax while everybody's smiling, shaking hands, laughing and just being happy.

These are my friends. My family. This love, this friendship, so strong and so bound, like the knot, is something that was so special in

Hawthorne and something that I will miss. For a moment, that makes my tears turn a little bitter.

Then, on the patio, I see a vision. A witch in a black cloak is standing alone. She stands there as if to bear witness to the ceremony, holding a single candle by her chest. The candle is just bright enough to show the face on the hooded shadow. Alondra. Alondra is with me again. And her presence isn't scary; it's soothing. Pleasant. I wave and she nods with a smile. Then she fades.

Her presence eases me. Despite there being only a few months left in my final school year, things are not ending. Since Lammas, I've been dreading the end of the school year. But nothing's ending. It's beginning. And, really, beginnings and endings are just an illusion. Only the moments with people we love are important. Those moments, when quiet and reflective, never end.

Bryce jumps into my arms, startling me from my deep thoughts. I'm back with everyone, hearing their raucous shouts and laughter. Dad, Maddie, Aunt Jane, Mira, Damie, Frida, Tammy, and everyone from my coven rush over.

We chose Ostara as the day of our marriage. Ostara is the witch holiday for Easter. Bryce and our marriage are a new beginning for all of us.

THE END

EPILOGUE

BRYCE IS SITTING ON THE BED IN THE MASTER BEDROOM OF ALONDRA'S house, my house, taking off his black shoes. It's our third night here. The bedroom doesn't feel spooky anymore. And after my talk with Alondra, it feels like *my* bedroom. He's laid his white pants and dress shirt on a chair and is wearing only a T-shirt, underwear, and socks. It's late, but a full moon and the view through the floor-to-ceiling window of the master bedroom still reveal a very messy backyard. The white chairs are still in rows, and Mira's podium is still there, but no one's outside. I've already showered and am wearing a white lace nightgown, writing in my book, *Broomstick.*

"What are you doing, babe?"

"Huh, husband?"

"Whatcha doing?"

"Writing."

He removes his socks. He hasn't showered yet, but his hair is still gorgeous. He partied late with his friends at the reception.

"I like writing in this book," I say with a shrug. "It's like my diary. But I'm running out of space. It's so full and there's only one page left."

"Give me," he says and jumps on the mattress, grabbing for it. I laugh and quickly close the book and stash it under me in the covers.

"It's private!"

"I thought the book creeped you out," he says, holding me. "Why do you write in it?" Then he kisses my lips. At first, it's a peck; then it's passionate. I play with his tongue, and I feel so close to him. But while we kiss passionately, I feel him reach under my back and grab the book.

"Hey!" I say.

He snatches it and opens the book to the last page. His eyes open wide. "Weren't ... weren't you just saying this? How do you do that?"

"Magic," I say with a big grin.

We stare at each other. His lips slowly curl into a larger and larger smile. Then he jumps on me again, leaning over my body and touching my lips to his while we laugh. He pulls me very close.

"I love you so much, Katie," he whispers between kisses.

"And I, you. And..." I take off his T-shirt. "Isn't tonight the start of our honeymoon?"

His tongue dances with mine and we stay like this for a while, just enjoying our touch. I feel the fingers of his free hand inside my nightgown, running along my side and pressing along my skin, reaching over the curves of my breasts and nipples. He rubs me, kissing me hard on the lips. I enjoy his weight and reach under his shirt, rubbing his back, then lower, along his butt. Then—

Everything fades.

What do you expect? It's our wedding night. Geesh. Give me some privacy.

WITCHY ADVENTURES ARE CONTINUED IN THESE NEXT BOOKS
IN THE HAWTHORNE UNIVERSITY WITCH SERIES

- WITCH MIRROR
- RAVENS
- SHADOW CAST

SHORT STORIES AND PREQUELS

- BELTANE FIRE short story prequel (Book 0.5)
- SAMHAIN WITCH (Book 3.5)
- CANDY CRONE (Book 6.5)
- ALONDRA 20 yr prequel

THE NEXT BOXED SETS

- THE HAWTHORNE UNIVERSITY WITCH SERIES (4-6)
- THE HAWTHORNE UNIVERSITY WITCH HOLIDAY
  COLLECTION

***DON'T FORGET, EVERY BOOK IS NOW PERFORMED IN
AUDIOBOOK FORMAT, NARRATED BY ALEXA ELMY (& PRESTON
GEER IN ALONDRA)

ACKNOWLEDGMENTS

I want to thank my beta readers Natalia Ramirez-Avila, Rob C., and George B. for their input in all three books. Stephanie Ward and Eliza Dee for their editing and shaping of my works. And Regina Wamba for dressing the books beautifully. I was so lucky to have this team. This series would not have been the same without you. Thank you!

PARTING WORDS

What did you think of my Hawthorne University Witch Series? By placing a book review, you can inform others of your thoughts and help spread the word about my book.

Want more? Periodically I like to send news regarding current or new projects. If you'd like to be privy, I encourage you to sign up to my email newsletter. Your information will remain private and you can cancel any time.

Sign up at www.alhawke.com or scan the following QR code:

AFTERWORD

With the ending of my trilogy, I thought I'd add a word about how it came to be. So, if interested, here we go …

Broomstick was inspired on a whim to write a novel on Halloween. That's it. Boring, right? But I had thought of the basis for the story many years before when listening to music by the band Dead Can Dance. The original idea involved a virgin introduced to adulthood by skeletons in a dark tower. I'll let your mind wander over that. Needless to say, the story could have turned into horror.

Then came Halloween in 2019. I was playing around with a fantasy while drinking a green tea latte in a coffee shop. The idea of stealing a cup of coffee and a virginal girl's reaction blossomed into the character Cadence. Once I liked the character, her innocence and sweetness, the rest was history. In my writing, characters are central and supersede plots. Mostly, I write my stories *around* my characters. I then endeavored to create *Broomstick*, my paranormal romance, with as much realism as possible.

After *Broomstick*, the sequels, *Windstorm* and *The Hawthorne Witch,* were challenging. I wanted to hold the same tenor of Cadence's thoughts and actions as in the first book. To achieve this, I decided to write all three books consecutively in one year without a break. Believe it or not, I don't outline. I had as much foreknowledge of the ending as you did. Well, the finished products, I believe, were three independent books that felt like one unified story.

I wrote *Windstorm* as a book of acceptance. Cadence finally accepted her job as a witch, her love for Bryce, and her place as a student in Hawthorne. The final book was designed to be the culmination of everything. Her acceptance at being, literally, *The Hawthorne Witch*. Her acceptance of her identity: a "witch" or an adult.

Completing the trilogy so soon makes me a little sad. But, who knows, there may be more adventures in Katie's life that she'll want to write about. After all, she might have finished *Broomstick*, but she can write a new Book of Shadows. She's a witch, you know.

ABOUT THE AUTHOR

A.L. Hawke torches the midnight candle over lovers against a backdrop of machines, nymphs, magic, spice and mayhem. The author specializes in fantasy romance and science fiction.

Visit A.L. Hawke at www.alhawke.com

Email: contact@alhawke.com

ALSO BY A.L. HAWKE

PARANORMAL ROMANCE

- THE HAWTHORNE UNIVERSITY WITCH SERIES (4-6)
- THE HAWTHORNE UNIVERSITY WITCH HOLIDAY COLLECTION
- CANDY CRONE (Book 6.5)
- BELTANE FIRE short story prequel (Book 0.5)
- SAMHAIN WITCH (Book 3.5)
- ALONDRA 20 yr prequel

- SHADES
- HAUNTING JOY
- PHANTOM MASQUERADE

- MY EVIL EYE
- THE GUARDIAN
- NECTAR OF AMBROSIA
- CORA

FANTASY: THE AZURE SERIES

- HARMONIA
- CORA: RISE OF THE FALLEN GODDESS
- AZURE BLUE
- CORAL RED
- PRINCESS SOJOURN

SCIENCE FICTION

- CANDY SAVANT SERIES

Books available at https://alhawke.com/books